The rider removed his steel mask and bowed deeply

The crowd jumped to its feet, cheering.

Amid the tumult, something on the far side of the center ring caught Ryan's eye. Something flashed behind the mirror wall of the facing trailer. And for a fraction of a second, the silver reflective glass became vaguely, hazily transparent, as if through a pall of oily brown smoke.

Then it was over.

In that frozen moment Ryan glimpsed a ghostly figure whose afterimage was burned deeply into his brain. Spindly-limbed. Slouching. Menacing. Even if he hadn't seen the glare of the light on the steel, he would have known who it was.

The Magus.

**Other titles in the
Deathlands saga:**

Pilgrimage to Hell
Red Holocaust
Neutron Solstice
Crater Lake
Homeward Bound
Pony Soldiers
Dectra Chain
Ice and Fire
Red Equinox
Northstar Rising
Time Nomads
Latitude Zero
Seedling
Dark Carnival
Chill Factor
Moon Fate
Fury's Pilgrims
Shockscape
Deep Empire
Cold Asylum
Twilight Children
Rider, Reaper
Road Wars
Trader Redux
Genesis Echo
Shadowfall
Ground Zero
Emerald Fire
Bloodlines
Crossways
Keepers of the Sun
Circle Thrice

Eclipse at Noon
Stoneface
Bitter Fruit
Skydark
Demons of Eden
The Mars Arena
Watersleep
Nightmare Passage
Freedom Lost
Way of the Wolf
Dark Emblem
Crucible of Time
Starfall
Encounter:
   Collector's Edition
Gemini Rising
Gaia's Demise
Dark Reckoning
Shadow World
Pandora's Redoubt
Rat King
Zero City
Savage Armada
Judas Strike
Shadow Fortress
Sunchild
Breakthrough
Salvation Road
Amazon Gate
Destiny's Truth
Skydark Spawn

JAMES AXLER

DEATH LANDS®

Damnation Road Show

A GOLD EAGLE BOOK FROM

WORLDWIDE®

TORONTO • NEW YORK • LONDON
AMSTERDAM • PARIS • SYDNEY • HAMBURG
STOCKHOLM • ATHENS • TOKYO • MILAN
MADRID • WARSAW • BUDAPEST • AUCKLAND

First edition June 2003

ISBN 0-373-62572-3

DAMNATION ROAD SHOW

Printed in U.S.A.

O eyes, no eyes, but fountains fraught with tears;
O life, no life, but lively form of death;
O world, no world, but mass of public wrongs,
Confused and filled with murder and misdeeds.

—Thomas Kyd,
1558-1594

THE DEATHLANDS SAGA

This world is their legacy, a world born in the violent nuclear spasm of 2001 that was the bitter outcome of a struggle for global dominance.

There is no real escape from this shockscape where life always hangs in the balance, vulnerable to newly demonic nature, barbarism, lawlessness.

But they are the warrior survivalists, and they endure—in the way of the lion, the hawk and the tiger, true to nature's heart despite its ruination.

Ryan Cawdor: The privileged son of an East Coast baron. Acquainted with betrayal from a tender age, he is a master of the hard realities.

Krysty Wroth: Harmony ville's own Titian-haired beauty, a woman with the strength of tempered steel. Her premonitions and Gaia powers have been fostered by her Mother Sonja.

J. B. Dix, the Armorer: Weapons master and Ryan's close ally, he, too, honed his skills traversing the Deathlands with the legendary Trader.

Doctor Theophilus Tanner: Torn from his family and a gentler life in 1896, Doc has been thrown into a future he couldn't have imagined.

Dr. Mildred Wyeth: Her father was killed by the Ku Klux Klan, but her fate is not much lighter. Restored from predark cryogenic suspension, she brings twentieth-century healing skills to a nightmare.

Jak Lauren: A true child of the wastelands, reared on adversity, loss and danger, the albino teenager is a fierce fighter and loyal friend.

Dean Cawdor: Ryan's young son by Sharona accepts the only world he knows, and yet he is the seedling bearing the promise of tomorrow.

In a world where all was lost, they are humanity's last hope....

Prologue

Evening hung dead still and oppressively humid over the shallow, five-acre, seep-fed lake, the lavender dome of sky perfectly reflected in its mercury-smooth surface. Encircling the muddy bank was a fringe of stripped, bleached skeletons of trees. The intense quiet was neither peaceful nor serene; the very air seemed to vibrate in anticipation and dread. Terrible forces of nature were about to make themselves known.

Swish-swish.

Swish-swish.

From the north end of the lake came a rhythmic sound.

Not a bird, not an insect. Sensing the impending hell show, the birds and insects had gone to ground.

A tall human figure stood on the bank in hip boots, waving a nine-foot-long, flexible rod back and forth. And as he did so, he sailed a bright-yellow line through the air, forward and back, forward and back, in a tight loop, out over the purple mirror of sky. The man wore a long, pointy, black goatee and his black hair was loosely tied in a ponytail, which hung to the middle of his back. On his head was a tatter-brimmed straw cowboy hat. His eyes were hidden behind wraparound sunglasses.

What face was visible was long, gaunt, perhaps tragic, certainly suffering, certainly world weary.

As the man cast, the water in front of him swirled and gurgled. The head of a huge mutie lungfish appeared in the middle of the ripples. The fish looked up at the man, then struggled out of the pool, walking on the bony spikes of its pectoral fins. Greenish-gray on the back with a light cream-colored belly, the mutie was easily five feet long and weighed more than sixty pounds. As it dragged itself from the world of fish into the world of men, its large, rubbery lipped mouth and its gill covers opened and closed, breathing air. Grunting from the effort, the lungfish crawled up beside the man. An odor rose up along with it—the smell of a slaughterhouse in August.

"You have no fly on the end of your line," it said in a strange, gravelly voice that was half croak, half belch. "You can't catch anything that way."

"I'm not fishing for anything," the bearded man said as he continued to cast far out over the smooth water, in the direction of the evening star.

"You're fishing for nothing?" the lungfish said.

"That's right."

"Are you catching any?"

"I'm catching and releasing nothing," the man replied.

As he continued to cast, to his left, a two-wheeled cart drawn by three men appeared over the rim of the slope. The lake sat on a stair-step rise in the land. Above it was mountainside; below it, the ground—mostly bare, eroded limestone—angled three hundred feet down to a broad flat spot between surrounding peaks. There, in a grove of low, scrubby trees, stood the remote ville. Even by Deathlands standards, it was a scab-assed place: dirt-floor shacks and lean-tos built up against the outer wall of the ville's only permanent structure, a predark concrete blockhouse. Most of these shanties were big enough to house one or two people, and not tall enough to stand in.

The three men took axes and a heavy-bladed machete from the cart and started hacking away at its contents. They laughed as they sprayed one another with flying gore. After a few minutes of extreme effort, they paused to catch their breath, then started throwing human arms, legs and quartered torsos into the water. The erratic splashes broke the metronomic swish-swish, swish-swish of the fly rod.

The lungfish turned back from the commotion and asked the bearded man, "Am I real to you?"

The man let his line fall and settle. He pushed his sunglasses down the bridge of his nose, looked at the talking fish and said, "Nothing is real."

As more body parts landed in the pool, swirls appeared in the water near the splashes. Other lungfish were rising to feed.

"That dinner looks pretty real to me," the fish said. "Eat my body, become my body…"

"Yeah, yeah," the man muttered distractedly.

As the lungfish slithered back to the water and to its share of the chow, it half turned and said, "Try some bait next time, Baron Kerr."

The bearded man remained silent and threw a loop into his floating line that allowed him to sweep the entire length of it back into the air.

Swish-swish.

Suddenly the entire surface of pool shivered before him, the lavender mirror shattering into a billion fragments. Like glittering confetti, the first spores of the evening lifted gracefully into the air. It was just the overture. In seconds, dense clouds of the freed genetic material boiled up from the water. Pale-green fingers of fire crackled and sparked from the pool's undulating surface, making the clouds glow and shimmer from within.

As the ministorm grew in intensity, the blood-spattered men hurried down the slope with their empty cart, determined to get under cover before spore fall.

Swish-swish.

Swish-swish.

The heat from the electrical discharge made the air temperature jump twenty-five degrees and sent the spore clouds billowing upward. The higher they rose, the more ferocious the strange lightning storm became: blistering, eye-aching bolts fired up from earth to sky, their prodigious thunder rattling the ground.

Baron Jim Kerr quickly wound in his line and headed downhill for cover. He recognized the evening's ominous signs. The much heavier than normal spore hatch. The absolute frenzy of bioelectric discharge. That told him the food supply was dwindling, even now barely sufficient for survival. Something would have to be done, and soon. He knew better than to frustrate the burning pool. He remembered what had happened the last time.

Chapter One

A little girl in a faded cotton dress sat atop Bullard ville's dirt-and-concrete defensive berm, watching distant plumes of yellow dust spiral up from the vast, barren flood plain—man-made tornadoes back-lit by the hard glare of the late-afternoon sun. She sat with her skinny, sun-browned legs drawn up, her elbows propped on scabbed knees. The hand-me-down garment she wore was way too big for her. Every time she moved, it slipped off one or the other of her thin shoulders.

During the hour that Leeloo Bunny had been keeping vigil, the ville's other children had joined her at intervals, scrambling up the back side of the berm for a look-see. After less than a minute of quiet reconnoiter, the pushing and pinching started. Squealing, they raced back down to resume an extrafrantic, extrashrill game of Chill the Mutie.

Only Leeloo had the patience to stay, to sit in silence and allow the promised miracle to unfold. She wanted to be first to see it, and to be able to remember every second as long as she lived.

Nothing this exciting had ever happened in Bullard ville.

It was without a doubt one of the two most dramatic moments in Leeloo's eight years of life.

It towered above sneaking peeks through the windows of the gaudy house to see the mostly naked men and women fight on the pallets laid on the floor. Leeloo had sometimes watched her own ma, Tater Bunny, fight men on those mattresses. It was a safe bet that one of Tater's adversaries was Leeloo's father; there were a lot of candidates for the distinction, but no one had ever stepped forward to claim the little girl as his own.

Because Leeloo didn't fully understand the aim of the gaudy house mattress fights, she had yet to figure out how to judge winners and losers. To her it seemed the combatants usually parted on friendly, if not affectionate terms. Some of the women fought ten or twelve men a night, and didn't seem the worse for wear, at least not any place that showed.

It was a different story for her ma. Tater Bunny had died more than a year ago when a drunken drifter choked her a bit too hard.

That was Leeloo's life-changing, dramatic event number one.

The man who'd chilled her ma had tried to run away afterward, but the ville's menfolk caught him and dragged him back. They hung him from an old basketball stanchion with his pants pulled down around his boot tops and his willy sticking out. Leeloo had sometimes gone to look at the man who chilled her ma, to look through the hot, blurry screen of her tears and throw rocks at him as hard as she could. After a while, she had to stand upwind because the smell got so bad. The ville's men cut down and buried the corpse only when they needed the stanchion to hang someone else.

Leeloo Bunny had no interest in eventually following in her ma's professional footsteps. Not because of the nature of the work, which held no particular stigma in Bullard ville, or the danger of injury, which was considerably less than other jobs to be had, but because of the required confinement. Leeloo liked to be outdoors in the sun, not indoors, lying in tangled, sticky bedding. She liked planting seeds in the raised beds under sheet-metal awnings and tending the young plants until they grew big enough to eat. She liked picking bouquets of the bitter-tasting, little wild daisies that seemed to pop up everywhere. She made delicate ornaments for herself out of them by knotting the stems together. This day, she was decked out with a daisy circlet on the crown of her head, and tiers of bracelets dangled from her slender wrists.

Her anticipation of specialness on this day had begun three weeks earlier, when the carny's advance scout had roared up to the berm gate in an armored Baja Bug.

The little wag had outsized knobby tires and a roll cage around the driver's seat made of heavy pipe. Over the empty front, rear and side window frames were hinged, blasterproof metal shutters that could be dropped during an attack, leaving only a view slit for the driver to steer by.

The carny scout had called himself Azimuth. A giant with cascading woolly dreadlocks, every muscle and sinew was visible beneath his glossy ebony skin. He wore a sleeveless vest of mutie coyote pelt, turned hair side out, and gray army pants tucked into the tops of scuffed and scraped, steel-toe-capped, lace-up, shin-high, black leather boots. Grimy goggles hung around his wide, muscular throat.

Leeloo could close her eyes and recall how the man smelled: a sweet, feminine perfume mixed with sharpish body odor. Azimuth had either slathered himself with great quantities of the flowery scent, or he had been in a prolonged fight with a gaudy slut who had. Leeloo also remembered the way his front teeth were filed to points, top and bottom, and that the inside of his mouth was as red as blood, as was his tongue and the insides of his nostrils.

Azimuth had been greeted by Bullard ville's most important people, including its headman, the lumbering, overweight, perpetually sweating Wilbur Melchior, who had adopted Leeloo right after her ma died. The black giant's mission was to determine whether the ville would be willing to pay for the privilege of seeing Gert Wolfram's World Famous Carny Show. If so, Azimuth said, the troupe would stop there for a night or so en route to another engagement. He quoted them a steep price for this entertainment, in water and fresh food.

When asked by Melchior what the show consisted of, Azimuth threw back his head and let out a howl that so startled the delegation of dirt farmers, they stepped back and grabbed for their blaster butts.

But there was no threat.

It was a howl of sheer exuberance.

When things calmed down, Azimuth assured them that Gert Wolfram's World Famous Carny offered genuine miracles and wonderments, gathered at great expense and hazard from the farthest corners of the Deathlands and beyond, all for their private amusement and edification. On his long, thick fingers, he listed some of the various, incomparable attractions: singing, dancing stickies; fantastical mutie beasts trained to do amazing tricks; feats of norm superstrength and daring; the most beautiful norm women this side of Hell walking around in next to nothing; unparalleled exhibitions of music, comedy and drama.

Something to tell your grandchildren about, Azimuth said. A once-in-a-lifetime opportunity.

At that point, Melchior and the other leaders of the ville withdrew to the shade of a nearby sheet-metal awning and conferred. Leeloo edged close enough to overhear their conversation. Her adoptive father said it was a matter of pride, that Bullard ville deserved this admitted luxury. Their hosting the World Famous Carny would indicate to anyone with half a brain that the remote agricultural enclave had finally come into its own. Around the circle, heads nodded in agreement.

The only word of caution came from the gaudy master, Skim O'Neil. He said there could be a big risk in letting so many strangers inside the berm at once. The protest fell on deaf ears. Melchior spoke for the rest when he bragged that Bullard ville wasn't afraid of anything that walked. Mopping his sweat-beaded jowls with a big wad of cotton rag, he reminded O'Neil how they had turned back the attempted takeovers of two different barons and chilled their sec men.

A vote was taken, and it was unanimous.

When they returned to where the scout waited, Melchior put his hand out and told him that he had a deal. They shook on it. Then Melchior and the other leaders took Azimuth on a guided tour of Bullard. Leeloo tagged along behind, unnoticed.

As was common in Deathlands, the isolated ville had sprouted up at the edge of a ruined interstate highway. The overpass that had once connected high-speed travelers with an oasis of fast food and fast gas had collapsed across four lanes of traffic on the day the world changed. The center of Bullard ville was formed around the shambling remnants of those predark fast-food franchises. Their dilapidated plastic signs still beckoned: Mergen's Family Restaurant, Taco Town, Burger Stravaganza, Fish 'n' More—now the gaudy house.

The four-lane highway had once paralleled a lush river valley that stretched for many hundreds of miles, bordered by rugged, steep, dark mountains to the east and rolling hills to the west. The flat valley, postnukecaust, was parched, burned yellow, turned to dust by sun and chem rains. Postnukecaust, the slow, meandering river that had watered trees and grass and cultivated fields decided it no longer liked the looks of things and burrowed deep underground.

The river's disappearance saved Bullard ville from extinction. Of course, there were no more pre-breaded steaks, fish fingers, burger patties or ice-cream novelties to lure tired, hungry travelers to Bullard. Yet the travelers still came and stopped and parted with whatever valuables they had, because there was water. The underground river ran right under the ville. Hand-operated pumps provided water for drinking, for very occasional bathing and for travelers to take away.

Grub could be had, but it was whatever was on hand. Travelers ate whatever bush meat the residents could chase down and kill. Usually mutie jackrabbits, or snakes, or birds of all sizes, from sparrows to turkey vultures. These were either spit-roasted over an open fire or parboiled in caldrons made of salvaged, fifty-five-gallon oil drums.

With the virtually endless supply of clean water, the ville folk grew a variety of edible crops year-round, under the shelter of metal awnings to keep off the chem rain. For fertilizer, they composted and used their own excrement. They cultivated beans, hot peppers, onions and garlic. They grew corn primarily for the sugar, which was used to make joy juice. There wasn't enough surface area inside the defensive berm to produce food for mass export. And there weren't enough people in Bullard to defend an expansion of crop growing outside the barrier.

Considering the miserable, hammered-down state of the world, the little hamlet was doing quite well. During the tour, Melchior hinted as much to Azimuth, but as Leeloo noticed, he gave no specifics.

As she well knew, the treasure of Bullard was safely locked away in the basement of Mergen's Family Restaurant, under twenty-four-hour armed guard. It consisted of miscellaneous objects of value traded for water: weapons, ammunition, canned food, predark medicine, first-aid supplies, wag fuel, oil, grease, batteries, transmission fluid, antifreeze, tires, matches, clothing, boots and shoes, hand tools, auto parts, various bits of repair material, duct tape, bailing wire, nails, screws, rope and electrical wire. There was no jolt, though. The ville leaders drew the line at hard drugs.

The contents of the warehouse were tangible proof of the water's worth. And anything worth more than a few drops of piss in Deathlands was worth chilling someone over. Two barons had tried and failed to annex Bullard ville, which stood in disputed border zone at the edges of their respective territories. Neither baron could muster and transport a large enough force to defeat the villagers. Every person over the age of twelve carried a loaded blaster all the time, whether working on the crops or sleeping. The youngest ones packed well-cared-for .36-caliber, black-powder, Italian-reproduction Colts. They wore the 5-shot, 1862 Police models in canvas, snap-flap hip holsters. The entire volunteer sec force trained regularly in marksmanship and tactics.

Leeloo Bunny was too young and still too physically frail to control a blaster that weighed more than a pound and a half, unloaded. But she was very much looking forward to the day when finally she got her own blaster. Not because she wanted to shoot anything in particular, but because it was a symbol of her growing up.

After the guided tour, the ville's leaders fed Azimuth a massive meal, got him stinking drunk and then let him fight three women at once in the gaudy.

All free of charge.

Melchior had called this extraordinary generosity "the famous Bullard ville hospitality."

As the dust plumes on the plain grew closer, Leeloo could just make out tiny, dark shapes at their bases, and her heart leaped. The shapes became more and more distinct until she could see the gaily painted wags, racing with strings of bright pennants whipping from their radio masts.

A man standing at the berm gate shouted, "The carny's here! The carny's here!"

Every man, woman and child dropped whatever they were doing and rushed to the ville's entrance, forming a dense double line, a gauntlet of well-armed Bullard ville welcome.

The fifteen-wag caravan slowed to a crawl as it approached the defensive berm. Leeloo saw that some of the wags were towing big tarp-covered cages on flatbed trailers.

Then the music started.

Taped music, scratchy with age and thousands of playings. Loud enough to wake the nukecaust's dead, a powerful male baritone boomed above the insistent crash of cymbals and drums. The words he sang rolled like thunder. Leeloo had taught herself to count to a hundred, so she knew what "76" signified. She wasn't sure whether a "trombone" was animal, vegetable or mineral, but the raucous, cheerful beat of the predark music thrilled her to the core.

As the dust clouds drifted away to the south, with the convoy slowly advancing, men began to jump out of the wags. They threw back the tarps covering the trailered cages, revealing the collection of creatures within.

Leeloo sucked in an astonished breath. It was more wonderful than her wildest imaginings! Behind the bars of the first cage lurked a two-headed scalie. One head was normal sized; the other looked like a baby's. The next trailer cage held a gaggle of stickies, naked but for plastic collars in bright colors, like open flower petals.

They showed their needle teeth and dilated their flat nostril holes as they took in the scent of the ville. Another cage contained a huge mutie mountain lion with scythe-shaped horns jutting on either side of its neck. It raised its head and yowled balefully along with the marching song. On the trailer behind the mountain lion was the biggest desert rattler Leeloo had ever seen. The thing was mebbe ten feet long, and its body was as big around as her waist. Its flat, triangular-shaped head was even wider, and the mouth could have easily swallowed two of her whole.

There were lizard birds with leathery wings and fangs so sharp they scored the steel bars of their cages.

Leeloo turned her attention to the carny folk walking alongside the trailers. The men wore slitted masks over their eyes. Their leather jerkins and shorts exposed bulging arm and leg muscles. They all carried bullwhips, which they smacked against the bars of the cages, making the mutie creatures howl in complaint. The carny women were long legged, their faces and heads concealed by brightly sequined hoods. But for thigh-high, high-heeled boots and a tracery of string over their privates, they were naked. The women also used whips to stir up the rolling menagerie.

Once inside the berm, the caravan of wags circled twice, to Leeloo's way of thinking, most majestically. Then it stopped.

A tall, muscular man in a worn red satin tailcoat, and with tight white pants tucked into hard-used black riding boots, climbed out of the largest wag. On one hip he wore a holstered, blue-steel, .45 Government Colt blaster; on the other he carried a coiled black bullwhip. His short, wiry hair was a rusty red, as was his six-inch-long goatee. A jagged ring of scar marked the left side of his face, perhaps made by a broken neck of a bottle, or Leeloo thought, by an attack from one of his ferocious muties.

As the tailcoated man walked toward the ville's leaders, a tiny stickie, not more than four years old, trotted along at his left heel. It was naked and barefoot, and there were bruises all over its pale body. Around its neck was a choke chain dog collar that wasn't tethered to a leash.

"Welcome to Bullard ville," Melchior said, extending a damp, callused hand to the carny master. "A pleasure to have Gert Wolfram and his famous troupe as our guests."

"I speak for my entire company," the tailcoated man stated, "when I say we are most honored to have the opportunity to entertain you."

The young stickie, eyes as dead as black stones, sniffed through the two holes in its face, taking the measure of the overweight Melchior. And having done that, the baby mutie made soft kissing noises in his direction, and began to drool copiously. Melchior's right hand reached across his pendulous chest and came to rest on the rubber butt of his shoulder-holstered Ruger Single Six.

"Oh, don't worry about Jackson," the carny master said, stroking the creature's hairless skull. "Unless you corner the little tyke, he's not the least bit dangerous."

At the hand-to-head contact, the immature stickie closed its eyes with pleasure; its jaw gaped, exposing tightly packed rows of needle teeth.

"When is the show going to start?" Skim O'Neil asked.

This question was met with wild cheers and whistles from the assembly.

"It takes us a while to stake out and set up the main tent," the carny master said.

"I'm afraid it's already too late in the day to get started on it. With your permission, we'll set up camp inside the berm tonight, then start raising the tent tomorrow morning. That will give my people a chance to rest up, too. They need a break before they perform. We've been on the road three days getting here."

Leeloo was crushed to hear this. She wasn't alone. A chorus of groans rippled through the crowd.

"Couldn't you give us a little taste of what's to come?" Melchior asked. "We've all been waiting for this day for weeks and weeks."

The carny man scratched his red chin beard, briefly considering what taste he might offer. "All right," he said, "I'll give you fine folks a preview of what's in store for tomorrow. But I warn you now, once you see it, you won't sleep a wink tonight."

He looked down at the baby stickie and said, "Sing!"

As the order echoed off the berm walls, the people of Bullard ville blinked at one another in amazement. It was common knowledge that the mouth parts of stickies were so primitive, so unevolved, that most could barely make mewling noises, let alone make music.

Yet, at its master's command, the little stickie opened its round, practically lipless mouth, threw back its bald head and sang, in perfect pitch, in a high, clear soprano, a predark song even older than the one caught on tape. "Ave Maria" burst forth from between rows of mutated needle teeth.

Most of the folks in the crowd closed their eyes and simply listened to the exquisitely pure tones, like bell chimes. Each word of the lyric was perfectly formed and enunciated.

There were no cries of sacrilege because no one understood the words, which were in Italian. Even if the Deathlands dirt farmers could have translated the lyric into English, its meaning and references would have been a mystery to them. Despite the yawning gap in the audience's understanding, the music itself was so moving that by the time Jackson finished the a cappella performance, there were tears of wonder in the eyes of men and women alike.

While Bullard ville rendered wild applause, the carny master patted the little stickie on the head, and it nuzzled its cheek against the side of his riding boot, leaving behind a shiny smear of saliva.

After the tumult had died down, a beaming Melchior pointed out a likely spot for the company to spend the night. The carny master thanked him, then returned with Jackson to the biggest wag, which pulled out of file to lead the convoy to the campsite. The marching music started up again as the wags and trailers rolled forward. Dust boiled up from their tires, swirling in thick, yellow clouds through the open gate of the berm.

Out of the corner of her eye, Leeloo caught more movement on the plain. Shadowy figures advanced through the man-made dust storm, making for the ville's entrance. They were hard to see with the all dust and the sunlight slanting hard behind them.

She counted seven.

Mebbe stragglers from the carny? she thought.

When they stepped out of the cloud, Leeloo knew at once they weren't carny folk. They were hunters. The man in the lead carried a scoped longblaster on a shoulder sling. He was tall, with dark hair falling to his broad shoulders. A black patch concealed his left eye socket. As he came closer, she noticed the color of the other eye.

It made her think of a cloudless morning sky.

Infinite blue.

Infinite cold.

Chapter Two

Ryan Cawdor shifted the sling, transferring the weight of his scoped Steyr SSG-70 sniper rifle from his right shoulder to his left. Six dusty companions followed single file behind him, heading for the crude gate cut into the twelve-foot-high berm wall. For the last third of a mile, they had been breathing and eating the drifting grit thrown up by the wag caravan. For the last third of a mile, they had been listening to the predark marching music, its sprightly cheerfulness like a dull dagger jammed in their guts, then twisted. For the last third of a mile, it had taken every bit of Ryan's self-control not to break into a dead run. Just as it not took all of his inner reserve not to sprint up the face of the perimeter barrier, drop belly down on the summit with the 7.62 mm longblaster and start bowling over the carny folk.

Suicide wasn't part of the plan.

The plan was to make damn sure what they all suspected was true, and then to act in stealth, lowering the odds from eight to one against before showing their hand. The mechanics of the operation had been hatched over four days of one of the hardest forced marches Ryan and the others had ever endured. They had approached Bullard ville from

the west, cross-country, over seemingly endless rolling hills and scrub forest, breaking their own trail,
sleeping only a few hours each night. They had
pushed themselves mercilessly because they didn't
want to risk arriving too late and uncovering another
horror.

For the thousandth time, the image of the hand
came into Ryan's mind. A grisly, ruined, black hand
jutting from the earth in the middle of long patch of
churned-up ground. The flesh had been torn away
by teeth or beak, or both. Three fingers were missing
down to the knuckles. Right off, he knew it was a
woman or a child's hand because it was so small
and slender. Somehow, whoever it was had survived
long enough to claw up through the smothering
clods of earth. It had to have taken a superhuman
effort.

They had discovered why after they had carefully
scraped back the top layer of soil.

Cradled in the young woman's other arm was a
dead infant.

Her strength had come from desperation.

The companions peeled back more dirt, exposing
other bodies. Many, many bodies piled on top of
one another. Both sexes, old, young, strong, weak.
As soon as Ryan saw the tangle of limbs and torsos,
he sent his twelve-year-old son, Dean, away from
the pit to recce the rest of the ville. The boy left
gratefully, but he would have remained to prove to
his father and the companions that he was made of
the same rock-hard stuff that they were. Ryan had

no doubt about the boy's stuff; as far as he was concerned, Dean had nothing to prove.

There were close-range blaster wounds on a few of the corpses, but most were unmarked by obvious acts of violence. They never did find the bottom of the mass grave. The stench of death rained like hammer blows against the sides of their heads, and they staggered from the trench, bent over, retching.

"Bastards chilled the whole ville," Krysty Wroth gasped as Ryan put a strong, gentle hand on her shoulder. The titian-haired, long-legged young woman was his lover and soul mate. They had seen many hard things during their wanderings over the hellscape, but rarely had they seen such wanton wholesale slaughter as this.

"Not all, mebbe," said Jak Lauren, pointing at the cluster of shabby dwellings. It was a false hope. And from the expression in the albino's ruby red eyes, he knew it. But Jak, like everyone else, wanted to be away from the pit and its rotting horrors. A thorough search showed the nameless little ville had been looted of everything of value, just like the dead folk buried in the ditch. The huts and lean-tos had been stripped, the underground storage pits emptied. All that remained was the trash in the ville's midden too heavy to be blown away by the howling wind.

Uncovering the mass grave had flipped a switch in Doc Tanner's head. He had stopped talking the moment they found the bodies of the mother and child. Which was unusual, because normally Doc never shut up. At the time, Ryan figured the discovery had triggered memories of Doc's own terrible loss of his long-dead children and wife, of the time-trawling whitecoats from the future who had snatched him from the natural course of his life in the year 1896, then played with him before bumping him further down the timeline, to the living hell called Deathlands.

Doc hadn't participated in the speculation about what had happened in the ville, about who could have committed such a bastard evil deed, and how the deed was done. Nor did Doc vote when it came time to decide what in rad blazes they should do about it—if anything.

Some hours later, as Ryan and the companions tracked the overlaid tire prints of many heavy wags leading out of the ville, Doc had suddenly started walking stiff-legged, like a tall, scarecrow zombie in his frock coat and high boots. After he had taken several hard falls, despite the support of his sword-stick, J. B. Dix had safety-lined him to his waist with a fifteen-foot length of rope to keep him from wandering off and breaking his neck.

A week had passed since they came on the looted ville and the mass grave. A week of walking, first in the wheel ruts of the presumed chillers to the ville of Perdition, then overland to try to intersect the path of the already departed convoy. In that time, Doc hadn't improved, and J.B. still towed him, out of duty and friendship.

The peeling sweat on J.B.'s face cut stripes of clean skin through the caked yellow grime; his wire-rimmed spectacles were smeared with a mixture of both. The stocky man wore his precious fedora hat screwed down on his head as he strained forward. Seeing the determination on his face made a flicker of a smile cross Ryan's lips. He had known John Barrymore Dix since their wild and woolly days with the legendary Trader. J.B. had been that operation's Armorer, a nickname that had stuck. They were best friends then, as now.

J.B. never said he was sorry when he wasn't.

And he never gave up.

As Dr. Theophilus Algernon Tanner was dragged along, he railed at a god who was either absent, or oblivious, or malevolent. Or some of each. Doc was an educated man. He used big words. Complicated arguments chased his thoughts, rather than vice versa, like angry wasps trapped inside his skull. He made leaps in logic, dropping out pivotal points, speaking from opposite points of view. At times he seemed to be taking on the persona of his own grand inquisitor.

The only companion with the background to unscramble his philosophical ravings was Mildred Wyeth, and she had long since given up the game. The solidly built black woman was a medical doctor, and aside from Doc, had the most formal education of any of them. She had been cryogenically frozen after a botched surgery just before skydark, and reanimated by Ryan and the others nearly a hundred years later.

Mildred's diagnosis of Doc's current condition

was grim. She had said his overwhelmed mind had twisted in on itself. Anger reflecting anger, which led to agonizing flashbacks, which reduced him to sobbing into his palms. The man was suffering from an unspeakable, unending ordeal—a price paid for no crime of his, other than the exquisite bliss of his former life. The life he had been born to live, and had been denied. In Mildred's medical opinion, Doc's rambling, often shouted, diatribes to imaginary gatherings of Oxford dons allowed him to flee the crushing reality of the present, where he was doomed to exist without his beloved wife and children.

Though Mildred sometimes acted as if she had little love for the old man, it was plain to Ryan that she found it hard to watch and be helpless to slow his further mental and physical disintegration.

The one-eyed man remained cautiously confident that Doc would come out of the tailspin eventually. As he always had before.

As they neared the ville entrance, Ryan saw a little girl in a loose-fitting, faded cotton print dress staring at them from inside the gate. A very pretty little girl with a headband of daisies. Her gaze swept past Ryan to rest upon Dean. The boy sensed he had a rapt audience of one. Though exhausted, he drew himself to his maximum height and flashed a smile at the girl. Ryan was amused to see that his son managed a bit of a manly swagger, with the 9 mm Browning Hi-Power blaster prominently strapped to his hip.

Krysty gave Ryan a nudge. "Like father, like son," she commented.

A trio of armed men in bill caps stood behind a pile of concrete boulders and rubble that served as both a checkpoint and traffic barrier. Beyond them, Ryan caught his first glimpse of Bullard ville: an oasis of brilliant green that sprouted miraculously from the sunbaked yellow earth. In rows of raised beds, under slanting, corrugated metal roofs, the crop plants grew lush and tall. On the far side of the beds, simmering in the valley heat, predark plastic-and-metal signs on tall poles dangled precariously above a line of low buildings.

"Man, oh, man, could I ever go for a cheese-burger and a strawberry shake," Mildred said.

Ryan grinned. "We'll be lucky to get a plate of beans and a swig of green beer."

"I know, I know. But a girl can still dream, can't she?"

As they stepped up to the checkpoint, one of the bill caps shouted in an unpleasantly high voice, "And just who might you folks be?" Without giving them time to answer, he asked a second question. "What is your business here?" The two other sentries held sawed-off, 12-gauge, double-barreled shotguns at waist height. The range was such that, by discharging all four stubby barrels at once, they could cut the strangers not so neatly in two.

Ryan showed the guards open hands. "We're just travelers on the long road north," he said. "Come to water and rest, and willing to pay for it."

The head sentry, a very short man with a full brown beard, gave them a hard once-over. He looked especially long at their complement of weapons, appraising them for possible threat and commercial value. When he came to Doc, he couldn't help but notice the slack rope that connected him around the waist to the man with the smeared eyeglasses.

"What's with the geezer?" the guard leader chirped. "He sick? He looks sick to me. He better not have the fucking oozies!"

Ryan and the companions knew he was referring to an incurable, mutated brain virus, much feared and believed to be transferred by cannibalism.

"He's just old," Krysty said. "Very, very old."

"Oughta leave him to meet his maker, then."

"Ain't his time, yet," Ryan said, the look on his face telling the guard to mind his own bastard business.

Unable to contain himself any longer, one of the shotgunners excitedly blurted out, "We got a carny come to town."

"That so?" J.B. said.

The sentries shared wide grins.

"Best rad-blasted carny in all the Deathlands," the head guard added. "Big show's tomorrow."

"We'll have to stick around, then," Ryan said. "Something like that you don't see every day."

"You'd better believe it," the shotgunner said. "Gert Wolfram's carny only plays the most important, big-time villes."

"You can stow your gear over where the carny is putting up camp," the head guard said. "As long as you got something to trade, you got the run of Bullard ville. There's food, water, joy juice and the best damn gaudy house this side of Perdition. When you run out of trade goods, we will escort you out of the berm. We don't give no charity here. And we don't take no guff from those who don't belong."

With that warning, the guards lowered their scatterguns and allowed the companions to enter Bullard ville.

Once inside, there was no mistaking the proposed campsite. Not with fifteen wags parked in a broad circle on the baked yellow dirt. On the side of the largest wag was a crudely painted sign that read Gert Wolfram's World Famous Carny Show. Lots of ville folks were standing around gawking while dozens of carny roustabouts worked to set up camp. The heavy protective tarps were pulled back from the trailered cages so the gawkers could see in. Only from a goodly distance, though. The newcomers appeared to have set up a kind of invisible perimeter that the ville folk weren't crossing. Mebbe they'd been warned to steer clear? Mebbe they didn't need to be.

As they approached the mob of spectators, a strange sound split the air. Two very loud tones, a high note sliding to low. Only Mildred made the connection to a foghorn; none of the others had ever heard one. To them it sounded like a baleful howl.

Beside Ryan, Jak cranked his head around and

stiffened, as if ten thousand volts had just shot through him. The youth's reaction surprised the one-eyed man. It was just an animal noise. A very large animal.

Before Ryan could raise a hand to stop him, the albino took off, running at full tilt for the cages. Some of the carny folk saw him coming and tried to block his way with widespread arms, but he feinted, swinging his white head one way, then squirted past them. Staring at his rapidly accelerating back, the empty-handed roustabouts yelled for someone to get him.

"Dark night," J.B. muttered, "we were supposed to go in nice and quiet, and recce first."

"Better back his play," Ryan said, waving the companions after him.

J.B. pulled Doc along like a stubborn calf.

Suddenly the howling got a whole lot louder, and it changed in timbre. Instead of coming from deep in a huge set of lungs, it came from high in the throat.

It went from misery to absolute joy.

Then it stopped altogether.

There was no one left to try to turn back the companions. All the carny folk had rushed over to one of the trailered cages.

And with good reason.

It appeared that the agile intruder was getting eaten alive.

Jak had his head stuck between the bars of the cage, holding on to them with both hands. For a split second, Ryan's heart dropped in his chest. He thought the young albino was a sure goner, his head half inside the great carnivore's open maw. But then he saw Jak wasn't getting chewed.

He was getting licked.

The mutie mountain lion's tongue slathered his face so hard that even holding on to the bars with all his might, Jak couldn't keep his boots on the ground.

The great cat made a loud purring sound, like a wag's big diesel engine fast idling, as it scrubbed the albino's face and neck with a wide pink tongue that had to be a foot and a half long.

"What the nuking hell?" J.B. exclaimed as he came to a stop beside his one-eyed friend.

"It's the lion, J.B.," Ryan said. "They've got the lion."

The companions—except Doc, who was still wearing the thousand-yard stare—needed no further explanation. Some time ago, Jak had been made a prisoner in Baron Willie Elijah's mutie zoo. He had been caged up with a mutie mountain lion. After an initial, violent and lengthy misunderstanding, the two had got on famously. They were both wild things, so well matched physically and spiritually that they could communicate without words, with their eyes and with touch. Brother beasts of the hellscape.

Once freed, the big lion hadn't run off, but had followed Jak and the companions. Only when it refused to enter a mat-trans unit was it left behind.

This, it seemed certain, was that selfsame noble beast.

"A captive again," Mildred said glumly.

"Unlucky," Krysty said.

"Mebbe," J.B. stated. "Mebbe not."

"What do you mean?" Krysty asked.

"Found Jak again, didn't he?"

"Step back from the cage, mutie," one of the roustabouts shouted as he shouldered up to the bars. He was a big, thick-bodied man with a heavy blue-black shadow of beard stubble, and matted black hair on the tops of his shoulders and the backs of his arms. He outweighed Jak by more than a hundred pounds.

The albino paid him no mind.

"I said, step back!"

With no one to stop them, the ville folk pressed forward for a good view of the action. The show was starting a day early.

Jak pulled his head out from between the bars but didn't move away. His fine, shoulder-length white hair was plastered to the side of his head.

"Let cat out," Jak said, his ruby-red eyes glittering.

"Yeah, right," the roustabout replied sarcastically.

Then he turned to address the gathered carny people. "Turn loose a thousand pounds of man-eater on your say-so."

This remark was met with peals of laughter from the ville and carny folk alike.

"Let him out," Jak repeated. His voice was flat, calm, controlled.

The smile melted off the hairy man's face.

"Get closer," Ryan told the others.

Even as they began to move, the hairy guy snarled, "You're begging for a major ass-kicking, Snowball." He looked around to make sure he had backup, then added, "And by skydark you're gonna get it!"

Before the hairy roustabout and his pals could take a step forward, the albino's right hand was up and full of .357 Magnum Colt Python. He showed them all the dark hole in the crowned muzzle, the hole where death slept, until called.

Jak spoke again. This time it wasn't a polite request; it was a threat. "Open cage now...."

Ryan lunged and used his momentum to throw a shoulder into the hairy man from behind. The blindsiding impact sent the roustabout stumbling to his knees, hard. He cursed as he immediately jumped back to his feet. He was very nimble for a big man.

In the next instant, weapons were out all around.

The carny folk waved nine mill semiauto blasters, mostly KG-99s and Llamas. Blue-steel, high-capacity cheapies, in excellent condition.

Ryan held his scoped Steyr SSG-70 rifle at waist height. Krysty had her Model 640 Smith & Wesson .38-caliber revolver in a double grip. Dean likewise braced his Hi-Power. Mildred one-handed her .38, a Czech-built, ZKR 551 target pistol. J.B. balanced his 12-gauge Smith & Wesson M-4000 pumpgun against his hip. Seeing the deadly turn of events, the ville gawkers turned and ran, scattering for the cover of the plant beds like so many jackrabbits.

The tense moment stretched on and on.

No one on either side wanted the shooting to start. They were standing way too close to each other to miss. Once the blasting began, there weren't going to be any survivors.

Nobody moved.

Nobody even blinked.

Then, from over by the circle of wags, someone shouted, "What in the rad-fucking-blazes is going on here?" A tall man in a red tailcoat stormed out of the side door of the biggest wag. At his side was a naked, three-foot-tall, immature stickie.

The tailcoated man and his little shadow slowed their charge as they approached the fracas.

With his KG-99's sights locked on Ryan's chest, the hairy roustabout explained the deadly stalemate. "Snowball there," he said out of the corner of his mouth, "wants us to let the nukin' lion out. Started waving his blaster in our faces."

As if it understood what the albino was trying to do, the mountain lion reached a huge paw between the bars and placed it lightly on his slim but powerful shoulder.

"Not gonna happen, son," the red-haired, red-goateed carny master told Jak. "That's one smart cat. The smartest, meanest, damnedest mountain cat in all of Deathlands. He's playing you for a triple stupe. Open that cage door and he'll gut you from windpipe to goobers with one swipe of that big old friendly paw of his. Then he'll carve up the rest of us, just for fun, before we can do jack shit about it. Same way he chilled three of my best handlers over the past two months. One second they were alive, and the next they were torn clean in half—legs here, the rest of them way the fuck over yonder.'' To illustrate, he gestured over his shoulder with a hooked thumb.

Ryan sidestepped over to Jak and whispered in his ear, ''It's not the time for this fight…we got other business first.''

The albino youth didn't give a flying fuck for the wishes of most other human beings, but he always paid close attention to Ryan Cawdor, whose battle smarts had never proved wrong, and whose courage never failed.

Ryan stared hard into the bloodred eyes and nodded, to underscore his point.

Jak smiled, then swung the ventrib sights of the Python across the chests of his adversaries, counting and marking targets, left to right. Prep for a rapid-fire, cylinder-emptying fusillade.

A visible shudder passed through the pack of roustabouts.

Having made his point, Jak holstered his blaster.

After a pause, all weapons were lowered.

''You ain't Gert Wolfram,'' J.B. said to the man in the tailcoat.

The baby stickie started making kissing sounds at the Armorer, who shifted and planted his back foot, bracing himself to swing up the shotgun and take the sucker-fisted squirt's spongy little head off at the neck.

"What makes you say that?" asked the carny master.

"Gert Wolfram is fat, fifty and fucked," J.B. replied. "Last time we saw him, he had two broken ankles and his stickie slaves were pulling him apart like a sweet dough pudding."

"Even if Wolfram survived the appetites of his pets," Mildred added, "he couldn't have lost twenty years in age, two hundred pounds in weight and gained six inches in height."

"You got me there," said the red-haired man with a disarming grin. "Actually I never claimed to be old Wolfram. People just assume that it's so. Sure doesn't hurt the business to let them keeping thinking that. I'm committed to keeping the show's original fine reputation. I'm called the Magnificent Crecca, for obvious reasons." He reached down to adjust the soft but prominent bulge in the front of his white pants. Then he leered at Krysty.

"Do we call you Magnificent, or just Crecca?" she asked.

"I answer to either, or to M.C., or carny master, or in your case—" he leaned closer to her to add "—to lover man."

Krysty's prehensile hair reacted to the unwanted advance, drawing up into tight coils.

Crecca's eyes widened when he saw this. "My, my," he said, "aren't you the special one?" He pulled at his chin beard, looked her up and down salaciously, then said, "Wonder what else you've got hidden away for me?"

Krysty put her hand on the butt of her wheelgun. "I've got six hollowpoints, all for you," she said, staring him down.

For a second Ryan thought things were going to escalate out of control again, but Crecca just looked amused. "I hope you're all going to be here tomorrow so you can see the carny show," he said. "You'll never forget it. I promise you that."

Neither will you, lover man, Ryan thought. Neither will you.

Chapter Three

"Ain't you never heard about the man with the black eye patch?"

From the luxury and comfort of an executive office chair bolted to the sheet metal floor—the rips in the brown leatherette on the arms, seat, and headrest repaired with overlapping strips of frayed duct tape—the Magnificent Crecca gestured impatiently for the big man breathing wolf-nasty in his face to take a step back. Something more easily ordered than obeyed.

Floor space in the carny master's cabin in the big wag was at a premium, largely because its side walls were lined with built-in, sway-proof racks and shelves. Jammed on these shelves were select items taken either in trade for performances, or looted after a mass chilling and burial. Among the more important trinkets were unfired, Brazilian-made handblasters still wrapped in their protective Cosmoline; several .223-caliber, full-auto, military carbines; a scoped Remington 700 longblaster; and factory-loaded ammo in their original metal boxes. There were tall bottles of the very best joy juice and plastic bags of uncut jolt. There were lidded glass jars packed with bright bits of jewelry and dozens of cardboard boxes full of single-serving-sized containers of predark candies. There was also a barely functioning mini-TV and VCR, a small number of video- and audio-tapes and a black boom box. The electricity to power the carny master's home entertainment center came from movable solar panels on the wag's roof.

Along the front wall, below the room's only decoration, a quartet of flyspotted, discolored, girly magazine centerfolds, was Crecca's narrow bunk. Jackson lay curled up in the corner in a nest of rags. A pale, sleeping pillbug. His choke collar was chained to an eyebolt in the wall. The cabin smelled strongly of unwashed male, cigar butts and paper-trained stickie.

Of course Crecca had heard about the man with the eye patch.

Every triple-stupe droolie who wasn't deaf had heard about him.

The gaudy houses up and down Deathlands were full of stories about that particular coldheart. About how he had run with Trader in the bad, bad old days. About how he had matured into a full-blown, human chilling machine. Norms. Muties. It didn't matter to him. Rumor had it, because of that rad-blasted single blue eye, he could only see things one way: his way. Not a man to cross, unless you were looking to book a quick ride on the last train west. More convincing than the always exaggerated whore-shack gossip, Crecca knew that even the Magus, Gert Wolfram's steel-eyed, half-mechanical former business partner, wanted no part of him.

Showing no emotion, the carny master said, "So, you think he's One Eye Cawdor?"

"Damn straight!" Furlong exclaimed. "Right down to the zigzag scar on his eyebrow where the knife cut took his peeper!"

His outburst disrupted the rhythmic, wet snoring coming from the corner behind him. Furlong jerked his head around at the sound of chain rustling on the floor, making double-nuking-sure he was out of reach of the little stickie's needle teeth and sucker fists. The relief on his face when he turned back was almost comical.

Crecca had to admit that the latecomer fit Cawdor's description. "What would he want with us?" he asked.

"Mebbe he knows what we've been doing," Furlong suggested. "Mebbe he wants to take our booty."

"With a force of seven?" Crecca said incredulously, stroking his red chin beard. And seven was being real generous, considering one was old and brain-fucked, and another was so young his balls hadn't even dropped yet. On the other side, the carny master had a virtual miniarmy, fifty-nine-strong, all hand selected and personally trained by him, hardened, efficient chillers who took pride in their work.

Only one creature in all of Deathlands had the

power to make that bloodthirsty bunch wet their pants. And do his bidding.

The Magus.

The Magus had done things to people that gave even Crecca's chill crew wake-up-sweating nightmares. Things that made the objects of his unwanted attention squeal like pigs and offer their own children's lives in exchange for a quick and merciful death.

If the Magus had ever had an ounce of mercy in him, he had had it cut out a long time ago. Cut out and replaced with clockwork metal gears.

The new and improved carny operation was large scale, large profit and held together by fear and greed—the hellscape's twin wellsprings of motivation.

That someone was after the accumulated spoils of mass murder came as no surprise to the Magnificent Crecca. With a setup as sweet as this one, he'd known it had to happen, sooner or later. It had happened later rather than sooner due to the fact that Deathlands folk generally kept their heads down and minded their business. They had more than enough trouble just making it through another night, without looking for a little something extra that belonged to strangers.

"I think we ought to take them out tonight," Furlong said, his dark, close-set eyes eager beneath bristling black eyebrows. "I can send a couple of my best boys to chill them all while they're sleeping."

Being the head roustabout in the most famous

carny in Deathlands didn't require much in the way of smarts—just straightforward, dependable brutality. The Magnificent Crecca sometimes wondered if Furlong could tie his own bootlaces, or if he had to bully someone else into tying them for him.

For years prior to his promotion to carny master, Crecca had worked for the late Gert Wolfram, but never as a roustabout. He had been an advance scout and collector of specimens for the fat man's menagerie of living oddities. He trapped wild muties in the Darks, using rope snares or pitfalls. In and around the villes, he bought or kidnapped the tame ones. He'd find a particularly disgusting freak that he knew old Wolfram would like, then he'd shove a bag over its head and steal it from the bosom of its loving family. If the family caught him in the act and objected too strenuously, he chilled the whole lot of them. He was paid by the pound in those days. Wolfram had a thing about the size and weight of his attractions, said "the big uns" drew better crowds—a rule of showmanship that the new carny master still followed. While on the road, Crecca often had to force-feed his severely depressed captives at blasterpoint to maintain their redemption value. If they still wouldn't take nourishment, he ditched them to make room for more profitable cargo. Dumped them in the middle of nowhere to starve or be eaten. Their lives weren't worth the price of a centerfire bullet or the trouble of resharpening a bone-nicked knife blade.

"What are you going to do with the bodies afterward?" Crecca asked his head roustabout.

"Drag the pieces of shit outside the berm and bury 'em on the plain."

"And tomorrow morning nobody's going to notice seven people who upped and vanished?"

Furlong shrugged. "Somebody might notice, but there'd be no proof, so what could they do?"

"What if one of them yells out as your boys attack or gets hold of a blaster? What then?"

Furlong was silent under knit brows, straining to come up with a good answer. He might as well have been trying to explain gravity. But he was too stupid to see the futility of the effort.

"Bullard ville's gonna be the best pickings we ever had," Crecca told him. "If we try anything on One-Eye and his crew and it goes sour, it will queer the whole deal. And I won't risk that."

The hairy man started to restate his case for a surgical strike, but Crecca cut him off. "Do nothing," he said. "Do absolutely fucking nothing. Understand?"

It took a long moment for this to sink in, but Furlong finally, reluctantly nodded.

"Get out," Crecca said, dismissing him with a wave of his hand.

After Furlong left, the carny master assured himself that even if One-Eye had come to pay them a visit, that even if he knew about the spoils of mass murder, it didn't matter. Cawdor didn't know how the chilling was done. He couldn't know because there had never been a single survivor left to tell the tale. Cawdor and his six fellow travelers would die like dogs along with the rest of the Bullard ville hayseeds.

Crecca twisted the ends of his goatee into a point. It was too bad about the bitch, though. Her mutation—the squirming strands of flame-red hair—wasn't flashy enough for her to make a sideshow attraction, but she had real potential as a sex slave. Ah, well, the carny master thought, sex slaves, even ones with legs as long as hers, could be had anywhere.

He reached in his tailcoat side pocket and took out a small beige cardboard box. On the box were printed the words Choco Duds. He shook a few of the predark candies onto his palm. They looked like ossified rat turds. Their milk-chocolate coating had crystallized to a floury white. More than a century of storage had turned once soft caramel centers to amber glass, unchewable by norm teeth and jaws.

Crecca flicked one of the Choco Duds across the cabin. It hit Jackson on the cheek with an audible whack. The stickie's eyes popped open at once. It sniffed the air, mewled in delight, then rooted in the heap of rags until it found the treat.

Jackson had no trouble eating the pellet. The dead eyes begged for more.

"First we've got work to do," Crecca said, getting up from his chair. He put a videocassette in the player and powered up the TV.

Jackson watched his every move with rapt attention.

Loud, hard-driving, backbeat-heavy music erupted from the speakers, and bright colors and dancing females appeared on the screen. Crecca fell into step with the lead singer-dancer—a dewy-eyed, teenage blonde with a bare midriff—and her troupe of four bare-bellied dancers. Their moves were complex and violent. And there wasn't much room to work. Tails of red satin coat flapping, the carny master pivoted left and spin-kicked right.

"Come on, Jackson," he called, teasing the creature with the offer of another treat. "Let's go!"

The stickie began to follow along with its master. Singing, sort of. Unable to precisely vocalize the new words, which dealt with virginal angst, Jackson soprano-droned along with the video's megastar. Dancing, sort of. The stickie waved its spindly arms, snapped and ground its narrow hips, a hair behind the beat.

"Good stickie," he said, smacking the creature on the forehead with another well-aimed Choco Dud.

It was part of the Magnificent Crecca's job, and the real, chilling-robbing operation's cover, to keep audiences in the larger villes coming back every time the company circuited through Deathlands. This required the invention of new and ever more spellbinding acts. The carny master's latest idea for a big-top finale was an all-stickie rock-dance number, with music and routines lifted from the video, and Jackson singing and dancing in drag—long blond wig, bare belly, tight miniskirt. As a Tiffany-imitator, the stickie had a long, long way to go.

"That's okay, Jackson," Crecca said patiently, after the little creature's spin move went awry, and it crashed into the wall. "Let's take it from the top...."

Chapter Four

The Clobbering Chair smiled and waved at Baron Kerr, beckoning him to come sit. To take the load off.

The plain piece of metal office furniture stood in the middle of the ville's tiny, pounded-dirt, central square. It had been dragged out of the low blockhouse across the way. Leather straps hung from the armrests and looped around its front legs. Leaning against its back was a club made of three and a half feet of heavy iron pipe, one end wrapped with strips of rag to form a handle.

For a shimmering instant, the baron could see a smiling victim seated there. A smiling executioner, standing behind, club in hand. A smiling audience surrounding all, patiently waiting its turn.

Baron Kerr had long since given up trying to keep the faces of any of them separated. For him the individual members of the army of the dead blurred into one another, and into the few still living, who were just as eager as those who had gone before to feel the weight of the falling club.

Kerr never had visions of the ghosts of those carted up to the pool, quarter sawn and chucked in. But often, living people appeared to him—indeed, everything that he saw, heard, touched, tasted and felt—as puffs of colored smoke rising up in front of a wall of infinite blackness. At other times, the baron experienced just the opposite perception, that everything that existed was unified, a universe-spanning, living singularity that invaded and permeated the void like the tendrils of a rad cancer. When in this latter mode, as he was now, the clear divisions between objects, the boundaries between animate and inanimate, between human and tree and stone no longer existed.

He dimly remembered that there had been a time—or he imagined that he dimly remembered—when his perception of things had been different, when he was someone else, somewhere else. Though the details were beyond him, he could recall that creatures like those of the pool and surrounding woods hadn't always spoken to him in his own language, and that the earth and water and sky hadn't always heaved and shuddered with stirrings only he could see and understand.

The world, itself, hadn't always been entirely alive.

The pale-yellow snow of spore fall, as fine as table salt, lay in scattered drifts as Kerr trudged across the square, toward the dirt-floor shacks and lean-tos built against the outer wall of the blockhouse. A half-dozen people stood around a fifty-five-gallon fire drum, watching their dinner cook on a red hot steel grate. One of them turned over the sizzling, pale, roast-shaped blob with a sharp-pointed

stick. The baron's grimy, raggedy, bright-eyed subjects all grinned and nodded a subservient greeting
to him as he passed.

Kerr didn't acknowledge their presence. He
walked down the short, narrow flight of concrete
stairs to the below-ground-level blockhouse entrance. The door, a massive, welded-steel bulkhead,
had been twisted and wrenched away from the frame
by crowbar and chisel. Scraped back on its sprung
hinges, it no longer closed; it had never closed for
as long as Kerr had been resident royalty in the
blockhouse palace.

Though there were no windows, it wasn't dark
inside. Greenish light coruscated from the beads of
condensation sweat on the concrete-block walls. It
glowed from the accumulated puddles along the
floor seam of the central hallway. Most of the acous-
tic tile ceiling lay scattered about on the floor. The
low ceiling's fluorescent light fixtures dangled lopsidedly from rusting chains and rotten wires.

Four of the seven small rooms off the main corridor were packed with squat, yellow-enameled, in-
operative machines of unknown function. These machines were lagbolted into the floor. Thick nests of
pipes of varying diameters fed into and out of them,
and vanished into holes cut into the block. Dials and
gauges with cracked faces and missing indicators
dotted the walls of these rooms.

Kerr's quarters were in the largest of the blockhouse's three offices. He made his baronial bunk on
the gray plastic laminated top of the built-in desk

that ran the full length of the back wall. His pallet was a duct-tape-patched, flaccid, plaid-flannel-lined Coleman sleeping bag that hadn't been cleaned since skydark. The work space's computers, printers and monitors had been pushed off onto the floor and left there in a shattered heap.

Though the building looked like a pump house complex connected to the shallow lake on the mountain ledge above, it had been much more than that. The baron couldn't read a lick, but even he realized the framed diplomas and certificates screwed into the walls of the offices meant whitecoats had worked there. Heavy-duty whitecoats. And the machines and electronic gear and miles of perforated computer spreadsheet covered with rows of numerical data meant government research jack. The bales of used printout paper were just about gone. For many years, the ville residents had used sheets of it to start their cook fires. Because of this, the site's original purpose would probably always remain a mystery.

The baron hung his straw cowboy hat on a wall hook next to the neatly arranged predark fishing gear he had found in a metal cupboard. He figured it had belonged to one of the whitecoats. Rods. Reels. Aluminum boxes of tiny flies. Wiped down. Oiled. Polished. Cased. They were the only items in the place so meticulously tended.

His evening meal had already been set out on a crude wooden platter on the end of the desk. The mound of sliced, roasted fungus was crispy and brown on the outside and still white, creamy, almost molten in the center. From it arose a delicious and intoxicating smell of cardamom and cinnamon spice.

Kerr wasn't hungry, but he ate. He ate every bite. And as he ate, he looked down at himself from somewhere near the ceiling, watching as his body satisfied the hunger that wasn't his own. It was eating of the body by the body—its flesh, his flesh, inseparable.

After he was done, he felt the familiar weight of exhaustion descend, infiltrating his limbs, his torso and finally his brain. On the desktop, his sleeping bag quivered in anticipation of holding him. The surrounding walls of concrete block maintained their slow, steady breathing. Kerr let himself fall back onto the pallet, and there began to weep. Tears spilled out from under his wraparound sunglasses and trickled into the edges of his beard. Overhead, the partially collapsed ceiling flinched and grimaced in sympathy.

If the baron, too, yearned to sit in the Clobbering Chair, he had learned long ago that the burning pool would never let him. Of all those it had drawn unto itself, he was different.

Chosen.

Pampered.

Held apart.

For reasons that were unfathomable, James Kerr had been made baron of an ever changing, joyous, obedient flock that was oblivious to its cruel poverty, its physical suffering and the absolute certainty of its doom.

There was nothing his subjects wouldn't do for him.

Except chill him.

And for as long as he could remember, that was all he had ever wanted.

Chapter Five

Ryan and the companions laid down their packs and bedrolls in the slanting shade of one of plant bed awnings, a good distance from the carny's campsite. Doc knelt on the ground, tethered by his waist to one of the awning's support posts. The old man's eyes were vacant, and his fingers raked furrows in the yellow dirt. As Ryan watched him, he felt a growing sadness in his heart. If the old man didn't snap out of his stupor, there would come a time for a mercy chilling. And he would have to be the one to do it. It was his responsibility as the undeclared leader of this group of friends.

A sound from the circled wags behind them made Ryan look over his shoulder. Blocked from view by the angle of its cage and trailer, the lion began to yowl mournfully—strange, high-pitched, flutelike noises.

Ryan glanced at Jak, and his stomach tightened into a hard knot. The albino was staring in the direction of the mutie cat. He stood flat-footed and rigid. The sinewy muscles in his dead-white, bare upper arms twitched from the strain; his hands were clenched into fists. The shock of each piercing cry rippled through his whipcord body like a wave.

Ryan sensed that if the tension wasn't released, and quickly, his young friend was going to shake apart.

"I go…" Jak announced to no one in particular.

With that, he loped away from the companions, crossing the pounded dirt in long, easy strides, making for the ville's defensive perimeter. When he reached it, the slope didn't slow him. The sun flashed once on his mane of white hair as he disappeared over the top of the berm.

"What's with him?" Mildred said in dismay. "Where's he off to now?"

Ryan shrugged as he smoothed out his bedroll and carefully set down the Steyr SSG-70. "Got some private business to attend to, I guess."

"Are we going to have trouble with Jak?" Mildred asked him point-blank, hands braced on her sturdy hips. "Is he going to lose it on us? Has he already lost it? That's the last thing we need."

"Mildred, keep in mind that Jak has saved your life more than once," Krysty cautioned her.

"And vice versa," the black woman replied. "Jak and that mutie mountain lion have a connection that's downright spooky. It's been so long since we parted ways with that horn-necked monster, I'd almost forgotten just how spooky. It reminds me of the psychological case studies I've read about the psychic bonds between human twins. Only in this case it involves creatures of very different species. It isn't natural, Krysty. It doesn't make sense, biologically or physiologically."

"You're talking like a whitecoat."

"I can't help that," Mildred said. "I was trained to think like a scientist. And the scientist in me says, we have no way of predicting with any sort of confidence what Jak is going to do next. Think about it. We no more than got inside the berm and he had us facing off against a dozen blasters...all over that mutie cat."

"She's right about the trouble," J.B. told Ryan as he took off his glasses and polished the lenses with the hem of his shirt. "The big question is, can Jak keep to the plan we made? Or is he going to blow it for all of us by trying to get that critter out of its cage?"

"As it stands," Mildred added, "this whole deal is balanced on a knife edge."

J.B. nodded in agreement. He slipped his glasses back on. "Every one of those carny chillers over there has a centerfire blaster," he said. "The odds were bastard bad even before we lost Doc. If the rest of us aren't at one hundred percent, and on the same page, we don't have a chance in hell here. We're all gonna end up in a shallow hole with dirt in our faces. Mebbe the smart thing would be to slip over there once it gets dark and put a slug in the back of that big cat's head."

"Jak won't let us down," Ryan said with conviction. "He never has and he never will. He knows what we have to do, and why." The hard edge to his voice said for the time being the discussion was over.

Inside, Ryan was as concerned as Mildred and

J.B., and for the same reasons, but he couldn't show it. His confidence had to shore up theirs; it was a simple matter of survival. He had to be the calm in the eye of the storm.

He sat cross-legged on his bedroll and with a scrap of lightly oiled rag began to brush the dust from the scope and action of his treasured predark longblaster. In silence, the others started going through the contents of their packs, sorting and gradually assembling a small pile of trade items so they could all eat and drink at the ville's hostelries.

Ryan's hands moved over the rifle automatically, his fingers programmed by countless repetitions of the same vital task. Trader had taught him that a fully functioning weapon was the difference between being dead and cold by the side of the road, and walking on. As he worked, Ryan thought about their long journey, about how they had followed the wheel tracks from the looted hamlet to Perdition ville. The trail ended on the outskirts of Perdition where they found a wide circle of deep holes pounded into the ground, holes made by carny tent's massive stakes. Exactly the same circle they had found in the looted ville.

From a stooped old man poking around in the pile of worthless, half-burned trash the show had left behind, the companions had learned that the Gert Wolfram show had spent three days and nights entertaining the good folks of Perdition. The trash picker had described the strange and wonderful acts, the rousing music, the feats of strength and daring.

There had been a terrible joy and satisfaction in his rheumy eyes as he told them about his favorite part of the show: the part where the two-headed scalie ate a live goat from both ends at once.

Legs first.

If the troupe hadn't stopped over for those extra days, Ryan and the companions never would have caught up to them. The question was, why were the folks of Perdition still breathing air, and not buried in a ditch?

Compared to the unnamed ville where the mass chilling had been done, Perdition was a major metropolis. Which led Ryan to speculate that mebbe it was just too big for the chillers to tackle, and that's why they had left it alone. Or mebbe they just skipped some villes along their route to throw any possible pursuit off the track.

The carny's performance schedule had been posted on the side of a fire-gutted, semitrailer near the circle of tent holes. It turned out that the circus company was heading to a large ville several days southwest of Perdition before moving up the long, dry valley to an engagement at another big hamlet at its northern end.

The companions had taken the difficult, cross-country shortcut to try to intersect the caravan's route. The hills and mountains that framed the dry valley were impassable by wags; once the carny entered at the southern end, the only exit was far to the north. When Ryan and the others had seen the towering spirals of dust in the distance, they knew they had found their quarry.

By the time Ryan had finished detailing his long-blaster, the mound of trade goods on Mildred's bed-roll had grown impressively. She had put in a few .38-caliber cartridges. J.B. had added two empty mags and a minitoolkit for an M-16—a weapon they didn't carry. Krysty had tossed in a pair of compact binocs with a cracked left lens, and Dean had given up a plastic-handled can opener that was near mint.

J.B. scowled at the carny's circled wags and said, "Mebbe the Magus himself is hiding over there. Like a nasty old spider, waiting for the fun to begin."

"Be just like him," Krysty said. "Crouching in the deep shadows while his puppets do all the dirty work."

"The Magus may not have anything to do with the carny anymore," Ryan said. "Not since Wolfram went west."

"From what it looks like the carny is doing," J.B. said, "it seems right up his street to me."

"Mebbe," Ryan said. "But looting the odd, shit-poor ville would be a big step down for him. The Magus has always been into mass slavery of muties and norms, mostly to support his mining operations and his jolt factories, but also for breeding stock."

The companions all knew the Magus was into animal husbandry. He specialized in the careful cross-breeding, and perhaps bioengineering, of new mutie races. Rumors abounded that he had "made" the first stickies. It was also rumored that he had acquired the power to travel forward and backward in time. That he had done evil deeds long before any person now alive had been born, and would do evil long after they were dust.

Deathlands was a place of little certain truth and much wild speculation. The only thing anybody knew for sure was that the Magus was a league of chiller above and beyond the run-of-the-mill, gaudy house backstabber.

"He's back!" Dean exclaimed, pointing at the berm gate. "Jak's back."

The albino trotted across the compound at the same easy pace. Over his shoulder, its short front and long back legs trussed, was a skinned, dressed-out, thirty-pound mutie jackrabbit.

There had been no gunshot echo rolling over the valley. Ryan figured Jak had used one of the many leaf-bladed throwing knives hidden on his person to dispatch the rabbit.

"Why did he bring us dinner?" Dean asked his father. "I thought we were going to eat at the gaudy?"

The lion let out a blood-curdling roar that put an end to conversation.

It became clear that it wasn't their dinner the albino had brought when he turned hard left and made a beeline for the row of trailered cages. Ignoring the crudely lettered Danger: Don't Feed The Muties sign, Jak passed the fresh carcass through the bars to his brother beast.

The mountain ate the offering greedily, crunching up the bones with no more effort than he used to chew the flesh. A thirty-pound jackrabbit was a mere snack for an animal his size—it was gone in a few seconds. But it had to have been mighty tasty if the diesel-wag purring noise the cat made as it licked the blood from its huge paws was any measure.

"Say, Dean," Ryan said, nudging his transfixed son with a gentle elbow. "I think someone's trying to catch your eye...."

Dean turned to look. Instantly, a wide smile lit up his face.

Standing at the far end of the plant bed was a sun-browned little girl in a too big cotton dress with a crown of daisies in her golden-streaked brown hair. She smiled back at him, tooth for gleaming white tooth.

Chapter Six

"My name's Leeloo. What's yours?"

The twelve-year-old boy beamed down at her. "Dean," he said.

"That's a great blaster you've got, Dean."

He glanced at the blue-steel weapon strapped to his hip. "It's a 15-shot, nine mill Browning. Want to hold it?"

Leeloo nodded enthusiastically.

Dean dumped the staggered-row magazine onto his palm. Then he cracked back and checked the breech for a chambered round. After making sure the weapon was safe, without a second thought, he handed over what she knew had to be his most prized possession in all the world.

Leeloo very carefully took the Browning Hi-Power from him and held it in both hands, making a shaky, wavering attempt to aim. "Oh," she said in dismay, "it's heavier than I thought."

Dean stepped around behind her and helped her raise the blaster to firing position. "You want to hold it about here," he said.

Something new happened to Leeloo Bunny as young Dean reached his arms around her, enfolding her. In kindness. She felt suddenly safe and protected; she felt the urge to lean back against his chest, to feel the strength and the energy he gave off.

It was an urge she didn't allow herself to give in to.

With great patience, Dean showed her how to work the Hi-Power's safety. He made her adjust her stance to brace herself for the recoil. And he showed her how to hold her finger outside the trigger guard until she was ready to fire.

Nobody had given her any blaster training before. And certainly not with such a sophisticated and deadly predark weapon. She wasn't old enough. Dean Cawdor, whose long, dark hair tickled the back of her neck as he leaned over her, thought she was. He cocked back the hammer with his thumb and told her to dry-fire the Browning.

"Go ahead," he said, "squeeze the trigger."

The firing pin made a twig-snap sound.

"Does it make a lot of noise when it really shoots?" she asked him.

"Sure does."

He took back the blaster, lowered the hammer with his thumb, put the safety on and reholstered it.

"My ma got chilled," Leeloo told him.

Dean looked at her for a long minute. She wasn't sure whether she had said something bad without meaning to. Something that would make him not like her anymore.

She was about to apologize when he said, "Mine,

too. She died of cancer. She was sick a long time. What happened to your ma?''

''My ma got choked in the gaudy while she was wrestling.''

''Wrestling?'' Dean said, puzzled.

''On the bed.''

''Oh,'' Dean said.

Leeloo stared at him closely, and as if she could read his mind—or heart—said, ''Did your ma wrestle in the gaudies, too?''

''Sometimes,'' the dark-haired boy said, staring down at his dusty boot tops. Though his lips moved, his face was expressionless. ''But only when we didn't have anything to eat, or nowhere safe to sleep. She was so pretty she could always find work in a gaudy.''

''They strung up the geezer who chilled my mom,'' Leeloo told him. ''I saw them do the whole thing. They yanked his pants down first. When his neck broke, it made a loud crack and his willy stuck out, like in wrestling. One time, before they cut him down, I clonked it good with a rock.''

''What about your dad?'' Dean asked.

''Never had one that I know of. You're lucky 'cause you've got one. And a good one, too. I can see that from the way he looks out for you.''

''Who takes care of you, then?''

''Fat Melchior, the headman of the ville. He took me in after Ma got chilled.''

''Is he nice to you?''

''Sure. But there's not enough nice to go around.

He has too many other kids of his own and the cabin is small.''

''You sound sad, Leeloo. Are you sad a lot?''

''I try not to be. I do things that make me happy, mostly by myself.''

''Me, too,'' Dean said. ''I like scouting ahead for the others when we're on the move. Jak, he's the one with the white hair, he's teaching me how to read signs. He doesn't say much, but I think I'm starting to get good at it.''

''You must have wonderful adventures with your dad and your friends. I'm still too young for adventures, I guess.''

''You'll have some, though. Mebbe even better ones.''

''Do you really think so?''

''I'm sure of it.''

From the other side of the compound came the sound of her name being called. ''Leeeee-looooo Bunny!''

''Dinnertime,'' she said, destroyed at the prospect of being pulled away from something so exciting and extraordinary by something so boring and ordinary.

''You'd better go, then,'' he told her. ''Don't want to be late, not with all those other kids at the table. You won't get anything to eat.''

''Are you staying for the carny?'' she asked him.

''Sure.''

''Then mebbe I'll see you tomorrow?''

He smiled at her. "Of course," he said. "I'll look for you in the morning."

With a totally mystifying combination of pain and joy sitting upon her heart, Leeloo Bunny descended the berm. She had never had a crush on a boy before. Had never wanted to kiss a boy before. In part, this was due to the awakening of her physical self; in part it was due to the fact that none of the ville boys interested her in the least. And for good reason. After watching the goings-on through the gaudy windows, the older ones got all panting and grabby handed, trying to insinuate their dirty fingers into very private places. Other girls in the ville, some even younger than Leeloo, let them do that, and more. Not Leeloo, though. The younger boys in Bullard ville were even more dismal crush prospects. They all had snot caked on their cheeks, and their breath smelled like creamed corn.

When she got back to Fat Melchior's cabin, the chaos of dinner for ten was well under way. She didn't compete for food, hardly ate any to speak of, and later, when she finally curled up on her tiny cot, she found she couldn't sleep a wink. And the cause, strangely enough, wasn't her excitement over the carny.

Chapter Seven

With Jackson trotting at the heels of his jackboots, the Magnificent Crecca headed back to the rear of the big wag, down the narrow, windowless, low-ceilinged corridor.

As the carny master approached the closed metal door at the far end, he felt a wave of the familiar, powerful unease he always felt just before entering the Magus's lair. Gert Wolfram had been afraid of the Magus, too. At the time, Crecca had thought it hysterically funny to see that huge mountain of blubber tiptoeing around, trying to avoid even the most incidental contact. Wolfram had never shown his fear to the Magus's face, if what he had could even be called a face—more like the jumbled contents of butcher and machine shop trash cans. The Magus loved to induce terror. And when he saw its first tender sprout, he nourished it and made it grow.

Crecca was much more comfortable when the puppet master wasn't along for the ride. The carny picked him up and dropped him off at different locations on the route. No explanation was ever given. They never knew where he went or how he got back. All they knew was that he was privy to ultrasecret, predark whitecoat technology, and that he had developed some unique refinements of his own.

The Magus had a distinctly unpleasant smell. Crecca had always figured it had something to do with the unnatural combination of flesh and stainless steel. The worst thing by far, though, were the eyes. Like a pair of chromed hen's eggs, with pinhole pupils. You could never tell for sure what they were looking at.

Crecca ordered Jackson to sit and stay outside the door. The Magus had been known to bite the heads off baby stickies on a whim, and Crecca had put in far too much time on this one to start over. He raised his balled fist and pounded on the door.

"Come!" said a strange, thready voice from the other side.

When Crecca entered the wag's rear salon, he was slammed by the odor of machine oil, fried brake linings and spilled blood. The dim, smoky room was surrounded by one-way, blasterproof, glass windows. It was five times the size of his cabin, and it had a hundred times more junk in it. Unsorted junk. Littering the floor were piles of gears, pipe, wire, housings, glass beakers, lamps, conduit, parts of wag engines and computer motherboards. Sitting on the salon's built-in rear-window sofa was living nightmare cast in decaying flesh and stainless-steel struts.

One of the rules of survival with the Magus was to not let him catch you staring.

Crecca tugged hard at his red chin beard, pretending to study with interest the vivisection that had been left abandoned on a crude wooden table. It was impossible to tell whether the half-dissected body was norm or mutie, as its layers of skin and muscle were now peeled back and tacked down to the tabletop, exposing a great yawning hole in the middle of its chest, lungs that still labored, a heart that still beat desperately.

"What do you want?" the Magus demanded. "As you can see, I am fully occupied at present." He was screwing together a contraption made of plastic tubing and metal fittings. He kept turning the thing over in his hands, then holding it up to the gaping chest as if measuring its fit.

What the gizmo's angles and ridges might do inside that tortured anatomy the carny master had no clue. He shifted his boot soles and felt the stickiness underfoot. Gear grease or guts, he couldn't tell. Crecca cleared his throat before he spoke, afraid his voice might break. "I just wanted to let you know that the valve problem on the canisters has been repaired," he said. "It was a rubber gasket that failed. We jury-rigged replacements. You said you wanted to be kept informed."

The Magus got up from the sofa. Lurching forward on knee joints made of Teflon and titanium, he wasn't a pretty sight.

Even though the carny master knew that to turn and run would have meant the end of him, it took every ounce of nerve to stand his ground. And as the creature clicked past him, he couldn't help but let go a sigh of relief.

The Magus had to have heard the exhalation.

He stopped in midstep, his head rotating as if on massive ball-bearing swivels, his eyes spearing the carny master's very soul.

Crecca opened his mouth, but no sound came forth. All he could see was the pupil holes in the chrome eggs narrowing to tiny pinpoints. He felt as if he were falling into them, drawn down as if by a whirlpool into spinning metal blades.

"So One-Eye has come for the world-famous show, has he?" the Magus said. "And brought his spawn to see it, too? How very, very convenient for me. To finally dispense with both the infuriating cyclops of a father and the annoying simp of a son. Poof!"

Crecca said nothing.

"Make sure he gets a good seat," the Magus ordered. "Make sure his son is sitting beside him. And make sure they don't get out of the tent."

"Of course, Magus."

"Death comes to all of us," the Magus said brightly as he moved to the dissection table. "Well, most of us, anyway." Then he threw back his head and made a noise.

Because Crecca had been the creature's pawn for so long, he recognized the racket as laughter and stifled the urge to cover his ears. To anyone else, it would have sounded like a wag engine throwing a piston rod—shrieking, clanking, before rattling to a stop.

The Magus reached a steel-claw hand into the chest cavity and took hold of the beating heart.

"This ville is fat and ripe for the plucking," the Magus said, weighing the pound of wet muscle on his palm. "There can be no mistakes."

Crecca nodded.

"Mistakes will be costly."

To prove his point, the Magus crushed the heart in his fist, making hot blood squirt in all directions. The body made a grunting noise, then its heels began to drum on the tabletop. Working in an absolute frenzy, the Magus fit the plastic-metal contraption into the ravaged chest. Muttering to himself, he seized a soldering iron and plunged the red-hot tip into the cavity. The smell of scorched flesh and burning plastic billowed from the gash.

He had no more time for carny masters, or canisters.

As the Magus began to hum—not from his throat, as a flesh-and-blood person might do, but from his round, spider belly—Crecca carefully and quietly backed over the piles of junk and out of the room.

As soon as he shut the door, Jackson jumped up and started licking the spatters of blood from the toe of his boot. Still a bit dazed, Crecca watched the little monster feed for several moments before backhanding it hard against the wall. Jackson ended up on its butt on the floor, face slack, vacant eyes slowly blinking.

Stickies had to be treated with firmness, and all instructions had to be repeated countless times before they sank in. Crecca was in charge of when, how and what Jackson ate. Left to its own primal instincts, the immature mutie would have chewed right through the tip of the boot, and once it tasted his blood, Crecca would have had to put a slug in its head to stop the chomping jaws and needle teeth.

Safely back in his own quarters, the carny master rushed to a waiting jar of joy juice and had a long, steadying pull. It was only then that he realized he had crapped himself.

Chapter Eight

Ryan and the companions were among the throng of ville folk watching the roustabouts lay out rolled sections of the big tent on the ground. Predark music blared from a row of black speakers on the roof of one of the wags. It was the same raucous show tune Ryan and the others had marched to the day before.

The head roustabout shouted orders over the insistent drumbeat. One of his men made measurements using a long piece of chain bolted to a stake that had been driven into the yellow dirt. The fixed length of this device allowed him to draw a great circle. As he moved the chain around the center-stake, at even intervals he tapped in perimeter stakes. When the floor plan had been laid out, two other men began digging a narrow, deep hole at the midpoint to act as a footing for the tent's main upright support.

When this was done, the roustabouts hauled the tent sections into final position, like the spokes of a wheel, and began snapping them together and folding the double, overlapping seams. From the strain and sweat on their faces, the rolls were very heavy.

In a matter of minutes, the big tent began to take shape on the ground. Easily two hundred feet across, it was striped in gay red and white, and made of some heavily coated fabric.

The cheery music and the festive colors made Ryan's skin crawl and his trigger finger itch. As did the expressions of delight he saw on the faces of the onlookers.

Like lambs led to slaughter.

Ryan was by no means a do-gooder, and life in Deathlands was survival of the fittest. But some things just had to come to a stop.

A worker with a wheelbarrow passed out tent stakes to men who waited at the perimeter markers with sledgehammers. The thick, cylindrical metal spikes were almost four feet long. The roustabouts grunted and swung in time to the music. The twenty-pound heads of their hammers sent showers of sparks flying as they slammed the spikes deep into the earth. When the broad ring of side stakes was set, ropes were tied, loosely connecting them to the tent's lower wall. A seventy-five-foot-long steel pole, also made up in shorter sections, was assembled, then eight men crawled inside the flattened bag with it.

At the hairy roustabout's direction, a heavy rope was attached to the tent's peak. A dozen workers then yarded it over the top of the tallest wag as the men inside the tent angled up the center pole in a series of steps timed to the music's beat.

The crowd of bystanders sent up a wild cheer as the pole's butt slipped into place and the tent was finally raised. Red-and-white pennants on the peak of the roof and around the top of the side wall hung down limply in the still, already scorching air.

"There's only the one exit," J.B. said to Ryan. "And no window vents that I can see."

"It's like we thought," the one-eyed man said. "Whatever it is that they're doing to folks, it all happens inside the tent."

"And nobody's getting out," Krysty added.

"From the looks of the fabric," Mildred said, "the tent could be a Kevlar weave, or something like it. But with a plasticized coating on the outside. If it is made of Kevlar, even blaster slugs won't tear it. With those double seams, it's got to be virtually airtight."

"A candy-striped, portable death house," Krysty said softly.

"All the evidence we've seen points to an inhalant," Mildred went on. "They've got to be using some kind of poison gas."

"Mebbe we don't want to go in there, Dad," Dean said, his voice tight with concern.

"The boy's right," J.B. said. "Once we're inside that tent, we're trapped along with everybody else."

Ryan grimaced. They had gotten themselves in a bind; that was for sure. But it wasn't unexpected. They had known that once they entered the ville, circumstances would be fluid. That whatever plan they had hatched over the long march might have to be thrown out.

A key part of it already had.

The original idea had been to take out some of

the chillers in the night, using their knives to quietly reduce the odds. But once they were on-site in Bullard ville it became clear that plan wouldn't work. For one thing, the caged sideshow muties acted like an army of watchdogs, alerting the carny folk with squeals and bellows when anyone approached their circled wags. For another, the dispatched roustabouts would have been missed on the work crews that morning. Search parties would have been sent out. Perhaps the shallow graves would have been discovered. Either way, the companions' hands would have been tipped. Outnumbered as they were, without the element of surprise, they had no chance at all.

Having caught up with the traveling troupe at last, and having gathered a sense of the people involved, Ryan had no doubt that it was the carny doing the mass chilling. The moment he had looked into the Magnificent Crecca's eyes, all other possibilities vanished.

To loot an entire ville down to the pots, pans and shoelaces called for manpower, which the carny had. To loot an entire ville required heavy-duty transportation for all the stolen goods. The only tracks of sufficient number and size leading from the place had belonged to the carny. To chill that many people at once called for confinement, isolation, no escape.

Which the tent provided.

After they had examined the bodies in the unnamed ville, Mildred had guessed that a poison had been used, but she couldn't tell what kind or how it had been administered. Though some of the victims had been shot in the head, most had no evidence of wounds. The bullet holes were either mercy shots or the result of a pack of chillers taking random target practice on a pile of corpses. It made sense that the lethal weapon would be a gas, although where it came from and how it was delivered was still a puzzle.

There was, of course, also still the possibility that the carny would just do its show and move on, without chilling anyone. As it had done in Perdition, and elsewhere.

Ryan thought this outcome was unlikely, as did the other companions. Bullard ville was made-to-order for another mass wipeout. It was isolated. It was unknown, except for being an established water stop along a very long, very dry road. If all the residents vanished overnight, the travelers up and down the valley would just conclude that the water supply had finally dried up, forcing folks to abandon their huts and disperse. No one would care one way or the other. No one would look any deeper.

Once more, Ryan took in the excited faces of the crowd. It wasn't just made up of kids, but people of all ages, and the leaders of the ville, too. Dirt farmers, cooks, housewives and sluts had deserted their work in order to gawk at the wonder of Wolfram's World Famous Carny. Their rapt expressions said this was the biggest thing to ever hit Bullard ville.

Unless something was done, it was also probably going to be the last thing to ever hit Bullard ville.

"We've got to go in," Ryan told the others. "We've got no choice. We've got to go in with everyone else, just like nothing's up. It's the only way to make sure we get everyone out alive. We've got to keep a low profile until the time comes to make our move."

"If we wait just a tetch too long, Ryan, things could get bastard ugly in a hurry," the Armorer said.

For a long moment there was silence between them.

The silence indicated a mutual understanding of the situation, and a mutual consent to proceed as exactly as Ryan suggested.

It was only broken when Dean looked around, and said, "Where's Jak?"

OUT OF THE COMPANIONS' direct view, around the curve of the sideshow trailers, Jak once again had his head thrust through the bars of the mountain lion's cage. Once again that great, hot tongue lovingly washed his face and neck.

The pale, ruby-eyed youth had few words to describe even the simplest moments of his violent and tragic life. For Jak, things were good or they were bad. He was happy or he wasn't. Hungry or not. Loaded or reloading. The complexity of his feelings at that moment was impossible to translate into a neat, black-white duality.

Only the lion understood what he felt.

And that was because he and the lion shared. Everything.

Without words.

Jak pushed back from the bars and wiped the viscous slobber from his cheek with the back of his forearm. He took in the enormity of dense, soft, beige fur; the long, lashing tail as big around as his bicep; the fat, black-fringed ears, rounded beautifully at the tips. Jutting from the sides of the creature's massive neck was the pair of curving, pointed horns that served to protect the throat against attack from the sides, and as offensive weapons. The canine fangs exposed by the lion's wide grin were longer than the blade of Ryan's panga; the lion's claws were cruel black gut hooks, fully extended in pleasure now, cutting shallow, bright grooves into the steel floor of its cage. The smell of meat breath and musk gusted over Jak's face.

He couldn't explain how the creature's thoughts and emotions came into his head, or how he knew that likewise the lion experienced what he experienced. It was as if an invisible tunnel connected them, and through the tunnel ran a torrent of exquisite tenderness.

The albino gripped the bars again and stared into the beast's huge, pleasure-slitted, yellow eyes. The sound of its purring rattled the steel in his hands like an earthquake. The tremendous heat given off by its body blasted him like a black basalt boulder sitting in the midday sun.

You free soon, he thought. Then we hunt.

Jak's mind was slammed with gratitude and joy,

and then a caress, a voiceless voice, a soundless sound that resonated in the very pit of his stomach: I know you will free me, Little Brother. I know you will.

Chapter Nine

After the companions' meeting broke up, Dean went
looking for Leeloo Bunny. He found her standing in
front of one of the trailered sideshow cages.

"Hi, Leeloo," he said as he walked up.

"Hi, Dean." From the light in her eyes, she
seemed real glad to see him. She had put a crown
of fresh daisies in her shining hair.

"What're you doing?" he asked.

"Just looking at this one," she said.

The painted nameplate on the bars read Baldoona,
The Two-Headed Scalie. The male mutie inside the
cage sported a pair of heads that sprouted side by
side in the middle of its wide shoulders. Shoulders
that seemed to stoop from their combined weight.
One head was full-sized, as if from a grown-up person. It looked mebbe forty years of age. Its coarse,
gray-blond hair was matted and greasy, its face
florid, beardless and unlined. Bloodshot eyes glow-
ered at them from beneath a heavy, eyebrowless
ridge of bone.

The other head was a baby's, small, bald and
perched on a short neck. Its skin was flushed with
infantile frustration. The eyes on the little head were
black and glittered behind squinty, puffy eyelids.

The scalie was exhibited stripped to the waist. It had a massive torso, wide and thick, and there were big muscles under the layers of sagging fat. As it moved slightly, the angled light caught the rows of tiny scales that covered its skin, giving it an iridescent grayish cast.

The cage was fouled by the smell of urine and excrement; brown mounds of the latter lay clumped along the cage's rear wall. Clouds of flies buzzed amid the miasma.

"Do you think they like each other?" Leeloo asked Dean.

"You mean the two heads?"

"Uh-huh. They don't look like they like each other at all."

When Dean examined the creature more closely, he saw that it was true. The baby head was scowling. The normal head was scowling. And they were glancing sidelong at each other, out of the corners of their nearest eyes, which were separated by no more than eight inches.

"I wonder if they both get hungry at the same time?" he said. "Do you think if one head eats, the other one gets full?"

"If one has to pee, does the other one, too?" Leeloo added, grinning.

The adult head glared at her. "Pipsqueak gets hungry every four hours," it said, its voice deep and liquidy in the wide chest. "Wakes me up in the middle of the night with his squalling. And then thanks me by pissing and shitting in my pants. A pain in the ass that you wouldn't believe. I'd have had someone take an ax and chop him off me years ago, but the shock of doing that would chill me, too. Our nervous systems are all grown together.''

Dean and Leeloo stood there, flatfooted, stunned that the thing before them could actually talk and make sense.

"Close your mouths," it said. "You're going to catch flies…and you know where they've been."

When neither of the children said anything, the creature continued, ever more irritated. "What are you two looking so surprised for? Just because my captors keep me sitting in my own shit and feed me with a shovel, do you think I'm some kind of wild animal?" Baldoona held up its powerful but flab-encased arms and let the sunlight play and flash on the rows of tiny scales. "My brain isn't mutated," it said, "just my skin."

Dean couldn't help but glance at the baby head, which was like a huge, purpling mushroom springing from its shoulder.

The scalie noticed what he was looking at. "Of course there's the other head," it said, "but that's something that could have happened to anyone— even you—under the right conditions."

Dean wondered if Baldoona knew about the mass chilling. The only way it could keep from knowing was if the cage was covered up with a tarp during the murdering and burial.

As one of the roustabouts came down the line of

cages toward them, the scalie shut up and slumped into a sullen slouch.

"Keep a good ways back from them bars, you two," the carny man warned them. "That lizard-skinned piece of nukeshit ripped the arm off a kid in Perdition, sat there and ate it in front of the parents while the poor little critter bled himself to death."

Dean looked at the scalie, who shrugged sheepishly, as if to say, "Ah, well…there you go…."

After the roustabout had moved on, Leeloo said to the mutie, "You're a mean thing to have done that to a child. A cruel, mean thing."

"And your point is…?"

"Dean should put a nine mill in the middle of your big, ugly face. Not the baby's, though. It's kind of cute the way it fusses, and it can't talk."

The scalie's double sets of eyes turned on young Cawdor. It gripped the bars in both hands, and the adult head said, "Well, Deanie boy, you gonna do it, or what? Shit or get off the pot."

The baby head mewled along in high harmony, echoing the other head's sentiment, even if it didn't know how to form the words.

The mocking contempt in the mutie duet riled Dean in a big way. He didn't like the idea of being insulted, and definitely not in front of Leeloo Bunny.

Dean drew himself up to his full height, then brought the Hi-Power out of hip leather in a blue-steel blur. He raked the handblaster's fixed front sight across the scalie's exposed knuckles, making him yelp from both mouths and jump back to the rear of his cage, where he raged and hopped in pain, clutching his damaged hand.

The baby was still squealing as the adult head snarled at the top of its lungs, "I'll get you for that, you little bed wetter! See if I don't! I'll eat the flesh from your bones!"

"Shut up," Dean told him as he reholstered the Browning. "Can't you see you're scaring the baby head?"

"Yeah," Leeloo chimed in. Then she slipped her thin arm in his and said, "Come on, Dean, let's go look at some of the other cages."

Dean liked her a lot, he realized with a start. Not in a sexual way, but he liked how she looked at him. As if he were her hero. And she wasn't any sort of quivery-lower-lip girl, either. The kind who was afraid of spiders and sorrow. Leeloo was a little girl, but Dean could tell she was as hard as flint. And in a strange way, she reminded him of Krysty. It was something about her certainty, something in the way she carried herself. He could tell even now that she was going to grow up to be a stunningly beautiful woman. Strong. Proud. Compassionate. Honest. It made him feel absolutely wonderful to be looked up to by her. It made him want to protect her.

As they walked to the next cage, he started to think about the tent, and what was going to happen inside, and it made his face go dark with worry. He wanted to tell Leeloo to skip the performance altogether, to just go someplace out on the plain and hide there until it was over, but he knew he couldn't do it. Everything depended on secrecy and surprise. Though he instinctively trusted her with his life, he couldn't place the lives of the companions in her hands.

Which left him only one alternative.

"Where are you going to sit for the show?" he asked her.

"Dunno. Anywhere I can, I guess."

"Would you sit next to me and my dad if I asked you to?"

Leeloo's face lit up instantly. "Are you asking me?"

"Yes. I want to watch the show with you."

Though it seemed impossible before it happened, her face lit up even brighter. "That'll make it extra good," she said.

Chapter Ten

With both hands on the steering wheel, Azimuth wound out the Baja Bug on the long straightaway, loving the way the oversize off-road tires juddered, the vehicle's independent suspension gobbling up the ruined highway's ruts and rills. The engine howled at redline; in his rearview mirror was a wall of yellow dust. He had his APC-crew, polarized goggles up. The hot valley wind pressed against his face like the palm of a great gritty hand. Gobs of dried white spittle were stuck in the corners of his grinning mouth.

In his lap was a predark portable CD player, one of the perks of traveling with the carny; the headset earphones clamped down over his dreadlocks. His head juked and bobbed to Bob Marley's greatest hits. From playing the same compilation CD over and over, he had picked up some curious and archaic mannerisms of speech.

One of the best parts of Azimuth's scouting-advance-man job for Gert Wolfram's World Famous Carny was having plenty of wag fuel to burn in the Bug, no boss man hanging over his shoulder and the right to go as fast as he pleased. The other good parts happened when he arrived at the performance sites, where he was fed and liquored bastard well, and then fucked seven ways from Tuesday, all for free. This day, he was headed up valley, to Perdition's sister ville of Paradise at the northern end, where in two days the carny's next scheduled performance was to take place. Paradise was renowned for having the best gaudy sluts west of the Shens, both in terms of talent and raw enthusiasm.

Azimuth didn't see the rude barricade that completely blocked both sides of the road until he was almost on top of it. Made of a pile of broken chunks of concrete, it had a sign propped up in front of it.

"Fuckin' B!" he growled, taking his foot off the accelerator and locking up the brakes. As the Baja Bug slewed right, its rear end swinging out, he steered into the skid with one hand. With the other, he yanked the KG-99 handblaster from its leather scabbard under the dash.

The Bug was like an extension of his big, hard body. He could make it do whatever he wanted, whenever he wanted.

Clutch in, hard, shifter dropped into third gear, as smooth and silky as a gaudy house sex sandwich, clutch popped out.

Its engine screaming an octave above redline, the Baja Bug's nose dipped sickeningly from the sudden deceleration, and Azimuth's stomach likewise lurched forward.

With the blaster's vented barrel sleeve braced against the rim of the missing windshield, and the Wailers still wailing sweet and mellow in his head,

Azimuth howled at the male figure standing beside the sign, "Doan mess wid me, mon!" He brought the Bug to a sideways skidding stop right in front of the tall, bearded man in wraparound sunglasses and a tattered straw cowboy hat. The skid made the big knobby tires dig in, and sent a wall of dust flying over the lone sentinel, who neither backed away nor jumped aside.

Azimuth jerked down his goggles and ripped off his headset, holding the sights of the KG-99 on the man. He poked the weapon out the passenger door's windowless frame until the dust cleared. "What you up to, mon?!" he shouted. "What you fuckin' wid me road for?"

The man in the sunglasses and straw hat raised his empty hands and started to walk slowly toward the passenger door. The sign leaning against the barricade was a delaminating, irregular chunk of plywood, a painted arrow pointing to the right. "There's a problem up ahead," he said.

"There be a bigger problem right here, mon, if you doan clear me way, and quick like."

"Got cave-ins up ahead," the tall man said. "The old highway has been undermined by the river."

"Ain't no river here, mon."

"You can't see it anymore. It runs underground now, in some places right below the road. Up ahead, the flowing water has eroded all the earth from under the road metal. Just the thin skin of concrete is left. It won't take the weight of your wag. The road will fall out from under you, and you'll either die in the crash or drown as you drop in the river and get swept underground.''

"Fuckin' C!" Azimuth said, killing his engine and scrambling out the driver's door. He swung the handblaster up over the little wag's roof, and its welded-on bar of high-intensity floodlights, to keep the bearded guy covered as he moved for the front bumper. "Stay where you be, goddammit!"

He stormed over to the barricade and stared down the road, keeping the barrel of the KG-99 pointed at the sentinel's chest.

"I doan see no fuckin' holes, mon."

"Around the curve," the bearded man told him. "By the time you'd have made the turn, it'd would have been too late. You'll be rolling over rotten ground. We lost an entire caravan this morning. Eighteen people and five wags. Swallowed up and gone in the blink of an eye."

Azimuth looked at the man carefully for the first time. He noticed how gaunt his face was under the beard, and how even though the sunglasses completely hid his eyes, they couldn't hide the suffering he radiated. Perhaps from losing family and friends to the sinkholes. Despite this, the scout remained suspicious. It was his job.

"And you be in charge of warnin' people?" Azimuth asked dubiously. "You come from another planet, mon? Or mebbe you just lose your fuckin' mind?" He raised his left hand and pinched his index finger and thumb together. "I come dis close to chillin' you, mon."

"Someone had to mark the detour," the man in sunglasses said.

"Detour?"

He pointed to his left, to a two-rut track that ran perpendicular to the highway, leading off in the direction of the darkly forested, savage-looking mountains to the east.

"Looks like de wrong bloody way to me," Azimuth said. "And narrow as worm shit."

"The road loops up through the foothills and comes back to the highway on the other side of the cave-ins," the man said.

"Shit! I got me a whole damn carny mebbe a day behind on the road. Big wags. Trailers. Heavy loads. How dey gonna make it up dat pissy little track?"

"I'm no expert on that," the man said, "but I suppose it would depend on how good the drivers were. I'll tell you this, though, there's no turnarounds once you start up that way. You've got to go all the way to the end before you can come back."

"Fuckin' D!" Azimuth snarled as he lowered his weapon. Part of his responsibility as carny scout was to make sure the roads were passable for the convoy. The standard operating procedure in a detour situation like this, given the opportunity for ambush and robbery, was for him to leave a marker at the turnoff, which would indicate to those who followed that he had tested the alternate route, returned and marked it safe. Unknown to head roustabout Furlong and carny master Crecca, to increase his enjoyment of the many perks at the other end of the journey, what Azimuth actually did most of the time was to mark the route as safe, and if it wasn't, he would turn back and retrieve the sign.

When he leaned into the back seat of the Bug, Azimuth wasn't thinking about the potential risks to himself and his caravan. He had never heard of a problem along this stretch of road. The lack of water, the crushing heat, and the sheer distance kept organized chillers and robbers from setting up shop. And it would take a highly organized and large crew to threaten the carny. As he leaned into the back of the Bug, he was thinking about the various attractions of the Blue Moon gaudy in Paradise, and specifically a set of quadruplet sisters, aged nineteen, who worked in tag-team fashion, around the clock, until the customer cried for his or her uncle. On the Bug's floorboards was a collection of smooth, white quartzite rocks. He selected one of about three pounds and placed it at the foot of the barricade, next to the detour sign.

"What's that for?" the man in sunglasses asked him as he straightened.

"To let me people know I've gone ahead."

"How many folks are in the carny?"

"More dan sixty," Azimuth boasted. "And dat's widout countin' all de sideshow muties. It be de biggest damn carny in all de hellscape."

"Maybe I'll get a chance to see the show," the man said.

"You woan be disappointed, dats for sure," Azimuth said as he climbed back in the Bug's driver's seat.

Azimuth climbed back in the Bug and rescabbarded the KG-99. He cranked over the engine, then backed up to give himself room to make the right turn.

"Mebbe I'll see you den in Paradise," he shouted gleefully to the bearded man as he slowly drove past him. "Look me up at de Blue Moon gaudy. I be under a pile of blondes. Ha!"

The man just tipped the frayed brim of his cowboy hat in salute.

Azimuth pulled up his goggles and pulled on his headset as he rolled off the roadway and onto the track. He got the Bug into second gear, and had to keep it there as the trail wound back and forth through a series of tight switchbacks that climbed up and away from the predark interstate.

The bearded man hadn't been shitting him about there being no place to turn around.

Although the one-wag road was wide enough for even the biggest carny vehicle to pass, no way could even Azimuth back the Bug down it by himself. The turns were too tight and road's downward angle was too steep. Getting back down in reverse could be done, but it would take a very long time, at virtual crawl speed while men walking behind shouted directions for brakes and steering.

And if one of the wags in the line broke down, it would bottleneck the whole caravan.

Azimuth drove on doggedly, and didn't start to

get an antsy feeling until he was about half an hour from the highway, and he saw the lower fringe of the forest ahead. He stopped the Bug in the sunlight, set the parking brake, ripped off his headset and got out.

Above him were towering, densely packed coniferous trees. The two-rut track made a turn just inside the edge of the forest and vanished in among the shadows and the dark, massively thick trunks.

"Bloody hell!" he shouted up at the wall of trees.

When he turned around to look for the highway, he saw it was the thinnest of thin ribbons running down the middle of the valley.

"You'd best no be fuckin' wid ol' Azimuth, mon!" he roared in what he knew to be the general direction of the barricade and the bearded man. "'Cause I be backin' down dis bloody snail trail an' fuckin' wid you right back!"

Kicking at the dirt with his steel-toe-capped boot, he hopped back in the Bug and headed into the shadows. In order to see, he had to switch on his headlights and roof lights. The road continued to climb and twist and turn around the huge trunks. Occasionally low branches whipped across his empty windshield frame. So far there was no problem with getting the big wags up the road.

The question was, would it ever return to the interstate?

As he continued on, Azimuth kept thinking that on the next turn, the track would wind back on itself and start to descend, but it showed no inclination of doing anything of the sort.

"You be takin' me to da summit, you rat bastard!" he cried out the driver's door window frame.

Azimuth told himself if that was the case, he would go no farther than the crest of the mountain. And once there, by hook or by crook, he'd find a way to get the Bug's nose turned the way he'd come. And when he got back to the sign and the barricade, he would pick up the bloody three-pound marker rock and use it to bash in the bearded man's head.

It occurred to him that there were no animals in these woods. No birds. Not even bugs. The heat was smothering, and there didn't seem to be enough air to breathe. Beyond the range of his head- and floodlights was a wall of darkness. Then he saw sunlight breaking through ahead. The backlit trees sent a wave of relief passing through him.

"About bloody time!" he said.

When the Bug crested the top of a rise, it rolled into the open. Azimuth stopped the wag and got out. Just below him was a small lake, surrounded by a dead zone of stripped, barkless trees and muddy bank. On the hillside below the body of water, on a shelf of flat land, was a small ville.

There was plenty of room to turn down there.

And as he watched the jumble of shanties and lean-tos, he saw a few people moving in and out. Folks he could ask about the best way to get back to the highway.

Feeling much better, Azimuth put on the headset and drove down to the lake. He paused at the shoreline to lean out the driver's door and look over the placid water. The sky reflected in it without a ripple.

Then something caught his eye.

A quivering shadow.

At first he couldn't tell whether it was something in the water or something in the sky reflected by the water.

It was in the water.

The spot of darker color began to grow, and as it grew it bubbled and churned. Silvery bits, like tiny mirrors, started to rise from the water, forming a churning cloud. Then came the pale green lightning, shooting the wrong way, from the surface of the churning water to the underside of the cloud.

"I be damned," he said, unable to take his eyes off the phenomenon.

The cloud got larger and larger and the lightning became more and more violent. When the strange ministorm started to drift across the lake toward him, Azimuth decided he had seen enough.

Even as he reached for the parking brake, the first of the pale spores swept over the Bug, angling in through the glassless window frames. They made a rustling, scratchy sound as they rained down on the sheet metal.

Azimuth sniffed at the air, once, and it was all over. His brain exploded in vibrating waves of color, color so pure and so intense that it obliterated everything else. He couldn't feel his body, which had gone rigid with shock.

The carny scout sat there for the better part of ten minutes, his eyes rolled back in their sockets, quietly convulsing. Ten minutes, ten hours, ten years, the concept of passing time ceased to be part of his mental framework.

When the deluge of colors finally faded, Azimuth came to. Out the empty windshield frame he saw someone appear out of the twinkling cloud and the falling, fine, pale snow. The someone was walking toward him. He automatically started to reach for the KG-99, but it wasn't there anymore. In the scabbard, instead, was a tropical flower with heavy, waxy red petals, a golden stamen and a perfume so rich and heady it made his mouth water.

When he looked up from the dash, the approaching man was close enough to make out. A thin black man with a snake nest of dreads and a baggy, crocheted, red, yellow and green hat. He was smoking a fat, foot-long, ganja stogie. Azimuth madly scrabbled on the floorboards at his feet for the CD's protective case and, finding it, stared at its much faded color picture.

"Fucking Z!" he exclaimed, tearing off the headset. He hardly noticed that even without it, reggae music was still hard rocking inside his brain.

"What's shakin', mon?" Bob Marley asked, leaning his skinny elbows on the window frame of the driver's door.

"You are, mon. You are."

"Soon you be, too," Marley said, laughing as he took a tremendous pull on the stogie, and then blew a fog of thick ganja smoke straight into the carny scout's upturned face.

The hot smoke blinded him and made his eyes run with tears. Over the sound of his own strangled coughing, Azimuth clearly heard Bob Marley say, quite close to his ear, "You gon sit dere an' cry like a l'il girl, or come meet de fellas in de band?"

Chapter Eleven

The Magnificent Crecca chained Jackson to one of the tent's steel stakes, then raised a flap at the rear of the candy-striped enclosure and ducked under it. Before him was a short tunnel made of the same airtight fabric as the main tent. The passage ended in a flight of metal steps that led up to a door set in a sheet-steel wall. A heavy rubber gasket and metal plate sealed the seam between the wall and the edge of the tunnel.

As he mounted the steps, the carny master felt that special unease once again. Fighting back a combination of vertigo and nausea that accompanied absolute dread, he knocked twice on the door.

From the other side, the familiar, thready voice called for him to enter. Crecca opened the door and looked in on the Magus's private viewing box. The twelve-by-eight-foot room sat on a trailer inside the perimeter of the main tent. The box wall that faced the crowd was made of one-way mirror glass, painted around the edges of the frame with a scene of predark clowns and lion tamers. The center of the picture window was clear; beyond it, in the bright lights of the main tent's floods, the people of Bullard ville were filing in to their doom. Seated before the window in a fully reclined reclining chair, his metal-and-flesh legs comfortably crossed, was the steel-eyed monster.

"Don't just stand there," the Magus barked. "The light's ruining my view. Come in and close the door."

The carny master did as he was ordered. Being trapped in an airtight box with the creature was much, much worse than being in the same wag salon with him. The unusual smell given off by the Magus—scorched machine oil and fleshly decay—was a thousand times more concentrated. That, coupled with his proximity and the fact that there was nowhere to run, made Crecca go soft in the knees. Conscious of that fact that the last time he had been in the Magus's company his body had betrayed him, the carny master made an extra effort to maintain a tight sphincter.

On the other side of the mirror window, Ryan Cawdor and his party were being ushered down to the front row by a pair of nearly naked female roustabouts. There were no seats. The audience sat on plasticized tarps spread on the ground. This made the cleanup much easier. The red-haired beauty sat next to Cawdor. On his right sat his son and a young girl from the ville. Beside the girl was the albino, then the black woman, the man in the fedora and the old one.

The Magus swiveled in his recliner. As he turned to face Crecca, his wide smile, half white bone and half stainless steel, curdled the carny master's blood.

"I want this to be a very special performance," the Magus told him. "I want the entire crowd on its feet, cheering at the moment the lights go out and the music swells."

Crecca knew the Magus could see in the dark. He had had some kind of microminiature infrared sensors built into his steel eyes. So as not to miss a thing. Even the Magnificent Crecca, a born chiller, a leader of other chillers, a man who had personally opened the nozzles on the poison-gas canisters more than once, couldn't stand to watch the final agonies of so many. The times he had been forced to remain in the viewing box, to stand beside the laughing thing in the recliner, to wear a pair of predark, Soviet night-vision goggles, he had shut his eyes tight against the horror. Because of the goggles' lenses, the Magus couldn't see his lack of enthusiasm.

The carny master had often wondered about the source of the Magus's horrendous appetites, which were as much a mystery as everything else about him. Did they spring from his being able to move back and forth through time? A consequence of some expanded, vengeful-godlike perspective he had acquired? Or were they the result of a progressive dementia brought on by the physical changes of decades of such travel? And then again, Crecca knew, it was possible that they had nothing whatsoever to do with time jumping. But rather, with the replacement of his various human parts with gear boxes and servo mechanisms. It was possible that as the Magus became less human physically, he became less human spiritually.

That the creature demanded the carny audience always received a rocking good show before they were chilled was a case in point.

Crecca knew there was no strategic need for this deception, this extra effort on the part of his crew. As soon as all the residents were seated, the tent entrance could have been sealed and the gas released. No pain, no strain. But because the Magus understood, and it seemed to the carny master, even fed off the dark, dark energy of human despair, he insisted that the exits remain open, even though the rousties not involved in the show were already systematically looting the ville; he insisted that the crowd be lifted up to the heights of joy before being dropped into the abyss.

Only at the grand finale, when the floodlights in the tent suddenly went out, when the canisters were opened, when the center-ring performers made their hasty exits; only when Mozart's *Requiem* began to boom at deafening volume from dozens of surrounding speakers, would the stunned audience realize it was all a trap.

And that there was no way out.

With glee, the Magus rubbed his palms together, his steel fingers clicking like castanets. "Oh, this is going to be good," he said. "This is going to be very good."

Chapter Twelve

Leeloo Bunny looked up at Dean, who sat close beside her, cross-legged on the ground. As the carny folk rushed around making last minute checks of their equipment, the boy seemed to be scanning everything and everyone with those intense eyes of his. She sensed a coiled tightness in him that she didn't really understand and couldn't put a name to. His mood under the circumstances seemed strange to her, though. For sure, it wasn't the same wild excitement she felt in the big tent with the big show about to begin.

Dean caught her staring at him, and smiled.

Oh, my, she thought as her heart melted into a small, throbbing puddle in the center of her chest.

"Everything's going to be fine," he said.

Leeloo felt a twinge of confusion. Since when was there any question that things were going to be fine?

Then the recorded overture started up. Through surround speakers, "Tah-Rah-Rah-Boom-Ti-Ay" blared forth. No one in the audience knew the long history of the song, nor did anyone recognize this particular version as belonging to the Grateful Dead.

The red-haired carny master jumped over the low

bumper of the center ring and into the spotlight. Behind him trailed a naked baby stickie on a long chrome chain fastened to a choke collar.

"Huzzah!" the Magnificent Crecca shouted a greeting to the crowd, throwing his arms open wide. "Welcome, Bullard ville, to Gert Wolfram's World Famous Carny!"

The Dead's shambling, sour-note-filled opus swelled deafeningly, then faded to a whisper.

"This afternoon," the carny master went on, "you will be treated to miracles and wonderments beyond compare. You will experience sights and sounds that you will take with you to your graves. Bullard ville, I give you the Fearless Flying Stickies!" Music up. Through the tent's loudspeakers, a live-recorded Jerry Garcia noodled up the chromatic scale, more or less, while eight male stickies in a line crossed into the center ring. They were all naked, except for broad, limp, brightly colored plastic collars that draped over their shoulders, chests and backs. The stickies did three turns of the ring, high-stepping in unison, skinny arms pumping in unison, genitalia flopping in unison. While they were strutting, roustabouts lowered a trapeze bar from the tent's peak. It wasn't lowered very far—just enough to allow it to swing freely.

"What is that?" Leeloo asked Dean, pointing at the wheeled contraption being pushed forward from the wings by a half-dozen roustabouts.

"A cannon," Dean told her. When she still

looked puzzled, he added, "Like a giant longblaster. Shoots big slugs."

Not in this instance, it turned out.

The smallest of the eight stickies raced over to the muzzle and climbed down it, feet first. The music suddenly stopped and was replaced by a loud, recorded drumroll as the roustabouts used a handwheel to crank up and aim the barrel at the tent's peak.

"Should we do it?" the carny master asked the audience. "Should we blow the little mutie bastard straight to hell?"

The answer from the assembled residents of Bullard ville was a resounding "Yes!"

Leeloo flinched when the cannon roared and flashed. Out of a cloud of dense gray smoke shot the little stickie, its spindly arms thrust forward. The pale, living missile arced high in the air. When the stickie's sucker fingers made contact with the trapeze bar, they locked on. It hung suspended, seventy-five feet above the center ring.

"Hoopa!" the Magnificent Crecca said, again throwing his arms wide. "If one was fun, folks, how about three?"

Bullard ville was all for that.

As the trio of muties climbed, one by one, down the cannon barrel, packing themselves in on top of one another, the carny master baited the crowd. "I have to warn you, good people," he said, "this trick doesn't always come off exactly as planned. A little too much blaster powder. A bit of a breeze. Too much humidity in the air. Those of you sitting in the front row should be ready to move quickly if it starts to rain stickies.''

Leeloo flinched again when the cannon discharged. Even though she knew it was coming, she couldn't help herself; it was that loud. To her amazement, the three muties came out of the barrel in a living chain, the second and third stickies having fastened their sucker hands onto the pair of ankles in front of them. As the trio rocketed up into the air, the audience let out a single gasp.

It didn't look as if they were going to make it.

It looked as if they were going to come up mebbe a yard short.

But the lead stickie stretched and stretched and somehow made contact with the feet of the little one hanging from the bar, and then all four of them swung from the trapeze, connected at the ankles.

"Whew, close one!" Crecca proclaimed, flicking an imaginary drip of perspiration from his forehead. "Shall we go for four?"

The audience shouted its assent.

"Lower the sights," the carny master commanded his gun crew.

The remaining naked stickies scrambled down the still smoking barrel as the roustabouts changed the point of aim to the legs of the lowest of the four suspended muties, some fifty feet above the center ring.

Again, the cannon boomed and jolted, and another living chain of bodies vomited from its muzzle and hurtled toward the tent's peak. The crowd groaned in unison as the first stickie missed the legs of its target by a good five feet. The groan stretched on as the four-car, runaway mutie train arced past the steel tent pole and, veering off to the right, crashed sideways into the far wall of the tent. Still stuck together by sucker and secretion, the stickie quartet crashed in a heap on the ground. For a long moment, none of the muties moved. Then, one by one, they stirred, untangling and unsuckering themselves.

Stickies were bastard tough to chill.

A few in the Bullard ville audience—perhaps those who had lost loved ones to this particular subhuman species—actually booed the miraculous survival, but everyone else cheered the spectacle. Some folks rose to their feet to clap as the entire acrobatic troupe took their waggle-weenie bows in the spotlight.

As thrilled as Leeloo was by the performance, in the pit of her stomach was a small knot of dread. She couldn't tell if the cannon miss had been on purpose or not, but she thought it hadn't. And that gave her the distinct feeling that the outcomes of the carny's acts weren't set in stone. That anything at all could happen, at any time, this afternoon. It was scary, but the fear made it all the more exciting.

The carny master waved an arm toward the wings. Grunting from the strain, masked roustabouts pulled and pushed a trailer bearing a tarp-covered cage into the center ring. Alongside the trailer, four beautiful, long-legged women danced and mugged for the crowd. From the rear, their nearly invisible costumes made it look as if they were naked but for thigh-high, high-heeled, black leather boots.

"Lesser carnies drag around carloads of snakes," the Magnificent Crecca bellowed. "They brag about how many deadly reptiles they've got and expect you to part with your hard-earned jack. I'll tell you this for free. Numbers don't matter. It's size that counts. There's only one snake in this carny. It's been here since the very first ticket was sold. Bullard ville behold, Wolfram's Worm!"

The tarp was thrown back, revealing the twelve-foot-long, three-foot-wide mutie rattlesnake. Worm slithered into a vast, diamond-backed coil and, hissing like a volcanic steam vent, struck at the inside of the bars. At the impact, the cage rocked on its trailer. The snake's dripping fangs looked like a pair of back-curving, yellow scimitars jutting from its upper jawbone.

"The good thing about Worm," the carny master said as he jumped on the front edge of the trailer and tiptoed along it to the middle of the cage, "is that he only eats twice a month." He had to shout the last part over the buzzing roar made by the snake's huge rattles.

Leeloo sucked in and held her breath as Crecca took hold of the pin that held shut the cage door.

Everyone in the audience saw him grip the pin, and everyone knew what was going to happen next.

They couldn't believe their eyes, but they knew it was going to happen.

"The bad thing," the carny master said, "is that it's a week past his dinnertime."

With that, he jerked the pin from the hasp and leaped out of the way as the barred door swung open. Worm was a lot faster than he looked. He was out of the cage and on the ground before anyone could even scream.

Then everybody was screaming.

Bullard ville's mothers grabbed for their children; Bullard ville's menfolk went for their blasters.

The folks closest to the rear started to run for the exit.

Dean was up in the blink of an eye, thrusting his body between the huge snake and Leeloo. With his feet shoulder width apart, he held the cocked, nine mill Browning in both hands.

"Don't shoot!" the carny master yelled over the din. "Everyone stay right where you are! Stay where you are and no one will be hurt. Everything is under control. The snake charmers are in position."

With that, the recorded music changed to something slow and sinuous, flutes and drums, drums and flutes.

Even the spectators halfway out the door stopped and turned to look.

Leeloo grabbed hold of Dean's arm; she couldn't help it.

The four beautiful norm women had surrounded the giant rattler, which now sat coiled in the middle of the center ring, its yard of rattles raised, buzzing mightily, its flat boulder of a head shifting as it tasted the air with a black forked tongue as long as a bullwhip. The snake charmers never stopped moving, never gave Worm a solid target to lock on to.

Even so, perhaps out of anger and frustration, the snake struck anyway. It launched itself forward, mouth agape, hollow fangs oozing thick streamers of poison.

The charmer that Worm had targeted did a hip feint and reverse, and with long legs jumped well out of the way.

The crowd cheered the clean miss.

Worm regrouped in the center ring, rattles buzzing even louder. The four women then took turns rushing at the flat, scaly head, drawing gaping strikes, and as they dodged and ducked the fang points, gasps rose from the audience. If there was so much as a stumble, if there was the slightest hesitation, one of the lovely women was going to die before their eyes.

Every time the snake struck, it extended itself to its full length on the ground. As it lay outstretched, after a dozen or more futile launches, a pair of the charmers ran right up the middle of its back. The one in front held a contraption made of chain link and padlocks. Before the snake could draw its body back beneath itself, the women had their long legs astraddle its neck, and with their combined body weight drove its chin into the dirt.

The crowd jumped to its feet, cheering.

The charmer in front slipped the chain muzzle

over Worm's broad snout, the muscles in her back jumping as she dug her heels in the ground and hauled back hard to seat the device behind his eyes. She locked the muzzle in place and dismounted with a flourish, pirouetting away hand in hand with her sister charmer.

They got out of range just in time.

Unable to open its mouth and free its lethal weapons, Worm went crazy, rolling and thrashing like a flesh-and-blood cyclone. It took many minutes for this display of animal power and fury to wind down. When the great snake had finally exhausted itself, with help of four burly roustabouts, the charmers dragged the defeated Worm back to its cage by the tail.

As the cage rolled away, the carny master vaulted over the center ring's bumper and cried, ''Bring on the swampies!''

Leeloo had never seen a real swampie before, only heard tell. How dirty they were. How bad they smelled. How bastard mean they were. She was surprised at their small stature. They were heavily built for their size, though, with stout, stumpy legs, wide, blocky hips, stocky torsos, thick arms and hands, and big, bony heads. The weight of the bone of their foreheads and brows gave them all, male and female, a perpetually sour, scowling appearance.

Even as they tumbled and rolled around the ring to sprightly, upbeat music of clarinets and cymbals, there was nothing playful or lighthearted in their performance. Somersaults, cartwheels, handstands, headstands, mutie pyramids, all were delivered with the same dour distaste.

Crecca let the mirthless gamboling continue for a few more minutes, then stepped back into the center of the ring and waved his arms. The swampies stopped tumbling and circled around him. "Time for some juggling!" he announced. "Not red-hot coals. Not flaming torches. Not razor-sharp swords. But these…"

He held aloft in either hand a clutch of small, round, flat-black-painted metal objects.

"Frag grens," Leeloo said. "Those are frag grens."

"Probably not real, though," Dean told her.

As if the carny master had heard the words, he pulled the pin on one of the grens and lobbed the armed explosive toward the tent's only exit. The crowd ducked…as if ducking would do any good. A roustabout at the exit caught the grenade and pitched it outside.

"Three, two, one…" Crecca counted aloud.

The ground under Leeloo rocked from the explosion.

"Now, let's have some real fun," the carny master said. With that, he pulled the pin on a grenade, then tossed the gren one way and the pin the other. Swampies on the opposite sides of the circle caught the thrown objects. The one who'd grabbed the gren quickly flipped it to the one who had the pin. That swampie put the pin back in, disarming the explosive.

"Get the picture?" Crecca asked his audience. Then he started yanking pins and throwing the armed grens and pins around the circle. In a moment or two, all five were flying back and forth.

It made Leeloo dizzy to watch.

And she was plenty scared, too.

She was in the front row.

Everything was okay for a while, but when the juggling act fell apart, it did so on a grand scale. Somehow, all the pulled pins ended up on one side of the ring, and all the armed grens on the other, at the feet of a particularly grouchy-looking swampie.

He threw back his matted head and bawled, "Mama!"

All the grens all blew with a loud whack! Instead of steel splinters, multicolored confetti flew through the air, drifting down onto the audience.

When the crowd settled down, the Magnificent Crecca wound in the long chain that connected him to the baby stickie. He put the palm of his hand on the mutie's hairless head, and said, "Sing, Jackson!"

Once again, the little stickie opened its lipless mouth, and beautiful music rushed out. Every a cappella note was in perfect pitch. Every word of the predark song was perfectly clear, and it was all in English.

After the first couple of bars, Jackson had the whole audience locking arms and swaying along in time.

Leeloo and Dean swayed, too, arm in arm.

The music was lovely and haunting, but the lyrics puzzled Leeloo.

She knew what the color blue was, but she had no idea what was meant by a "bayou."

Chapter Thirteen

As the tent's house lights went up and the carny intermission began, Ryan rose to his feet, as did the other companions. So far, there were no obvious signs of danger, yet he could whiff it, like the scent of a miles-distant cook fire riding on the wind. Only about half of the carny folk were visible and directly involved in the performance.

What the rest of the chillers were doing he could only guess.

And when he studied the roustabouts as they stared at the milling audience of farmers and shop-keepers, he saw both contempt and glee on their faces. The carny folk thought they knew what was going to happen to every person inside the tent, and they delighted in that secret, terrible knowledge.

It didn't cross Ryan's mind to wonder how human beings could be so callous and so unfeeling. He had lived in Deathlands all his life; he had seen and done things nearly as bad as what was planned for Bullard ville. Because he'd been there, because he, too, had wallowed in it, he understood the place of manifest evil, the heart of darkness. The difference between Ryan Cawdor and the carny chillers was that he had found his moral center, his personal bedrock, and he wouldn't be budged from it. Not even in the face of ten to one odds. "As soon as the show starts," he told Krysty and Mildred, "move for the exit. No matter what else happens, you've got to keep it open."

"Got it," Mildred said.

Krysty nodded in agreement, then said, "There may be other escape routes for the carny folk. Secret ways out that we don't know about."

"Makes sense," Ryan agreed. "It means that you're going to have to clear the way inside and outside the tent. Otherwise, they'll just chill us with blasters as we come through the exit."

"Mebbe Jak should come with us, then?" Mildred suggested.

Ryan looked at the albino, who was staring in the direction of the lion's cage, which was outside the tent. "No," he said. "We're going to have our hands full in here when the shooting starts. Can't do the job with less than four blasters."

"Some of the ville folks aren't gonna make it to the exit," J.B. said softly. "One way or another, either from poison or stray slugs, innocent blood is gonna flow."

"Some is better than all," Krysty said.

"Way better," Mildred agreed.

As the theme music resumed, Ryan swept his one-eyed gaze over the assembled crowd, their joyful faces, their anticipation of even more spectacular events to come. As they took their seats on the ground, some glanced at the windowless, rubber-coated walls of the tent without really seeing them, without understanding the implications of ''airtight.'' They had no clue that this was meant to be their death chamber.

''Stay together,'' Ryan told Dean and the others. ''Stay together, stick to the plan, and we'll all get out.''

The Magnificent Crecca and his pet stickie once again entered the ring. ''I trust you all enjoyed our first act?'' he asked the seated mob.

Bullard ville applauded and whistled enthusiastically.

''Well, the second act of our show is even better. Without further ado, I give you the ever popular, always satisfying, Deathlands Last Man Standing! You all know the rules. No closed fists. No bared claws. And biting is optional.''

Over the years, Ryan and J.B. had seen versions of this particular entertainment many times before. Troupes of professional hand-to-hand fighters toured the larger gaudies along the main trade routes, giving exhibition bouts and offering paying spectators the chance to bet on the outcomes.

What made this particular bout different were the gene pools of the combatants who faced off. It wasn't norm against norm, as was usually the case in the gaudies. In Wolfram's carny, it was norm against mutie.

The first bout featured a giant of a man with a shaved head and spiraling, concentric brandings over his shoulders and upper back, the raised welts like an angry red shawl. His mutie opponent was a head shorter, but as powerfully built. He was completely hairless. Cascading down the back of his skull and along the ridge of his spine were thousands upon thousands of pale, six-inch-long, tentacle-like growths. This mane of flesh had erectile function, the individual, dermal villi moving in response to stimuli, rippling like a field of strange wheat.

Crecca gestured for the fighters to come together in the middle of the ring and shake hands. When they touched bare knuckles, the mutie's mane flared instantly upright, like a spiky sail.

Which made the crowd ooh and ahh.

The contest consisted of three rounds, the standard for Deathlands Last Man Standing fights. The first three-minute round was "contact optional," which meant that the fighters could move, feint and land open-handed blows whenever the opportunity presented itself. The second round was "contact mandatory." Which meant that each fighter could move at will, but had to match the other blow for blow or be disqualified. The last round was toe-to-toe, with no moving whatsoever. If one of the combatants shifted his feet as he struck, or was staggered as he and his opponent traded full-power, forehand and backhand bitch slaps, the contest was over.

The final round was always bloody, always ugly and always a big crowd pleaser.

This case was no different.

A minute and a half into the third round, both fighters' faces were drenched in gore from numerous shallow cuts on foreheads and cheekbones, their eyes swollen to slits. The bigger man seemed to have the upper hand, and was in fact grinning a wide, bloody-toothed grin as he smacked the mutie on the side of the head and made the creature's mixed spittle and gore erupt in a pink mist. The mutie's mane sagged lifelessly; his eyes were dull and vacant. It looked as if he was going down. The giant cocked back his arm for the finishing blow.

When the tables turned, they turned in an eye blink.

As the hand shot forward, the mutie's mane sprang fully erect. When the hand reached the target, the target had moved. Juking his head, the mutie caught the giant by the wrist and gave a perfectly timed pull, using the bigger man's weight and momentum against him. The norm lost his balance and stumbled forward.

Contest over.

Well, not quite.

As Crecca rushed up to declare the winner, the giant let out a furious growl and scrambled up from his knees. From his expression it was clear the rules were off the table. But before he could rise to his full height, the maned mutie landed a wicked, cracking elbow shot to the middle of his face, which sent the giant to the ground, hard on his butt. He sat there for an instant, fists clenched at his sides, face contorted, trying to keep from passing out. Trying and failing. He slumped to his back, his arms and legs spread wide, his mouth drooping open and drooling blood.

The two other matches that followed were cut from the same melodramatic cloth.

Powerful fighters.

Lots of blood.

Sore losers.

In the last bout, the sore loser chased the winner out of the tent swinging a length of heavy chain.

Ryan hardly noticed. His attention was elsewhere. Whenever a roustabout came or went, he tracked him or her to see what was being carried. Whenever a trailer moved in or out, he watched it closely. So far, everything that had come into the tent had gone out again.

Well, almost everything.

The only trailer that hadn't moved sat on the other side of the center ring. It had been there, in the same spot, when the companions had entered the tent—an oblong box on a wheeled bed, with a facing mirror wall on which was painted a mural of predark circus scenes.

When the competition ended, the carny master announced the next act. "Friends, prepare yourselves to witness the strangest thing you will ever see. Something so unusual, and so startling that I guarantee you will never forget it as long as you live." Then he waved to the wings and gave the order, "Roll in Baldoona."

The cage containing the two-headed scalie was dragged on its trailer into the center ring. When it was in position, one of the moving crew tossed Crecca a long, metal-tipped pike and he used it to viciously prod the great lump of scale-covered flab.

In outrage, Baldoona's heads snarled and squealed respectively.

"Bastard fat, isn't it?" Crecca said to the crowd. "And if you're all wondering how it got that way, you're all about to find out." He turned to the wings again and shouted, "Bring in his dinner!"

Two roustabouts trotted in a half-grown pig that weighed roughly one hundred pounds. It walked like a dog beside them, with a long, coiled leash of rope around its neck. The men used some kind of white grease from a tub to coat the pig's body head to foot, then they tied the end of the rope to a stake that had been pounded deep into the dirt. When they walked away, the pig tried to follow them, but was brought up short by the end of the rope.

"I don't want any of you to panic when we let out the scalie," the Magnificent Crecca told his audience. "Pig is its favorite food, so it won't pay you any mind until it's done. And there's another thing...old Baldoona knows there's a time limit." On cue, a pair of roustabouts carried what looked like a giant stopwatch to the tent pole and hung it from a hook there, in plain sight of all the seated spectators. Obviously predark, it had a black minute hand and a thin red hand that counted seconds.

"Baldoona has to catch and eat as much of the pig as it can before the clock's alarm goes off," Crecca continued. "Once the bell starts ringing, it knows it either steps away from the carcass, or it gets the shit kicked out of it by my rousties.''

With that the music swelled, a different theme now, a happy but tension-building, tick-tock song. One of the crew very carefully opened the scalie's cage door, and the carny master started the time clock.

There was much laughter and thigh slapping from the crowd as the obese mutie pursued the greased but tethered pig around the center ring. The act's opening antics were undeniably comical, but once Baldoona got a firm grip on the animal's left rear hock, things quickly took a turn in a different direction.

Some things are harder to watch than others.

Baldoona ate the pig from the feet up, its adult head attacking at the front, baby head working on the rear, both mutie mouths gobbling for all they were worth, with the pig shrieking like a steam whistle the whole time. It didn't stop shrieking until the adult head bit out its heart.

When Ryan looked over at his son, Dean was shielding the face of the little girl from the ville against his chest, a gentle hand resting on her slender shoulder. The boy wasn't looking at the macabre spectacle; he was glaring at the carny master.

A look that Ryan knew well.

It was his look. His legacy.

Cold fire.

The two-headed scalie, its faces, necks and massive, flabby chest smeared with gore, was threatened back into its cage by four roustabouts with clubs and the carny master with his long prod.

As Baldoona was rolled out, it gripped the bars in both hands and belched sonorously in defiance. Then another tarp-covered cage was rolled in.

"You all have heard the legend of the Wazl bird," Crecca said. "A ferocious mutie strain found only in the darkest, grimmest mires of Deathlands. Half crocodile, half condor. All chiller. The legend says the Wazl can't be tamed, can't be taught, can't be defeated. It lives only for the joy of tearing apart living flesh and drinking living blood. It drops out of the night sky like a meteor and takes the unwary from behind with talons and teeth. It is my honor and privilege, dear Bullard ville, to present to you, the Wazl!"

Crecca threw back the tarp, exposing a pair of huge, featherless bird creatures. Their bodies and wings were covered with what looked like thin, aged, well-tanned leather; their long, straight, reptilian beaks were lined with tight rows of serrated teeth; their tri-talons black and curving like great fish hooks. As the two creatures took in the crowd, and the crowd's fear, their eyes were full of savagery and insane fury.

First one of the muties opened its maw and let out a shrill, sawing cry, then both of them were doing it. The noise required no explanation from the carny master; its meaning passed through the ears and into the marrow.

It was the Wazls' call to taste blood.

A moment later, a large, strangely attired figure stepped into the center ring. A steel-mesh fencing mask concealed the man's face and head, his body was protected by a chain-mail suit, his hands and arms by mesh gauntlets. He wore a monumental black codpiece strapped to his hips.

Of all the bad ideas ever come to fruition, letting the Wazls out of their cage was right up there with the nukecaust.

But from what had gone before, Ryan knew, as did everyone else in the crowd, that that was exactly what was going to happen. The only question was, how? Six roustabouts used long metal poles to trap and pin the Wazls against the inside of the bars. The bird creatures' screams of outrage drowned out the music from the tent's speakers, and made many of the Bullard ville folk cover their ears with their hands. Once the Wazls were securely pinned, the cage door was opened and the man in the steel helmet and suit stepped inside.

The mutie birds wanted him.

They snapped their beaks and hissed in blood lust.

The man bent, spread his arms and took hold of the birds' ankles, trapping both feet of both birds in his gauntleted hands.

The Wazls didn't like that one bit, and it was all the roustabouts could do to keep them hard against the bars.

"Are you ready?" the Magnificent Crecca asked the man in the cage.

His reply was a nod.

"Then fly!" the carny master cried.

The instant the roustabouts let off the pressure on their prods, the two mutie avians exploded out the open cage door, their long, leathery wings snapping like unfurled sails caught in a shifting gale. Behind them came the man, out of the cage and into the air.

Chaos erupted inside the carny tent.

The Wazls shrieked even louder. Dragged down by their two-hundred-pound burden, they flew low and fast, circling the walls of the tent. The man's heels, as he was carried aloft, grazed the heads of the stunned spectators.

People screamed.

People threw themselves flat on the ground.

The lizard birds beat the air, raising clouds of dust from the dirt floor. As they flew, they tried to bite their rider, cocking their heads this way and that, looking for an opening to wound, to maim, to chill. The gauntlets protected the man's hands and arms, and the birds couldn't get at his head and continue to fly. Their instinct to fly away was stronger than their need to be rid of him.

Around and around, the three of them circled. Ryan marveled at the man's grip strength and stamina. They were all that kept the Wazls from feasting on the audience.

Gradually, the birds' frantic, sweeping spirals grew narrower and dropped in altitude. Their cries became desperate and despairing. As the man was borne around, his boot heels cut furrows in the dirt. When the Wazls were finally exhausted, they just dropped from the air, crash-landing in the center ring. The man took a hard landing, too, bouncing forward on his face and chest. He didn't loosen his grip, though.

Before the Wazls could recover from the impact, a dozen roustabouts set upon them with long poles and ropes, trussing their beaks and legs together, then carrying them on the poles back to their cage.

Their rider removed his steel mask and took a low bow.

The crowd jumped to its feet, cheering.

Amid the tumult, something on the far side of the center ring caught Ryan's eye. Something flashed behind the mirror wall of the facing trailer. And for a fraction of a second, the silver, reflective glass became vaguely, hazily transparent, as if through a pall of oily brown smoke.

Then it was over.

In that frozen moment Ryan glimpsed a ghostly figure, whose afterimage was burned deep into his brain. Spindly limbed. Slouching. Menacing. Even if he hadn't seen the glare of the light on the steel, he would have known who it was.

Chapter Fourteen

When the Magnificent Crecca opened the door to the Magus's private viewing booth, a crack of light from the tunnel speared the gloom, flaring off the wall of glass. Before the carny master could get the door shut behind him, the half-metal monster who was his lord and master snapped around in his recliner, steel eyes glaring.

"Sorry," Crecca said. His words hung in the air, the half-whispered apology unaccepted. He kicked himself for saying anything at all. Over the years he had learned that silence was always the best response. Contrite silence.

With the viewing booth's door closed and darkness surrounding them, the one-way mirror again became transparent from their direction.

"I see you brought your goggles, as I requested," the Magus said. "Go on, put them on."

Crecca hefted the massively overbuilt ComBloc infrared sensors by their wide head straps. They were powered by a radium battery, and came installed with a small warning plate in Russian that the carny master couldn't read. Translated, the warning said: Extreme Radiation Hazard. He placed the heavy instrument on top of his head, with the stubby

goggle lenses pointing up at the ceiling like ant-
ler buds.

On the other side of the glass, roustabouts were
pushing the Wazls' cage out of the tent. A moment
after they disappeared through the lone exit, another
trailer entered, this one tightly tarped over and
dragged forward by men in black masks that covered
their heads from crown to throat.

The masks protected them from the effects of a
chemical gas, the death-producing agent known as
Zyclon B.

How the Magus had discovered the stockpile of
lethal gas was unknown. Crecca presumed that he
had found the canisters during his wanderings back
and forth through the timescape. Somehow he had
arranged to steal it, and had left it in a place where
it could be recovered more than a century later.
There was no way to prove this, of course. However
the Magus had come by the information, he had led
the carny right to the burial spot.

The carny master watched the one-eyed man stare
at the cage and at the masked men pushing it. His
blood ran suddenly cold.

"He knows!" Crecca exclaimed. "Cawdor
knows!"

"Of course he knows," the Magus said, chuckling.

The noise grated on Crecca's nerves, like stripped
gears grinding.

"That doesn't worry you?"

"No," the Magus said, "it doesn't. What it does
is make what is about to happen all that much
sweeter. The one-eyed man knows, and there is ab-

solutely nothing he can do about it. Nothing he can do to save the good and innocent people of Bullard ville. Nothing he can do to save his traveling companions, his own son or even himself. Ryan Cawdor has a date with death today that he isn't going to miss." After a pause, the Magus said, "I hope you impressed on our looting teams the need for speed and selectivity."

"They know what to take, and they're already taking it," Crecca assured him. "By the time we're filling in the burial pit, they'll be done with the sacking, and all the booty will be safely packed away."

In the tent's center ring, one of the masked roustabouts loosened the edge of the tarp that covered the trailered cage. He ducked out of sight under the flap to open the nozzles of the pile of poison-gas canisters.

"Get ready to cut the lights and bring up the *Requiem*," the Magus told his carny master.

As Crecca reached for the switch box beside the door, the creature added a warning, "And if I catch you closing your eyes this time, I'll pluck them out and feed them to the Wazls."

On the other side of the center ring, at the front row of spectators, there was a blur of movement, then came star-burst muzzle-flashes and staccato blasterfire. Before the Magus could move from his recliner, the mirror glass wall before him exploded in a wild spray of bullets.

Crecca threw himself out the door and down the steps, nearly crushing Jackson, who sat chained to the foot of the rail.

Chapter Fifteen

At the signal from Ryan, Krysty and Mildred broke ranks from the cheering crowd and sprinted for the tent's exit, which was guarded by three big, bare-chested men in full-head, black masks. All three carried blue-steel 9 mm KG-99s on lanyards. As the two women bore down on the exit, one of the guards stepped up to meet them, his empty hands raised with palms out, pressing forward.

A slow-down-and-stop gesture.

Mebbe because of the mask's narrow eye slits, mebbe because he was looking at Krysty's long, scissoring legs, mebbe because he had started to take the outcome of these special performances for granted, the roustie didn't notice what she had in her right hand until it was too late.

As she charged, Krysty raised the short barrel of the .38-caliber Smith & Wesson and pointed it between his hairy pecs, straight at his heart.

The Model 640 cracked twice, and the man staggered backward, fingers clutching frantically at his chest as if trying plug up the small, dark holes to keep the gout of blood inside.

Behind him, the other masked men were already untying the flaps of the exit, getting ready to seal the death chamber nice and tight. The sounds of the blastershots made them freeze. Blastershots weren't part of the show, not until later when there would be a few survivors to dispatch.

As Krysty vaulted the masked man's slumping form, a blaze of blasterfire erupted from near the center ring. Blasterfire and breaking glass. The flurry of rounds could have been either Ryan or Dean, or both. The baritone boom-boom-boom was definitely J.B.'s pump shotgun, and the mind-numbing roar of Jak's .357 Magnum blaster was likewise unmistakable.

Mildred had meanwhile dropped to one knee. With her gun hand braced, she squeezed off two groups of two shots, quick but well aimed. The first pair of jacketed .38 slugs caught the guard on the left just under the point of his chin, and turned him. He twisted sideways into the tent wall and, leaning against it, hands to his throat, slid to the ground, kicking and jerking.

The second guard was already moving, already halfway out the exit, when Mildred brought her Czech target pistol's sights to bear. The first shot hit him in the left shoulder; the second smacked into the tent fabric.

It plucked mightily at the rubberized cloth, but made no through-and-through hole.

As she had thought, it was Kevlar.

By the time Mildred was up and running, Krysty was already at the exit. They both knew they had to control the way out, and they had to control it now.

There would be no second chance. Their commitment to the task at hand was total. Without slowing, without considering what might have been waiting for her on the other side, the redhead dived through the opening, hitting the ground in a low shoulder roll, and came up kneeling with her blaster tracking in the direction the wounded roustie had fled.

He wasn't moving very fast, and his left shoulder hung down like the broken wing of a bird. He had his blaster clutched in his good hand. Hidden around the curve of the tent in the direction he was going were the circled carny wags. Reinforcements.

Krysty didn't hesitate. She shot him in the back once, below the shoulder blade. A clean chill shot, right through the center of the heart. He fell on his face in the dirt and didn't move again.

From inside the tent came the sound of a raging gun battle, a battle sawing back and forth, and people screaming.

As Mildred and Krysty knelt beside the opening, the folks of Bullard ville started spilling out into the daylight, their eyes wide with terror.

They didn't understand what was going on, what had been about to happen to them, how close they had come to horrible death. All they knew was that some strangers in the audience had opened fire on the carny crew, and that the crew had returned the favor.

And that they were caught in the middle.

THE MOMENT RYAN SAW the men in the black, hoodlike masks enter the tent, he knew the waiting was finally over and the time for action had come. He knew because he'd personally looted antichem warfare gear from stockpiles when he was traveling with Trader.

When push came to shove, there wasn't all that much you could do to disguise a mil-spec gas mask.

Ryan glanced over at J.B., who was looking at him. The Armorer knew, too. He had seen it at the same instant Ryan had. He put his hand on Jak's shoulder and the albino nodded.

Dean noticed this gesture and response, and immediately looked up at his dad, concern on his face. Ryan gave him a smile, which the boy instantly returned. Whatever happened next was in speed of hand, and in the hand of fate.

And what flowed between father and son in that second before battle was wider than the widest river. A great, brawling planet and its circling, perfect moon.

There was no reason not to smile.

He who had everything, who wanted nothing, had nothing to fear.

When the tarp-covered cage was in the center of the ring, one of the masked rousties loosened a tie-down, raised the edge of the tarp and ducked his head and shoulders under it. The other masked men waited, their arms crossed over their chests, for him to finish.

The Bullard ville audience waited for the Magnificent Crecca to reappear before them and in his dulcet tones to announce the next amazing act, to tear back the tarp and reveal the caged wonders concealed beneath.

In the trailered box on the other side of the ring, behind the wall of mirrored glass, a creature half of flesh, half of steel waited for his victims to start dying. Ryan Cawdor waited for no one.

With his shoulders squared on the chosen target, he cleared the SIG-Sauer P-226 from its holster.

A pair of .38-caliber blastershots popped from behind, from the direction of the tent's exit. The heads of the masked men in the center ring jerked around in surprise. At the same instant, the predark weapon in Ryan's fist bucked as it fired.

The bulge of tarp concealing the head and torso of the masked roustie took three tightly spaced rounds at its upper end. A millisecond later, the half-concealed man dropped out from under the flap, dropped as limp as jelly to his knees, and then fell forward. Inside the black hood that could fend off the terrible corrosive power of Zyclon B but that offered no protection from full metal jackets, what little remained of his head rested against the hub of the trailer's wheel.

Without pause, even as the last of the trio of 9 mm slugs thumped flesh and bone, Ryan swung his aimpoint and to the right and fired repeatedly.

As fast as he could pull the trigger, he poured round after round into the front of the mirrored box, hoping to nail the unspeakable spectator, the force behind the evil that was planned for Bullard ville.

The creature known as the Magus. Bullet holes stitched across the mirror's silver surface.

From across the center ring, the tiny dark holes looked like pinpricks. Pinpricks that cracked and crazed into each other, dropping and shattering huge pieces of glass.

Under his ravening fusillade, the entire mirror wall crashed from its frame, allowing him to see inside. Among the litter of silver shards, there was an overturned armchair, its backrest pocked with many slug holes, the stuffing blasted out the back in handfuls. The door to the rear of the viewing box stood open. No corpses littered the floor.

Beside him, the other companions opened fire, the din of the simultaneous shooting making his head reel. Dean had the little girl standing behind his back. She clung to his narrow hips as he blasted away, scattering the masked rousties. Jak bowled over one of the running men with his .357, sending him flying end over end.

The rousties were more disciplined than Ryan had figured. They didn't try to make a beeline for the exit, spraying random fire to clear the way. With their blasters out, they dashed behind the cover of the tarped trailer.

The plan was obvious: release the gas, chill the opposition and everyone else in the tent.

Ryan couldn't let that happen. He turned and shouted to the astonished audience, "Everybody out! Everybody out, now!"

J.B.'s scattergun roared, drowning out the one-eyed man's words before he could repeat them.

It didn't matter.

Bullets from the concealed roustabouts whined over his head. From the back of the crowd came a high, shrill cry of pain.

In seconds, the 150 or so residents of Bullard ville were madly stampeding for the exit.

Ryan signaled for Jak to circle wide, while he charged the near corner of the cage. J.B. kept blasting the dirt under the front of the trailer's frame, with his scattergun, keeping the rousties from firing at them from beneath its undercarriage. Dean likewise provided steady covering fire as Ryan closed on his targets.

If there hadn't been poison gas in the tarped cage, Ryan would've shot right through it to hit the men on the other side. But as it was, he couldn't risk blind fire. He had to wait until he rounded the end of the trailer.

One of the rousties was hoping he'd do just that.

As Ryan neared, the man stepped out, his KG-99 barking. The stick mag held a lot of rounds, and the roustie was trying to burn them all. He took wild, barely aimed shots that sailed high over Ryan's head or skimmed the dirt at his feet. The one-eyed man didn't slow, didn't blink.

Sometimes the first shot didn't win the contest.

Sometimes not even the tenth shot.

Ryan put a single slug from the P-226 into the

middle of the black mask. The roustie crashed to his back and stayed there.

The other gas-masked men crouching behind the cage had thrown up the tarp in back. They couldn't get inside the barred box because the cage door was on the other side, and exposed to J.B.'s and Dean's fire. As Ryan cleared the corner of the trailer, he saw two of the men frantically trying to pull around the nozzle ends of the pile of long, gray canisters so they could open them.

Before Ryan could fire, one of the two men took a ricochet hit off the dirt from a load of double-aught buckshot. The blast shattered both his shins. Howling in pain, he fell away from the cage and tried to crawl away. The other man had his arm through the bars. His hand was on a nozzle, and he was turning it.

Jak's Colt boomed twice from the other end of the cage. Two of the rousties jerked as if flicked by a giant finger, and were slammed sideways and down. Ryan drew a bead on the man who had his hand inside the cage. Hand in the cookie jar. Hand drawing back. Ryan couldn't see the roustabout's smile because of the mask, but he knew the chiller was smiling. He couldn't hear the hiss of the deadly gas escaping from the canister, or see it in the air, but he knew that's what was happening. Both he and Jak shot the last roustie at the same instant, their shots angled so no matter how the bullets deflected off bone, neither of them would be hit by friendly fire. The combined impact ripped the man off his feet and sent him crashing to his face on the ground. His legs were still kicking as Ryan closed the gap to the canisters.

"No!" he shouted at Jak. "Stay back! The poison is loose! Get out! Get everybody out!"

The albino stopped, and for a moment it looked as if he were going to protest or defy the order, but he thought better of it. He turned and ran back the way he'd come.

Ryan sucked down a quick breath and rushed over to the spot where the roustie had been standing. What with the screaming and shouting in the tent, he couldn't detect the hiss that might have told him which canister had been opened. Standing with his chest pressed against the bars, he reached through and ran the palm of his hand in front of the nozzles turned toward him.

Nothing from the first.

Nothing from the second.

Cold.

Cold that burned like a blowtorch.

He jerked his hand back. Ignoring the blisters that had been instantly raised on his palm, ignoring the growing, burning pain in his chest, he screwed down the wheel that sealed the nozzle.

Then he spun away, running around the trailer for the exit. He could see the tent was almost empty of people. Dean and the little girl, J.B. and Doc and Jak were bringing up the rear, driving out the stragglers.

How far did he have to run to be safe?

How much gas had escaped?

How much would it take to chill him?

Hand of fate, he thought. Hand of fate.

He ran until his legs gave out, and that wasn't far. Fifteen steps. Mebbe twenty. Just over the center ring's bumper, he dropped to his knees. Should have taken a deeper breath, he told himself. Then he gasped for air and choked on a lungful of razor blades.

Chapter Sixteen

Strong hands reached under Ryan's armpits and pulled him to his feet.

When he opened his eyes, he stared into irises the color of blood.

Jak ducked his head under the one-eyed man's left arm. J.B. did the same on the right, and they half carried, half dragged him to the exit. As Ryan labored to breathe, it felt as if Baldoona the scalie were jumping up and down on his chest.

Outside the tent, while he sat on the trampled earth beside the entrance, Mildred quickly looked him over, testing his pupils, pulse, and examining the inside of his mouth.

"Your mucous membranes are blistered from some kind of corrosive poison," she said. "If you'd gotten a little bit bigger dose, it would have turned your lungs to rags."

As Ryan fought to catch his breath, he focused on the berm wall opposite the tent entrance and about 150 feet distant. On this side of the big top, the people of Bullard ville were nowhere to be seen. And there weren't any carny chillers in evidence, either.

From the ville, out of sight on the far side of the

tent, came a sudden crackle of blasterfire. The hollow booms of black-powder blasters mixed with the sharp, rapid reports of automatic weapons. People started yelling and screaming. Then a gong sounded, over and over.

The Bullard ville call to arms, Ryan had no doubt.

He knew a running firefight when he heard one. So did the other companions. And this battle quickly increased in intensity.

"What's happening?" Leeloo asked Dean, her eyes wide. If the little girl wasn't afraid before, she was afraid now. The blasterfire wasn't part of any show. It was real.

In a few clipped phrases, Dean explained it to her. The poison gas. The mass chilling that had been in store for every man, woman and child, all to allow the robbing of the dead.

"They're gonna be sorry they ever started this," Leeloo said angrily. "Everybody in the ville knows just what to do, even the kids too young to carry blasters. We train all the time to drive off chillers and robbers. Sometimes we drill in the middle of the night. We use real bullets, too. Whenever that bell rings, everybody is ready to fight."

"How many rousties did we get?" Ryan asked J.B., his voice cracking and hoarse.

"Six or eight."

"Plenty left, then." He hawked and spit to clear his throat.

"'Fraid so," J.B. answered.

"The Magus is behind this whole operation,"

Ryan said. "And he's here. He was watching the show, sitting there like a big fat spider, waiting for the gas to be released."

"You saw him?" Krysty asked.

"Just for a second. I had a shot at him, but I couldn't make it. He got away."

"The Magus isn't gonna let us quietly slip away after what we just did to his plans," J.B. commented. "He never lets things like this slide."

"The carny chillers are going to regroup and come after us, that's for sure," Krysty said.

"We can't count on the ville folks for any help, either," Mildred quickly added.

"They don't understand what happened in the tent. All they saw was us shooting first, without provocation. They don't know what we saved them from. And there's no way to tell them now. They're going to be as eager to blast us to pieces as the roustabouts."

"In a situation like this, as far as the locals are concerned, every outlander has a target on his or her back," Ryan said.

At that moment, blasterfire barked at them from the top of the berm. Well-concealed and well-protected shooters lying prone along its ridge sent a volley of bullets smacking into the sides of the tent, forcing the companions to scramble for cover.

There was no telling to which side the attackers belonged.

And under the circumstances, it didn't matter a nukin' damn.

J.B. and Jak put up covering fire, spraying the face of the berm with buckshot and Magnum slugs as they all ducked inside the protection of the tent entrance.

"Is it okay for us to be in here?" Krysty asked Mildred. "Aren't we going to get poisoned?"

"Very little of the gas got loose," the black woman said. "And what was released has been diluted by the volume of air in here. It shouldn't hurt us, except for maybe minor skin rashes and burning eyes."

"It might be safe to breathe in here, but we can't stay," Ryan said. "We've got to make our break, and we've got to make it now, before the other sides get themselves organized."

"Mebbe they are already organized," J.B. speculated. "Could be those shooters along the berm out there are set up to herd us into an ambush."

"That's a chance we've got to take," Ryan said. "We've lost the element of surprise, and that was our only advantage. We're way outnumbered and way outgunned. The folks who live here can defend themselves against the looters. But all we can do at this point is beat a fighting retreat. We've got to get out of this ville."

"And we sure can't do it on foot," J.B. added. "The rousties will run us down in minutes with their wags."

"Our only hope is to steal a fast one and roll out of here in it," Ryan agreed.

"If we can, we'd better find a way to disable the

other wags before we take off,'' J.B. added. ''Otherwise, all we're doing is changing the location of our funerals.''

Ryan drew a broad circle in the dirt with his fingertip. ''Tent,'' he said, marking the entrance with a slash. ''The shortest route to the wags is to the right, past the rows of sideshow trailers, over here.''

''If I was planning an ambush,'' Mildred said, ''that's right where I'd set it up. With hard cover for my shooters from the berm and the trailers, and the targets caught out in open ground between.''

''Sounds like we've got to go the other way, then,'' Krysty said. ''The long way.''

''That puts us in plain sight of the ville and whatever's happening there,'' J.B. said.

''From the sound of it,'' Ryan said, ''everybody in Bullard is pretty well occupied. Let's just hope they stay that way.''

''What about Leeloo?'' Dean asked his father.

The little girl stood beside Dean, her back straight, her eyes unblinking, her crown of daisies slightly tilted.

''He's right, Ryan,'' Krysty said. ''We can't just leave her here with all these chillers on the loose.''

''We'll find a way to get her safely back to her people,'' Ryan said. ''But first, we've got to deal with the shooters from the top of the berm so we can circle around the other side of the tent.''

''I draw fire other way,'' Jak said, already moving in a blur.

''Jak, wait!'' Ryan cried, reaching for him.

Too late.

The albino slipped out of the tent, his Colt Python raised in his fist. No sooner had he vanished than a torrent of slugs slapped the wall of the tent in the direction he had fled. The direction of the mutie menagerie.

"Move!" Ryan shouted to the others. "Move, now!"

J.B. burst out the exit first, his scattergun thundering at his hip, dragging the zombielike Doc behind him.

JAK COULD RUN like the wind.

Something in his genes had given him coiled steel springs for legs, with just the right balance of muscle to bone, just the right kind of muscle. As he ran, sucking air all the way down into his boot tops, bullets flew at his head like angry wasps and whacked the side of the tent, raising puffs of dust. He ignored them. The curve of the tent loomed before him; the curve was cover if he got far enough, fast enough.

From behind him came rocking, consecutive blasts of J.B.'s scattergun. For an instant, the blaster-fire aimed at him stopped. An instant was all he needed. He rounded the perimeter of the tent, out of the line of pursuing fire.

If there were more shooters along the berm in front of him—and from the way his scalp and neck were prickling, Jak felt sure that there were—they were keeping their heads and blasters down. He figured they were holding fire, waiting for the rest of the companions to blunder into the killzone.

As the rows of trailered cages came into view, the lion roared. Joy exploded in Jak's chest.

Joy shared.

The lion knew he was coming.

Jak sprinted to close the gap between them. The great cat awaited him, pacing wildly back and forth in its cage. He holstered the Colt and used the hub of a wheel to scramble onto the trailer's bed.

Freedom. The thought exploded in the albino's mind like a frag gren. And then a wave of tremendous emotion swept through him—gratitude to the nth power.

He unbolted the cage door and pushed it wide open. The mutie mountain lion jumped out, landing softly on the dirt despite its tremendous weight. When Jak hopped down from the trailer, the cat gave him a swat with a huge, soft paw. The blow drove Jak hard to his knees. Then a hot, scratchy tongue slathered his face and neck.

There are others, close, Little Brother. They lie in wait.

Jak could almost sense their terrible confusion and panic. It had never occurred to the chillers hiding on top of the berm that upon reaching safety the first act of their adversaries' pointman would be the release of a half-ton of man-eater. They didn't know whether to open fire to protect their comrades concealed among the trailers from the lion, or to wait for the rest of the designated targets to appear, according to the plan. It was a problem they had no time to consider, let alone solve.

Jak felt the rage building in the great cat's body, the rage and the raw power, unquenchable and bottomless. The carny master's words of warning about the true nature of this superintelligent, supercunning predator beast flooded back to him.

And through him to the mind of the lion.

Don't be afraid of me. I will never hurt you.

Not afraid.

Good. Now we hunt.

The lion ducked under the trailer that supported its cage, out of the line of sight of the berm shooters. It pulled itself forward with its front legs and claws, belly dragging on the ground. Jak followed on his knees, the Colt Python in his hand. On the far side of the trailer's undercarriage, in the aisle between the first and second rows of cages, Jak could see legs. Seven sets of legs. Five belonged to men and two to women. Seven pairs of feet shifted anxiously. Jak ducked his face lower and got a glimpse of the semiauto handblasters the ambush crew held. High-capacity stick mags jutted from the blue-steel weapons' receivers. Big-time firepower—210 rounds versus his six.

Me first, Little Brother.

The thought came to him in the same instant the lion moved.

Jak lost the cat in a cloud of dust as it sprang out from under the trailer. The albino thrust himself forward, the cocked .357 Magnum blaster in front, seeking targets.

Before he could do that, staccato blasterfire roared, as the roustabouts and snake charmers, caught standing practically shoulder to shoulder, tried to put bullets into a tornado of fang and claw moving way too fast to track. The beige blur, five feet tall at the shoulder, slipped between them, wound around them, brushing them electric with the tips of its soft fur and its black-tasseled tail. The ambushers' volleys of wild shots banged into cages and trailers, and set the trapped sideshow muties screaming. Jak saw Baldoona the scalie throw himself into a corner and cover both his heads with his arms as slugs sparked off of and rattled the bars of his cage.

Jak held his own fire. There was no need for him to shoot. The lion hadn't even scratched the carny chillers, and their ship was already sinking. Mebbe they had seen what the lion had done when it had gotten loose before, he thought. Or mebbe just the idea of what the beast was capable of made them crazy with terror. Bottom line: semiauto, high-capacity weapons, blind panic and no clear firing lanes were a recipe for self-inflicted disaster.

One of the rousties, his eyes bulging with fear, squeezed the trigger of his KG-99 over and over as he whirled, spraying a tight string of single shots through the chest of the man standing flatfooted and helpless in front of him. The multiple, close-range impacts lifted the guy off his feet and set him down four feet away, a look of astonished horror on his face. As his knees buckled and his shirtfront bloomed red, he managed to return fire. His two shots went wide of the guy who'd accidentally blasted him, but they hit one of the leggy women in the hip and thigh. She twisted away and dropped, unable to stand with a shattered pelvis. She writhed in the yellow dirt, her face ashen with shock, her mouth open, screaming.

The lion still didn't chill. Ignoring the blaze of blasterfire, it played with the surviving five like a housecat with a brood of very stupid, very slow mice. One by one, it swept their legs out from under them, or batted them on the back of the head just hard enough to stagger them. It let them run a few yards toward cover, then hooked a single cruel claw in the back of their waistbands and dragged them back into the middle of the aisle. With dismissive, precise blows of its paw, it flattened them, one after another, facedown on the ground. The battering went on for several minutes until finally, all five chillers were on their hands and knees, unable to rise. Having lost their weapons, they gasped and sobbed, tears streaming down their cheeks.

Jak could see it in their eyes: they knew they lived or died at the whim of something far more terrible, far more merciless than they. Theirs were the faces of people lost at sea, floating far from shore.

Doomed.

But the lion didn't take their lives. It stood over them for a moment, panting softly, its long tail lashing, then it sat back on its haunches and began to clean itself. It wet the top of its huge paw with its tongue and rubbed it against its cheek and brow. As it did this, the idling-wag-engine sound rumbled up from its throat.

After a few seconds, one of the rousties began to stir. Jak drew a bead on the slowly moving man with the Python, but held his fire. He could see the chiller was unarmed and had no fight left. Head down, the roustie crawled over to Baldoona's trailer and meekly climbed into the cage. After he pulled the door shut, he threw himself belly down in the semi-solid piles of scalie shit on the floor and tried his best to become invisible.

The four who were left on the ground were playing possum. Seeing one of their number make it to safety, realizing that this was their last opportunity to escape, they struggled to their feet and staggered away. Jak and the lion followed them around the end of the trailer. They watched the beaten quartet limp across the compound. As the chillers neared the foot of the berm, they started yelling at their comrades hidden along its ridge. They yelled for them not to shoot, then started clawing their way over the rubble to the top.

Jak raised the big Colt in a two-handed grip, bracing himself to take out targets of opportunity as the other group of ambushers laid down covering fire for their friends. Heads and weapons popped up, all right, but there was no shooting.

Wait.

Jak had already let off pressure on the wide combat trigger. He sensed that none of the rousties on the berm wanted to fight the lion. They didn't even consider taking cover and massing their fire because they knew they couldn't defend themselves. All they wanted was to get as far away as they could, as fast as they could. The berm-top shooters abandoned their hide and set out across the plain on a dead run, with their injured companions trailing behind.

I can't talk to them the way I can talk to you, Little Brother. That's the problem. I can't explain to anyone else what I am. I can only use this physical form to dominate. A weak form of communication, at best.

The lion smiled. *But things could be worse, I suppose. If I were a daisy, I couldn't communicate at all.*

A baleful moan from the trailers behind them made Jak pivot, weapon up and ready. He looked at the roustie cowering on the nasty floor of Baldoona's cage. The man was alone in the enclosure; the sideshow mutie was nowhere to be seen.

What happened to scalie? the albino thought as he stepped closer.

Then he saw the door standing slightly ajar and the spawl of a bullet impact—a bright splash of lead where the cage's locking bolt had been.

Chapter Seventeen

Ryan raced out of the tent after the Armorer and Doc. As J.B. sidestepped, squaring his shoulders to the target, scattering fléchettes across the top of the berm, Ryan ran past him, turning left around the candy-striped tent's perimeter, taking the point.

The sounds of concentrated small-weapons fire rolled over him in waves. As he rounded the curve of the big top, clouds of black-powder gun smoke interspersed with sickly yellow muzzle-flashes obscured his view of the ville. Bullets whined across the compound, ricocheting and kicking up dirt.

Ryan could make out three carny wags parked in the ancient road that ran between the first of the rows of raised, awning-covered plant beds and the building that had once housed Burger Stravaganza. The wags were predark RVs, Winnebagos refitted for the hazards of Deathlands. Rousties fired from behind the steel-armored wheel wells and from around the massive I-beams that were replacement bumpers, front and rear. The carny chillers were absorbing fire from a small group of ville folk strung out along and shooting from the low cover of the plant beds. The ville folks had their backs turned to the tent, and to the companions.

Even though he was running full tilt, Ryan could see dead and wounded rousties on the ground around the wags. The loot they'd been carrying when they were hit lay in the dirt beside them. Caught with both hands in the Bullard ville cookie jar. The ville had dead, as well, some of them shot to pieces.

Other rousties, blocked from most of the sec force's fire by the wags, were still moving booty from the jumble of cabins and shacks built alongside the prenukecaust fast-food restaurant, and hurriedly loading it into the rear of the Winnebagos.

At first glance it was hard to say which side was winning the war. One thing was for sure, though— the looters were concentrating all their attention on the ville people, and vice versa.

There was no safety for the companions along the tent perimeter; the stakes that held up the guy wires were the only cover, and they were useless. If the ville sec men caught them trying to sneak past in plain view, it was going to be instant chilling. Ryan broke away from the tent wall, leading the others across the stretch of open ground to the far side of the first row of raised plant beds. They bellied down behind the protective berm.

Two rows over, through the lower branches of overgrown tomato plants, Ryan could see a small portion of the ville sec crew systematically popping away at the looters with handblasters. From the care they were taking with their shot placement, and the number of bodies already strewed around the wags, they were no doubt the most skilled marksmen in Bullard.

Ryan and the others ducked as a wave of return fire from the rousties behind the wags trimmed clumps of leaves and stems and exploded ripe tomatoes above their heads.

Crawling to the end of the bed, Ryan saw where the rest of the ville sec force was headed. With covering fire from their sharpshooting pals, they were carefully filtering through the rows of beds at the far end of the compound. From there, they were crossing the ville's main street and the leaders of the pack were already circling the other fast-food buildings to outflank the looters and attack them from behind.

As Leeloo said, they knew what they were doing.

The fighting force of Bullard ville advanced like a seasoned army, leapfrogging with precision from hard cover to hard cover. The younger kids carrying black-powder blasters were keeping well to the rear, in a position to put up shielding fire if the folks forward had to suddenly pull back.

Ryan glanced along the row they were in. Right off he could see the companions needed to move to two beds down, as that would block the sec men's line of sight of their only route to the convoy of parked wags, and escape.

Ryan led Dean, Leeloo and Krysty across the five-foot gap between the beds. They made it without a problem. When J.B., Mildred and Doc followed, all hell broke loose.

One of the sec men shouted over the din of the shooting, "It's the other ones! They're tryin' to get behind us!"

As J.B. shoved Doc facedown in the dirt, withering fire poured onto the front of the bed. The range was only about forty feet. In the hail of bullets, half the sheet-metal awning ripped loose and tumbled onto Dean and Leeloo. Ryan kicked it aside. He and Krysty could only fire blindly over the top of the bed; they didn't dare raise themselves up to take proper aim. Slugs from the opposition were chewing great hunks of wood out of the top edge of the frame inches over their heads. Ryan stopped firing and pulled back the SIG P-226. Down the row, J.B., Mildred and Doc were likewise pinned. In the space of a few seconds, everything had gone to shit.

"Ryan, what are we going to do?" Krysty shouted as she jammed a speed loader into her Smith & Wesson's open cylinder. "These people want our heads."

"The sec force is about to flank the looters," he told her. "Once they close in and lower the hammer, the carny chillers are dead meat. And when that happens, we're going to have a whole bunch more pissed-off folks waving blasters in our faces. I'd say we've got four or five minutes, tops, before that happens."

"But what are we going to do?" Krysty repeated.

By way of an answer, Ryan turned to his son and said, "Dean, make a break for the circled wags. Take the little girl with you. We can't leave her here.

She'd be cut to pieces. Find Jak. He's there somewhere. Go with him, get out of the ville. Even if
you have to go on foot. We'll track you down and
meet up later.''

The last part was very unlikely, given the circumstances. The boy's face dropped.

"But, Dad…" he began.

"No argument, son. When we commit ourselves,
it's going to be all out, everything on the line to get
you to the wags. You've got to take Leeloo and run.
Don't stop for anything. You wait for my signal, and
then you go. You understand?''

With great reluctance, unable to conceal his hurt,
Dean answered, "Yes, Dad.''

"Good boy.''

Ryan reached over and gave his son's shoulder a
gentle squeeze. Then he signaled to J.B., pointing at
Dean and the girl, then behind them in the direction
of the tent and the parked wags. J.B. got the picture
at once, and nodded in agreement. He spoke to Mildred, who looked at Ryan and also nodded. The Armorer then took out his Tekna knife and with a single swipe cut himself free of Doc. The old man was
down on his hands and knees, swaying back and
forth, mouth in constant motion, seemingly unaware
of the hellstorm that surrounded them.

That J.B. and Ryan would attack the ville shooters
from opposite directions went without saying. It was
their standard skirmish procedure since the days
with Trader. The intent was to divide the opposi-

tion's fire, to come from unexpected angles, to startle and confuse them.

There was no time for goodbyes.

Ryan and Krysty shared a look that only lasted an instant, but said everything that needed to be said.

The one-eyed man held up his hand so J.B. could see it. Five fingers extended. Then four, then three. On none, he rolled to his right and came up running.

"Now, Dean!" he cried, rounding the end of the bed.

Krysty was right on his heels as he charged into the wide aisle that separated the rows.

The ville shooters hiding behind the bed in the next row gave up their cover to get a clear shot at the rapidly closing targets. As they popped up over the greenery, they had expressions of righteous fury on their faces. Nobody was going to steal from them; nobody was going to bushwhack them; nobody was going to trick them.

If Ryan felt sympathy for the people of Bullard ville, he had to crush it, to bury it under the weight of his own determination to survive. This wasn't the fight he had wanted, not the fight he had intended. But survival was on the line for him and the companions. If he ended up chilling the very folks he'd come to help, it was because he was left no choice in the matter.

Crossing the strip of open ground, Ryan wondered why the Bullard ville sec force hadn't kept to its cover. There was such a thing as being too confident; there was such a thing as mistaking dumb luck for skill, letting a few successes go to your head. And there was such a thing as liking the heat of battle way too much. No matter how you spun it, jumping up to shoot was a bonehead move.

As the sharpshooters' blasters blazed, so did Ryan's. He ignored the hot lead roaring past his ears. The SIG in his fist bucked and cycled, bucked and cycled as he pulled the trigger as fast as he could. It was impossible to shoot fine and tight while sprinting for your life. The best he could do was to lob slugs at the sec force. A 9 mm slug from his handblaster ripped a big chunk out of a tall man's upper arm. For a split second, a mist of red hung in the air around his shoulder. The tall man stopped firing and twisted away, clutching at himself, his hand on the wounded side dangling uselessly at his hip. Ryan's next shot hit him in the right cheek, just below the eye. The decompression shock as the back of his head blew away popped the eyeball from its socket.

A fraction of a second later, a guy in patched bib-front overalls standing next to him absorbed a center body hit, doubling over around the bullet impact, clutching at his stomach and showing Ryan the bald top of his head. The one-eyed man was already tightening down on a follow-up shot as the man started to bend over. He put the second round in almost the same place relative to the ground, but because the man had moved while the bullet was in flight, it crashed through his skull instead of his mid-section. As the bib-front guy toppled backward, a torrent of blood rushed from his nose and mouth, and it geysered high and red out the top of his head.

Two strides later, Ryan was vaulting the still kicking bodies and cutting around the end of the bed. As he did so, Krysty's .38 barked in rapid fire.

Six hollowpoint slugs clipped through the greenery—two sailed on, high and wide, but four made solid thwacks as they hit flesh and bone.

The flesh and bone belonged to the whoremaster of Bullard ville and two of his best gaudy sluts. The women were all dressed up for the carny show in long, shiny ball gowns, their bosoms bare to the nipples, their faces feverishly rouged, lips thickly painted. Suddenly single, small, round beauty spots appeared near the centers of each of their foreheads, and big cratering holes in the backs of their skulls where the mushrooming hollowpoints exited. The sluts dropped their battle-scarred Walther PPKs and made stiff, awkward curtseys as their knees buckled. Their bottoms struck the ground at almost the same instant, dead before they hit the dirt.

The whoremaster O'Neil was slammed twice in the chest, .38 slugs coring both lungs. As he fell, he discharged his mini-Uzi into his own boots, pinning the trigger on full-auto, sending up flurry of yellow dust mixed with blood and bone chips.

Ryan rounded the end of the bed. As he did so, Melchior and two other ville bigwigs, having stood up to confront their attackers, were now backing up at top speed, trying to retreat to the cover of the next row, firing wildly as they went. Melchior's ponderous bulk lurched to the side as a blast from J.B.'s scattergun caught him in the torso, under the left arm. The Armorer had loaded the weapon with lead pellet rounds, and the impact made the flab of the headman's face shudder. He lost his grip on his Ruger revolver, and it went flying, end over end. A smaller man would have gone flying along with it.

Before Melchior could recover his balance, he was struck again, this time at the knees. Clutching at his ruined legs, he went down, the scattergun's roar drowning his cries.

As J.B. advanced, he worked the M-4000's butter-smooth slide. Holding the trigger pinned, he hammered the other two bigwigs, sending one pinwheeling into the plant bed headfirst, and blowing the other off his feet with a center chest hit.

Kneeling at the corner of the bed, Mildred followed up on three more retreating figures—an extremely heavyset woman in a shapeless gunnysack of a faded, calf-length, print dress, and two lanky boys in their late teens. The heavy woman was packing a .32 Beretta blaster. One of the teenagers carried a Government Colt remake, the other a .38 Smith & Wesson with a five-inch barrel. As the trio backed up, they fired without aiming, hoping to somehow hit J.B., Ryan, Krysty and Mildred with lucky shots.

Mildred, on the other hand, took very careful aim. She fired three quick rounds from her ZKR 551. The first hit the heavyset woman high in the flabby forearm of her gun hand. The little .32 tumbled from fingers numb with shock. Mildred hadn't been trying to hit bone, but bone had been hit. And shattered. The second round passed through the Government Colt boy's bicep. The third clipped the shoulder of the other teenager. Two more gun-hand hits. Both boys managed to hold on to their weapons, but neither could raise them to return more fire.

Realizing they were helpless to defend themselves, all three turned and ran.

Mildred was pleased to see them able to run.

The other companions drew beads on their retreating backs, easy shots to make, given the distance, but no one fired. It was obvious that these three were no longer in the contest.

Ryan glanced over his shoulder at the tent and was relieved that Dean and Leeloo were nowhere in sight. Whatever else happened, at least they had made it safely to the circled wags.

As he turned back to the action, blasterfire erupted from beside the looter wags. Dirt puffed up all around the fleeing woman and two boys as they tried to cross the ville's main street and rejoin their people. They went down in a tangled heap in the middle of the road, the heavy woman crashing on top of the teenagers.

"Shit!" Mildred cried, returning fire.

Krysty joined in, as well.

As J.B. scrambled back to retrieve Doc, Ryan unslung the Steyr longblaster and flipped up the lens protectors on its telescope. With the forestock braced against the frame of the plant bed, he swung the sight post over the nearest looter wag. A roustie peeked around the front bumper, KG-99 in hand, looking for something else to chill. Ryan held the top of the post way low to adjust for the short distance to target, and squeezed off a shot.

The man kneeling behind the bumper jerked upright as if flicked by a giant, invisible finger. Arms flying wide, he did a midair half twist and hit the ground hard. He wasn't dead. Back arching, he kicked his legs and thrashed his arms.

Nobody rushed out to help him.

Ryan was searching the line of wags for a second target when he saw bullet impacts from the opposite direction kicking up dust. The ville folks' flanking attack had begun. The carny chillers were about to get themselves sandwiched. He flipped down the lens caps on his scope. He didn't need ten-power magnification to see what was going on downrange.

The ant line of looters moving between the cabins and the wags disintegrated as small-weapons fire swept over it. From the hard cover of Taco Town, the ville sec force sent volleys of lead down the narrow lanes between the low shacks, through the walls of the shacks themselves. The blasting was indiscriminate; the folk of Bullard were in an outraged frenzy at having their personal belongings taken. The looters caught flatfooted by the barrage dropped where they stood, hit by dozens of rounds at once. Arms heaped with clothing, tools, utensils opened and spilled what they held. Other rousties managed to dump their booty and run, only to be cut down after taking a few steps. The only chillers who had half a chance were the ones closest to the wags. At least they could dive into the wags for cover.

Bullets rained down on the three Winnebagos.

"These folks aren't going to be satisfied until they've chilled every outlander," Krysty said to the others. "They're going to grind up the rest of the rousties and then they're going to roll over us."

"Time for us to try and pull back, Ryan," Mildred said. "While we still have a prayer of making it."

"It's now or never," J.B. agreed.

Before Ryan could speak, the engine of the second Winnebago roared to life, and an instant later, with spinning rear wheels, it swerved out of line. It accelerated, fishtailing wildly.

"Fireblast!" Ryan growled as the driver regained control and the looter wag shot across the road.

As if it was locked on a target, the RV barreled down on them.

Chapter Eighteen

Baldoona's adult head peeked out from the shadows between a pair of trailers. The boy and girl had stopped running, but were still moving its way. If they continued on their current course, they would pass within a yard of its hiding place. The adult head ducked back, out of sight.

The baby head was drooling and chuckling. It had been drooling and chuckling like that for more than forty years. It had always been a baby head. The adult head had started out that way, but it had matured along with the rest of the body.

For more than forty years, Baldoona had lived in a cage. Even among scalies, the birth of a huge, two-headed infant was altogether too frightening and bizarre.

When Gert Wolfram's scouts had spotted the young scalie, they'd attacked and captured the freak of nature. None of the pack had tried to defend the youngster against its kidnappers.

Despite the adult head's whining complaints about the unsanitary accommodations and rough treatment, despite the fact that it was momentarily free of its cage, it had no intention of ever escaping from the carny. The adult head wasn't smart by any stretch of the imagination, but it was smart enough to understand that freedom for Baldoona the Two-Headed Scalie meant a slow death by starvation. Baldoona had never made its own way in the world. Chow came to it regularly, instead of it having to chase down the chow, which because of its weight it could never catch unless said chow was staked and tethered, or blindsided. The two tender young morsels walking his way were a case of the latter. If it could surprise and stun them, it could have them. As Baldoona's adult head drew even deeper into the shadows, it considered the moist, succulent flesh, the sweet blood, the crisp bones. It wiped the drool from its chin, then from the baby chin.

Contemplating at extreme close range the ruddy, contorted face of its shouldermate, the puffy eyelids, the ever-wet-from-snot upper lip, the perpetual puke breath, the adult head allowed itself to admit the real reason that it hadn't somehow arranged to have the ugly, messy knob chopped off decades ago. The baby head, whatever else it was or wasn't, was the adult head's only friend in the world. Even though it couldn't talk, even though it woke him up four times a night, even though it crapped in what the adult head considered its pants, even though it regularly barfed all over the adult head's shirtfront, without the baby head Baldoona would have had to actively make its own living in the world. It would have been just another big, fat, dumb scalie.

The adult head could hear the footfalls of its quarry drawing nearer; it could hear the children whispering to each other as they approached. It prepared itself to spring.

As it continued to slobber a bubbling waterfall, the baby head started making a funny noise. A kind of soft, rhythmic chirping from deep in its throat. It was the same noise it made whenever they got their hands on a live pig or a goat.

"Quiet," the adult head warned its counterpart, nose to nose. "If we do this right, we can eat them both."

"Goo," whispered the baby head.

Chapter Nineteen

The Magnificent Crecca hurried down the command wag's narrow corridor. In his arms was a bundle of ghastly, cold limbs. A violently twitching bundle of limbs. A head too heavy for its size leaned against his shoulder. The rest of the Magus's body was as light as a feather, this a product of hollow stainless-steel replacement bones and Teflon joints. Having to actually touch the creature he so feared, to feel its cold metal and its feverish flesh, made his skin crawl. In order to keep from vomiting at the smell, Crecca had to make a conscious effort to suck in every breath through his mouth.

Sounds of blasterfire raging outside accompanied them to the salon-workroom. The Magus, who was fully awake as Crecca deposited him on the autopsy table, paid no attention to the battle, or what it portended for the future of this incarnation of Gert Wolfram's World Famous Carny Show. His only concern was ending his own pain and insuring his own immediate survival, which was in jeopardy.

The steel-eyed monster hadn't completely escaped the dozen or so steel-jacketed handblaster rounds that had imploded his private viewing box's mirror. Momentarily frozen in his recliner chair, he had been caught in the hail of lead. Through the glittering whoosh of shattered glass, Crecca had seen the sparks fly and heard the ricochets whine from bullet strikes on the creature's tempered metal parts. In the midst of the surprise barrage, the Magus had managed to turn and bail from the chair. He had hit the floor with a dull thud, barely able to crawl hand over hand, and spurting vile-smelling internal fluids of various colors and densities.

Because of his boss's unnatural, composite physiology, as Crecca had looked back from the doorway, he couldn't tell whether any of the wounds were fatal. If the carny master had been sure, he would have left the Magus to die alone on the floor of the box. Even now, Crecca would have chilled the monster himself if he could have been certain of pulling off the deed. Though the Magus was obviously seriously injured, there was no way to judge his ability to defend himself. It was widely rumored among carny folk that once his metal jaws clamped shut on something they could never be pried loose; they would hold on like grim death until the second coming of skydark. In the end, what stayed Crecca's hand was his fear of failure and its consequences, which were too terrible to imagine.

"Roll the tool cabinet over here," the Magus commanded, his voice unusually high-pitched, like a tape recording played too fast.

Crecca unlocked the wheels of the tall, red, multi-drawer toolbox and quickly pushed it to the side of the table. As he did so, he saw that the Magus was using both hands to compress one of the prominent, artificial veins that festooned his chest. Between his fingers, the steel flex-piping oozed what looked like dirty transmission fluid.

More disturbing to the carny master than the spreading brown goo was the erratic movement of the creature's left leg. A mechanical servo located above the synthetic knee joint had been damaged by a bullet hit. There was a deep dent at one end of its titanium housing, and it leaked an oily green liquid mixed with blood. The injury made it impossible for the Magus to control the leg. It jerked and spasmed madly, donkey kicking in the air. In its cage of stainless steel, the Magus's human calf muscle seized up into a rock hard lump, sinews straining, real veins bulging, then it relaxed, then it seized up again, as if it had a mind of its own.

A demented mind.

The tense-relax cycle was reflected, most horribly, in the few remaining human features of the Magus's face.

The spectacle of human-machine interface gone awry might have been funny to Crecca if he had been watching from say, forty or fifty yards away, while hiding behind a large boulder, and if a battle royal for control of the ville hadn't been going on just outside the wag. As it was, the carny master could only stand there in the shambles of the big salon, grim faced, trying not to show his impatience and growing concern over the deteriorating tactical situation, while he awaited further orders from his commander in chief.

He didn't have to wait long.

"Give me a speed wrench!" the Magus cried.

Crecca handed over the adjustable crescent.

With wet steel fingertips, the Magus fitted and tightened the jaws of the wrench over the coupling nut on the ruptured steel-mesh vein. "Replacement tubing," he snarled. "Third drawer of the cabinet. Fast! I'm losing pressure to my head!"

The carny master didn't see fit to point out that there was also an alarming knocking sound coming from inside his boss's torso. He grabbed a twelve-inch length of preassembled tubing from the drawer and ripped it free of its hard plastic shrink-wrapping.

The Magus loosened the nuts at either end of the broken vessel. "Finger, here," he ordered Crecca, indicating the lower end of the vein, where it joined a stub of rigid steel pipe.

When the Magus freed the bottom coupling, Crecca jammed his thumb over the threaded hole, stopping the gush of tranny fluid.

The Magus fitted the new coupling and vein to the top, torquing it down. After he had Crecca move his thumb, he attached the length of tubing at the bottom. This repair completed, the steel-eyed monster turned his attention to his madly jerking leg.

To Crecca, the problem didn't seem life-threatening, or even important—a painful inconvenience, mebbe—but when he suggested that perhaps he was needed to supervise the rousties in the battle for Bullard ville, the Magus would have none of it.

"Let Furlong deal with rad-blasted dirt farmers!" the creature snarled. "I need your help to deactivate the servo's internal power supply. I can't afford to lose any more of my calf muscle."

The Magus rarely explained anything, so the carny master was somewhat surprised when he continued. Carefully, as if to a slow child, he said in the unusually high-pitched voice, "There is a balance, precarious at best, between my living and my nonliving parts. I know you think that eventually I will become an entirely mechanical being, but that just demonstrates your profound ignorance of the energy dynamics of biological systems. The steel and plastic parts I have accumulated over the years allow me to survive, but they are clumsy and inefficient, and the replacements are only useful below a certain number. Above that total number, they become a serious liability. My ratio of human tissue to mechanism is already so low that if I exert myself to any degree the nutrient supply to the living flesh is challenged, and I risk massive cell death of my remaining tissue."

Though the Magnificent Crecca very much liked the sound of "massive cell death" when it was applied to the Magus, he understood nothing else of what had just been said. Because he understood nothing, he didn't dare make a sound or even a facial expression.

When he made no response, the Magus barked

GET FREE BOOKS and a FREE GIFT WHEN YOU PLAY THE...

Lucky 7

SLOT MACHINE GAME!

Just scratch off the silver box with a coin. Then check below to see the gifts you get!

YES!
I have scratched off the silver box. Please send me the 2 free Gold Eagle® books and gift for which I qualify. I understand I am under no obligation to purchase any books, as explained on the back of this card.

366 ADL DRSG   **166 ADL DRSF**

FIRST NAME   LAST NAME

ADDRESS

APT.#   CITY

STATE/PROV.   ZIP/POSTAL CODE

7	7	7	**Worth TWO FREE BOOKS plus a BONUS Mystery Gift!**
🍒	🍒	🍒	**Worth TWO FREE BOOKS!**
♣	♣	♣	**Worth ONE FREE BOOK!**
🔔	🔔	🍒	**TRY AGAIN!**

(MB-01/03)

DETACH AND MAIL CARD TODAY!

more orders at him, demanding a succession of tools from the rollaway box. The titanium housing on the servo had been partially crushed by the slug impact, and two of the retaining bolts had been badly twisted. Because of this, and because the Magus couldn't keep his leg still, the removal of the outer case not only required Crecca's hands-on assistance, but that he sit on the ankle to pin it down on the autopsy table while they worked.

The bent case bolts proved difficult to extract with hand tools. As the moments stretched on, and the din of blasterfire continued, Crecca's urge to look out the window grew until it became almost intolerable, but he couldn't leave the operation. As the Magus worked on one of the two bolts with a socket wrench, he cursed Ryan Cawdor. "He did this to me! That one-eyed son of a swampie jolt whore!"

In Crecca's opinion, unasked for and unexpressed, the Magus had done it to himself by insisting that One-Eye and his son sit in the tent where he could watch them die with the farmers. And he had done it to the rest of the carny by insisting that the looting begin before the mass chilling was over. The Magus had been obsessed with the idea that in the case of Bullard everything had to happen quickly, the ville cleaned of its extralarge cache of valuables, the bodies buried and the caravan moving on, all before a bunch of new travelers along the long, dry road wandered onto the scene and complicated things.

If Crecca knew nothing of biology, from his life experience roving through the Deathlands, he had acquired a fine grasp of what made people tick. It didn't take much to realize that the Magus took an unholy pleasure in playing the puppet master. The steel-eyed monster's idea of fun was diverting and deceiving the doomed suckers in the gas tent while his crews stripped their humble cabins of furnishings, clothing, tools, food, utensils, weapons and ammunition, and tore up floor- and wallboards looking for other predark treasures. The Magus had assigned twenty-five rousties to this task, supervised by Furlong.

Dividing the force had been a big mistake, but it was understandable.

The carny had run this operation successfully so many times that once the crowd was seated, the canisters in position and exit guards in place, all the rest seemed a sure thing. The tent was Kevlar and couldn't be cut or torn with anything less than a blowtorch, and there were armed rousties to seal off the only way out. The Magus hadn't even considered the possibility of a mass breakout of his intended victims, so he hadn't been prepared to defend against it. Nor had he considered the consequences to follow with all the ville sec men alerted, and everyone older than twelve years packing a blaster, and the good folk of Bullard catching the rousties in the act of looting their cabins and storehouses.

Given the switch in odds, which was suddenly three to one against the rousties, and the fact that these farmers had trained to defend themselves and had been successful doing so in the past, it was no surprise to Crecca that the whole thing had gotten way out of hand in a hurry.

Some of the carny crew had been chilled in the tent by Cawdor and his bunch, which left another twenty or so to guard the wag convoy. And that was before the shooting from the ville folks started. There was no way of telling how many rousties were still alive. Certainly not enough to beat back the farmers. In which case, the best Crecca and the carny survivors could hope for was to exit Bullard with whole skins. Which meant abandoning pretty much everything to escape, and doing it before they were overrun.

As the carny master finally wrenched free the bent bolt, it occurred to him that even now the Magus was jerking his strings, making him act against his own interests. And that there was nothing he could do about it.

Once the cover to the servo was off, the Magus attacked the leads to the microminiature nuke battery that powered the unit. The ruined device couldn't be replaced; there was no spare on hand. A new one needed to be machined from titanium bar stock, something that couldn't be done in Bullard. Or anywhere else in Deathlands that Crecca knew about. There weren't any functioning precision machine tools readily available. Even if there were, no one was alive who could figure out how to run one. In the present, all the Magus could do was shut off the unit. When the connection to the battery was broken, his calf muscle relaxed, but without the servo to coordinate its movements, the half-steel leg was just so much deadweight.

The Magus didn't seem worried. One leg or two, he always managed to get away. Jumped dimensions or time traveled, or whatever it was that he did.

To get himself a new servo made, Crecca thought as he hurried to the salon's rear window, mebbe the Magus would jump backward in time, to before the nukecaust.

One glance across the compound told Crecca his worst fears had come true. Everything had gone wrong. Most of the looter crew lay sprawled on the ground. As the ville sec force advanced on the three parked wags, blasters blazing, one of the wags swerved out of line and came roaring his way.

Chapter Twenty

"What the fuck is that?!" Furlong snarled from the Winnebago's swivel-mounted driver chair.

The man who was about to dump an armload of spoils into the stripped RV's built-in booty bins froze as the head roustie lurched out of the shabby throne and bore down on him.

Furlong snatched a crudely framed object from the top of the load. It was a hair painting, made of twisted and braided lengths of human and animal hair in different colors, knotted into flowers and vines. It was stuck to a square board with little globs of translucent yellow glue.

"This is worthless shit!" he said, tossing the painting out the open rear cargo doors. "So is this...and this...and this...." Furlong grabbed other items from the roustie and tossed them out onto the ground, as well. Handmade wooden eating utensils, raggedy clothing, holed-out boots. In a matter of seconds, he had stripped the man of his loot.

The only items Furlong didn't throw out were a handful of dubious predark trinkets: a broken metal wristwatch without a band, a pair of thick glasses with scratched lenses and some junk jewelry with stones missing from the settings. Gesturing at the heap on the ground, he told the roustie, "Haul back another bunch of crap like that, and you'll be digging graves. I'm not gonna warn you again. And you tell the others the same. We only want tradeable stuff. No more of that garbage." As Furlong lumbered back to the captain's chair, he heard familiar music faintly drifting over from the big top. The swivel throne was turned to the rear so he could oversee the grunt-and-carry work of his subordinates. Overseeing was what he did best. Every time rousties returned to the RV, he gave them the hard once-over, looking for suspicious lumps under their clothing, making sure they weren't hiding valuable items on their persons. And he kept his eye out for anything especially nice and concealable that he could appropriate for himself when all backs were turned.

So far, there'd been nothing worth the risk. The pickings from Bullard ville had been pathetic.

The clothing liberated from the cabins was patched and threadbare, and even when apparently clean, reeked of composted human manure. The flatware used by the dirt farmers was roughly carved from tree branches. The hand tools and edged weapons were made of rebar chipped out of the fallen highway overpass, and of salvaged, ground-down wag leaf springs. The farmers' personal-grooming items were likewise homemade: corn-cob-and-pig-bristle hairbrushes, snaggle-pronged bone combs, toothbrushes that were nothing more than furred-out twigs. Hut furnishings consisted of small, irregular pieces of mirror, faded predark photos, handmade wooden toys, curtains made of strung small and large animal vertebrae. The predark "keepsakes" consisted largely of broken small electronic items and parts of same; plastic and metal odds and ends that 150 years earlier would have been tossed aside. So far, no weapons or ammo had been found. The dirt farmers had all carried their blasters and cartridge belts into the tent.

Furlong figured a ville this well-organized had to have hidden away all the good stuff in a safe place, probably under armed guard. The roustie crews just hadn't uncovered the main storehouse yet. Because Bullard ville was the carny's biggest target so far, both in terms of population and the number of buildings, the plan was to work systematically, moving from one end to the other, ransacking every hut and lean-to along the way. The looters were under orders to take only the choicest stuff; otherwise the wag bins would get filled up with worthless junk, which would just have to be dumped once they hit the motherlode.

In the wake of their previous mass chillings, booty other than food, blasters, ammo and fuel, the stuff they couldn't use in the near term, they had either stashed in caches well off the main roads along their performance circuit or carried to one of Deathlands' primitive trading outposts.

Gert Wolfram's World Famous Carny wasn't the kind of operation that could make a roustie rich. Nobody in Deathlands was getting rich, except mebbe the barons. And the Magus. But the carny folk sure weren't starving, and that set them apart from most other denizens of the hellscape. They had two square meals a day, a shelter over their heads and some regular excitement. Each chiller got a share of the profit, the share determined by the carny master. This was taken out in stolen property, allowing the rousties to occasionally upgrade their blasters and stabbers, and to maintain their jolt and joyjuice habits.

The chillers' other options for gainful employment, given their skill base, were slim. They could work for a baron as part of a sec force, or work as solo robbers, ambushing and picking off the weakest individuals, or join a band of coldhearts that could occasionally tackle and overpower a small wag convoy, or attack a remote single-family cabin.

Furlong had tried the sec man job for a while. It didn't work out. He liked to use the stick too much, and he liked to steal whenever the opportunity arose. In short order he had made enemies of the very ville folk he was supposed to protect. Personally, he considered the itinerant-robber lifestyle too dangerous, even in a band of coldhearts. Robber packs were usually only a half-dozen strong. When it came to chilling for a living, there was safety in numbers. Big numbers. In organization. In the kind of deception and cover the carny provided.

When the first crackle of blasterfire erupted from inside the carny tent, Furlong didn't think anything of it. A few times before in other targeted villes, right after the gas had been released, when the folks in the front rows started foaming at the mouth, going into convulsions and dropping dead, some of the suckers at the rear had guessed what was going on. They had held their breaths and charged the exit with drawn blasters. What with the poison circulating inside the tent and the armed rousties in gas masks, the shooting had never lasted more than a minute.

This time the blasterfire didn't stop.

It dwindled momentarily, then resumed in a frenzy of back-and-forth reports.

"Nukin' hell!" Furlong snarled, even as his stomach sank to somewhere around his boot tops.

Something had gone wrong with the plan.

A few heartbeats later, bullets started slamming into the side of his wag that faced the tent. They passed completely through the Winnebago's cargo compartment, thundering on the metal walls above the armor plate, punching ragged holes in the thin sheet steel. A looter caught standing at the rear of the box was hit by many slugs at once. The top of his skull exploded spectacularly as he was hurled backward, into and over the edge of a bin. His upper body was hidden, but his legs, which stuck up in the air, kicked reflexively as they absorbed more impacts from the hail of lead. The bastard couldn't feel the slugs plowing into and ripping chunks out of his calves. What was left of his brains dripped down the side wall in a pink smear. The two other rousties working in the back managed to dive to the deck and the safety of the low wall of tempered-steel plate, covering their heads with their hands.

Furlong immediately dropped the louvered steel shades that protected the front and side windows of the RV's driver compartment. Through the slats, amid the flurry of dust puffs kicked up by the waves of bullet strikes, Furlong watched his looting crew fall dead in their tracks, cut down by withering blasterfire from the rows of plant beds.

The head roustabout jammed the front half of his Llama 9 mm semiblaster through the driver's-side window shade's gun port and fired back. The opening was so small that he couldn't look down the blaster's sights. There was just enough room for the action to cycle. To aim the weapon, he had to peer through louver slit eight inches above the firing hole.

Because Furlong had put in a lot of practice shooting through the port, it only took him two bracketing rounds to find the range to the nearest occupied plant bed. The dirt farmer shooters crouching there had found him, too. Their bullets spanged harmlessly off the outside of the armored window shade. Grinning, Furlong pumped slug after full-metal-jacketed slug into the stand of nearly ripe corn, aiming at the muzzle-flashes that winked at him from between the densely packed stalks.

After the fifth shot, a bib-front-overall-clad dirt farmer came tumbling out from behind the curtain of green. He crashed through the stalks, flattening them as he fell, arms outstretched, handblaster slipping from his fingers. He hit the ground and lay sprawled, head down, over the lip of the bed for a moment, then as he regained consciousness, started thrashing his arms, struggling to get out of the line of fire. Struggling in vain.

Furlong shot him again. The bullet plucked at the fabric of his T-shirt six inches below the base of his skull, just above the crisscross of his bib-front straps. The arms stiffened and then went limp.

An instant later, the head roustie was surprised to see the body scoot backward a foot, back between the corn stalks. Then he realized that someone had hold of the dirt farmer by the ankles and was trying to drag him back behind cover. Furlong dropped his aimpoint and touched off five more rounds. Ears of corn exploded juicily, broad leaves went flying, and the stalks parted for a second, revealing a second bib-fronted man, spurting jets of red from a devastating head wound as he slumped over the legs of his dead pal.

Autofire from behind the front and rear bumpers of the wags mowed down the six or eight ville sec men trying to advance to the closest of the plant beds. The rousties whistled and taunted the surviving sec men, even as their friends twitched in the dirt, trying to make them mad enough to charge into the killzone. Nobody charged. The farmers had discipline. After that, there was a lot of random shooting from both sides. A lot of gray smoke drifted about, but no chilling.

Everyone had taken hard cover.

There were no clear targets for Furlong out the

gunport, so he held his fire. It appeared that only a few of the ville folk were attacking them. Less than a dozen shooters were hidden behind the beds. He was relieved at that. He couldn't see out the windshield more than ten feet because of the wag parked in front of him. He had no way of knowing that the driver of the lead wag hadn't gotten his steel shades down quickly enough, and had been hit several times in the face and neck by high-powered slugs, and was unconscious and rapidly bleeding out on the floor of the driver's compartment. Because the lead wag completely blocked Furlong's view of the main road ahead, he couldn't see all the armed, angry folks slipping across it, then filtering between the predark buildings in order to circle behind him.

How a few of the dirt farmers could've escaped the death tent puzzled the head roustie, but it didn't worry him much. Once the other carny folk had figured out what happened, they would close in from the rear and wipe out the stragglers.

The looters weren't all that worried, either. The two guys in the back slipped off to resume their robbing. Because the carny chillers were partially protected by the three parked wags, blocked from the view and aim of the shooters, the flow of stolen goods from the huts continued to trickle into the rear bins. If anything, the rousties worked a bit faster because of the threat of being hit by random fire.

Gradually the shooting from the beds and the thunk of bullets rattling through the wag's rear compartment slowed to a steady trickle.

Then the potshots stopped altogether.

When Furlong first saw the ville folks breaking from cover and firing the other way, he thought for sure the carny side had finally launched an overdue counterattack. Several dirt farmers dropped in their tracks and three others sprinted away, two boys and a fat woman in a baggy dress.

"Now you're gonna get it!" he shouted over the roar of looter blasterfire that had already begun. He angled the muzzle of the Llama toward the fleeing trio suddenly caught in the middle of a cloud of yellow, bullet-raised dust.

Furlong aimed at the fat woman and fired four quick shots. What with the flying dirt and all the other bullet strikes, he couldn't tell if he'd hit her. Not that it really mattered. In the space of a heartbeat, all three lay in a dead heap in the middle of the road.

The shooting from both sides stopped.

The head roustie expected the counterattackers to show themselves then, to stand up and wave the all-clear. When that didn't happen, he was again at a loss to explain it.

Then three things happened almost simultaneously: a hollow thunk came from the left front bumper, a mist of red sprayed through the Winnebago's windshield louvers and a heavy-caliber roar erupted from the far side of the plant beds.

Furlong jerked back from the gun port, choking on the coppery smell of blood mixed with cordite. When he glanced down at himself, the gunshot still echoing through the compound, he saw the dense black hairs on his forearm were beaded with tiny drops of blood.

Not his.

Longblaster, Furlong thought at once. From the sound of it, a 7.62 mm. Firing from the cover of the beds, the rifle had picked off one of his guys with surgical precision, which meant there had been no carny counterattack on the dirt farmers. Furlong could remember seeing only one rifle like that in Bullard ville, and it had belonged to Ryan Cawdor. Only someone who'd practiced long and hard with a scoped longblaster could put the first slug in the ten ring. Furlong knew instinctively, deep in his guts that the one-eyed man wasn't only alive, but had also caused the disaster that was unfolding.

Even as that realization hit him, bullets started slamming into his wag from the other direction. Furlong hopped into the passenger chair to look out the louvers on that side. Whatever slim hope he still had of things working out evaporated in that instant.

There had to be a hundred ville shooters. They had the wags completely flanked and were massing their fire from the hard cover of the Taco Town building. Meanwhile, Furlong's crews were dumping their booty and returning wild fire as they ran for their lives.

Bullets rained down on his rousties in a hellstorm. They had no chance against so many blasters. Those caught out in the narrow lanes between the huts were hit by dozens of slugs. Those ducking into the huts in search of cover found none. The dirt farmers shot through the flimsy walls of their own cabins, nailing the looters crouching there. The Bullard ville sec men knew exactly what they were doing. Under the barrage of blasterfire, they pushed forward to the edge of the rows of shanties and the back side of the Burger Stravaganza.

As far as Furlong was concerned, the handwriting was on the wall. The opposition was too strong, and they were too well armed and trained. As he flipped up the driver's ob port and cranked over the engine, a pair of ashen-faced rousties jumped in the back of the RV. He didn't wait for them to shut the rear doors. Revving the engine, he cut the steering wheel hard over, then dropped it into gear. With a roar, the Winnebago lurched around the end of the wag in front. There was a jolting hop on the right side as the big wag's front wheel crunched over a fallen man, then Furlong accelerated, heading for the tent and the circled wags.

The first row of plant beds came up in a hurry.

Through louvered shade's ob port, Furlong caught a blur of movement to his right as people standing there scattered. He glimpsed the scoped longblaster first, then the black eye patch and dark curly hair. At the very last instant, he swerved the Winnebago at Ryan Cawdor, who was caught flatfooted in the open, with nowhere to run.

The look on the about-to-be-dead-man's face burned into Furlong's brain. There was no fear in it. No panic.

Nothing but calm.

The head roustie didn't give a damn how Cawdor took being squashed to a pulp.

"You're mine now!" he cried, pinning the gas pedal to the floor. "You one-eyed, fucking bastard!"

WHEN RYAN SAW the middle wag pull out of line and start heading their way, he knew it was a golden opportunity, and that it might be their last. It all depended on the driver seeing a way to rack up an easy last chill while he beat feet. "Spread out and take cover!" he ordered to the others.

"Here!" he shouted to J.B., as he tossed the Steyr longblaster to him.

With the companions scattering out of the way and the RV bearing down, Ryan just stood there like a mutie jackrabbit frozen in headlights.

He couldn't see the driver because of the armored screen that completely covered the windshield. Of course, that meant the driver couldn't see him that well, either, trying to steer while peeping out of the narrow ob port. At a glance, from the size and position of the slit, Ryan figured it had to have a blind spot to objects up close. At least that was what he was hoping for.

When the RV was ten feet away, he dived to his right, beyond the reach of the front bumper, rolling and coming up in a crouch. As the Winnebago rushed straight past him, he leaped for the driver's-side mirror strut. His left hand closed on the steel tubing, and the Winnebago's momentum whipped him around. His body weight broke the grip of the adjustment nut and the entire mirror assembly swung back, slamming him so hard into the outside of the driver's door that he concaved it.

Somehow he held on.

As the wag picked up speed, Ryan managed to get a toehold on the narrow step below the bottom of the door frame. In the middle of the louvers over the side window was a round hole, about two inches across. He yanked the SIG-Sauer P-226 from its holster and rammed its blunt nose through the blasterport. As fast as he could pull the trigger, Ryan fired into the driver's compartment, swinging the weapon's muzzle in a narrow arc. The driver started to swerve wildly back and forth to try to throw him off.

Ryan held on and kept shooting.

Because of the angle of the louvers he couldn't see if he was hitting anything. He could hear the sickly whine of ricochets zigzagging inside the armored box. The RV suddenly swung even more crazily, first to the left, then the right. It glanced off the end of a plant bed, tearing away twenty feet of corrugated chem rain awning and tipping over onto two wheels for an instant before slamming back down.

The impact almost threw Ryan off the door. It forced him to stop firing. Before he could resume, the Winnebago started to slow down, as if the driver had taken his foot off the gas.

After ten yards, the heavy RV was barely crawling along, which allowed the companions to catch up to it. It was still rolling as they rushed the open rear door. There was no hesitation on their part. They knew it was all or nothing, that the wag was their only hope of getting out of Bullard ville alive.

As the furious, close-range shootout raged at the back of the RV, Ryan tried to get the driver's door open, but it was locked from the inside.

He heard J.B.'s scattergun boom, and the sharp reports of Mildred's and Krysty's handblasters. The trapped rousties returned fire with their autopistols. With blasterfire pouring in through the open door, the steel plate that lined the box was a big negative. Buckshot and .38-caliber slugs cat's-cradled back and forth between the side walls.

After mebbe fifteen seconds, the shooting stopped.

"We got 'em," J.B. shouted to Ryan from inside the driver's compartment. The one-eyed man hopped down from the door's step.

After a moment, the driver's door opened and Ryan stared up at the Armorer's sweaty face and smeared glasses.

He climbed into the RV, and he and his old friend dragged the driver out from between the seats. The head roustie was paralyzed but alive, his spine shattered, the wounds in his hairy back leaking red. They dragged him out of the Winnebago like a roll of old carpet and dumped him on the ground, leaving him there to stare up at the sky, his mouth moving and the weakest of sounds coming out.

If Furlong had some famous last words, nobody was interested in hearing them.

Ryan climbed behind the steering wheel, which was no longer circular, having been almost half blown off by a load of buckshot, it was more a U shape. He glanced to the rear to see that everyone was okay. Mildred and Krysty nodded to him. Doc sat with his back against the crudely welded, quarter-inch steel plate that lined the lower third of the interior wall. His chin sagged to his chest, his eyes were closed, but he was breathing. Above Doc, the wall of the RV had so many bullet holes in it, it looked like a cheese grater. The wag had been completely stripped on the inside to make room for stolen cargo. The rear door was another crude bit of customizing; it was wide enough to get really big things inside. From the looks of things, the built-in bins contained more dead carny chillers than Bullard ville loot.

"Dump those bodies," Ryan said as he quickly eyeballed the controls of the RV.

"What about the loot the bastards collected?" Krysty asked him. "What should we do with it?"

"Keep the food and the ammo," he replied. "Everything else, shove out the back." He put his foot down on hard the gas pedal, heading for the big tent and Dean, Jak and Leeloo.

As Krysty and Mildred heaved the last of the three corpses over the back bumper, the sec men who had moved up to Burger Stravaganza finally found the range, and bullets started spanging into the rear door.

Chapter Twenty-One

At his father's command, Dean grabbed Leeloo's hand and they broke from cover on a dead run. Blasterfire blazed behind them as they sprinted across the stretch of open ground between the plant beds and the red-and-white-striped tent. Dean followed his dad's orders to the letter and didn't look back, no matter how much he wanted to. This wasn't the first time he'd been sent away from danger because of his age and his lack of experience. Usually, there was never anyone to look after but himself. This time his feelings of helplessness over leaving his dad and his friends to their fate and allowing them to sacrifice themselves were made easier to swallow by the responsibility he had been given. It was his job to get Leeloo Bunny to safety.

He took some comfort from the knowledge that the companions had always managed to beat the odds before. Someday, he thought, his father wouldn't make him go when things looked blackest. Some day, there'd be no question of letting him stand and fight with the others.

Dean ran hard and Leeloo ran stride for stride beside him. She was fast and strong for a person of her age. As they neared the side of the tent, slugs whined low overhead. He slowed and ushered her in front of him, shielding her from bullets with his own body.

The blaze of shooting wasn't the only ruckus going on.

The clatter of the pitched gunbattle had sent the mutie zoo creatures into a panic. The Wazl birds shrieked like shattering plate glass. The Worm hissed and shook its rattles. The naked stickies mewled in a terrified chorus. The swampie jugglers yelled for help, begging at the tops of their lungs to be released from their dung-encrusted cage. The entire Wolfram menagerie seemed to sense, and rightly so, that there would be no justice and no mercy if they were abandoned to the care of the revenge-seeking Bullard ville norms.

Dean was relieved to hear the din they made. The way the muties were all carrying on at once, no way could they sound an alarm over the presence of him and Leeloo. How many armed carny folk were still lurking among the wags? The boy had no clue. His plan was simple: slip under the trailers. He figured he and Leeloo could crawl below the rows of cages and stay out of sight until they found Jak.

As Dean and Leeloo raced past the first trailer, a great, flabby arm lunged out from the shadows, and before they could duck or dodge, it clotheslined them both. Dean ended up flat on his butt, with the muzzle of his Hi-Power blaster rammed deep in the soft yellow dirt. The impact of bone against bone, of forearm against chin made him see stars. He shook his head to clear it, looked over between the trailers, and his blood froze.

Baldoona, the two-headed scalie, its massive bulk seated on the ground, held Leeloo Bunny at arm's length, snatched up by a handful of hair, like a plaything. An unhappy plaything. The little girl was fighting like a demon, but her nails couldn't scratch the glittering, reptilian skin, and her kicks were futile against the creature's well-padded exterior.

Dean jerked up his handblaster, giving its slide a quick, hard thump with the heel of his hand to clear the barrel of dirt. Then he dropped the safety and put his finger inside the trigger guard, and drew a careful bead on the adult head. "Let her go!" he shouted.

By way of answer, the mutie soundly backhanded the wildly struggling child once across the face. It was a hard blow. Leeloo went instantly limp, a ragdoll held off the ground by sixteen inches of light brown hair.

"Bastard!" Dean snarled, thumbing back the blaster's hammer and jumping to his feet. "I said, let her go, you sack of shit!"

The two-headed scalie did nothing of the kind. Instead, it gathered up the unconscious girl in both hands, holding her by the wrists and ankles, and raised her to its mismatched mouths like an ear of roasted corn.

"Try to bite her and you're dead meat!" Dean warned.

"Do you really think you can chill me before I

chill her?'' Baldoona's adult head asked him with a
smirk. From the way the baby head was lopsidedly
grinning, it, too, was amused at the idea.

Dean said nothing. His finger tightened on the
trigger, taking up the slack to the break point. The
cap was about to snap.

''Think you can stop me with just one shot?'' the
adult head went on. ''Because that's all you're going
to get. And it won't be enough. In case you forgot,
I've got two brains, Bed Wetter.''

Dean grimaced, sighting the Browning first at one
nasty drooling head, then the other. From the only
shot angle he had, he couldn't hit both with a single
9 mm slug, through one head and into the other,
which was the only hope he had of taking out the
scalie before it could hurt the girl. He racked his
brain, trying to think of what his father would have
done in the situation, and came up with a gigantic
blank. There were no options as long as the monster
had hold of Leeloo.

Baldoona's adult head licked the unconscious
girl's cheek and ear, tasting her skin, and then
smacked its lips appreciatively. ''Cinnamon spice,
very nice,'' it said.

The baby head gibbered and chattered excitedly,
puckering its mouth, stretching its neck to the limit,
trying to get its lips and then its tiny teeth wrapped
around one of the little girl's bare feet, her sun-
browned toes, which were just out of its reach.

''No, don't!'' Dean cried, lowering his weapon.
''Don't!''

"'Don't'?" the adult head said, giving him an irritated look. "I'm about to eat this tender little morsel's face off, and you think I'm interested in your 'Don't'?"

"Let her go and take me instead," Dean told the monster. "You can eat me. I'm bigger than she is. There's more meat. I won't fight you, I promise. Just let her go."

"Yeah, sure…" the adult head said dubiously, opening its mouth, moistening its lips as it prepared to take the first bite.

"Look," Dean said, "I'll prove it. I'll put down my blaster." He carefully placed the weapon in the dirt at his feet. Parting with the Browning under these circumstances was one of the hardest things the boy had ever had to do. But the memory of what the scalie's two heads had done to the live pig in the big top was still very fresh in his mind. Dean couldn't bear to witness it doing that to Leeloo. He needed the scalie to put the girl down. That was step one.

Baldoona smiled with both its wet mouths. "You got yourself a deal, Piss Pants," the adult head said. The scalie then gently set the still unconscious Leeloo on the ground, smoothing her faded dress, then securely trapping her there by laying its grotesquely fat thigh across the small of her back. It extended both its arms to Dean, then snapped its fingers impatiently at him. "Chow time for Baldoona," it said.

There had never been a doubt in the boy's mind

that Baldoona would try to double-cross him, that it would eat them both, if it could.

Dean's plan was born of desperation. Get in close enough and use his legs and feet. Get inside the creature's guard and kick for the heads. Boot the adult head first, then the baby head. Boot them until they were knocked out.

But before he could plant his back foot and get off a kick, the scalie had him fast by the scruff of the neck. It was much quicker than it looked. And much, much stronger. As the fingers vise-gripped his neck, Dean realized the monster could break his spine with a sudden twist, like a dog with a rat. And when Baldoona squeezed a little harder, cutting off the blood flow to Dean's brain, all the strength went out of his legs.

The baby head started to coo as its suddenly helpless, living meal was drawn tantalizingly closer.

Dean smelled the mutie's huge, and hugely soiled, underpants as Baldoona grabbed his right hand by the wrist and raised to its adult head. The jaws opened wide, exposing short, wear-blunted fangs and a mossy, vaguely reptilian tongue. Dean tried to draw back his hand, but the scalie increased the pressure on his neck, and his arm went dead in the creature's grasp.

In the near distance, over the sounds of the shooting, Dean heard the engine of a big wag starting up, then getting louder and louder as it rumbled his way. Something hot and wet slithered between and around his fingers. The scalie was licking him. Dean cringed, anticipating the horrible pain to follow.

But Baldoona didn't start crunching on his fingers. The scalie's grip suddenly slackened on Dean's neck. Below him, Leeloo had regained consciousness, and was trying to claw her way out from under the weight of the mutie's thigh. It snagged Leeloo's slender shoulder, dragged her back under its leg and sat on her.

"Get out of here!" Baldoona's adult head bawled. "This is mine! All mine!" Dean turned his head and glimpsed a huge beige shape poised, as still as a statue, not five feet away.

The mountain lion, uncaged.

Its stare was locked on the scalie, and the stare was having its desired effect.

Dean saw that Baldoona was paralyzed. Both heads knew it couldn't run and hope to escape from the lion. Both heads knew it couldn't fight the lion and win. But neither head wanted to give up the food it had captured. The monster's four eyes glittered with fear. With gluttony. With anger.

Given its show-stopping big-top act, the scalie had had considerable practice in eating live prey against the clock.

In a flash it made up its minds.

But before it chomp down on either of its captives, the lion sprang. A beige blur rushed past Dean. Its front paws landed high on the scalie's sagging chest, knocking the air from its lungs and bowling it over onto its back. Dean was slammed to the ground but rolled free as Baldoona lurched up to defend itself from the attack of the giant cat.

Defense was futile, comical, even, and certainly brief.

As big as the scalie was, as quick as it was, it was no match for this adversary. Baldoona lunged for the lion's horned throat, and its fingers closed on air. Dean blinked in amazement. The big cat was standing behind the scalie, whose hands were clenched together, strangling nothing. With a single blow of its paw, the lion sent Baldoona crashing onto its hands and knees.

Dean had witnessed mountain lion kills before, but always at a distance, through the telescopic sight on his father's longblaster. Dog style was the position lions preferred for chilling man or beast.

It offered access to the prey's throat. In this case, it had a choice of throats.

Dean had no idea how big the lion's mouth was until it opened wide. It was so big that it could wedge the scalie's adult neck between its back teeth. As the lion squeezed down its jaws, cutting off air and blood and shrill cries of terror, the adult head turned a deep plum purple, eyes bulging out of their sockets, quasireptilian tongue protruding obscenely. The baby head, stabbed by the cat's stiff whiskers, began squealing, not unlike the live pig it had so recently consumed.

The lion didn't use its prodigious fangs on Baldoona. It used its back molars and started sawing, grinding away with them, twisting its thousand pounds of muscle and bone, digging into the dirt with its claws for added leverage, this while the scalie frantically bucked and jerked.

Dean grabbed Leeloo by the arm and pulled her away from the struggle. As they stood, Jak appeared from between the trailers, his Colt Python raised in a two-handed grip. The albino lowered the .357 blaster at once; it wasn't needed.

The power of the big cat's bite was in those back teeth, where the muscles of its jaws and neck could apply the most pressure. The vertebrae of the adult head's neck made a crunching sound as they shattered, and Baldoona's body went rigid, as if touched by a high-voltage wire. A thick spurt of blood escaped from the corner of the cat's mouth. The lion then turned its head slightly and with slitted eyes kept chewing, angling the points of its molars to shear the sinew and gristle that was all that was holding the head to the body. The severed adult head of Baldoona dropped to the dirt between its feet.

The baby head, suddenly all alone in the world, and facing at close range a nightmare of gory saber fangs, squealed even more shrilly. Six inches from the tip of its button nose, blood from the neck stump, a rude knob of red meat and bone, sprayed in a superfine mist, sprayed in time to the pounding of its no longer shared heart. The terrible crushing power of the lion's jaws had at least temporarily sealed off the clusters of severed arteries and veins.

The mutie cat made no move to bite off the little head on the big body. It stood there, watching, as the great, flabby scalie lurched to its feet and tried to run. Baldoona took a single step before falling to the ground. It lurched up again, the baby head grimacing from the effort.

And fell again.

"Look!" Leeloo said. "The baby head doesn't know how to walk."

It was true.

Baldoona struggled up again, its monumental bulk teetering horribly for a second, arms flailing for balance, then it crashed to its knees and started to crawl. The exertion and the repeated impacts broke open the compression-sealed vessels in its neck stump. As the baby head tried to pull itself away from danger, a gusher of gore spewed forth, bathing the side of its face, splattering into the dirt before it. The blood loss was massive. Baldoona managed to crawl only a few more feet before collapsing in a heap.

The lion burped, licked its paw, then scrubbed at the side of its face where blood had spurted, seemingly oblivious to the armor-shuttered Winnebago coming full speed around the curve of the tent.

As the RV bore down on them, Dean pivoted and swung up the Hi-Power, preparing to fire.

"Not shoot," Jak said, clamping his hand over the blaster's slide and pushing it away, "Ryan. See him take wag."

The albino wasn't the only one who'd seen it. Bullard ville sec men charged out from the cover of the plant beds, firing wildly at the RV as they ran.

The Winnebago skidded to a sideways stop ten feet from Dean and the others, shielding them from the bullets. The rear door opened at once. Krysty waved everyone in from the back bumper. She didn't have to tell them to hurry.

Dean followed Leeloo into the wag. The girl, uncharacteristically it seemed to him, immediately sought shelter in Mildred's open arms. Mebbe her close call with Baldoona had really scared her? he thought. She was tough, but she was still just a little girl.

The mountain lion hopped in last. Even though it did so almost silently, on its huge soft pads, the wag's springs and shocks creaked and the entire cargo box shifted from the additional half ton of weight. If any of the companions objected to its presence, no one said a word.

As the wag began to move, Dean climbed forward to the driver's compartment and braced himself between the driver's and front-passenger chairs. His father accelerated past the doomed menagerie, cutting around the perimeter of the circled wags. A flurry of bullets sparked and zinged off the steel shutter that protected the windshield. Blasterfire from the rousties still scrambling about, Dean presumed.

"How many of the carny wags did you wreck?" J.B. asked Jak from the shotgun seat.

"Cut tires on eight," Jak said.

"That's all?"

"No time more."

"Shit," J.B. said.

"We have to let the girl off before we bail on this place," Mildred said.

"She's right, Ryan," Krysty said from beside the rear door. "Leeloo needs to stay here with her own people. We can't take her with us."

"We can put her out on the other side of the tent, near the entrance," Mildred stated. "She should be safe there."

"Come over here now," Krysty said to the girl. "We aren't going to be able to stop for long. You're going to have to jump out quick."

Dean and Leeloo shared a look as she stood up. He smiled at her and nodded; she nodded back. Then Leeloo moved beside the rear door with Krysty.

As Ryan slowed to stop near the tent entrance, Krysty opened the door. She held Leeloo's arm as the girl prepared to jump off the back bumper. Before she could do that, once again bullets sang all around them. The ville sec men had anticipated their exit route and circled around the far side of the tent. They were lined up in a double row, massing their fire to catch the RV as it came around the curve of the tent, and before it could head for the break in the berm wall.

"No!" Dean cried.

But Krysty had already pulled Leeloo back inside.

"Everybody on the floor back there!" Ryan shouted over the clatter, stomping the gas pedal. "Get behind the armor!"

Bullets rattled the sides of the stripped Winnebago, howling as they passed through and through
overhead, slamming into the tempered-steel plate
with solid whacks.

Ryan steered for the berm entrance as the RV
picked up speed. The Winnebago vibrated over the
rough ground as if it was going to come unriveted,
unscrewed and unglued.

"Fireblast!" Ryan swore as the break in the perimeter wall came into view of the ob port.

No further explanation was necessary.

Bullets rained down on the armored shutters. The
ville sec men had already manned the top of the
berm wall on either side of the only exit, and now
they were cutting loose with everything they had.
The shooters' angle of fire meant that their slugs cut
through high in the walls and roof, and sliced into
the middle of the cargo box's deck. The companions
pressed their backs hard against the armor to keep
from being cut to pieces.

Ryan didn't give the sec men time to correct their
aim. When he passed through the gap and the choking pall of black-powder smoke, he was going seventy-five miles per hour.

For a full thirty seconds, as Ryan made for the
ruined interstate, bullets whined at them. Then the
shooting suddenly stopped. The range from the berm
was better than a half mile and growing, and the sec
men had realized they were just wasting bullets.

As Dean released his pent-up breath, Ryan and
J.B. raised the armored shutters, letting in the glare

of bright sunlight. The rutted highway stretched ruler straight for miles ahead. Over the engine and road noise, there was a crackle of small-arms fire from the ville behind them.

"Suppose they're finishing off the last of the rousties," J.B. speculated. "Mebbe the sideshow freaks, too."

"So much for Gert Wolfram's World Famous Carny Show," Krysty said.

"Good riddance," Mildred added.

Ryan reached over and tapped the twin fuel gauges with a fingernail. Dean noted that one was dead empty, the other jiggling above the one-third-full mark. His father eased off the gas. Dean knew he was trying to conserve as much fuel as possible, and put the maximum distance between them and Bullard ville before the tank ran dry.

"What are we going to do about the girl now?" Mildred asked.

"We can't take her with us," Krysty said. "She's too young. She's got to go back to her ville."

There was no argument from the other companions. Not even from Dean. "I can't just stay?" Leeloo asked him.

Dean shook his head. She was much safer inside the berm.

The little girl heaved a sigh.

"Trouble is," J.B. said, "how do we get her back to Bullard without getting ourselves all shot to hell?"

"We can wait until the smoke clears," Ryan said.

"Let everybody back there settle down. She can stay with us for a week or two, then we'll sneak her back."

Leeloo looked pleased at the idea.

"Uh-oh, Ryan," J.B. said as he glanced into his side mirror. "We got company."

Dean peered over his shoulder into the dirty glass, past the dust cloud they were raising. About a half mile behind them was a second dust cloud, and in the middle of it was an RV just like the one they were riding in.

"I count four carny wags chasing us," the Armorer stated, "including the biggest wag in their convoy."

"Who's driving them?" Mildred said. "Did the carny folk manage to escape, too?"

"Can't see," J.B. told her. "They're still too far back to tell. Probably got their armor down, anyway."

"Rousties or sec men," Ryan said, "it doesn't make much difference. You can bet they're after our hides." He pressed the accelerator to the floorboard and held it there.

Even so, the trailing wags were closing distance. Dean could see that.

Ryan was unable to make the RV go faster than seventy-eight miles per hour. The front end started to shimmy and shake. It didn't like going that fast, particularly on a chem-rain-etched roadway. The Winnebago sounded as if it was about to come apart.

The engine noise was tremendous, as was the whistling of the wind through hundreds of bullet holes.

"Start looking for a place to make a stand," Ryan shouted to J.B.

The flat plain offered little in the way of defensive prospects. With the river gone underground, there were no trees or even bushes. They had to keep going. Soon the lead wag was close enough to try to shoot at them. Dean could hear muffled blasterfire, but the bullets weren't making contact.

Yet.

"We got trouble ahead, Ryan!" J.B. cried.

Dean could see it. A pile of big chunks of concrete rubble stretched completely across the four-lane road. And was coming up fast.

Too fast.

His father cursed and slammed on the brakes. The Winnebago skidded on the rotted tarmac, its rear end fishtailing to the left.

Dean held on to the seatback with both hands as the world slewed sickeningly and clouds of dust boiled through the holed-out walls.

The RV hit the rubble barrier sideways, and in what seemed like slow motion, bounced off and came down with a jarring crash beside the crude arrow sign. Ryan punched the gas pedal, and the wag roared off the roadway. He had no choice.

"Dark night!" J.B. exclaimed when he saw the narrow track before them.

Which matched Dean's thoughts exactly.

Chapter Twenty-Two

The rutted lane was just wide enough for the RV. It ran flat and perpendicular to the interstate for thirty yards or so, then it started to climb up the steep slope. The series of switchbacks had been hacked out of beige sandstone bedrock.

"Got to be what's left of a predark road," J.B. said.

Ryan grunted in agreement. There was no road-grading machinery in operation postskydark. Highway departments worldwide had gone spinning down the toilet along with everything else. And as far as Ryan knew, in Deathlands there was no army of slave laborers large enough to carve even this crude one-lane track.

"Could have been some kind of service road," Mildred suggested. "For firefighters. Or power line crews." She pointed at the blue dark forest and mountains towering above them. "Had to have been National Forest up there. Could have been part of that."

Whatever its original purpose, the detour was an endurance course for the aged and now shot-up Winnebago. The hairpins were tight and the grade in some places was forty-five degrees, which forced the companions to brace themselves against floor and walls, or end up in a pile of tangled arms and legs in front of the rear door.

Negotiating the zigzags took some very careful driving on Ryan's part. Keeping the wag's momentum going with an automatic tranny was tough, and if he gained too much speed and lost control, there was no margin for error—he'd drop a wheel off the edge of the road. The unpaved track was badly rilled out in spots. The weight of the RV caused these parts to crumble, and the spinning rear tires cut deeper potholes and ruts. The lion sitting over the back wheels helped big time as far as traction was concerned.

As the Winnebago climbed, Ryan and the others could hear a chorus of engines below, roaring ominously as they lumbered up the track after them. They couldn't see the wags, though. They were about a quarter mile behind. Any hope of the pursuit giving up once they saw the grade and the narrow road had long since evaporated.

"Whoever they are," Krysty said, "they sure got a giant bug in their butts over us."

"If they were ville folk," Mildred said, "you'd think they would have turned back long before this. After all, they won the fight, even though a few of them got chilled in the process. Seemed like they would write it off as part of the cost of doing business…and building their reputation as a big-time, take-no-shit ville."

"Makes me think it's got to be the Magus who's after us," Ryan said. "We caused him a good bit more trouble than we did the farmers. We didn't just upset his plans for Bullard ville—we put an end to his carny operation. Mebbe forever.''

''And Magus doesn't give up until he's dead square even,'' J.B. added. ''That's a proven fact.''

As the grade continued to steepen, the RV lost so much speed that they probably could have outpaced it on foot, but abandoning their wheels at this point was out of the question. If they did that, once the ground flattened out, or turned downhill, the pursuers in wags could run them down. Nor was there any discussion of some of the companions getting out and trying to slow down or stop the miniconvoy with small arms or hastily rigged deadfalls. They were already outnumbered and outgunned. To have split up their force would have been suicidal.

Ryan was keeping an eye on the fuel gauge, as was J.B. Because of the angle of the road, the tank sensor was misreading the level. They both knew it had to be wrong. It showed more gas now than when they'd started.

''Look up there,'' Dean said, pointing out the side window. ''We're almost at the edge of the forest.''

All that separated them from the wall of hundred-foot-tall trees were a few switchbacks.

''What do you think, Ryan?'' J.B. asked.

From J.B.'s tight-lipped expression, Ryan knew the two of them were on the same wavelength. In a few minutes, the RV's fuel tank was going to run dry and they'd end up stopping somewhere, but not by choice. And mebbe not in the right spot to permanently slow the pursuit.

''I think the next hairpin is as far as we go in this wag,'' he said. ''I'm going to wedge it across the road. Make our friends down below come after us on foot. Everybody get ready to bail out.''

He had to park the Winnebago so it couldn't be budged, rammed or dragged out of the way. He knew the other wags couldn't back up without going over the edge, so there was no way they could pull it free. The lead wag could only push it. And the road leading up to the hairpin was so steep, there was no traction to do this. ''Everybody out!'' Ryan shouted when he reached the spot he was looking for. ''Head up the road for the tree line. Triple quick!''

As the companions ran ahead, he turned the front wheels hard over, put it in reverse and goosed the gas pedal, backing up until he bashed the rear end into the facing slope. Then he shifted into Drive, cutting the wheels as far as they'd go the other way, and moved forward a half yard. He put it in reverse again and repeated the process. After shifting into forward gear, he very carefully edged the nose of the Winnebago off the road, dropping it hard onto its front axle, with its rear bumper brushing the sheer wall on the other side.

Foot traffic could pass, if it hopped over the bumper.

But nothing else.

Below him, the sounds of the other wags' engines were getting louder. Ryan climbed out the driver's door, slung his Steyr longblaster and beat feet up the road, past the last switchback, up to the edge of the dense forest where the others were waiting.

As he approached the wall of trees, he sensed something unnatural. Ryan had come across a few other forests like this during his wanderings, lifeless except for the tightly packed trees. In this case some kind of mutated evergreen. There were no other types of trees, or vegetation for that matter. There was no undergrowth. Just pale-gray dust that shaded the seemingly endless sprawl of trunks. Smothering heat and silence. No air. Little light. It was the kind of place that gave children wake-up-screaming nightmares, and that grown men and women avoided like the bloody flux.

The rumble of engines coming up the grade suddenly stopped.

"They're at the barricade," Ryan said. "Let's go...we've got to hurry now."

He waved the others up the road that vanished into the immense stand of trees. J.B. went first, pulling Doc behind him on a tether. Mildred followed, then Dean and Leeloo and Krysty. Everyone but Doc and Leeloo had a weapon up and ready to fire. Jak stood beside the mountain lion, who hung back at the edge of the darkness, as if reluctant to set foot in the woods. Its huge nostrils flared, as if it had caught the scent of something filtering down through the trees.

"What's the matter with your pet?" Ryan asked Jak.

"He's afraid," the albino said.

Chapter Twenty-Three

The Magnificent Crecca plowed the biggest of the carny wags through the quarter-mile-long dust cloud swirling in the wake of Ryan Cawdor's RV. The red-haired, red-bearded man had lost virtually everything. Three-quarters of his convoy's chillers and wags had been left behind at Bullard ville. As had all of the mutie menagerie collected by Gert Wolfram and him over the years, except for Jackson, the singing stickie, who sat on the floor at his hip.

Not that Crecca had feelings for the collection of nukecaust-deformed critters—he didn't even have them for Jackson, who followed him around like a dog. What irked him was the wasted effort and missing income. In the blind rush to escape the wrath of the ville folk, all of the carny gear had been abandoned; it represented the sum total of his working life. Crecca had gone from being somebody important, from carny master, to master of nothing, in the space of a couple of hours; from anticipating the biggest score of his life to the kind of devastation he had only in his worst, sweat-soaked nightmares dreamed possible.

Much of the blame for his current predicament he laid at the feet of the creature who sat coiled across from him in the Winnebago's duct-tape-patched shotgun chair. The Magus was arrogant, parasitical and evil beyond imagining. And it had been his hubris and lust for the pain of others that had allowed Cawdor to turn the tables and beat him.

The steel-eyed monster's calf muscle continued to spasm intermittently, despite their disconnecting the damaged leg sensor. The contortions of his half-mechanical face in response were gruesome indeed. A once-human spirit was trapped in layers of metal and plastic, layers that seemed suddenly fragile. Yet, even wounded, he couldn't be disregarded.

The Magus was still in control of the situation. Crecca knew he had the capacity to replace all that had been lost. The wags. Gear. Muties. Chillers. But the Magus could also just limp away, jump into the past, or wherever it was that he disappeared to, and leave the Magnificent Crecca to a less than magnificent fate. As much as Crecca wanted to, he couldn't take his rage out on the Magus.

He didn't dare.

His was not the only anger boiling over in the Winnebago's driver's compartment. The Magus didn't like to be thwarted, in even the smallest, the least important of things. One-Eye Cawdor had been a thorn in his side for a long, long time. That Cawdor had outthought and outfought him, even though he and his friends had been trapped in the death tent, that Cawdor had perhaps managed to cause the Magus some permanent physical damage, wasn't something that would ever be forgotten or forgiven.

It was something that demanded retribution. ASAP.

It had been the Magus who, after they had escaped Bullard ville's perimeter, had ordered Crecca to turn and chase the hijacked wag toward Paradise ville. It had been the Magus who had ordered the rousties to begin firing on the RV ahead, even though he had known it was out of range.

Old Steel-Eyes had wanted to let Cawdor know a pack of wolves was howling up his backside. Wanted to make him and his companions afraid. It was more of the same, Crecca realized. It was the same primitive urge. Answered in the same way. The carny master was no whitecoat, certainly. He had no education whatsoever. And he possessed only the most rudimentary understanding of human psychology. But having dealt with robbers and chillers, and having been one himself for most of his life, the Magnificent Crecca thought he knew what drove the creature to do what he did: the Magus had to instill fear in others in order to quiet his own. Crecca found himself wishing that Ryan Cawdor had nailed the monster in the head with that sideways rain of full-metal-jacketed slugs, turning the brains and gears inside to a pile of bloody metal shavings.

"Rad blast!" the carny master said as a couple of hundred yards in front of him Cawdor nearly ran head-on into the concrete barricade across the highway. Crecca tapped his brakes, slowing in plenty of time to keep the wags behind from plowing into his rear end, and to make the hard right turn. As he did, he saw the white signal rock below the detour sign.

So did the Magus.

"Your scout's been up the detour and back, and left his mark," the monster said. "Which means there's probably a way out for Cawdor. Go faster! You've got to catch him!"

The big wag was a tight fit down the two-rut, dirt road. And things got even dicier as the track started to climb through a series of tight switchback turns. And as Winnebago gained altitude above the valley and the interstate, as the road grew ever steeper, Crecca's hands began to sweat on the steering wheel. Beads of perspiration ran from his wiry red hair, down the sides of his face and along the scar on his cheek. Wet marks appeared under the arms of his ringmaster's coat.

There was no going back. There wasn't enough room on the track for even the smallest of the four wags to reverse course, let alone turn. The drop-off at the edges of the unpaved road was precipitous. And there was nothing to stop the big wag if it tumbled over and started to roll. The RV and its occupants would be turned to scrap by the time it stopped at the bottom of the slope.

Jackson sensed its trainer's terror, even if it didn't understand the reason for it. Sitting between the driver's and front-passenger throne chairs, it gazed up at Crecca with black, dead eyes and began to whimper softly. Clear snot bubbled and popped at its nose holes.

"Shut that thing up, Crecca," the Magus said, "or I'll damn well strangle it."

Crecca had no doubt that his boss could and would do just that. "Jackson!" he snapped at the little mutie. "Get in your bed!"

With a chastened, hangdog expression, the stickie retreated to the pile of stiff rags behind the driver's seat.

The trio of rousties sitting on Winnebago's bench seat gave Jackson their full attention, hands on pistol butts. The needle-toothed critter was wearing its choke collar, but it wasn't chained up.

"Where is this blasted road going?" the Magus said. "We're headed up over the bastard mountain! I swear I'll cut out Azimuth's heart if he foxed us on this."

You'll have to stand in line for that privilege, Steel-Eyes, Crecca thought. He'd already started to wonder if his scout had even tried to tackle this road before setting down the all-clear marker. In the back of his mind, the carny master had begun to envision a further narrowing of the already too narrow track. And somewhere up ahead, mebbe just around the next turn, a collapse of the roadway, brought on by wash water from the chem rains and the weight of Cawdor's RV. Mebbe Cawdor and company were already down at the bottom of a ravine? Mebbe the RV was lying on top of Azimuth's crushed Baja Bug.

That would end the chase, but leave them in a

sorry fix. They'd have no way to retreat, except on foot.

Which meant the stinking Magus would have to be carried.

Crecca knew he'd have to do the nasty job himself. The Magus would demand it of him, because he knew how much touching him filled Crecca with fear and loathing.

The carny master gave the creature in the shotgun seat a quick sidelong glance. He looked away before the Magus could catch the flat, murderous expression in his eyes. Before he'd touch that hideous contraption of metal and flesh again, he vowed he'd put a .223-caliber tumbler in the back of its skull and boot it off the side of the mountain.

"Shit! Shit!" Crecca exclaimed as he negotiated a hairpin and suddenly came upon the stolen RV, turned sideways with its front wheels hanging off the road. He braked hard. "Could be an ambush!" he shouted over his shoulder to the rousties. After setting the parking brake, he reached up and deftly dropped the steel louvers that protected the Winnebago's cab.

There was no blasterfire.

It wasn't an ambush.

It was a blockade of the road, and it was perfect.

"What are you waiting for?" the Magus demanded of him. "Go on, clear the road. Push that damn wag over the edge."

Crecca released the emergency brake and crawled the huge RV up the grade. There was no question

of his building any real speed to bump the other
wag. There wasn't enough distance between them,
and he couldn't back up any farther because of the
turn and the wags stopped behind. On top of that,
the grade was too steep, and the road surface too
loose to get good traction. So Crecca merely crept
up and nudged the smaller wag. His front bumper
hit the middle of the cargo box. The back end of the
wag tipped a bit, but not the front, which was sitting
on its axle. He gunned the engine and the abandoned
wag moved a little, its undercarriage scraping over
the sandstone bedrock. Then it stopped. The back
wheels of the big wag started to spin, and its rear
end swerved toward the drop-off.

Crecca let off on the gas.

"What are you waiting for?" the Magus howled.
"Ram it!"

Much easier said than done.

Crecca let the RV roll back fifteen feet, as far as
he could go without hitting the wag behind, then he
tromped the gas pedal. The Winnebago struggled up
the slope, banged into the wag, deeply denting the
sidewall, but didn't budge it out of position even an
inch. If anything, the blocking RV seemed to be
wedged more firmly into the face of the uphill road.

"Get out!" the Magus cried. "Get out and find a
way to move the damn thing!"

Crecca ordered the three rousties out first. They
exited with their blasters ready. The carny master
waited a minute or two, then followed with a chain-

clipped Jackson at his side and an M-16 in his hands.

Crecca carefully watched his young stickie, who stretched out its neck and sniffed at the air. From Jackson's lack of blood lust, he knew that Cawdor and his pals were nowhere around. He waved for the other drivers and rousties to exit their wags. All in all, just fifteen chillers had survived Bullard ville, not counting the Magus.

A brief look-see told Crecca that they couldn't use the other wag to push or pull the obstacle out of the way. He climbed into the abandoned wag's driver's compartment and tried to start the engine. It cranked over, but when he put it in gear and tried to power forward, all he managed to do was dig holes in the road with the back wheels. Then the engine died, and he couldn't restart it. The gauges on both fuel tanks read empty.

The Magus wasn't happy when he got the news that pursuit of Ryan Cawdor would have to proceed on foot. With his bad leg, he couldn't walk, let alone run to keep up with the others. And if they carried him it would only slow the chase.

It meant he would miss the fun, unless the fun was brought to him.

Standing in the RV's open passenger doorway on his good leg, the Magus gave Crecca his marching orders. "I want three rousties to stay here with me. Take the rest and all the excess ammo, and track down Cawdor and the others. I don't care what you do to his friends, but I want you to bring Cawdor back here alive, even if he's barely breathing." He paused for a pain spasm to pass, then added, "And his kid, too."

Crecca chose three men to stay behind. As twelve of his rousties hurried to gather up the surplus ammo, the carny master stared at the lucky ones who weren't going ahead on foot. They were trying hard not to look too relieved. Though it had gone unsaid, he knew their job was going to be carrying the Magus to safety if he and the others didn't make it back. If Ryan Cawdor chilled them all, the monster left himself an exit option.

With Jackson securely leashed, the carny master led his men past the roadblock and up the road. He could see the wall of blue dark forest ahead, and above the tops of the nearest trees, the savage-looking ridge of the mountain.

Tactically speaking, Crecca knew the situation had changed. In the terrain ahead, the rousties' advantage in numbers was negated. Once inside the woods, they would be open to ambush. To hit-and-run strikes. To that scoped longblaster Cawdor carried.

Crecca payed out the full length of Jackson's chain, letting his mutie bird dog enter the forest first. Jackson strained hard at the leash, sniffing the air. Long strands of drool swayed from its chin as it made soft kissing sounds.

The stickie had caught Cawdor's scent.

back here after twenty miles before crackup?" He
paused for a while, about to pour ahoit edin... And
his side, the

Chapter Twenty-Four

From his vantage point, some six hundred feet above
the ruined interstate, Baron Kerr watched and
waited. The secondary fire road on which he hun-
kered ran over the top of the mountain and down its
west-facing slope, intersecting the ancient freeway a
quarter mile from the barricade, on the Paradise ville
side. Parked in the shadows behind a large sandstone
boulder a short distance uphill was the Baja Bug
Kerr had commandeered from the carny scout. From
the direction of Bullard, he could make out a series
of dust devils, twisting high into the windless afternoon sky.

The promised convoy approached the barricade.

The baron looked over at his three helpers, men
whose names he had never bothered to learn. He had
long since given up such formalities. Their hair,
their faces and their hands were black with encrusted
grime. As were his.

Their clothes hung in greasy tatters, showing
peekaboo filthy knees and elbows. As did his.

All three were grinning at the line of onrushing
wags, but in the backs of their eyes was a terrible,
hooded fear.

Kerr didn't ask himself if the terror he saw in their

faces was real or whether he was just imagining it.
He knew it was real because he felt it, too, the fluttering in the depths of his heart. It was the same
paralyzing fear that kept him from taking the Baja
Bug, which had more than enough gas to get him to
the safety of Paradise ville, from just driving away
and leaving the burning pool and all its horrors behind. The part of him that had been born James Kerr,
the pre-burning pool James Kerr, wanted more than
anything to make his break while he had the chance,
or failing that, to simply die. But that part of him
no longer had control over the body it inhabited.
That James Kerr had shrunk in size and influence,
until it had become like a lone passenger on a cruise
ship commanded by someone else. By something
else. The something else could steer the ship. Could
make it run faster or slower. Could, on a whim, run
it aground on some rocky shore, or scuttle it over
bottomless seas. And it did all this by manipulating
reality.

Or to be more precise, by manipulating the glandular secretions that determined his reality.

Kerr understood none of this, and not just because
he was ignorant of the complex biological principles
that were involved. His brain had been permanently
rewired by its long-term exposure to the spores' mutagenic chemicals. This rewiring had dug deep circular ruts in his already limited powers of thought.

The surviving scrap of the original James Kerr
saw the burning pool as a conscious, malevolent
force that had swallowed him alive, a whirlpool of

impossible power and perfect evil that had held him trapped, that had manipulated him like a puppet for longer than he could remember.

The larger portion of himself, the vast fleshy ship that carried him and that he observed with what seemed to be some degree of emotional detachment, had a much different view of the situation. The SS *James Kerr* found indescribable peace and contentment in living close to the pool and its lovely, twinkling spores. That James Kerr found serenity in tending the fungus in its moist grottoes, in following the pool's grisly, unspoken commands, in being one with its infinite majesty.

It was this larger James Kerr who, standing on the edge of the fire road, felt the crushing fear of separation and loss. He longed to be back in the pool's all-encompassing embrace.

Though passenger Kerr could only vaguely remember it now, there had been a time when he had been a whole, undivided being. He remembered traveling from Paradise ville to the pool and the blockhouse and the shanties. He had come on purpose, and he had brought many others with him. Like-minded others. Kerr had belonged to an extended family—religious cult of nearly a hundred members who had migrated from the east in a handful of rusted-out school bus wags. They came in search of a new eden, unpolluted land and water, freedom from the moral depravity that typified Deathlands, and personified Paradise.

In their view, the thriving ville, with its rows of

scabrous, twenty-four-hour gaudies and its lice-infested flophouse shacks, with its thieving, murderous residents, was nothing short of hell. After many weeks of enduring the indecencies and indignities of this postnukecaust Sodom, Kerr had located and purchased a crudely drawn map that, according to the traveling trader who had sold it to him, purported to show the way to exactly the sort of place the members had come looking for: isolated, protected, unsullied.

Kerr had then taken the map around the better sections of Paradise, in search of someone trustworthy who they could pay to lead them to the hidden high mountain valley.

No one trustworthy in Paradise would have anything to do with the journey. On seeing the map, most of the prospective guides just spit in the dirt and walked away. The few who would talk to Kerr repeated gruesome campfire stories about what went on in those cruel, dark mountains. About people going up there and never being seen or heard from again.

Because Kerr and his fellow cult members believed they were righteous in their faith and that their god wouldn't lead them astray; because they were desperate to leave Paradise, they chose to ignore the ominous signs and set out to find the place marked on the map on their own.

Inside of ten minutes of their arrival at poolside, the green lightning began to crackle and the spores fell upon them in a pale-yellow blizzard. It was so beautiful, so remarkable that the people cheered and rejoiced on the bank, taking it for a sign from God. Afterward, they had wandered down to the deserted shacks, to the ready-made, if shabby, little town. Within half an hour, the Clobbering Chair had been dragged out of the blockhouse and into the center of the ville's pounded-dirt square. The first victims had laughed as they pushed and shoved one another to win a seat and be strapped down. There was more cheering and rejoicing from these morally upright folk as the lead pipe smashed down and brains began to fly.

That day Kerr himself had swung the bloody pipe and led the cheers, and had supervised the butchery that followed on the muddy banks. His curse from the very beginning had been his receptivity to the pool's needs. It was what kept him alive. Even when he no longer wanted to be.

"Only five," one of the men standing near him said.

The words snapped Baron Kerr out of his dismal reverie. He refocused his eyes and saw that that was true. Just five wags. One was a ways ahead of the others. It was a much smaller convoy than the scout had described, but there was no way of knowing how many people were inside each one. There was room for sixty, for sure, if they were packed in tight.

Once all five wags had taken the detour and turned up the main fire road, Kerr led the three men back to the Baja Bug. He drove them down to the valley floor, then to the barricade across the interstate. At his command they got out and started dismantling the barrier, throwing the chunks of concrete onto the shoulder. It was the work of a couple of hours to pull it apart.

The baron didn't remember how many times he had temporarily diverted traffic in this way, but he had always diverted just enough to fill the pool's needs. Only so many could be accommodated in the ville. Only so many could be nourished by the fungus.

How long would sixty fresh souls last in the hidden valley? Kerr no longer tried to predict such things. Survival time was different for every individual. And sometimes, for reasons beyond his understanding, the pool chose to gorge shamelessly, taking a dozen or more unto itself in a single day.

Chapter Twenty-Five

Jak peered around the bend in the downhill road, squinting his ruby-red eyes to slits as he listened hard for the sound of pursuit. All he could hear was the rasp of his own breath in his throat. The oppressive and airless stillness of the deep forest pressed against the sides of his head; it felt as if his ears were plugged up with cotton. The albino shifted the Colt Python to his left hand and wiped the sweat on his right palm on his pants leg. His mission wasn't to fight a rearguard, delaying action, but to verify that the carny chillers had abandoned their wags and come after them on foot. And to try to get a head count if he could.

Jak had been the natural choice for the job because he was the fastest runner of the companions. But he was as slow as molasses compared to the lion, who sat on his back legs on the road beside him, its huge head cocked, its round ears upright and at full attention.

They are coming, Little Brother, the big cat said without making a sound, the words appearing in Jak's mind.

Knew would be, Jak thought back. How many?

Fourteen pairs of feet.

That all? We seven, eight with you...

I cannot help you fight them.

Jak was astonished by this revelation.

Only men with blasters, he thought. You stronger. You faster. Is it this place? Bad place?

It has nothing to do with them, or with these woods. It is what's coming, what waits for you all over the mountaintop.

The lion gently placed its huge paw on his shoulder. Little Brother, I am not afraid. I just know how it ends, and I know I have no part in it.

How know? How can know if hasn't happened yet?

Time as we know it is an illusion. It's an artifact of the physical forms we currently inhabit, of their hardwiring, if you want to look at it that way. The truth is, everything that has ever happened, that ever will happen, is always happening. All of history takes place in the same endless instant. There is no past, no present, no future.

If can see it, tell what happens.

I cannot tell you.

I live? You live?

It doesn't matter. Don't you understand? Nothing ever dies, Little Brother.

Wife Christina, baby? Jak thought at once, a great lump rising in his throat.

They are with you, and with me.

The albino shook his head, grimacing. They weren't. If he knew anything, he knew that much. He had buried them with his own hands.

Not understand.

But you will, Little Brother. Listen. They are close now.

A second later, Jak heard footsteps crunching on road. Many men were running uphill in a skirmish line.

We go, Jak thought as he holstered his hand-blaster. He ran soundlessly up the road, sprinting on his toes and high kicking. The lion loped easily along a few steps behind.

When Jak rounded a turn and glanced back over his shoulder, the great cat was gone. Simply gone.

There was no crashing noise as it plunged deep into the tangle of deadfall.

No twinkling dust trail spiraling up into the slanting rays of sunlight that pierced the forest canopy.

No goodbye.

"It's JAK," Dean called softly to his father's back.

Ryan stopped jogging and turned in the middle of the road, as did the others, watching as the albino raced up to him, out of breath. The lion was nowhere to be seen.

The one-eyed man said nothing about the lion; he had other, much more important questions. He listened, grim faced, to the answers Jak gave. They were pretty much what he had expected. The carny chillers were still pursuing them. They were on foot and about a quarter of a mile behind. There were as many as fourteen in the band.

Ryan had three choices, as he saw things. The first

was to lead the companions over the mountain at top speed and keep on running, figuring that the coldhearts would eventually wear down and abandon the chase. That outcome was something he knew he couldn't count on, especially with the Magus giving the orders. There was also the problem of his not knowing the terrain; with a full-out run there'd be no time for recce, and he could get his people boxed in.

Permanently.

His second choice was to find the highest ground and spread his force out to defend it. This would work, he knew, but only if they had enough ammo to do the job, and enough time to reach the peak. Ryan couldn't tell how far off the summit was because of the densely packed trees. It was possible that the pursuit could overrun them before they reached it.

His last option was to locate a suitable place for an ambush and bushwhack the murdering bastards as they came up the road. That seemed the best course of action to him. At the very least, it would reduce the number of the opposition, and the massed fire might scatter, or even turn the rest back. There was also the possibility that the companions might nail them all—the odds were only two to one. It also gave him the choice of the chilling ground, which was a big plus as far as he was concerned.

"Okay, let's move," he said, waving the others up the road after him.

They jogged in a single file along the steeply angled track, which wound back and forth through the clustered trunks. There was dust underfoot, and there was stifling heat, but there were no signs of life other than the trees. Here and there, shafts of light speared through breaks in the canopy of branches, spotlighting the blue-gray, bone-dry litter of fallen needles and limbs.

As he trotted up the road, despite the suffocating heat, a chill passed down Ryan's spine, and he felt a sudden tension at the back of his head, as if the skin had drawn drum tight. It was the same feeling he had experienced when they uncovered the death pit in the nameless ville.

In the grim, eerie forest, he sensed the presence of the dead. Multitudes of the dead, swarming around him.

With an effort he shook off the sensation. He had more than enough flesh-and-blood trouble on his plate without worrying about legions of ghosts. J.B. ran behind him, straining to pull along the roped Doc. After Doc came Dean and Leeloo, then Mildred and Krysty. Jak brought up the rear. Ryan dropped back to jog alongside the Armorer.

"Got to quickly find us a place to chop down these bastards," Ryan said in a low voice to J.B.

"Anyplace along here will do," he replied as they rounded a right-hand bend that led to a long, dark, uphill straightaway. "Split up on either side of the road. Sandwich 'em."

Ryan held up his hand, signaling for the column to stop. "This looks like a good spot for an ambush," he told them. "We let 'em get to the straight part, then cross fire them from behind. If we work fast, we can keep them from getting to cover in the trees."

"They'll be tracking us, for sure," J.B. said. He pointed at the jumbled footprints in the soft dirt of the road.

"By the time they figure out we've doubled back on them," Ryan said, "they'll be caught in the kill-zone."

He then split up the companions, sending Dean, Leeloo, Mildred and Krysty to the left side of the road. He led Jak, J.B., and Doc to the right, into the stand of trees on the inside of the bend.

He didn't have to tell any of them to make their shots count.

Underfoot, the dry twigs and branches snapped and crackled. Puffs of talc-fine dust rose like smoke into the shafts of light.

From the other side of the road came a tiny squeak of a smothered sneeze.

Leeloo, Ryan thought as he watched Jak and J.B. slide belly down in the litter beside the dark trunks. The Armorer made Doc lie down beside him, then followed Jak's example and pulled some of the crumbling forest litter over them both, creating a double-wide hide.

Before burrowing into the deadfall himself, Ryan carefully placed the Steyr longblaster behind a tree. The range was going to be too close to use it, and the bolt action was way too slow for the shoot-out he envisioned. The idea was to keep the chillers from reaching cover, and that meant cyclic rate. He dropped the SIG's magazine into his palm, making sure it was topped off. Then he set out a second and a third full mag in front of him, hoping to hell he wouldn't have to reach for them.

Chapter Twenty-Six

As he trotted up the road, the Magnificent Crecca carried his .223-caliber assault rifle by its plastic pistol grip, with his trigger finger braced outside the trigger guard, just behind the thick curve of the 30-round magazine. The rifle's fire selector switch was on full-auto. The carny master was ready to whip-saw with hot lead anything that moved among the seemingly endless ranks of tree trunks.

Nothing moved on either side of him, nor on the road ahead.

Not yet, anyway.

Even after his eyes had become adjusted to the darkness of the forest, the road before him was dim. Fifty feet ahead, it blended in with the dismal shadows. There were a few bright patches where sunlight penetrated the branches, but they actually made things worse. They made the surrounding shade seem even darker, more impenetrable.

That's why he had brought Jackson along. What the little stickie couldn't see, it could sniff out.

Because Crecca had been concerned about Jackson's breaking free and running off to hunt solo, he had reeled in all but five feet of the leash, keeping the mutie on a short lead. He kept the rest of the chain coiled in reserve. He could pay it out if the creature made a sudden lunge, taking the strain off the leash, but still keep the stickie under control.

Sensing the excitement of his trainer and the impending bloodshed, Jackson was no longer the singing, dancing puppet that so fascinated the hicks and hayseeds. Under conditions of the hunt, the real Jackson, the pure stickie, bubbled to the surface. The raw chiller instinct that could never be beaten away.

Eyes bulging, whipcord muscles straining, needle teeth bared, it was a perfect example of a stickie on the prowl, a thing that drops from a tree limb into your path with sucker-tipped fingers reaching for your face; a thing that crawls through the half-open cabin window and makes soft kissing sounds under your bed before it crawls in with you, who are too scared to move or cry out.

If either of the prevailing legends was true, if the Magus had constructed the stickies using predark whitecoat technology, tinkering with the minute components of human sperm and egg, or had simply snatched a few breeding pairs from the future, then he had peopled—*monstered* was a better word—the nightmares of every Deathlands child.

As the carny master and Jackson rounded a turn, the stickie made a sudden surge forward. It dropped onto all fours and scrabbled madly at the dirt, trying to break free, straining at the chain. The prey was close. Very close. Despite the pronged choke collar, it was hard for Crecca to hold the stickie back with his left hand. To get Jackson's full attention and

cooperation, Crecca had to forcefully apply the butt
of the M-16.

Twice.

He then drew his men together on the right side
of the road. They were all breathing hard and dripping with sweat from the heat and the uphill run.
They weren't scared; Crecca could see that. These
were hard-eyed, hard-bitten, longtime professional
chillers. They had willingly dug mass graves, administered mercy bullets to the survivors of the poison tent and robbed the huts of the still warm dead.
They'd gotten all pumped up for the big chilling at
Bullard, but had been denied their fun and their
spoils. Like Crecca, they had lost everything in the
debacle. Not just gear and livelihood, but friends and
lovers, too. And the blame for all of it could be laid
at the feet of Ryan Cawdor and his pals.

The rousties wanted payback. As did he.

Crecca spoke in a hushed whisper, so softly that
the chillers had to huddle around him to hear.
"From the way the stickie's acting," he said,
"looks like Cawdor and company are waiting for us
up around the next bend. They've probably got both
sides of the road covered, expecting us to walk into
their sights. Not gonna happen that way, though."

The carny master drew a rough sketch in the dirt
with a fingertip. It showed the right-hand turn in the
road that they could see the start of from where they
stood. He pointed at the three best shots of his crew.
Each had a high-capacity, semiauto handblaster. "I
want you to sneak up to the edge of the bend on

this side of the road," he said, pointing at his sketch. "Don't show yourselves until you hear the first shots. Then move out around the curve and nail anyone running down the road." He tapped the point of the curve. "From this spot," he said, "you've got control of the KZ. If no one breaks and runs, locate the shooters in the cover on the left side. For sure, they'll be potshotting at us from across the road. Pin 'em down and chill 'em."

Crecca waved for the other men to huddle even closer. "The rest of us are going to work our way through the brush and get behind the shooters on the right. It's going to be tough for us to move quietly through all the fallen branches. Go slow and watch your step until we're in position. When I give the attack signal, we'll charge them from the rear—the more noise we make the better, and either we kill the bastards outright or drive them onto to the road, where they can be picked off easy by our sharpshooters."

As Crecca straightened, Jackson let out a soft whine. The mutie was quivering, head to foot, with excitement. That wouldn't do. Not at all. The carny master showed the stickie the rifle butt.

Jackson immediately dropped to its back in the dirt and offered its trainer its soft underbelly.

"That's better," Crecca said. He unclipped the chain from the choke collar and pointed at his heel.

The little stickie meekly obeyed.

Crecca shouldered his M-16, then stepped off the road and into the trees. The thick, rough-barked trunks were unevenly spaced. Some grew only inches apart while others were a double arm's length from their closest neighbor. Blocked from sunlight, most of the lower branches had withered and fallen off. Around the base of each tree was a ring of rotting debris: a rat's nest of dusty needles, twigs and small and large limbs. Some of these brush piles stood as high as Crecca's waist.

By staying as close as possible to the trunks, he avoided most of the tinder-dry material. He was forced to advance at a snail's pace, watching the placement of each step, occasionally toeing a rotted branch out of the way when he couldn't safely see past it.

The nine carny chillers moved in a widely spaced line behind him. They followed his trail exactly, keeping close to the tree trunks, stepping in his steps. Because they were pros at both chilling and stalking, they made only the slightest rustling noise as they advanced; Crecca could hardly hear it over the thudding of his own pulse in his ears.

The carny master couldn't see the road because of the wall of trees, but he knew that he had to be close to it—no more than thirty or forty feet away. He also knew that he had to be just about on top of Cawdor and the other ambushers...if they were really there.

As Crecca paused for a moment, his back pressed to a tree trunk, Jackson started acting nervous. The stickie wasn't whimpering or mewling; it was making the softest of soft kissing sounds while gazing

warily at the butt of the M-16. The expression on
the little stickie's face said it was trying hard to keep
quiet but couldn't.

Cawdor was near, all right.

Crecca turned around the trunk, holding the assault rifle at hip height, his finger inside the trigger
guard, lightly resting on the trigger. As he brought
down his right foot, something unseen crunched under his heel. With the weapon poised, he froze, scanning the row of trees in the gloom directly ahead.
He saw nothing, and was about to make another
jump forward when, not ten feet away, leaning
against the base of a tree, he caught the shape of the
scoped Steyr longblaster.

A hair-raising jolt of adrenaline coursed through
his veins.

As Crecca opened his mouth, before he could get
out a warning shout, a hand appeared from under
the pile of debris, grabbed the sling and snatched
the rifle away.

RYAN LAY BURROWED under a brush pile of his own
making, with a peekaboo view of the empty road.
From his position, he couldn't see Krysty or any of
the others on the opposite side. The heat under the
debris was sweltering. Beads of sweat ran down his
spine and trickled in rivulets over the sides of his
rib cage. Dust mixed with body oils and perspiration
had turned the backs of his hands ash-gray.

Ever since he and the others had taken cover, he
had been counting the elapsed time in his head. He

had figured it would take the chillers mebbe four minutes to close the quarter-mile gap if they were moving at a quick pace. And under the circumstances he couldn't see them doing anything but double time to catch up. At that rate, they should have been in his sights more than two minutes ago. With every second that passed, his concern grew.

It wasn't a sudden noise that first alerted him to the danger they were in. It was an awareness. A vague presence. A pressure. From behind. He had been counting on the dry deadfall to give them plenty of advance warning of an enemy approach from the rear. Listening hard, he could hear the rustle of branches not twenty feet away. The enemy was closing in, and there had been no alarm. He picked up a twig and flicked it at J.B. to get his attention. The Armorer immediately reached over and nudged Jak, who turned to look Ryan's way. Doc looked at him, too, but his eyes were unfocused.

Ryan jerked a thumb toward the woods behind them. The gesture was urgent and emphatic. And to the companions the meaning was obvious.

They'd been foxed.

J.B.'s jaw dropped in disbelief, but he recovered at once, grimacing as he thumbed his wire-rimmed glasses back up the bridge of his nose. Ryan pointed across the road, toward Krysty and Mildred's position. J.B. and Jak nodded in agreement. The ambush was scrapped. They had to rejoin their forces, and quickly.

Ryan gathered up his extra mags and tucked them

inside his waistband. As he started to reach back to grab the Steyr, a branch cracked ten feet away. No way was he going to leave his precious sniper rifle behind. He caught hold of the longblaster by its shoulder sling and jerked it away from the tree, using his momentum to roll up onto his knees.

A fraction of a second later someone shouted, "Get 'em!" Then all the chillers were yelling as they crashed through the brush. Ryan brought up the SIG. He couldn't make out any targets, but as gunshots barked and bullets thudded into the trunks all around him, he returned fire, spraying a line of 9 mm death in front of him at waist height.

Behind him, the rocking boom of J.B.'s scattergun was followed by the roar of Jak's .357 Magnum blaster.

The yelling abruptly stopped. The attackers broke off their charge and took cover.

Ryan waved for Jak, J.B. and Doc to beat feet. He caught up to them as they reached the road. As they started to cross, three rousties appeared around the bend and, dropping to kneeling positions, opened fire on them.

"Go!" Ryan said as bullets whined overhead. "Go!"

He and the others returned fire on the run.

The roustie on the far right took a slug very low in the chest. From the way it blew him off his pins, it had to be one of Jak's .357 Mags. It lifted and slammed the man onto his back. Screaming, kicking, he clawed at his guts as the companions dived into the cover of the trees.

Blasterfire from Krysty, Dean and Mildred sent the two survivors scurrying back around the bend.

Ryan cupped his hand and shouted to them, "Frog it!"

It was their signal for a full-out, fighting retreat, which meant the two groups would retreat by leap-frogging each other, one group defending the bend while the other ran up the straightaway to take up a firing position at the next turn.

They were already in high gear up the road by the time the chillers got themselves reorganized. As they withdrew, the companions used sparse blaster-fire to keep the opposition back at least a hundred feet. They weren't trying to make perfect shots. The gloom of the forest made pinpoint accuracy next to impossible. The idea was to stall the enemy until the companions could reach a place they could success-fully defend. And they were trying to use up as little ammo as possible in getting there. J.B. didn't shoot at all, but concentrated on keeping Doc moving up-hill; there was no point in wasting his scattergun rounds on a long-distance delaying action.

As Ryan raced past Mildred, she knelt at the side of the road and fired her Czech-made target pistol from a braced stance. Her skillful potshotting brought a shrill yelp from the shadows far down-slope. Then a wail filtered through the forest. She had nailed one of the chillers with a .38 slug. Nailed him good, from the racket he was making.

The flurry of answering gunshots echoed off the trees. As Ryan made for the next bend in the road, bullets spanged into the surrounding trunks and clipped off branches. The road above them continued to wind back and forth among the dark trunks. There was no choice but to keep on running until they reached the summit.

Which, he knew, couldn't be far away now.

Then the opposition shooting slowed.

Two possibilities occurred to Ryan as he knelt, the SIG's sights aimed downhill. Mebbe the chillers had realized that the running gun battle was burning up ammo that they were going to need when they caught up to their quarry. Or mebbe they had finally figured out that if the companions made the summit they might have a defensive position too strong to overcome no matter how much ammo they had.

When a moment later the shooting stopped altogether, Ryan knew the chillers were concentrating on closing the distance before the companions could reach the high ground.

"Forget the frog!" he told Mildred, Dean, Leeloo and Krysty as they dashed past him. "Straight to the top! Triple fast!"

Ryan sent J.B., Doc and Jak up ahead of him. The albino grabbed Doc under one armpit and J.B. took the other. They half carried the old man as they ran.

After three more bends, the track straightened. Ryan could see the light breaking through the tops of the trees above them. The road rose even more steeply as it approached the summit. By the time he reached the edge of the tree line, Mildred, Krysty and Jak were on their bellies on the crown of the road, sighting their handblasters down the straight stretch. He moved past them and joined J.B. who was already doing a recce of the summit.

There was no hardsite for them to defend. The crest of the summit was rock, all right, but it was as flat as a pancake. The densely forested ridge bracketed the top of the road, which continued steeply down on the other side of the crest.

Words weren't necessary between the two long-time trail buddies.

It was bad.

Bastard bad.

They both knew the chillers could filter through the ridgetop trees and flank them if they tried to make a stand on the summit.

"Get up!" Ryan told the others as he turned back from the table of rock. "We can't stay here. We've got to keep running. Cross the summit and take the road down the other side."

One hundred fifty feet below him, at the start of the straightaway he'd just climbed, four rousties tried to cross the road.

In a single, fluid movement, Ryan shouldered the Steyr, dropped the safety and snap fired.

The longblaster boomed like a cannon under the canopy of tree branches.

A heavy-caliber bullet skipped harmlessly off the road between the chillers, but the near miss made them throw themselves headfirst into the brush. And,

Ryan thought, as he broke from the crest and ran after the others, it would give them something to worry about as they worked their way up through the trees.

As he sprinted down the descending road, he got his first glimpse of the little lake. From the high angle of view, it looked like a predark painting or advertisement—serene, pastoral, inviting.

What appeared to be steam or fog hung over part of its mirrorlike surface. With chillers at his back, Ryan had no time to examine the placid panorama more closely. He raced to catch up with his companions, who were already nearing the muddy shore.

Chapter Twenty-Seven

Thick brown muck sucked at Mildred's boot-soles as she struggled around the denuded perimeter of the lake. She couldn't run through the mud; it was too deep. And trying to run made her boots sink in past her ankles, which slowed her even more. She wasn't alone; the other companions had the same problem.

Inside the dead zone of the lake's shoreline, the few remaining trees were long dead, barkless, bleached, eroded smooth. Like gigantic, stripped bones jutting from the wet earth.

What could have caused it? she wondered.

Something to do with the lake, obviously. Some localized toxicity or disaster perhaps springing from skydark. It occurred to her that the lake might be sitting over a volcanic vent. But there was no telltale aroma of sulfide. The smell was of intense biological decay. Not just swamp, though. Latrine. Abattoir.

She noted other scattered boot prints and the deep wheel tracks in the soft ground. Someone else had been here, and recently, she thought. So the place was probably safe enough.

While the other companions trudged slowly ahead, Mildred paused for breath. She turned and glanced up at the summit. She saw Ryan coming down the steep road in great strides, his longblaster in his hand. There was no sign of the chillers yet. She took the opportunity to lever open the cylinder of her ZKR 551 target revolver and dump out its two spent shells. She thumbed in a pair of live bullets, then snapped the cylinder shut. This done, she stuck her hand back in the bag pocket of her fatigue pants and counted the loose .38-caliber cartridges. There were eight left.

Mildred felt no wave of panic at this discovery. She wasn't afraid of dying, and she wasn't afraid of pain. She had already lived through both.

And through resurrection, thanks to Ryan and the companions.

Though she didn't fancy dying again, she had hopes of a different kind of resurrection the next time.

Then she caught a flash of green out of the corner of her eye, out over the smooth surface of the lake, green that seemed to climb from water to sky. Even though she heard the crackle of the electrical discharge, she thought she had imagined it. She shook her head to clear it. Lightning didn't travel in that direction. Not normal lightning, anyway. Perhaps the heat and the exertion were making her mind play tricks she thought.

But there were more flashes, much stronger ones. Even in broad daylight, they underlit the clouds of dense fog or mist that were rising like steam from the placid surface. The zapping sound of electricity was followed by a baritone rumble of thunder that she could feel in her guts.

"Did you see that?" she said to J.B., who had stopped twenty feet away with Doc at his side.

"Yeah, I saw it. Don't understand it, but I saw it. What's going on out there?"

Krysty, Dean, Leeloo and Jak had momentarily stopped, too, and were staring at the micro-weather system.

"It's kind of pretty," Leeloo remarked. "I like the green lights."

"Look!" Jak said, pointing at the water under the cloud.

A strange sort of disturbance had appeared directly under it. A riffling on the water. A dark, churning circular patch about 150 feet wide, as if billions tiny fish were schooling. Or large predatory creatures below were herding them into a vast, panicked ball.

Something wasn't right.

Something definitely wasn't right.

"Everybody," Mildred said urgently, waving her arms, "move back from the water."

The others didn't move. They all seemed mesmerized by the strange, localized electrical storm. All of them but Doc. The old man wasn't even looking at the lake. He was staring fixedly at his own muddy boot tops and mumbling to himself.

Then a blast of withering heat sucked Mildred's breath away as the low-hanging clouds began to surge toward them.

"Triple red!" Mildred cried over the fresh round of rolling thunder. "Triple red! Run!"

Still nobody moved.

Deep shadow swept over them as the clouds blocked the sun.

Cursing, Mildred slogged over to Leeloo and Dean, grabbed their arms and tried to pull them away from the shoreline.

Too late.

The snow came down slanting, driven sideways by the scorching wind.

The pale-yellow precipitation was the size of snowflakes, but it wasn't snow, she realized at once. It was hard. More like tiny hail. Or bird shot. Hard enough to bounce a foot in the air as it hit the mud. The deluge of spores peppered Mildred's plaited hair, head, face and shoulders. Instinctively she held her breath.

Dean and Leeloo went rigid under her hands. Though she used all of her strength, she couldn't budge them. They seemed to weigh a thousand pounds each, their feet rooted to the earth. When Mildred took in the expressions on the children's faces, she was horrorstruck. Their mouths hung down slack, their eyes open wide, the pupils hugely dilated.

There was something in the snow, she thought, or whatever the hell it was. Something bad.

Mildred knew if she was going to help Dean and Leeloo, if she was going to help any of her friends, she had to get clear of the downpour. She had to escape its effects and regroup. The deep mud sucked at her boots as she tried to run from the bank, which made her exert more energy and burn more of her limited air.

The cloud moved with her, tracking her.

And along with it came the pale snow.

Mildred looked back over her shoulder and through the blizzard saw Ryan coming, on the double. He had reached the start of the shoreline and was hurling himself through the muck. She wanted to wave him off, but what with the thunder and the heavy downfall, he was still too far away for her to warn. And he was way too far away to help her.

She managed another few steps before her legs gave out. On her knees in the mud, with tears of rage running down her cheeks, her last thought before she inhaled was Oh, fuck!

Then she sucked down air.

And her brain melted.

As Ryan charged down from the top of the road, he took in the desolation surrounding the tiny lake. He also saw the companions standing there on the bank. Doing the opposite of what they were supposed to be doing, which was running for hard cover. Instead, they were gawking.

Under the strange clouds forming over the small body of water, something twinkled, then flashes of green reflected in the lake's mirror surface. Over the thuds of his footfalls, he heard the snap and crackle of lightning. A fraction of a second later, there was thunder.

Big-time thunder.

The unnatural was natural in Deathlands. The unexpected was to be expected. But this storm brewing in miniature caught Ryan completely off guard. The lightning was green and blindingly bright. It didn't spear down from the clouds to the lake; it traveled upward, from the water to the billowing mist. The savage intensity of the electrical discharge filled him with dread. It appeared that he had done the last thing he had wanted to do: he had led his friends into something far worse than a box canyon.

"Nukin' hell!" he swore, running faster.

As fast as he ran, he couldn't beat the clouds. Blown by a jet wind from hell, they rushed from the lake to the land. Waves of pale yellow snow sheeted over the companions, who, except for Mildred, still didn't move. The stocky black woman was trying to drag Dean and the little girl away from the shoreline. After a moment, she gave it up, and before Ryan could reach her, turned to run for the edge of the lower slope. The snowstorm engulfed her. For an instant, she disappeared behind a pale curtain. When the curtain shifted, she reappeared. Ryan saw her stagger and fall. She didn't get up.

By the time Ryan got to the bank, the snowfall had already stopped. The earth around the waterline was heaped with foot-high yellow drifts, which seemed to shrink even as he walked through them. The tiny particles crunched like rice underfoot. They were rapidly dissolving into nothing. Over his head, the clouds dissipated into fine cottony wisps. Along the bank, the smell was of a slaughterhouse, of ancient, multitudinous butcheries.

The storm had been short-lived but devastating. All of the companions had been struck to stone, either left standing, riveted to the boggy ground, or facedown in the muck, like Mildred.

His own heart trip-hammering, Ryan checked Dean's throat for a pulse. As he felt the steady beat under his fingertips, a gunshot cracked from high above. A slug slapped the soggy ground two feet away.

When he looked up, he saw a half-dozen chillers spilling over lip of the summit, charging down the road toward him.

More gunshots rang out from the rim. For the chillers' short-barreled blasters, the range was extreme. They couldn't hit the side of a barn. Bullets smacked into the mud, plunking into the water. Ryan glanced over his shoulder to see if anyone had been wounded. It was hard to tell. One thing was certain, though. If the companions were still alive, they weren't going to be for long. The rousties were rapidly closing the distance.

Ignoring the hot lead screaming by him, Ryan slogged over to the nearest dead tree. He flipped up the lens caps on his scope and used a forked limb as a shooting rest.

Aiming the Steyr uphill, Ryan took a stationary lead on the man running in the middle, holding the sight post way low to compensate for the shooting angle. He tightened down on the trigger, and the longblaster bucked and barked. He rode the rifle's recoil wave, cycling the bolt action to put another live round under the hammer, recovering his target as it ran headlong into the heavy caliber bullet. The chiller's arms flung wide and loose. His handblaster went flying as he was hurled backward and down. Ryan glimpsed the soles of his boots as his legs bounced limply in the dirt.

Stone dead.

The rest of the chillers kept coming, as if the danger hadn't sunk in yet.

Ryan aimed low and fired again.

His second target had to have realized he was in trouble, as he slowed a fraction of an instant before the firing pin snapped. Instead of running into the arc of the speeding bullet and meeting it square midchest, he met it square midshin. His right leg buckled under him, the long bones shattered and he sprawled on his face in the road.

The others took cover then, scurrying behind the boulders on either side of the road.

As Ryan cycled the Steyr's action, he was hit from behind by an intense blast of heat and another wave of rolling thunder. He looked back to see that the strange clouds had already re-formed in the middle of the pool and were rushing toward him, pushed by the hot wind. As the yellow, snowlike substance began to fall over the lake, Ryan rushed to Dean's side. The boy still stood like a statue, seemingly as dead as one of the stripped trees. Ryan was trying to scoop him up into his arms when the spore blizzard swept over them, making a rattling sound as it bounced off the earth, and off his head and shoulders.

Ryan took a breath.

And he smelled flowers.

A billion flowers.

It was as if he had been dropped into fields of ripe blossoms that stretched in all directions as far as the eye could see. The concentrated sweet perfume overloaded and short-circuited his nervous system.

No longer aware of the flurry of bullets zipping past him, Ryan dropped the Steyr muzzle-first into the mud.

WITH THE ENEMY longblaster controlling the short stretch of road leading up to the summit, Crecca and crew had had no choice but to bust brush. After the carny master split the rousties into two groups, they circled through the trees from opposite sides of the road, coming out on the flat bit of table rock that was the mountain's peak.

Cawdor and company were nowhere in sight.

Peering over the edge of the summit, Crecca saw their quarry, by now already a good distance away, down by the shore of the little lake. He paid no attention to the clouds, nor to the thunder and lightning. He immediately dispatched six of his chillers to go after the bastards. He kept the best long-range shots with him, and ordered them to fire, but sparingly, from a prone position along the peak, this to keep Cawdor and the others pinned along the shore.

Even though the carny master was expecting the longblaster to bark again, when it came, he flinched at the boom. Out the back of one of the rousties on the road beneath him came a puff of red mist. His shredded lungs and heart gusted from a fist-sized exit hole, spraying over the side of a boulder. The big-bore rifle slug exploded against the sandstone.

Before Crecca could react, before the other men on the road could react, the longblaster spoke again. A second chiller was hit in the leg and fell to the ground. The rousties ducked for cover as the wounded man crawled after them, screaming. Then the sharpshooters Crecca had lined up along the summit resumed firing, with gusto, at the man behind the dead tree. The roar of their weapons drowned out the thunder from below.

Crecca saw Cawdor drop his weapon. The carny master completely misread what was going on beside the lake. Because all of the companions were standing still or were down, he thought they'd given up, that they were surrendering.

"Stop!" he shouted at the men on either side of him. "Stop firing!"

They obeyed, albeit grudgingly.

"But we've got 'em cold!" one of the rousties complained. "We can cut 'em to pieces from here!"

"The Magus wants Cawdor and his son alive," Crecca told the man. "He's made big plans for them. Do you want to tell the Magus how you spoiled his fun?'' The chiller's face blanched, and he shook his head.

Truth be told, Crecca wanted to take them alive, too. He intended on doing some serious, prolonged, but nonlethal ass-whipping before he turned them over to the whims of old Steel-Eyes.

The carny master yanked Jackson to its feet and led his men down the hill, stepping over bodies of their fallen comrades. The man wounded in the leg had already bled to death. For the first time, Crecca really took in the run-down shanty ville below the lake. It looked deserted, and he wondered why Cawdor and the others hadn't tried to make it down there. They could have at least made a fight of it then. As Crecca neared the lake, he warned his men to keep their blasters ready and the targets in their sights, in case it was some kind of trap.

Thunder rolled from the clouds over the lake. Crecca ignored it. Jackson, on the other hand, became highly agitated at the noise, more agitated than Crecca had ever seen it. The stickie started hopping about nervously, from one foot to the other, and it strained at the limit of the chain, digging furrows in the mud as it tried to get closer to the water's edge. It sputtered and coughed on its own outpouring of saliva.

Crecca gave the little stickie a hard, snapping jerk on the choke collar to bring it back in line. By way of answer, Jackson turned and bit him, a single savage, needle-toothed chomp and release.

"Bastard!" the carny master cried, wrenching back his torn and bleeding left hand and dropping the end of the leash. He managed to keep hold of his M-16, but no way could he shoulder it and take aim at the fast-moving little mutie. Jackson made a beeline for the lake, dragging the length of chain behind it. Without a pause, it jumped in, feet first, and then started to run, thrashing into deeper water, toward the minisquall that was forming.

Crecca had never seen the stickie swim before.

And it turned out it couldn't.

After Jackson had battled its way to neck height in the water, its hairless head slipped under, popped up and went under again, ever farther from shore, as if the stupe creature were trying to continue to walk along the bottom. It was then that big swirls appeared all around it. Brown back and tail fins knifed up through the surface. The smallest of the fish circling Jackson looked to be about six feet long. As Crecca watched, the little stickie was buffeted and knocked about by lunging fish. Jackson surged backward, its head throwing a bow wave, as it was half lifted into the air by something huge beneath the surface that had hold of it.

"They're eatin' the ugly little fuck!" one of the chillers exclaimed. "Tearing the living shit out of him!"

Crecca cradled his injured hand. The needle teeth had punctured the webbing between his thumb and forefinger. It looked as if it had been caught in the gears of a machine. He was lucky not to have lost a few fingers. On the other hand, his investment in Jackson was a total write-off. Only a triple-stupe droolie, or someone contemplating suicide, turned his back on a stickie that had tasted human blood.

"They can have him," Crecca said. "It'll save me the cost of a bullet."

The carny master walked away, leaving Jackson to its fate. As he moved closer to Ryan and the companions, he waved with his assault rifle for the chillers to follow.

"Are they dead, or playing dead, or what?" said the man beside him.

The carny master didn't answer. His quarry seemed to be frozen in position, but he could see the slight rise and fall of their chests. They were breathing, and they were making little movements of the face: their closed eyelids twitched, as if they were asleep on their feet and dreaming.

"Not dead," Crecca announced.

He moved in for a closer look at Cawdor.

"What are you and your pals playing at, One-Eye?" the carny master asked.

There was no response.

Crecca jammed the muzzle of the M-16 against Ryan's cheek.

No response.

"They sick?" a chiller asked. "If not, I'll make 'em sick." With that, he slammed J.B. in the lower back with the sole of his boot. The Armorer grunted at the impact, which knocked him off his feet. He fell into the mud near the waterline, but didn't move.

Out on the lake, another storm was brewing. Green lightning crackled and lit up the bleached trees.

Crecca was so preoccupied with Cawdor that he didn't bother to look over his shoulder. Because of that, he missed seeing Jackson pushed ashore by the pod of lungfish. The little stickie crawled out of the shallows on its hands and knees, sputtering and gasping.

"Let's have a peek at what you've got under this," Crecca said, reaching out and flipping up Ryan's eye patch.

"Rad blast!" exclaimed the chiller peering over his shoulder.

The carny master grinned. "Now that is what I call—"

A wave of scalding heat slammed Crecca's back. Then it started to snow spores, and the carny master not only forgot what he was about to say, but he also forgot who he was.

SLOWLY, RYAN BECAME aware of his surroundings. He had no idea how long he'd been unconscious. It could have been a minute or an hour. But no longer than that because the sun was still high and hot.

He remembered the perfume, and remembering brought a flashback of the amazing sensation it had wrought. An instantaneous, almost orgasmlike disconnect of his normal consciousness, as if sheared away by a blow from a longblade. He recalled drifting upward, joyous, freed of his body and all its restraints.

Though he was certainly back in his body now, some of the detachment remained. He felt like a spectator. And he couldn't summon up the strength or the desire to fight what was happening to him, to return to the way he was, before the perfume.

Ryan's head turned, though he had no sense of having willed it.

And couldn't stop it.

He saw the others around him. Not just his companions, but the carny chillers, too. As his head moved, things appeared to him in a series of freeze-frames. Instead of shadows on faces, he saw bands of beautiful pure colors. Lavender. Blue. Yellow. He wanted to pull his SIG from its holster, but he couldn't make his hand reach for it. The failed effort was exhausting. He didn't need the blaster anyway. No one was fighting. Everyone looked dazed and barely able to move.

Dean stood right where Ryan had left him. And the little girl was there, too, by his side. Their eyes were open and blinking. They appeared to be all right. A sound intruded on his thoughts, a banging noise, as if a muffled gong was being struck over and over.

As this was happening, he caught a whiff of a wonderful scent riding on the breeze. Not the flowers' perfume again, but the aroma of food. Delicious food. Until he smelled it, he hadn't realized how hungry he was. And then the gnawing ache in his stomach was more than he could bear.

Ryan wasn't the only one so affected.

Companions and chillers alike roused themselves and began shuffling away from the lake. The violent storms over the water had subsided. The lightning was no more. The low-hanging clouds had vanished. Its surface was a gentle, rippleless mirror of sky.

As Ryan walked beside his son, a hand gripped his shoulder from behind. A weathered hand. Doc stepped up alongside him. Words came out of the old man's mouth in a language that Ryan didn't understand. They angered him. He shrugged off the hand.

Ryan, Dean, indeed everyone marched in time to the gong beat echoing up from the ville below. Ryan felt disjointed and clumsy, as if he had great soft pillows for feet. Though they were all famished, no one hurried to be first. They all moved at the same rate, which was dictated by the rhythmic banging.

The lake sat on a plateau of sorts. Beyond the mud bank was a long incline of limestone bedrock. Ryan and the others climbed carefully over the moss and tufts of spike grass that rimmed the edges of the deep, crumbling fissures and yawning holes dotting the slope. There was flowing water, too. It seeped steadily from the bottoms of the fissures and the cracks. It was as if the whole face of the hillside leading down to the ville were weeping.

When he and Dean reached the bottom, Ryan ignored the little hamlet. He followed his ears and his nose to the center of the pounded-dirt square, where a black man with dreadlocks was hammering on the side of a fifty-five-gallon steel barrel with a chunk of firewood. As he drummed, he danced, shaking his hips and bobbing the tangled mass of his woolly curls to the backbeat. He had a raging hot fire burning in the barrel, and a metal grate was pulled over the flames.

Heaped on the grate like a stack of cannonballs were the sizzling sources of the delicious aromas.

"Come on, now, doan be shy," the cook sang as the new arrivals approached. "I got plenty here. It's real Jamaica jerk, an' that's no lie. Getcha good stuff while it's hot!"

Even though Ryan wanted what was on that grill more than he'd ever wanted anything, he didn't push. No one did. Everyone seemed to be in the same state.

Able to move, but rockily.

The detached part of him knew that things were very wrong. That he should have long since gone for the eighteen-inch panga sheathed below his knee, and started cutting chiller throats. That his companions should have been doing likewise. But the proximity of their mortal enemies no longer seemed to matter to any of them. The need for revenge and the need to stop the butchery had become irrelevant. They were possessed of only one desire: to eat what was being offered. For all the black smoke coming off the grate, and the folks standing in line in front of him, Ryan couldn't even see what he was waiting for.

That didn't matter, either.

The line slowly advanced. Dean reached the head of the line in front of Ryan. The boy shuffled off without a word, juggling between his hands a smoking, char-roasted glob that his father barely got a glimpse of.

It was big, though.

The size of a ripe melon.

Using the piece of firewood, the cook rolled another glob out of the flames, across the grate, this time in Ryan's direction. It looked like a twenty-pound meteorite that had just crashed to Earth. "There you go, mon," he said. "Best you'll ever eat."

Ryan grabbed it up with eager fingers. It burned him, but he wouldn't let it drop. He, too, juggled the smoking glob and sat in the dirt beside his son. Dean was already tearing into his food, as was the little girl from Bullard. They were making animal noises of pleasure.

The first bite made Ryan groan. It was roast beef. And more succulent than any he had ever eaten. The outer part was crispy and tasted as if it had been rubbed with spices. The charred flesh came off in juicy shreds under Ryan's teeth. Inside, the roast was so tender it melted in his mouth.

The more he ate of it, the more he wanted. The thought that mebbe it was too much to consume in one sitting, of mebbe saving some for later didn't even enter his mind. Ryan ate the whole thing and when he was done he licked the sweet grease from his fingers. Stomach bulging, he lay back on his elbows. Dean curled up on his side, unable to budge after packing so much into his gut. Everyone else was on the ground, too. Most were flat on their backs with their eyes closed.

Ryan was no longer hungry, but he was getting sleepy. In a disinterested way he took in the immediate surroundings. The only building of note was the low concrete blockhouse across the square, which was obviously predark. The rest of the ville was a shit heap of ramshackle, dirt-floored lean-tos barely tall enough to crawl into. Clouds of black flies swarmed over the open latrines and trench sewer.

In a corner of the square stood a predark metal chair. It had straps looped around both arms, and on the chair back was a dark, broad stain that looked like dried blood. Flies hovered over it, and over the long piece of iron pipe that leaned against it.

Ryan dozed off to the seesaw, droning buzz. He was awakened with a start a few minutes later by a sound that he couldn't place. He sat up and looked around; others were stirring, as well.

He realized that the noise was coming from a wag engine when he saw the approaching Baja Bug. To him it sounded as if it were underwater. And it had a strange, shimmering halo, or aura around it, a purple-and-rose glow that had nothing to do with its flat gray paint job. When the Bug stopped beside the square and the driver got out, Ryan's jaw dropped in astonishment. He opened his mouth to speak, but words failed him.

He thought he'd never see Trader again.

Chapter Twenty-Eight

When Doc awoke, he was standing by the fetid lake-side, tethered by the waist to John Barrymore Dix with a length of nylon rope. He felt that a terrible burden had been lifted from his shoulders, if only temporarily. It wasn't the first time that he had shaken free from a nightmare of grief and personal tragedy.

Nor the hundredth.

Even when he was fully functional, Dr. Theophilus Tanner walked an emotional tightrope.

The whitecoats of Operation Chronos had trawled him from the bosom of his family, from his wife, Emily, from his young children, Rachel and Jolyon, in November 1896. They had removed him against his will to the year 1998, and had kept him prisoner while they experimented with him. He was never to see his loved ones again or to know their fates.

After two years of poking and prodding, of drawing blood and giving him electrical shocks, the whitecoats had decided to be rid of him and his infuriating truculence. In December 2000, just before the world flamed out forever, Doc was sent forward in time to a destination unknown. The grim future he found himself trapped in was called Deathlands.

In terms of his own biological age, Doc Tanner was still in his thirties, but he looked twice that old. A man could only take so much pain, so much loss, so much truth about the real nature of existence. The lack of control over anything that mattered. Once that limit was reached, the only refuge was the abyss of madness. And it was over that bottomless chasm that Doc's tightrope was stretched.

Though his memories of the most recent events were largely blurred, he retained a few clear images. He recalled the nameless ville the companions had happened upon, and the pit of the dead marked by the upraised hand of the female corpse. He recalled the infant and its mother, whose final, desperate agonies had shocked him into reliving his own mind-shattering loss.

Less clearly, he remembered the start of the companions' long overland pursuit of the carny villains, and how with every step along that trail, his anger at being trapped in a universe so infinitely perverse seemed to build, and finally to turn inward. More vaguely, he recalled J.B. towing him and caring for him like a child.

Gradually, over the next few minutes, Doc's full power of thought returned to him. He was a man with a classical education. A highly accomplished scholar of the nineteenth century, a trained scientific observer. As such, he saw that all of his companions seemed to be stricken by the same malady: Ryan, Dean, J.B., Jak, Krysty and Mildred appeared dazed and confused, as did the little girl. And the others, the coldhearts from the carny, were in the same state. The immature stickie was in the worst shape of any of them. Doc had never seen a terrified stickie.

It was an unnerving sight.

He untied the rope from his waist and reached down to help J.B. up from where he lay sprawled in the mud. For his trouble, he was roughly shoved away.

"What's wrong, John Barrymore?" he said with concern. "Are you injured?"

As he rose, the Armorer pointedly turned his back on Doc.

Doc tried to thank the man who had saved his life, who had protected him, but the Armorer refused to acknowledge his existence. Behind his wire-rimmed glasses, J.B.'s eyes were narrowed to slits, and his jaw was set hard. Doc looked at Mildred and Krysty, hoping to get a more friendly reception, if not some sympathy or an explanation for the rejection.

"Dr. Wyeth, Krysty, what in heaven's name has come over John Barrymore?" he asked.

Evidently the same thing had come over them.

Neither of the women would speak to him. Not a word. They looked through him as if he weren't even there.

Muttering to himself, Doc bent and retrieved his precious ebony swordstick. J.B. had dutifully carried the antique weapon for him this far, only to let it drop on the bank when he fell. Its ornate silver lion's-head handle had landed in the mud along the waterline. He carefully wiped it clean on the hem of his frock coat. Doc then removed himself from the company of his infuriatingly silent friends and leaned against the trunk of one of the stripped trees. For a painful moment he considered the possibility that what he was experiencing was just another mental aberration, another waking nightmare, that this time he had perhaps slipped even more deeply into madness. He was jolted by the memories of seeing the yellow snowfall and the bizarre storm on the lake—snowfall and storm that no longer were in evidence. Memories that supported a diagnosis of insanity.

Doc had to know whether he was still dreaming. He unsheathed the sword hidden in his stick and drew its razor edge ever so lightly across the back of his middle finger just above the knuckle. The blade tugged at his skin, then cleanly sliced through. He grimaced at the pain. And the wound bled.

He wasn't dreaming. This was all real, all horribly real.

From the distance there came an insistent, repetitive banging. It was accompanied by an odor that Doc couldn't place, but something unpleasant was burning. The combination of stimuli seemed to animate both the companions and the carny chillers. Everyone started moving slowly away from the bank, in the direction of the banging and the caustic smell.

Doc caught up with Ryan as he, too, fell into line.

Taking hold of his broad shoulder, Doc said in a pleading voice, "Ryan, dear boy, can you understand me? I fear we are all in terrible danger. We must get away from this place at once. Can you hear what I am saying?"

The one-eyed man roughly pushed his hand away. The expression on Ryan's face made Doc draw back. Ryan had never given him a look like that. It said Touch me again and I'll chill you.

As hurt to the core as he was puzzled, Doc let all the others shuffle past him like zombies. Why was he alone unaffected? he wondered. He could come up with no answer to the question.

Bringing up the rear, Doc followed the ragged line down the mountainside. The steep limestone slope had fractured into huge, smooth blocks, and it had been eroded from within, hollowed and honeycombed by centuries of seeping groundwater. As Doc descended, he kicked loose an avalanche of rock that tumbled into one of the gaping potholes. After a few seconds, he heard splashes and clunks as the stones hit bottom. It was a long way down, and a hard landing.

At the base of the slope was a ville of sorts. To Doc it looked like a trash midden heaped up around an ancient concrete blockhouse. Ahead of him, the others crossed the dirt square and lined up in front of the flaming burn barrel and the wildman pounding on its side with a round chunk of firewood. Doc stepped wide to the right and moved closer so he could get a better look at the goings-on.

Shouting and dancing to his own erratic rhythms, the black giant bent to pick up a big gray glob from a pile sitting in the dirt, and threw it on the grate where other globs sizzled and smoked. The objects being seared were the size and shape of predark bowling balls. Or adult human heads. The black flies seemed especially partial to the ones on the ground.

When Doc's turn came to partake, he quietly gathered up his share of the charred stuff. He wasn't hungry, just curious. Moving away from the others, he used his swordstick to cut the glob in two. Even on close inspection of one of the halves, he couldn't identify the material as animal or vegetable. It had a slippery, rubbery texture like raw liver, and it was laced with branching veins and tough sheets of sinew. The powerful aroma of urea it gave off so turned his stomach that he had to hold it at arm's length.

Then something moved on the cut surface.

"By the Three Kennedys!" he exclaimed. "What have we here?"

With the edge of his fingernail, Doc pried loose a translucent, wormlike creature. Eyeless and spineless, it was eight inches long when fully stretched, and when released, it sprang back into a tight coil.

Doc dropped the parasite in the dirt and with difficulty—it was tougher than it looked—crushed it to a pulp under his heel. He pushed the two halves of the glob back together and rolled them into the doorless entry of a lean-to made of tattered, opaque plastic sheeting.

Turning back to the square, the sight of his dearest friends eagerly gorging on the contaminated food made his skin crawl. He hurried over to Krysty and tried to take her half-eaten meal away from her.

"It's full of parasites!" he said as she mightily resisted.

For his concern, Doc received a quick, hard punch in the solar plexus that doubled him up and sent him staggering away. As he gasped for breath, Krysty tore off another greasy chunk with her teeth and poked it into her mouth with her fingertips.

Chastened and humiliated, Doc retreated to the scant shade along the front of the blockhouse, where he could observe and absorb, and perhaps form a plan of action. It appeared that his companions were suffering from some kind of sudden-onset mass mental illness. They all presented the same symptoms, which could have been caused by a shared trauma or by exposure to some infectious agent. Doc knew he had to uncover the cause before he could come up with a cure.

After the huge, if monotonous meal, everyone in the square except for Doc and Jackson fell asleep where they lay. As it turned out, the only other creature who wouldn't eat the awful stuff was the young stickie, which was most curious. A picky stickie was something Doc had never seen nor heard tell of. The naked mutie stood resolute guard over its snoring, red-coated master.

After a few minutes, Doc heard the sound of a wag approaching from the north, apparently traveling a different route than the one he and the companions had taken.

A battleship-gray Baja Bug rumbled over a rise and roared over to the square. Like a pack of dogs, the sated diners stirred from their beds in the dirt. They rose to their feet as the Bug stopped. Its doors opened and four men piled out. Doc's attention was drawn and held by the driver, a tall thin man in a tattered straw cowboy hat and scratched wraparound sunglasses. He wore his dark hair in a long braid and had a snaggly goatee beard. His clothes were ripped and filthy. His hands were filthy, too.

From the way the black cook prostrated himself in greeting the driver, Doc assumed that he had to be the hammered-down ville's headman.

Doc was struck by the way the faces of the companions and chillers lit up in his presence. Everyone seemed thoroughly delighted to see the man for no reason that Doc could fathom. As far as he knew, none of them knew him from Adam.

If Ryan beamed at the driver as if he were a lifelong hero, Mildred's response was even more surprising, and unsettling. The middle-aged black woman sidled up to the man in the cowboy hat and slipped her arm around his lanky waist. She fawned on him in an overtly sexual way that was absolutely contrary to her nature, as Doc thought he understood it. The Dr. Mildred Wyeth that he knew was a self-contained and self-sufficient human being, whose stoic and clinical reserve was the stuff of legend, and she never fawned over anything or anyone.

While Doc pondered this development, the crowd moved away from the Baja Bug, leaving it unguarded. With no one to stop him, the old man wandered over to the driver's door and looked inside the open window. There were no keys in the ignition. Keys weren't needed. The ignition had been pulled apart, leaving the ends of two bare wires hanging under the dash.

Doc straightened and looked over the Bug's roof. Before anyone could stop him, he knew he could easily slip behind the wheel, start it up and drive away. And once he got rolling, he was free. Doc had the means to escape, but he made no move to do so. He couldn't abandon his friends to whatever fate had in store. No more than they could leave him when he was out of his mind.

The situation he faced was much more difficult, however. He couldn't simply lasso the companions and tow them away. There were too many of them. And it appeared from recent events that they would resist his intervention, and do so with all their might. His predicament was colossal, yet he was determined to succeed. From the middle of the square, the driver addressed the rapt crowd in a soothing voice. "My name is Kerr," he said. "I am baron here. Now that you have been fed and rested, there is work to be done. Most rewarding work, as you will soon discover. Follow me."

The throng set off to the foot of the limestone slope. Everyone but Doc was animated, even cheerful at the prospect.

Baron Kerr stopped at a wide gash in the rocky hillside, the entrance to a natural tunnel. "Everything comes from the burning pool above us," he said. "It is the wellspring of our existence here. Its flesh becomes our flesh, and our flesh becomes its flesh. Our meaning and destinies are intertwined.

"Everything you will see inside the caves belongs to the pool. It lives both inside and outside the mountain. Its miraculous filaments wind through solid rock. Growing. Nourishing. Enlightening."

From his academic experience at Harvard and Oxford, Doc guessed that they were being treated to a stock speech that had been given many times before. The baron was like an aged professor droning out the same lecture for decades. Kerr's deadpan delivery didn't bother any of the others; on the contrary, they hung on his every word and appeared eager for more.

Kerr removed his sunglasses and seated them firmly on the brim and crown of his straw hat. It was then that Doc noticed the man's eyes were different colors, one yellowish-brown, the other blue, which gave him a decidedly deranged look as he waved his arm and led the flock into the huge grotto.

Jackson refused to enter the cave. No one tried to coax the stickie in. No one seemed to care or notice his extreme agitation. Doc found it difficult to feel sympathy for the creature, knowing full well its genetic predilection for violence and bloodshed. Like the others, he wished the stickie would just go away.

Inside the cave, what with the white limestone

walls and the fissures in the ceiling, there was plenty of light to see by. Water steadily trickled across the floor; in the depressions it pooled ankle deep. Along the right-hand wall, caught in a shaft of sunlight, was a stack of wooden implements. They reminded Doc of flensing knives, the tools used in the whaling trade to carve blubber. Only these had short handles. The outwardly curving, scimitar-like blades were sharpened on one edge.

"These are your tools," Baron Kerr said. "With them you will tend the bounty of the pool. They are made of wood because the touch of metal taints the bounty and makes it unfit to eat. Take one and come with me."

Doc was the last to pick up a tool. He tested the edge, which was barely sharp and nicked in many places. Whatever it was meant to cut was very soft indeed. He and the others tracked the baron deeper into the hillside. The passage grew narrower and much darker. So dark that Kerr paused to light a torch, one of many that lay on a ledge well above the waterline. After more torches were lit, they proceeded down the winding tunnel.

Beads of strange, faintly luminous moisture appeared on the cave walls. Doc felt a tightness building in his chest that had nothing to do with the torch smoke or the dank-smelling cave or the rapid rise in the air temperature. He sensed that he was walking into the core of something more powerful and more evil than his mind could grasp. An evil that cast a shadow in the darkest corners of the dripping cave.

The only thing that kept him from turning and running for daylight was the knowledge that his companions walked ahead of him, unaware, perhaps bewitched, and at the mercy of that selfsame evil.

Deep under the mountain, the cave widened into a low-ceilinged antechamber that was roughly circular. It was there that Baron Kerr stopped and gave instruction on the harvesting of the pool's "bounty."

Only when the baron actually pointed out the tendrils did Doc see them. They were mottled gray, and in the dim and flickering torchlight, they blended in with the colors of the stained and shadowy bedrock. The glistening, interlacing, tapering growths pushed through splits in the stone; they encased the walls and roof of the antechamber. Some were as big around as a man's waist, others the size of little fingers.

At least at present they were immobile, and Doc was thankful for that.

"Go on and touch them," the baron urged the crowd. "Feel the pool's majesty."

When Ryan, Krysty, J.B., Mildred, Jak, Dean and Leeloo laid hands on the tentacles, they uttered gasps of delight. The carny chillers had exactly the same reaction.

Doc touched one, as well, to satisfy his scientist's mind. He got no particular thrill from the contact. He found the tendril moist to his fingertips, either from something secreted through its pores or from the water dripping down the wall, and the outer skin was coarse, like shark hide. When he pressed on the tendril, the flesh beneath yielded, but it didn't contract or in any other way respond to his touch. From this, he concluded that it was either vegetable or fungal in nature.

The baron brandished his wooden flensing knife and said, "This is how we tend the bounty."

Carefully he used the edge of the knife to pry a thigh-sized tendril free of its grip on the rock. He lifted it up and draped it over his shoulder in order to show his audience the thousands of tiny, hairlike, adhesive-coated fibers on the underside that allowed it to cling to and grow along the solid surface. Thin strands of clear liquid drooled from the broken fibers, soaking through the back of his shirt. At the place where the tentacle exited the rock there was a large nodule. Doc recognized it as one of the globs.

"For the bounty to form and fully ripen," Kerr continued, "the filament must be freed. Part of your work is to search the caverns for mature filaments of this size and loosen them from the rock."

Heads nodded all around.

"The other part of your work is to harvest the bounty," the baron said. "In doing this, you must be careful not to damage the filament. The edge of the blade should slide in this way." He placed the knife along the underside of the tentacle he had freed, then pushed its edge against the join of nodule. "If the bounty is ripe," he continued, "it will come off easily. Like this."

With a wet pop, the glob separated from the tendril and Kerr caught it in his free hand.

A sudden waft of highly concentrated urea filled the antechamber. Doc averted his head and smothered a cough with his fist, but the sharp, unpleasant stench brought smiles to the faces of the others. Clearly, Doc thought, something had altered their most basic perceptions.

The baron held up the tentacle and showed the throng how the circular wound seeped the same viscous, clear liquid, then gradually puckered closed, sealing itself.

"Take only one ripe bounty for yourself," Kerr told them. "It is your ration. Spend the rest of your time in these caverns identifying and tending the filaments."

That was the end of the training session.

The baron didn't invite questions from the floor. He simply turned and walked away, leaving companions and chillers to fend for themselves.

Though there were many things Doc wanted to ask him about the pool, the snow and the tendrils, he knew better than to open his mouth and draw attention to himself.

His hard experience at the hands of the predark whitecoats, and at hands of Jordan Teague, told Doc how to lay low until the right time came.

If it ever came...

Chapter Twenty-Nine

Ryan's face hurt from smiling as he listened to Trader's explanation of how things worked in the caverns. Trader had been like a second father to him. He had taught him leadership, discipline and how to surpass his own limits.

Now Trader was teaching him the way. The way that answered all questions. It was so clear. So clean. So simple.

Even as Ryan took in the details of the harvesting, of his responsibilities to the burning pool, the shrunken, the virtually incapacitated part of him—Ryan Cawdor the indomitable fighter, the hard-eyed realist—insisted that the Trader he knew and loved was lost to him, mebbe chilled. Trader and Abe. That diminished Ryan insisted that he couldn't be seeing him or hearing his voice.

But the evidence of his single eye told him that he was.

And the light that shone from Trader's face was like a beacon in the darkness.

It wouldn't be denied.

Ryan took up his wooden flensing knife and a lit torch and set off down a passage that twisted and narrowed until it was barely wide enough for his shoulders. All along the corridor, the filaments hung from the dripping walls, as gray and thick as tree trunks.

The larger part of him saw that Trader was right, that there was much important work to be done here. Much love to impart. Much care. Being in the caves was like being in fields of blooming flowers.

So much beauty.

On all sides.

Ryan chose a mature filament and began loosening its grip on the cave wall. The hairlike fibers made faint snapping sounds as he broke their connection with the limestone with the blade. The gray tentacle came free from its delicate, pointed tip to the wide root that exited from the rock face. The severed hairlets bathed his hands in their ooze.

He lifted up the freed tendril, but there was no ripe bounty at its widest spot, the place where it emerged from the stone. Instead he found a small, hard nodule no bigger than his fist. The fruit of the pool needed time and room to grow.

As Ryan the cruise ship stood there admiring the bud, Ryan the passenger, the spectator, had a sudden sense of the burning pool as an individual creature, of its mountainous vastness, of its hundreds of miles of intruding, interlacing filaments.

Of its infinite hunger.

Of its infinite evil.

"There is nothing to be afraid of, Ryan," said a familiar voice behind him.

A gruff man's voice.

Ryan smelled cigar smoke. He turned and Trader was standing there beside him. His old friend's face seemed younger than Ryan remembered. The hair wasn't quite as grizzled.

"You're not dead," Ryan said. "Thought Abe and you might have bought the farm."

"Mebbe I am dead," Trader said.

Ryan picked up the torch and held it closer to get a better look. "You're a ghost?"

Trader laughed, but he didn't answer. "I brought you here for a reason. I brought you here to show you that there is joy beyond all the hard living. That beyond the gate, joy awaits you."

Ryan's cheeks suddenly felt as if they were going split, his grin was that wide. Why in rad blazes am I smiling? Passenger Ryan thought. None of this is real.

"We are all here to show you...." Trader said, gesturing down the narrow tunnel behind him.

Ryan saw then that Trader hadn't come alone.

Behind Trader in the passage were many figures, half in shadow and half in dancing torchlight. All of them were smiling; all of them he knew. Some were people Ryan had loved, while some were people he had chilled. Friends and enemies alike. His father, Baron Titus Cawdor, was there, as was his mother, Lady Cynthia, and his brothers. Lori Quint. Cort Strasser. Bessie and Cissie Torrance. And so many others. A line of familiar faces that stretched off into the darkness.

All dead.

All very happily dead, it seemed.

He could tell from their expressions that none of them blamed him for anything that he had done to them or hadn't done for them. They forgave him completely. They understood him completely. They had overcome the shortsighted yearnings and judgments of the flesh.

In their gleeful faces was an invitation to join them, an invitation that held the promise of ultimate redemption.

Until it was actually offered to him, Ryan hadn't known that he even desired such a thing. But now, while searching the eyes of those who had gone before him, he felt the same sort of intense, uncontrollable yearning that he had felt for the roasted globs: a marvelous scent on the wind drew him closer and closer, like a puppet on a string, to death.

Below the decks of the great, storm-tossed ship called *Cawdor,* a tiny voice screamed, ''No!''

LEELOO BUNNY WALKED hand in hand through the caverns with her mother, Tater. Neither carried a burning torch because it wasn't dark in the narrow passage. Their winding path was lit by hundred-foot-high bright tentacles in orange, pink, red and yellow. The rock walls and ceiling had turned transparent; all Leeloo could see were the filaments. And she could see them twisting all the way up to the summit, like the root ball of some enormous plant with the dirt knocked loose.

The tendrils blurred and shifted, and became

candy trees and popcorn bushes. In the distance, she could faintly hear cymbals and brass playing a lively marching song.

"Please don't leave me again," Leeloo said to her mother.

"But I never left you."

"I couldn't see you. We weren't together. I was lonely."

"We will always be together now."

"And Dean?"

"You like him, don't you?"

"Uh-huh."

"He's your Prince Charming."

"He's wonderful. He's brave and smart. I don't want to lose him. Can he come with us? Please?"

"He'll be with us, too. When you get released, and he gets released, we'll all be together."

Leeloo understood without being told that "released" meant being freed from her body. "But what happens then?" she asked.

Tater Bunny put a hand on her daughter's head.

Leeloo beamed up at her adoringly.

The facial resemblance between mother and daughter was uncanny. Daughter could have been mother at age eight. Mother could have been daughter at age twenty-six. And their expressions mirrored each other exactly, reflecting absolute joy.

"You will climb," Tater said, "like a cloud of smoke. Straight up into the sky. You will be everywhere at once. Flying."

"Like a bird?"

"Much better than a bird. Faster. Freer. There will be no wind you can't fly through. No height you can't soar to. No place you can't go by just thinking about it."

"You can do all those things?"

"I can. And so will you."

"Will I have to wait long?"

"No, my darling. Not long."

"And will I always be safe?"

"Always."

Leeloo reached up and with her wooden tool pried free a huge lollipop, the flat disk of candy much bigger than her face. It was red and green and white, the colors swirling in a pinwheel shape. She closed her eyes tightly and touched it with the tip of her tongue.

"It's peppermint!" she exclaimed.

Leeloo eagerly licked the scratchy gray skin of the nodule, the clear sap from its cut surface sheeting off her tiny chin.

JAK SENSED that he was being stalked, and by something big. He advanced alone through the dark cave; the light of the torch he carried dwindled away fifteen feet ahead of him and fifteen feet behind. Deep inside the mountain, there were no openings to the sky to let in light or air. The farther and deeper he went, the warmer it became. The cave he had picked to follow angled down into the earth. The water that trickled over the cave floor ran in the direction he was headed. He paused to listen for his pursuer. Although his hearing was very sharp, it picked up no scrape of boot on rock, no rustle of dirt as a body brushed a wall. There was only the steady hiss of the burning torch in his hand, and the babbling-brook sound of the water flowing around his boots.

Jak pressed on, looking for what he had been told to look for and was eager to find. Whether it was called "bounty" or "dinner," what he'd been given at the burn barrel was some of the best roast pork he'd ever eaten. He was looking forward to stuffing himself with more.

After he had traveled perhaps ten yards, the sensation of being followed returned. He felt it as a tingling at the back of his neck and across his shoulders. It didn't make him nervous that he was being trailed. It made him curious. He adjusted the ride of the Colt Python in its holster.

When he found a likely looking tendril, he stuck the end of the torch in a cleft in the rock and started prying on it with the wooden tool. It didn't take him long to break the thing free from the wall. Under its armpit was a bounty the size of his head. As he plucked the ripe nodule, he knew that someone or something was watching him from behind. He put the bounty on the floor and picked up the torch. Holding the flame out in front of him, he took several steps toward it.

"Who there?" he demanded.

There was no answer.

Then in the shadows of the next bend in the walls, he saw something shift. It was big. The same size as the lion. As he advanced on it, whatever it was retreated out of the reach of the torchlight.

"That you?" he said.

He recognized the voice that entered his mind.

Of course it's me.

Said couldn't come, Jak thought. Said knew how ended and you not part of it.

I just wanted to surprise you. Are you surprised?

Yeah, guess so. You help me fight?

Fight who?

Carny chillers.

There is nothing and no one to fight. Not anymore. You've got to get your mind around that. You've got to put the lid down on your killer instinct. It will only get in the way from here on.

How?

This isn't Deathlands. This is the border of someplace else. Someplace far better. If you want to cross over, you've got to stand in the snowstorm, and eat your bounty.

Why want go someplace else?

So that you can see Christina again.

Dead.

There's no such thing. I've tried to explain that to you many times before. You don't listen.

Listen. I not understand.

Life as you know it doesn't exist. Life as you know it is an illusion. You must shed the scales over your eyes. You must know the truth. You must see the other side. I can help you. Come closer to me.

No.

Jak's right hand automatically reached for the Python, but his holster was empty. His fingers dipped under his shirt. The leaf-bladed knives were gone, too. Jak felt a shiver of fear. Unaccountable. He wasn't afraid of the lion.

Come to me.

Jak's legs began to move, stiffly. He couldn't stop them. As he approached the bend in the cave, and the thing that waited for him there, he could see that the details of the shape were wrong. The ears were long and stiff and pointed. The eyes were small and luminous green. The skin was hairless, as was the tail. A pair of leathery wings lay folded along the jutting knobs of the spine.

Not lion, Jak thought. Enemy.

No, I am the victor.

With a great effort, Jak managed to retreat a step, then two. Then he turned and ran.

Don't forget your bounty!

Cruel laughter rolled through Jak's head as he stopped and scooped it up.

Chapter Thirty

It was getting on into evening when Doc followed
the others out of the caves and back toward the ville.
The sun was just starting to dip below the fringe of
trees along the ridgeline; from the mountain above
came a threatening growl of thunder. Everyone was
carrying their "bounty." Everyone but Doc. He was
starting to get hungry, but he knew he'd never be
that hungry.

All around him, his friends and the rousties were
talking, but not to one another. They spoke only to
themselves, or to imaginary companions. Each was
wrapped up in his or her own world. Some were
agitated to the point of shaking their fists. Some
were beatific. Some were morose.

They reminded Doc of inmates of an insane asylum, out for a bit of exercise and fresh air.

There was more thunder as the others deposited
their wormy prizes on the ground beside the already
roaring drum fire. The rumbling grew steadily louder
and louder. Doc could feel the storm's intensity
building. In a matter of minutes, a bank of churning
clouds appeared above the ville. Darkness descended. There was no lightning, but there was a
blistering wind and snow. Sideways sheets of yellow

snow as fine as table salt swept down the mountainside and over the square.

It was dry.

It wasn't cold.

It stung Doc's face like windblown sand. He
hunched his shoulders and turned his back to it.

The others in the square made no concessions to
the strange downpour. They leaned against the driving wind and let it hit them straight on. The tiny
granules bounced off their heads and shoulders.

And then the clouds dropped lower and grew even
thicker, the snow came down even harder and it became difficult to breathe. Doc was forced to take
refuge in one of the nearby scabrous lean-tos, crawling on elbows and knees over the pounded-dirt floor.

Outside, the storm crescendoed. The winds
whipped the tattered plastic sheeting and crudely
lashed cross members above Doc's head, threatening
to flatten the flimsy structure. The nearly constant
thundering shook the ground beneath him. The snow
came down in a blizzard of yellow, rapidly building
into ankle-deep drifts. Doc's visibility out the lean-
to's entrance dropped to five feet or less. Then, as
quickly as it began, it was over. The thunder
stopped, as did the snowfall. The darkness lifted.

When Doc crawled out of the hut, he saw a clear,
turquoise sky above and the sun dipping below the
tree line. The ville's square was peopled by living
statues, everything dusted with pale yellow.

All around him, the snowdrifts were visibly
shrinking. He bent and scooped up some in his hand.

It wasn't made of flakes, as he had thought, but individual grains. Like pollen. Or crystals.

In seconds, the pile of stuff on his palm grew smaller. He could see it wasn't melting into a liquid; nothing was dripping off the heel of his hand. It was just disappearing, which was impossible. Doc knew the basics of physics and chemistry. He knew that matter couldn't disappear, couldn't be created or destroyed; however, it could be made to change form. In this case, it appeared that solid matter, the snow, was turning into a gas, perhaps upon contact with air. According to the laws of physics, this required the application or release of some kind of energy. But the material wasn't hot.

What he was observing seemed to violate the most fundamental principles of science.

Doc dumped what was left of the snow on the ground and brushed off his hands.

Moments later, he began to notice a tingling numbness in his fingers and feet. It spread rapidly to his mouth and lips. He clenched his fists, heart pounding up under his chin as he anticipated being turned to stone like the others. But the numbing sensation didn't travel any farther. He quickly rubbed back the circulation in his hands and face.

Doc hurried across the square, walking between the rigidly upright human forms. The snowfall had produced immediate and total paralysis in every other person present. Even the baron, the black man who had tended the cookfire and three who had come out of the Baja Bug were frozen.

When he reached Ryan, Doc laid his hand on his friend's chest. The one-eyed man was breathing, but only just barely. His heartbeat was very slow, but steady. The pupil of his eye was dilated, and its blink reflex was stifled. Doc took hold of Ryan's arm and shook him, then he shouted in his ear.

Nothing.

No response.

It was the same with all the companions. He couldn't rouse them from their stupor.

Doc retreated to the front wall of the blockhouse, despairing and at a loss as to how to help his friends.

After a few minutes passed, he was relieved to see the paralysis starting to wear off. Gradually everyone began to stir. As they regained their faculties, there was a noticeable change in their behavior. They were all quiet, tranquil and smiling. Behavior that the circumstances hardly called for. It seemed to Doc they were now all suffering from the same variety of madness. He sensed that whatever was influencing them had reestablished complete control. The evidence so far pointed to some chemical in the snow.

Doc reflected on what the baron had said about the pool being the source of everything here. He had no doubt that a complex system was in operation. A living system. Its size, its power and its menace were almost tangible. If it existed as a single entity, as the baron had suggested, it was the largest creature Doc had ever encountered, indeed had ever heard of. Of course, the baron's view wasn't nec-

essarily accurate. He was as impacted by the snow
as the others. And he was not trained as a scientist.

If the tendrils were fungal, as Doc had speculated,
then the snow would be fungal spores. If they were
vegetable, the snow would be plant pollen. Either
way, they were the entity's genetic material.

Doc could recall no sign of anything growing in,
on or around the pool. That didn't mean much.
Fungi and plants could be living out of sight and in
profusion on the pool's bottom. Because fungi were
such simple structures, and tended to grow so
closely together, it was sometimes difficult to separate one individual from others of the same type in
the same area. Whether it was one gigantic creature
or a population of ten thousand smaller ones, the
danger was palpable.

Doc asked himself why he hadn't been paralyzed
by the spore fall. Was it because he was already
stark raving mad when exposed to the stuff? It
seemed to have had the opposite effect on him as it
had on everyone else: it had straightened out his
thinking instead of confusing it. And the spores had
only brought a mild numbness to his hands, feet and
face. Perhaps he was immune to the chemicals they
contained. Perhaps that immunity had something to
do with his time travel. With the rearrangement of
his atomic structure. Perhaps everyone else's sus-
ceptibility had to do with skydark-produced mutations in their genetics. Mutations that he didn't have
since he had been born one hundred and forty years
before it had occurred. None of these speculations
satisfied him.

As the others turned to face the baron, Doc pushed away from the wall and moved to the back of the crowd.

"Bring out the chair!" Kerr said.

Two of the men who had ridden in the Baja Bug with the baron pulled a metal office armchair out into the middle of the square. The third rider placed a long pipe with the rag-wrapped handle in a four-wheeled cart and pushed it near the chair. Everyone pressed in closer until they were shoulder to shoulder, ringing the center of the square. They seemed expectant and eager, as if they knew what was coming. They all wore stiff, unnatural grins on their faces.

Doc wasn't grinning. He didn't understand what was about to happen, but he had a very bad feeling about it, a premonition that turned out to be well-founded.

Baron Kerr waved the black man over to his side and slapped him in the middle of his broad, muscular back.

"The burning pool is hungry," Kerr said to the circled crowd. "And we must feed it. As it feeds us. Eat the body. Become the body."

Doc was taken aback when the audience, without prompting, immediately picked up the chant, "Eat the body. Become the body. Eat the body. Become the body."

Even the notoriously closemouthed Jak added his voice to the chorus, his ruby-red eyes wide with excitement.

"This evening we celebrate three departures,"
Kerr said, pointing at the men who'd been passengers in the Bug. "The road to where they're going
starts right here." The baron patted the back of the
chair. Then he asked, "Who's going to be first to
take the load off?"

The question started a shoving match between the
three men to see who would take the seat. The pushing escalated into full-power punches and kicks.
When one of the men fought his way to the chair,
the others stopped wrestling on the ground and
quickly strapped down his wrists and ankles. The
winner smiled as this was happening, showing his
bloodied teeth to the crowd. The black man with the
dreadlocks took the iron pipe from the cart and made
a whistling practice swing. Overhead and down, he
drove the end of the pipe into the dirt.

Doc watched as the cook then moved to the back
of the chair. Planting his feet, he reared back on one
leg and swung the pipe over and down, putting all
his weight behind the blow and grunting from the
effort.

Like pounding in a tent stake with a twenty-pound
mallet.

At the last second, Doc instinctively averted his
gaze. But he didn't have time to stop up his ears.
He heard the hollow whack of the pipe and the
sound of crunching bone.

Dean, who stood next to him, flinched at what he
saw, but didn't look away.

From the crowd there was a unison gasp of amazement.

I am imagining this, Doc thought, shaking his head to clear it. This can't be real.

But when he looked back, there was no doubt that it was. The top of the seated man's head was caved in, his body jerking and kicking against the restraints. The old man's stomach heaved mightily, and he knew he was going to be sick. As he gritted his teeth, stumbling to the side of the blockhouse to vomit, the others were just standing there, staring at the horror that sat quaking in the chair, and smiling. It was as if they were seeing something completely different than he was. Leaning against the blockhouse with a hand, Doc retched into the dirt. He didn't have much to retch.

He was still bent over, dry heaving when one of the two remaining men pulled the body out of the seat and dumped it over backward into the waiting cart. The third man took the opportunity to slip past the other and sit in the chair, firmly gripping the arms and wrapping his shins around the front legs. When the second man couldn't drag him out of the seat, he buckled down the wrist and ankle straps. The man in the chair beamed at the audience as if he were about to be crowned king of the world.

Instead of being simply crowned.

As RYAN MADE his way out of the caves, the entourage of people from his past trooped alongside and behind him. Their happy chatter began to fade as he approached the exit. And when he turned to look at Trader and his father, he saw their shapes rippling, then disintegrating like campfire smoke in a breeze. A terrible sadness struck him. He didn't want them to go, but he couldn't make them stay. Outside the cave, Ryan the passenger became Ryan the captain, the sole commander of his own body. Fully conscious as he filed along with the others toward the square, he understood that he had been hallucinating, that he had been talking to ghosts, to imaginary presences. That he had been utterly lost in those hallucinations. It was worse than any jump nightmare he had ever suffered because it was real. And because he knew without a doubt that he was being held against his will, and made to perform like a puppet or a mutie in the zoo.

He wasn't alone.

Krysty, J.B., Mildred, Jak and Dean stumbled along beside him, lost in their own inner worlds, raving to themselves.

Something terrible had gripped all of the companions, and it was toying with them.

Ryan knew he had to gather Dean and the others and get out of there while the getting was good. Even as he shook free of the leadenness that still hung upon his limbs, thunder boomed at his back, then came the hot wind, then the sting of the pale-yellow snow.

He stopped walking and turned to face it.

The initial jolt this time, the plunge into the perfume of the flower fields, was less shocking to his system. He slid into it like a well-worn pair of boots. And almost at once, he had a profound sense of well-being. All the wrinkles, the doubts were smoothed away.

He stood there, eye shut, head tilted back, mouth wide open, letting the spores fall on his tongue and dissolve there. They tasted like grains of sugar. Time passed, the snow drifted over his ankles and up to his shins, but he didn't care.

He was happy. He was content.

Trader and his father, Baron Titus, were by his side again.

Passenger Ryan knew this couldn't be. But the body in which he was trapped felt their presence, their physical warmth. It even smelled Trader's cigar smoke. When everyone moved in close to the chair, Ryan's body moved along, too. When they grinned and chanted, it grinned and chanted. It knew that bloody murder was about to be done.

In all his days, in all his battles, Ryan had never seen men fight each other in order to be the first to die. He had never seen men rejoice at the prospect of their own destruction. Passenger Ryan felt the body rejoice, as well, and was disgusted. Not only did he have no control over the emotions that it felt, but also they weren't and never could be his emotions.

He wanted to look at the others, but he couldn't make the head turn; it was locked straight ahead, at the man scrambling into the chair. Ryan sensed that his friends were feeling the same thing that he was, that they were smiling like he was. The insanity was like an infection. Not just out of character. For the companions he knew, it was out of the question. And yet none of them could break free and stop the horror.

The man strapped in the chair was filthy and raggedy, beard matted. His eyes burned like blue coals in his head; he was missing most of his front teeth. With all the dirt that encrusted him, it was hard to guess his age, but he was probably somewhere between twenty and thirty years old.

It all happened very quickly. The black man stepped behind the chair, cocked himself, then brought down more than a yard of metal pipe. The impact drove the man's head between his shoulders. His skull crunched lopsidedly. Brains flew. Blood sprayed. And his right eyeball popped out of its socket and dangled on his cheek.

Along with everyone else, Ryan let out a gasp.

From the cratering wound twinkling points of light streamed upward, circling mebbe five feet above the body, building in volume and turbulence. The light continued to stream until the corpse heaved its last jerk. Then the pinpoints drifted farther and farther apart, until they finally disappeared.

Ryan the passenger was stunned by the detail and realism. Had it been a hallucination? Or had he witnessed the spirit flowing out of the dying body, the soul freed?

After dumping the corpse in the cart, the two men left squabbled and struggled over who would take the seat next. The guy who won was strapped down by the guy who lost. The lucky winner glanced over his shoulder at the waiting black man, a gleeful expression on his face. Then he turned back and shut his eyes as if he was in store for a pleasant surprise.

The black man swung the pipe down again. At the impact Ryan was jolted to the core, as if he had been the one who had been struck. And again, from the devastating wound, he witnessed the streaming of nonsubstance, of ectoplasm, of soul.

"This is the real carny," Trader whispered into his ear.

THE MAGNIFICENT CRECCA grabbed the bloody end of the pipe with one hand and gave Azimuth a hard shove in the chest with the other. "Give it to me," he said. "I want a turn swinging the pipe."

The black man refused to let go of the weapon.

"In case you forgot, you work for me, Azimuth," Crecca said, giving him another hard push. "Me and the Magus." He put a heavy emphasis on the last two words.

"I used to work for you, mon," the carny scout said. "No more. Now I do just what ol' Marley says."

Crecca glared at Baron Kerr, who stood with his arms crossed over his chest. Then, without warning, he ducked forward and head-butted Azimuth. The black man's nose crunched under the blow, and bright blood gushed from his nostrils. As the carny master tried to wrench the pipe away, his scout fought back. Azimuth landed a hard right to the side of Crecca's head, then jammed the end of the pipe into his solar plexus.

Crecca doubled over and went down, but he pulled the off-balance Azimuth along with him. The two big men crashed to the ground and began rolling around in the dirt. Over the next thirty seconds, they each had their moments. Crecca hammered the black man's face with consecutive rights and lefts. Azimuth got his big hands around the carny master's throat and squeezed until his face turned purple. It was the baron who finally broke up the scuffle. He picked up the pipe that Azimuth had dropped and gave each of the men a solid whack in the legs with it.

Crecca got to his feet first. "I want to take my turn on the last guy," he said to Kerr, holding out his hand. "Azimuth has already done two."

The baron stared at him hard for a few seconds, then half smiled in a strange, sad way. "I like how he handles the pipe," Baron Kerr said. "A sweet swing."

With that, to Crecca's fury, he handed the weapon back to the black man. The carny master was then forced to watch with the others as Azimuth wound up and hit another long ball. When the shuddering from the chair had stopped, he shouldered in beside the black man to help him load the last body into the cart.

"You're dead meat," he warned his former scout.

"We're all dead meat, mon," Azimuth said with a laugh.

The baron threw a couple of axes and machetes and a tree-limb saw on top of the corpses. Then he set off across the square, gesturing for the crowd to push the cart after him.

On the north side of the ville was the start of a narrow track that led up the mountainside in a series of winding switchbacks between the fallen blocks of limestone. From the wheel ruts, which were deep and matched the tires perfectly, the cart had been the only vehicle to traverse it in a very long time, and had traversed it often.

Crecca didn't do any of the cart pushing. He walked a short distance behind, and he stopped to look back when the procession was halfway up the slope. What he saw wasn't what Ryan or Mildred or Doc saw.

There were no shabby huts below, no open sewers, no mind-numbing poverty and starvation. What Crecca saw instead was a place of enormous wealth and luxury homes, a suburban development that had apparently, miraculously been left untouched by the fires of skydark and the ravages of the decades of nuclear winter that followed. And for the most part it was deserted.

All there for the taking.

And there was only one person keeping Crecca from taking it: Baron Kerr. The last of Kerr's men lay dead in the cart.

So far the job of baron looked butt simple to

Crecca. Much simpler, and much less dangerous than running a carny and mobile gas chamber.

Pick some bounty.

Slam some heads.

And the last bit was especially easy since the folks getting their heads slammed wanted it to happen.

He stared at the low concrete-block building at the foot of the slope. It was the most secure structure in the ville, and where he knew its most valuable treasures would be kept. He recognized the building as a predark pumphouse because he'd come across others like it before. From the oblique and downward angle of view, he could see the huge pipes running down the mountainside to the back of the building. No doubt they had something to do with the pool's water level.

A tug at the tail of his ringmaster coat made Crecca turn. He looked down to see Jackson staring up at him with dead black eyes.

"Get away from me," the carny master said.

The naked stickie started to sing and dance, to try to make up for biting the hand that fed it. Jackson did a rendition of the Tiffany music video that they had been rehearsing in the big wag, complete with head jukes and hip thrusts.

The singing sounded like screeching to Crecca, and the dancing wasn't like dancing at all, more like a perpendicular grand mal seizure. The carny master wasn't amused and wanted no part of it. He hauled off and booted the stickie in the backside, sending it tumbling down the road.

When Jackson didn't go away, but rather resumed its irritating caterwauling and pelvic thrusting at a safe distance and with a pleading look on its pale face, Crecca reached down and picked up stones, with which he pelted the creature.

Struck and bleeding, Jackson slunk away over the hillside, still in its choke collar and trailing its chain leash.

With Crecca bringing up the rear, the procession crested the rise, then followed Baron Kerr downhill to the muddy bank beside the pool, where he signaled for them to stop. When the baron handed out the cutting tools, Crecca was first in line to take one of the axes.

The job was messy, but not difficult, because the tools had been honed to razor-sharpness.

After the first body had been chunked, Kerr started lobbing the pieces into the pool. Almost at once the huge lungfish rose to the bait, swirling and splashing on the surface as they fought over their dinner.

Crecca enthusiastically returned to the chopping. As he did so, he noticed Kerr staring at him. The carny master smiled at the ville's headman as he brought down the ax.

You're next, Baron, he thought.

Chapter Thirty-One

Baron Kerr had learned not to trust rays of hope. Like everything else in his ever shifting world, they had always proved to be illusions, cast by the burning pool for its own inexplicable ends.

Yet, as he watched the man in the red coat struggle on the ground with the black scout over the right to brain the strapped-down-and-beaming sacrificial lamb, he had the first inkling of what might be possible. While it wasn't unusual for people to fight for the right to be next to sit in the Clobbering Chair, and so to sooner exit the grasp of the pool, no one had ever before demanded the right to be executioner. To test his suspicion, he had given the pipe back to the black man, then studied Red Coat's reaction when it was used shortly thereafter to crush the victim's skull. Kerr saw fury in the man's eyes. Fury at having been denied pleasure. Fury directed at him, the denier.

Which was good.

Which was very good.

If the anger the baron had witnessed was real, and not some figment of his own imagination, it was also a first. The spores and the bounty had always produced slaves who were compliant. Not demanding.

Not impatient. And above all, not envious. They would take up the pipe and wield it joyfully when the time came, but only when ordered to do so.

The black man had only battled to keep the pipe because the pool entity, speaking through Kerr, had commanded him to use it.

Assuming that the pool had absolute control of Red Coat, a safe assumption under the circumstances, it was making him behave differently than anyone else ever had, allowing him an element of personality that it had refused all the others. Whatever his hallucinations were, they, too, had to be markedly different than anyone else's.

The baron kept his eye on Red Coat as he led his flock and the corpse cart up the zigzag trail to the pool. He noticed when the red-haired man paused and looked back at the ville. The expression on the newcomer's face was one of desire, of greed, even.

What was he seeing down there? Kerr asked himself. Or, more properly, what was the pool making him see? It had a way of finding the weakest point in a human being's psychology, and attacking it. How it did this was a mystery. As far as the baron could tell, the pool wasn't capable of thought; it just did the things it did.

It was.

As Kerr moved up the grade, he swam in a sea of the dead. Vague floating specters surrounded him, drifted through him, over his head. These were the innumerable ghosts of the pool; he could see them through closed eyelids. He couldn't match names with faces, but every one of them had drawn his or her final breath in the Clobbering Chair. Every one bore the mark of the iron pipe on their skull.

Although the baron's world and this spectral world of the pool's victims overlapped visually—he could see them, but they could not see him—they didn't overlap tangibly. There was no sensation of contact as the gauzy forms passed through or brushed against him. Kerr had become so used to the horrors of these hallucinations that they had become nothing more than an annoyance. Especially when the sun was going down. The angled, softened light made it difficult to see through the randomly shifting apparitions.

Though the pool could be subtle in its manipulations, it wasn't in this case. His visions of the legions of dead were meant to demonstrate how close the ones who had gone before were, how close freedom was, and yet always just beyond his reach. It was a constant, minute-by-minute reminder that he who wanted more than anything to escape could not.

Once Kerr had had a life, though he could barely remember it. Once he had had faith, though that was dead to him. The pool had taken everything. It had taken his soul.

When the procession reached its denuded bank, the pool was quiet. It reflected the peach and turquoise of the sunset, and the black fringe of the trees along the ridgeline above.

The flock looked to Baron Kerr for further instructions.

"The body is never alone," he told them. "It has gathered and keeps a web of creatures around it. A family connected by the chain of life. Each member of the family performs a different task, or set of tasks, all to insure the body's health and well-being. And the body, in return, insures the health and well-being of all its family members."

He pointed at the tools in the cart and the corpses under them. "As loyal members of that family, we have one more job to perform. The dead must be cut up in small pieces, so the fish in the pool can eat them."

Several of the newcomers grabbed the implements and immediately set to hacking up the corpses into chunks. Red Coat showed a particular zeal for the task, and he kept looking up from the gruesome work, wiping the spattered blood from his face with his coat cuff, and shooting Kerr a look of absolute hatred.

"Do you really think that one's your ticket on the last train west?" said a croaking voice from the waterline behind him.

Kerr glanced down and saw a six-foot-long lungfish bobbing in the shallows. Its back and tail were three-quarters out of the water as it rested on its pectoral spikes, and breathed air. "Could be," the baron answered. "If nothing is possible, then anything is possible."

The lungfish chuckled, lowering its head and making a bubbling noise underwater that Kerr found most irritating. "You've got to be kidding," the fish said. "How many times have you thought you had a way out of this place? A hundred? A thousand? Face facts, the pool is never going to let you go, Baron. You're its A-Number-One Boy, forever."

"What do you know?" Kerr snapped back. "A talking fish? You might not even exist. You might be just another hallucination."

"Well, this hallucination is getting mighty hungry. How about tossing me some chow?"

Kerr walked over to the cart, picked up some of the pieces that had fallen on the ground and flung them as far out into the lake as he could.

"You could have just handed me one," the lungfish complained. Then, with a swish of its wide tail, it turned away from the shore and swam to join the feeding frenzy that had already begun.

The baron watched Red Coat continue to work on the remaining bodies, and to shoot him more of the evil looks. Despite the lungfish's prediction of another failure, Kerr became more and more hopeful that the man with the red hair had the right stuff for a much more difficult job than quartering a torso, that he had both the homicidal tendencies and the unique brand of delusion necessary to end his own intolerable suffering.

Standing there, Kerr had a sudden, chilling realization. After killing him, Red Coat would most certainly throw him into the pool.

The baron had never considered the likely consequences of his being chopped up and fed to the fish. All he'd wanted was to be dead and gone. But now that he saw that dying might really be possible, it became clear to him that dying might not mean escape.

The lungfish were the intermediate processors, the predigesters of the pool's food. Their guts broke the tissue and bone into a simpler form. What they excreted, and what drifted down, was what sustained the fungal entity that carpeted the bottom and sent fingers of itself worming down through the mountainside. If his life force was consumed by the pool, assimilated by it, Kerr realized he could still be part of it. Conscripted into the army of ghosts that swirled around him. If that was the case, the fish was right—he would never get away.

When the chopping and feeding were completed, the baron waved the crowd back down the trail to the ville. As they began to move, he cut overland, climbing over the fallen blocks of stone. Kerr had a goal in mind, if not an exact plan. He made for the edge of one of the deepest of the hillside's potholes, a circular opening more than thirty feet across. When he reached his destination, he stopped, picked up a rock from the ground at his feet and dropped it into the hole. It took seven seconds for the stone to splash.

The blackness below him promised what he sought: true and eternal oblivion. If he stepped off the edge, there was no way his body could be recovered by Red Coat and turned into fish food. And even though the filaments of the pool probably decorated the walls of the yawning cavern, they

couldn't dine on his corpse. The tendrils had no
feeding apparatus; they were the fungis' fruiting
bodies, whose only function was to produce bounty.
And even if they did have a way of digesting things
that he was unaware of, without the intercession of
the lungfish, his body was in the wrong form for
them to use.

Kerr stood on the edge, poised to end his life, but
he didn't take the fatal step.

He couldn't take it. His legs wouldn't move forward.

If stepping off into one of the potholes and chilling himself had actually been possible, Baron Kerr
would have done it long, long ago. It was impossible
because the pool would not allow him to injure himself. It kept him safe because it needed him.

Kerr heard the sounds of rocks shifting and the
scraping of boot soles. Someone was coming up behind him.

"You've got a pretty sweet operation going for
yourself here," said a voice to his back.

The baron turned and faced Red Coat, who was
smiling in an unfriendly way.

"Mebbe it's too much for you to handle," the
red-haired man suggested as he moved closer. He
reached up and scratched at his scraggly red goatee.
"Mebbe you need a partner."

"I don't need a partner," Kerr said, letting Red
Coat get within arm's reach. The pool forced him to
shift to the right; Red Coat countered. And when he

did that, the baron had no place left to retreat to. His heels were a foot from the edge of the pothole.

"How about a hostile takeover, then?" the red-haired man suggested, leaning closer still.

It was then, and only then, that Kerr smiled back. The broadest, most infuriating smile he could muster.

Red Coat's arms came up, and the heels of his hands slammed into the baron's chest. As he went off balance, the pool made him flap his arms to try to regain it.

But the push was too hard.

James Kerr went over backward, somersaulting into the blackness.

His victory cry lasted exactly seven seconds.

Chapter Thirty-Two

Crecca stood on the rim of the pothole and listened as the echoes of Baron Kerr's final cry and splashdown faded away. Then he did a celebration dance, loosely adapted from the choreography in the Tiffany video, complete with head jukes. Nothing stood between him and the baronship.

Nothing.

"I am Baron Magnificent Crecca," he shouted into the cavern below, the words booming.

He liked the sound of it so much that he shouted it again.

It was an announcement to the world, a taunt to his newly dead predecessor and a self-coronation.

The triumphant Baron Magnificent Crecca no longer had a human—or partly human—overlord he had to answer to. No more Magus. No one to be afraid of. No one he had to hand over the lion's share of the spoils to. The pool had shown him his heart's true desire, his true mission; his entire life he had been waiting for, and working toward this very end. All he had ever wanted was to rule over his own private kingdom. Not some fly-by-night gypsy tent carny, but a real kingdom, with real territory and real influence that he could build on and expand. He had never had the means to get what he wanted before. He had always had to compromise his desire, to give up dominion in order to seize a small part of his dream. Now he had all the power he needed to make it happen.

All the power and then some.

He peered into the darkness of the pothole and couldn't see the bottom, or Kerr's body. It angered him that the former baron's corpse was lost to harvest because the pool was still very hungry. Even with his eyes averted, Crecca could sense its lingering agitation. He felt it as a prickling sensation on the back of his neck and a faint fluttering in the pit of his stomach. Without looking he knew that from the surface of the water, a mist was starting to rise, and mixed in were twinkling bits of silver confetti.

Another spore fall wouldn't be long in coming.

Crecca knew instinctively, and with absolute certainty, that the pool's unappeased appetite had to do with its having been semistarved for weeks. He also knew that the previous baron had allowed the ville's human population to slowly dwindle. Of late, Kerr hadn't done a good job of recruiting new residents, and he had phased out the sacrificing of the people that were here. It was almost as if he had wanted the pool to suffer.

That was all going to change now.

Under Crecca's stewardship, the burning pool would never be hungry again. If it needed more bodies to satisfy the hunger it had built up under the Kerr regime, it would have them. At once.

When the new baron looked back to the trail, he saw the crowd had gone on without him and was already almost at the bottom of the hillside. The evening light that surrounded him was turning purple and beginning to fade to night. He traversed the blocks and circled the yawning pitfalls of the slope, regaining the crude road and descending it at a trot. He caught up with the others shortly after they reached the square.

Azimuth was standing behind the burn barrel, busy cooking the fresh bounty. Flames leaped from the barrel as he rolled the gray globs into position on the grate with a block of wood. The crowd stood in a long, orderly line, waiting for the meal to be handed out.

They would have to wait a little bit longer.

The pool demanded to be fed first.

The former carny master picked up the iron pipe and stepped onto the seat of the Clobbering Chair. He banged the pipe on the chair's arms to get their attention. All heads slowly turned his way.

"Baron Kerr is dead," he told them. "I have been chosen to be the new baron of this place."

There was no reaction from the crowd. No groans of shock or sadness upon hearing of the old baron's demise. No cheers or applause at the announcement of a new leader to take his place. Their smiles were the same, before and after the announcement.

As Crecca reviewed his grinning subjects, he wondered if the information he'd just imparted had even penetrated their spore-and-bounty-befuddled brains. And if it had penetrated, how had their brains translated and interpreted his words? How had the meaning been distorted by their individual delusions? In the end, it didn't matter. The line of people accepted him as their new ruler as they accepted everything else: without blinking an eye.

"The body isn't satisfied," he said. "The body needs more." He tapped on the arm of the chair. "Who would like to volunteer?"

Everyone, it seemed.

The food line broke up, and its members encircled the Clobbering Chair and the baron. From the mountain above came a roll of thunder and faint flashes of green light. Azimuth left a clutch of bounty to burn to cinders on the grill, threw down his block of wood and joined them.

"You!" Crecca said, pointing at the black man with the end of the yard-long pipe. "Come over here and take the load off."

The choice of sacrifice had nothing to do with any lingering bad feelings Crecca had over their struggle earlier in the afternoon. In fact, he had no lingering feelings, one way or another, about the incident. The choice was made on the basis of seniority. The choice had been made by the pool itself. Azimuth had been in the ville longer than any other surviving person. He had inhaled and ingested more spores, eaten more bounty; he was the best prepared—having undergone a kind of a mental and physical tenderizing—to meet the very specific needs of the body.

The carny scout thrust both arms above his head, danced in a circle and cried, "Yes!"

As if he had just won the big prize.

Bingo!

Crecca hopped from the chair, making room for Azimuth to take his seat. As the big man sat down, he rounded the back of the chair and got into position for the clobbering.

Some of the rousties rushed in to buckle down the wrist and ankle straps. As they did, Azimuth slapped out a reggae rhythm on the chair's arms, bobbing his head and shaking his dreads.

"I never thought I'd ever get to sit in with you, my brother," he said over his broad shoulder, addressing the new baron. "It's my biggest dream come true. I am so bloody stoked, mon."

Crecca gripped the length of pipe like a baseball bat. It was much heavier than a bat, though. And when he took a practice cut with it, the thing whistled through the air and slammed into the dirt.

"Play that tune," Azimuth entreated him with a grin so wide that it showed every one of his hand-sharpened yellow teeth. "Wail on me, Marley!"

Crecca swung from the soles of his boots, putting the full weight of his body behind the blow. The impact jolted up his arms and deep into his shoulder joints. The pipe sounded a dull clunk as it bounced high off its target.

Baron Magnificent Crecca stepped nimbly aside as blood from the massive scalp wound he had inflicted jetted in a fine spray three feet in the air.

Azimuth's body convulsed violently. It jerked so hard and so erratically that it set the chair rocking, then tipped it over sideways. Both the chair and the body hit the ground in a cloud of dust. For a long moment, the unconscious black man spasmed in the dirt.

Then Azimuth's eyes popped open, and he began to scream. As he fought against the straps, his shrill cries were blood-curdling.

Crecca moved forward and hit him again.

And again.

It took a half-dozen full-power blows of the pipe to dispatch the huge man. And by the time it was over, his head from the ears up was an undistinguishable mass of shattered bone, brains and dreads.

Puffing from the effort he'd expended, the former carny master lowered his head and leaned on the handle of the pipe for a couple of minutes. He was the only one in the audience who was resting. His rousties unfastened the straps holding down the scout's body, then lifted the corpse and dumped it headfirst into the cart. When he'd recovered his breath, Crecca bent, grabbed the fallen chair by an arm and set it upright. Azimuth was a big man, but he wasn't quite big enough to fill the pool's requirements. As the baron looked over his beaming subjects, he said, "Who's next?"

The crowd edged closer. Everyone wanted to be next.

Crecca's glance swept past, then returned to the young son of Ryan Cawdor. He was just the right size. He aimed the bloody pipe at the boy. "How about you, then?" he said.

Crecca didn't have to ask twice.

Dean raced over to take a seat in the gore-splattered chair. He looked very, very happy as the rousties cinched him down.

Crecca put a hand on the boy's shoulder and said, "I promise to try to do a neater job of it this time."

Chapter Thirty-Three

Doc hung back at poolside while the others started back down the hill with the empty cart. When they were out of sight over the lip of the slope, he slogged over to where Ryan had dropped his long-blaster. He pulled the Steyr from the mud and used the tail of his frock coat to wipe some of the dirt from the barrel, scope and stock. The weapon had gone in muzzle first, so he had to assume the bore was blocked. There was no time to clear it. And he had nothing to clear it with. He slung the bolt-action rifle over his shoulder and hurried down the trail. By the time he caught up the rest of the group, they were lining up in front of the burn barrel to get another ration of the wormy chow. His own stomach growling, Doc carefully hid the Steyr against the wall at the far end of the blockhouse.

As the old man walked across the square to join the others, the carny master climbed on the bloody chair and banged on its arm with the metal cudgel to get everyone's attention.

Doc had hoped that the chilling was over for the day. He had counted on having the entire night to work out a plan for getting his companions away from the gruesome horror of this hellhole.

But it wasn't to be.

The red-haired carny master announced a coup d'état and proclaimed himself baron. Looking at the man, Doc had no doubt that he had dispatched the former ruler personally. Because both men were in the control of the pool, because both were coldheart chillers of the lowest order, it didn't matter who was baron. The agenda was the same.

Doc's heart leaped into his throat when the new headman said the pool wasn't satisfied and called for volunteers. Of which there were plenty, including his own dear friends.

Doc's window of opportunity was rapidly slamming shut.

The simplest course of action was to break the spell of the pool, but he had tried that without success. There was nothing he could do to the companions themselves to snap them out of it. He had noticed that their respective dazes seemed to wane at times, that they appeared to be struggling against the reins. He also noticed that their resistance to control ended with the paralysis that followed each spore fall. If this wasn't an illusion on his part, it meant that the confused state of mind was temporary, and maintained only by regular redosing with spores, and perhaps with bounty. From the thunder and lightning coming over the ridge above, another downpour was imminent, as was another meal of fungal nodes.

If Doc couldn't shake them out of their state, and he couldn't remove them forcibly, then he knew he only had one course left. And that was to try to chill whatever it was that lived in the pool.

On the face of it, a much more daunting undertaking. The thing was vast and inconceivably powerful. Still, Doc knew he had to try.

As he racked his brain to come up with something, anything of use in that regard, the carny scout volunteered to sit in the chair.

The black man was all smiles as he let himself be strapped down. It was difficult to tell for certain, but he seemed to have a change of heart when the first blow landed and it didn't kill him outright. Lying in the dirt, he wasn't screaming words; he was just screaming. Doc had the feeling, though, that the shock had awakened him at the last instant, when it was already far too late to do anything about it.

Tanner turned away from the follow-up mayhem and stared at the low concrete blockhouse. The blows were still sounding behind him when he started to put the whole thing together.

He was fairly sure that for whatever reason, for pure science or to develop a new military weapon, predark whitecoats had created the pool and its ecosystem. And that they had done it from the ground up.

He asked himself why then had the laboratory been sited here, so far below the pool. Certainly, it made more sense to build the lab next to the system they were studying. That told Doc the whitecoats probably knew it was dangerous, and that they wanted to be a safe distance away. Which offered support for the bioweapon hypothesis. But that wasn't the whole story.

He could see that the laboratory was connected to the pool through the pipes at the base of the slope. As there were no pipes in evidence at the lakeside, at least none that he had seen, they had to be in place under it. Which supported the idea that it wasn't a naturally occurring body of water. The pool had been created. But that didn't explain what the pipes were there for. Could the whitecoats have used them to sample the pool's contents? Doc thought that unlikely. A pipe five feet across was overkill for taking samples. As he examined the base of the hillside, he noticed two other structures that seemed to be artificial. The rounded humps looked like culverts that had been buried by rock and dirtfall. They were twice as big as the blockhouse pipes.

What was all the underground plumbing for? Doc asked himself. Was it because the whitecoats knew even in the planning stages the potential danger of the pool? Was it because they wanted their fingers on the trigger of a fail-safe device that could deactivate or terminate the project?

From the position of the blockhouse and the pipe connections, Doc had a clue as to the function if not the exact construction of the device. It involved draining the lake above. Draining it suddenly and completely. The trouble was, they hadn't designed it as a dead man's switch. The nukecaust had taken them by surprise, as it had everyone else.

Doc grimaced. It was all supposition, of course.

As he started for the steps leading to the blockhouse
entrance, the rousties pulled the body of the dead
scout from the chair and pitched it into the cart.
When he looked back he saw young Dean taking a
seat in the death chair.

It stopped him cold in his tracks.

"By the Three Kennedys!" he cried, and he
broke into a run, not for the bunker, but for the boy.
Doc threw himself between the numbed spectators,
trying to reach Dean and drag him free before harm
could be done.

Powerful hands roughly grabbed Doc by the arms
and hurled him back. The crowd closed in more
tightly around the chair, effectively blocking another
attempt on his part.

Doc gripped the handle of his swordstick, but he
didn't draw the blade. He knew he could skewer
more than a few of the bodies before him, but he
could never chill enough of them to free Dean in
time. And in the process, he would have had to mor-
tally stab his friends, even Ryan, who appeared to
be willing to stop him from rescuing the boy.

The old man reversed course and sprinted across
the square. He ran down the blockhouse steps and
through its open door. His boots splashed in the
faintly glowing puddles on the floor of the central
hallway. As he ran, he ducked and dodged the dangling, rusting light fixtures. The smell of mildew and
rot was almost overpowering.

Doc charged into the first room he came to, skidding on the concrete floor. Before him was a row of

squat, heavy-looking machines. They looked like pumps of some kind. In the dim light, he quickly examined them. Yes, they were definitely pumps. He located the starter switch on one of them and depressed it. Nothing happened.

He tried the others with same result. He kicked aside some of the debris from the fallen tile ceiling and saw the thick electrical cable on the floor. They were electric powered.

There was no generator in the room. The wall opposite the hallway was laced with rows of heavy pipe. He scanned the various dials and gauges set at intervals along the wall. Some had cracked faces and missing indicators. All the others read zero. The system was off-line, either because it was simply broken, or because of the lack of operating power.

Doc was slammed by a crushing sense of hopelessness. Without a blueprint or a schematic of some kind, how was he ever going to figure it out? He smothered the thought and moved on. If there was a generator in the building, he had to find it.

And quickly.

It wasn't in the next room he checked, but in the one after it. There was no mistaking it, either. It was the size of four refrigerators, stacked one on top of the other. Doc located the ignition switch, pressed it and got nothing. If there was a battery in the system, it was long dead. The pull-start rope produced nothing, although the engine did turn over.

He found the generator's gas tank and discovered the root of the problem. It was empty.

"Hell's fire!" he cursed, slamming his fist on top of the tank.

He knew that whitecoats sitting on a biological time bomb wouldn't leave themselves a single way to deactivate it. They wouldn't completely depend on electrical power that could be shut off at a critical moment by any number of mechanical failures. There had to be a more direct method. He thought about the lake above, and the pressure of thousands of tons of water. Perhaps the deactivation system was gravity powered. Perhaps it could use the water pressure to physically or hydraulically move a barrier out of the way.

Doc rushed on. Now that he had a clue what he was looking for, he wasted no time on the offices where it appeared people had been living. The last room in the corridor had more of the squat pumps, and the pipes along its wall were much bigger in diameter.

When he saw the red steel wheel, and the sign above it, he knew he had found the drain plug. The wheel was part of a massive valve set in a bend in a thick pipe. The peeling red-on-white sign was stained with rust but it was still legible. It read: Extreme Danger: Emergency Use Only! System Test and Certification Required Every Thirty Days. Secure Escape Route And Evacuate All Downstream Personnel Before Operating Valve.

There was a dusty clipboard hanging on a hook below the valve. The faded top page was a maintenance record. It'd been almost a hundred years since the system had been checked and certified.

Not that that mattered. It either worked or it didn't.

And there was no way to evacuate anybody.

Doc untwisted a loop of steel wire that locked the rim of the wheel to the valve. When he tried to turn the wheel, it wouldn't budge. He jammed his swordstick through the spokes and used it like a lever.

With a crack and a creak the wheel moved an inch or two, then the turning became easy. From somewhere on the other side of the wall came a squeal. The squeal grew louder as he spun the valve open.

Then something boomed. The floor rocked violently and the air was ripped by a deafening noise. The roar sounded as if he had just unleashed Niagara Falls.

Everything continued to shake, and as it did, to shake apart. Concrete dust streamed from the ceiling above him; he knew it was going to come down, and before he could reach the doorway, it did. Doc lost his grip on his swordstick as the debris buried him.

Chapter Thirty-Four

Ryan the passenger watched from the wheelhouse of the S.S. *Cawdor* as Baron Crecca beat the scout's head to a pulp. He was standing close enough to be hit by some of the back splatter, brains or blood, or both. He could feel it dripping down the side of his face, but he couldn't make his hand move to wipe it away.

The hallucinations of his father and Trader had faded into the gathering darkness, so he knew that the combined effects of the spores and the bounty were wearing off. However, the odor of the bounty that was roasting unattended on the burn barrel was making his mouth water. His body wanted its share. Passenger Ryan fought against the urge. Fought successfully.

Thunder rolled and flashes of green lit the slope above the ville. The sky started to spit a few tentative spores.

It was coming again, he knew. The pool was about to reestablish control over its slaves.

Ryan forced his fingers to move. A twitch was all he could muster, but it was a start.

Then Crecca called for another volunteer, and Dean stepped forward. Ryan wanted to cry out a warning, but couldn't. His hands closed into fists at his side. Dean took a seat in the chair and allowed himself to be strapped down. There was a commotion to his left. He managed to turn his head far enough to see Doc Tanner fighting to break through the crowd and save his son from execution. Ryan tried to help, but only got a step or two in the right direction before the rousties seized Doc and threw him back.

The other companions were struggling as he was; Ryan could see that from the strain and anguish in their faces.

Ryan turned the full force of his effort to reaching the chair and the red-coated chiller before he could bring down the pipe. It was like walking through molasses. He had to beat back the heaviness and lethargy that infused his limbs. But with each step, it got a little easier.

The new baron watched his slow-motion approach with amusement. "What do you think you're doing, Cawdor?" he said. "Do you think you can get here in time to stop me?"

Ryan didn't answer. He didn't want to waste his energy or divert his focus from what he had to do.

"Well, you'd better hurry up, then," Crecca told him. "Get a fucking move on."

It took minutes for Ryan to cross the short stretch of ground. Minutes while the former carny master watched and waited with a leer on his face, confident that he had the upper hand, confident that he could smash the boy's skull with a single blow, even as his father reached out to save him.

Sweat poured off Ryan's face, chest and back. Though it hadn't started to snow in earnest yet, the tiny granules were peppering the square, and the thunder was an almost constant rumble.

He was still ten feet away, and moving at a crawl, when Crecca lightly tapped the top of Dean's head with the end of the pipe, measuring the range to his target. Then he reared back, cocking the bludgeon over his shoulder, coiling himself to swing for the center field fence.

A deep growl shook the ground, making Crecca stagger and lose his balance. He caught himself on the chair back to keep from falling.

Earthquake! Ryan thought as he continued to move.

But it wasn't.

With a howitzer-like boom, water and dirt exploded from the base of the mountain, about one hundred yards from where they all stood. Ahead of the twin plumes of black water, flying through the air like artillery shells, were chunks of broken limestone. As the rock crashed down and bounced around them, the water's howl grew much louder. Seventy-five feet from the mouths of the hidden culverts that had unleashed them, the two torrents coalesced, funneling, twisting together, plowing headlong into the earth with their combined might. They blasted through, sending a wall of water and debris ten feet high racing downhill toward the square.

Baron Crecca was no longer intent on caving in the back of Dean's head. Riveted by the sight of the onrushing wave, he didn't seem to notice Cawdor closing the distance between them, either.

Ryan could feel his strength and his physical control returning. For the last few feet, his legs drove forward with real power, as if their overdrive had suddenly kicked in. His right hand did his bidding, unsheathing eighteen inches of panga from its scabbard below his knee.

As the one-eyed man reached the foot of the chair, Crecca bolted away from it and the boy, cutting across the square toward the blockhouse entrance, well ahead of the leading edge of the flash flood.

There was no time for Ryan to hack through the four leather straps that held Dean pinioned. Grunting from the effort, he picked up the chair by the arms and started lugging it and Dean away. He'd gone no more than few yards when J.B. caught up to him and grabbed one of the arms. The two of them then ran with the chair and the boy between them.

Mildred and Krysty ran ahead, as did Jak, who had picked up the girl, Leeloo, and was carrying her in his arms. The companions raced to their left, away from the water, beyond the far end of the square, and along the curve at the base of the mountain.

When they were far enough away to be safe, Ryan and J.B. stopped, put down the chair and looked back.

The wall of water had gouged its own deep channel in the dirt, dividing the square and separating its occupants. The rousties who could run had gone the opposite direction and were out of sight. Those still partially paralyzed by the spores managed to move away, but slowly, like their legs were encased in ice—a feeling Ryan and his companions would never forget. The edge of the flood-choked channel eroded away at the chillers' heels. As the undercut bank gave way beneath them, their bodies twisted and fell, disappearing into the churning blackness. The main thrust of the torrent had swung past the front of the blockhouse, missing it entirely. But it was rampaging full-tilt into and through the hammered-down shanty ville. With falling darkness, it was impossible for Ryan to see clearly, but it looked as if the entire place had already been washed away, scoured off the landscape. He looked up at the sky and saw that the spore fall had stopped; the threat of blizzard was gone. The thunder, if there was any, was drowned out by the roar of the draining lake.

Beside him, Jak and J.B. were busy unstrapping Dean from the chair. Mildred and Krysty were comforting the little girl. Ryan was relieved to see them working as a team again.

"Is everybody all right?" he yelled over the noise of the cataract. He counted heads as they each nodded, and came up one shy.

"Where's Doc?" he shouted at them. "Did anybody see what happened to Doc?"

BARON CRECCA STOOD transfixed by the sight of two monumental gushers exploding from the hillside. Twin streams of water ten feet in diameter jetted through the air before burying themselves in the earth, sending dirt and spray flying. The sound it made was like some gigantic engine running wild. It took a second or two for the full import of what he was seeing to sink in.

Then a cold finger touched the center of his heart.

The source of the water was the burning pool.

It had to be.

The pool was being emptied.

Without the protective layer of water, without the lungfish who lived in it, the entity at its bottom couldn't survive. Without entity's continued existence and assistance, Crecca's was going to be one of the shortest-lived baronies in Deathlands history. He had to stop the drop in water level, before the pool was completely drained.

Crecca left the boy in the chair and sprinted toward the blockhouse. He was almost there when a ripple passing through the earth made him stumble over his own feet and fall. As he scrambled back up, to his right he saw the flash flood rip a fifty-foot-wide trench in the ground.

Somewhere behind him in the failing light, his handful of subjects were running for their lives. If they were screaming in terror, he couldn't hear it over the water's roar.

Crecca dashed down the stairway and into the corridor. Inside the hallway, the effect of the ground shaking was much worse. Plaster and concrete dust rained on him from the remains of the collapsed ceiling. As he ran down the corridor, splashing through the puddles, the back-and-forth tilting of the floor made him careen into and bounce off the walls.

The baron had known from the get-go that this catastrophe couldn't have been an accident. Hallucinations or not, massive floodgates didn't just open by themselves. Not suddenly, after a hundred years. Someone had to have done it on purpose. Since he hadn't seen anyone come out of the blockhouse, he was fairly sure that the someone was still inside. He had to find him or her and reverse whatever had been done.

Pipe in hand, and ready to clobber, he ducked his head inside the first few rooms along the hall. The dim light was made even dimmer by the airborne dirt and dust, but he saw no one.

In the last room, ninety-five percent of the ceiling had fallen onto the floor. It lay in a jumbled heap, from wall to wall. In a far corner something caught his eye.

Something bright and reflective along the back wall.

He climbed over the piles of rubble to reach it. The silver lion's head was on the end of a wooden walking stick that had been thrust through the spokes of a red metal wheel. The kind of a wheel that opened or closed a valve. Crecca read the warning sign.

Or a floodgate.

He pulled out the stick and flung it aside. Then

he started to crank the wheel over clockwise, shutting the valve.

"Not the best of ideas," said a loud voice to his right.

Crecca whirled to face a glaring scarecrow of a man. He recognized him at once as one of Cawdor's party. It was the old, babbling bastard who had to be led around on a rope. The baron's laughter was muffled by the dull roar coming through the walls.

"So, old man," he shouted back, "looks like you've got your brain on straight...just in time for me to beat it in." To demonstrate he bashed the end of the pipe into the concrete wall.

His adversary scampered over the rubble and out into the hall. He had picked up the stick Crecca had tossed aside.

"You aren't going to get away from me!" the baron called to him as he followed.

The old man was waiting for him in the corridor. "If you think I am trying to escape, you are sorely mistaken, sir," he yelled. "I just require some room to work." With that the old bastard did something to the silver handle, and the wood sheath of the stick came away in his left hand, revealing a long, tapering, double-edged blade of steel.

"I don't have time for games," Crecca shouted. And then he charged, holding the pipe out in front of him like a lance.

The tremors that still rippled the floor made his course erratic at best. As he veered toward his target, a fluorescent light fixture hanging by a thread gave up the ghost and crashed down in front of him, spoiling his aim.

The old man was more agile than he had any right to be. He sidestepped the charge and pivoted, and as Crecca rushed past him, the baron felt something molten-hot lance through the back of his tall boot and into his left calf.

"First blood!" the old man cried. With a back-and-forth slash of the sword, he cut down the light fixtures that blocked his view.

He now stood between Crecca and the room with the wheel. To reach it and stop the draining of the pool, the baron was going to have to go through him. The former carny master realized he had been outmaneuvered and outfoxed. Infuriated, Crecca made a blind thrust with the end of the pipe, aiming for the old man's face.

The sword parried the blow, metal scraping metal, then before the carny master could withdraw, he felt the sharp bite of razor-honed steel deep in his right shoulder. "Fucker!" he howled as blood flowed down his arm. He banged the pipe on the floor in frustration.

"Is something wrong, sir?" the old man demanded. "Would you to like to pass by me?"

Crecca charged again, this time swinging. He brought the pipe around at waist height, slashing from right to left, figuring the bastard couldn't possibly escape the blow.

The end of the pipe threw a shower of sparks as it hit the concrete wall.

The wall was all it hit.

The old man stepped back into the doorway, out of range, and as he did, with an ease that a man of his apparent age shouldn't have been able to muster, he squatted low and thrust upward with his sword.

The point plunged into Crecca's right thigh, a quick in-and-out stab that wrung a scream from his throat. He staggered back, flailing with the pipe to keep his opponent from following up with a second thrust.

"You look surprised, Baron," the old man yelled.

The Magnificent Crecca clapped a hand over his most recent injury and scowled at him.

"Why should it surprise you," Doc hollered, "that a man carrying a weapon like this—" he paused to flourish it "—could actually use it?"

Time was running out.

With his good leg, Crecca kicked the fallen light fixture into the old man's chest and lunged with the pipe. His opponent blocked the hunk of metal and glass with his sword, sweeping it aside, but before old man could bring the blade's point back, Crecca was on top of him.

The former carny master never saw the blow that felled him.

He was within a few inches of getting his big hand wrapped around the old man's scrawny throat when he caught a flash of silver from below, as the sword's heavy carved metal handle snapped up in a crisp, accurate, backhanded strike that he couldn't deflect.

He heard the crunch of his own cheekbone shattering and felt hot blood spraying down his suddenly numbed face. Falling forward as his knees buckled under him, he took another blow from the sword's pommel, this time on the crown of his head. For a second it made him see black. He crashed to the floor on his knees, knowing there would be more, and much worse to come, and unable to raise his arms to defend himself.

The third blow nailed him square in the back of the head. Everything went black.

Crecca toppled to the floor on his face.

DOC CRADLED the palm of his right hand, which bled from a long, shallow cut that he'd given himself by gripping the swordstick barehanded. There had been no time to get the blade's point around, so he'd had to make use of the pommel.

Effective use.

And once he'd gotten started, he'd had to follow up with successive, similar blows before the baron could recover.

Doc took a soiled linen handkerchief from the pocket of his frock coat and tightly bound his wound, then knelt beside the fallen man. There was blood everywhere. Crecca's blood. His blood. He tried to locate a pulse in the man's neck and couldn't find it.

As he leaned over the baron, the ceiling tiles on the floor around him started to move. They were floating, bobbing. The water in the corridor was no longer standing in puddle; it was flowing in a current. It was already an inch deep. Doc looked toward the hallway's entrance and saw the steps had been turned into a series of low, feeble waterfalls. The river he had created was starting to flood the blockhouse. He dashed into the room behind him and spun the red wheel, reopening the emergency drain valve as far as it would go.

When he returned to the hallway, the water had risen over the prostrate baron's mouth and nose.

The Magnificent Crecca wasn't blowing any bubbles.

Doc splashed down the corridor and up the stairs. As he climbed out of the entry well, he glimpsed the destruction he had wrought. A deep, dark torrent had gouged away the ville and the square and was undermining the near edge of the blockhouse. He could see no one moving, and a terrible thought struck him: had he drowned the very people he had been trying to save?

He drew his Civil War–era handblaster from its holster, the LeMat, and ran along the face of the building, away from the rushing water. Doc found the Steyr longblaster where he had hidden it. As he shrugged into its shoulder strap, he saw shadowy figures hurrying toward him from the base of the mountain. He primed the LeMat's shotgun barrel, ready to spray any enemies with smoking shrapnel.

"Do not come any closer!" he warned, aiming the old blaster at the running figures.

"Doc! It's us!" someone shouted back.

"John Barrymore," Doc said with relief, lowering his weapon. "And Ryan! Is everyone else all right? Did they all make it away safely?"

"We got lucky," Ryan told him. "Just scrapes and bruises. Come on, see for yourself. They're waiting for us."

"I trust our carny friends were not so fortunate," Doc said as they moved toward the hillside.

"We saw a few of them go down in the flood," J.B. said. "The rest are somewhere on the other side of all that water."

"The baron is probably under it by now," Doc said. "He is no longer a matter of concern." The old man unslung the Steyr and handed it over to its rightful owner.

"Glad you picked that up," Ryan said, giving the stock an affectionate slap. "I feel naked without it."

"Do not try to fire it before you check the bore," Doc warned him. "The muzzle is probably blocked with dried mud."

As they neared the foot of the slope, figures rushed out of the shadows to greet them. Doc received a hearty slap on the back from Mildred and a kiss on the cheek from Krysty. Jak nodded to him, a silent yet eloquent acknowledgment of his courage and heroism.

When the congratulations were over, they got right down to business.

"Are we still danger?" Krysty asked. "Should we try to move out of here tonight?"

"The pool seems to have stopped its activity, at

least for the time being,'' Mildred said. ''No more
storm clouds. No more spores. But there's no guarantee that it won't start up again before it's run completely dry.''

''How long before the lake is empty?'' Dean said.

''That could take all night,'' Ryan said. ''There's
no way of telling how deep it is. ''

''We can't leave here,'' J.B. told them. ''Not in
the dark. Not knowing the terrain. Not knowing
where the rousties went. We've got to hunker down
and ride it out until sunrise.''

''J.B.'s right,'' Ryan said. ''We'll take turns
standing watch. Dean, Leeloo, Doc and Krysty can
sack out first. We'll wake you in three hours. We
move out at dawn.''

Doc stood with Ryan and watched young Dean
escort the little girl to a safe, relatively comfortable
place among the boulders. After they had sat down,
the boy removed his coat and draped it over her
shoulders. She curled up with her head against his
chest and his protective arm over her.

''The reports of chivalry's demise appear to be
greatly exaggerated,'' Doc said.

''He's a good boy, with a good heart,'' Ryan
agreed. ''And he's going to grow into an even better
man.''

Chapter Thirty-Five

At first light, Ryan led the companions to what little was left of the ville's square. The roaring river had become a feeble creek. The shantytown was gone; the blockhouse full to the ceiling with standing water. They jumped down into the muddy channel the torrent had left behind, and moved in fighting formation with weapons drawn to the other side. When they climbed out of the riverbed, they found nothing to shoot at.

There was no sign of life.

Ryan and the others had been hoping that the Baja Bug had survived the flood. The little wag, even if overloaded with bodies, would have made it much easier for them to get back to the interstate. But the Baja Bug had vanished. Somewhere downstream it was overturned, perhaps buried in mud.

The companions had no choice but to walk out, to return Leeloo to Bullard. They voted unanimously to take the route past the burning pool. When they reached the bank where the evil had first touched them, they stopped and stared for a long time at what was revealed. The bottom of the lake was gray, a solid mass of lusterless gray that followed the contours of the bedrock beneath.

There were small standing puddles on its surface. It didn't move. Nothing on its surface moved.

"But it's just goo," Leeloo said.

Then a high-pitched sound filtered down from the forest above. Because it was intermittent, Ryan didn't recognize it as singing at first.

But it was.

A familiar bell-like soprano drifted through the dense trees along the ridgeline, and it grew stronger and more distinct: "'Baby, baby, it's a wild world....'"

The companions strained to hear, barely breathing, until it faded to silence.

James Axler
Outlanders

SEA OF PLAGUE

The loyalties that united the Cerberus warriors have become undone, as a bizarre messenger from the future provides a look into encroaching horror and death. Kane and his band have one option: fix two fatal fault lines in the time continuum—and rewrite history before it happens. But first they must restore power to the barons who dare to defy the greater evil: the mysterious new Imperator. Then they must wage war in the jungles of India, where the deadly, beautiful Scorpia Prime and her horrifying bio-weapon are about to drown the world in a sea of plague....

In the Outlands, the shocking truth is humanity's last hope.

MODERN STUDIES IN PHILOSOPHY

ARISTOTLE

A Collection of Critical Essays

EDITED BY J. M. E. MORAVCSIK

ANCHOR BOOKS
DOUBLEDAY & COMPANY, INC.
GARDEN CITY, NEW YORK
1967

CONTENTS

Introduction   1

I. LOGIC

Aristotle and the Sea Battle, G. E. M. ANSCOMBE   15
Aristotle's Different Possibilities,
    K. JAAKKO J. HINTIKKA   34
On Aristotle's Square of Opposition, M. THOMPSON   51

II. CATEGORIES

Categories in Aristotle and in Kant,
    JOHN COOK WILSON   75
Aristotle's *Categories*, Chapters I–V: Translation
    and Notes, J. L. ACKRILL   90
Aristotle's Theory of Categories, J. M. E. MORAVCSIK   125

III. METAPHYSICS

Essence and Accident, IRVING M. COPI   149
Tithenai ta Phainomena, G. E. L. OWEN   167
Matter and Predication in Aristotle, JOSEPH OWENS   191
Problems in *Metaphysics* Z, Chapter 13,
    M. J. WOODS   215

IV. ETHICS

The Meaning of *Agathon* in the *Ethics* of Aristotle,
    H. A. PRICHARD   241
Agathon and *Eudaimonia* in the *Ethics* of Aristotle,
    J. L. AUSTIN   261
The Final Good in Aristotle's *Ethics*,
    W. F. R. HARDIE   297
Aristotle on Pleasure, J. O. URMSON   323

Notes on Contributors   334

Selected Bibliography   335

ARISTOTLE

INTRODUCTION

What is it for us to understand Aristotle?[1] In order to grasp the difficulties involved in answering such a seemingly simple question, it is necessary to consider, briefly, some of the features of the history of philosophy and some of the characteristics of Aristotle's philosophy. Even if this necessarily sketchy introductory discussion fails to yield answers satisfactory to everyone, it should at least help to make clear why this volume is the way it is, and how it is viewed by its editor.

The mere existence of recent and contemporary commentaries on Aristotle might seem to call for an explanation if not an apology. At first glance at least, it might seem that after more than two thousand years Plato and Aristotle should be as well explained as they are ever likely to be, and that historians of philosophy should be turning their attention to the interpretation of less well known figures. And yet the facts are that there is exciting work being done on Aristotle today, that in the view of numerous philosophers and historians of philosophy much of the interpretation done in the past, even when of excellent quality, is not wholly satisfactory for our understanding, and that

[1]The views expressed in this introduction about the nature of the history of philosophy and about Aristotle are those of the editor and are not to be imputed to the contributors to this volume. The editor wishes to express his gratitude to Professor William Dray for a helpful discussion of some of these matters.

future generations are likely to view with dissatisfaction much of the work done today, while doing good and interesting historical work themselves. Under these circumstances the question arises: Why do men feel the need to rewrite the history of philosophy over and over again? One should attempt to answer this question, even if it turns out to be merely a special case of the tantalizing general question: Why must history be rewritten over and over again? In the case of philosophy, this question is sharpened by the fact that the repeated attempts at reconstructing the past are rarely occasioned by the appearance of drastically new empirical evidence. Once an ancient temple or palace is unearthed, it is there for all to see; subsequent excavations seek new targets. The interpreters of ancient philosophy, however, do not behave this way.

Faced with a bewildering variety of materials, one might be tempted to conclude that each school of philosophy feels the need to rewrite the history of the profession in its own image. Perhaps with each so-called "revolution" in philosophy—of which we have recently had such an uncomfortably large number that one is strongly inclined to doubt the genuineness of some—new emphases are given to different aspects of the thinking of the past. Such a line of thought leads to two popular conclusions, which this introduction is intended to combat. One of these is the claim that there is little if any objectivity in histories of philosophy written by philosophers. The other is the view that in order to gain unprejudiced, real insight into the philosophies of classical writers the best thing to do is to turn to the writings of those historians who have little or no systematic interest in current philosophy or at least hold no controversial positions upon this subject.

One way of showing these conclusions to be non sequiturs is to demonstrate that the peculiarly perennial nature of the history of philosophy can be accounted for on the basis of four considerations. First, an illuminating historical account involves comparisons (not necessarily evaluative ones) between the thought of the past and that of the present. (It is, after all, mostly by contrast and comparison that we learn about the thoughts of contemporaries as well.) Such comparisons tend to cast light both ways, and function as a conceptual bridge. Second, much of the explaining of a classical philosopher's thought involves explanations in our own terms, or at least in terms familiar to us. No historical interpretation of an author's works can be complete and adequate if it never breaks out of the circle, no matter how wide, of that author's terminology. These two ingredients of the historian's work, ingredients that link the past to a perpetually changing "present," and a perpetually changing set of terms, "our terms," help to explain the need for rewriting history without abandoning the claim of objectivity.

A third ingredient of the interpreter's task is the tracing of implications and consequences of some of a classical author's key claims. Such logical analysis is aided by the cumulative experience of the centuries, and it is an unending task, since such implications and consequences have no natural boundary. Finally, if we give a wide enough interpretation to the notion of empirical evidence, one can say that the appearance of new evidence fairly frequently plays an important role in new efforts at historical reconstruction. Such evidence may be a large number of quotes embedded in later texts that escaped notice for a long time, or new findings concerning the predominant mode of communication, oral or written, of a certain period. New discoveries in such related fields as the history of science or the history of literature also may lead to revisions

in the history of philosophy. In view of these four factors, one may hold that the history of philosophy is
an empirical enterprise with a corresponding claim of
objectivity,[2] partly cumulative in its progress and partly repetitive for reasons not necessarily linked to lack
of objectivity or the influence on the historian of contemporary philosophic positions.

At the same time these considerations begin to show
the complexity of the task of the historian of philosophy, and they hint at the variety of skills required for
success. Both the complexity and the variety can be
better appreciated if one considers the differences
among the related but distinct questions that a historian can ask about a given text. Examples of these
questions are: (i) What did Aristotle have in mind
when he said that ... ? (ii) What did Aristotle's statement that . . . mean to his contemporaries? (iii) To
what did Aristotle commit himself when he said
that ... ? (iv) How should one take Aristotle's statement that . . . in relation to the problems of our own
times?

What skills are required in order to answer these
questions? In the context of this brief introduction
only one thing needs special emphasis, namely that one
of the requisite skills is that of being a good philosopher. How else, except by being a good philosopher
in his own right, can a historian construct a sufficient
variety of interesting possible interpretations adequate
to the original thought of the subject? Robert Lowell
once said that no translation of a classic in poetry is
adequate unless the translation of a fine poem yields
what is a fine poem in its own right. This point could
easily be extended to the interpretation of classic phi-

---

[2]Some of what Aristotle said is likely to be true or false *a priori*,
but when the historian claims that Aristotle expressed such and
such an *a priori* claim, the historian's claim is empirical.

losophers. Such an extension, however, must meet the possible objection that while poetry is, in a sense, timeless, in an interpretation of a classic philosopher we must distinguish between (a) the treatment of, e.g. Aristotle, as an attempt to rediscover certain thoughts, and (b) the attempt to use this treatment as part of a general inquiry into expressions of timeless verities. With regard to (a) the "Lowell criterion" need not hold, for what is good philosophy in one period might, when viewed from the vantage point of a later period, appear no more than an "adolescent version" of a promising view. Against this objection it can be said that the sharp dichotomy implied by (a) and (b) has already been undermined by our discussion of the interrelatedness of questions (i) to (iv). With regard to the claim that some of the earlier philosophic views may seem "adolescent" to us, the following must be said. Most of the philosophy of our civilization has been organized around a set of loosely connected problems, most of which are not empirical in nature, at least in their original formulation. At times the accumulation of new empirical evidence leads to a reformulation of some of these problems so that they are seen either as not genuine, or as admitting of empirical solutions. In other cases the advances in logic or the availability of other tools of conceptual clarity allow us to arrive at reformulations which have greater clarity in the sense that these reformulations suggest answers that would not have been conceivable under the earlier formulations. There are still other problems, however, which remain with us through the centuries in spite of continuous reformulations. Thus philosophy is cumulative in some ways while in others it is not; some of its problems are perennial while others are not. Much of what Aristotle wrote is centered around issues which are alive today, and thus Robert

Lowell's criterion of adequacy is applicable to most interpretations of Aristotle.

This part of the introduction sheds, one may hope, some light on the nature of the history of philosophy. Our last point also sheds some light on some of the considerations that have guided the construction of this volume. For one of the key considerations in the selection of the material has been that the interpretations should be not only fine pieces of scholarship, but also fine pieces of philosophizing in their own right.

Aristotle's life and its historical context will not be considered here; these matters are discussed adequately in scores of other books. Nor will this introduction summarize Aristotle's views; it may be gathered from what has been said so far, and it will become even clearer from what follows, that according to the editor's view Aristotle's philosophizing does not admit of a summary. Instead, an attempt will be made to elucidate the following questions: (a) Why should one regard Aristotle as a classic philosopher? (b) How does the nature of Aristotle's philosophizing compare with the ways in which more modern philosophers have conducted their inquiries? (c) To what extent and in what ways does Aristotle's philosophy have unity?

With regard to the first question, one should note the variety of ways in which Aristotle's influence has been significant. One of these is manifested in the frequency with which his successors react, positively or negatively, to his writings. Regardless whether the topic is the rules for deductive inferences, or the proper analysis of what it is to explain natural phenomena, or the alleged primacy of material substances, in almost every age philosophers dealing with these topics have conducted a dialogue with Aristotle or with an Aristotelian view. Another manifestation of his influence is that he has been associated, rightly or wrongly, with a coherent view of reality which is supposed to give philosophic foundations to Christian doctrines about God, man, and nature. One may rightly question the extent to which this view can be attributed to Aristotle, but that he inspired it is undeniable. A third, and perhaps most important, way in which Aristotle's influence has been crucial can be seen when we realize the extent to which he set the problems of subsequent philosophy. These problems set for philosophy tasks that have yet to be completed. Such tasks are: collecting in a systematic fashion all the rules of valid inference, giving a proper analysis of the notion of responsibility, clarifying concepts basic to our understanding, such as the concepts of change, action, thing (or object), mass (or heap), and delineative proper ways of classification. This manifold nature of Aristotle's influence explains why he is a figure to be dealt with by the logician and semantic analyst as well as by the Thomistic theologian, by the student of metaphysics as well as the philosopher of science.

This partial answer to our first question also gives us some conception of the breadth of Aristotle's philosophy, and this—in turn—tells us something about the nature of his philosophizing, the subject of our second question. Aristotle is one of those rare philosophers who wrote about an enormous range of topics within the fields of logic, ethics, philosophy of education, philosophy of science, philosophy of art, philosophy of language, epistemology, and metaphysics. But it is a mistake to think that his philosophizing adds up either to a system or to a world view within which all the answers within all these fields are organized and interrelated. Some of the topics with which Aristotle deals, and his corresponding solutions, are only loosely connected with one another, and he repeatedly emphasizes that different types of topic require different types of approach. Still, neither are we to think of his philosophizing as fragmentary, or as designed only to catch glimpses here and there of the nature of things. In his philosophizing Aristotle seems to have kept in mind the ideal of the self-sufficient man, an ideal that both Plato and he espoused in their ethical writings; a self-sufficient man ought to be able to deal with any problem that he encounters even though he may not organize his answers into an axiomatic pattern, and even though he may come to the conclusion that different types of question require different types of answer. Among his problems epistemological questions did not occupy a central position, and when he came to set for himself questions about knowledge these often cut across the dichotomy of justification and explanation which has dominated most of philosophy since Descartes. But this is only a partial explanation of why he cannot be classified among either the empiricists or the rationalists. Another part of that explanation would be that from his vantage point—as from the vantage point of many philosophers today—these positions seem neither mutually exclusive nor exhaustive of the possibilities. We fare no better if we try another dichotomy, made familiar by Professor I. Berlin,[3] and applicable mainly to the contrast between the dreamers and ideologists of the nineteenth century, and the careful piecemeal thinkers dominating professional philosophy in the twentieth century in England and the United States. Aristotle could be described neither as a hedgehog of the type familiar from the post-Kantian philosophy of the nineteenth century, nor as the intellectual ancestor of that variety of philosophic thought which flourishes in the twentieth and is

[3]*The Hedgehog and the Fox. An Essay on Tolstoy's View of History* (London, 1953).

commonly referred to as "analytic philosophy." Perhaps this elusiveness of Aristotle's philosophy with respect to subsequent classifications helps to account for the fact that both hedgehogs and foxes are often indebted to him. If this brief discussion does not give much of a positive picture of what Aristotle's philosophy was like, at least it should suffice to make the important negative point, that in its nature it was very different from the dominant ways of philosophizing of the last four hundred years.

The foregoing also gives, in outline, the answer to the question about the unity of Aristotle's thought. Today most people tend to think of the great philosophers of the past as system-builders who laid down definitions and basic axioms, and then tried to account for all the salient features of nature, man, and the rules of conduct by means of these basic "truths" and the theorems that can be derived from them. Or, perhaps more loosely, people think that classical philosophers tried to account for all the salient features of the world and man's role in it in terms of an explanation that blends these features into an interrelated organic whole. It is very important to note that neither Aristotle, nor his teacher Plato, was a system-builder of this type. Though some of their concepts ranged over more than one problem, there is no simple truth which either Plato or Aristotle would have regarded as a key to all their answers and suggestions. The only sense of unity that applies to a discussion of Aristotle's views is that of consistency, and even this should be regarded as a desideratum—both Aristotle's and the interpreter's—rather than a fact to be taken for granted. It could be said that Aristotle's metaphysical suggestions were intended to underlie some of what he says about the proper way to explain natural phenomena, but it would be wrong to say that they underlie all

his philosophy. (It was reported to me that the late
Professor John L. Austin said on one occasion that
one of the refreshing features of Aristotle's ethics is
its almost total lack of connection with his metaphysics.)

These reflexions suggest that the proper approach to
Aristotle's philosophy is a piecemeal, or pluralistic one.
What Aristotle says as an answer to one question may
not relate to his answers to other questions similar in
appearance. Thus acceptance of some of Aristotle's
suggestions does not commit one to a wholesale acceptance of his philosophic claims. This remark applies both to content and to methodology. Furthermore, even if it did not have other support, this approach suggests itself as a heuristic principle, for it fa-
cilitates the emergence of dialogue between the philosophers of the past and those of the present. The
conception of a classic philosopher as a system-builder
carries with it the implication that if you reject a part,
you must reject all; or conversely that partial acceptance must lead to wholesale acceptance. The approach
favored by the editor makes it possible for us to claim
with plausibility that one may understand some parts
of Aristotle's thought while finding others obscure, that
some of his suggestions are acceptable while others do
not seem to be, that some of his results seem naïve
in the light of subsequent research, while in some other ways (e.g. in his discussion of the variety of types
of predication, his analysis of responsibility, and his
views on the nature of pleasure and enjoyment) his
suggestions are far more profound and far more fruit-
ful than those made by the vast majority of philosophers in the twentieth century.

Right or wrong, these meditations on the nature of
the history of philosophy and on the nature of Aristotle's philosophy have influenced the construction of

ARISTOTLE AND THE SEA BATTLE
De Interpretatione, Chapter IX
G. E. M. ANSCOMBE

1   For what is and for what has come about, then,
it is necessary that affirmation, or negation, should
be true or false; and for universals universally
quantified it is always necessary that one should
be true, the other false; and for singulars too, as
has been said; while for universals not universally
quantified it is not necessary. These have been
discussed.

For what is and for what has come about: he has in
fact not mentioned these, except to say that a verb or
a tense—sc. other than the present, which he regards
as the verb *par excellence*—must be part of any proposition.

it is necessary: given an *antiphasis* about the present
or past, the affirmative proposition must be true or
false; and similarly for the negative. An *antiphasis* is
a pair of propositions in which the same predicate is
in one affirmed, in the other denied, of the same subject. Note that Aristotle has not the idea of the negation of a proposition, with the negation sign outside
the whole proposition; that was (I believe) invented by
the Stoics.—What Aristotle says in this sentence is ambiguous; that this is deliberate can be seen by the con-

From *Mind*, LXV (1956), 1–15. Newly revised by the author.
Reprinted by permission of the author and the editor of *Mind*.

trast with the next sentence. The ambiguity between necessarily having a truth-value, and having a necessary truth-value—is first sustained, and then resolved at the end of the chapter.

for universals universally quantified: he does not mean, as this place by itself would suggest, that of "All men are white" and "No men are white" one must be true and the other false. But that if you take "All men are white" and "No men are white" and construct the antiphasis of which each is a side, namely, "All men are white—Not all men are white" and "No men are white—Some man is white," then one side of each antiphasis must be true, and the other side must be false.

for singulars too, as has been said: sc. of "Socrates is white—Socrates is not white" one side is necessarily true, the other necessarily false. (This is what a modern reader cannot take in; but see the "Elucidation.")

for universals not universally quantified: his example rendered literally is "man is white—man is not white." From his remarks I infer that these would be correctly rendered "men are. . .". For, he says, men are beautiful, and they are also not beautiful, for they are ugly too, and if they are ugly they are not beautiful. I believe that we (nowadays) are not interested in these unquantified propositions.

These have been discussed: i.e. in the immediately preceding chapters, by which my explanations can be verified.

2   But for what is singular and future it isn't like this. For if every affirmation and negation is true or false, then it is also necessary for everything to be the case or not be the case. So if one man says something will be, and another says not, clearly it is necessary for one of them to be speaking truly, if every affirmation and negation is true or

3   false. For both will not hold at once on such con-

ditions. For if it is true to say that something is
white or is not white, its being white or not
white is necessary, and if it is white or not white,
it is true to say or deny it. And if it is not the
case, then it is false, and if it is false, it is not the
case; so that it is necessary as regards either the
affirmation or the negation that it is true or false.

singular and future: sc. There will be a relevant discussion tonight; this experiment will result in the mixture's turning green; you will be sent down before the
end of term.

it isn't like this: namely, that these propositions (or
their negations) must be true or false. Throughout this
paragraph the ambiguity is carefully preserved and concealed.

*it is also necessary for everything to be the case
or not be the case:* the Greek "or" is, like the English, ambiguous between being exclusive and being non-
exclusive. Here it is exclusive, as will appear; hence
the "or" in the conditional "if every affirmation and
negation is true or false" is also exclusive, and to point
this he says "every affirmation and negation", not, as
in (1) "every affirmation or negation"; that "or" was
non-exclusive.

For both will not hold on such conditions: namely,
on the conditions that every affirmation is true or false.
This condition is not a universal one; it does not apply
to the unquantified propositions, though if the "or" is
non-exclusive it does. But if the conditions hold, then
just one of the two speakers must be speaking the
truth.

It is true to say or deny it: ἦν is the common philosophical imperfect.

4   So nothing is or comes about by chance or
'whichever happens'. Nor will it be or not be, but
everything of necessity and not 'whichever hap-

pens'. For either someone saying something or
someone denying it will be right. For it would
either be happening or not happening accordingly. For whichever happens is not more thus or
not thus than it is going to be.

'whichever happens': the Greek phrase suggests both
"as it may be" and "as it turns out". "As the case
may be" would have been a good translation if it
could have stood as a subject of a sentence. The 'scare-
quotes' are mine; Aristotle is not overtly discussing the
expression "whichever happens".

is not more thus or not thus than it is going to be:
as the Greek for "or" and for "than" are the same, it
is so far as I know a matter of understanding the argument whether you translate as here, or (as is more
usual) e.g.: "isn't or (sc. and) isn't going to be rather
thus than not thus". But this does not make good
sense. Aristotle is arguing: "We say 'whichever happens' or 'as the case may be' about the present as well
as about the future; but you don't think the present
indeterminate, so why say the future is?" Or rather (as
he is not talking about the expression): "Whatever
happens *will* be just as determinately thus or not thus
as it *is*."

5   Further, if something is white now, it was true
       earlier to say it was going to be white, so that it
       was always true to say of any of the things that
       have come about: "it is, or will be." But if it was
       always true to say: "it is, or will be", then: im-
       possible for that not to be or be going to be. But if
       it is impossible for something not to come about,
       then it is unable not to come about. But if some-
       thing is unable not to come about it is necessary
6   for it to come about. Therefore it is necessary
       that everything that is going to be should come
       about. So nothing will be 'whichever happens' or
       by chance. For if by chance, then not by necessity.

But if it is impossible for something not to come about, then it is unable not to come about: the reader who works through to the end and understands the solution will examine the dialectic to see where it should be challenged. It will turn out that the point is here, in spite of the equivalence of the two Greek expressions. It is impossible for the thing not to come about, i.e. necessary that it should come about by *necessitas consequentiae,* which does not confer the character of necessity *necessitas consequentis,* on what does come about. A necessary consequence of what is true need not be necessary.

> Still, it is not open to us, either, to say that neither is true, as: that it neither will be nor will
> 7 not be. For firstly, the affirmation being false the negation will not be true, and this being false the affirmation won't be true. —And besides, if it is true to say that something is big and white, both must hold. And if they are going to hold to-morrow, they must hold tomorrow. And if something is neither going to be nor not going to be tomorrow, 'whichever happens' won't be. Take a sea-battle, for example: it would have to be the case that a sea-battle neither came about nor didn't come about tomorrow.

Still, it is not open to us, either, to say that neither is true: And yet Aristotle is often supposed to have adopted this as the solution.

For firstly: this goes against what he has shown at the end of (3): "if it is false, it does not hold." So much, however, is obvious, and so this is not a very strong objection if we are willing to try whether neither is true. What follows is stronger.

And if they are going to hold tomorrow: from here to the end of the paragraph the argument is: if it is the case that something will be, then it will be the

case that it is. In more detail: you say, or deny, two
things about the future. If what you say is true, then
when the time comes you must be able to say those
two things in the present or past tenses.

'whichever happens' won't be: i.e. 'whichever happens' won't happen.

8   These are the queer things about it. And there
         more of the sort, if it is necessary that for every
         affirmation and negation, whether for universals
         universally quantified or for singulars, one of the
         opposites should be true and one false, that there
         is no 'whichever happens' about what comes
         about, but that everything is and comes about of
         necessity. So that there would be no need to
         deliberate or take trouble, e.g.: "if we do this,
9   this will   happen, if not, not." For there is noth-
         ing to prevent its being said by one man and
         denied by another ten thousand years ahead that
         this will happen, so that whichever of the two was
         then true to say will of necessity happen. And in-
         deed it makes no difference either if people have
         said the opposite things or not; for clearly this is
         how things are, even if there isn't one man saying
         something and another denying it; nor is it its
         having been asserted or denied that makes it
         going to be or not, nor its having been ten thou-
         sand years ahead or at any time you like. So if in
10   the whole of time it held that the one was the
         truth, then it was necessary that this came about,
         and for everything that has been it always held,
         so that it came about by necessity. For if anyone
         has truly said that something will be, then it can't
         not happen. And it was always true to say of
         what comes about: it will be.

These are the queer things about it. And: I have di-
verged from the usual punctuation, which leads to the
rendering: "These and similar strange things result,
if...." This seems illogical.

E.g.: often rendered "since": "since if we do this, this will happen, if not, not." This does not appear to me to make good sense. The Oxford translator sits on the fence here.

So if in the whole of time it held: one must beware of supposing that Aristotle thinks the conclusion stated in the apodosis of this sentence follows from the condition. It only follows if the previous arguments are sound. He is going to reject the conclusion, but there is no reason to think that he rejects the condition: on the contrary.

11 Now if this is impossible! For we see that things that are going to be take their start from deliberating and from acting, and equally that there is in general a possibility of being and not being in things that are not always actual. In them, both are open, both being and not being, and so also both becoming and not becoming. And plenty of
12 things are obviously like this; for example, this coat is capable of getting cut up, and it won't get cut up but will wear out first. And equally it is capable of not getting cut up, for its getting worn out first would not have occurred if it had not been capable of not getting cut up. So this
13 applies too to all other processes that are spoken of in terms of this kind of possibility. So it is clear that not everything is or comes about of necessity, but with some things 'whichever happens', and the affirmation is not true rather than the negation; and with other things one is true rather and for the most part, but still it is open for either to happen, and the other not.

take their start: literally: "there is a starting point of things that are going to be." The word also means "principle". A human being is a prime mover (in the engineer's sense), but one that works by deliberating. As if a calculating machine not merely worked, but was, in part, precisely *qua* calculating, a prime mover. But Aristotle's approach is not that of someone enquiring into human nature, but into causes of events and observing that among them is this one.

acting: he means human action, which is defined in terms of deliberation; see *Nicomachean Ethics* VI 1139: there he repeats the word "ἀρχή": "ἡ τοιαύτη ἀρχὴ ἄνθρωπος": the cause of this sort is man. An animal too or a plant, is a prime mover. Hence his thought is not that there are new starting points constantly coming into existence; that would not matter. It is first of all the nature of deliberation that makes him think that the fact of human action proves the dialectic must be wrong. I cannot pursue this here; though I should like to enter a warning against the idea (which may present itself): "the nature of deliberation presupposes freedom of the will as a condition." That is not an Aristotelian idea.

things that are not always actual: things that are always actual are the sun, moon, planets and stars. Aristotle thought that what these do is necessary. The general possibility that he speaks of is of course a condition required if deliberation and 'action' are to be possible. If what the typewriter is going to do is necessary, I cannot do anything else with the typewriter. Not that this is Aristotle's ground for speaking of the general possibility. That is shown in his consideration about the coat: the assumption that the coat *will be* worn out does not conflict with our knowledge that it *can* be cut up. We know a vast number of possibilities of this sort.

in terms of this kind of possibility: I take it that we have here the starting point for the development of Aristotle's notion of potentiality. The sentence confirms my view of the point where he would say the dialectic went wrong.

with other things one is true rather and for the most part: as we should say: more probable.

14   The existence of what is when it is, and the non-existence of what isn't when it isn't, is necessary. But still, for everything that is to be is not necessary, nor for everything that isn't not to be. For it isn't the same: for everything that is to be of necessity when it is, and: for it simply to be of necessity. And the same for what isn't. And the same reasoning applies to the antiphasis. For it is necessary that everything should be or not, and should be going to be or not. But it is not the

15   case, separately speaking, that either of the sides is necessary. I mean, e.g. that it is necessary that there will be a sea-battle tomorrow or not, but that it is not necessary that there should be a sea-battle tomorrow, nor that it should not happen. But for it to come about or not is necessary. So that since propositions are true as the facts go, it is clear that where things are such as to allow of 'whichever happens' and of opposites, this must hold for the antiphasis too.

The existence of what is when it is . . . is necessary: i.e. it cannot be otherwise. A modern gloss, which Aristotle could not object to, and without which it is not possible for a modern person to understand his argument, is: and cannot be shown to be otherwise. It will by now have become very clear to a reader that the implications of 'necessary' in this passage are not what he is used to. But see the "Elucidation".

simply to be of necessity: there is a temptation to recognise what we are used to under the title "logical necessity" in this phrase. But I believe that Aristotle thought the heavenly bodies and their movements were necessary in this sense. On the other hand, he seems to have ascribed something like logical necessity to them.

But it is not the case, separately speaking, that either of the sides is necessary: the ambiguity of the opening "it is necessary that an affirmation (or negation) should be true or false" is here resolved. And we learn that when Aristotle said that, he meant that if p is a statement about the present or the past, then either p is necessary or not-p is necessary. But this means that in order to ascribe necessity to certain propositions (the ones, namely, that are not 'simply' necessary) we have to be informed about particular facts. So, one may ask, what has this necessity got to do with logic? —Aristotle, however, states no facts, past, present, or future. (I do in what follows; I hope this will not prove misleading: the purpose is only didactic.) His results could perhaps be summarised as follows: we use indices $_p$ and $_f$ to the propositional sign to indicate present and past time references on the one hand, and future time reference on the other. Then for all p, p vel not-p is necessary (this covers the unquantified propositions too) and p_p is necessary vel not-p_p is necessary; but it is not the case that for all p, p_f is necessary vel not-p_f is necessary.

16   This is how it is for what is not always existent or not always non-existent. For such things it is necessary that a side of the antiphasis should be true or false, but not this one or that one, but whichever happens; and that one should be true rather than the other; but that does not mean that it is true, or false. So it is clear that it is not necessary for every affirmation and negation that this one of the opposites should be true and that one false; for it does not hold for what does not exist but is capable of being or not being; but it is as we have said.

whichever happens: sc.: it is a matter of whichever happens.

that one should be true rather than the other: cf.

"rather and for the most part" above; note that this is governed by "it is necessary"; I infer that Aristotle thought that correct statements of probability were true propositions.

but that does not mean: ἤδη, logical, not temporal;[1] ἤδη works rather like the German "schon" (only here of course it would be "noch nicht"). ἤδη in a non-temporal sense is, like οὐκέτι, frequent in Greek literature. English translators of philosophical texts usually either neglect to translate it or mistranslate it. For examples, see *Theaetetus* 201e4, *Physics* 187a36, *De Interpretatione* 16a8, *Metaphysics* 1006a16. Bonitz gives some more examples.

AN ELUCIDATION OF THE FOREGOING FROM A MODERN POINT OF VIEW

A. The Vice Chancellor will either be run over next week or not. And therefore either he will be run over next week or he will not. Please understand that I was *not* repeating myself!

B. I think I understand what you were trying to do; but I am afraid you were repeating yourself and, what is more, you cannot fail to do so.

A. Can't fail to do so? Well, listen to this: The Vice Chancellor *is* going to be run over next week ...

B. Then I am going to the police as soon as I can.

A. You will only be making a fool of yourself. It's not true.

B. Then why did you say it?

A. I was merely trying to make a point: namely, that I have succeeded in saying something true about the future.

[1] I am indebted to Miss M. Hartley of Somerville College for pointing this out to me.

B. What have you said about the future that is true?

A. I don't know: but this I do know, that I have said something true; and I know that it was either when I told you the Vice Chancellor would be run over, or on the other hand when I said he wouldn't.

B. I am sorry, but that is no more than to say that Either he will or he won't be run over. Have you given me any information about the future? Don't tell me you have, with one of these two remarks, for that is to tell me nothing, just because the two remarks together cover all the possibilities. If what you tell me is an Either/Or and it embraces all possibilities, you tell me nothing.

A. Can an Either/Or be true except by the truth of one of its components? I seem to remember Quine speaking of Aristotle's "fantasy", that "It is true that either *p* or *q*" is not a sufficient condition for "Either it is true that *p* or it is true that *q*." Now I will put it like this: Aristotle seems to think that the truth of a truth-functional expression is independent of the truth values of the component propositions.

B. But that is a howler! The "truth" of Either p or not p is determined, as you know very well, by its truth value's being T for all possible combinations of the truth *possibilities* of its components; that is why its "truth" gives no information. Having set out the full truth-table and discovered that for all possibilities you get T in the final column, you need make no enquiry to affirm the truth of $p \lor \sim p$—any enquiry would be comic. If on the other hand you tell me $p \lor \sim q$ (q being different from p) you do give me some information, for certain truth-combinations are excluded. There is therefore the possibility of enquiring whether your information is correct. And that I do by discovering which of the truth-possibilities is fulfilled; and if one of the combinations of truth-possibilities which is a truth-condition for p∨∼q is fulfilled, then I discover that your information is correct. But to tell me "It will rain, or it won't", is not to tell me of any truth-possibility that it is—or, if you like, will be, satisfied. Now will you actually tell me something about the future?

A. Very well. Either you are sitting in that chair or it will not rain tomorrow.

B. I agree, that is true, because I am sitting in this chair. But still I have been told nothing about the future, because since I know I am sitting in this chair I know what I have been told is true whether it rains tomorrow or not—i.e. for all truth possibilities of "It will rain tomorrow." But do you mind repeating your information?

A. Either you are sitting in that chair or it will not rain tomorrow.

B. (*Having stood up.*) I am glad to be told it will be fine—but is it certain? Do you get it from the meteorologists? I have heard that they are sometimes wrong.

A. But surely we are talking about truth, not certainty or knowledge.

B. Yes, and I am asking whether your information —which I agree is information this time—is true.

A. I can't tell you till some time tomorrow; perhaps not till midnight. But whatever I tell you then will have been so now—I mean if I tell you then 'True', that means not just that it will be true then but that it was true now.

B. But I thought it was the great point against Aristotle that 'is true' was timeless.

A. Yes—well, what I mean is that if I tell you—as I shall be able to—'True' tomorrow—I mean *if* I am able to, of course—why, then it will have been, I mean is now correct to say it is true.

B. I understand you. If it is going to rain tomorrow it is true that it is going to rain tomorrow. I should be enormously surprised if Aristotle were to deny this.

A. But Aristotle says it isn't true that it is going to rain tomorrow!

B. I did not read a single prediction in what Aristotle said. He only implied that it didn't have to be true that it will rain tomorrow, i.e. it doesn't have to rain tomorrow.

A. What? Even if it is going to rain tomorrow?

B. Oh, of course, if it is going to rain tomorrow, then it necessarily will rain tomorrow: $(p \supset p)$ is necessary. But is it going to?

A. I told you, I can't say, not for certain. But why does that matter?

B. Can't you say anything for certain about tomorrow?

A. I am going to Blackwell's tomorrow.

B. And that is certain?

A. Yes, I am absolutely determined to go. (Partly because of this argument: it is a point of honour with me to go, now.)

B. Good. I fully believe you. At least, I believe you as fully as I can. But do I—or you—know you will go? Can nothing stop you?

A. Of course lots of things can stop me—anything from a change of mind to death or some other catastrophe.

B. Then you aren't necessarily going to Blackwell's?

A. Of course not.

B. Are you necessarily here now?

A. I don't understand you.

B. Could it turn out that this proposition that you, NN., are in All Souls today, May 7, 1954, is untrue? Or is this certain.

A. No, it is quite certain—My reason for saying so is that if you cared to suggest any test, which could turn out one way or the other, I can't see any reason to trust the test if, situated as I am, I have any doubt that I am here. I don't mean I can't imagine doubting it; but I can't imagine anything that would make it doubtful.

B. Then what is true about the present and the past is *necessarily* true?

A. Haven't you passed from certainty to truth?

B. Do you mean to tell me that something can be certain without being true?—And isn't what is true about the present and the past quite necessary?

A. What does 'necessary' mean here, since it obviously doesn't mean that these are what we call necessary propositions?

B. I mean that nothing whatever could make what is certain untrue. Not: if it is true, it is necessary, but: since it is certainly true it is necessary. Now if you can show me that anything about the future is so certain that nothing could falsify it, then (perhaps) I shall agree that it is necessarily true that that thing will happen.

A. Well: the sun will rise tomorrow.

B. That is so certain that nothing could falsify it?

A. Yes.

B. Not even: the sun's not rising tomorrow?

A. But this is absurd! When I say it is certain I am here, am I saying it wouldn't falsify it for me not to be here? But I am here, and the sun will rise tomorrow.

B. Well, let me try again: Could anything that can

happen make it untrue that you are here? If not,
I go on to ask: Could anything that can happen
make it untrue that the sun rises tomorrow?

A. No.

B. If we continued in darkness, the appearance of
the night being continued for the rest of our lives,
all the same the sun will have risen; and so on?

A. But that can't happen.

B. Is that as certain as that you are here now?

A. I won't say. —But what does Aristotle mean when
he says that one part of the antiphasis is necessarily true (or false) when it is the present or the
past that was in question? Right at the beginning,
when I said "The Vice Chancellor will either be
run over or not, therefore either he will be run
over or he will not" you said that I was repeating
myself and could not fail to be repeating myself.
And then you referred to the Truth-table-tautolog-
ical account of that proposition. But does not precisely the same point apply to what Aristotle says
about "Either p or not p" when p is a proposition about the present or the past?

B. You could have avoided repeating yourself if you
had said "The Vice Chancellor will either be run
over or not, therefore either it is necessary that he
should be run over or it is necessary that he should
not be run over." But as you would have been disinclined to say that—seeing no possible meaning
for an ascription of necessity except what we are
used to call 'logical necessity'—you could not
avoid repeating yourself.

Thus Aristotle's point (as we should put it) is that
'Either p or not p' is always necessary, and this necessity is what we are familiar with. But—and this is from
our point of view the right way to put it, for this
is a novelty to us—that when p describes a present or

past situation, then either p is necessarily true, or ~ p is necessarily true; and here 'necessarily true' has a sense which is unfamiliar to us. In this sense I say it is necessarily true that there was not—or necessarily false that there was—a big civil war raging in England from 1850 to 1870; necessarily true that there is a University in Oxford; and so on. But 'necessarily true' is not simply the same as 'true'; for while it may be true that there will be rain tomorrow, it is not necessarily true. As everyone would say: there may be or may not. We also say this about things which we don't know about the past and the present. The question presents itself to us then in this form: does "may" express mere ignorance on our part in both cases?

Suppose I say to someone: "In ten years' time you will have a son; and when he is ten years old he will be killed by a tyrant." Clearly this is something that may be true and may not. But equally clearly there is no way of finding out (unless indeed you say that waiting and seeing is finding out; but it is not finding out that it will happen, only that it does happen.)

Now if I really said this to someone, she would either be awe-struck or think me dotty; and she would be quite right. For such a prediction is a prophecy. Now suppose that what I say comes true. The whole set of circumstances—the prophecy together with its fulfilment—is a miracle; and one's theoretical attitude (if one has one at all) to the supposition of such an occurrence ought to be exactly the same as one's theoretical attitude to the supposition that one knew of someone's rising from the dead and so on.

As Newman remarks, a miracle ought not to be a silly trivial kind of thing—e.g. if my spoon gets up one day and dances a jig on my plate, divides into several pieces and then joins up again, it qualifies ill as a miracle, though it qualifies perfectly well for philosophical

discussion of naturally impossible but imaginable occurrences. Similarly if one were discussing impossible
predictions one would take such an example as the
following: Every day I receive a letter from someone
giving an accurate account of my actions and experiences from the time of posting to the time I received
the letter. And whatever I do (I do random, absurd
actions for example, to see if he will still have written
a true account) the letter records it. Now, since we are
dealing in what can be imagined and therefore can be
supposed to happen, we must settle whether this would
be knowledge of the future: its certainly would surely be a proof that what I did I did necessarily.

It is interesting to note that Wittgenstein agrees
with Aristotle about this problem, in the *Tractatus*.
"The freedom of the will consists in the fact that future actions cannot be known. The connexion of knowing and the known is that of logical necessity. 'A
knows that p' is senseless, if p is a tautology." We are
therefore presented with the logical necessariness of
what is known's being true, together with the logical
non-necessity of the kind of things that are known.
The "logical necessity" of which he speaks in the remark on knowledge is thus not just truth-table necessariness. It is the unfamiliar necessariness of which
Aristotle also speaks. "A knows that p" makes sense
only if p describes a fact about the past or present;
so it comes out in Wittgenstein, and in Aristotle: past
and present facts are necessary. (In more detail, by the
Tractatus account: if A knows p, for some q (q ⊃ p)
is a tautology, and q expresses a fact that A is 'acquainted' with.)

Then this letter about my actions would not have
been knowledge even if what it said was always right.
However often and invariably it was verified, it would
still not be certain, because the facts could go against

it. However Aristotle's considerations are not about knowledge and certainty but about necessity and its correlative possibility. They have probably been made more difficult to understand because they are an instance of his willingness to deny what it does not make sense to assert—for the affirmation of the necessity of p is equivalent to a denial of the possibility of not-p. The possibility in question relates only to the future, hence by some current conceptions the negation of such possibility also relates only to the future.

E.g. 'This plaster can be painted for the next eight hours and not after that since by then it will have set too hard.' Neither the affirmation nor the negation of this sort of possibility can be constructed relative to the past. 'It can be painted yesterday' demands emendation perhaps to 'It may have been painted yesterday,' perhaps to 'It could have been painted yesterday.' (The contingency of the past is that something was possible, not that it is possible. The openness of the future is that something is possible. This is not the same as saying that it *will* be possible, since the possibility may be extinguished. It is a present state of affairs that the plaster can be painted for the next few hours.) Now Aristotle who readily uses 'No men are numbers' as a premise would pass from the denial that possibility of this sort holds in relation to the past (or present) to asserting that the past and present are necessary.

ARISTOTLE'S DIFFERENT POSSIBILITIES

K. JAAKKO J. HINTIKKA

1. *The interrelations of modal notions in Aristotle.*
The results of our examination of the varieties of ambiguity in Aristotle (see *Inquiry*, [1959], 137–51) can be used to analyze his notion of possibility. This notion is closely connected with the other modal notions, notably with those of necessity and impossibility. Since these notions are somewhat more perspicuous than that of possibility, it is advisable to start from them.

Aristotle knew that the contradictory (negation) of 'it is necessary that *p*' is not 'it is necessary that not *p*' but rather 'it is not necessary that *p*' (*De Int.* 12, 22a4 ff.). The last two phrases are not contradictories, either, for they can very well be true together (*De Int.* 13, 22b1 ff.), the latter being wider in application than the former. By parity of form, 'it is not necessary that not *p*' is wider in application than 'it is necessary that *p*'.

These relations are conveniently summed up in the following diagram (which is not used by the Stagirite):

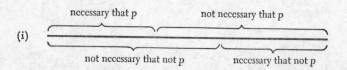

(i)

necessary that *p*   not necessary that *p*

not necessary that not *p*   necessary that not *p*

From *Inquiry*, III (1960), 18–28. Reprinted by permission of the author and the editors of *Inquiry*.

According to Aristotle, 'impossible' behaves like 'necessary' (*De Int.* 12, 22a7 ff.). We can therefore illustrate it by means of a diagram similar to (i). In fact, the diagram will be virtually the same as the one for 'necessary', for "the proposition 'it is impossible' is equivalent, when used with a contrary subject, to the proposition 'it is necessary'." (See *De Int.* 13, 22b5.) In other words, 'impossible that *p*' is equivalent to 'necessary that not *p*', 'impossible that not *p*' equivalent to 'necessary that *p*', etc. We can therefore complete the diagram (i) as follows:

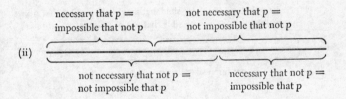

(ii)

necessary that *p* = impossible that not *p*

not necessary that *p* = not impossible that not *p*

not necessary that not *p* = not impossible that *p*

necessary that not *p* = impossible that *p*

2. *The two notions of possibility.* The problem is to fit the notion of possibility into the schema (ii). In this respect, Aristotle was led by two incompatible impulses. On one hand, he was naturally tempted to say that 'possible' and 'impossible' are contradictories; something is possible if and only if it is not impossible (See e.g. *De Int.* 13, 22a16–18, 32–38.) Under this view, we get the following diagram:

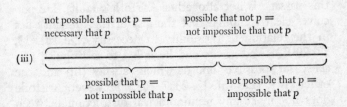

(iii)

not possible that not *p* = necessary that *p*

possible that not *p* = not impossible that not *p*

possible that *p* = not impossible that *p*

not possible that *p* = impossible that *p*

But this temptation is not the only one. In ordinary discourse, saying that something is possible often serves to indicate that it is *not* necessary. Aristotle catches this implication. For him, "if a thing may be, it may also not be" (*De Int.* 13, 22b20; see also 22a14 ff.). Essentially the same point is elaborated in the *Topica* II 7, 112b1 ff. There Aristotle says that "if a necessary event has been asserted to occur usually, clearly the speaker has denied an attribute to be universal which is universal and so has made a mistake."

Under this view, our diagram will have this look:

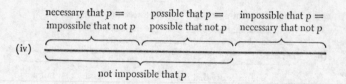

It is seen that (iii) and iv) differ in that in (iii) the range of possibility comprises everything that is necessary, while in (iv) possibility and necessity are incompatible.

It appears from *De Interpretatione* that Aristotle did not immediately see that the assumptions underlying (iii) and (iv) are incompatible. Not surprisingly, he ran into difficulties which he discusses in a not entirely clear way in *De Int.* 13, 22b11–23a7 (although I suspect that the confusion of the usual translations of this passage is not altogether Aristotle's fault). He perceives clearly enough that the gist of the difficulty lies in the relation of possibility to necessity (*De Int.* 13, 22b29 ff.). And at the end he is led to distinguish two senses of 'possible' one of which satisfies (iii) and the other (iv). (*De Int.* 13, 23a7 – 27.) However, Aristotle does not make any terminological distinction between the two. Insofar as the distinction is vital, I shall call the notion of possibility which satisfies (iii) 'possibility proper' and the notion which satisfies (iv) 'contingency'.

3. *Homonymy v. multiplicity of applications.* Now we can see why the distinction between a diversity of applications and homonymy is vital for this essay. We have found a clear-cut case of homonymy: the notions of contingency and of possibility proper have different logical properties. They cannot be covered by a single term 'possibility' except by keeping in mind that this word has different meanings on different occasions. Their relation is therefore one of homonymy (cf. section 10 of the first paper).

But in addition to this duality of 'contingency' and 'possibility proper', there is a different kind of distinction. One of these two logically different notions, viz. possibility proper, covers *two kinds of cases.* When one says that *p* is possible (in the sense of possibility proper), one sometimes could also say that *p* is contingent and sometimes that *p* is necessary. This does not mean, of course, that the term 'possible' is ambiguous; it merely means that its field of application falls into two parts. It was for Aristotle therefore a typical case of multiplicity of applications as distinguished from homonymy (cf. section 10 of the first paper). The following diagram makes the situation clear:

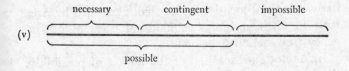

(v)

The distinction between the different applications of 'possibility proper' loomed large for Aristotle because he tended to emphasize the distinction between

necessity and contingency. Thus Aristotle argues in
Met. X 10 that the perishable and the imperishable
are different in kind (εἶδος and γένος). In an earlier
paper ("Necessity, Universality, and Time in Aristotle," *Ajatus*, XX [1957], 65–90), I have argued that the
distinction between contingency and necessity is for
Aristotle equivalent to that between what is perishable and imperishable. The field of application of 'possibility proper' therefore falls into two parts which are
different in kind. We have already seen in sections 10
and 12 of the first paper that Aristotle viewed situations of this kind with suspicion, although he grudgingly admitted that no logical harm need result. This
is probably one of the reasons why Aristotle in *Analytica Priora* preferred the notion of contingency to
that of possibility proper.

4. *Aristotle's definition of contingency.* According to
the results of our examination of the ambiguities of
Aristotelian ambiguity, we may expect that the Stagirite usually refers to the distinction between possibility proper and contingency by means of ὁμωνυμία
and that he always refers to the distinction between
the different cases of possibility proper (i.e. between
necessity and contingency) by means of some other locution, e.g. διχῶς λέγεται, κατὰ δύο τρόπους λέγεται
or πολλαχῶς λέγεται. An examination of the text
will bear out this expectation as far as the first, the
second, and the fourth expressions are concerned. Similarly, the third locution is, we shall find, used by Aristotle in distinguishing two kinds of cases of contingency (see section 6 below).

In Aristotle's discussion of the notion of possibility,
the key passage is in *An. Pr.* I 13, 32a18–21. It is referred to by Aristotle repeatedly as the definition of
possibility (e.g. *An. Pr.* I 14, 33b24; 15, 33b28; 15, 34b
28; 17, 37a27). The 'definition' is clear enough (I shall

not discuss here why Aristotle thinks of it as a definition):

> I use the terms 'possibly' and 'the possible' of that which is not necessary but, being assumed, results in nothing impossible.

This is clearly the notion I have called contingency. However, it is not the only variant of possibility, for Aristotle continues:

τὸ γὰρ ἀναγκαῖον ὁμωνύμως ἐνδέχεσθαι λέγομεν

That is, to say of the necessary that it is possible is to use the term 'possible' homonymously. This explanation obviously serves to motivate the qualification "which is not necessary" in Aristotle's definition. The use of the word ὁμωνύμως shows that he knows that he is making a choice between two incompatible meanings of ἐνδέχεσθαι (to be possible). The second meaning, under which even necessary things are called possible, is the notion of possibility which satisfies (iii) and which I have called possibility proper.

We have thus reached two important conclusions: (a) the main notion of possibility employed by Aristotle in *An. Pr.* is what I have called contingency; (b) Aristotle is aware of the existence of the other notion (possibility proper) which is different from contingency to the degree that the same term can be applied to them only homonymously.

These results are confirmed by other passages. A glance at (iv) shows that contingency is symmetrical with respect to negation: p is contingent if and only if not-p is also contingent. They are therefore convertible to each other. Aristotle makes the same observation and applies it to syllogistic premises in *An. Pr.* I 13, 32a30 ff. This shows that his 'possibility as defined' agrees with my 'contingency'. Essentially the same point is made in *An. Pr.* I 17, 37a22 ff.

Aristotle's awareness of the ambiguity of possibility is also demonstrated by the development of his syllogistic. He frequently points out that the conclusion of a certain syllogism is valid only if one does not understand possibility in the sense defined (i.e. in the sense of contingency) but in a sense in which it is the contradictory of impossibility (e.g. *An. Pr.* I 15, 33b30–33; 15, 34b27–32; 16, 35b33; 17, 36b33; 20, 39a12).

5. *An analysis of An. Pr. I 13, 32a21–28.* The fact that Aristotle was aware of the different logical properties of contingency as distinguished from possibility proper seems to me to be in agreement with what Aristotle writes immediately after the passages I have quoted (*An. Pr.* I 13, 32a21–28). This passage has been censured by the recent commentators in spite of the fact that it occurs in all the MSS and is recognized both by Alexander and by Philoponus (W. D. Ross, *Aristotle's Prior and Posterior Analytics* [Oxford, 1949], p. 327). However, it seems to me that the passage can be understood as it stands by making due allowance for Aristotle's conspicuous conciseness. I shall offer a paraphrase of the passage, enclosing explanatory additions as well as my own comments in brackets. The superscripts refer to further comments.

Aristotle has just explained his sense of ἐνδεχόμενον (possible) and distinguished it from the homonymous notion of possibility proper. He goes on:

That this [= Aristotle's definition] is the meaning of 'possible' is obvious from the opposing affirmations and denials.[1] For [in the other sense of 'possible'] 'it is not possible to apply', 'it is impossible to apply' and 'it is necessary not to apply' are either the same or imply each other.[2] Consequently their contradictories[3] 'it is possible to apply', 'it is not impossible to apply' and 'it is not necessary not to apply' are the same or imply each other. For either the affirmation or the negation always applies. [This is not correct, however, for we mean by possibility something more than the absence of impossibility.[4]] That which is necessary will therefore not be possible, and that which is not necessary [nor impossible[5]] will be possible.

Further comments: (1) This elliptic sentence poses two questions:

(a) What are these affirmations and denials affirmations and denials of?

(b) What kind of opposition is Aristotle here referring to?

As regards (a), the sequel shows that Aristotle is not dealing with affirmations and denials of possibility in the sense (of contingency) just defined. It turns out (cf. (2) below) that the affirmations and denials pertain to the other sense of possibility (possibility proper). Since Aristotle is obviously trying to justify his own definition, it may be concluded that he is here starting a *reductio ad absurdum* argument.

As regards (b), a comparison with the occurrences of ἀντικείμενος later in the passage (cf. (3)) suggests that this word—which is Aristotle's vaguest and most general term for opposition of any kind—here refers to contradictory opposition. The alternative would be to understand the sentence as referring to the opposition between the two kinds of possibility; this would suit my interpretation quite as well as the other reading.

(2) This is exactly what we get by accepting the other sense of ἐνδεχόμενον, i.e. by not excluding necessity from the range of possibility: 'not possible that p' will be equivalent to 'impossible that p' which is (cf. diagram (ii)) tantamount to 'necessarily not p'.

(3) The following sentence shows that these contradictories are the ἀντικείμενα referred to here.

(4) It was already pointed out above (in section 2) that Aristotle took this view. See especially the reference to the *Topica*, loc. cit. It appears from the φανερὸν

in 32a20 that Aristotle thought of this point as being perfectly obvious; so obvious, indeed, that he neglected to make it explicit here.

(5) The second part of the last sentence seems strange. The addition I have indicated is a most tempting way of making the passage correct. It is very likely, however, that the passage is Aristotle's as it stands. He knew that his notion of possibility (i.e. contingency) is symmetrical with respect to negation in the sense which best appears from diagram (iv). He may have thought that this symmetry justifies the transition from 'what is necessary is not possible' to 'what is not necessary is possible'. This leads to a reading of 'not necessary' as an elliptic form of 'not necessary either way', i.e. 'neither necessary nor impossible'. In the sequel, we shall find more indications that this was Aristotle's reading; see section 7 infra.

Here I shall only point out that my interpretation is supported by what we find in De Interpretatione. If it is true that 'not necessary' sometimes does duty for 'neither necessary nor impossible', it may be expected that 'not necessarily not', i.e. 'not impossible', will sometimes mean 'neither impossible nor necessary'. When this is so, 'not impossible' will entail (in fact, it will be equivalent to) 'not necessary'. And this is exactly what we find in De Int. 13, 22b14–16, where Aristotle infers 'not necessary' from 'not impossible'. This inference is very difficult to explain otherwise. The inference is based on the sequence of implications (equivalences?) set up by Aristotle in De Int. 13, 22a16 ff., where again μὴ ἀδύνατον εἶναι entails μὴ ἀναγκαῖον εἶναι.

6. *A subdivision of contingency.* Having made these distinctions, Aristotle goes on to say (in An. Pr. I 13, 32b5 ff.) that possibility has two applications (the expression he uses is κατὰ δύο τρόπους λέγεται). On

one hand, it is used to describe what generally happens but falls short of being necessary, on the other hand it is used to describe the indeterminate, that which can be 'thus or not thus' without the prevalence of either alternative. Now the distinction plainly has nothing to do with the difference between possibility proper and contingency. Neither of the two uses distinguished by Aristotle covers what happens necessarily. What we have here is therefore a *subdivision of contingency*. Aristotle's use of the expression κατὰ δύο τρόπους λέγεται suggests that he is not distinguishing two meanings of ἐνδεχόμενον but rather two kinds of cases to which it can be applied. This is verified by his remarks on the conversion of statements of contingency. He says that in both cases the possible premise can be converted into its opposite premise, i.e. '*p* is contingent' into 'not-*p* is contingent'. This is trivial in the case of a *p* which is contingent because it is 'indeterminate'. But Aristotle also holds that the conversion applies to contingency in the sense of that which 'generally happens'. This may seem mistaken; if *p* happens generally but not necessarily, we certainly cannot infer that not-*p* happens generally. What Aristotle means is that even in this case not-*p* is neither necessary nor impossible and hence contingent in the sense of his definition. If 'what happens generally but not necessarily' were one of several meanings of 'contingent', Aristotle would not be able to say that 'contingent' always converts with its opposite. What he means is that in each of the different cases that fall under the term 'contingent' we have a conversion to the opposite of some case—not necessarily of the same case— covered by the term.[1] Hence, he is not dealing with

[1]Aristotle's awareness of the fact that a case of a concept may be converted into another case of the same concept is also shown by his remarks on τὸ εἰκός in *Rhet.* II 23, 1402a9 ff.

different meanings of ἐνδεχόμενον, but only with different applications of the term. 'Contingent' is not homonymous although it covers different kinds of cases.

7. *An analysis of An. Pr. I 3, 25a37–25b19.* Some of the passages I have just discussed are referred to by Aristotle earlier in *Analytica Priora* in connection with the conversion of problematic (possible) premises (*An. Pr.* I 3, 25a37–25b19). We are now in a position to understand the context of these references.

In *An. Pr.* I 3, 25b18 Aristotle refers to his later discussions of the conversion of problematic premises. All the remarks on this subject later in *Analytica Priora* pertain to contingent premises. This suggests that the notion Aristotle has in mind in 25b18 is his 'possibility as defined' or contingency. This is confirmed by the way Aristotle explains the notion of possibility which he is here dealing with: "But if anything is said to be possible because it is the general rule and natural ..." (*An. Pr.* I 3, 25b14 ff.). This recalls one of the different cases of contingency discussed in *An. Pr.* I 13, 32b5 ff. (*vide supra*). And when Aristotle says that this "is the strict sense we assign to possible" (Ross's translation), he is obviously anticipating his definition of contingency, in 32b18–20.

I conclude, therefore, that in *An. Pr.* I 3, 25b14–18 Aristotle is thinking of contingency rather than possibility proper. Now the passage which was just quoted shows that this variant of possibility is contrasted to the one employed in the immediately preceding passage (*An. Pr.* I 3, 25b8–13). We may therefore expect that this latter notion of possibility is what I have called possibility proper. Aristotle's examples show that this is in fact the case. In one of his examples the term 'man' necessarily does not apply to any horse, while in another the term 'white' does not necessarily apply to any coat. This shows that the meaning of possibility which is used here covers cases of necessity as well as cases of contingency. (The examples are both negative in form because he is discussing the conversion of negative premises.)

Although the testimony of Aristotle's examples thus unambiguously shows that in 25b8–13 he is discussing possibility proper, one may still be puzzled by his own explanation of the variant of possibility he is using: "Whatever is said to be possible because it is necessary or because it is not necessary admits of conversion like other negative statements. . . ." For what one would expect here is 'neither necessary nor impossible' instead of 'not necessary'. Some commentators have tried to emend the passage by inserting the negative particle μή so as to make it read 'not necessarily not', although there is no real support for such an insertion in the MSS (see Ross, op. cit.). Moreover, this insertion has the disadvantage of making the clause 'because it is necessary' superfluous. In any case, the emendation is quite unnecessary, for we have already found independent reasons for suspecting that Aristotle sometimes uses 'not necessary' (τὸ μὴ ἀναγκαῖον) and, by analogy, 'not necessarily' (μὴ ἐξ ἀνάγκης) as elliptic expressions for 'neither necessary nor impossible' and 'neither necessarily nor impossibly', respectively (see section 5, comment (5) supra). This suspicion is now confirmed by the fact that the same explanation works here: on my reading the quoted passage says just what one is entitled to expect.

Here one may ask whether my reading is contradicted by the fact that in his second example Aristotle says that it is not necessary that 'white' applies to any coat (τὸ δὲ οὐκ ἀνάγκη ὑπάρχειν). If Aristotle were consistently using the elliptic mode of expression, should he not use double negative οὐκ ἀνάγκη μὴ ὑπάρχειν, since he is here dealing with negative premises? To this it may be answered that 'neither necessary nor impossible' is symmetrical with respect to negation, so that no extra μὴ is needed even if the elliptic mode of expression is used. Besides, one of Bekker's MSS as well as Philoponus do have the missing μὴ (see Ross, op. cit.), so that Aristotle may very well have been even pedantically consistent in his usage.

We may conclude that in his treatment of the conversion of negative problematic premises Aristotle first discusses premises in which the notion of 'possibility proper' is used and then those in which the notion of contingency is used. In contrast, both these notions are lumped together in Aristotle's discussion of the conversion of positive problematic premises (25a37–25b2). He indicates this as follows: . . . ἐπειδὴ πολλαχῶς λέγεται τὸ ἐνδέχεσθαι (καὶ γὰρ τὸ ἀναγκαῖον καὶ τὸ μὴ ἀναγκαῖον καὶ τὸ δυνατὸν ἐνδέχεσθαι λέγομεν). . . . Here the words πολλαχῶς λέγεται suggest that he is not exclusively concerned with the different meanings of ἐνδεχόμενον. In fact, it has been pointed out by Ross that the three cases listed in the parenthetical clause cannot possibly be as many different meanings of ἐνδεχόμενον. However, it seems to me that it cannot be said, either, that they are just three different cases to which the notion of possibility can be applied. The first two are clear; we have encountered τὸ ἀναγκαῖον and τὸ μὴ ἀναγκαῖον before as the two cases covered by the notion of possibility proper. The recurrence for the fourth time of the elliptic expression τὸ μὴ ἀναγκαῖον (or of one of its variants) where one expects 'neither necessary nor impossible' gives further support to my interpretation of this phrase. But τὸ δυνατὸν cannot very well be a third case to which the notion of possibility is applied, for there is no third case comparable with the two already listed. Rather, we must understand τὸ ἀναγκαῖον καὶ τὸ μὴ ἀναγκαῖον as referring to the notion of possibility proper, and understand τὸ δυνατὸν as referring to the other notion of possibility, viz. contingency. This, in fact, seems to be the way Ross understands the passage. Its meaning may hence be expressed somewhat as follows: "... seeing that possibility has many applications (for we call possible both that which is necessary or is not necessary either way and that which is capable of being)...."

This interpretation is supported by the fact that the context shows that Aristotle is here treating both the variants of possibility at the same time. If they are here mentioned in the same order in which they are subsequently treated (in the connection of the conversion of negative problematic premises) we can scarcely separate Aristotle's references to the two variants in any way different from the one just suggested.

Our interpretation also agrees with the way δυνατόν is used elsewhere in *Analytica Priora*. The most important passage in which this term occurs is *An. Pr.* I 15, 34a6 ff. And it is indicated by Aristotle (in 34a14) that the arguments he there gives pertain to possibility with respect to generation. Now this variant of possibility is very likely just our contingency. For something which is generated will sometimes be (viz. after having been generated) and sometimes not be (viz. before it is generated). It is therefore possible in the very sense (in that of contingency) which we wanted to give δυνατόν in *An. Pr.* I 3, 25a39.

8. *Remarks on An. Pr. I 13, 32b25–32.* What we have found in this paper and its predecessor confirms my earlier analysis of *An. Pr.* I 13, 32b25–32 (in "Necessity, Universality, and Time in Aristotle," pp. 86–88). Here I shall only briefly outline the argument, adding such new evidence as was not mentioned in the earlier paper.

In the passage under discussion Aristotle seems to be saying that

(P)   it is possible for A to apply to all B

is ambiguous in that it may mean either

(P₁)   it is possible for A to apply to everything
       to which B in fact applies

or

(P₂)   it is possible for A to apply to everything
       to which B possibly applies.

This cannot be his meaning, however. For one thing, he never seems to use (P₁) but only (P₂) in his subsequent discussion of syllogisms from possible premises. He seems even to say that (P₂) is what (P) was defined to mean (*An. Pr.* I 14, 33a24–25). For another, the term Aristotle uses is διχῶς, which strongly suggests that he is not at all distinguishing two different meanings of (P). Rather, he is saying that (P) covers two kinds of cases, i.e. that (P) is tantamount to the conjunction of (P₁) and (P₂). This suffices to explain everything that Aristotle says and does. It may be expected that the variant of possibility Aristotle is using in (P₂) is the one he usually employs, viz. contingency. Expressed as explicitly as possible, Aristotle's point therefore is that (P) is equivalent to the conjunction of (P₁) and (P₂₁), where the latter is

(P₂₁) it is possible for A to apply to everything
       to which B applies contingently.

Now this conjunction is clearly equivalent to what we get by assuming that the variant of possibility used in (P₂) is my 'possibility proper':

(P₂₂) it is possible for A to apply to everything
       to which B possibly applies (in the sense of

'possibility proper'), i.e. to everything to which B applies necessarily or contingently.

This explains why Aristotle seems to deal exclusively with (P_2) in his syllogistic theory; for what he is really dealing with is (P_{22}) which is equivalent to the conjunction of (P_1) and (P_{21}) and therefore also to (P).

Further evidence is perhaps found in *An. Pr.* I 29, 45b31–32. Having just explained how the different kinds of assertoric syllogisms are established, Aristotle goes on to say that apodeictic (necessary) and problematic (possible) syllogisms are established in the same way. But he adds a warning:

> In the case of problematic propositions, however, we must include those terms which, although they do not apply, might possibly do so; for it has been shown that the problematic syllogism is effected by means of these. . . . (H. Tredennick's translation in the Loeb Library edition)

Prima facie this is completely tautologous. For problematic syllogisms contain by definition terms which do not apply but may apply. What can Aristotle mean here? It is clear that the *predicate term* A of a premise like (P) may apply possibly but not actually. But it is not equally obvious whether the *subject term* B is to be taken to apply possibly or actually; whether, in other words, (P) is to be understood as being equivalent to (P_1) or to (P_{22}). Unless we assume that Aristotle's statement is pointless, we can scarcely interpret it except as a repetition of the point which we found him making in *An. Pr.* I 13, 32b25–32, viz. as identifying (P) and (P_{22}). Notice in particular that there is no semblance here of a distinction between two meanings.

9. *Concluding remarks.* We have discussed the most important passages of *An. Pr.* I which turn on the dis-

tinction between the various notions of possibility used by Aristotle. Insofar as we have been successful in applying the results of my earlier analysis of the ambiguities of ambiguity in Aristotle, our success conversely serves as a further confirmation of the earlier analysis. In particular, it supports what was said in section 10 of the first paper. Aristotle's own definition of contingency (see *supra*, section 4) establishes a connection between contingency and possibility proper: contingent is that which is (properly) possible but not necessary. If homonymy were tantamount to the absence of any common element in definition, contingency and possibility proper would not be homonyms. The fact that Aristotle calls them homonyms shows that there is more to his notion of homonymy than that.

ON ARISTOTLE'S SQUARE
OF OPPOSITION

M. THOMPSON

Arguments have recently been offered that purportedly save Aristotle's square of opposition from the charges which modern logicians have brought against it.[1] The main argument in this defense, as I understood it, is the contention that the principle of excluded middle, or the principle that "every meaningful statement is either true or false," is subject to certain qualifications. These qualifications have nothing to do with multivalued logics or the adoption of some new formal principle, but concern an alleged "feature of ordinary speech." In brief, this feature is that in order for an empirical descriptive sentence to be meaningful it is not necessary for it to yield a true or false statement on *every* occasion of its utterance. Thus, the sentence "All Smith's children are girls" is meaningful because it would yield a true and not also a false statement if uttered on an occasion when Smith had

From *The Philosophical Review*, LXII (1953), 251–65. Reprinted by permission of the author and the editor of *The Philosophical Review*.

[1]The most lengthy statement of this defense of Aristotle is given by H. L. A. Hart, "A Logician's Fairy Tale," *The Philosophical Review*, LX (1951), 198–212. Hart says he owes the "substance" of his criticism of "modern logical doctrine" to P. F. Strawson, and refers to the latter's article, "On Referring," *Mind*, LIX (1950), especially pp. 343–44. For a shorter statement of a similar defense of Aristotle, see P. T. Geach, "Subject and Predicate," *Mind*, LIX (1950), esp. 480.

children all of whom were girls. It would likewise yield a false and not also a true statement if uttered on an occasion when Smith had at least one child who was a boy. But if uttered on an occasion when Smith had no children at all it would yield neither a true nor a false statement—"the question of its truth or falsity simply would not arise."

Bearing in mind this feature of ordinary speech, we are to interpret Aristotle's square of opposition as applicable to empirical descriptive sentences only on those occasions when their utterance would yield a statement that it is either true or false but not both. Thus, when an Aristotelian logician affirms that the logical relation of "All ogres are wicked" to "Some ogres are wicked" is one of super-implication, he is not also affirming that some ogres exist. He is merely affirming that the two sentences are so related that on any occasion when an utterance of the first yields a true statement, an utterance of the second must also yield a true statement. The fact that we believe there could be no such occasion is beside the point. The sentences are meaningful because we can imagine what would have to obtain on such an occasion. An Aristotelian logician is then no more guilty of affirming ogres into existence than is the teller of a fairy tale who makes statements about ogres. For the logician like the story teller speaks only of what would be the case *if there were* ogres.

The modern interpretation which permits us to say that "All ogres are wicked" is true though "Some ogres are wicked" is false is thus not only unnecessary in order to avoid the paradoxes of existential import, but it also leads to a misunderstanding of ordinary speech. For it assumes that every meaningful empirical descriptive sentence yields a true or false statement on every occasion of its utterance, and overlooks those occasions when common sense would say that the question of its truth or falsity simply does not arise. If we interrupted the story teller with the question, "But is it true that all ogres are wicked?" this would be a clear indication that we had misunderstood his use of language. Similarly, if we argued about the truth or falsity of "All Smith's children are girls" when we knew that Smith had no children, we could hardly be said to have understood the conditions under which this statement would ordinarily be taken as true or false.

Now I want first of all to argue that these proposed qualifications of the principle of excluded middle are of dubious value since they make any application of the supposedly simple and elementary logical relations in the square of opposition extremely complex.

I

Classical logicians from Aristotle on have taken the relations in the square of opposition as connecting entities which must be either true or false, even though these entities have been variously identified as linguistic expressions, as propositions, and as judgments. While the relations themselves may on occasion have been defined without reference to truth or falsity, such a mode of definition does not mean that sometimes the relations may hold when neither truth nor falsity is applicable. The prerogative of the logician extends only to the point of not having to specify in a given case which one obtains, truth or falsity; it does not extend to the point of casting aside the question of truth and falsity altogether. Yet the latter appears to be what the new defenders of Aristotle are proposing. For according to the new defense, we are to say that "All ogres are wicked" and "Some ogres are not wicked" are related as contradictories, even though neither truth nor falsity is applicable to either of them.

Any assertion here of the commonplace that one of a pair of contradictories must be true and the other false will take the form of a contrary-to-fact conditional. If there were ogres, i.e. if the question of the truth or falsity of these statements were to arise, then one would have to be true and the other false.

Thus, what has traditionally been a simple and straight-forward specification of relations of truth conditions has now been made to involve the complicated logical distinctions required to cope with contrary-to-fact conditionals. Even if we succeed in defining the relations in the square without reference to truth or falsity, we must resort to contrary-to-fact conditionals in order to specify how any of the relations are applicable to all ordinary statements in a way that logical relations have traditionally been supposed applicable. The decision of modern logicians to regard the truth conditions of a universal affirmative statement as satisfied when nothing of the kind named exists enables us to preserve the traditional simplicity in the application of the relation of contradictoriness. Even though this decision does away with the applicability of contrariety, sub-contrariety, and super- and sub-implication, it seems preferable to a decision which makes the application of any of the relations exceedingly complex. The traditional square can be retained as a valid schema relating by contradictoriness four of the most frequent types of quantified statements. The remaining relations indicated by the square can be defined by other schemata in accordance with which they are always applicable, and the traditional simplicity of application for any of the relations can be retained.

Even if we agree with the new defenders of Aristotle that the decision which leads to the modern analysis is repugnant to ordinary speech, we can still argue that this is more desirable than a decision repugnant to logical analysis itself. For surely a decision which makes any specification of the conditions under which a simple logical relation is universally applicable take the form of a contrary-to-fact conditional sins against our conception of what logical analysis should achieve. It seems to me fairly easy to show that the sin is against Aristotle's as well as against our modern conception.

I propose in the remainder of this paper to argue (a) that the account of the square of opposition given in Aristotle's *On Interpretation* is fundamentally different from what is usually taken as the traditional analysis of the square,[2] and (b) that Aristotle's account is free from the contradictions and absurdities which arise from the latter, this freedom being achieved, not by qualifying the principle of excluded middle, but by Aristotle's own peculiar restrictions on the existential import of statements. For reasons that should soon become apparent, I shall begin with some remarks about singular statements.

II

The applicability of truth or falsity to statements when the subject named does not exist is explicitly declared by Aristotle to hold for singular statements.[3]

---

[2]By "traditional analysis" I mean simply the sort that is presented today in most logic texts as the Aristotelian one. As will be made clear in the sequel, the essential features of this analysis are (1) the usual doctrine of immediate inferences, including obversion, contraposition, and inversion; (2) all the logical relations purportedly expressed in Aristotle's square of opposition. When I speak of contradictions and absurdities in this analysis, I do not mean to deny that some classical logicians may have intended some special assumptions not in Aristotle (such as the proposed qualifications of the excluded middle) which keep the analysis consistent. I am concerned only with the analysis as it stands without such assumptions.

[3]*Cat.* 13b26–35. All quotations from Aristotle, unless otherwise specified, are from the Oxford translation.

But in the case of affirmation and negation, whether
the subject exists or not, one is always false and the
other true. For manifestly, if Socrates exists, one of the
two propositions 'Socrates is ill,' 'Socrates is not ill,' is
true, and the other false. This is likewise the case if he
does not exist; for if he does not exist, to say that he is
ill is false, to say that he is not ill is true.

This clearly suggests that any affirmation about a singular subject implies that the subject exists, while a
negative statement about such a subject cannot have
this implication. Yet in another passage Aristotle seems
to contradict what he says here by arguing that "Homer
is a poet" does not imply "Homer is." "Take the proposition 'Homer is so-and-so,' say 'a poet'; does it follow that Homer is, or does it not? The verb 'is' is
here used of Homer only incidentally, the proposition
being that Homer is a poet, not that he is, in the independent sense of the word."[4]

The crucial point in understanding this second passage is the meaning of "is, in the independent sense
of the word," i.e. of "is per se." Clearly this is "is" in
the substantive sense of the word and means the same
as "is a substance." What Aristotle is denying in this
passage, then, is that "Homer is a substance" follows
from "Homer is a poet." Now in the first passage
quoted above the word "exists" is used to translate
ontos, which of course literally means just *being* and
not necessarily *being a substance*. Hence we should
take "exists" as meaning the same as "being" without
the specification of the sense of being, as being a substance or being an accident, and then there is no con-
tradiction. "Homer exists" does follow from "Homer
is a poet," since if Homer did not exist, i.e. if he were
simply nonbeing, it would not be true to say that he
is anything. This point is suggested by Aristotle's re-

[4]*On Interpretation* 21a26–28.

marks almost immediately following the second passage quoted above. "But in the case of that which is not, it is not true to say that because it is the object of opinion, it is; for the opinion held about it is that it is not, not that it is." In other words, the fact that a non-existent Homer may be the object of opinion, as he would be if we were to construct a myth about him, does not mean that it is true to say Homer is something.[5] The assertions "Homer is merely the object of opinion" and "Homer is a mythical being" are about Homer only in the sense of denying that he is in fact anything. While we might say that "Homer is a poet" is true in fiction, what is true in this case is true of the myth and not of Homer. And the myth does exist, even though not per se as a substance does.[6]

An affirmation about a singular subject, then, is false and its contradictory is true when either of the following conditions obtains.

C-1   The subject exists, either per se as a substance or as something dependent on a substance (as an accident of a substance), but does not possess the predicate affirmed of it (e.g. when Socrates exists and is healthy, "Socrates is ill" is false, and when the color of this table exists but is not dull, "The color of this table is dull" is false).

[5]The Oxford translation of the passage just quoted above (21a32–33) obscures the fact that the question is whether non-being is *something* because it is the object of opinion. The Greek just before the semicolon in this translation reads *on ti*. The Loeb translation gives "it is not true to say that it 'is' somewhat, because it is matter of opinion."

[6]The myth may be said to exist as an artificial substance, dependent on its maker. With this interpretation of the text, we must of course deny that Aristotle would allow a realm of fictitious things as a realm of being. This point admittedly calls for further consideration, but it will be passed over here as simply one of the assumptions required in order to make sense out of Aristotle's remarks that are relevant to his account of the square of opposition.

C-2   This subject does not exist, i.e. is neither a sub-
      stance nor something dependent on a substance.

There is thus no need to qualify the principle that
every meaningful statement is either true or false, as
this principle applies to statements about singulars.

There is one further point to be considered before
we turn to the square of opposition. What about the
relation of "Socrates is not-ill" to "Socrates is not ill"?
As Aristotle analyzed this relation it is an implication
with the first statement as antecedent; it is not an
equivalence. "Socrates is not-ill" counts as an affirmation, although one of a very peculiar sort. For the predicate "is not-ill" is not strictly what Aristotle calls a
verb, and after complaining that there is no specified
name for such a predicate, he proposes to call it an
indefinite (or infinite) verb, since it applies "equally
well to that which exists and to that which does not."[7]
Thus, we might say "Socrates is not-ill" when we wish
to affirm that Socrates is a not-ill man, though we
might also use this same affirmation when we want
merely to deny that Socrates is ill. When C-2 obtains,
our assertion is false in the first case but not in the
second.[8] We, of course, could overcome this indefiniteness by adopting the convention that in logic a singular statement with an indefinite verb as predicate
will always be taken in one sense and not the other.
But this would be to retreat from the problem rather
than solve it. Statements of the sort in question are

[7]16b12–16.
[8]Aristotle remarks in 20a25–27 that if the negative answer to
"Is Socrates wise?" is true, then an inference affirming that Socrates is unwise (or not-wise) is correct. In the light of 13b26–35
(quoted above) we must interpret this remark as assuming that
the question would not be asked if Socrates were nonexistent.
The purpose of such an assumption at this point is to show a
difference between universal and singular statements. Even though
men exist, a negative answer to "Is every man wise?" does not
allow the inference that every man is unwise.

logically indefinite and the logician must accept them as such and make what he can of them. Aristotle pointed out that if "Socrates is not-ill" is true, then, whether this is equivalent to affirming that Socrates is a not-ill man or merely to the denial that he is ill, "Socrates is not ill" must be true. However, because of the indefiniteness of the antecedent in this implication the relation does not hold the other way around. When C-2 obtains, the antecedent is false in its strictly affirmative sense while the consequent remains true, and the relation thus cannot be an equivalence.[9]

The recognition of statements with indefinite terms as peculiar entities for the logician to cope with rather than to obliterate by convention is essential to Aristotle's account of the square of opposition.

Aristotle does not say explicitly that a universal affirmative or A statement is false when nothing of the kind named exists, but what he does say about the logical relations of quantified statements seems to me to make the best sense when we take this interpretation of the universal affirmative. Let us see, then, how far we can go toward making sense out of Aristotle's account when we begin with the seemingly rash assumption that an A statement is false when either of the following conditions obtains.

C'-1   At least one thing of the kind named exists, i.e. is either a substance or something dependent on a substance, but does not possess the predicate affirmed of it.

C'-2   Nothing of the kind named exists, i.e. is either a substance or something dependent on a substance.

We must first make sense out of saying that the corresponding O statement, the contradictory of A, is

[9]This point is made in the *An. Pr.* 51b36–52a17.

true when C'-2 obtains. Now it is clear that Aristotle regarded O as denying precisely what A affirmed, and that he took these statements as forms of simple affirmation and denial, respectively. Yet the usual rendering of O as "Some S exists and is not P" certainly does not express what Aristotle meant by a simple denial. We have instead a compound statement in which one thing is affirmed and another denied. A literal translation of his examples of O gives "Not every S is P," which is to be taken as simply the denial that P is truly affirmed universally of S. In this simple denial we do not affirm anything, and hence if C'-2 obtains, our denial is true because if there are no S's, it is not true to affirm P universally of them, any more than it is true to affirm illness of Socrates when Socrates does not exist. We must next explain how the corresponding E statement, the contrary of A, is likewise true when C'-2 is the case. For if E is false its contradictory I must be true and we would have the absurdity that "Some S is P" is true when there are no S's. But E and O do not differ in being more or less simple, or more or less a denial. They are both simple denials, though E denies that P can be particularly affirmed (affirmed in at least one instance) of S while O denies that P can be universally affirmed. But clearly, then, if C'-2 obtains E is true since P cannot be particularly affirmed.

With this interpretation of the square, the existential import of a statement is determined by its quality rather than its quantity.[10] While this means that

[10]C. S. Peirce remarks, "It is probable that Kant also understood the affirmative proposition to assert the existence of its subject, while the negative did not do so: so that 'some phoenixes do not rise from their ashes' would be true, and 'All phoenixes do rise from their ashes' would be false" (*Collected Papers*, Vol. II, par. 381). Peirce refers, Vol. III, par. 178, to the view that ex-

in any case at least one of the two particular statements in the square must be true, it does not result in the absurdity of forcing us to affirm the existence of whatever may be the subject of a statement. In all cases where C'-2 obtains, both affirmative statements are false and we do not affirm the existence of anything.

This interpretation of the square, however, is impossible if we accept the usual treatment of what Aristotle called indefinite (or infinite) nouns and verbs. As they are normally used in logic books these indefinite terms permit us to assert equivalences between affirmative and negative statements, so that the quality of a statement remains relative to a particular mode of expression and clearly cannot serve as the determination of its existential import. But Aristotle seems to deny these equivalences in his discussion of indefinite terms as they occur in universal and particular statements.

We noted above that, according to Aristotle, the logical relation between a singular affirmation with an

istential import is determined by the quality of the statement as a view "usually understood" in the traditional account.

Peirce does not cite evidence in support of this interpretation of Kant, but it is not difficult to find passages in the *Critique of Pure Reason* that suggest it. For example, "As far as *logical* form is concerned, we can make negative any proposition we like; but in respect to the content of our knowledge in general, which is either extended or limited by a judgment, the task peculiar to negative judgments is that of *rejecting error*" (A 709, B 737; tr. N. Kemp Smith; italics in original). Viewed in this way, then, negative judgments simply reject affirmative judgments as erroneous and affirm nothing about objects in the world. The remark that, as regards logical form, we can make negative any proposition we like, is relevant to the considerations in the remainder of the present paper. We should note in passing that in accordance with this remark the quality of a statement as determining its existential import is not, for Kant, to be identified with its quality as determined by its logical form.

Evidence that Kant assumed affirmative statements to have existential import may be found in his well-known denial that "existence" is a predicate, plus his insistence on the distinction between categorical and hypothetical judgments.

indefinite verb as predicate and the corresponding denial with respect to the same subject was not equivalence but implication with the first statement as antecedent. Although Aristotle's account of universal and particular statements with indefinite terms is difficult in its details and the text seems corrupt at a few places, I believe there is little room for doubt about the following two points. (1) Whenever a statement containing no indefinite terms and representing one of the four categorical forms is logically related to another statement containing indefinite terms, the relation seems to be implication rather than equivalence.[11] (2) In every case the affirmative statement is the antecedent of the implication.

The following four implications are clearly indicated by Aristotle's remarks in Chapter X of his *On Interpretation* (the implications run horizontally and the antecedent is always first).

(1) Every man is just.   Not every man is not-just.
(2) Every man is not-just.   Not every man is just.
(3) Every man is not-just.   No man is just.
(4) Some men are just.   Not every man is not-just.

The first two pairs in this list occur in a context where Aristotle is concerned primarily with the contradictory oppositions indicated by the diagonals rather than the implications and the latter emerge from the schema of

---

[11]The verb used to express this relation is *akolouthein*, which means literally "to follow," "to go after," or "with." The most obvious translation when the verb occurs in a logical treatise is "to follow from," "to be implied by," and this is the practice followed by the Oxford and Loeb translators. However, many commentators have read Aristotle as often using the verb with the force of "to be equivalent to." This reading is ruled out by the present interpretation of Aristotle, but the exclusion rests on an attempt to make sense out of his logical doctrine rather than on the claim that it is necessitated by the Greek alone. When, on the other hand, the text gives *tauton semainein* the logical relation must of course be equivalence rather than implication.

oppositions. The last two pairs are stated separately as
implications and are not presented as part of a schema
of oppositions. Since an A statement with an indefinite verb as predicate implies both an O and E statement, a definite A statement would also seem to have
two corresponding implications. Further, since the list
of antecedents includes both the definite and indefinite
forms of A it would seem that this list should also include both forms of the I statement. It might thus
appear that we can add the following two implications
which are not explicitly stated in the text.

(5) Every man is just.   No man is not-just.
(6) Some men are not-just.   Not every man is just.

However, I believe we can argue plausibly that, with
Aristotle's analysis, these two additional implications
are fundamentally different from the preceding ones,
and that his failure to include them here is probably
not an oversight. We should note first of all that in
none of the four implications listed by Aristotle is there
a statement with an indefinite term as subject. All the
indefinite terms are predicates. Secondly, the two categorical statements that convert *simpliciter*, viz. E and
I do not occur in the list with an indefinite term. Yet
our proposed additions to the list involve such occurrences. By simple conversion, we get the following
equivalent forms of our new implications.[12]

(5.1) Every man is just.   No not-just is a man.
(6.1) Some not-just is a man.   Not every man is just.

The difficulty here is in explaining how indefinite
nouns function as subjects. We should note next that

[12]It is assumed here that for Aristotle simple conversion (as
distinct from obversion) yields an equivalent statement. Justification for this assumption can be found in Aristotle's use of conversion in the reduction of syllogisms. He of course did not use
obversion in the reductions.

after (1) and (2) are presented as pairs of opposites Aristotle lists two more such pairs that occur
when "not-man" is taken as "a kind of subject." He
cautions that this new set of opposites "should remain distinct from those which preceded it, since it
employs as its subject the expression 'not-man'." The
two further pairs of opposites (with oppositions indicated by the diagonals) are:

(7) Not-man is just.   ╳   Not-man is not not-just.
(8) Not-man is not-just.   Not-man is not just.

Aristotle does not comment on the quantification of
these statements, nor does he give any explicit indication that implications hold here as in (1) and (2), but
a little later in the same chapter he gives the following
pair as equivalents.[13]

(9) Every not-man is not just.   No not-man is just.

Yet if treated as an ordinary categorical statement, the
first member of this equivalence is ambiguous and
might mean "Not every not-man is just" instead of
"No not-man is just." In order for the equivalence to
hold, "every" and "no" must be taken with the force
of "everything" and "nothing." We should thus understand the equivalence as between

(9.1)   Everything that is   Nothing that is not man
        not man is not just.   is just.

The necessity for this interpretation of "every" and
"no" arises from the indefiniteness of the subject "not-
man." With this term as subject the only things about
which we can make assertions are those which are not
some definite kind of thing. We can thus never make
an assertion about every member of a collection, but

---

[13]The Greek here is *tauton semainein* as opposed to *akolouthein*. Cf. note 11. The translation in (9) is literal. The Oxford
translation is that given in (9.1).

only about every member that is not such and such. Our assertions will be like the statement a teacher might make after collecting examination papers. "Every paper in this group that does not receive a score of 50 or above is not passing," or in other words, "Every not-50-or-above-paper is not passing." But when we use an indefinite noun as subject without reference to some particular collection, such as a group of examination papers, we make a reference to the collection that comprises the totality of real things. Thus, the statements in (9) and (9.1) are equivalent to "Everything in the totality of real things that is not a man is not just." This reference to the totality of real things results from the peculiar way that an indefinite term signifies things.

These considerations should make it apparent that the statements in question do not have existential import in so far as they are assertions about those members of a collection that are not such and such. The teacher's statement does not imply that there is at least one not-50-or-above-paper in the group nor do (9) and (9.1) imply that there is at least one not-man. From this point of view, the statements are compound denials rather than affirmations—they deny that there is at least one member of the collection which is both not-50-or-above and passing, both not-man and just. This equivalence to a compound denial is again a result of the peculiar signification of indefinite terms, and is no less the case when the statement appears to be a universal affirmative. "Every not-man is just" is equivalent to the denial that there is at least one thing which is both not-man and not just. Particular statements with indefinite terms as subjects, on the other hand, are always equivalent to compound affirmations of existence, even though they appear to be particular negatives. "Not every not-man is just" is equivalent to "Something in the totality of real things is both not-

man and not just." The statement must be construed
in this way if it is to contradict the compound denial
expressed by "Every not-man is just."

The above remarks may suffice to explain why Aristotle regarded indefinite terms as providing only "a
kind of subject," and cautioned that the resulting statements should remain distinct from the ones previously
considered. His failure to comment on the quantification of the statements in (7) and (8) is perhaps due
to the fact that the contradictory oppositions, which
seem to have been his primary interest here, are not
altered when the statements are quantified as in (1)
and (2). A list of the quantified forms would have
been superfluous unless he intended also to add a specific account of the peculiarities which resulted from
the indefinite subject.

A similar explanation may be given for the failure
to mention the implications stated in (5) and (6). Unlike any of the preceding, each of these implications
related a simple affirmation or denial to one whose subject is an indefinite term. Had Aristotle mentioned
these two implications, it certainly would have been
an oversight on his part if he had then omitted the
other implications of this sort. But since he did not
give the two in question, it seems fair to conclude
that he did not intend here to consider any of them.

In light of the above considerations, we now have
the following account of the immediate inferences that
arise from the introduction of indefinite terms, i.e. of
the processes usually called obversion and contraposition.

An A statement implies, but is not equivalent to,
its obverse, its partial contrapositive, and its full contrapositive. Thus, "If every S is P, then no S is not-P,
no not-P is S, and every not-P is not-S." Each of these
three statements in the consequent is equivalent to the

other two. "No not-P is S" is equivalent to its obverse, because unlike the original A or a simple E, it has an indefinite term as subject so that neither it nor its obverse has existential import. The inference from "Every not-P is not-S" to "Some not-P is not-S," the so-called full inverse of "Every S is P," is illegitimate because the antecedent in this case does not have existential import while the consequent does.

An E statement is implied by, but is not equivalent to, its obverse, just as the definite denial "Socrates is not ill" is implied by the indefinite affirmation "Socrates is not-ill." Hence the inference from an original E to its contrapositive or its inverse (whether these are full or partial) is never permissible. We cannot infer from "No mathematicians are circle-squarers" that some nonmathematicians are circle-squarers. In order to obtain this conclusion we need independently the premise, "Every circle-squarer is a nonmathematician." This premise is the obverted converse of the original E, and while with the present analysis it implies the E, it is logically independent of the obverse of E, since "Every mathematician is a noncircle-squarer" does not affirm anything about circle-squarers.

An I statement implies its obverse but is not equivalent to it (see (4), while an O statement is implied by its obverse but is not equivalent to it (see (6)). An O is also implied by its partial and full contrapositives, which are both equivalent to its obverse. These equivalences obtain because particular statements with indefinite terms as subjects always have existential import, in contrast to the original O, which asserted a simple denial.

The fundamental difference between this account of immediate inferences and the one which is usually accepted as characteristic of traditional logic is the treatment given the distinction between statements with

definite and indefinite subjects. Before we consider
how this account avoids the contradictions and absurdities in the traditional analysis, there is one further
point to be noted about Aristotle's analysis.

Aristotle seems to have begun construction of his
square with an A statement taken as a simple affirmation about every member of a collection rather than
about every member that is not such and such. In
other words, with a statement like "Every man is
just" as opposed to "Everything that is not a man is
just." As we have already indicated, with Aristotle's
analysis we should take the first but not the second of
these statements as having existential import. Yet
granting this point, we still have the problem of deciding which of the following two statements we shall
take as the contrary of our A statement.

(10)   No man is just.
(10.1)   Every man is not-just.

Either of these statements is so related to our original A that it cannot be true when the A is true,
though it can be true or false when the A is false. If
this reference to truth conditions is our only criterion
for determining the contrary, we should have to admit both statements, even though they are not equivalent, as contraries of our original. Yet clearly, (10) is
the only one that will satisfy the present interpretation of Aristotle's square of opposition. If this interpretation is correct, we would expect Aristotle to offer
arguments for selecting (10) rather than (10.1), and
this is precisely what he does in the last chapter of
On Interpretation. He devotes this chapter to the problem he poses in the opening sentence: "The question
arises whether an affirmation finds its contrary in a denial or in another affirmation; whether the proposition
'every man is just' finds its contrary in the proposition

'no man is just', or in the proposition 'every man is unjust'."[14]

It is unnecessary for our purposes here to analyze separately each of the various arguments Aristotle offers for selecting the denial rather than the affirmation as the contrary. His main point may be summed up by saying that since (10) is implied by but does not imply (10.1), (10) is more opposed to the original A because when the latter is false (10) may be true even though (10.1) is also false. I do not propose to debate the logical merits of this decision, as the relevant point here is simply that with Aristotle's analysis, (10) and (10.1) are not equivalent and that (10) alone represents an E statement in the square of opposition. This determination of E does not prevent it from implying O, since the latter is likewise a simple denial without existential import. Thus, the logical relations which Aristotle claimed for his square of opposition hold if we grant that the statements related in the square are of the peculiar sort that he seems to have intended them to be.

We may now turn to the contradictions and absurdities in what is usually taken as the traditional analysis of the square. When an A statement is taken as equivalent to its obverse, Aristotle's distinction between statements with definite and indefinite terms as subjects is ignored. A statement which has existential import with his analysis is made equivalent to one that cannot have this import as he construed it. The traditional analysis then becomes inconsistent by ac-

[14] 23a28–31. The logical relations in question here remain the same if the privative "unjust" is replaced by the indefinite "not-just." Cf. *An. Pr.* 52a15–17. While one might intend by this replacement to make the statement equivalent to (10), he does not succeed in doing so because the result, (10.1), remains an affirmation and thus, like the original "every man is unjust," implies but is not implied by (10).

cepting *in toto* Aristotle's account of the square of opposition along with this equivalence which Aristotle
rejected. It must then be affirmed that "Every S is P"
implies "Some S is P," and denied that "Every S is
P" can be false while "No S is not-P," "No not-P is
S," and "Every not-P is not-S" are all true. This procedure becomes inconsistent when one admits, as Aristotle does, that any of these last three statements is
compatible with the falsity of "Some S is P." Inconsistency is avoided in Aristotle's account, not by qualifying the principle of excluded middle, but by restricting existential import in accordance with the quality
of the statement and the definite or indefinite character of the subject term.

The traditional procedure also leads to the absurdity
that any object of opinion (anything thinkable) must
be said to exist. We have characterized statements
with indefinite terms as subjects as like statements
about every member that is not such and such in a
certain collection, but clearly as far as existential import is concerned, they are also like statements about
every member that is such and such. "Every paper in
this group that scores 50 or above is passing" is just
as free of existential import as our former example.
There is obviously something absurd about a logic that
allows us to infer from this that some paper in the
group scores 50 or above and is passing. Yet this is
analogous to what the traditional account allows us to
do. For a statement like

(11)   Every ogre is wicked.

is construed as equivalent to "Every not-wicked is not-
ogre," which clearly means the same as "Everything
in the totality of real things that is not wicked is not
an ogre." But then with this equivalence (11) must
mean the same as

(11.1)   Everything in the totality of real things that is an ogre is wicked.

We thus end with the absurdity that we cannot assert (11.1) without implying that ogres exist. And even worse, we cannot deny (11.1) without making the same implication. For

(12)   Not every ogre is wicked.

is also assumed to have existential import.

Aristotle's account avoids such absurdity by denying the equivalence between (11) and (11.1) and holding that (12) has existential import only when taken as the contradictory of the latter. In this way there is no need to qualify the application of the principles of excluded middle. In order to preserve Aristotle's square *in toto* we must of course deny the equivalence between (10) and (10.1), and accept only the former as properly an E statement. The contradictory of such a statement has existential import and is implied by the corresponding A. In contrast, modern analysis accepts the traditional position that (10) is equivalent to (10.1), and (11) to (11.1), but remains consistent and avoids absurdity by refusing to accept Aristotle's square without qualification.

I do not propose here to examine the adequacy of the Aristotelian account or to subject it to criticism in the light of modern analysis. But it should be noted in conclusion that if the present interpretation of Aristotle is correct, his analysis cannot, as the traditional one can, be taken simply as an inconsistent account which modern analysis has rectified. In accepting the equivalences mentioned above, the traditional doctrine of immediate inferences has already taken an essential step toward the modern position. Consistency can be restored (without special assumptions, such as that restricting the applicability of the principle of excluded middle) only by completing the break with Aristotle or by returning to his analysis. There is thus a fundamental difference between the Aristotelian and modern analyses which I believe it would be profitable to examine. This difference is concerned in part at least with the role of indefinite terms in procedures of quantification and with the existential import of affirmations as distinct from denials. When we say that "-(x)fx" is equivalent to "($\exists$x)-fx," or that "-($\exists$x) fx" is equivalent to "(x)-fx," we have replaced what seems to be a denial by an affirmation with an indefinite predicate, and we are not talking about the categorical statements Aristotle intended when he constructed his square of opposition.

II. CATEGORIES

CATEGORIES IN ARISTOTLE
AND IN KANT

JOHN COOK WILSON

§ 438. If our reasoning is correct, the universalities
of the various species of a genus are not particulars of
the universality of the genus but kinds (or parts) of it.
Suppose now an abstraction beginning from individual
things till we come to so-called *summa genera*, or, as
they would be more correctly termed, *summae species*.
The universalities of all other universals would be
comprised in the universalities of these, not as their
particulars but as kinds, forms, parts, or aspects of
them. If, then, we considered these *summae species* as kinds which Being or Reality must take,
where Being is more accurately the Being of Things
(that is, the universal of which Things are the particulars), the Being of Things is in the position of *genus*
to these *summae species* and their several universalities
are all comprised in the universality of this genus. In
regard to this we must avoid the fallacy of creating a
universal of universalities, with an infinite regress. That
fallacy has been already sufficiently exposed. There is
no universal of universalityness of which the universalities of universals would be particulars, for the universality of one genus universal as distinguished from
that of another lies not in its being a unity which is

From *Statement and Inference* (Oxford, 1926), Vol. II, pp.
696–706. Reprinted by permission of the Clarendon Press, Oxford.

particularized but in being particularized in these precise individuals, in being the particularization of its
own peculiar quality or characteristic; but this is precisely itself, and its universality is indistinguishable
from itself in the fullness of its being. Thus the classification of universalities can only be, if possible at
all, the classification of universals; there is no universal
of universalityness of which the universalities of universals would be particulars.

§ 439. This genus, then, of the *summae species* is
not mere Being but the universal of the being of
Things or Substances, and is therefore the generaliza-
tion of Substance, Substanceness, or Substance-in-gen-
eral. Now in this system every universal has things for
its particulars, and thus the universals of attribute and
relation will not appear in the system. Nevertheless,
every variety of being, attribute, and relation as well
as substance, must be comprised in the system, because all these are comprised in the existence of things.
The nature of substance involves in itself attributes
and relations; its universal therefore involves the universal of possession of attributes and the universal of
relatedness. We have now to consider the relation of
such a universal as attributeness in general or the universal of a particular attribute such as colour(edness)
to the universal of substance in general and to the universals of substances. We may note in passing that we
can understand why Aristotle said that Being was not
a genus if we remember that the genera *par excellence*
(in the *Categories*, for example) are in fact universals
whose particulars are substances.[1]

Attributeness means being an attribute of a substance, hence the universal of substance involves in its
own being the being of attributeness. Nevertheless,
the latter is not an element in the universal substance-

---

[1]*Cat.* 2a11 ff.

ness, the corresponding element is 'having-attributes'-ness. Moreover, the latter is not a differentiation of substanceness. The question, then, is whether these universals are capable of being unified by any unity beside the unity that one involves the existence of the other. They cannot be differentiations of one and the same universal because differentiations of the same universal must have identical particulars with that universal. Nor can they be particulars of the same universal, for if two universals are particulars of the same universal, they must be differentiations of a common universal though not of that universal. Thus, though we can state of attributeness and substanceness that they are, Being is not a universal of which they are differentiations, nor is Being a universal of which they are particulars.

§ 440. Thus the form 'S is', which as opposed to 'S is P' does not occur in ordinary linguistic usage whether in ancient Greek or in modern languages, does not represent in its subject particulars of a universal which is Being or Beingness. If, then, Aristotle had carried out fully the thought which appears to be implicit in chapter 5 of the *Categories*, with the distinction there made between 'said of a particular subject' and 'existing in a particular subject', the result would have been a system of universals classified as in the section above and based on his view that the only true independent reality is the individual thing (or person). The *summum genus* would be Thingness, and for this the only word in his terminology that appears to be suitable is Being (οὐσία), a word which both in the *Categories* and in *Metaphysics*, Book Z, is sometimes the name for Thing as such, or First (Primary) Being. This, however, is nowhere unmistakably stated; he appears indeed to have virtually stopped in his classification at certain highest genera and his own expression, 'the highest of the genera',[2] favours this interpretation.

§ 441. For his view that Being is not a genus, the important passages are three in the *Metaphysics* with which one in the *Topics* agrees, a passage in the *De Interpretatione*, and one in the *Posterior Analytics*.[3] The first of the passages from the *Metaphysics* does not turn on his view that the genera *par excellence* are secondary essences and is a little difficult to interpret. It runs as follows: 'But it is not possible for One or Being to be a genus. For each difference of a genus must have one and being said of it (sc. when we speak of it), whereas it is impossible that either the species of the genus or the genus without the species should be said of the differences. Thus, if One or Being were a genus, none of their differences could have one or being stated of it'. By difference he here means not the differentiated universal (e.g. rectilinearity) but the *differentia* (straight, etc.).[4] This suggests that he had not realized that, according to his own theory, Being would be the proper name for the highest genus. The passage from the *Posterior Analytics*, 'to exist is not the being (essence) of anything, since the being existent (that which exists) is not a genus', does seem to be connected with his doctrine that the individual is the only real existent and that the true genera have 'beings' for their particulars. Finally, the passage in the *De Interpretatione* runs as follows: 'for not even "to be" or "not to be" is a sign of a thing, not even if you mention "being" by itself merely. In itself it is nothing, but it signifies in addition a kind of compounding which cannot be understood without the

[2]*Met.* 998b18.
[3]*Met.* 998b22, 1053b23, 1059b30; *Top.* 121a16; *De Int.* 16b22; *An. Po.* 92b13.
[4]Cf. his language in the *Topics* 144a37 ff.

things so compounded'. This is most important for the linguistic point involved in our problem.

It is singular that Aristotle, who in the *Metaphysics* is attacking those who made Being and Unity the essence of things, does not adopt the seemingly clear and decisive argument based upon his own theory of true being as the individual and the true genus as that of which the individuals are the particulars. His argument, however, and this is important, is directed to showing that Being as a universal cannot be differentiated, though he has not realized what seems to be the direct proof required (he gives instead a single *reductio ad absurdum*), viz. that if being were the genus or class universal of the universals which we say 'are', those universals, as we have shown, would necessarily have the same kind of particulars as it and consequently the same kind as one another. But, obviously, the universals of a substance, an attribute, a relation, cannot have the same particulars. To reach this positive point of view Aristotle would have required to have had before him the point of view from which a universal could be represented as a particularization, not a differentiation, of another universal.

§ 442. We miss, then, two things in Aristotle's discussion. The line of thought which led him to say 'being is not a genus', at least when it took the shape it seems to have in the *Posterior Analytics*, might have made him recognize that though the universal 'being' was not a highest genus, yet in his own terminology such a genus was exactly 'essence' as the being of things or, more accurately, 'the being a thing'. How far he was from this may be seen when he says,[5] 'Unity cannot be a genus for the same reasons that neither being (existent) nor essence can be'. Secondly, he might have been led to see that though Being is not a clas-

[5]*Met.* 1053b23.

sifying genus which unified everything in that way, yet there is a unifying principle in all reality. Instead he rested content with the negative statement that Being is not such a principle, where being is that 'is' which is universally predicable. He may have been prejudiced by his justifiable criticism of Plato who had sought this unifying principle in the Idea of goodness. Had he followed up his thought he might have reflected that just as a genus demands its own differentiation into species and individuals, so by the same inward necessity the unity of reality demands the kinds and things into which reality actually is differentiated.

§ 443. Taking his own categories, they are obviously unified in the reality of (primary) Being or Substance, and he does elsewhere recognize that the other categories depend on the first. But he never put this as the unity and the real unity which corresponds to what is common to the statement of 'being'. In fact he never cleared up his mind about it, or he could not, so to speak, have so degraded 'being', as he does in the passage translated from the *De Interpretatione*, and have merely left it at that. What he has said there is true and important, but it is misleading, as it stands.

Moreover, the formula 'Being is not a genus', although it shows from one point of view an accurate insight into the nature of classification, is extraordinary and misleading when considered in relation to his own terminology. He must speak of the categories as categories of being; this being cannot be merely the common predicate of everything, if we are to take categories literally as predicates. For we cannot state of this 'being-in-general' that it is a substance. On the other hand, if it does mean 'being-in-general', categories would surely have to mean species or kinds, so that being would indeed be a genus and the formula be contradicted. It is most natural to leave category its proper meaning and then 'being' will stand for 'that which is', not for being in general. This again, if all the categories are asserted of it, as the formula 'categories of that which is' naturally implies, could only be complete being, that which is in the fullest sense. Now that with Aristotle is the individual thing. This agrees with the fact that the categories are given not as abstract universals in the noun form (whiteness, as an example of quality) but in the adjectival form (white, double, etc.). If so, what is meant by the categories of being (that which is) is that each of them is an attribute of the true and real being of the individual thing, the primary being of this treatise. It is the thing in fact of which we can properly state that it is a substance, two cubits long, in the market-place, etc. The only word form which causes any difficulty in this interpretation is that of the adverb of time (e.g. yesterday). This, however, is again not put as an abstract universal but as it would occur in a statement, and it is true (and the truth) that as every happening belongs to a substance, so the temporal qualification ultimately also belongs to a substance (e.g. this substance was in the market-place yesterday). This appears, then, to be the meaning, for it is difficult to see how anything else could be meant.

§ 444. But now, if this is so, in the categories of being, of 'that which is', the latter expression is used in the general sense, and 'that which is' represents the universal of all particular 'beings' and so is the universal of substanceness. It is just in relation to the distinction of the categories that the meaning of 'being is not a genus' becomes of great importance. On the above view 'that which is' is equivalent to substance (being) when the categories are termed categories of that which is. Thus 'that which is' is not only a genus of which real complete things are the particulars (com-

plete, that is, in the Aristotelian sense as equivalent
to things) but the highest and most comprehensive
genus, though *not* the genus of the categories, including all reality whatever. This discussion seems to con-
firm the hypothesis that Aristotle did not pursue the
train of thought which his view that 'being' taken in
one sense is not a genus might have suggested to him.

§ 445. What, then, is the fallacy in Aristotle's proof
that being is not a genus? He contemplates two ways
of stating the genus X in regard to a given subject S.
Either a species AX is stated in S is an AX and therefore mediately the genus S is an X, or the genus is
stated 'without its species', and we say immediately S
is an X. In neither way, he says, can we state the genus
of the difference A. He seems to mean that odd being
the differentia of odd number, we can't say that odd
is an odd number and so a number, nor directly that
odd is a number.

But is the argument free from verbal fallacy? When
we state that S is a species, we mean that S is an AX,
and when we say that the genus belongs to the species, we state X, the genus universal of a *member* of
the species AX, we mean an AX is an X. If, then,
we state the species of the differentia we ought to
mean that we state that an A is an AX. Now if the
differentia necessarily presupposes X the genus, the
statement must be true. We do not say that odd numberness is numberness, but that an odd number is a
number. So if we state odd number of odd, we mean
that an odd thing is an odd number, which is necessarily true. It looks as though Aristotle meant that
linearity cannot be predicated of straightness because
straightness is not a line; but neither is rectilinearity
a line, and thus he would appear to have fallen into a
verbal fallacy.

§ 446. There is a danger that in appreciating the

insight shown by Aristotle in his dictum 'being is not a genus', we may ourselves fall into the same one-sidedness. There are certain characteristics of Being which, if not identical with those of a true genus, are parallel to them in a remarkable way and must therefore not be neglected. These characteristics are not destroyed by the discovery that being is not a true genus; only a certain way of regarding them, i.e. as particularizations or differentiations of a universal, is destroyed. An attribute or a relation may rightly be said to have being as well as a substance, and this being is not identical with that of substance. We can study the attribute in abstraction from the subject, as we do in the mathematical sciences, and this proves that it is distinguishable in being. So of relation, it is essential to relation that it should be 'between' things which have some other nature than that of standing in a given relation. Hence it is natural at first sight to say that Being is a genus with its species 'being of attribute', etc. Again we think that Being in its own nature necessitates these forms of itself, and this is parallel to the self-determination of a universal in its differentiations. If, then, the forms of Being are not species nor kinds as ordinarily understood, nor of course particulars of a universal, how should they be described accurately? We have to revise one of our usual conceptions and either to refuse to call these universals or to admit universals which have no particulars and no differentiation, the universality of one quality (attribute) being identical in kind with the universality of every other. In this difficulty we may provisionally term them common principles. They are live universals because they are a unity in a manifold; universality in each universal, particularity in each particular, and so on, but different from true universals because the manifold is not a particularization or differentiation of the common principle. This will meet the difficulty we found in regard to classes. We say of every class that it is a class, yet we saw that classness is not a true universal of which classes are particulars. Class has no differentiation and no particulars. We have a unity in a manifold, but the manifold is not a particularization of the unity. Instead, then, of our ordinary view we have to recognize that there are some universals which admit of differentiation and particularization but not of individualization, and that some (which we have called common principles) do not admit of either particularization or differentiation.

§ 447. In Being, then, called provisionally a common principle, we recognize a unity in a manifold which is *sui generis*, just as much as the unity of a true universal in its particulars and its species is *sui generis*. Being, like a true universal, also determines its own manifoldness but in a different manner. If we are to seek an illustration or analogy we may refer to the self, which is an absolute unity in its different thoughts, or a body, which is identical in its different positions and aspects, but neither the self nor the body is the universal of those differences nor they its particulars.

§ 448. If we now consider the forms of Being, the manifold which it must assume and which simulates the differentiation of a universal, we may perhaps find the true significance of the philosophical classifications called systems of categories. These categories are obviously of a very special kind and are philosophical and not scientific. They are, that is, though comprehensive, not a classification and could not be reached by abstracting successively from the whole field of individual substances. In this way we should attain to the classifications of the natural sciences but not to categories. Now Kant's criticism of Aristotle's categories has shown that while there may be agreement about some of the main categories, there may be the greatest disagreement about the real meaning and object of them as a whole. Kant believes that Aristotle was led to his grouping of the categories without realizing its true character, and that in consequence he did not carry it out consistently. Whether, then, Kant's own view of the categories was right or wrong (and surely it was not right) this suggests that there may be a certain instinctive impulse to search for categories, without full consciousness of its nature. The impulse will lead to an arrangement of a quite peculiar kind, and reflection must then supervene in order to understand the impulse and to correct its imperfect work. Kant naturally makes the categories forms of the unifying understanding, because of his dominant confusion of the apprehension and the apprehended. Aristotle's tendency is far sounder, for necessity of apprehension can, after all, only mean apprehension of a necessity in the object.

The explanation, then, of systems of categories may well be that we come in time, by reflection on the use of the verb 'to be', to recognize a corresponding unity of being, that the totality of particulars in all their variety is a unity. Long before we have recognized this unity in particular sets or varieties of being. Then comes the philosophic impulse to determine the forms which *being in general* must take, suggested by the analogous determination of such a unity as the section of a cone, and so to cover exhaustively the differentiations of being in general in the whole of existence. This impulse need not be fully aware of itself. Aristotle, for example, doesn't consciously go to work in this way or, if he did so begin, he probably gave it up when through his clear idea of differentiation and classification he realized that Being is not a genus. Still it may have been the fact that we state of everything that it *is*, which suggested the idea of an absolutely unified system of being.

§ 449. Thus the characteristic of Aristotle's system is that it is a sort of exhaustive attempt to cover the whole variety of reality. 'Everything is either substance or an affection of substance' is its implicit meaning. These are in fact his two main categories. But he gets into difficulties about substance, so that his thought in the end is that everything is either substance, or quality of substance, or quantity of substance (or of what belongs to substance), or relation of substance (or of what belongs to it), and so on. Now it is clear from our analysis above that the impulse to determine a sort of differentiation of Being must produce an altogether unique system. For the general forms of Being are not true differentiations of it, nor are the individuals, which 'are' particulars of Being but of other universals. This explains the fact that the classification (as it first seems to be) of all being could not be attained by any abstraction from individuals or any classification of them; because this, the natural form which classification first takes, proceeds to universals of which the original particulars are those very individuals, and the successive universals are differentiations of one another in succession. This systematization is by means of differentiation and particularization, the other (the system of the categories) is achieved by neither. Hence the latter acquires its uniqueness; for the ordinary scientific method, even when carried to the utmost unity, will not bring to light one single category except substance itself. If continued ideally upwards, it cannot even bring to light the universal 'mere being' of which the categories are the unfolding. The same is of course true of any classification proper which starts from the individual, whether thing or individual attribute. Attributeness, for instance, if regarded as the universal of individual attributes, is neither a differentiation nor a particularization of being; the most general universal which could have individual attributes for its particulars is just attributeness. Now substanceness, attributeness, relationness, etc., cannot be treated as *summa genera* because they would then be members of the same classification; this they can never be, for such genera must have the same sort of particulars, and here the particulars of the one would be substances, the particulars of the other attributes.

§ 450. If, then, this is the true account of the philosophic impulse under discussion, we see that it is a most serious and fatal mistake to regard it as a classification, when once we understand what a classification truly is. (That leads to the further error of vainly attempting to adapt the system of categories to the ordinary classifications and to make them departments of it.) Properly understood, it is simply the just endeavour to determine the manifoldness in which Being in general must unfold itself, and Aristotle proceeded correctly when he exhibited as categories such general forms as those of Substance, Attribute, Relation, etc. Contenting himself, however, with pointing out that Being is not a genus and therefore could not constitute the essence of things, he seems by his merely negative attitude to have missed the true significance of his own list of categories.

§§ 438–50. *Translation of principal passages referred to in the above investigation.*

[Arist. *Cat.* 2a11. 'Substance most properly and primarily and especially so called is that which is neither said of a particular subject nor is in a particular subject, for instance, a particular human being or a particular horse. Secondary substances are what the species are called, in which the substances primarily so called exist, and besides them the genera of these species; for instance, while a particular human being exists in the species human being, the genus of the species is animal. These, then, are called secondary substances, for example, both human being and animal'.

De Int. 16b22. 'For not even "to be" or "not to be" is a sign of a thing, and not even if you mention "being" by itself merely. In itself it is nothing but it signifies, in addition, a kind of compounding which cannot be understood without the things compounded'.

An. Po. 92b13. 'Again we say that it is necessary that everything be proved to exist by demonstration, unless it be essence. But to exist is not the essence of anything, since the being existent (that which exists) is not a genus. That a thing exists therefore will be (subject of) demonstration. This is what the sciences in fact do. The geometrician assumes what triangle means, but proves that it exists'.

Met. 998b22. 'But it is not possible for either being one or being existent to be a genus of existents. For while it is necessary that the differentiae of each genus should each both exist and be one, it is impossible either for the species of a genus to be said of the appropriate differentiae or the genus <to be said of them> without its species. Therefore if we assume being one or being existent to be a genus, no differentia will either be or be one'.[6]

The same argument is used in *Met.* 1059b30, and *Top.* 121a16. In *Met.* 1053b23 he says, 'being one cannot be a genus for the same reasons that neither being existent nor essence can be'.

___

[6]J. C. W. translated: 'It is not possible for One or Being to be a genus. For each differentia of a genus must have one and being said of it (in statements), whereas it is impossible that either the species of the genus should be said of its differentiae or the genus without the species. So if One or Being were a genus, none of their differentiae could have one, or being, stated of it.'

Met. 1017a22. 'Whatever the forms of predication signify are said to be essentially. For to be has as many significations as there are forms. Inasmuch, then, as the predicates signify what the subject is, others its quality, etc., . . . to be has a signification equivalent to each of these (for there is no difference between "the man is walking" and "the man walks)".]

ARISTOTLE'S *CATEGORIES*

TRANSLATED BY J. L. ACKRILL

CHAPTER 1

1a1. When things have only a name in common and
the definition of being which corresponds to the name
is different, they are called *homonymous*. Thus, for
example, both a man and a picture are animals. These
have only a name in common and the definition of being which corresponds to the name is different; for if
one is to say what being an animal is for each of them,
one will give two distinct definitions.

1a6. When things have the name in common and
the definition of being which corresponds to the name
is the same, they are called *synonymous*. Thus, for example, both a man and an ox are animals. Each of
these is called by a common name, 'animal', and the
definition of being is also the same; for if one is to
give the definition of each—what being an animal is
for each of them—one will give the same definition.

1a12. When things get their name from something,
with a difference of ending, they are called *paronymous*. Thus, for example, the grammarian gets his name
from grammar, the brave get theirs from bravery.

From *Aristotle's Categories and De Interpretatione*, tr. with
notes by J. L. Ackrill (Oxford, 1963), pp. 3–12 and 71–91. Reprinted by permission of the Clarendon Press, Oxford.

CHAPTER 2

1a16. Of things that are said, some involve combination while others are said without combination. Examples of those involving combination are 'man runs', 'man wins'; and of those without combination 'man', 'ox', 'runs', 'wins'.

1a20. Of things there are: (a) some are *said* of a subject but are not *in* any subject. For example, man is said of a subject, the individual man, but is not in any subject. (b) Some are in a subject but are not said of any subject. (By 'in a subject' I mean what is in something, not as a part, and cannot exist separately from what it is in.) For example, the individual knowledge-of-grammar is in a subject, the soul, but is not said of any subject; and the individual white is in a subject, the body (for all colour is in a body), but is not said of any subject. (c) Some are both said of a subject and in a subject. For example, knowledge is in a subject, the soul, and is also said of a subject, knowledge-of-grammar. (d) Some are neither in a subject nor said of a subject, for example, the individual man or individual horse—for nothing of this sort is either in a subject or said of a subject. Things that are individual and numerically one are, without exception, not said of any subject, but there is nothing to prevent some of them from being in a subject—the individual knowledge-of-grammar is one of the things in a subject.

CHAPTER 3

1b10. Whenever one thing is predicated of another as of a subject, all things said of what is predicated will be said of the subject also. For example, man is predicated of the individual man, and animal of man; so animal will be predicated of the individual man also—for the individual man is both a man and an animal.

1b16. The differentiae of genera which are different[1]
and not subordinate one to the other are themselves
different in kind. For example, animal and knowledge:
footed, winged, aquatic, two-footed, are differentiae of
animal, but none of these is a differentia of knowledge; one sort of knowledge does not differ from another by being two-footed. However, there is nothing
to prevent genera subordinate one to the other from
having the same differentiae. For the higher are predicated of the genera below them, so that all differentiae
of the predicated genus will be differentiae of the subject also.

CHAPTER 4

1b25. Of things said without any combination, each
signifies either substance or quantity or qualification
or a relative or where or when or being-in-a-position or
having or doing or being-affected. To give a rough idea,
examples of substance are man, horse; of quantity: four-
foot, five-foot; of qualification: white, grammatical; of
a relative: double, half, larger; of where: in the Lyceum,
in the market-place; of when: yesterday, last-year; of
being-in-a-position: is-lying, is-sitting; of having: has-
shoes-on, has-armour-on; of doing: cutting, burning; of
being-affected: being-cut, being-burned.

2a4. None of the above is said just by itself in any
affirmation, but by the combination of these with one
another an affirmation is produced. For every affirmation, it seems, is either true or false; but of things
said without any combination none is either true or
false (e.g. 'man', 'white', 'runs', 'wins').

CHAPTER 5

2a11. A *substance*—that which is called a substance
most strictly, primarily, and most of all—is that which

[1]Read τῶν ἑτέρων γενῶν.

is neither said of a subject nor in a subject, e.g. the individual man or the individual horse. The species in which the things primarily called substances are, are called *secondary substances*, as also are the genera of these species. For example, the individual man belongs in a species, man, and animal is a genus of the species; so these—both man and animal—are called secondary substances.

2a19. It is clear from what has been said that if something is said of a subject both its name and its definition are necessarily predicated of the subject. For example, man is said of a subject, the individual man, and the name is of course predicated (since you will be predicating man of the individual man), and also the definition of man will be predicated of the individual man (since the individual man is also a man). Thus both the name and the definition will be predicated of the subject. But as for things which are in a subject, in most cases neither the name nor the definition is predicated of the subject. In some cases there is nothing to prevent the name from being predicated of the subject, but it is impossible for the definition to be predicated. For example, white, which is in a subject (the body), is predicated of the subject; for a body is called white. But the definition of white will never be predicated of the body.

2a34. All the other things are either said of the primary substances as subjects or in them as subjects. This is clear from an examination of cases. For example, animal is predicated of man and therefore also of the individual man; for were it predicated of none of the individual men it would not be predicated of man at all. Again, colour is in body and therefore also in an individual body; for were it not in some individual body it would not be in body at all. Thus all the other things are either said of the primary substances as subjects or in them as subjects. So if the primary substances did not exist it would be impossible for any of the other things to exist.

2b7. Of the secondary substances the species is more a substance than the genus, since it is nearer to the primary substance. For if one is to say of the primary substance what it is, it will be more informative and apt to give the species than the genus. For example, it would be more informative to say of the individual man that he is a man than that he is an animal (since the one is more distinctive of the individual man while the other is more general); and more informative to say of the individual tree that it is a tree than that it is a plant. Further, it is because the primary substances are subjects for all the other things and all the other things are predicated of them or are in them, that they are called substances most of all. But as the primary substances stand to the other things, so the species stands to the genus: the species is a subject for the genus (for the genera are predicated of the species but the species are not predicated reciprocally of the genera). Hence for this reason too the species is more a substance than the genus.

2b22. But of the species themselves—those which are not genera—one is no more a substance than another: it is no more apt to say of the individual man that he is a man than to say of the individual horse that it is a horse. And similarly of the primary substances one is no more a substance than another: the individual man is no more a substance than the individual ox.

2b29. It is reasonable that, after the primary substances, their species and genera should be the only other things called (secondary) substances. For only they, of things predicated, reveal the primary substance. For if one is to say of the individual man what he is, it will be in place to give the species or the genus (though more informative to give man than animal); but to give any of the other things would be out of place—for example, to say 'white' or 'runs' or anything like that. So it is reasonable that these should be the only other things called substances. Further, it is because the primary substances are subjects for everything else that they are called substances most strictly. But as the primary substances stand to everything else, so the species and genera of the primary substances stand to all the rest: all the rest are predicated of these. For if you will call the individual man grammatical it follows that you will call both a man and an animal grammatical; and similarly in other cases.

3a7. It is a characteristic common to every substance not to be in a subject. For a primary substance is neither said of a subject nor in a subject. And as for secondary substances, it is obvious at once that they are not in a subject. For man is said of the individual man as subject but is not in a subject: man is not *in* the individual man. Similarly, animal also is said of the individual man as subject but animal is not *in* the individual man. Further, while there is nothing to prevent the name of what is in a subject from being sometimes predicated of the subject, it is impossible for the definition to be predicated. But the definition of the secondary substances, as well as the name, is predicated of the subject: you will predicate the definition of man of the individual man, and also that of animal. No substance, therefore, is in a subject.

3a21. This is not, however, peculiar to substance; the differentia also is not in a subject. For footed and two-footed are said of man as subject but are not in a subject; neither two-footed nor footed is *in* man. Moreover, the definition of the differentia is predicated of that of which the differentia is said. For example, if footed is said of man the definition of footed will also be predicated of man; for man is footed.

3a29. We need not be disturbed by any fear that we may be forced to say that the parts of a substance, being in a subject (the whole substance), are not substances. For when we spoke of things in a subject we did not mean things belonging in something as parts.

3a33. It is a characteristic of substances and differentiae that all things called from them are so called synonymously. For all the predicates from them are predicated either of the individuals or of the species. (For from a primary substance there is no predicate, since it is said of no subject; and as for secondary substances, the species is predicated of the individual, the genus both of the species and of the individual. Similarly, differentiae too are predicated both of the species and of the individuals.) And the primary substances admit the definition of the species and of the genera, and the species admits that of the genus; for everything said of what is predicated will be said of the subject also. Similarly, both the species and the individuals admit the definition of the differentiae. But synonymous things were precisely those with both the name in common and the same definition. Hence all the things called from substances and differentiae are so called synonymously.

3b10. Every substance seems to signify a certain 'this'. As regards the primary substances, it is indisputably true that each of them signifies a certain 'this'; for the thing revealed is individual and numerically one. But as regards the secondary substances, though it appears from the form of the name—when one speaks of man or animal—that a secondary substance likewise signifies a certain 'this', this is not really true; rather, it signifies a certain qualification, for the subject is not, as the primary substance is, one, but man and animal are said of many things. However, it does not signify simply a certain qualification, as white does. White signifies nothing but a qualification, whereas the species and the genus mark off the qualification of substance—they signify substance of a certain qualification. (One draws a wider boundary with the genus than with the species, for in speaking of animal one takes in more than in speaking of man.)

3b24. Another characteristic of substances is that there is nothing contrary to them. For what would be contrary to a primary substance? For example, there is nothing contrary to an individual man, nor yet is there anything contrary to man or to animal. This, however, is not peculiar to substance but holds of many other things also, for example, of quantity. For there is nothing contrary to four-foot or to ten or to anything of this kind—unless someone were to say that many is contrary to few or large to small; but still there is nothing contrary to any *definite* quantity.

3b33. Substance, it seems, does not admit of a more and a less. I do not mean that one substance is not more a substance than another (we have said that it is), but that any given substance is not called more, or less, that which it is. For example, if this substance is a man, it will not be more a man or less a man either than itself or than another man. For one man is not more a man than another, as one pale thing is more pale than another and one beautiful thing more beautiful than another. Again, a thing is called more, or less, such-and-such than itself; for example, the body that is pale is called more pale now than before, and the one that is hot is called more, or less, hot. Substance, however, is not spoken of thus. For a man is not called more a man now than before, nor is anything else that is a substance. Thus substance does not admit of a more and a less.

4a10. It seems most distinctive of substance that what is numerically one and the same is able to receive contraries. In no other case could one bring forward anything, numerically one, which is able to receive contraries. For example, a colour which is numerically one and the same will not be black and white, nor will numerically one and the same action be bad and good; and similarly with everything else that is not substance. A substance, however, numerically one and the same, is able to receive contraries. For example, an individual man—one and the same—becomes pale at one time and dark at another, and hot and cold, and bad and good. Nothing like this is to be seen in any other case.

4a22. But perhaps someone might object and say that statements and beliefs are like this. For the same statement seems to be both true and false. Suppose, for example, that the statement that somebody is sitting is true; after he has got up this same statement will be false. Similarly with beliefs. Suppose you believe truly that somebody is sitting; after he has got up you will believe falsely if you hold the same belief about him. However, even if we were to grant this, there is still a difference in the *way* contraries are received. For in the case of substances it is by themselves changing that they are able to receive contraries. For what has become cold instead of hot, or dark instead of pale, or good instead of bad, has changed (has altered); similarly in other cases too it is by itself undergoing change that each thing is able to receive contraries. Statements and beliefs, on the other hand, themselves remain completely unchangeable in every way; it is because the *actual thing* changes that the contrary comes to belong to them. For the statement that somebody is sitting remains the same; it is because of a change in the actual thing that it comes to be true at one time and false at another. Similarly with beliefs. Hence at least the way in which it is able to receive contraries—through a change in itself—would be distinctive of substance, even if we were to grant that beliefs and statements are able to receive contraries. However, this is not true. For it is not because they themselves receive anything that statements and beliefs are said to be able to receive contraries, but because of what has happened to something else. For it is because the actual thing exists or does not exist that the statement is said to be true or false, not because it is able itself to receive contraries. No statement, in fact, or belief is changed at all by anything. So, since nothing happens in them, they are not able to receive contraries. A substance, on the other hand, is said to be able to receive contraries because it itself receives contraries. For it receives sickness and health, and paleness and darkness; and because it itself receives the various things of this kind it is said to be able to receive contraries. It is, therefore, distinctive of substance that what is numerically one and the same is able to receive contraries. This brings to an end our discussion of substance.

NOTES ON THE CATEGORIES

CHAPTER 1

1a1. The word translated 'animal' originally meant just that; but it had come to be used also of pictures or other artistic representations (whether representations of animals or not).

The terms 'homonymous' and 'synonymous', as defined by Aristotle in this chapter, apply not to words but to things. Roughly, two things are homonymous if the same name applies to both but not in the same sense, synonymous if the same name applies to both in the same sense. Thus two things may be both homonymous and synony-

mous—if there is one name that applies to both but not
in the same sense and another name that applies to both
in the same sense. From Aristotle's distinction between
'homonymous' and 'synonymous' one could evidently derive a distinction between equivocal and unequivocal
names; but it is important to recognize from the start that
the *Categories* is not primarily or explicitly about names,
but about the things that names signify. (It will be necessary in the translation and notes to use the word 'things' as
a blanket-term for items in any category. It often represents the neuter plural of a Greek article, pronoun, etc.)
Aristotle relies greatly on linguistic facts and tests, but his
aim is to discover truths about non-linguistic items. It is
incumbent on the translator not to conceal this, and, in
particular, not to give a misleadingly linguistic appearance
to Aristotle's statements by gratuitously supplying inverted
commas in all the places where *we* might feel that it is
linguistic expressions that are under discussion.

The contrast between synonyms and homonyms, between same definition and different definition, is obviously very crude. Elsewhere Aristotle recognizes that the different meanings of a word may be closely related. Thus
at the beginning of *Metaphysics* Γ 2 as he points out that
though the force of 'healthy' varies it always has a reference to health: a healthy person is one who enjoys
health, a healthy diet one which promotes health, a
healthy complexion one which indicates health. Similarly, he says, with 'being': it is used in different ways when
used of things in different categories, but there is a primary sense (the sense in which *substances* have being) to
which all the others are related. Though the *Categories*
gives emphatic priority to the category of substance it
does not develop any such theory about the systematic
ambiguity of 'being' or 'exists'. Chapter 1 makes it seem
unlikely that Aristotle had yet seen the importance of
distinguishing between words that are straightforwardly
ambiguous and words whose various senses form a family
or have a common nucleus. (See Aristotle's suggestions
about 'good' at *Nicomachean Ethics* 1096b26–28.)

1a12. 'Paronymous' is obviously not a term co-ordinate

with 'homonymous' and 'synonymous', though like them it is applied by Aristotle to things, not names. A thing is paronymous if its name is in a certain way derivative. The derivativeness in question is not etymological. Aristotle is not claiming that the word 'brave' was invented after the word 'bravery'. He is claiming rather that 'brave' *means* 'having bravery'; the brave is so called because of ('from') the bravery he has. For an X to be paronymous requires both that an X is called X because of something (feature, property, etc.) which it has (or which somehow belongs to it), and that 'X' is identical with the name of that something except in ending. To say that an X gets its name from something (or is called X from something) does not necessarily imply that there is a name for the something (10a32–b2), or that, if there is, 'X' has any similarity to that name (10b5–9). But only if these conditions are fulfilled does an X get its name from something *paronymously*.

Paronymy is commonly involved when items in categories other than substance are ascribed to substances. If we say that generosity is a virtue or that giving one's time is a (kind of) generosity, we use the name 'generosity'; but if we wish to ascribe generosity to Callias we do not say that he is generosity, but that he is generous —using a word identical except in ending with the name of the quality we are ascribing. Sometimes, indeed, the name of an item in a category is itself used to indicate the inherence of that item in a substance. In 'white is a colour' 'white' names a quality; in 'Callias is white' 'white' indicates the inherence of the quality in Callias. Here we get homonymy or something like it, since the definition of 'white' in the former sentence cannot be substituted for 'white' in the latter: Callias is not a colour of a certain kind (2a29–34, 3a15–17). There are also the possibilities mentioned above: an adjective indicating the inherence of something in a substance may have no similarity (or not the right kind of similarity) to the name of the something, or there may be no name for the something. So the ascription of qualities, etc., to substances does not always involve paronymy; but it very often does.

The whole idea of an X's being called X *from something* (whether paronymously or not) is of importance in the *Categories*. The categories classify things, not words. The category of quality does not include the words 'generosity' and 'generous'; nor does it include two things corresponding to the two words. It includes generosity. 'Generosity' and 'generous' introduce the very same thing, generosity, though in different ways, 'generosity' simply naming it and 'generous' serving to predicate it. Aristotle will frequently be found using or discussing distinctly predicative expressions like 'generous', because though they are not themselves names of items in categories they serve to introduce such items (e.g. the item whose name is 'generosity'). The person called generous is so called *from* generosity.

CHAPTER 2

1a16. What does Aristotle mean here by 'combination' (literally, 'inter-weaving')? The word is used by Plato in the *Sophist* 262, where he makes the point that a sentence is not just a list of names or a list of verbs, but results from the combination of a name with a verb; this line of thought is taken up in the *De Interpretatione* (16a9–18, 17a17–20). In the present passage Aristotle's examples of expressions involving combination are both indicative sentences, and his examples of expressions without combination are all single words. Yet he ought not to intend only indicative sentences (or only sentences) to count as expressions involving combination. For in Chapter 4 he says that every expression without combination signifies an item in some one category; this implies that an expresion like 'white man' which introduces two items from two categories is an expression involving combination. Nor should he mean that all and only single words are expressions lacking combination. For he treats 'in the Lyceum' and 'in the market-place' as lacking combination (2a1), while, on the other hand, a single word which meant the same as 'white man' ought to count, in view of Chapter 4, as an expression involving combination. There seem to be two possible solutions. (*a*) The necessary and sufficient condition for an expression's being 'without combination' is that it should signify just one item in some category. The statement at the beginning of Chapter 4 is then analytic, but the examples in Chapter 2 are misleadingly selective, since on this criterion a single word could be an expression involving combination and a group of words could be an expression without combination. (*b*) The distinction in Chapter 2 is, as it looks, a purely linguistic one between single words and groups of words (or perhaps sentences). In Chapter 4 Aristotle neglects the possibility of single words with compound meaning and is indifferent to the linguistic complexity of expressions like 'in the Lyceum'. Certainly he does neglect single words with compound meaning in the rest of the *Categories*, though he has something to say about them in *De Interpretatione* 5, 8, and 11.

1a20. The fourfold classification of 'things there are' relies on two phrases, 'being in something as subject' and 'being said of something as subject', which hardly occur as technical terms except in the *Categories*. But the ideas they express play a leading role in nearly all Aristotle's writings. The first phrase serves to distinguish qualities, quantities, and items in other dependent categories from substances, which exist independently and in their own right; the second phrase distinguishes species and genera from individuals. Thus Aristotle's four classes are: (*a*) species and genera in the category of substance; (*b*) individuals in categories other than substance; (*c*) species and genera in categories other than substance; (*d*) individuals in the category of substance.

Aristotle's explanation of 'in a subject' at 1a24–25 is slight indeed. One point deserves emphasis. Aristotle does not define 'in X' as meaning 'incapable of existing separately from X', but as a meaning 'in X, not as part of X, and incapable of existing separately from what it is in'. Clearly the 'in' which occurs twice in this definition cannot be the technical 'in' of the definiendum. It must be a non-technical 'in' which one who is not yet familiar with the technical sense can be expected to understand.

Presumably Aristotle has in mind the occurrence in ordinary Greek of locutions like 'heat in the water', 'courage in Socrates'. Not all non-substances are naturally described in ordinary language as *in* substances, but we can perhaps help Aristotle out by exploiting further ordinary locutions: A is 'in' B (in the technical sense) if and only if (*a*) one could naturally say in ordinaryy language either that A is in B or that A is of B or that A belongs to B or that B has A (or that . . .), and (*b*) A is not a part of B, and (*c*) A is inseparable from B.

The inseparability requirement has the consequence that only *individuals* in non-substance categories can be 'in' individual substances. Aristotle could not say that generosity is in Callias as subject, since there could be generosity without any Callias. Only this individual generosity—Callias's generosity—is *in* Callias. Equally, white is not in chalk as subject, since there could be white even if there were no chalk. White is in body, because every individual white is the white of some individual body. For a property to be in a kind of substance it is not enough that some or every substance of that kind should have that property, nor necessary that every substance of that kind should have it; what is requisite is that every instance of that property should belong to some individual substance of that kind. Thus the inherence of a property in a kind of substance is to be analysed in terms of the inherence of individual instances of the property in individual substances of that kind.

Aristotle does not offer an explanation of 'said of something as subject', but it is clear that he has in mind the distinction between individuals in any category and their species and genera. (Aristotle is willing to speak of species and genera in any category, though, like us, he most often uses the terms in speaking of substances.) He assumes that each thing there is has a unique place in a fixed family-tree. What is 'said of' an individual, X, is what could be mentioned in answer to the question 'What is X?', that is, the things in direct line above X in the family-tree, the species (e.g. man or generosity), the genus (animal or virtue), and so on. Aristotle does not explicitly argue for the view that there are natural kinds or that a certain classificatory scheme is the one and only right one.

It is often held that 'said of' and 'in' introduce notions of radically different types, the former being linguistic or grammatical, the latter metaphysical or ontological; and that, correspondingly, the word translated 'subject' (literally, 'what underlies') means 'grammatical subject' in the phrase 'said of a subject' and 'substrate' in 'in a subject'. In fact, however, it is perfectly clear that Aristotle's fourfold classification is a classification of things and not names, and that what is 'said of' something as subject is itself a thing (a species or genus) and not a name. Sometimes, indeed, Aristotle will speak of 'saying' or 'predicating' a *name* of a subject; but it is not linguistic items but the things they signify which are 'said of a subject' in the sense in which this expression is used in Chapter 2. Thus at 2a19 ff. Aristotle sharply distinguishes things said of subjects from the names of those things: if A is said of B it follows that the name of A, 'A', can be predicated of B, though from the fact that 'A' is predicable of something it does not follow that A is said of that thing. At 2a31–34 Aristotle is careless. He says that white is in a subject and is predicated of the subject; he should have said that white is in a subject and its name is predicated of the subject. But this is a mere slip; the preceding lines maintain a quite clear distinction between the things that are said of or in subjects and the names of those things. Being said of a subject is no more a linguistic property than is being in a subject—though Aristotle's adoption of the phrase 'said of' to express the relation of genus to species and of species to individual may have been due to the fact that if A is the genus or species of B it follows that 'A' can be predicated of B.

As regards 'subject', it is true that if virtue is said of generosity as subject it follows that the sentence 'generosity is (a) virtue'—in which the name 'generosity' is the grammatical subject—expresses a truth. But 'virtue is said of generosity as subject' is not about, and does not mention, the names 'virtue' and 'generosity'. It would be absurd to call generosity a *grammatical* subject: it is not generosity but 'generosity' that can be a grammatical subject. Again, if A is in B as subject then B is a substance. But this does not require or entitle us to take 'subject' in the phrase 'in a subject' as *meaning* 'substance' or 'substrate'. It is the expressions 'said of' and 'in' (in their admittedly technical senses) which bear the weight of the distinctions Aristotle is drawing; 'subject' means neither 'grammatical subject' nor 'substance', but is a mere label for whatever has anything 'said of' it or 'in' it. Thus at 2b15 Aristotle explains his statement that primary substances are subjects for all the other things by adding that 'all the other things are predicated of them or are in them'.

The distinctions drawn in this chapter are made use of mainly in Chapter 5 (on substance). In particular, it is only in his discussion of substance that Aristotle exploits the distinction between individuals and species or genera. He seems to refer to individuals in non-substance categories at 4a10 ff., but they are not mentioned in his chapters on these categories. Why does Aristotle not speak of primary and secondary qualities, etc., as he does of primary and secondary substances?

CHAPTER 3

1b10. Aristotle affirms here the transitivity of the 'said of' relation. He does not distinguish between the relation of an individual to its species and that of a species to its genus. It does not occur to him that 'man' functions differently in 'Socrates is (a) man' and '(a) man is (an) animal' (there is no indefinite article in Greek).

1b16. In the *Topics* (107b19 ff.) Aristotle gives this principle about differentiae as a way of discovering ambiguity. If sharpness is a differentia both of musical notes and of solid bodies, 'sharp' must be ambiguous, since notes and bodies constitute different genera neither of which is subordinate to the other. At 144b12 ff. he argues for the principle, saying that if the same differentia could occur in different genera the same species could be in different genera, since every differentia 'brings in' its proper genus. He goes on to water down the principle, allowing that the same differentia may be found in two genera neither of which is subordinate to the other, provided that both are in a common higher genus. In later works Aristotle preserves it as an ideal of classification and definition that the last differentia should entail all preceding differentiae and genera, although he recognizes that in practice we may fail to find such definitions and classifications (*Metaphysics* Z 12). In the *Metaphysics* Aristotle is motivated by a desire to solve the problem of the 'unity of definition' (*De Interpretatione* 17a13), but no such interest is apparent in the *Topics* and *Categories*. Here he is probably influenced by the obvious cases of ambiguity like 'sharp', and also by the evident economy of a system of classification in which mention of a thing's last differentia makes superfluous any mention of its genus. Certainly the *Categories* gives no argument for the principle here enunciated. The principle may help to explain what Aristotle says about differentiae at 3a21–28, b1–9.

The last sentence probably requires emendation. As it stands it is a howler, unless we take 'differentiae of the predicated genus' to refer to differentiae that divide it into sub-genera (*differentiae divisivae*) and 'differentiae of the subject genus' to refer to differentiae that serve to define it (*differentiae constitutivae*). But there is nothing in the context to justify such an interpretation. Only *differentiae divisivae* are in question. A correct point, following naturally from what goes before, is obtained if the words 'predicated' and 'subject' are transposed. That Aristotle is willing to describe the differentiae of a genus X as differentiae of the genus of X is clear; for he mentions two-footed as well as footed as a differentia of animal at 1b19, though the genus of which two-footed is an immediate differentia is not animal but a sub-genus of the genus animal.

CHAPTER 4

First, some remarks about the translation. 'Substance': the Greek word is the noun from the verb 'to be', and 'being' or 'entity' would be a literal equivalent. But in connexion with categories 'substance' is the conventional rendering and is used in the present translation everywhere (except in Chapter 1: 'definition of *being*'). 'Quantity': the Greek is a word that serves both as an interrogative and as an indefinite adjective (Latin *quantum*). If Aristotle made use also of an abstract noun it would be desirable to reserve 'quantity' for that; since he does not do so in the *Categories* (and only once anywhere else) it is convenient to allow 'quantity' to render the Greek interrogative-adjective. 'Qualification': Aristotle does use an abstract noun for 'quality' and carefully distinguishes in Chapter 8 (e.g. 10a27) between qualities and things qualified (Latin *qualia*). So in this translation 'quality' renders Aristotle's abstract noun, while his corresponding interrogative-adjective is rendered by 'qualified' or 'qualification'. 'A relative': Aristotle has no noun meaning 'relation'. 'A relative' translates a phrase consisting of a preposition followed by a word which can function as the interrogative 'what?' or the indefinite 'something'. In some contexts the preposition will be rendered by 'in relation to' or 'related to'. 'Where', 'when': the Greek words serve either as interrogatives or as indefinite adverbs ('somewhere', 'at some time'). 'Place' and 'time' are best kept to translate the appropriate Greek nouns, as at 4b24. 'Being-in-a-position', 'having', 'doing', 'being-affected': each translates an infinitive (which can be used in Greek as a verbal noun). The examples of the first two suggest that Aristotle construes them narrowly (posture and apparel), but the labels used are quite general. 'Being-affected' is preferred to alternative renderings because of the need to use 'affected' and 'affection' later (e.g. 9a28 ff.) as translations of the same verb and of the corresponding noun.

The labels Aristotle uses for his ten categories are, then, grammatically heterogeneous. The examples he proceeds to give are also heterogeneous. Man is a substance and cutting is a (kind of) doing; but grammatical is not a quality and has-shoes-on is not a kind of having. 'Grammatical' and 'has-shoes-on' are predicative expressions which serve to introduce but do not name items in the categories of quality and having.

How did Aristotle arrive at his list of categories? Though the items in categories are not expressions but 'things', the identification and classification of these things could, of course, be achieved only by attention to what we say. One way of classifying things is to distinguish different questions which may be asked about something and to notice that only a limited range of answers can be appropriately given to any particular question. An answer to 'where?' could not serve as an answer to 'when?'. Greek has, as we have not, single-word interrogatives meaning 'of what quality?' and 'of what quantity?' (the abstract nouns 'quality' and 'quantity' were, indeed, invented by philosophers as abstractions from the familiar old interrogatives); and these, too, would normally collect answers from different ranges. Now Aristotle does not have a category corresponding to every one-word Greek interrogative, nor do all of his categories correspond to such interrogatives. Nevertheless, it seems certain that one way in which he reached categorial classification was by observing that different types of answer are appropriate to different questions. This explains some of his labels for categories and the predicative form of some of his examples. The actual examples strongly suggest that he thinks about answers to questions about a *man*. Certainly he will have thought of the questions as being asked of a *substance*. This is why he often (though not in the *Categories*) uses the label 'what is it' as an alternative to the noun 'substance'. For what this question, when asked of a substance, gets for answer is itself the name of a substance (cp. *Categories* 2b31). One must not, of course, suppose that in so far as Aristotle is concerned to distinguish groups of possible answers to different questions he is after all engaged in a study of expressions and not things. That 'generous' but not 'runs' will answer the question 'of-what-quality?' is of interest to him as showing that generosity is a different kind of thing from running.

Alternatively, one may address oneself not to the various answers appropriate to various questions about a substance, but to the various answers to one particular question which can be asked about any thing whatsoever—the question 'what is it?'. We may ask 'what is Callias?', 'what is generosity?', 'what is cutting?'; that is, we may ask in what species, genus, or higher genus an individual, species, or genus is. Repeating the same question with reference to the species, genus, or higher genus mentioned in answer to the first question, and continuing thus, we shall reach some extremely high genera. Aristotle thinks that substance, quality, etc., are supreme and irreducibly different genera under one of which falls each thing that there is. This approach may be said to classify subject-expressions (capable of filling the gap in 'what is . . . ?') whereas the previous one classified predicate expressions (capable of filling the gap in 'Callias is . . .'), though, as before, the point for Aristotle is the classification of the things signified by these expressions.

The only other place where Aristotle lists ten categories is in another early work, the *Topics* (I 9). Here he starts by using 'what is it' as a label for the category of substance. This implies the first approach, a classification derived from grouping the answers appropriate to different questions about some individual substance. But later in the chapter the other approach is clearly indicated. It is plain, Aristotle says, that 'someone who signifies what a thing is sometimes signifies substance, sometimes quantity, sometimes qualification, sometimes one of the other predicates. For when a man is under discussion and one says that what is being discussed is a man or is an animal, one is saying what it is and signifying substance; whereas when the colour white is under discussion and one says that what is being discussed is white or is a colour, one is saying what it is and signifying qualification; similarly, if a foot length is being discussed and one says that what is being discussed is a foot length, one will be saying what it is and signifying quantity'. In *this* passage, where the question 'what is it?' is thought of as addressed to items in *any* category, Aristotle can no longer use 'what is it' as a label for the first category but employs the noun for 'substance'. The whole chapter of the *Topics* deserves study.

It is not surprising that these two ways of grouping things should produce the same results: a thing aptly introduced in answer to the question 'of-what-quality?' will naturally be found, when classified in a generic tree, to fall under the genus of quality. The two approaches involve equivalent assumptions. The assumption that a given question determines a range of answers that does not overlap with any range determined by a different question corresponds to the assumption that no item when defined *per genus et differentiam* will be found to fall under more than one highest genus. The assumption that a certain list of questions contains all the radically different questions that may be asked corresponds to the assumption that a certain list of supreme genera contains all the supreme genera. It should be noticed, however, that only the second method gets *individuals* into categories. For one may ask 'what is it?' of an individual in any category; but items introduced by answers to different questions about Callias are not themselves individuals, and a classification of such items will have no place for Callias himself or for Callias's generosity. It has, indeed, been suggested that individuals have no right to a place in Aristotle's categories because the Greek word transliterated 'category' actually means 'predication' or 'predicate' (it is in fact so rendered in this translation, e.g. 10b21). However, it is substance, quality, quantity themselves which are the 'categories', that is, the ultimate predicates; items belonging to some category need not be items which can themselves be predicated, they are items of which that category can be predicated. Thus the meaning of 'category' provides no reason why Callias should not be given a place in a category, nor why non-substance individuals should be left out.

Some general points: (1) Aristotle does not give argument to justify his selection of key questions or to show that all and only the genera in his list are irreducibly different supreme genera. When speaking of categories in other works he commonly mentions only three or four or five (which nearly always include substance, quantity, and quality), but often adds 'and the rest'. In one place he does seek to *show* that 'being' cannot be a genus, that is, in effect, that there must be irreducibly different kinds of being (*Metaphysics* 998b22). (2) Aristotle does not seem to doubt our ability to say what answers would be possible to given questions or to determine the correct unique definitions *per genus et differentiam* of any item we consider. When he looks for features peculiar to a given category (4a10, 6a26, 11a15) he does not do this to suggest criteria for categorial classification; his search presupposes that we already know what items fall into the category in question. He assumes also that we can tell which words or expressions signify *single* items rather than compounds of items from different categories. He does not explain the special role of words like 'species', 'predicate', etc., nor warn us against treating them, like 'animal' or 'generosity', as signifying items in categories. (3) Aristotle does not adopt or try to establish any systematic ordering of categories. Substance is, of course, prior to the rest; and he argues in the *Metaphysics* (1088a22) that what is relative is farthest removed from substance. (4) Aristotle does not in the *Categories* indicate the value of the theory of categories either for dealing with the puzzles of earlier thinkers or for investigating new problems. Nor does he, as elsewhere, develop the idea that 'is', 'being', etc. have different (though connected) senses corresponding to the different categories (*Metaphysics* 1017a22–30, 1028a10–20, 1030a17–27; *Prior Analytics* 49a7).

CHAPTER 5

2a11. The terms 'primary substance' and 'secondary substance' are not used in other works of Aristotle to mark the distinction between individual substances and their species and genera, though the distinction itself is, of course, maintained. The discussion of substance in *Metaphysics* Z and H goes a good deal deeper than does this chapter of the *Categories*. Aristotle there exploits the concepts of matter and form, potentiality and actuality, and wrestles with a whole range of problems left untouched in the *Categories*.

Aristotle characterises primary substance by the use of terms introduced in Chapter 2. But he does not, as might have been expected, go on to say that secondary substances are things said of a subject but not in any subject. Instead he describes them as the species and genera of primary substances and only later makes the point that they are said of primary substances but not in any subject. The reason for this may be that he is going to say (surprisingly) that the differentiae of substance genera, though not themselves substances, are nevertheless said of the individuals and species in the genera, and are not in them.

'Called a substance most strictly, primarily, and most of all': does Aristotle mean to suggest that 'substance' is used in two different *senses*? It would be difficult for him to allow that without upsetting his whole scheme of categorial classification. Aristotle is no doubt aware that the distinction between primary and secondary substances is not like that between two categories or that between two genera in a category; 'Callias is a primary substance' is unlike both 'Callias is a man' and 'Callias is a substance'. But he fails to say clearly what type of distinction it is.

2a19. 'What has been said' presumably refers to 1b10–15, which is taken to explain why, if A is said of B, not only the name of A but also its definition will be predicable of B. The first part of the paragraph is important as showing very clearly that the relation 'said of . . . as subject' holds between things and not words. The fact that A is said of B is not the fact that 'A' is predicable of B. The fact that A is said of B is not even the fact that both 'A' and the definition of A are predicable of B. This is a fact about language that follows from that fact about the relation between two things.

The second part of the paragraph is also of importance.

It shows that Aristotle recognizes that, for example, 'generosity' and 'generous' do not serve to introduce two different things (we should say 'concepts'), but introduce the same thing in two different ways. In saying that usually the name of what is in a subject cannot be predicated of the subject he obviously means more than that, for example, one cannot say 'Callias is generosity'. He means that there is something else which one does say—'Callias is generous'—by way of ascribing generosity to Callias. His point would be senseless if 'generous' itself were just another name of the quality generosity or if it were the name of a different thing altogether.

2a34. Someone might counter the claim in the first sentence by pointing out that, for example, animal is said of man and colour is in body, and man and body are *secondary* substances. Aristotle therefore examines just such cases. It is somewhat surprising that he says: 'were it predicated of none of the individual men it would not be predicated of man at all.' For in view of the meaning of 'said of' he could have made the stronger statement: 'were it not predicated of *all* of the individual men. . .'. However, what he does say is sufficient for the final conclusion he is driving at, that nothing else could exist if primary substances did not. As for colour, Aristotle could have argued to his final conclusion simply by using the definition of 'in' together with the fact, just established, that the existence of secondary substances presupposes the existence of primary substances: if colour is in body it cannot exist if body does not, and body cannot exist if no individual bodies exist. What is Aristotle's own argument? It was suggested earlier that to say that colour is in body is to say that every instance of colour is in an individual body. If so, Aristotle's present formulation is compressed and careless. For he does not mention individual instances of colour; he speaks as if, because colour is in body, colour is in an individual body. Strictly, however, it is not colour, but this individual instance of colour, that is in this individual body; for colour could exist apart from this body (though this instance of colour could not). Aristotle's use of a relaxed sense of 'in' may be connected with his almost complete neglect, after Chapter 2, of individuals in non-substance categories.

In drawing his final conclusion in the last sentence Aristotle relies partly on the definition of 'in' ('. . . cannot exist separately . . .'); partly on the principle that if A is said of B, A could not exist if B did not. The closest he comes to arguing for this principle is at 3b10–23, where he insists that secondary substances are just *kinds of* primary substance.

Aristotle's conclusion is evidently intended to mark out primary substances as somehow basic (*contra* Plato). But the point is not very well expressed. For it may well be doubted whether (Aristotle thinks that) primary substances could exist if secondary substances and items in other categories did not do so. But if the implication of existence holds both ways, from the rest to primary substances and from primary substances to the rest, the statement in the last sentence of his paragraph fails to give a special status to primary substances.

2b7. The two arguments given for counting the species as 'more a substance' than the genus—for carrying into the class of secondary substances the notion of priority and posteriority already used in the distinction between primary and secondary substances—come to much the same. For the reason why it is more informative (2b10) to say 'Callias is a man' than to say 'Callias is an animal' (though both are proper answers to the 'what is it' question, 2b31–37) is just that the former entails the latter but not vice versa: 'the genera are predicated of the species but the species are not predicated reciprocally of the genera' (2b20). The point of view is different at 15a4–7, where it is said that genera are always prior to species since they do not reciprocate as to the implication of existence: 'if there is a fish there is an animal, but if there is an animal there is not necessarily a fish'. For this sense of 'prior' see 14a29–35.

2b29. Here the connexion between the 'what is it' question and the establishment of categorial lines is made very clear.

The second argument (from 'Further, it is because . . .') is compressed. Primary substances are subjects for everything else; everything else is either said of or in them (2a34, 2b15). Aristotle now claims that secondary substances are similarly related to 'all the rest', that is, to all things other than substances. This must be because all those things are *in* secondary substances. All Aristotle says, to establish this, is that 'this man is grammatical' entails 'a man is grammatical'. He means to imply that any non-substance that is in a primary substance is necessarily in a secondary substance (the species or genus of the primary substance). Since he has already argued that all non-substances are in primary substances he feels entitled to the conclusion that all non-substances are in secondary substances. But it will be seen that a further relaxation in the sense of 'in' has taken place. It is now implied, not only that generosity can be described as in Callias (though generosity could certainly exist in the absence of Callias), but also that generosity can be described as in man simply on the ground that some one man is generous (and not, as it strictly should be, on the ground that all instances of generosity are in individual men).

3a7. Why is it 'obvious at once' that secondary substances are not *in* primary substances? It is not that they can exist separately from primary substances (2a34–b6). Nor does Aristotle appear to rely on the fact that a given secondary substance can exist separately from any given individual, that there could be men even if Callias did not exist, so that the species man can exist separately from Callias and is, therefore, not in him. Aristotle seems rather to be appealing to the obvious impropriety in ordinary speech of saying such a thing as 'man is in Callias'. It was suggested in the note on 1a24–25 that Aristotle made it a necessary condition of A's being in B that it should be possible to say in ordinary non-technical discourse such a thing as 'A is in B' ('belongs to B', etc.). Now Aristotle is pointing out that this condition is not satisfied in the case of man and Callias. If this is his point he could have extended it to other categories; no genus or species in any category can naturally be described as in (or belonging to or had by) any subordinate genus, species or individual. What distinguishes secondary substances from non-substance genera and species is not that they are not in the individuals, species, and genera subordinate to them but that they are not in any *other* individuals, species, or genera; virtue is not in generosity, but it is in soul, whereas animal is not in man and not in anything else either.

One cannot say 'hero is in Callias' or 'father is in Callias'; but if Callias is a hero and a father the definition of 'hero' and 'father' can also be predicated of him. So it might be suggested that the considerations advanced by Aristotle in this paragraph imply that hero and father are secondary substances. But Aristotle is not claiming that any predicate-word which can be replaced by its definition is the name of a secondary substance (or differentia of substance, see below), but that a predicate-word can be replaced by the definition of the item it introduces if and only if the item is a secondary substance (or differentia of substance). 'Generous' can be replaced by definitions of 'hero' and 'father', but not by definition of the item which 'generous' introduces, the quality generosity. Similarly, 'hero' and 'father' can be replaced by definitions of 'hero' and 'father', but not by definitions of the items they serve to introduce, heroism and fatherhood. Aristotle gives no explicit rules for deciding which common nouns stand for species and genera of substance (natural kinds) and which serve only to ascribe qualities, etc., to substances. He would presumably rely on the 'what is it' question to segregate genuine names of secondary substances from other common nouns; but the question has to be taken in a limited or loaded sense if it is always to collect only the sorts of answer Aristotle would wish, and an understanding and acceptance of the idea of natural kinds is therefore presupposed by the use of the question to distinguish the names of such kinds from other common nouns which serve merely to ascribe qualities, etc. Surely it would often be appropriate to say 'a cobbler' in answer to the quesion 'What is Callias?'.

3a21. The statement that something that is not substance is nevertheless said of substance is a surprising
one, which can hardly be reconciled with the scheme of
ideas so far developed. If the differentia of a genus is not
a substance (secondary substances being just the species
and genera of substance), it ought to belong to some other
category and hence be in substance. That an item in one
category should be said of an item in another violates the
principle that if A is said of B and B of C then A is said of
C. Aristotle, indeed, positively claims that the definition
as well as the name of a differentia is predicable of the
substance falling under it, but this too seems very strange.
In a definition *per genus et differentiam* the differentia is
commonly expressed by an adjective (or other non-sub-
stantive), and this should surely be taken to introduce an
item named by the corresponding substantive (as 'generous' introduces but is not the name of generosity). If
we say that man is a rational animal 'rational' brings in
rationality, but neither the name nor the definition of
rationality can be predicated of man. Thus the differentiating property satisfies a test for being *in* substance (cp.
2a19–34).

Aristotle is no doubt influenced by the following facts.
(1) Species and genera of individual substances are themselves called substances because 'if one is to say of the
individual man *what* he is, it will be in place to give the
species or the genus' (2b32). If we now consider the
question 'what is (a) man?' we shall be strongly inclined
to mention not only the genus animal but also the appropriate differentia. The differentia seems to be *part of*
the 'what is it' of a secondary substance, and this provides a strong motive for assimilating it to substance even
while distinguishing it from species and genera. (2) The
principle enunciated at 1b16 implies that mention of a
differentia-words words which function naturally in Greek
true classification of things) any mention of the genus.
To ascribe the differentia 'two-footed' to man is as good
as to say that he is a two-footed land animal. Thus the
differentia is, in a way, the *whole* of the 'what is it' of
a secondary substance. (3) Aristotle uses as examples of

differentia-words words which function naturally in Greek as nouns (though they are strictly neuter adjectives). At 14b33–15a7 he uses the same words when speaking explicitly of *species* (and so they are translated there by 'bird', 'beast' and 'fish'). Moreover, there are in Aristotle's vocabulary no abstract nouns corresponding to these neuter adjectives (as 'footedness', 'two-footedness'). Such facts are far from establishing that the definition as well as the name of a differentia is predicated of substances. For not all differentiae are expressed by nouns or words used as nouns, and abstract nouns corresponding to differentia-words are not always lacking. In any case, there are plenty of nouns (like 'hero') which Aristotle would insist on treating as mere derivatives from the names of the things they introduce ('heroism'); and the fact that there is no name for, say, a quality does not exclude the possibility that some predicative expression serves to ascribe that quality (though not, of course, paronymously: 10a32–b5). Thus, that 'footed' is (used as) a noun and no noun 'footedness' exists is not a justification for refusing to treat 'footed' in the same kind of way as 'hero' or 'generous', as introducing a characteristic neither the name nor the definition of which is predicable of that which is footed. Nevertheless, the above features of the examples he hit upon may have made it somewhat easier for him to say what he does about differentiae without feeling the need for full explanation. For deeper discussion of the relation of differentia to genus, and of the connected problem of the unity of definition (referred to at *De Interpretatione* 17a13), see especially *Metaphysics* Z 12.

3a33. 'All things called from them are so called synonymously': Aristotle is not denying that there are words which stand ambiguously for either of two kinds of substance (like 'animal' in Chapter 1). Things to which such a word applied in one sense would not be 'called from' *the same substance* as things to which it applied in the other sense; and Aristotle is claiming only that all things called from any given substance are so called syn-

onymously, not that all things called by a given substance-
word are necessarily so called synonymously.

Aristotle is drawing attention again to the following
point (it will be convenient to assume that there is no
sheer ambiguity in the words used). There are two ways
in which something can be called from the quality virtue:
generosity is a virtue, Callias is virtuous; neither the name
nor the definition of virtue is predicable of Callias. There
are two ways in which something can be called from the
quality white: Della Robbia white is (a) white, this paper
is white; the name but not the definition of white is
predicable of this paper. There is only one way in which
something can be called from man: Callias is a man,
Socrates is a man, and so on; both the name and the
definition of man are predicable of Callias and Socrates
and so on.

It is not quite clear that Della Robbia white and this
paper are homonymous with respect to the word 'white',
in the meaning given to 'homonymous' in Chapter 1. For
there the case was that the word (e.g. 'animal') stood in
its two uses for two different things with two different
definitions. Now, however, we have 'white' in one use
standing for a thing (a quality) which has a certain definition, but in the other use not standing for a different
thing with a different definition but introducing differently the very same thing. However, an easy revision of
the account in Chapter 1 would enable one to say that
'synonymously' in the present passage contrasts with both
'homonymously' and 'paronymously': most non-substances
(like generosity) generate paronymy, a few (like the quality white) generate homonymy; no substance generates
either.

'From a primary substance there is no predicate': there
is no subject of which Callias is said or in which Callias
is. In the *Analytics* Aristotle speaks of sentences in which
the name 'Callias' is in the predicate place, and says that
this is only accidental predication (43a34; cp. 83a1–23).
He does not make any thorough investigation of the different types of sentence in which a proper name may occur in the predicate place. Nor does he discuss such uses

as 'he is a Socrates', 'his method of argument is Socratic'. He would no doubt allow that these are cases of genuine predication but deny that the predicates are 'from a primary substance': the connexion between the characteristics ascribed by '. . . is a Socrates' and '. . . is Socratic' and the individual Socrates is purely historical and contingent; we should not have used '. . . is a Socrates' as we do if there had been no Socrates or if Socrates had had a different character, but we could perfectly well have used a different locution to ascribe the very same characteristics. A similar answer would be available if someone claimed that there are after all two ways in which something may be called from a secondary substance since while Tabitha is *a cat* Mrs. So-and-so is *catty*. It is because of real or assumed characteristics of cats that the word 'cattiness' names the characteristics it does; but the characteristics themselves could have existed and been talked about even if there had never been any cats.

3b10. Aristotle has contrasted individual substances with their species and genera. He has labelled the latter 'secondary' and has argued that their existence presupposes that of primary substances. Nevertheless, much that he has said provides a strong temptation to thing of species and genera of substance as somehow existing in their own right like Platonic Forms. In the present passage Aristotle tries to remedy this. It is careless of him to speak as if it were substances (and not names of substances) that signify. More important, it is unfortunate that he draws the contrast between a primary substance and a secondary substance by saying that the latter signifies a certain qualification. For although he immediately insists that 'it does not signify simply a certain qualification, as white does', yet the impression is conveyed that secondary substances really belong in the category of quality. This, of course, Aristotle does not mean. 'Quality of substance' means something like 'kind' or 'character of substance'; it derives from a use of the question 'of what quality?' different from the use which serves to classify items as belonging to the category of quality. 'Of what quality is Callias?' (or 'what kind of person is Callias?') gets answers from the category of quality. But 'what quality of animal is Callias?' (or 'what kind of animal is Callias?') asks not for a quality as opposed to substance, quantity, etc., but for the quality-of-animal, the kind-of-animal. It is a result of the limitations of Aristotle's vocabulary that he uses the same word as a category-label and to convey the idea of a kind, sort or character of so-and-so. (Cp. *Metaphysics* 1020a33 – b1, 1024b5–6, where 'quality' refers to the differentia—in any category—not to the *category* of quality.) It is also clear that he is at a disadvantage in this passage through not having at his disposal such terms as 'refer', 'describe', 'denote', 'connote'; and that he would have been in a better position if he had from the start examined and distinguished various uses of expressions like '(a) man' instead of embarking at once upon a classification of 'things there are'.

3b24. Aristotle raises the question of contrariety in each of the categories he discusses. On the suggestion that large and small are contraries see 5b11 – 6a11.

3b33. The question of a more and a less is raised in each category. 'We have said that it is': 2b7. There is a certain ambiguity in 'more', since to say that a species is more a substance than a genus is to assign it some sort of priority but not to ascribe to it a higher degree of some feature as one does in saying that this is more hot than that.

The point Aristotle makes here about substances applies also, of course, to sorts which he would not recognize as natural kinds: one cobbler or magistrate is not more a cobbler or magistrate than another.

4a10. What Aristotle gives here as distinctive of substance is strictly a characteristic of *primary* substances. For he is not speaking of the possibility of man's being both dark and pale (of there being both dark men and pale men), but of the possibility of one and the same individual man's being at one time dark and at another time pale. (It will then be distinctive of secondary substances that the individuals of which they are said are capable of admitting opposites.) Correspondingly, Aristotle must be meaning to deny, not that species and genera in other categories may in a sense admit contraries (colour may be white or black), but that individual instances of qualities, etc., can admit contraries while retaining their identity. His first example is not convincing. An individual instance of colour will necessarily be an instance of some specific colour and will be individuated accordingly: if X changes from black to white we first have X's blackness and then X's whiteness, *two* individuals in the category of quality. (To this there corresponds the fact that one and the same individual substance cannot move from one species to another.) What is required is to show—not that X's blackness cannot retain its identity while becoming white, but—that X's blackness cannot retain its identity while having contrary properties at different times. The sort of suggestion Aristotle ought to rebut is, for example, the suggestion that one and the same individual instance of colour could be at one time glossy and at another matt, this variation not making it count as different instances of *colour*. Aristotle's second example is of the right kind, since the goodness or badness of an action does not enter into the identity-criteria for an individual action in the way in which the shade of colour does enter into the identity-criteria for an individual instance of colour. However, the example is still particularly favourable for him. For 'good' and 'bad' are commonly used to appraise an action *as a whole*, and for this reason one would not speak of an action as having been good at first and then become bad. There are clearly very many cases which it would be less easy for Aristotle to handle (cannot an individual sound sustain change in volume and tone?). The question demands a fuller scrutiny of cases and a more thorough investigation of usage than Aristotle attempts. It would seem that the power to admit contraries is not peculiar to individual substances but is shared by certain other continuants, so that a further criterion is required to explain why these others are not counted as substances.

4a22. Aristotle of course treats the truth and falsity of statements and beliefs as their correspondence and lack of correspondence to fact (4b8, 14b14–22; *Metaphysics*

1051b6–9). Here he first points out that it is not through a change in itself that a statement or belief at one time true is at another time false, whereas an individual substance itself changes; so that it remains distinctive of primary substances that they can admit contraries *by changing*. He next argues (4b5) that strictly a thing should be said to admit contraries only if it does itself undergo a change from one to the other; so that, strictly speaking, it is not necessary to qualify what was said at 4a10–11: only individual substances can admit contraries.

Aristotle might have argued that the alleged counter-examples, individual statements or beliefs which change their truth-value, fail, because my statement now that Callias is sitting and my statement later that Callias is sitting are not the same *individual* statement even if they are the *same statement* (just as 'a' and 'a' are two individual instances of the same letter). Thus they are not examples of the very same individual admitting contraries. Alternatively, Aristotle could have denied that the statement made by 'Callias is sitting' when uttered at one time *is* the *same statement* as that made by 'Callias is sitting' when uttered at another time. The sameness of a statement or belief is not guaranteed by the sameness of the words in which it is expressed; the time and place of utterance and other contextual features must be taken into account.

ARISTOTLE'S THEORY OF CATEGORIES

J. M. E. MORAVCSIK

In several of his writings Aristotle presents what came to be known as a "list of categories." The presentation of a list, by itself, is not a philosophic theory. This paper attempts a few modest steps toward an understanding of the theory or theories in which the list of categories is embedded. To arrive at such understanding we shall have to deal with the following questions: What classes of expressions designate items each of which falls under only one category? What is the list a list of? and What gives it unity? To show this to be a worthwhile enterprise, let us consider a few passages in which the list of categories is introduced or mentioned.

In *Topics* 103b20 ff. the list is introduced as containing certain kinds (*gené*) within which one can find the accidents, genus, properties, and definition of anything. Thus apparently all (simple?) elements of the nature of any entity are to be found in one of the categories. In *Metaphysics* 1028a10 ff. we are told that 'is' has as many senses as there are categories. Thus we see that Aristotle analyzes the ambiguity of 'is' with the list of categories as an assumed background. What he takes to be the systematic ambiguity of 'is' provides one of the cornerstones of his metaphysical speculations. In *Physics* 225b5 ff. Aristotle analyzes the concept of *kinésis* and concludes that instances of this can be found in three of the categories.

Each of these passages presents problems; some of these will be taken up later in this paper. This brief preliminary survey is intended only to show that the list of categories plays an important role in several of Aristotle's theories, and thus it is reasonable to assume that the list has constitutive principles and unity.

I

Which parts of language designate an item in one of the categories? In Categories 1b25 ff. the list of categories is introduced as containing the kinds (e.g. quality, quantity) of those items (e.g. white, grammatical, three cubits long) which are signified by "things said without any combination" (Ackrill's translation, contained in this volume). Chapters 2 and 4 of the Categories taken together make it quite clear that the "things" in question are linguistic items. Our first task is to determine which parts of language Aristotle is referring to in the passage under consideration. Earlier, in 1a16 ff. we read that "Of things that are said, some involve combination while others are said without combination. Examples of those involving combination are 'man runs', 'man wins'; and of those without combination 'man', 'ox', 'runs', 'wins'."[1] In view of the meagerness of the examples, the key term in this account is "combination." As Ackrill,[2] and a century ago Trendelenburg,[3] pointed out, the Greek term sumploké used here by Aristotle had been previously used by

[1] J. L. Ackrill's translation here is far superior to the old Oxford version, which renders the first part of this passage as: "Forms of speech are either simple or composite." This suggests, wrongly, that Aristotle is saying something about all forms of speech, and, equally wrongly, that the distinction to be drawn is a surface distinction between what is syntactically simple or analyzable.

[2] J. L. Ackrill, Aristotle's Categories and De Interpretatione (Oxford, 1963), p. 73. (See earlier in this volume p. 102.)

[3] A. Trendelenburg, Geschichte der Kategorienlehre (Hildesheim: Olms, 1846 [1963]), p. 11.

Plato to refer not to mere conjunction or juxtaposition, but rather to the interweaving of words and phrases into sentences.[4] This would suggest that the uncombined elements are parts of language from which sentences can be formed. This is confirmed by 2a4 ff., where Aristotle says that the combination of these items produces a true or false sentence. (Aristotle regards sentences as the bearers of truth-value.) There is an interesting parallel to this passage in *Topics* 101b26–28, according to which the key elements in a statement are property, genus, definition, and accident, and it is emphasized that none of these by themselves make up a statement. Thus as a reasonable first approximation we can say that Aristotle is interested in potential elements of sentences that are true or false, or definitions. One is tempted to add the qualification: "sentences of subject-predicate form," for neither in the examples given nor in the subsequent discussions are sentences expressing identity or existence treated. Their inclusion in the discussion would raise some interesting questions about the extent to which these types of sentence could be regarded as "interweaving," and about the senses of 'is' involved. The addition of this qualification would be in harmony with Trendelenburg's remark that Aristotle in this context seems to have in mind what Kant called judgments,[5] (a notion which carries similar limitations).

Having specified the relevant class of sentences, we should investigate whether the Aristotelian theory entails that every element of such a sentence designates an item, and whether every element that designates is supposed to designate an item falling into only one of

---

[4]On Plato's views on this see J. M. Moravcsik, *"Sumploké Eidoon," Archiv für die Geschichte der Philosophie*, XLII (1960) 117–29; also "Being and Meaning in the *Sophist*," *Acta Philosophica Fennica*, XIV (1962), especially pp. 61–65.

[5]Trendelenburg, op. cit., p. 12.

the categories. An affirmative answer to either question would place the theory in jeopardy. There is, however, evidence that:

(i) Aristotle does not think that every word or phrase which could be part of a sentence of subject-predicate form has the function of designating an entity.

As both Steinthal and Trendelenburg remarked,[6] Aristotle does not ascribe the same type of significance to every word within a sentence, and he does not think that every word has a designative role. In *Poetics* 1456b38 ff. he separates from nouns and verbs (to which he also assimilates adjectives) the so-called connectors or auxiliary expressions. These are said to include particles and prepositions, but in order to complement the theory of categories they ought to include a great deal more: logical constants, articles, and the ordinary language equivalents of quantifiers must also be members of this class. There is evidence to support the view that Aristotle intended the connectors to include a great deal more than he explicitly mentions. For one thing, what he says about them applies to a much larger group than his examples would suggest, for he says that these expressions (a) do not designate and (b) do not contribute to the content of a new (larger) linguistic unit, i.e. the sentence. These criteria are interesting, for they show that Aristotle did not mark off the connectors on purely syntactic grounds. The criteria can be taken as foreshadowing the characterization of what were later called the syncategorematic expressions. In any case, these conditions would allow all the above-mentioned types of expression to qualify. It is impossible to say how many of these Aristotle had in mind when he wrote the *Poetics*, but the

[6]Trendelenburg, op. cit., pp. 24 ff. and H. Steinthal, *Geschichte der Sprachwissenschaft* (Hildesheim: Olms, 1890 [1961]), Vol. I, pp. 263 ff.

fluidity of the classification is witnessed by *Rhetoric* III 5 where—as Steinthal saw—Aristotle blends articles, pronouns, and conjunctives into one class. Steinthal's interpretation of what Aristotle thought of as the main parts of speech is of further relevance here, for it is claimed that apart from nouns and verbs Aristotle recognized only one more class, i.e. the connectors.[7] None of this is direct evidence, but taken all together it renders plausible the interpretation of the class of connectors on the suggested broad basis.

With this we have narrowed down the candidates for the "uncombined elements" to the members of the class of designative expressions which can be elements of those sentences that are definitions or are of subject-predicate form. Still, further restrictions are obviously needed. Fortunately there is evidence to support additional qualifications.

(ii) Aristotle does not think that every noun or verb designates an item in one of the categories.

In *De Interpretatione* 16a13 ff. Aristotle lists as a necessary condition for the production of what is true or false the combination of verb and noun, and in this context treats "being" as a verb. We see, however, from his treatment of being in the *Categories* and the *Metaphysics* (see the reference in the beginning of this paper) that he does not construe being as falling into only one of the categories. His claim that being is not a genus, and the argument backing up this claim,[8] are sufficient ground on which to base the interpretation that 'being'—and similar terms like 'same', 'one', etc.— have either no designative role or a divided designative role.

[7]Steinthal, op. cit., pp. 260 ff.

[8]The most profound discussion of this argument is to be found in John Cook Wilson's paper "Categories in Aristotle and in Kant," *Statement and Inference*, Vol. II, pp. 696–706 [above, pp. 75–89].

Before we consider further qualifications, let us look briefly at the interesting status that definitions had for Aristotle. It is not clear whether he regarded definitions as true or false, and whether they counted as instances of combination. The passage quoted from the *Topics* above casts doubt on their counting as combinations. Now in *De Interpretatione*, chapters 4 and 5, he argues that what is true or false must contain such interweaving or combination. Again in *Poetics* 1457a25 ff. Aristotle says that, though definitions are sentences, they need not contain a verb. This passage, however, can be construed as saying only that no verb need appear explicitly in a definition; the same is true in Greek for many other types of sentences. Again in *De Anima* III 6 it is pointed out that a definition does not involve a mental task of synthesis as an assertion does. All of this together supports the interpretation according to which Aristotle did not regard definitions as true or false or as produced by combination. Nevertheless, we must assume that he thought of parts of definitions as falling under one category.

(iii) There are some noun- or verb-phrases (other than words like 'being', etc.) that designate items falling under more than one category.

An obvious example of a phrase designating a complex that spans two categories is the expression 'incontinent man'. In order to rule out such cases we have to introduce further qualifications. The restriction to be put forward here is not backed by direct textual evidence, but it is supported by what we took to be the significance of *sumploké* and the proposed broad delineation of the class of connectors: it is to rule out as not completely uncombined all those phrases which the mere addition of connectors can transform into a sentence. For though 'red colored' and 'incontinent man' are not sentences, they can be expanded into the sentences 'all red things are colored' and 'some men are incontinent' by the mere addition of connectors. Here one can see the importance of our previous qualification that only sentences of subject-predicate form are under consideration. Without it our current restriction would turn out to be so strict as to leave no word in the "uncombined" class, since the addition of "there are some . . . things" will render 'white' or 'heavy' into sentences; yet 'white' and 'heavy' are known to be expressions which Aristotle regards as "in no way combined."

Throughout this discussion we have taken the notion of a sentence for granted. It is time to see what Aristotle has to say on this topic. But his account of a sentence as significant sound, some part of which is significant in separation as an expression (*De Interpretatione* 16b26 ff. and *Poetics* 1457a23 ff.), is obviously inadequate since it fails even to separate sentences from clauses. The reason for this seems to be that Aristotle finds himself in a curious predicament. He cannot accept the Platonic account of a sentence as the interweaving of noun and verb since he recognizes counterexamples to it. On the other hand, he knows that he cannot use the theory of categories to explain a sentence as an intercategorial connection, since he knows that a sentence like 'all men are animals' does not combine elements from different categories. Thus he lacks a conceptual framework that would enable him to give an adequate account of what a sentence is. In view of this, we shall have to continue in this discussion to take the notion of a sentence for granted.

We are not yet finished with the required restrictions, for we must admit the following:

(iv) Not all relevantly simple nouns and verbs designate items falling into only one category.

As Aristotle saw, one can simply define a word x as 'incontinent man' and thereby create a word which our previous restrictions allow as uncombined but which designates something that spans two categories. What is clearly needed is a further restriction that would rule out expressions like x as somehow ill-formed. There is evidence that Aristotle did have such a qualification in mind, for in *De Interpretatione*, chapters 8 and 11, he discusses the problem of the extent to which a predicate expression may or may not designate a "genuine unity." The discussions are sketchy and no adequate interpretations of them have so far been offered. Thus Ackrill wrote[9] that the difficulty of deciding what Aristotle regards as a genuine unity "corresponds" to the difficulty of deciding which simple phrases are supposed to designate items falling into only one category. Ackrill is quite correct in emphasizing the magnitude of the task facing the interpreter, but this should not keep us from seeing that the notion of a genuine unity could still be invoked by Aristotle in an account of the "uncombined" elements of language. For as 18a18 ff. shows, there are certain predicates, e.g. that which is the equivalent of 'horse and man', which designate items falling into one category only, which nevertheless Aristotle would not regard as having genuine unity. Thus whatever the correct account of genuine unity is, the passage under consideration shows that it does not presuppose the correlation between uncombined elements and the list of categories, and thus it could be invoked without circularity to place further restriction on what is to count as an uncombined element.

In view of these considerations it is not unreasonable to suppose that Aristotle could describe x defined as 'incontinent man' as an expression not designating a genuine unity; that he could do so without assuming anything about its correlation with any of the categories, and that he could on this ground rule that it is not one of the legitimate uncombined elements. This

[9]Ackrill, op. cit., p. 126.

final restriction leaves us with the following formulation of Aristotle's view:

(v) Those elements of sentences of subject-predicate form, or definitions, which (a) are not connectors; (b) are not, like 'being', otherwise non-designative in nature; (c) cannot be turned into sentences of subject-predicate form, by the mere addition of connectors; and (d) designate genuine unities, are "uncombined elements" of language, and designate items falling into one and only one category.

Intuitively restated, Aristotle's principle says that by what we would call semantic and syntactic analysis[10] we can discover certain basic units among the elements of sentences of subject-predicate form, and that these turn out to designate those simple elements of reality which fall into only one category. Thus the designative link between these simple parts of language and the simple parts of reality which fall into only one category is, according to Aristotle, the key link between the structure of language and the structure of reality.

This account is not without difficulties. The main problem is the as yet unexplained doctrine of genuine unity. Another problem is the fact that the restriction ascribed to Aristotle that rests on the possibility of expanding certain phrases into sentences with the help of connectors is not supported by direct evidence. But it is not a weakness of the interpretation that it seeks to connect what is said in the *Categories* with some of what is said in the *Poetics* and the *Rhetorics*. On the contrary, to show that under a certain interpretation these passages complement the views of the passages in the *Categories* is to give that interpretation added plausibility.

Given the difficulties, we might cast around for alternative interpretations. In this connection it is worth not-

[10]Aristotle, like Plato, did not distinguish between these.

ing that both the possible solutions listed by Ackrill,[11] and perceptively criticized by him, turn out to be inferior to the account presented in this paper. One of these solutions takes "without combination" to mean "designates an item falling into only one category." The main difficulty with this view is that—as Ackrill observes—it construes the statement introducing the list of categories in chapter 4 as analytic. If the statement that the elements which are in no way combined designate items falling into only one category is analytic, it is deceptively so; for this would imply that there is no way of sorting out the uncombined elements of a sentence except by observing whether their designata fall into only one category. Thus the beginning of chapter 4 could just as well have started: "some sentential elements designate ... and we regard these as being without any combination." Furthermore, according to this interpretation what Aristotle says about the combined and uncombined parts of language rests entirely on metaphysical grounds and thus cannot be connected with what he says elsewhere about the structure of language.

The other possible solution fares hardly better, since according to it the distinction between what is and what is not combined is identical with the distinction between simple words and more complex sentential elements. In order to accept this view we would have to assume that in chapter 4 of the *Categories* Aristotle forgets about the possibility of simple terms with complex meanings. However, we saw above that this possibility is discussed in *De Interpretatione*, and to suppose that Aristotle is not aware of this issue in a context in which it is vital is to accuse him of too gross a mistake. Moreover, this version suggests that Aristotle's distinction among different parts of language rests on purely superficial features, whereas the passages

[11]Ackrill, op. cit., pp. 73–74 [pp. 102–103 above].

quoted from the *Topics* and the *Poetics* assure us that this is not so.

To sum up, if we can regard the evidence presented in support of the interpretation argued for in this section as adequate, the interpretation recommends itself on the following grounds: it links Aristotle's metaphysical speculation with his view on the structure of language; it relates the *Categories* to what is said in other works on language; it helps to explore Aristotle's views on language, which turn out to be far from simple-minded; and it sketches the structure of an explanation that Aristotle would be likely to give as justification of the claim that there are certain "uncombined" elements in language with a—to him—vital designative role.

II

The unity and completeness of the list of categories. In the beginning of chapter 4 of the *Categories* we find a list of ten categories. The labels given to them are oddly heterogeneous. Some are philosophical constructs, some are ordinary questions, and some are lifted out of simple singular sentences of subject-predicate form.[12] Thus at first glance it is not clear whether the list is supposed to yield an ontological classification or an analysis of the structure of propositions. Some interpreters have gone as far as accusing Aristotle of having failed to give the list sufficient unity. Perhaps the most famous of these critics is Kant,[13] who assumes that Aristotle was interested in the same task that he was—i.e. to give a set of necessary conditions under which judgments are possible—and then concludes that Aristotle failed in this task. A comparison of Kant's categories with those of Aristotle, however, suggests the not too surprising alternative that Kant and

[12]Ackrill, op. cit., p. 73 and Trendelenburg, op. cit., p. 13.
[13]*Critique of Pure Reason* B 105–107.

Aristotle designed their categories with different purposes in mind. Many of Kant's categories must be construed as properties of judgments or ideas (e.g. universality or singularity). Aristotle's list, on the other hand, cannot be so construed. His items are either very general properties of objects or not properties at all. There is no reason why the two lists should coincide, and once the difference in their aims has been discerned, the two need not be regarded as conflicting.[14]

One way of explaining the heterogeneity of the labels is to assume that Aristotle is concerned primarily with the types to be designated, and not with the manner of designation. As we shall see, the adoption of this assumption is rewarding. We must note at this point, however, that it leads us to reject a claim like that made by Trendelenburg, according to which the list of categories is derived from grammatical considerations.[15]

Let us begin by considering one commonly accepted characterization of the categories, the one that describes them as the "highest predicables."[16] In order for this view to be even initially plausible, we must construe 'predicable' in a technical sense. For not only is the first category ambiguous between primary and secondary substance, but some of the examples given for the other categories, e.g. 'in the Lyceum' and 'yesterday', cannot be regarded as predicables in the ordinary sense of the term. What this technical sense of 'predicable' wide enough to embrace everything falling under each of the ten categories could be is far from clear. But

[14]For a different view of the relation between Aristotle and Kant see H. W. B. Joseph, *An Introduction to Logic* (Oxford, 1916), pp. 63–65. Also Cook Wilson, op, cit,, p. 704 [p. 85].
[15]Trendelenburg, op. cit., p. 33.
[16]As remarked but not endorsed by W. D. Ross in *Aristotle*, pp. 27–28. According to Joseph, op. cit., pp. 48–49, the Greek word for category (κατηγορία) means 'predicate,' but for counterexamples see H. Bonitz, *Über die Kategorien des Aristoteles* (Vienna, 1853), pp. 30–31.

even if such a sense could be found, further difficulties arise in connection with the term 'highest'. There are two ways in which the metaphorical value of this term could be captured by logical analysis. On one interpretation predicate p' is higher than predicate p'' if and only if all members of the class which makes up the range of application of p'' are also members of the class which makes up the range of application of p', but not the other way around. In this sense *animal* is higher than *man*. The other interpretation takes p' as higher than p'' if and only if p' is an attribute of p''. In this sense *category* would be a higher predicate than *quality* or *quantity*, and *colour, quality, category* would constitute a hierarchy. It is clear, however, that Aristotle does not want such a pyramid. He denies the ontological reality of the higher strata here indicated. Not to do so would leave him far closer to Platonism than he would find comfortable. Thus the sense in which the categories would have to be "higher" is the former sense—as Cook Wilson noted.[17] That is to say, as we go to wider and wider genera, the particulars contained in any one genera are on the same level as the particulars contained in the wider genera. Given this characterization of the categories, one is confronted with the question: where must one stop? Why call the categories the "highest" (actually the "widest") genera? The only plausible Aristotelian reply is: "because by some principle the genera that would have even wider comprehensions are not genuine genera; i.e. they have no ontological status." Such a reply takes us back to a metaphysical principle, and it is the explication of that principle, rather than the phrase "highest predicables," that will shed light on the nature of the categories.

Another current interpretation could be characterized

as the "linguistic view." Among its advocates are Ryle[18] and Anscombe.[19] According to this view Aristotle uses the list of categories to mark off the different kinds of fairly simple things that can be said about a substance. As such, the list could not be regarded as final or complete, since there may be an indeterminate number of ways in which one can raise questions about substances. The most important achievement of the list turns out to be—according to this interpretation—the anticipation of the concept of semantic category and the notion of a "category-mistake," a confusion which supposedly underlies a type of semantically deviant sentence. (E.g. an answer in terms of food to a question about the size of a substance allegedly does not make sense, even though the sentence expressing the answer is—on the surface at least—syntactically well formed.)

This is not the place to hold autopsy over the notion of a category-mistake as used by recent analytic philosophers. To show that this could not be the correct interpretation of Aristotle's theory will have to suffice. Three considerations prove fatal to this account. First, according to this view once the significance of the list is properly understood, questions about completeness could not arise. But, as some of the passages quoted at the beginning of this paper show, Aristotle committed himself to claims which entail that the list should contain mutually exclusive categories which are jointly exhaustive of reality. (More on this point below.) Thus either this interpretation is incorrect, or we must

[18]G. Ryle, "Categories," *Logic and Language*, second ser., ed. A. Flew (Oxford, 1955), pp. 65–81. Ryle—like Kant—thinks that Aristotle was really interested in what he, Ryle, is interested in doing but that he did not do it so well. I find deeply depressing this tendency of philosophers to think that the great men of the past tried to do what they are doing but that they did not do it so well.

[19]G. E. Anscombe, in *Three Philosophers* (Oxford, 1961), pp. 14–15.

suppose that Aristotle himself completely misunderstood the significance of his own theory. Such an assumption should be adopted by a historian only as a last resort. Secondly, the only basis for the individuation of the categories would be the linguistic intuition which allows us to detect category-mistakes. It is clear, however, that Aristotle does not leave the individuation of his categories to intuitions, linguistic or otherwise. He states their differentiating characteristics quite explicitly: e.g. quality is that in virtue of which things can be said to be similar; quantity is that which can be said to be equal or unequal.[20] These characteristics do not depend on the notion of semantic anomaly. Finally, it is difficult to suppose that had Aristotle been concerned with semantic anomaly, he would have missed the glaring fact that to describe a shape as red or blue is semantically odd, even though both shape and colour belong to the same Aristotelian category, i.e. that of quality. Thus the linguistic interpretation can be safely rejected.

Let us proceed to the consideration of the interpretation put forward by Professor Ackrill.[21] According to this view Aristotle arrived at the list of categories in two ways. One of these is the sorting out of the different types of question that can be asked about substances. The other is to start by asking what any given thing is and to continue by repeating that question with reference to whatever the previous answer revealed. Both these approaches are supposed to come to an end when irreducible genera are reached. Ackrill thinks that the two ways are exemplified in *Topics* I 9. He does not find it surprising that they should result in the same list, with the exception that only the second brings particulars into the classification. He leaves open the question of completeness, since he does not think

[20]*Categories* 11a15–20 and 6a26.
[21]Ackrill, op. cit., pp. 78–81 [pp. 109–12].

that Aristotle had any grounds, in the form of a general argument or principle, on which he could have concluded that his list includes all and only irreducibly different genera.

This summary shows that Ackrill's account has an element in common with the "linguistic view." Both interpretations assume that the list of categories is arrived at by the consideration of questions, or classes of properties, concerning substances. The only evidence in favour of this assumption is the fact that Aristotle's examples seem to be about a substance, i.e. man. We must remember, however, that Aristotle employed the category-structure in his attempt to show substances to be prior to all else. Thus if we accept this hypothesis, we must attribute to him the grand design of outlining a set of categories by classifying questions about substances, and then using this structure to show that substances are prior to all entities collected under the other categories. Such an outrageously question-begging procedure should not be attributed to any philosopher except in the face of overwhelming evidence. After all, the use of a pattern such as the one under consideration would make proofs of ontological priority surprisingly easy. For example, one could collect all the questions which can be raised about shadows, classify the relevant predicates gathered through the answers to these questions, and conclude that the items in the categories thus formed are posterior to shadows since they are specifications of shadows. As long as Aristotle's general account of his list and his characterizations of the several categories lend themselves to alternative accounts, which avoid such question-begging, these alternatives should be explored.

This objection leads to the observation that it would be surprising indeed if the two approaches described by Ackrill were to yield the same list. Why should the classification of the aspects of one kind of entity, e.g.

substance, coincide with an exhaustive classification of the essences of all entities that make up reality? Would this be true also of other types of entity, such as events, qualities, numbers, etc.? Such a correlation will not hold unless one views everything as a modification or relational accident of the type of entity preferred. These ways of viewing things are trivial.

Ackrill's second way of arriving at the list of categories also contains an inherent weakness. For there are an indeterminate number of ways in which we can classify things by the repeated asking of the question: What is it? Furthermore, how could one decide whether the highest genera have been reached? Intuitions, as we saw, are not enough. To take one of Aristotle's examples, why should one not arrive at change (*kinésis*) as one of the categories? It certainly answers a "what is it?" question. Yet, as we know, Aristotle does not think that this is one of the categories; on the contrary, he thinks that the list of categories must be presupposed by the adequate analysis of this concept which shows it to be cutting across three categories.

It does not, therefore, seem likely that Aristotle arrived at his list in either of the ways that Ackrill suggests. In view of this we should take a look at the passage in the *Topics* (103b22 ff.)—mentioned above—which Ackrill construes as containing the second way of arriving at the list. It states, among other things, that the essence of anything will be found in one of the categories. This statement does not entail Ackrill's second approach, but only that the categories make up such an exhaustive classification of reality that no real essence will cut across categories. Thus it is consistent with the possible claim that there are irreducible ultimate genera within the categories, or that the categories could be reduced in number. Most importantly, the statement is only a necessary condition for the correct list of categories; in itself it does not provide a pro-

cedure for arriving at the list. Nor does it give a principle of unity for the list of categories.

In turning to the more constructive task of spelling
out a plausible alternative interpretation, let us begin
by noting—partly on the basis of the negative discussion above—some necessary conditions for any adequate
interpretation. These conditions arise out of the ways
in which Aristotle employs the list of categories in his
philosophizing.[22] The passages quoted previously from
the *Topics*, *Physics*, and *Metaphysics*, together with
Metaphysics 1017a, show that Aristotle uses the list
in his analyses of key concepts such as being and
change, and also in his claiming priority for substances.
Thus the list has to be complete in the following ways:
(i) It must be exhaustive of all that Aristotle takes to
be existing. (ii) No reduction of the number of categories should be possible without violating the principle
upon which the list is constructed. (iii) No further
subdivision of the categories should be possible without
violating the constitutive principle. Without these
conditions Aristotle could not claim that *kinésis* can
be found in exactly three categories, or that by saying
that 'is' has as many senses as there are categories he
is giving a significant characterization of being.

These conditions help in resolving the question
whether the categories include only universals, or particulars as well. Underlying this issue is the debate
whether there are particulars and universals in each
category, or only universals in all but the first.[23] It is
difficult to conceive of each category as containing
universals; for example, what universal would correspond to 'in the Lyceum'? On the other hand, it is
equally difficult to conceive of particulars falling under

[22]"Da endlich jede Lehre erst in ihren Folgen ihre Stärke und
Schwäche offenbart, so wird es wichtig sein, die Kategorien in der
Anwendung zu beobachten." Trendelenburg, op. cit., p. 11.
[23]See Ross, op. cit., p. 28, n. 20.

each category. What particulars would we find under the category of relation? The conditions laid down above do not entail that each category must contain both universals and particulars; they entail rather, that the categories jointly must contain all the universals and particulars that Aristotle would acknowledge as existing. This leaves open the possibility that in some categories there may be only universals, in some only particulars, and in some both. In any case, events, processes, and abstract entities such as numbers must be contained within the categories. The analysis of *kinésis*, and the explanation of the category of quantity reveals how Aristotle conceived of this inclusion.

The constitutive principle which we seek is likely to be one that shows how the categories make up classes of predicates (in a very wide sense of 'predicate') to each of which some type of entity must be related. Apart from the issue of question-begging, our conditions of completeness guarantee that the type in question cannot be that of substance; for in order to be a sensible substance an entity must have both shape and weight, and these two properties fall under the same Aristotelian category of quality. Thus if the categories are those classes of predicates of which substances must partake, then the list as we have it would have to be subdivided to put weight and shape into different categories, a violation of the completeness conditions.

A more adequate interpretation can be given, based partly on Bonitz's suggestion[24] that Aristotle's list yields a survey of what is given in sense experience, and that each entity thus given must be related to some item in each of the categories. According to this interpretation the constitutive principle of the list of categories is that they constitute those classes of items to each of which any sensible particular—substantial or otherwise—must be related. Any sensible particular, sub-

[24]Bonitz, op. cit., pp. 18, 35, and 55.

stance, event, sound, etc. must be related to some substance; it must have some quality and quantity; it must
have relational properties, it must be related to times
and places; and it is placed within a network of causal
chains and laws, thus being related to the categories
of affecting and being affected. The only categories of
the complete list of ten that cause difficulties for this
interpretation are those of "having" and of "being-in-
a-position." In this connection the following should
be noted. First, these two categories are not always
included in the list Aristotle gives. Secondly, 'have'
is taken by Aristotle—as chapter 15 of the *Categories*
shows—in a variety of senses, one of which is the sense
of "having" parts. Given this construction, all sensible
particulars relate to that category. The category of
"position" is an obscure one, and it causes difficulties
for any interpretation, including the ones surveyed
critically above.

This proposed interpretation meets the completeness
conditions stated above. Neither a reduction nor a further subdivision would leave the list as definitive of
that to which sensible particulars must be related. The
account also meets the exhaustiveness condition, at
least as far as Aristotle is concerned. For the Stagirite
believed that all properties, including the second-order
ones, are ultimately related to what is presented by our
senses. Finally, this account construes the list of categories as the proper background for Aristotle's investigations of being, change, and priority relations. If it is
question-begging, it is so only in the same way that
one might construe Aristotle's general preference for
what is presented to the senses—a preference never
defended—as question-begging. Thus this interpretation
fulfills the promise made at the beginning of this paper;
we have shown how the list of categories can be construed as part of a theory and how this in turn serves
as a background for other Aristotelian theories.

Conclusion. The theory of categories is partly a theory about language and partly a theory about reality. With regard to language it states that certain elements of a language have key-designating roles, the full understanding of which requires that we understand the designata as falling within those classes which jointly form the set definitive of that to which a sensible particular must be related. We can see from this that Aristotle did not think of the structure of language as mirroring the structure of reality. But he did believe that there are specific items of language and reality the correlation of which forms the crucial link between the two.

III. METAPHYSICS

ESSENCE AND ACCIDENT

IRVING M. COPI

The notions of essence and accident play important and unobjectionable roles in pre-analytic or pre-philosophical thought and discourse. These roles are familiar, and need no elaboration here. Philosophers cannot ignore them, but must either explain them or (somehow) explain them away. My interest is in explaining them.

If they are taken seriously, the notions of essence and accident seem to me most appropriately discussed within the framework of a metaphysic of substance, which I shall accordingly assume. The account of essence and accident that I wish to set forth and argue for derives very largely from Aristotle, although it is not strictly Aristotelian. Where it differs from Aristotle's account it does so in order to accommodate some of the insights formulated by Locke in his discussion of "real" and "nominal" essences. My discussion is to be located, then, against the background of a substance metaphysic and a realist epistemology. The theory of essence and accident to be proposed seems to me not only to fit the demands of the general philosophical position mentioned, but also to be consistent with the apparent requirements of contemporary scientific development. I wish to begin my discussion with some historical remarks.

From *The Journal of Philosophy*, LI (1954), 706–19. Reprinted by permission of the author and editor of *The Journal of Philosophy*.

The earliest Western philosophers were much concerned with change and permanence, taking positions so sharply opposed that the issue appeared to be more paradox than problem. If an object which changes really changes, then it cannot literally be one and the same object which undergoes the change. But if the changing thing retains its identity, then it cannot really have changed. Small wonder that early cosmologists divided into warring factions, each embracing a separate horn of their common dilemma, the one denying permanence of any sort, the other denying the very possibility of change.

Aristotle discussed this problem in several of his treatises, bringing to bear on it not only his superb dialectical skill but an admirable, common-sense, dogged insistence that some things do maintain their identity while undergoing change. To explain the observed facts he was led to distinguish different kinds of change. A man does retain his identity though his complexion may change from ruddy to pale, or though he may move from one place to another. He is the same man though he become corpulent in middle life or his sinews shrink with age. In these types of change, called *alteration, locomotion, growth,* and *diminution,* the changing thing remains substantially or essentially what it was before changing.

Another type of change, however, was admitted to be more thoroughgoing. To take, for example, an artificial substance, we can say that if a wooden table is not just painted or moved, but destroyed by fire, we have neither alteration, locomotion, growth, nor diminution alone, but *substantial* change. The characteristic mark of substantial change is that the object undergoing the change does not survive that change or persist through it, but is destroyed in the process. The ashes (and gas and radiant energy) that appear in place of the burned table are not an altered, moved, or larger or smaller table, but no table at all. In substantial change its essential property of being a table disappears.

It seems clear that distinguishing these different kinds of change involves distinguishing different kinds of attributes. The basic dichotomy between substantial change and other kinds of change is parallel to that between essential attributes or *essences*, and other kinds of attributes, which may be lumped together as accidental attributes or *accidents*. (Here we diverge rather sharply from at least one moment of Aristotle's own terminology, in ignoring the intermediate category of "property" or "proprium.")

Of the various bases that have been proposed for distinguishing between essence and accident, two stand out as most reasonable. The first has already been implied. If we can distinguish the different kinds of change, then we can say that a given attribute is essential to an object if its loss would result in the destruction of that object, whereas an attribute is a mere accident if the object would remain identifiably and substantially the same without it. This basis for distinguishing between essence and accident, although helpful heuristically, is not adequate philosophically, for it seems to me that the distinctions among these kinds of change presuppose those among the different kinds of attributes.

The other, more satisfactory basis for distinguishing essence from accident is an epistemological or methodological one. Knowledge of the essence of a thing is said to be more important than knowledge of its other attributes. In the *Metaphysics* Aristotle wrote: "... we know each thing most fully, when we know what it is, e.g. what man is or what fire is, rather than when we know its quality, its quantity, or its place...."[1] It is the essence that is intended here, for a subsequent passage explains that: "... the essence is precisely what

[1] 1028a37–1028b2. Quotations are from the Oxford translation.

something *is*. . . ."[2] It is perhaps an understatement to say that Aristotle held knowledge of essence to be "more important" than knowledge of accidents, for he later says explicitly that: ". . . to *know* each thing . . . is just to know its essence. . . ."[3] And if we confine our attention to scientific knowledge, Aristotle repeatedly assures us that there is no knowledge of accidents at all,[4] but only of essences.[5]

Aristotle was led to draw an ontological conclusion from the foregoing epistemological doctrine. If some attributes of objects are epistemologically significant and others are not, the implication is that the former constitute the real natures of those objects, whereas the latter can be relegated to some less ultimate category. I must confess that I am in sympathy with the realist position which underlies and justifies such an inference, but to expound it in detail would take us too far afield.

As a biologist Aristotle was led to classify things into genera and species, holding that things belong to the same species if and only if they share a common essence. In remarking this fact we need not commit ourselves to any position with respect to the systematic or genetic priority of either logic or biology in Aristotle's thought. He apparently believed these species to be fixed and limited, and tended to ignore whatever could not be conveniently classified within them, holding, for example, that "the production of a mule by a horse" was "contrary to nature,"[6] a curious phrase. Some modern writers have tended to regard this shortcoming as fatal to the Aristotelian system. Thus Susan Stebbing wrote: "Modern theories of organic evolution have

[2]1030a1.
[3]1031b20.
[4]1026b4; 1027a20, 28; 1064b30; 1065a4. Cf. also *Posterior Analytics* 75a18–22.
[5]75a28–30.
[6]1033b33. But cf. 770b9–13.

combined with modern theories of mathematics to destroy the basis of the Aristotelian conception of essence. . . ."[7] It seems to me, however, that the fixity of species is a casual rather than an integral part of the Aristotelian system, which in its broad outlines as a metaphysical framework can be retained and rendered adequate to the most contemporary of scientific developments. A not dissimilar objection was made by Dewey, who wrote that: "In Aristotelian cosmology, ontology and logic . . . all quantitative determinations were relegated to the state of *accidents*, so that apprehension of them had no scientific standing. . . . Observe by contrast the place occupied by measuring in modern knowledge. Is it then credible that the logic of Greek knowledge has relevance to the logic of modern knowledge?"[8] But the Aristotelian notion of essence can admit of quantitative determination, as is suggested by Aristotle himself in admitting ratio as essence.[9] Hence I do not think that this criticism of Dewey's can be regarded as any more decisive than that of Miss Stebbing.

Having set forth in outline an Aristotelian philosophy of essence and accident, I propose next to examine what I consider to be the most serious objection that has been raised against it. According to this criticism, the distinction between essence and accident is not an objective or intrinsic one between genuinely different types of attributes. Attributes are really all of the same basic kind, it is said, and the alleged distinction between essence and accident is simply a projection of differences in human interests or a reflection of peculiarities of vocabulary. Let us try to understand this criticism in as sympathetic a fashion as we can.

The distinction between different kinds of change,

[7] *A Modern Introduction to Logic*, p. 433.
[8] *Logic: The Theory of Inquiry*, pp. 89–90.
[9] 993a17–20.

on this view, is subjective rather than objective. We happen to be interested, usually, in some attributes of a thing more than in others. When the thing changes, we say that it persists through the change provided that it does not lose those attributes by whose possession it satisfies our interests. For example, our interest in tables is for the most part independent of their colors. Hence that interest remains satisfiable by a given table regardless of any alteration it may suffer with respect to color. Paint a brown table green, and it remains substantially or essentially the same; the change was only an accidental one. If our interests were different, the same objective fact would be classified quite differently. Were our interest to lie in *brown* tables exclusively, then the application of green paint would destroy the object of our interest, would change it substantially or essentially from something which satisfied our interest to something which did not. The implication is that attributes are neither essential nor accidental in themselves, but can be so classified only on the basis of our subjective interests in them. Dewey stated this point of view very succinctly, writing: "As far as present logical texts still continue to talk about essences, properties and accidents as something inherently different from one another, they are repeating distinctions that once had an ontological meaning and that no longer have it. Anything is 'essential' which is indispensable in a given inquiry and anything is 'accidental' which is superfluous."[10]

The present criticism lends itself easily to reformulation in more language-oriented terms. That we regard a table as essentially the same despite alteration in color or movement from place to place is a consequence of the peculiar nature and limitations of our vocabulary, which has a single word for tables, regardless of color, but lacks special words for tables of dif-

[10]Op. cit., p. 138.

ferent colors. Suppose that our language contained no word for tables in general, but had instead—say—the word "towble" for brown table and the word "teeble" for green table. Then the application of green paint to a towble would be said to change it essentially, it might be argued, for no towble would remain; in its place would appear a teeble. Or if there were a single word which applied indiscriminately to tables and heaps of ashes, say "tashble," with no special substantive denoting either of them univocally, then perhaps the destruction of a table by fire would not be regarded as an essential change. That which appeared at the end of the process would admittedly be in a different state from what was there at the start, but it would still be identifiably the same tashble. C. I. Lewis regards the difference between essence and accident to be strictly relative to vocabulary, writing: "Traditionally any attribute required for application of a term is said to be of the essence of the thing named. It is, of course, meaningless to speak of the essence of a thing except relative to its being named by a particular term."[11]

I think that for our purpose these two criticisms can be regarded as variants of a single basic one, for the connection between human interests and human vocabulary is a very intimate one. It is an anthropological and linguistic commonplace that the concern of a culture with a given phenomenon is reflected in the vocabulary of that culture, as in the several Eskimo words which denote subtly different kinds of snow. In our own culture new interests lead continually to innovations in vocabulary; and surely it is the decline of interest in certain things that leads to the obsolescence of words used to refer to them.

Both variants of this criticism were formulated long ago by Locke, and developed at considerable length in his *Essay.* Locke paid comparatively little attention

[11]*An Analysis of Knowledge and Valuation,* p. 41.

to the problem of change, but where he did discuss it his treatment was very similar to Aristotle's. Thus we are assured in the *Essay* that: ". . . an oak growing from a plant to a great tree, and then lopped, is still the same oak; and a colt grown up to a horse, sometimes fat, sometimes lean, is all the while the same horse. . . ."[12] The oak ". . . continues to be the same plant as long as it partakes of the same life . . ."[13] and the identity of animals is explained in similar terms. Personal identity is explained in terms of sameness of consciousness.[14] If we ignore the Cartesian dualism implicit in that last case, and if we are not too critical of the reappearance of the term "same" in the explanation of *sameness*, we can recognize these answers to be the Aristotelian ones, for according to Aristotle the soul is the principle of life,[15] the life of a plant is the nutritive soul,[16] that of an animal its sensitive soul,[17] and that of man his rational soul,[18] these souls constituting the substantial forms or essences of the respective substances.[19] On the other hand, in his brief discussion of identity as applied to non-living things, Locke construes it very strictly to apply only to things which ". . . vary not at all. . . ."[20] But the following passage has a characteristically Aristotelian flavor: "Thus that which was grass to-day, is to-morrow the flesh of a sheep; and within a few days after becomes part of a man: in all which, and the like changes, it is evident their real essence, i.e. that constitution,

---

[12]Bk. 2, ch. 27, §3.
[13]Ibid.
[14]Bk. 2, ch. 27, §8, §9, §10, §16, §17, §23.
[15]*De Anima* 402a6, 415b8.
[16]432a29, 434a22–26; cf. also *De Plantis* 815b28–34.
[17]432a30.
[18]*Politics* 1332b5.
[19]*De Anima* 412a20, 412b13, 415b10.
[20]Bk. 2, ch. 27, §1.

whereon the properties of these several things depended, is destroyed, and perishes with them."[21]

Despite this partial similarity of their views, the bases for distinguishing between the essential properties and other properties of a thing are very different for Locke than for Aristotle. For Aristotle, the distinction is twofold: first, the essential properties of an object are those which are retained by it during any change through which the object remains identifiably the same object; and second, the essential properties of an object are most important in our scientific knowledge of it. For Locke, on the other hand, the *real* essence of a thing is a set of properties which *determine* all the other properties of that thing.[22] Since all other properties depend on its real essence, any change in an object entails a change in its real essence. Hence for Locke the essential properties of an object are not retained by it during any change. This view is very different from Aristotle's, on which the accidents of a thing are not bound to its essence but can change independently of it. The epistemological difference is equally striking. Whereas for Aristotle all scientific knowledge is knowledge of the essence, for Locke there is no knowledge of the real essences of things.[23]

Locke was more interested in what he called "nominal essences," which are more nearly analogous to the Aristotelian notion of essence. Our idea of a particular substance, according to Locke, is a complex idea composed of a number of simple ideas which are noticed to "go constantly together," plus the notion of a substratum "wherein they do subsist."[24] A general or abstract idea of a sort or species of substance is made

[21]Bk. 3, ch. 4, §19. But cf. Bk. 3, ch. 6, §4, §5.
[22]Bk. 3, ch. 3, §15.
[23]Bk. 3, ch. 3, §15, §17, §18; ch. 6, §3, §6, §9, §12, §18, §49; ch. 9, §12; ch. 10, §18.
[24]Bk. 2, ch. 23, §1.

out of our complex ideas of various particular substances that resemble each other by leaving out "that which is peculiar to each" and retaining "only what is common to all."[25] Such an abstract idea *determines* a sort or species,[26] and is called a "nominal essence,"[27] for "every thing contained in that idea is essential to that sort."[28]

The properties contained in the nominal essence of a thing can be distinguished from the other properties of that thing on the same basis as that on which the Aristotelian essence is distinguished from accidents. In the first place, a particular substance of a given species can change with respect to some property whose idea is *not* included in the nominal essence of that species, and will continue to be recognizably the same thing; whereas it must be regarded as a quite different thing if it changes with respect to some property whose idea is included in the nominal essence.[29] And in the second place, the nominal essence is more important in knowledge than other properties. To have knowledge of a thing is to know what *sort* of thing it is, and to know the nominal essence is to know the sort. Locke says, moreover, that the leading qualities of a thing, that is, the most observable and hence, for Locke, the most knowable, are ingredient in the nominal essence.[30] Finally, it is argued in the *Essay* that knowledge of nominal essences is required if we are ever to be certain of the truth of any general proposition.[31] Since Locke's nominal essences play so similar a role to that of Aristotle's essences, Locke's arguments intended to prove their subjectivity and relativity to human interests and vocabulary can be interpreted as applying to Aristotle's notion as well as his own.

[25]Bk. 3, ch. 3, §7.   [29]Bk. 2, ch. 27, §28.
[26]Bk. 3, ch. 3, §12.   [30]Bk. 3, ch. 11, §20.
[27]Bk. 3, ch. 3, §15.   [31]Bk. 4, ch. 6, §4.
[28]Bk. 3, ch. 6, §2.

One fairly minor difference should be noted before going on. Since Locke's nominal essences are abstract *ideas*, they are immediately subjective in a way that Aristotle's essences are not. But that difference is not decisive, for substances may well have objective properties that nominal essences are ideas of, or objective powers that correspond to them exactly.[32]

Locke urges that essences are subjective in a less trivial sense. Since they are "inventions"[33] or the "workmanship"[34] of the understanding, different persons in fashioning abstract ideas which they signify by the same term can and do incorporate different simple ideas into them. Acts of choice or selection are involved here, and people do make different choices, as proved by the disputes that so frequently arise over whether particular bodies are of certain species or not.[35]

That essences are relative to vocabulary is argued by Locke in terms of an example: "A silent and a striking watch are but one species to those who have but one name for them: but he that has the name watch for one, and clock for the other, and distinct complex ideas, to which those names belong, to him they are different species."[36]

That the "... boundaries of species are as men, and not as nature, makes them ...,"[37] proved by the verbal disputes already referred to, is explained by the fact that since we have "... need of general names for present use ..."[38] we "... stay not for a perfect discovery of all those qualities which would best show us their most material differences and agreements; but we our-

[32]Bk. 2, ch. 23, §7.
[33]Bk. 3, ch. 3, §11.
[34]Bk. 3, ch. 3, §12, §13, §14.
[35]Bk. 3, ch. 3, § 14; ch. 6, § 26, § 27; ch. 9, § 16; ch. 10, § 22; ch. 11, §6, §7.
[36]Bk. 3, ch. 6, §39.
[37]Bk. 3, ch. 6, §30.
[38]Ibid.

selves divide them, by certain obvious appearances, into species...."[39] Nominal essences are made for use, and different intended uses or interests will determine different essences. Even the *noticing* of similarities between distinct particulars is relative to our interest in them, so our selection of simple ideas for inclusion in a nominal essence is relative to such interests. These determining interests are not scientific, for as Locke observed, "... languages, in all countries, have been established long before sciences."[40] The situation is rather that the terms of ordinary discourse "... have for the most part, in all languages, received their birth and signification from ignorant and illiterate people...."[41] And for the purposes or interests of those practical people, the properties selected by them as essential to the objects they deal with are adequate enough. For "Vulgar notions suit vulgar discourses; and both, though confused enough, yet serve pretty well the market and the wake."[42]

Now do these arguments succeed in establishing that the distinction between essence and accident is subjective rather than objective, that is, relative to human interests and vocabulary?

I think that the objections are not utterly destructive of the Aristotelian doctrine, although they do call attention to needed modifications of it. Locke's case, it seems to me, depends upon his distinction between real and nominal essences, and his belief that real essences are unknowable. But his doctrine that real essences cannot be known flows from two peculiarities of his philosophy, which I see no reason to accept. One of the bases for his belief that real essences are unknowable is his view that the only objects of our knowledge are the ideas that we have in our minds.[43] Locke's

[39]Ibid.   [42]Bk. 3, ch. 11, §10.
[40]Bk. 3, ch. 6, §25.   [43]Bk. 2, ch. 1, §1.
[41]Ibid.

other basis for his belief that real essences are unknowable is his doctrine that experiment and observation yield only "...judgment and opinion, not knowledge...."[44] Here the term "knowledge" is reserved for what is *certain*.

I would reject these two doctrines on the following grounds. The first of them, that knowledge is only of ideas, is the germ of scepticism. Locke's premisses lead necessarily to Hume's conclusions, and the partial scepticism we find explicitly set forth in Locke is but a fragment of the complete scepticism that Hume later showed to be implicitly contained there. It seems to me that if a philosophy denies the very possibility of scientific knowledge, then so much the worse for that philosophy. As for reserving the term "knowledge" for what is certain, that usage has but little to commend it. It seems more reasonable to accept the results of experiment and observation, although probable rather than demonstrative, as knowledge nonetheless.

It must be admitted that the doctrine of the unknowability of real essences was not an unreasonable conclusion to draw from the relatively undeveloped state of science in Locke's day. For chemistry, at least, if we can believe what is said of it in the *Essay*, was in a very bad way in the seventeenth century. Locke tells us of the "sad experience" of chemists "...when they, sometimes in vain, seek for the same qualities in one parcel of sulphur, antimony or vitriol, which they have found in others. For though they are bodies of the same species, having the same nominal essence, under the same name; yet do they often, upon severe ways of examination, betray qualities so different one from another, as to frustrate the expectations of very wary chemists."[45]

Contemporary science, however, presents a quite dif-

[44]Bk. 4, ch. 12, §10; cf. also Bk. 4, ch. 3, §28.
[45]Bk. 3, ch. 6, §8.

ferent picture. Locke characterized the (allegedly un-knowable) real essences of things as the "... constitution of their insensible parts; from which flow those sensible qualities, which serve us to distinguish them one from another...."[46] Now modern atomic theory is directly concerned with the insensible parts of things. Through the use of his Periodic Table, interpreted as dealing with atomic number and valency, "... Mendeléev was enabled to predict the existence *and properties ...*" of half a dozen elements whose existence had not been previously known or even suspected.[47] And other scientists have subsequently been able to make similar predictions. Modern science seeks to know the *real* essences of things, and its increasing successes seem to be bringing it progressively nearer to that goal.

It must be granted that Locke's distinction between real and nominal essence is a helpful one, even though it is not absolute. The construction of nominal essences is usually relative to practical interests, and the ordinary notion of the essence of a thing is relative to the words used in referring to it. I think that Locke (and Dewey and Lewis) are correct in that contention. Surely different interests lead different people to classify or sort things in different ways, and thus to adopt different nominal essences, the more permanently useful of which receive separate names in ordinary language. Thus it is that: "Merchants and lovers, cooks and taylors, have words wherewithal to dispatch their ordinary affairs...."[48]

The distinction, however, is not absolute. Not every interest is narrowly practical. The interest of the scientist is in knowledge and understanding. The scientist desires to know how things behave, and to account

[46]Bk. 3, ch. 3, §17.
[47]J. D. Main Smith, in the *Encyclopaedia Britannica* (14th ed.; 1947), Vol. 17, p. 520 (my italics).
[48]Bk. 3, ch. 11, §10.

for their behavior by means of explanatory hypotheses or theories which permit him to predict what will occur under specified conditions. He is interested in discovering general laws to which objects conform, and the causal relations which obtain among them. The scientist's sorting or classifying of objects is relative to this interest, which is not well served by classifying things on the basis of properties which are either most obvious or most immediately practical. It is better served by classifying things in terms of properties which are relevant to the framing of a maximum number of causal laws and the formulation of explanatory theories. Thus a foodstuff and a mineral source of aluminum, common salt and cryolite, are both classified by the chemist as sodium compounds, because in the context of modern chemical theory it is this common characteristic which is most significant for predicting and understanding the behavior of these substances. In the sphere of scientific inquiry, the distinction between real and nominal essence tends to disappear. The scientist's classification of things is intended to be in terms of their *real* essences. And here, too, the process is reflected in vocabulary, not necessarily or even usually in that of the man in the street, but rather in the technical jargon of the specialist.

The essences which science seeks to discover, then, are real essences rather than nominal ones. Since the arguments for subjectivity or relativity to interest or vocabulary were concerned with nominal rather than real essences, they simply do not apply to real essences as either Locke or Aristotle conceived them.

In one passage of his *Essay*, though, Locke does make the further claim that even a real essence relates to a sort and supposes a species.[49] But on Locke's own account of real essence, the real essence of a particular must be that set of its properties on which all of its

[49]Bk. 3, ch. 6, §6.

other properties depend. And that can be investigated independently of any sorting or classifying we may do —although once its real essence is discovered, that will determine how we should classify it scientifically if the occasion for doing so arises.

At this point let me indicate the direction in which I think the Aristotelian doctrine of essence and accident might well be modified. Aristotle definitely held that there could be no scientific knowledge of accidents,[50] but contemporary science would admit no such limitation. It seems to me that both Locke's and Aristotle's views about unknowability should be rejected. Contrary to Locke, I should hold that real essences are in principle knowable, and contrary to Aristotle, I should hold that non-essential or accidental properties can also be objects of scientific knowledge.

It seems to me also that neither Locke nor Aristotle gives a satisfactory account of the relationship between essence and accident. For Locke, all (other) properties of a thing depend on its "real constitution" or real essence[51]; but it is not clear whether the dependence is supposed to be causal or logico-deductive. The former is obviously the more acceptable doctrine. Aristotle, on the other hand, held that some properties of a thing, namely, its accidents, do not in any way depend upon its essence. I think that Locke's view, understood as asserting a causal dependence of accident on essence, is the more plausible one, and that the Aristotelian doctrine ought to be so modified as to accord with that of Locke in this respect.

Now if both essences and accidents are scientifically knowable, on what basis are they to be distinguished from each other? I suggest that the epistemological or methodological distinction is still valid. For example,

[50]1064b30–1065a25.
[51]Bk. 3, ch. 3, §18.

common salt has many properties, some more obvious than others, and some more important than others relative to different practical interests. The scientist singles out its being a compound of equal parts of sodium and chlorine as its essential nature. In doing so he surely does not mean to imply that its chemical constitution is more easily observed than its other properties, or more important to either cook, tailor, merchant, or lover. He classifies it as sodium chloride because, within the context of his theory, that property is fundamental. From its chemical formula more of its properties can be inferred than could be from any other. Since the connection is causal rather than logical, the inference from essence to accident must make use of causal law premises or modes of inference as well as strictly logical ones. Hence to derive conclusions about *all* accidental properties of a substance, we should need to know both its real essence and all relevant causal laws. That is an ideal towards which science strives, rather than its present achievement, of course. To the extent to which one small group of properties of a substance can serve as a basis from which its other properties can be causally derived, to that extent we can be justified in identifying that group of properties as its real essence. This view, it should be noted, is in agreement with Aristotle's doctrine that the definition of a thing should state its essence,[52] and that definition is a scientific process.[53]

There is a certain relativity implied in this account, although it is quite different from those previously discussed. Our *notion* of what constitutes the real essence of a thing is relative to the science of our day. Centuries hence, wiser men will have radically different and more adequate theories, and their notions will be closer approximations than ours to the real essences

[52] 91a1, 101b21, 38.
[53] 1039b32.

of things. But it will still be the real essences of things that are destined to be known by Peirce's ultimate community of knowers.

There is one other and more radical sense of accident that I would agree to be relative. Each separate science is concerned with only some of the properties or aspects of things which it studies. Those left out will be accidental relative to the special science which ignores them. They will not be derivable from what that science considers to be the real essences of those things, although a different special science might be much concerned with them, and even include them in *its* notion of the thing's real essence. But as (and if) the sciences become more unified, no properties of a thing will be wholly accidental in this sense, and all will be causally derivable from the real essence.

In closing, I should like to refer once again to the topic of change. If all of a thing's properties depend on its real essence, then it would seem to follow that every change is an essential one. In my opinion, that unwelcome conclusion can be evaded in two ways. In the first place, with respect to common-sense, practical usage, our ordinary sortings will continue to be based on nominal rather than real essences, so that changes can continue to be classified as accidental or essential in the traditional way. And in the second place, with respect to scientific usage, we can say the following. The real essence of a thing will consist very largely of powers or, in modern terms, dispositional properties. An essential change in a thing will involve the replacement of some of its dispositions or powers by other dispositions or powers. But a change which is nonessential or accidental would involve no such replacement; it would rather consist in differently actualized manifestations of the same dispositional property or power. Unfortunately, lack of space prevents an adequate development of this suggestion.

ΤΙΘΈΝΑΙ ΤΑ ΦΑΙΝΌΜΕΝΑ

G. E. L. OWEN

The first part of this paper tries to account for an apparent discrepancy between Aristotle's preaching and his practice on a point of method. The second part reinforces the first by suggesting a common source for many of the problems and methods found in the *Physics*.

I

There seems to be a sharp discrepancy between the methods of scientific reasoning recommended in the *Analytics* and those actually followed in the *Physics*. The difference is sometimes taken to lie in the fact that the *Posterior Analytics* pictures a science as a formal deductive system based on necessary truths whereas the *Physics* is more tentative and hospitable both in its premises and in its methods. But this is too simple a contrast. It is true that for much of the *Physics* Aristotle is not arguing from the definitions of his basic terms but constructing those definitions. He sets out to clarify and harden such common ideas as change and motion, place and time, infinity and continuity, and in doing so he claims to be defining

From *Aristote et les problèmes de la méthode* (Symposium Aristotelicum; Louvain, 1961), pp. 83–103. Reprinted by permission of the author and Editions Nauwelaerts, S.P.R.L., Louvain.

his subject matter.[1] But after all the *Analytics* shows interest not only in the finished state of a science but in its essential preliminaries; it describes not only the rigorous deduction of theorems but the setting up of the ἀρχαί, the set of special hypotheses and definitions, from which the deductions proceed. And the *Physics*, for its part, not only establishes the definitions of its basic concepts but uses them to deduce further theorems, notably in books VI and VIII. The discrepancy between the two works lies rather in the fact that, whereas the *Analytics* tries (though not without confusion and inconsistency) to distinguish the two processes of finding and then applying the principles, the *Physics* takes no pains to hold them apart. But there seems to be a more striking disagreement than this. It concerns the means by which the principles of the science are reached.

In the *Prior Analytics* Aristotle says: "It falls to experience to provide the principles of any subject. In astronomy, for instance, it was astronomical experience that provided the principles of the science, for it was only when the *phainomena* were adequately grasped that the proofs in astronomy were discovered. And the same is true of any art or science whatever."[2] Elsewhere he draws the same Baconian picture: the *phainomena* must be collected as a prelude to finding the theory which explains them. The method is expressly associated with φυσική and the φυσικός,[3] and from the stock example in these contexts—astronomy—it seems clear

[1]*Phs.* III 1, 200b12–21.

[2]*An. Pr.* I 30, 46a17–22: διὸ τὰς μὲν ἀρχὰς περὶ ἕκαστον ἐμπειρίας ἐστὶ παραδοῦναι, λέγω δ' οἷον τὴν ἀστρολογικὴν μὲν ἐμπειρίαν τῆς ἀστρολογικῆς ἐπιστήμης (ληφθέντων γὰρ ἱκανῶς τῶν φαινομένων οὕτως εὑρέθησαν αἱ ἀστρολογικαὶ ἀποδείξεις), ὁμοίως δὲ καὶ περὶ ἄλλην ὁποιανοῦν ἔχει τέχνην τε καὶ ἐπιστήμην.

[3]*De Part. Anim.* I 1, 639b5–10 with 640a13–15; *De Caelo* III 7, 306a5–17.

that the *phainomena* in question are empirical observations.[4] Now such a method is plainly at home in the biological works and the meteorology;[5] equally plainly it is not at home in the *Physics*, where as Mgr. Mansion observes "tout s'y réduit en général à des analyses plus ou moins poussées de concepts,—analyses guidées souvent et illustrées par des données de l'expérience, plutôt qu'appuyées sur celle-ci."[6] In this sense of "*phainomena*" it would be grossly misleading for Aristotle to claim that he is establishing the principles of his physics upon a survey of the *phainomena*. And there his critics are often content to leave the matter.

But in other contexts similarly concerned with methods of enquiry "*phainomena*" has another sense.[7] In the *Nicomachean Ethics* Aristotle prefaces his discussion of incontinence with the words: "Here as in other cases we must set down the *phainomena* and begin by considering the difficulties, and so go on to vindicate if possible all the common conceptions about these states of mind, or at any rate most of them and the most important."[8] Here Sir David Ross translates φαινόμενα by "observed facts," a translation evidently designed to bring Aristotle's programme into conform-

---

[4] Cf. further *An. Po.* I 13, 78b39 with 79a2–6; *De Caelo* II 13, 293a23–30; 14, 297a2–6; *Met.* A 8, 1073b32–38; Bonitz, *Index*, 809a34 ff.

[5] *De Part. Anim.* II 1, 646a8–12, referring to *Hist. Anim.* I 7, 491a7–14; *Meteor.* III 2, 371b18–22 with Olympiodorus' scholium (217.23–27 Stueve. Olympiodorus' reference to *De Gen. et Corr.* is to I 5, not II 8 as Stueve and Ideler think).

[6] *Introduction à la physique aristolélicienne*[2], p. 211.

[7] There is a temptation to distinguish this sense as what φαίνεται εἶναι by contrast with what φαίνεται ὄν. But this overstates the difference; see pp. 174–76 below. Aristotle is ready to use φαίνεσθαι with the infinitive even of empirical observations, *De An.* I 5, 411b19–22.

[8] *NE* VII 1, 1145b2–6:   δεῖ δ', ὥσπερ ἐπὶ τῶν ἄλλων, τιθέντας τὰ φαινόμενα καὶ πρῶτον διαπορήσαντας οὕτω δεικνύναι μάλιστα μὲν πάντα τὰ ἔνδοξα περὶ ταῦτα τὰ πάθη, εἰ δὲ μή, τὰ πλεῖστα καὶ κυριώτατα.

ity with such passages as those already cited. But this
can hardly be its sense here. For, in the first place,
what Aristotle proceeds to set out are not the observed
facts but the ἔνδοξα, the common conceptions on the
subject (as the collocation of φαινόμενα and ἔνδοξα
in his preface would lead us to expect). He concludes
his survey with the words τὰ μὲν οὖν λεγόμενα ταῦτ᾽
ἐστίν,[9] and the λεγόμενα turn out as so often to be
partly matters of linguistic usage or, if you prefer, of
the conceptual structure revealed by language.[10] And,
secondly, after this preliminary survey Aristotle turns
to Socrates' claim that those who act against their
own conviction of what is best do so in ignorance, and
says that this is plainly in conflict with the *phainomena*.[11] But he does not mean that, as Ross translates it,
"the view plainly contradicts the observed facts." For
he remarks later that his own conclusion about incontinence seems to coincide with what Socrates wanted
to maintain,[12] and in reaching it he takes care to answer the question that he had named as a difficulty
for Socrates, namely what kind of ignorance must be
ascribed to the incontinent man.[13] So Socrates' claim
conflicts not with the facts but with what would commonly be said on the subject, and Aristotle does not
undertake to save everything that is commonly said.
He is anxious, unlike Socrates, to leave a use for the
expression "knowing what is right but doing what is
wrong," but he is ready to show a priori that there
is no use for the expression "doing what is wrong in
the full knowledge of what is right *in the given circumstances*."[14] It is in the same sense of the word that

[9]Ibid. 2, 1145b8–20.
[10]Especially Ibid. 1145b10–15, 19–20.
[11]NE VII 3, 1145b27–28.
[12]Ibid. 5, 1147b14–15.
[13]Ibid. 3, 1145b28–29; 5, 1147b15–17.
[14]Ibid. 5, 1146b35–1147a10, 1147a24–b14. But Ross's translation of φαινόμενα in the two passages 1, 1145b3 and 3,

all dialectical argument can be said to start from the phainomena.[15]

This ambiguity in φαινόμενα, which was seen by Alexander,[16] carries with it a corresponding distinction in the use of various connected expressions. Ἐπαγωγή can be said to establish the principles of science by starting from the data of perception.[17] Yet ἐπαγωγή is named as one of the two cardinal methods of dialectic[18] and as such must begin from the ἔνδοξα, what is accepted by all or most men or by the wise;[19] and in this form too it can be used to find the principles of the sciences.[20] Similarly with the ἀπορίαι. When the φαινόμενα are empirical data such as those collected in the biology and meteorology, the ἀπορίαι associated with them will tend to be questions of empirical fact[21] or of the explanation of such facts,[22] or the problem of squaring a recalcitrant fact with an empirical hypothesis.[23] In the discussion of incontinence, on the other hand, where the φαινόμενα are things that men are inclined or accustomed to say on

---

[15] 1145b28 is at any rate consistent and so superior to that adopted by most scholars from Heliodorus to Gauthier-Jolif, who see that at its first occurrence the word must mean ἔνδοξα (τοὺς δοκοῦντας περὶ αὐτῶν λόγους. Heliodorus *Paraphr.* 131.16 Heylbut) but suppose that at its occurrence 25 lines later it means the unquestionable facts (τοῖς φανεροῖς, ibid. 137.29–30).

[15]*An. Pr.* I 1, 24b10–12; *Top.* VIII 5, 159b17–23. Cf. *Ph.* IV 1, 208a32–34, where the *phainomenon* is the theory as contrasted with the facts (τὰ ὑπάρχοντα). At *De Caelo* II 5, 288a1–2; 12, 291b25; IV 1, 308a6; *De Part. Anim.* I 5, 645a5, it is the speaker's own view.

[16]*Meteor.* 33.6–9 Stueve.

[17]*An. Po.* II 19, 100b3–5; I 18, 81a38–b9.

[18]*Top.* I 12, 105a10–19.

[19]*Top.* I 1, 100b21–23.

[20]*Top.* I 2, 101a36–b4.

[21]*Meteor.* II 3, 357b26–30.

[22]*Meteor.* I 13, 349a12–14 with a 31-b2; II 5, 362a11–13; *De long. et brev vitae* 1, 464b21–30; *De Gen. Anim.* IV 4, 770b 28–30 with 771a14–17; *Hist. Anim.* VI 37, 580b14–17.

[23]*Meteor.* II 2, 355b20–32.

the subject, the ἀπορίαι that Aristotle sets out are not unexplained or recalcitrant data of observation but logical or philosophical puzzles generated, as such puzzles have been at all times, by exploiting some of the things commonly said. Two of the paradoxes are veterans, due to Socrates and the sophists.[24] The first of the set ends with the words "If so, we shall have to say that the man of practical wisdom is incontinent, *but no one would say this*" (not that it happens to be false, but that given the established use of the words it is absurd).[25] The last ends "But we say (i.e. it is a common form of words) that some men are incontinent, without further qualification."[26]

Now if the *Physics* is to be described as setting out from a survey of the φαινόμενα it is plainly this second sense of the word that is more appropriate. Take as an example the analysis of place. It opens with four arguments for the existence of place of which the first states what δοκεῖ (it appeals to established ways of talking about physical replacement),[27] the third states what certain theorists λέγουσι,[28] the fourth quotes what Hesiod and the majority νομίζουσι,[29] and the remaining one relies on the doctrine of natural places which is later taken as an ἔνδοξον. [30] Of the ἀπορίαι which follow, one is due to Zeno, one is due to an equally rich source of logical paradoxes of which I shall say more in a later section, and all ultimately depend on the convictions or usage of the many or the wise. Nor are these arguments merely accessory to the main

[24]*NE* VII 3, 1145b23–27, 1146a21–31.
[25]Ibid. 1146a5–7.
[26]Ibid. 1146b4–5.
[27]*Ph.* IV 1, 208b1, 5.
[28]Ibid. 208b26.
[29]Ibid. 208b32–33.
[30]*Ph.* IV 1, 208b8–25; 4, 211a4–6 with Ross's note on 5, 212b29–34 (*Aristotle's Physics*, p. 580).

analysis: those of the δοκοτῦνα which survive the preliminary difficulties are taken over as premises for what follows.[31] "For if the difficulties are resolved and the ἔνδοξα are left standing," as Aristotle says in both the *Physics* and the *Ethics*, "this in itself is a sufficient proof."[32] As for ἐπαγωγή, when it is used in the argument it proves to be not a review of observed cases but a dialectical survey of the senses of the word "in."[33]

By such arguments the *Physics* ranks itself not with physics, in our sense of the word, but with philosophy. Its data are for the most part the materials not of natural history but of dialectic, and its problems are accordingly not questions of empirical fact but conceptual puzzles. Now this reading of the work is strikingly reinforced, as it seems to me, when we recognize the influence of one other work in particular on the argument of the *Physics*. In a following section of this paper I shall try to show that in the *Physics* Aristotle over and again takes his start, not from his own or others' observations, but from a celebrated set of logical paradoxes that may well have appeared during his own early years in the Academy. Far more than that overmined quarry the *Timaeus*, it is the *Parmenides* which supplies Aristotle in the *Physics* not only with many and perhaps most of his central problems but with the terminology and methods of analysis that he uses to resolve them. But before turning to this evidence let us see whether we are yet in a position to explain the discrepancy from which we set out.

[31]*Ph.* IV 4, 210b32–211a7. Thus for instance the common conception of place as a container which is not part of what it contains (1, 208b1–8; 2, 209b28–30) must be rescued from Zeno's puzzle (1, 209a23–26; 3, 210b22–27) by a survey of the senses of "this is in that" (3, 210a14 ff.) and can then be taken as secure (4, 210b34–211al).

[32]*NE* VII 1, 1145b6–7; *Ph.* IV 4, 211a7–11. The verb for proof in each case is δεικνύναι.

[33]*Ph.* IV 3, 210b8–9 (ἐπακτικῶς σκοποῦσιν) with 210a14–24.

Can we appeal to this ambiguity in Aristotle's terminology in order to explain how such a generaliza-
tion as that quoted from the *Prior Analytics* could be
taken to cover the methods of the *Physics*? By now
the ambiguity seems too radical for our purpose. Even
within the second sense of φαινόμενα, the sense in
which it is equated with ἔνδοξα and λεγόμενα, some
essential distinctions lie concealed. For an appeal to a
λεγόμενον may be an appeal either to common belief
about matters of fact[34] or to established forms of language[35] or to a philosophical thesis claiming the factual virtues of the first and the analytic certainty of
the second.[36] And the broader ambiguity between the
two senses of the word was one which Aristotle himself had the means to expose. For when he wishes to
restrict φαινόμενον to its first sense he calls it expressly
a *perceptual* φαινόμενον and distinguishes it from an
ἔνδοξον.[37] And in the *De Caelo* it is this more precise
form of words that he uses to describe the criterion by
which the correctness of our principles in physics must
ultimately be assessed.[38]

I think such considerations show that it is a mistake
to ask, in the hope of some quite general answer, what
function Aristotle assigns to φαινόμενα, or to ἀπορίαι,
or to ἐπαγωγή; or they show how the function can
vary with the context and style of enquiry. But we
have pressed them too hard if they prevent us from
understanding how Aristotle could have taken the formula in the *Analytics* to apply to the *Physics* as well
as to the *Historia Animalium*. If there is more than one
use for the expression φαινόμενα, the uses have a
great deal in common. Thus for example it is not a

[34]E.g. *NE* I 11, 1101a22–24.
[35]E.g. Ibid. VII 2, 1145b19–20; 3, 1146b4–5.
[36]E.g. Ibid. I 8, 1098b12–18.
[37] τῶν φαινομένων κατὰ τὴν αἴσθησιν, *De Caelo* III 4, 303a
22–23.
[38]Ibid. 7, 306a16–17.

peculiarity of φαινόμενα in the second sense that they may fail to stand up to examination; for so may the φαινόμενα of perception,[39] and within this latter class Aristotle is careful to specify only the reliable members as a touchstone for the correctness of physical principles.[40] As for his favourite example, astronomy, Aristotle knew (or came to realize) how inadequate were the observations of the astronomers.[41] And of the biological "observations" many were bound to be hearsay, λεγόμενα, to be treated with caution.[42] Such φαινόμενα must be "properly established," ascertained to be "true data."[43] In the same fashion the ἔνδοξα must pass the appropriate scrutiny, but in doing so they too become firm data.[44] Nor, if Aristotle associates the φαινόμενα with ἐμπειρία, as he does in the text from the *Analytics*, must it be supposed that his words are meant to apply only to φαινόμενα in the first sense. Ἔνδοξα also rest on experience, even if they misrepresent it.[45] If they did not Aristotle could find no place for them in his epistemology; as it is, an ἔνδοξον that is shared by all men is *ipso facto* beyond challenge.[46]

Nor is it in the least surprising if Aristotle, writing in the tradition of Parmenides and Protagoras, tended to assimilate these different senses of φαινόμενα.

[39]*De Caelo* II 8, 290a13–24 and esp. *Met.* Γ 5, 1010b1–11. (On Protagoras cf. p. 176 below.)

[40]*De Caelo* III 17, 306a16–17: τὸ φαινόμενον ἀεὶ κυρίως κατὰ τὴν αἴσθησιν, "the perceptual *phainomenon* that is reliable when it occurs," *not*, as Tricot translates, "l'évidence toujours souveraine de la perception sensible": for κυρίως here cf. *Met.* Γ 5, 1010b14–19.

[41]*De Part. Anim.* I 5, 644b24–28.

[42]E.g. *Hist. Anim.* II 1, 501a25–b1.

[43]*An. Pr.* I 30, 46a20, 25.

[44]*Ph.* IV 4, 210b32–34, 211a7–11, *NE* VII 1, 1145b6–7.

[45]E.g. *De Div. per Som.* 1, 462b14–18.

[46]*NE* X 2, 1172b36–1173a1; cf. VII 14, 1153b27–28, *EE* I 6, 1216b26–35.

176   G. E. L. Owen

For Parmenides, the δόξαι βροτεῖαι include not only
the supposed evidence of the senses but the common
assumptions (and specifically the common uses of
language) which form men's picture of the physical
world.⁴⁷ As for Protagoras, both Plato and Aristotle
represent his theory as applying indifferently to perceptual phenomena and ἔνδοξα, and use φαίνεσθαι
in describing both these applications.⁴⁸ It is the same
broad use of the word that is to be found in the formula from the *Prior Analytics*. In the *De Caelo*, it is
true, Aristotle observes that it is the φαινόμενα of
perception by which we must ultimately test the adequacy of our principles in physics;⁴⁹ but this is said of
φυσική as a whole, a body of science in which the
analyses of the *Physics* proper are preliminary to other
more empirical enquiries and consequently must be
justified, in the last resort, by their success in making
sense of the observations to which they are applied.
But this is not to say (and it does not commit Aristotle
to supposing) that in the *Physics* proper the analyses
either start from or are closely controlled by our inspections of the world. Nor in fact is he liable to consider his analyses endangered by such inspections: if
his account of motion shows that any unnatural movement requires an agent of motion in constant touch
with the moving body, the movement of a thrown
ball can be explained by inventing a set of unseen
agents to fill the gap.⁵⁰ The *phainomena* to which the
Physics pays most attention are the familiar data of
dialectic, and from the context in the *Prior Analytics*
it seems clear that Aristotle's words there are meant
to cover the use of such data. For in concluding the

⁴⁷A conflation helped by talking as though data of perception
were themselves arbitrary assumptions (B 8, 38–41 Diels-Kranz).
On the "common uses of language" see B 8, 53; B 9; B 8, 38.
⁴⁸*Crat.* 386a1; *Met.* Γ 5, 1010b1, 1009a38–b2.
⁴⁹*De Caelo* III 7, 306a16–17.
⁵⁰*Ph.* VIII 10, 266b27–267a20.

passage and the discussion in which it occurs Aristotle observes that he has been talking at large about the ways in which the premises of deductive argument are to be chosen; and he refers for a more detailed treatment of the same matter to the "treatise on dialectic."[51] He evidently has in mind the claim made in the *Topics* that the first premises of scientific argument can be established by methods which start from the ἔνδοξα.[52]

II

I turn to the part played by the *Parmenides*, and specifically by the arguments in which "Aristotle" is the interlocutor, in shaping the *Physics*. Perhaps it is by misreading the *Physics* as a confused and cross-bred attempt at empirical science that critics have been led to look for its antecedents elsewhere and so to make excessive claims for its originality. So it is worth dwelling on this particular Platonic influence, partly for the light that it throws on the methods and interests of Aristotle's work, partly to call in question the claim that "the discussions in books III–VI . . . attack a series of problems for which there was little in Plato's teaching to prepare the way,"[53] and partly to establish, if this needs establishing, that the *Parmenides* was not read by the Academy either as a joke or as a primer of fallacies.[54] What the positive aims of the dialogue

[51]*An. Pr.* I 30, 46a28–30.

[52]*Top.* I 2, 101a36–b4. Ross seems to mistake the sense of the *An. Pr.* text (46a28–30) when he writes: "It is of course only the selection of premises of *dialectical* reasoning that is discussed in the *Topics*; the nature of the premises of scientific reasoning is discussed in the *Posterior Analytics*" (*Aristotle's Prior and Posterior Analytics*, p. 396). But in this passage Aristotle is concerned with finding the principles of scientific reasoning, and must be thinking of the claim made in the *Topics* to find such principles dialectically.

[53]Ross, *Aristotle's Physics*, p. 9.

[54]In this respect what follows can be read as complementary

may have been does not concern us; the present enquiry is a necessary preliminary to settling such questions.

Consider the celebrated account of the point. It is Plato in the *Parmenides* who argues first that what is indivisible (viz. the One, which cannot be plural and so has no parts) cannot have a location. For to have a location is to have surroundings i.e. to be contained in something; and this is to be contained either in something other than oneself or in oneself. But to be contained in something other than oneself is to have a circumference and to be in contact with that other thing at various points, and an indivisible thing cannot have various points or a circumference distinct from its centre. Nor can a thing without parts be contained in itself, for this would entail dividing it into container and contained, and no such division of it is possible. "Hence it is not anywhere, since it is neither in itself nor in another."[55] This concept of place as surroundings is normal in Greek philosophy, as the arguments of Zeno and Gorgias show (and in ordinary conversation, which has small use for plotting objects by Cartesian co-ordinates, it still is so). Aristotle took it over as an ἔνδοξον and made a more sophisticated version of it in the fourth book of the *Physics*. And one problem that he raises at the start of his argument depends on the assumption that if a point has any location it must be its own location, an assumption that flatly conflicts with the received view that place is a container distinct from the thing contained.[56] Aristotle does not argue the assumption; plainly he is drawing on Plato's argument that an indivisible cannot be contained in something else, nor yet can there be any distinction within it between container and

---

to Professor D. J. Allan's essay in *Aristotle and Plato in the Mid-fourth Century* (*Aristotle and the Parmenides*).

[55] *Parm.* 138a2–b6 (Burnet's lineation). The lack of shape and circumference is proved in 137d8–138a1.

[56] *Ph.* IV 1, 209a7–13.

contained. And he concludes that a point cannot be said to have a location.[57]

On the way to this conclusion, and as a preface to his general account of place, he lists the different senses in which one thing can be said to be in another,[58] and follows this with an argument to show that a thing cannot be said to be in itself except in the loose sense that it may be a whole having parts present in it.[59] This sense is sharply distinguished from the "strictest sense of all," that in which a thing is said to be in a place.[60] Why does he spend so much time on this? Because of further arguments in the *Parmenides*. Having maintained, in the first arm of his argument about the One, that an indivisible cannot be contained in itself, Plato goes on in the second arm to reduce his subject to a whole of parts and so, by dubious steps, to reimport the notion of place. For (a) since the subject is in itself in the sense that all its parts are contained in it,[61] it is always "in the same thing," i.e. in the same place and hence at rest;[62] and (b) since the subject is not in itself, in the sense that as a whole it is not contained in any or all of its parts, it must be always in something else[63] and so never at rest.[64] Among other eccentricities, the argument clearly relies on (and I think is clearly out to expose) an ambiguity in the form of expression "being in so-and-so": it shows that any sense of the phrase in which a thing can be said to be in itself cannot be the appropriate sense for talking of location, otherwise paradoxes result. Anaxagoras had traded on this ambiguity,[65] and no doubt

[57]*Ph.* IV 5, 212b24–25.
[58]*Ph.* IV 3, 210a14–24.
[59]Ibid. 210a25–b22.
[60]Ibid. 210a24.
[61]*Parm.* 145b6–c7.
[62]*Parm.* 145e7–146a3.
[63]*Parm.* 145e7–e3.
[64]*Parm.* 146a3–6.
[65]*Ph.* III 5, 205b1–5.

Plato wrote with Anaxagoras in mind; but that Aristotle's arguments are framed primarily with a view to those of the Parmenides is shown by the fact that he mentions Anaxagoras' thesis not in this context but elsewhere and by the clear echoes of Plato's language in his own.[66]

Points, then, cannot have location. And it is Plato who first proves the corollary, that something without parts cannot be said to move. But his reason is not just that what has no location cannot be said to change location. It is that to move to a certain place is a process, and there must be some intermediate stage of the process at which the moving body has arrived partly but not altogether.[67] And it is just this argument that Aristotle in the Physics takes over and generalizes, so that it applies to other forms of change besides locomotion.[68] Again, Plato prefaces his proof that an indivisible thing cannot change place by showing that it cannot even rotate in one place, since rotation entails a distinction between a centre and other parts;[69] and with this in mind Aristotle prefaces his argument by noticing the case in which a point might be said to move if it were part of a rotating body, but only because the whole body, which has a distinct centre and circumference, can be said to move in the strict sense.[70] Since it is often mistakenly said that Aristotle accepted the

[66]E.g. Ph. IV 3, 210a25–26 = Parm. 145d7–e1; Ph. IV 3, 210a27–29 = Parm. 145c4–7. Notice too that by μέρη here Plato means attributes of the subject, i.e. its being and unity and their derivatives (cf. 142d1–5); and that in the corresponding context of the Physics Aristotle corrects this use of the word by pointing out that attributes may be contained κατὰ μέρη in the subject not as being μέρη themselves (which he rejects, Cat. 2, 1a24–25) but as being attributes of μέρη (Ph. IV 3, 210a29–30).
[67]Parm. 138d2–e7.
[68]Ph. VI 10, 240b8–241a6.
[69]Parm. 138c7–d2.
[70]Ph. VI 10, 240b15–20.

definition of a line as the path of a moving point,[71] it is worth stressing how thoroughly he accepts Plato's reduction of this idea to absurdity—a *reductio* which no doubt counted as part of Plato's "war against the whole class of points."[72]

Again, consider the account of a connected concept, continuity. In the *Parmenides* Plato defines "contact" (ἅπτεσθαι) in terms of "succession" (ἐφεξῆς) and "neighbouring position" (ἐχομένη χώρα).[73] These terms Aristotle takes up in the fifth book of the *Physics*. "Contact" he defines as holding between terms whose extremities are together, i.e. in one and the same place;[74] an unhappy suggestion, since in themselves extremities can have no magnitude and so no position. And then, changing Plato's order of definition, he defines "neighbouring" (ἐχόμενον) in terms of "contact" and "succession."[75] From both accounts, it is clear, the same implication can be derived: Plato, by defining contact in terms of neighbouring position, and Aristotle, by defining it in terms of things having *extremities*, preclude the attempt to talk of a series of points as having contact with each other and so making up a line or any other magnitude. But this result only follows from Plato's definition if it is coupled with the argument that an indivisible thing cannot have position; and no doubt it was this that determined

[71]E.g. by Heath, *Mathematics in Aristotle*, p. 117; he cites *De An*, I 4, 409a4–5, where Aristotle is reporting someone else's theory. Of other passages which seem to imply this view *Ph*. IV 11, 219b16–20 can be read otherwise and *Ph*. V 4, 227b16–17 may represent an objector's view. But Aristotle does inconsistently credit points with location at *An. Po*. I 27, 87a36; 32; 88a33–34; *Met*. Δ 6, 1016b25–26, 30–31, and perhaps with the possibility of being in contact at *Ph*. V 3, 227a27–30 (but this seems to depend on the unaristotelian thesis in lines 27–28).

[72]*Met*. Α 9, 992a19–22.

[73]*Parm*. 148e7–10.

[74]*Ph*. V 3, 226b23. "Together" (ἅμα) is defined in 226b 21–22.

[75]*Ph*. V 3, 227a6–7.

Aristotle to reform the definition so that the conclusion would follow directly from the simple premiss that a point has no parts or extremities. This reordering of the definition would not have served Plato's purpose, for in this particular chain of reasoning in the *Parmenides* he reserves the right to treat his subject as indivisible[76] without committing himself to the conclusion that it can therefore have no location. His definition allows him to talk of an indivisible thing as having contact with something else, and when he proves that it cannot have contact with itself it is on other grounds than the mere lack of location.[77] As a result his proof is valid for all things and not merely for indivisibles. But it is plain that his definition of contact, taken together with his denial of location to indivisibles, produces exactly the conclusions which Aristotle draws from his own definitions at the beginning of the sixth book of the *Physics*,[78] namely that there is no sense in saying that lines are collections of points in contact. It was in the *Parmenides* that Aristotle found not only the general approach to his problem but the special ideas in terms of which he treats it.[79]

There is another point in these contexts at which Aristotle corrects Plato. For Plato, contact requires *immediate* (εὐθύς) succession in the contiguous terms,

---

[76]*Parm.* 147a8–b2; but earlier in the same movement he has treated it as divisible into parts and continues to do so later.

[77]*Parm.* 148e10–149a3.

[78]*Ph.* VI 1, 231a21–b10.

[79]Another such term in the same context is χωρίς (*Parm.* 149a5), taken over and defined by Aristotle. And there are other reminiscences of Plato's treatment of these ideas. One is the comment at *Ph.* I 2, 185b11–16, which Aristotle admits to be irrelevant to the argument in hand. Why does he introduce it? Because he has just mentioned continuity, and this reminds him to Plato's argument in this connexion that, since the parts can be distinguished from the whole, the whole can have contact with itself (*Parm.* 148d6–7, 148e1–3).

and this immediacy he explains by saying that they must occupy neighbouring positions.[80] But a little later he explains this requirement in turn by saying that there must be no third thing between the two terms;[81] and Aristotle is anxious to find room for this condition too in his definitions. He cannot use it to define "neighbouring," since he has another definition of that concept in view; so he uses it to define "successive,"[82] and in doing so he adds an important qualification: there must be nothing between the terms *of the same kind as themselves.*[83] If A B C are consecutive sections of a straight line, C cannot follow ἐφεξῆς after A, but it evidently can do so if B is merely a point. In correcting Plato here Aristotle may have in mind the treatment of limits in one passage of the *Parmenides* as parts of a thing, logically comparable with what lies between them;[84] but this is a treatment that Plato's own argument enables Aristotle to reject.

There is an embarrasing wealth of examples of this influence in the *Physics,* and I shall not bore you with them all. But one group is too important to omit. We saw earlier that, in arguing that an indivisible thing cannot move, Plato (and Aristotle after him) treated movement as a process taking time and having intermediate stages. As Aristotle would say, it is a continuous change, divisible into parts which are themselves changes taking time. But later in the *Parmenides* Plato argues that if a change is construed as the passage from not-A to A the change must be instantaneous; for there is no time in which a thing can be neither A nor not-A, neither at rest (for instance) nor in motion.[85] And this introduction of changes which are not

[80]*Parm.* 148e7–10.
[81]*Parm.* 149a6.
[82]*Ph.* V 3, 226b34–227a4.
[83]*Ph.* V 3, 227a1; cf. VI 1, 231b8–9.
[84]*Parm.* 137d4–5.
[85]*Parm.* 156c6–7: the whole context is 155e4–157b5.

processes is carefully prepared by some earlier arguments. Twice—once in each of the first two chains of argument about the One—Plato discusses the logic of growing older. In the first argument[86] he considers it as a special case of becoming different; and he argues that if X is becoming different from Y it cannot be the case that Y already is different from X, since otherwise X would already be different from Y and not merely becoming so. All that follows from "X is becoming different from Y" is another proposition about becoming, "Y is becoming different from X." The conclusion is applied forthwith to the particular case, to show that if X is becoming older than itself it is at the same time becoming younger. But on a later page the same example is taken up again.[87] Now Plato argues that at any moment during the process of growing older the subject must *be* older; at any stage of becoming different, the thing must already be different. For to say that it is becoming different is to say something about its future as well as its present; but so far as the bare present is concerned, it must already be something that it was becoming, given that the process of change is under way at all. Thus the argument relies heavily on the law of excluded middle: either the changing thing is already different, or it is not. If it is not, the process of change is not yet under way. And if it is, then the old conclusion, that from "X is becoming different from Y" we can infer only what X and Y are becoming and not what they are, breaks down. The old conclusion relied on inserting a *tertium quid* between "X is different" and "X is not different," namely "X is becoming different," something temporally intermediate between the first two; but such a *tertium quid* is ruled out by the law of excluded middle. Yet it is just this law that leads to the problem

86*Parm.* 141a6–c4.
87*Parm.* 152a5–e3.

of instantaneous change with which we began; for Plato goes on to argue that, if there is no time in which a thing can be neither A nor not-A, neither still nor moving, it baffles us to say when it makes the change from the one to the other.[88] When it changes from rest to motion it cannot be either at rest (for then the change would be still to come) or moving (for then the change would be past). Yet the change is not to be talked away: "if a thing changes, it changes."[89]

Here then is the problem, and the whole context of argument, taken over by Aristotle. It is generally held that Plato's purpose was to show that there can be no period of time during which a thing is neither A nor not-A, and consequently that the change from one to the other must occur at a moment of time.[90] But Aristotle evidently thought the puzzle more radical, and I think he was right. For by the same law of excluded middle not only is there no period but there is no point of time at which a thing can be neither A nor not-A. At any rate, whether Aristotle is enlarging or merely preserving Plato's problem, he gives it considerable space in the *Physics*. He agrees that some changes take no time at all.[91] Among other instances he cites the recovery of health, which is "a change to health and to nothing else";[92] in other words, although the process towards recovery may take time, the actual

[88]*Parm.* 156c1–7.

[89]*Parm.* 156c7–8: Ἀλλ' οὐδὲ μὴν μεταβάλλει ἄνευ τοῦ μεταβάλλειν. Cornford (*Plato and Parmenides*, p. 200, n. 2) mistakes the sense, insisting that the statement is "intelligible only if we suppose that Plato shifts here from the common use of μεταβάλλειν for 'change' in general to the stricter sense of 'transition' or passing from one state to another." What Plato means is like our truism "business is business"—sc. it mustn't be taken for anything else or explained away. He would probably regard Aristotle as explaining such changes away.

[90]Cornford goes so far as to call it a "businesslike account of the instant" (Ibid., p. 203).

[91]*Ph.* VIII 3, 253b21–30; cf. I 3, 186a13–16.

[92]*Ph.* VIII 3, 253b26–28.

recovery is simply the change from not-A to A.[93] In
any process of change to a given state there will be a
similar completion of the change, and this will take
no time:[94] the argument at once recalls Plato's discussion of the transition from movement to stillness.
Later, in the eighth book, Aristotle faces the problem
squarely. It will not help, he argues, to postulate a
time-atom between the period in which something is
not white and the subsequent period in which it is
white, with a view simply to providing a time for the
change to occur from not-white to white. For one
thing, time-atoms cannot be consecutive to periods of
time or to other time-atoms, just as points cannot have
contact either with lines or with other points. Moreover the suggestion would set a regress on foot. For
when we have postulated one time-atom to house the
change from not-white to white, there will be another
change to be accommodated in the same way: the
change from changing to being white.[95] In brief, Aristotle takes the puzzle to show that it is a mistake to
look for a special time-reference such that the subject
is then neither white nor not-white. The primary moment at which the subject becomes (or, as Aristotle
prefers to say, has become) white is the first moment
at which it is white.[96] And, given this moment, it
becomes improper to talk of the last moment at which

[93]Ross explains it otherwise; but for the treatment of ὑγίανσις
as the limit of a κίνησις cf. *Met.* Θ 6, 1048b18–23.

[94]*Ph.* VI 5, 235b32–236a7.

[95]*Ph.* VIII 8, 263b26–264a1.

[96]Ibid. 263b9–26, 264a2–4, cf. the earlier argument in VI 5,
235b32–236a7. The solution of Plato's puzzle given in *Ph.* VIII
8 is more trenchant than the earlier reply in VI 9 (240a19–29):
there Aristotle suggested that even between not-A and A a *tertium quid* could be inserted, viz. when the subject is neither
wholly not-A nor *wholly* A; but this is easily defeated by reformu-
lating the contradictions as "wholly A" and "not wholly A."
Just as the reply to Zeno which is given in VI 9 is admitted to be
inadequate in VIII 8 (263a15–18), so the reply to Plato's puzzle
given in VI 9 is superseded in the same later chapter.

the subject was not white, for the two moments would have to be consecutive.[97] Equally, given a last moment of stability there cannot be a first moment of change.[98] And Aristotle, having thus saved the situation and the law of excluded middle, can take over without qualms the moral of Plato's second analysis of growing older: namely that at any time during the period in which a thing is becoming different, it has already completed a change and to that extent is different from what it was.[99]

His reply to Plato's puzzle has side-effects on other discussions. To underline the paradox, Plato had called all change from not-A to A "sudden" change (ἐξαίφνης).[100] Aristotle restores the word to its proper use: it is used of what departs from its previous condition in an imperceptibly short time.[101] But all change, he adds, involves departing from a previous condition; and his motive for adding this is clear. He has in mind that because of this characteristic Plato had tried to reduce all change to sudden change, and he implies that this was a misleading extension of the word's use. There is nothing physically startling in most changes and nothing logically startling in any of them.

There is no need to go on. It might indeed be objected that the evidence does not necessarily show that Aristotle was indebted to the *Parmenides*; both Plato and Aristotle may have been drawing on a lost source. These problems were surely discussed in the Academy,[102] and the Academy in turn must surely have

[97]*Ph*. VIII 8, 264a3–4.
[98]*Ph*. VI 5, 236a7–27.
[99]*Ph*. VI 6, 236b32–237a17.
[100]*Parm*. 156d1–e3.
[101]*Ph*. IV 13, 222b14–16.
[102]We know for instance that others had tried to define continuity (*Ph*. III 1, 200b18–20), though they did not make use of the nexus of ideas common to Plato's and Aristotle's treatments

drawn on earlier arguments, in particular those of Zeno and Gorgias. The general purposes of this paper would be as well served by such a theory, but it cannot account for the intricate correspondence that we have seen in our two texts. Gorgias' part in the matter is guesswork: the evidence for his sole adventure into abstract thought has been contaminated, probably beyond cure, by traditions to which both the *Parmenides* and the *Physics* contributed. Of Zeno luckily we know more; we know that Plato does echo some arguments of Zeno, but that he transforms them radically for his own ends.[103] The *Parmenides* was not an historical anthology, and when Aristotle's words and ideas coincide closely with those of the dialogue he is under the spell of a work of astonishing brilliance and originality. A work, moreover, of logic or dialectic, not in the least a piece of empirical science; and the *Physics* is in great parts its successor.

This is not to say, of course, that Aristotle would call his methods in the *Physics* wholly dialectical. He, and his commentators on his behalf, have insisted on the distinction between "physical" and "dialectical," or "logical," or "universal," arguments; and no doubt

---

of the subject; hence Aristotle can take over their definition at the start of the *Physics* (I 2, 185b10–11) before producing his own revision of Plato's account.

[103]The *Arrow* underlies *Parm.* 152b2–d2, and the argument of B 1 and 2 in Diels-Kranz (the resolution of a thing into its fractions without ever reaching ultimate units) underlies *Parm.* 164c 8–d4 and 165a5–b6. I have not been convinced by Hermann Fraenkel's interpretation of B 3, nor therefore by his claim that it underlies the last-mentioned passages of the dialogue ("Zeno of Elea's Attacks on Plurality," *American Journal of Philology,* LXIII [1942], pp. 6, 198–99 = *Wege und Formen,* pp. 203, 227–28). Fraenkel is also inclined to see the Arrow behind *Parm.* 145–46 (art. cit., p. 13, n. 33 = *Wege und Formen,* p. 210, n. 1), where others will more readily detect Anaxagoras (cf. p. 94 above); and he sees B 4 behind *Parm.* 156c–d ibid. pp. 11–13 = pp. 207–9). He says all that is necessary for my purpose when he observes that in such echoes "Plato modifies the argument and . . . transfers it, as it were, to a higher order."

some of the reasoning in the *Physics* falls within the first class. Yet even if the distinction were (as it seldom is) sharp and fundamental in sciences where a knowledge of particular empirical fact is in question,[104] we need not expect it to be so in such an enquiry as the *Physics*. This is clear from the one major example of the contrast that is offered in the work, the dialectical and physical proofs that there can be no infinite physical body.[105] The dialectical proof is evidently distinguished by the fact that it proves too much: starting from a definition that applies to mathematical as well as to physical solids, it reaches conclusions that apply to both sciences.[106] Yet immediately after his promise to turn to physical arguments Aristotle produces a proof that no complex body can be infinite, and this proof shares the characteristics of its predecessor. It relies partly on quite general definitions of "body" and "infinite,"[107] partly on a treatment of the ratio between finite and infinite terms which could be formulated quite generally[108] and which in fact is later given a different application to speed and resistance;[109] and partly, perhaps, on the argument against an infinite number of elements which occurs in the first book and relies largely on quite general premisses.[110] Certainly there are other arguments in the context which seem

[104]E.g. *De Gen. Anim.* II 8, 747b27–748a16.

[105]*Ph.* III 5, 204b4–206a8. There is a second use of the same distinction (unnoticed by Bonitz s.v. λογικῶς) at VIII 8, 264a-7–9, and here too it proves elusive. The "logical" arguments can hardly be marked by their generality (the λόγος μᾶλλον οἰκεῖος at 264b1–2 itself applies to kinds of change other than movement) nor the "physical" by their reliance on the special theorems of physics (the "logical" also may do this, 264a24).

[106]*Ph.* III 5, 204b4–7, cf. Ross's notes on 204b4, 204b6.

[107]Ibid. 204b20–21.

[108]Ibid. 204b11–19: a particularly clear case of the artificial restriction of a general theorem of proportion so as to bring it within "physics."

[109]*Ph.* IV 8, 215b10–216a11.

[110]*Ph.* III 5, 204b12–13; I 6, 189a12–20.

to depend on special empirical claims, such as the
unfortunate hypothesis of natural places.[111] But the
impulse throughout the work is logical, and the restriction of its subject-matter to movable bodies and their
characteristics does not entail a radical difference of
method from other logical enquiries. It makes for better understanding to recall that in Aristotle's classification of the sciences the discussions of time and movement in the *Parmenides* are also physics.

[111]*Ph*. III 5, 205a10–12; but for the treatment of this too as an
ἔνδοξον see n. 30 above.

MATTER AND PREDICATION
IN ARISTOTLE

JOSEPH OWENS, C. SS. R.

§1 INTRODUCTION

In describing the basic matter of things, Aristotle removed from it all determinations and so all direct intelligibility. Yet he regarded the basic matter just in itself as a subject for predication. You can say things about it. You can say, for instance, that it is ingenerable and indestructible, and that it is the persistent substrate of generation and corruption. Still more strangely, Aristotle means that a substance or substantial form, like that of a man, of a plant, of a metal, can be predicated of matter.[1] How can this be, if matter is in itself wholly undetermined and entirely unintelligible?

From *The Concept of Matter in Greek and Medieval Philosophy*, ed. E. McMullin (Notre Dame, Ind., 1963), pp. 99–115. Reprinted by permission of the University of Notre Dame Press.

[1] See Aristotle *Met.* Z 3, 1029a20–30. The technical term used by Aristotle for matter was the Greek *hylê* or 'wood'. He seems to have been the first to coin a term for this notion, though the philosophic use of *hylê* for materials in general was prepared by Plato at *Ti.* 69A, and *Phlb.* 54C. In modern times the overall approach to the scientific notion of matter is hardly different; e.g.: "By the building materials I mean what we call matter, . . . ordinary matter is constructed out of two types of ultimate things called 'electrons' and 'protons.' " C. G. Darwin, *The New Conceptions of Matter* (London, 1931), p. 8. Aristotle, however, is approaching the question on a level that does not lead to electrons and protons but to very different principles; cf. Appendix. For texts, see Bonitz' *Index Aristotelicus*, 652b49–51, 785a5–43.

How can matter even be indicated, if it exhibits nothing that can halt the gaze of the intellect?

The above observations envisage two ways in which characteristics may be predicated of matter. One is essential (*per se*) predication. Matter is of itself ingenerable and indestructible, somewhat as man is animal and corporeal. The other way is through added forms. Matter is metallic, bovine, human through the forms of a metal, a cow, a man. But these forms are substantial, not accidental. Yet their predication in regard to matter resembles accidental predication, just as the specific differentia in the category of substance is predicated of the genus as though it were a quality. As changes within the category of substance are called by Professor Fisk in the present volume "qualified-like changes," this type of predication may correspondingly be designated "quality-like" predication. It is one type of the medieval *predicatio denominativa*.

In ordinary predication, as treated in Aristotelian logic, the ultimate subject is always actual and concrete. The universal, from a metaphysical viewpoint, is potential (*Met.* M 10, 1087a15–22). The concrete singular always retains its actuality as its various features are universalized and made potential. It cannot be treated as an undetermined residue that remains after its predicates have been removed. Logical analysis of predication, therefore, leads ultimately in Aristotle to the actual, and not to something wholly potential like matter. Ultimate matter is arrived at through the reasoning of the *Physics*. So reached, it poses problems for metaphysics. How does it have being, and how are forms predicated of it? The Stagirite had here to grapple with a refined concept attained by his scientific thinking and established to the satisfaction of that technical procedure itself, but which broke through the systematized logic presupposed by him for every theoretical science.

The solution reached by Aristotle in this question may or may not provide light for other disciplines when in the course of their reasonings they arrive at concepts that cannot fit into the grooves of the logic they have been using. Such new concepts may well appear self-contradictory when stretched on the Procrustean bed of a closed logical system. Certainly in metaphysics pertinent help for understanding the notion of essence can be obtained from studying Aristotle's procedure in establishing the notion of matter. Whether or not such help may be extended to other disciplines has to be left a question for investigators who specialize in them. But the contingency is one that can be encountered when any discipline pushes its concepts far past the experiences in which human thought commences. Concepts taken from immediate experience sometimes have to be refined in peculiar ways if they are to function in very remote areas of inquiry. The procedure of a first-rate thinker in meeting such a contingency belongs to the common treasury of achievements in the history of thought, and hardly deserves to be forgotten. Aristotle's method in this problem seems, then, *prima facie*, a subject worthy of investigation and critique.

§2 THE SUBJECT OF PREDICATION

First, what is the basic subject of predication in Aristotelian logic? As is well enough known, this ultimate subject of predication is the highly actual concrete singular thing. It is the individual man, or the individual horse, or the individual tree, according to the examples used in the Aristotelian *Categories*.[2] In a logical context, the real individual thing was called "primary substance" by the Stagirite. In Greek the term was *prôtê ousia*, primary entity. The term characterized the concrete singular thing as absolutely basic

2See *Cat.* V 2a13–14, 2b13.

among the subjects with which logic deals, and as the fundamental being that received the predication of all other perfections. Secondary substances, in that logical context, were *man, animal, body,* and the like, taken universally. They were all predicated of a primary substance, of a concrete individual man like Socrates or Plato, or of an individual horse or stone. Accidental characteristics, like *white, large, running,* and so on, were predicated of substances and ultimately of an individual substance. There was nothing more fundamental of which they could be predicated. For Aristotelian logic the concrete individual was the basic subject of predication. It was the primary entity upon which all logical structure was raised. In a logical context it was primary substance in the full sense of the expression.[3]

This doctrine of predication functioned without special difficulty when applied throughout the world of common sense thought and speech. Quite obviously the ultimates with which ordinary conversation deals are shoes and ships and sealing-wax and cabbages and kings, individual pinching shoes and flat-tasting cabbages and uncrowned office kings, as one meets them in the course of everyday life. These are all concrete individual things or persons. Aristotelian logic, it should be kept in mind, was expressly meant as a propaedeutic to the sciences. It did not presuppose knowledge of any theoretical science. Rather, it had to be learned before any theoretical science could be approached.[4] There should be little wonder, then, that Aristotelian logic was not geared to function smoothly in situations brought into being solely through the results of scien-

[3]*Cat.* V 2b4–6, 15–17. In a metaphysical context, on the other hand, the form and not the composite was primary substance, as at *Met.* Z 7, 1032b1–14; 11, 1037a28. On the category mistake occasioned by this twofold use of 'primary substance' in Aristotle, see my article "Aristotle on Categories," *The Review of Metaphysics,* XIV (1960), 83–84.

[4]See Aristotle *Met.* Γ 3, 1005b2–5.

tific analysis and construction. Yet those situations have to be expressed in concepts and in language. Logic has to be applied to them as they occur. Aristotle, as may be expected, could not go very deeply into any theoretical science without encountering situations that broke through the logical norms presupposed in his hearers. Was he prepared to meet such situations? Was he able to adapt his logic to them as they presented themselves in the course of his scientific investigations?

§3 THE PROBLEM OF MATTER

An instance that could hardly be avoided was that of matter. Matter quite obviously did not come under the notion envisaged for an ultimate subject of predication in a logic where that ultimate subject is the concrete singular thing. In the everyday universe of discourse the material or stuff out of which things are said to be made is always of the concrete individual stamp. The wood of which a house is constructed consists of individual pieces. The bronze in which a statue is cast is a piece of bronze in definite dimensions in a definite place at a definite time. In the later Scholastic vocabulary these concrete materials out of which more complex things were made received the designation, *materia secunda*, or 'secondary matter.' Bronze and wood and stone were indeed matter, in the sense that things were made out of them. But they were not the basic or ultimate matter out of which those things were made. That was signified by calling them secondary matter. The designation implied that there was a still more basic matter that was not concrete nor individual. Aristotle had not finished the first book of his *Physica* or philosophy of nature before he had established in sensible things a subject still more fundamental than the concrete individual. A visible, tangible, or mobile thing, the Stagirite showed, was necessarily composite. It was literally a *con-cretum*. It was composed of more fundamental elements. These ultimate constituents of sensible things, according to the Aristotelian reasoning, were form and matter. Matter played the role of ultimate subject, and a form was its primary characteristic.

The absolutely basic matter of the Aristotelian *Physics* became known in Scholastic terminology as *materia prima*, 'primary matter'. By Aristotle himself it was simply called matter. However, Aristotle uses the term 'matter' regularly enough to designate the concrete materials out of which artifacts are made, materials like bricks and stones and wood. So there was ground for the Scholastic insistence on the use of two expressions, 'primary matter' and 'secondary matter,' to mark the important distinction. For convenience in the present study the term 'materials' or 'material' will be used wherever possible to denote what the Scholastics called 'secondary matter', and the term 'matter' without any qualification will be used regularly for the absolutely basic substrate of things as established in the Aristotelian *Physics*. By 'matter', then, will be meant what the mediaeval vocabulary designated as 'primary matter'.

With matter in this sense established as subject, and form as its immediate though really distinct characteristic, you may readily expect to hear that the form is considered to be predicable of matter. You will not be disappointed; Aristotle actually does say that substance, in the sense of substantial form, is predicated of matter: "... for the predicates other than substance are predicated of substance, while substance is predicated of matter."[5] That is his express statement. What does it mean? At the very least, it means that matter is the ultimate subject with which predication is concerned. Everything other than substance you can predicate of substance. But what is intelligible about

[5]*Met.* Z 3, 1029a23–24; Oxford tr.

substance can in turn be predicated, denominatively of course, of matter. The principle of intelligibility in a substance is its form, and its form is the primary characteristic of its matter, from the "quality-like" viewpoint.

At first sight, perhaps, nothing could seem more natural than to predicate a form of its corresponding matter. Characteristics are regularly predicated of subjects. A new subject has been unearthed by the Aristotelian philosophy of nature. The substantial characteristic of that subject has been isolated. What is more normal, then, than to say that here as in other cases the characteristic is predicable of its subject?

Yet as soon as one tries to express this type of predication in any definite instance, linguistic and conceptual difficulties arise. How would you word a sentence in which a substance, or a substantial form, is predicated of matter? The first part of Aristotle's assertion was clear enough: "Predicates other than substance are predicated of substance." The predicates other than substance are the accidents. They are quantity, qualities, relations, activities, time, and place. They are predicated without difficulty of a concrete, individual substance. You may indicate a particular tree and say without hesitation that it is large, green, near to you, growing in the yard at the present moment. Each of these accidents is obviously predicated of a substance, the individual tree. But, the Aristotelian text continues: "the substance is predicated of matter." How would you express this in the case of the tree? You would have to say that matter is this particular tree. You would have to say that matter is likewise Socrates, or is Plato, or is this particular table or that particular stone. Such predication is unusual, and requires considerable explanation even to make sense.

Some light may be obtained from the way in which for Aristotle a thing may be defined in terms of the materials of which it is composed. If asked what a house is, you may answer that it is "stones, bricks, and timbers."[6] If that may be called a definition, it is surely the least perfect type of definition possible. But Aristotle does refer to it as a definition in terms of the materials that are able to be made into a house. From that viewpoint the house is the materials that constitute it, and conversely the materials are the house insofar as definition and thing defined are convertible. In general, then, in the way in which a thing may be said to be its materials, the materials themselves may be said to be the thing. Awkward though this predication is, what prevents it from being applied in the case of the basic matter of which things are composed? In each particular case it should allow you to say that matter is this individual man, this individual stone, this individual tree. Substance, even the individual substance, would in this way be predicated of matter.

The context in which the present doctrine occurs is one of the central books of the Aristotelian *Metaphys-*

[6]*Met.* H 2, 1043a15; Oxford tr. On this doctrine, and Aristotle's use of the expression 'primary matter' in connection with it, see W. D. Ross, *Aristotle's Metaphysics* (Oxford, 1924), II, 256–57. 'Primary matter' is found in various senses at *Ph.* II 1, 193a29; *GA* I 20, 729a32; and *Met.* Δ 4, 1015a7–10. 'Matter' in its chief or primary sense, however, meant for Aristotle the substrate of generation and corruption (*GC* I 4, 320a2–5), even though the designation 'primary matter' never seems to have been limited by him to that sense. The therapy required by the concept's genesis has to be kept applied in representing the absolutely undetermined matter as that of which things are composed. Such matter is not individual, like any of the materials of which a house is composed. Still less is it something universal, for the universal is subsequent to the individual in Aristotelian doctrine. Rather, it is below the level at which individuality and universality appear. Considered just in itself, it has nothing to distinguish it as found in one thing from itself as found in another. From this viewpoint it parallels the common nature of Duns Scotus, which of itself had nothing to distinguish it as found in Socrates from itself as found in Plato (see Duns Scotus, *Quaest. Metaph.*, 7, 13, No. 21; ed. Vivès, 7, 421b. In contrast to the Scotistic

ics. In a metaphysical context, the universal is not substance. When in this context substance is said to be predicated of matter, it can hardly mean just another instance of universal predicated of particular. From the viewpoint of logic, the secondary substance or the substance taken universally is predicated of the particular substance. Even though present as a condition, that logical doctrine can scarcely be what Aristotle meant in saying in the *Metaphysics* that substance is predicated of matter. It is not just another case of predicating universal of singular, as in the assertion: 'Socrates is a man.' Subject and predicate are really the same when a universal substance is predicated of a particular substance. If you say: "Matter is a man," however, you have a different type of predication. Matter does not coincide in reality with a man in the way Socrates does. A really distinct principle, the form of man, is added. From this viewpoint the predication resembles rather the assertion of an accidental form in regard to sub-

---

common nature, however, the Aristotelian basic matter lacks all formal determinations, and so not only individual determinations). The absolutely undetermined matter is accordingly one through the removal of all distinguishing characteristics. It is wholly formless in the *Physics* (I 7, 191a8–12) as well as in the *Metaphysics*. In this sense only, may it be regarded as common. When actuated, it differentiates by its very nature in making possible the spread of the same form in parts outside parts and the multiplication of singulars in a species. In that way it is an individuating principle without being of itself individual. As the substrate of substantial change, it may be said—with the appropriate therapy—to change from one form to another. So doing, it shows itself to be really distinct from its forms, since it really persists while the forms really replace each other. But it is not therefore a really distinct being from the form. In the individual there is but the one being derived from the form to the matter and the composite. Thus any single thing is differentiated from a "heap" (*Met.* Z 17, 1041b7–31). Subsidiary forms, for instance those indicated in water by the spectra of hydrogen and oxygen, would accordingly be accidental forms for Aristotle, and in a substantial change would be replaced by new though corresponding accidental forms.

stance, as when one says that a man is pale, or fat. The accidental form is really distinct from the substance, as the substantial form is really distinct from its matter. Such predication will be of the "quality-like" type.

That indeed is the way in which Aristotle presents the situation. As an accidental form, for instance quantity, is predicated of substance, so substance is predicated of matter. What is predicated of matter, accordingly should be the substantial form or act, and not the composite. Later in the same part of the *Metaphysics* it is stated in exactly that manner: ". . . as in substances that which is predicated of the matter is the actuality itself, in all other definitions also it is what most resembles full actuality."[7] As accidental forms are predicated of substances, then, so the substantial form is what is predicated of matter within the category of substance.

The doctrine clearly enough is that form in the category of substance may be predicated of its matter as of a subject. You may accordingly apply the form of man to matter, the form of iron to matter, and so on, and call it predication. But how can you express this in ordinary language? It can hardly be done. Ordinary language has not been developed to meet this contingency. The best you can do, perhaps, is to say that matter is humanized, equinized, lapidified, and so on, as it takes on forms like those of man, horse, and stone. To say that matter is human, equine, lapideous, or that it is a man, a horse, a stone, may be true enough in this context; but with all its linguistic oddity the way of speaking hardly brings out the full import of the situation. It tends to give the impression that matter is of itself these things. The Aristotelian meaning, on the contrary, is that matter is not of itself any of these things, but becomes them by receiving the appropriate substantial forms. As their real subject it

[7]*Met.* H 2, 1043a5–7; Oxford tr.

remains really distinct from them, somewhat as a substance remains really distinct from its accidents. The assertion that matter is humanized, equinized, lapidified by the reception of different substantial forms expresses the predication with less danger of being misunderstood, though with still less respect for linguistic usage.

The linguistic difficulties, however, turn out to be mild in comparison with the conceptual. The immediate context of the Aristotelian passage that gave rise to this discussion is enough to cause doubts about the very possibility of the predication. Matter had just been defined as "that which in itself is neither a particular thing nor of a certain quantity nor assigned to any other of the categories by which being is determined."[8] Matter is not anything definite. It is not a particular thing. It is not a "what" nor at all an "it." It exhibits nothing that could provide a direct answer to the question "What is it?" It has in itself none of the determinations by which a thing can be or be recognized or indicated or known or understood. The text states explicitly that it has no quantitative nor other categorical determination. Of itself, therefore, it has no length nor breadth nor thickness nor number nor parts nor position. It cannot at all be conceived in the fashion of the Cartesian concept of matter. In this concept, matter was identified with extension.[9] Nor can the Aristotelian matter be represented as anything capable of detection by means of a pointer-reading. There is nothing about it, in itself, that could register in quantitative terms. It belongs to a level on which neither quantitative nor qualitative physics has any means of functioning. It eludes quantitative and qualitative and other accidental determinations, as well as all substantial determinations.

[8] *Met.* Z 3, 1029a20–21; Oxford tr.
[9] See Descartes, *Principia Philosophiae*, 2, 4–9; A–T 8, 42.4–45.16 (9^2, 65–68).

Yet it cannot be expressed by negations of known characteristics, as for instance non-being is expressed negatively in terms of being.[10] The nature of matter cannot be represented in terms of what it is not. The same Aristotelian text continues:

> Therefore the ultimate substratum is of itself neither a particular thing nor of a particular quantity nor otherwise positively characterized; nor yet is it the negations of these, for negations also will belong to it only by accident.[11]

All categorical determinations are first denied to matter. They are outside its nature, and in that sense "belong to it only by accident." This has been expressed in the preceding paragraphs of the present study by saying that the forms are really distinct from matter somewhat as accidents are really distinct from substances. But, the Aristotelian text insists, the negations of all the different determinations are just as accidental to matter. None of them can express its nature, as the term 'nature' is used of matter in the *Physics* (II 1, 193a28–30; 2, 194a12–13). It eludes even negations. You can indeed say that matter is not something, or better still, that it is a "not-something." What you say is true. But you have not thereby expressed the nature of matter, even negatively. Negations are just as accidental to it as are the determinations it takes on in the actual world. You are still only skimming its accidental manifestations. You have not penetrated to its proper nature. Its nature eludes the negations.

In a word, matter as reached by Aristotle escapes in itself both determinative and negative characterizations.

[10]For Aristotle, predication of being is made through reference to the primary instance of being. Even the negation of being, namely "non-being," is asserted in this way. See *Met.* Γ 2, 1003b5–10.

[11]*Met.* Z 3, 1029a24–26; Oxford tr. 'Positively' refers here to determination; cf. a21.

It cannot be conceived or described in any direct fashion, either determinatively or negatively. It is not even a "what" nor an "it" that is capable of being indicated. In terms of modern logic, it is not the "referent" of any "demonstrative" (i.e. monstrative) symbol, because it cannot be presented directly to one's cognition. Nor can the referent be any property or set of properties, because such determinations are lacking to matter in itself.[12]

How, then, is the Aristotelian matter to be conceived and represented? How can it be set up as a subject for predication? Quite obviously, from the above considerations, no direct method, either affirmative or negative, is capable of grasping what Aristotle meant in this regard. The concept will have to be that of a positive subject, able to receive predication. No negation is able to express the nature of matter. Yet from that notion of positive subject every determination will have to be removed, even, or rather especially, the determination expressed by "something." Matter is explicitly not a "something" nor a "what" nor an "it." All determination, even the most elementary, has to be drastically eliminated from the notion of the positive in this concept. The concept that expresses the Aristotelian notion of matter will have to be the concept of a positive object that is wholly indeterminate. Is the human mind able to form such a concept? If so, upon what referents will it be based?

Presumably Aristotle could not have spoken so cogently about matter if he had not worked out its concept to his own satisfaction. The most likely way to

---

[12]"The referend of a demonstrative symbol (i.e. a word used demonstratively) is *the object directly presented to* the speaker. The referend of a descriptive phrase is a *property*, or *set of properties.*" L. Susan Stebbing, *A Modern Introduction to Logic* (6th ed.; London, 1948), p. 499. On the technical term 'referend,' cf.: "We shall find it convenient to use the word 'referend' to stand for *that which is signified.*" Ibid., p. 13.

learn how the concept is formed, accordingly, should
be to follow the steps by which the originator of the
concept reasoned to the presence of matter in sensible
things. In this context, of course, the referents will be
sensible things in themselves, and not Kantian phenomena.

§4 SUBSTANCE AND CHANGE

How, then, did Aristotle arrive at the notion of matter as a real subject, and as a subject denominatively
characterized by forms that remained really distinct
from it? In the first book of the *Physics*, the Stagirite
surveyed the teachings of his philosophic predecessors
on the basic principles of natural things. Things in the
world of nature were known by observation to be
capable of motion or change. In the course of his survey, attention is focused upon the universal requirements for change. Any change whatsoever needs three
principles. It has to have a subject that loses one form
and acquires another. The three principles necessarily
involved are therefore the form that is lost, the form
that is acquired, and the subject that undergoes the loss
of the old form and the acquisition of the new.[13]

The Aristotelian examples meant to illustrate this
doctrine are clear enough. They are concrete individual
materials that lose and acquire different forms. Bronze
is the subject that becomes a statue. At first the bronze

[13]See *Ph.* I 7, 189b30–191a7. The analysis of change or motion
is made by Aristotle without dependence on the notion of time.
Rather, motion is first defined, and then the notion of time is
worked out in terms of motion, that is, as the numbering of motion in respect of prior and subsequent (*Ph.* IV 11, 219b1–2).
Since Kant the tendency has been first to establish the notion of
time, and then to describe motion in terms of relation to time;
e.g.: "Change thus always involves (1) a fixed entity, (2) a
three-cornered relation between this entity, another entity, and
some but not all, of the moments of time." Bertrand Russell,
Principles of Mathematics (Cambridge, Eng., 1903), 1, 469.

has a nondescript form or shape. Then it is cast into the form of a statue, say of the Greek god Hermes. It is the subject that changes from one form or shape to another. The notion of form in this example is readily understood from its ordinary English use. It is the external shape of the bronze. Another Aristotelian example, however, uses 'form' in a more esoteric way. A man from an uneducated state comes to be educated. The man is the subject that changes from uneducated to educated. 'Uneducated' describes the quality of the man who has not had proper schooling. 'Educated' means the quality of adequate instruction and cultural training. Both 'educated' and 'uneducated' mean qualities; and in the Aristotelian vocabulary qualities are forms.

As can be seen in these examples, the original form from which the subject changes is more properly regarded from the viewpoint of a privation of the form to be acquired in the change. It is expressed in a privative way, as in the term 'uneducated.' Any of the Aristotelian categories, like the thing's quantity, its place, its time of occurrence, or any of its relations, is a form in this technical Aristotelian sense. Change can take place in any of the categories of being.[14] But in its very notion, as has emerged from the foregoing analysis, it involves indispensably the three principles —a subject that changes, a form that is lost, a form that is acquired.

This essential notion of change is reached from the changes that are observed in the accidental categories, like change from place to place, from size to size, from color to color. But the analysis of the notion establishes it as a general concept that will hold wherever change is found, regardless of the particular category. It is accordingly applied by Aristotle in the category of sub-

[14]*Ph.* III 1, 201a8–9.

stance. In all other categories the subject of the change
is observable. You can see the man who changes from
uneducated to educated. You can touch the bronze
that is cast from a nondescript form into a statue. You
can handle the wood that is made into a bed. But
with change in the category of substance you cannot
observe the subject that changes, even in principle.
This means that you cannot observe the subject changing. Change in the category of substance is accordingly
not observable, even in principle.

There need be little wonder, then, that Aristotle is
sparing in examples of change in the category of substance. Without too much enthusiasm he accepted the
tradition of the four Empedoclean elements as the
basic simple bodies, and admitted as generation the
change of any one of these bodies into another.[15] But
he is very circumspect in determining just where substance is found. Earth, air, and fire, three of the traditional elements, do not seem to him to have sufficient
unity in their composition to be recognized as substances. Living things seem to have that unity, yet just
where the unity is cannot be located too easily.[16] The
one instance that he does mention definitely, though
only in a passing way, is the change to plants and animals from seed.[17]

Today this Aristotelian example may not seem any
too happy an illustration of substantial change. Without having to call the fertilized ovum of a rhinoceros
a little rhinoceros, one may argue either for or against
the position that an embryo is the same substance as
the fully developed animal. To say that a tadpole is
not a frog does not commit you to the stand that the

[15]See *Cael.* I 2, 268b26–29; GC II 1, 329a2–8; 8, 334b31–
335a23.

[16]*Met.* Ζ 16, 1040b5–16.

[17]*Ph.* I 7, 190b4–5. Cf. GA I 18, 722b3–5, and St Paul's
simile, I Cor. 15:36.

one is a different substance from the other. In general, it may be easy enough to claim that the change from something non-living to something alive is a change in substance. But in regard to pinpointing the change from non-living to living substance, or even to showing definitely that there was change from the truly non-living, are we today in any noticeably further advanced position than was Aristotle? Similarly, with modern chemical knowledge, it is easy to show definitely that air, fire, and earth are not substances in the Aristotelian sense. We no longer share the Stagirite's hesitations in that regard. With respect to water, however, can a definite decision be given? In the higher kinds of living things, Aristotle's criterion was a unity that distinguishes the complex organism from a heap. It is the same criterion that enables us now to consider the ant a different thing from the sandpile. In man, consciousness adds a still more profound criterion of unity. Every man considers himself a different being from other men, a different being from the substances he absorbs in nutrition and from those into which he will be dissolved when he dies. Apart from preconceived positions arising out of conclusions in metaphysics or in modern physics, and illegitimately transferred to the domain of natural philosophy, the difference of one being from another and the change of one sensible being into another may in general be admitted. *The evidence of pertinent bearing either for or against, though, is scarcely any greater now than it was in Aristotle's day.*

However, the plurality of things in the universe will hardly be contested any more today in a properly physical context than in the Stagirite's time.[18] As long as a plurality of beings in the sensible universe is admitted without subjecting the term 'beings' to intol-

[18]See *Ph.* I 2, 184b25–185a16.

erable strain, the plurality of substances required for
the Aristotelian demonstration of matter is present.
'Substance' in Aristotle's terminology meant the entity
or *ousia* of things. Wherever you have a being, simply
stated, you have an *ousia*, a substance. Nor should there
be too much difficulty about the change of one thing,
macroscopically speaking, into another. Molecular compounds are changed into other compounds, transmuta-
tion of the elements is no longer a dream. The one
real difficulty might lie in the proposal to locate the
individuality of things in sub-atomic particles. In that
case might not all the changes taking place in the
physical universe be merely new combinations of the
particles, as in Democritean atomism? There would be
only accidental change, not substantial change.

The denial of any unifying principle in things over
and above the sub-atomic particles would leave the
behavior of every particle wholly unrelated to that of
the others. A cosmic puppeteer would have to cause
the regularity of the world processes. A principle of
unity in each thing itself, on the other hand, would
have to be deeper than the division into particles and
into quanta, and indeed would have to be of a different
order. It would have to function on a more profound
level, in order to dominate the polarity of the sub-
atomic particles and to maintain the statistical regularity of the quanta. Such a principle would function exactly as the Aristotelian substantial form. It would be
the deepest principle of unity in a thing, and so would
make a thing "a being" simply and without qualification. It would be the principle that rendered the thing
intelligible. It would be the thing's basic determinant,
making the thing one kind of thing and not another.
It would be deeper than the entire qualitative and
quantitative or measurable orders in the thing, and so
would enable the thing to exist and function as a unit
in spite of the common patterns of atomic and sub-

atomic motion that it shares with other things. When this formal principle gave way to its successors in changes like nutrition or death, a radically new thing or things would come into being, in spite of common spectra before and after the change and in spite of the equality of the total weight before and after. It would enable the thing to function as a nature and not just artificially at the hands of a cosmic puppeteer. In a word, this principle would coincide entirely with the Aristotelian form in the category of substance.

The argument for the change of one substance into another, accordingly, seems neither stronger nor weaker in any notable way than it was in fourth century Greece. If you grant that you are a different thing or a different being from the food you absorb in nutrition and from the substances into which you will dissolve in death, you have recognized the data necessary to understand the Aristotelian demonstration. When one substance changes into another, what disappears is the most basic principle of determination and knowability, the principle that most radically made food one thing and man another thing. Without it, nothing in the thing could be knowable or observable. It is of course immediately succeeded by the form of the new thing. But the change of the one thing into the other requires a common subject, according to the very notion of change. Such a common subject will be unobservable both in principle and in fact, because it is what loses and acquires the most basic of forms and so of itself has not even the most rudimentary principle of knowability or observability. It has to be known in virtue of something else. That "something else," quite naturally, will be the observable subject in accidental change, like the wood that becomes a bed or the bronze that becomes a statue. Some corresponding subject has to be present for substantial change. In that analogous way, then, the subject of substantial change, namely

matter, is indirectly known. It is known as the conclusion of scientific reasoning in the Aristotelian sense
of 'scientific'. In Aristotle's own words:

> The underlying nature is an object of scientific knowl-
> edge, by an analogy. For as the bronze is to the statue,
> the wood to the bed, or the matter and the formless
> before receiving form to any one thing which has
> form, so is the underlying nature to substance, i.e. the
> "this" or existent.[19]

The presence of matter is proven stringently from
the requirements for change, while the nature of matter is established through analogy with the subject of
accidental change. The demonstration presupposes the
universal notion of change and the two terms, but not
the substrate, of substantial change.

The original referent upon which the Aristotelian
concept of matter is based is therefore the subject of
accidental change, like wood or bronze. From that
notion of "subject," however, all determinations are
removed, with the proviso that the negations as well
as the determinations are accidental to it. In its own
nature, then, this refined notion of subject remains
as positive as ever. It was a positive notion from the
start, as seen in a positive subject like wood or bronze,
and all determinations were denied it under the express
condition that none of these pertained to its own
nature. In this way the notion *positive* is shown to be
independent of *determinate*. For Aristotle, 'actual' was
a synonym for 'determinate'. What lacked actuality,
or in technical language the potential, could therefore
be positive. By establishing the concept of the potential as positive even though non-actual or indeterminate, Aristotle has been able to set up matter as a
positive though entirely non-actual subject of predication. Because the potential is positive without being

[19]*Ph.* I 7, 191a7–12; Oxford tr.

determinate, this concept of matter is possible to the human mind. Its referent is any sensible thing considered potentially as substance. It is the concept of a principle wholly undetermined, yet necessarily posited in reality by any form that is extended, multiplied in singulars, or terminating substantial change.

§5 CONCLUSION

As should be clear from the foregoing considerations, matter in the category of substance can be an object of scientific inquiry only on the level of natural philosophy. It cannot at all be reached by qualitative or quantitative procedures like those of chemistry and modern physics. What is predicated of it, in itself, does not belong to the order of the measurable or the directly observable, even in principle. Its predicates are notions like *purely potential, unknowable of itself, incorruptible,* and so on. Its presence is still necessary to explain substantial change, if such change is admitted. In any case, its presence is absolutely required to account for the extension of a formally identical characteristic in parts outside parts, and for the multiplication of the characteristic in a plurality of individuals, without any formal addition whatsoever. The Aristotelian matter has not been superseded nor even touched by the stupendous progress of modern physics. Nothing that is measurable can perform its function in explaining the nature of sensible things, and by the same token it cannot be brought forward to account for anything that requires explanation in measurable terms. Any type of matter dealt with by chemistry or modern physics would in comparison be secondary matter, and not matter that is a principle in the category of substance. "Matter" in the basic Aristotelian sense is therefore in no way a rival of the "matter" that can be measured or of the mass that can be transformed into energy, but is rather a very different means of explanation for sensible things on another scientific level, the level of natural philosophy.

In distinguishing his two tables, the solid one he wrote on and the "nearly all empty space" table he knew as a physicist, Eddington failed to stress that his knowledge of his scientific table was constructed from his knowledge of the ordinary table.[20] The scientific construct was the result of understanding the ordinary table in quantitative terms. The same ordinary table can also be understood scientifically (in the traditional sense of knowledge through causes) in terms of substantial principles, form and matter, as is done in natural philosophy. It can also be understood in terms of entitative principles, essence and being, as is done in metaphysics. They are all different accounts of the same thing, given on different levels of scientific (again, in the centuries-old meaning of "scientific") investigation. All these different accounts are necessary for a well-rounded understanding of sensible things. None of these accounts can afford to despise any of the others, nor seek to substitute for any of them, nor to interfere with any of them. Each has its own role to play, a role that only itself can play. The Aristotelian matter is a principle for explaining things on the level of natural philosophy. On that level it has its own predicates, predicates that still have to be used today in the properly balanced explanation of nature.

[20]See Arthur Stanley Eddington, *The Nature of the Physical World* (Cambridge, Eng., 1928), pp. ix–xi. Cf.: "The whole reason for accepting the atomic model is that it helps us to explain things we could not explain before. Cut off from these phenomena, the model can only mislead, . . ." Stephen Toulmin, *The Philosophy of Science* (New York, 1953), p. 12.

APPENDIX

On the independence of these different scientific procedures, see my paper "Our Knowledge of Nature," *Proceedings of the American Catholic Philosophical Association*, XXIX (1955), 80–86. A widely accepted view at present is to regard natural philosophy as a sort of dialectic that prepares the way for genuine physics; e.g.: ". . . frontier physics, natural philosophy. It is analysis of the concept of matter; a search for conceptual order amongst puzzling data." Norwood Russell Hanson, *Patterns of Discovery* (Cambridge, Eng., 1958), p. 119. "Not so very long ago the subject now called physics was known as "natural philosophy". The physicist is by origin a philosopher who has specialized in a particular direction." (Arthur S. Eddington, *The Philosophy of Physical Science* [Cambridge, Eng., 1939], p. 8.) It is true that before physics was developed through quantitative procedure as a special science, its problems had in point of historical fact been given over to the non-mathematical treatment of natural philosophy. That way of dealing with its problems was entirely illegitimate. The specific *differentiae* of natural things remain unknown and impenetrable to the human mind. They cannot be made the source for scientific knowledge of the specific traits of corporeal things. For this reason any new attempt to treat the experimental sciences as a continuation of natural philosophy, e.g. C. de Koninck, "Les Sciences Expérimentales sont-elles Distinctes de la Philosophie de la Nature?" *Culture*, II, (1941), 465–76, cannot hope to be successful. On the other hand, the view that natural philosophy consists only in "a search for conceptual order amongst puzzling data" seems continuous with the trend that has given rise to the conception of philosophy in general as linguistic analysis, concerned with words and concepts and not with things. Similarly, the notion that natural philosophy is a frontier investigation rather than a full-fledged science in its own right, seems to stem from Comte's law of the three stages, in which speculative philosophy in general was but an immature stage in the unilinear development towards positive science. In this view, philosophical treatment "will naturally be expected to deal with questions on the frontier of knowledge, as to which comparative certainty is not yet attained." Bertrand Russell, *Introduction to Mathematical Philosophy* (London, 1930), p. v. This is nothing but a cavalier dismissal of natural philosophy as a science.

Theoretically, it is indifferent whether the substantial principles (matter and form) used for the explanation of things through natural philosophy are reached by way of substantial change, or of extension, or of individuation. In point of fact, the way used by Aristotle himself was through substantial change. To show that the same two principles are required to explain extension and multiplication of singulars, is not a *tour de force* to safeguard the principles against someone who does not admit substantial change. It is rather a global view of the whole approach, from a theoretical standpoint, to the problem of matter.

May I express my thanks to Msgr. G. B. Phelan for many helpful suggestions, and to Fr. Ernan McMullin for carefully reading the first draft of this paper and pointing out a number of deficiencies. These I have tried to remedy in the final draft. This draft, of course, benefits from the other papers and the discussions at the conference, and in particular from the clear statement of the issues in Professor Fisk's contribution. Friedrich Solmsen's recently published work, *Aristotle's System of the Physical World* (Ithaca, N.Y., 1960), with its illuminating discussion (pp. 118–26) on the historical background of Aristotle's wholly undetermined matter, reached me too late to be of help in preparing the present paper.

PROBLEMS IN
METAPHYSICS Z, CHAPTER 13

M. J. WOODS

The purpose of this paper is to attempt a clarification of the theory of substance which Aristotle had developed at the time when he wrote books Z, H, and θ of the *Metaphysics*, by considering a passage where he puts forward a number of arguments against a certain doctrine about substance. Some of my conclusions could, I think, be supported by an examination of certain other passages in Z. But in this paper I confine my discussion to Z 13.

As Ross points out in his edition of the *Metaphysics*, chapters 13–16 form a single section, the main upshot of which is summed up in 1041a3–5:[1] ὅτι μὲν οὖν τῶν καθόλου λεγομένων οὐδὲν οὐσία οὔτ᾽ ἐστὶν οὐσία οὐδομία ἐξ οὐσιῶν, δῆλον*

The suggestion that τὰ καθόλου λεγόμενα have claims to be regarded as substances is raised at the beginning of chapter 13, a discussion to which Aristotle looks forward in chapter 3 at 1028b34. It is in the course of these four chapters that the main, though

---

[1]Line references are all to Jaeger's Oxford text of *Metaphysics*. [For the convenience of the reader, translations of some Greek passages appear in footnotes. The translations used are those of W. D. Ross and J. L. Ackrill.—Ed.]

*"Clearly, then, no universal term (τῶν καθόλου λεγομένων οὐδέν) is the name of a substance, and no substance is composed of substances."

not the only, criticism of the Theory of Forms occurs in this book.

To turn to detailed discussion of chapter 13: the exact course of the argument is difficult, and at some points the text is disputed. However, it is fairly clear that the main part of the chapter ends at 1039a14. an appendix. Beginning ἔχει δέ τὸ συμβαῖνον ἀπορία a dilemma is presented; it is a firmly held doctrine that it is substance which is the object of definition; but the earlier arguments tend to show that no actual substance is composite (σύνθετον). So substances appear to be indefinable. This dilemma is clearly before Aristotle's mind in the succeeding three chapters.

It is important to make clear exactly what doctrine Aristotle was attacking in these chapters. He was opposing the view that a correct answer to the question, "What is οὐσία?" would be given by saying that it is τὸ καθόλου. Thus he is denying that something καθόλου is as such an οὐσία. To deny this is not to claim that nothing καθόλου is an οὐσία, only that being καθόλου is not by itself a sufficient ground for so describing something. I wish to argue that Aristotle was in fact maintaining that only some things properly described as καθόλου are to be regarded as οὐσίαι; something καθόλου iis an οὐσία only if it is not predicated universally (καθόλου λεγόμενον). That is, the main purpose of these chapters is to deny that anything καθόλου λεγόμενον is an οὐσία. I will return to the distinction between being a universal and being predicated universally later.

We notice that he begins his discussion by saying (1038b3 f.) that some have regarded τὸ καθόλου as an αἴτιον or ἀρχή,* and it therefore needs investigation. No indication of who holds this is given, but it is difficult to believe that Aristotle would not have regarded

---

*"Cause" or "principle."

the Platonic Theory of Forms as an example of the sort of theory he had in mind.[2] I shall refer to Aristotle's opponent for convenience as "the Platonist," without intending to beg any question by the use of this label.

He continues (1038b8–9) with the remark that it is impossible for anything which λέγεται καθόλου to be an οὐσία. For that which is predicated universally is necessarily something which can be common to many things (ὃ πλείοσιν ὑπάρχειν πέφυκεν) whereas the οὐσία of something is that which is peculiar (ἴδιος) to it. Τὸ καθόλου cannot therefore be the οὐσία of all the set of objects of which it is predicated; equally it cannot be the οὐσία of nothing. But if it is the οὐσία of one of them, then all the other members of the set will have to be identical with this one, which is absurd; for things which share one οὐσία and τί ἦν εἶναι are one.

According to Ross,[3] the argument has to be interpreted as follows: the Platonist seeks to satisfy the requirement that the universal be ἴδιον to a single thing of which it is the οὐσία by supposing it to be the οὐσία of just one of its particulars; but unfortunately it has as good a claim to be the οὐσία of the other particulars of which it is predicated; so if the requirement of uniqueness is to be fulfilled, these others must be identical with the one selected, which is absurd. (From now on I shall call the requirement that an οὐσία be ἴδιος to that of which it is the οὐσία "the uniqueness requirement.")

This interpretation, which requires us to supply a good deal, seems untenable. It is, of course,

[2]Cf. H 1042a15–16: Τῷ δὲ καθόλου καὶ τῷ γένει καὶ αἱ ἰδέαι συνάπτουσιν (κατὰ τὸν αὐτὸν γὰρ λόγον οὐσίαι δοκοῦσιν εἶναι) ["And with the universal and the genus the Ideas are connected (συνάπτουσιν); it is in virtue of the same argument (κατὰ τὸν αὐτὸν λόγον) that they are thought to be substances"].

[3]*Aristotle's Metaphysics* (Oxford, 1924), Vol. II, p. 210.

true that if the Platonist said that the universal
animal were the οὐσία of only one particular
ζῷον (say, Socrates), not of Callias, Bucephalus,
and Fido, his position is vulnerable and indeed
absurd. Any such selection would be arbitrary. But
nothing in the text suggests that Aristotle regarded
the argument as vulnerable in just this way. Moreover,
the very absurdity and indeed lunacy of the position
put into the mouth of the Platonist may be thought
to be an argument against the view that he is toying
with the possibility of satisfying the uniqueness requirement in this way. Also, as reconstructed by Ross,
the argument seems to beg the question. The Platonist
begins by supposing that a universal like ζῷον is the
οὐσία of just one animal, e.g. Socrates; he is then told
that he will be committed to regarding τὰ ἄλλα as
identical with him, since τὰ ἄλλα will also have τὸ
καθόλου as their οὐσία. But this is precisely what the
Platonist is desperately denying. Τὰ ἄλλα must, on
this view, refer to those particulars of which τὸ
καθόλου is predicated other than the one of which it
is the οὐσία; and the Platonist will not agree that they
have τὸ καθόλου for their οὐσία without argument,
for the position he has just taken up is the denial of
this. As the passage stands he is represented as agreeing
without argument that all particulars of which τὸ
καθόλου is predicated have it for their οὐσία, and not
simply one of them. So Ross's interpretation does not
really find any argument in the passage at all.

Cherniss interprets the passage in a different way.[4]
According to him, the sentence ἑνὸς δ᾽ εἰ ἔσται, καὶ
τἆλλα τοῦτ᾽ ἔσται* provides a reason for the dis-
junction stated in the first half of the previous sentence

[4] Aristotle's Criticism of Plato and the Academy (Baltimore,
1944), p. 318, n. 220.
*"If it is to be the substance of one, this one will be the others
also."

("either τὸ καθόλου is the οὐσία of *all* the particulars
falling under it or of none of them"); while
ὧν γὰρ μία ἡ οὐσία καὶ τὸ τί ἦν εἶναι ἕν, καὶ αὐτὰ ἕν*
provides a reason for saying that it cannot be the
οὐσία of all of them. This interpretation avoids the
difficulty mentioned just now in Ross's interpretation:
that no argument is presented which could lead the
Platonist to abandon his suggestion that τὸ καθόλου
might be the οὐσία of one thing. On the other hand,
it is hard not to take 11, 14–15 (ὧν γὰρ μία . . .)
as providing a reason for what is asserted immediately
before, especially as it is readily intelligible as a reason
for it. But even if we accept Cherniss' view, the passage concerned (11, 9–15) seems best interpreted, as
I shall argue, not as an argument which is decisive as
it stands, but as one which shows what a Platonist is
committed to if he insists on regarding τὸ καθόλου as
οὐσία. He will be committed to accepting it as the
οὐσία of all its particulars, and treating these as identical with one another.

In order to see how this and later passages in these
chapters are to be interpreted, we need to raise a major
problem which immediately faces anyone who reads
this passage in the light of Aristotle's criticism of
Plato. Aristotle's answer to the question, "What is
οὐσία?" is that what is οὐσία in the fullest sense is
the εἶδος or τὶ ἦν εἶναι of something. This comes
out very clearly in chapter 17, but it is already present
as a doctrine in the chapters of Z before chapter 13.
It emerges from the identification of εἶδος with
τί ἦν εἶναι and of this with πρώτη οὐσία at 1032b1–2.
Thus Aristotle is presumably committed to holding that the form of the species *man* is a substance. But this seems incompatible with the doctrine
that nothing καθόλου can be a substance: for *man*

*"For things whose substance is one and whose essence is one
are themselves also one."

is surely predicated universally of Socrates, Callias, etc. How can the species man be an οὐσία, if any οὐσία has to belong ὡς ἴδιον to that of which it is the οὐσία? It is clearly of no use to seek to avoid this difficulty by saying that, when discussing the suggestion that τὰ καθόλου are οὐσίαι, Aristotle has in mind only the higher genera into which species fall. For his own theory of substance may obviously still be open to the objections he makes to the claims of τὰ καθόλου λεγόμενα to be substances even if he himself only uses these arguments against the claims of higher genera to be οὐσίαι.

One way of escaping these difficulties is to suppose that in Z Aristotle, where he says that οὐσία is εἶδος, has in mind not the form common to all members of a species but something peculiar to an individual member. Thus the οὐσία of Socrates will be peculiar to him and will not be something predicated of anything universally. The thesis that, as well as the form of species, there is a form peculiar to each member of a species to be found, almost certainly, in Λ, and furthermore, the doctrine that in the case of animate objects their form is their soul is difficult to interpret without presupposing some such view as this. If this view can be found independently in Z, we shall have some grounds for interpreting chapter 13 along these lines. There will then be no conflict between the requirements for being an οὐσία stated at the beginning of 13 and the doctrine that οὐσία is form.

This question has been discussed in an article by Professor R. Albritton.[5] Albritton finds clear evidence that Aristotle believed in a distinct form for each individual substance in Λ and M of the Metaphysics and in the De Anima; but in Z and H of the Metaphysics the most he can find is some evidence that

[5]"Forms of Particular Substances in Aristotle's Metaphysics," Journal of Philosophy, Vol. LIV, No. 22 (October 1957).

Aristotle accepted that there was a distinct form for each living substance. This evidence lies in the passages in which the doctrine that the form and οὐσία of a man is his soul occurs. So whether or not these passages be regarded as evidence for the doctrine of particular forms depends on whether we regard the doctrine that the soul is the form of the body as intelligible only with such a view. But, in any case, the most that these passages could be said to point to is the doctrine that there is an individual form for each living individual. However, if Z 13, the passage with which we are immediately concerned, be interpreted as showing that Aristotle thought that there was a distinct form for each individual substance, it would show that Aristotle regarded the doctrine as holding for all individual substances, and not merely those with a ψυχή; for the argument would be a general one. Since nothing καθόλου λεγόμενον can be an οὐσία, and the form of the species is predicated of the plurality of individuals in the species, the οὐσία of each individual substance, whether animate or inanimate, must be a form which is peculiar to it.

Albritton considers the suggestion that chapter 13 implies a doctrine of particular forms and argues that there is nothing in the chapter which forces us to interpret Aristotle in that way. To quote Albritton (p. 706): "One might distinguish, as Aristotle does, ways of being 'one' and agree that things whose substance is one need not be one in every way but only in that of their substance. These are many in number. It follows that nothing one in number can be their substance. But the universal form of man is *not* one in number. . . . It is only one in form. And men are one in form. The one form of man *may*, therefore, be their substance."

This interpretation is very attractive, and I agree with the general approach. But as it stands, it seems to allow the Platonist a very obvious rejoinder. If the form of a species can be said to be an οὐσία, compatibly with the uniqueness condition, because the particulars are ἕν εἴδει, one might equally hold that the genus could be said to be an οὐσία also, in spite of being predicated of many things, since these things (species and particulars) though not ἓν ἀριθμῷ nor ἕν εἴδει are ἕν γένει.* Now it may be thought that the sense in which a group of things which belong to the same genus can be said to be one is weaker than the sense in which things in the same species can be so described, and that therefore the Platonist would at least have to admit that genera like animal are less fully entitled to be called οὐσίαι than species like man. But at least this defense would seem to show that τὰ καθόλου have some claim to be regarded as οὐσίαι; and this is something which Aristotle seems firmly to reject in this chapter. He insists roundly that nothing καθόλου λεγόμενον is a substance, and these assertions are difficult to reconcile with the position that they are substances of a sort, though less fully than certain other items. If he were prepared to concede that both man and animal qualify as οὐσίαι though the latter less than the former, we should have a position like the one he takes up in the Categories (2b7 f.: τῶν δὲ δευτέρων οὐσιῶν μᾶλλον τὸ εἶδος τοῦ γένους).† But it seems clear that this view is now abandoned. So we have the position that if we interpret the chapter along the lines that Albritton suggests, and make the fact that man is the οὐσία of many individuals compatible with the uniqueness requirement, the Platonist will be able, apparently, to find a comparable sense in which animal can be said to be

---

*"One in number," "one in form," "one in genus."

†"Of the secondary substances the species is more a substance than the genus, since it is nearer to the primary substance."

an οὐσία: and that is something Aristotle will not accept.

Although Albritton does not consider this way out for the Platonist, the next paragraph of his article suggests an answer that Aristotle might have made to the position. He says: "The argument would not allow any universal of species to be the substance of its species. The species of a genus, for example, are precisely many in form, not in number, and therefore this genus, which is one in form cannot be their substance." But where does Aristotle say that a genus is one in form? In order to find the argument acceptable we need to know that the genus *animal* is one in form in precisely the same way as that in which the species or individuals of which *animal* is predicated are not one in form. Only if that is so can we regard the argument as establishing a difference in the relation between *man* and the members of this species on the one hand and the relation between *animal* and the species and individuals of which it is predicated on the other.

Albritton does not mention any passage in which Aristotle says that a genus is one in form. But he draws attention a little earlier, amongst other passages, to the beginning of Book I of the Metaphysics. There Aristotle says that those things are one ὧν ἡ νόησις μία, τοιαῦτα δ' ὧν ἀδιαίρετος, ἀδιαίρετος δὲ τοῦ ἀδιαιρέτου εἴδει ἢ ἀριθμῷ (1052a30).* Again, a little later he says τὸ ἑνὶ εἶναι τὸ ἀδιαιρέτῳ ἐστὶν εἶναι.† Since he does not in this passage explicitly mention γένη as examples of things which are ἕν εἴδει we must consider whether he would in fact have allowed a γένος to be something which was

*". . . the other things that are one are those whose definition is one. Of this sort are the things the thought of which is one (ὧν ἡ νόησις μία) i.e. those the thought of which is indivis-indivisible (ἀδιαίρετος); and it is indivisible if the thing is indivisible in kind (εἴδει) or number."

†" 'To be one' means 'to be indivisible'."

ἀδιαίρετον εἴδει. It seems to me that he would not. When he says that something is ἕν εἴδει if it is ἀδιαίρετον εἴδει, he seems to have in mind the same idea that he expressed Z 1034a8 (for example). There he says that Socrates and Callias are ταὐτὸ δὲ εἴδει (ἄτομον γὰρ τὸ εἶδος).* An εἶδος is ἄτομον in the sense that it is not capable of further differentiation. This is precisely what is *not* the case with γένη. If ἄτομον in this passage means the same as 'ἀδιαίρετον' in Book I, then it seems that we are forbidden to treat a γένος as being ἕν εἴδει in the sense distinguished in that passage. Moreover, even if passages can be found in which a genus is described as ἕν εἴδει, this will presumably be in a wider sense of εἶδος in which it is not contrasted with 'γένος', and therefore *not* that sense in which the various species of a genus are not ἕν εἴδει. Again, if it is the case that a γένος is correctly described as ἕν εἴδει, presumably, derivatively from this, there will a sense in which the different species of the genus can themselves be ἕν εἴδει, which could be exploited by the Platonist.

I conclude that Albritton's suggestion does not provide Aristotle with a way of meeting the argument we have put in the Platonist's mouth: that if the form of a species can be allowed to be a substance compatibly with the uniqueness requirement, so can a higher genus. The difficulty seems to be that the suggestion does not take seriously enough Aristotle's several times repeated statement that nothing predicated universally (καθόλου λεγόμενον, κατηγορούμενον, ὕπαρχον) is an οὐσία. On the view we have just criticized, Aristotle is saying simply that nothing that is predicated universally can be a substance, unless the plurality of objects of which it is predicated can themselves be said to be one in a certain sense. This runs into the difficulty

---

*"The same in form; for their form is indivisible."

that the Platonists can provide a sense in which the things of which a genus is predicated can be said to be one. Albritton's suggestion implicitly makes the predication of a universal of many things compatible with the satisfaction of the uniqueness requirement. But what Aristotle says is that since τὸ καθόλου is common to many objects, it cannot be ἴδιον to one. He does not restrict himself to saying that nothing can be a substance which is common to plurality of objects, unless the many are also one. The suggestion under discussion waters down Aristotle's remarks considerably, since it treats the doctrine that nothing καθόλου λεγόμενον is a substance as one accepted by Aristotle only with considerable qualification.

If we take these remarks as they stand and wish still to hold that when Aristotle says that the εἶδος is οὐσία he has in mind a form common to all numbers of a species, we must suppose that he would have denied that the form *man* is predicated universally of Socrates, Plato, Callias. If genera, by contrast are predicated of a plurality of objects, we have found a way of interpreting chapter 13 which allows Aristotle, consistently with his own doctrine that substance is form, to deny that anything predicated universally is a substance. For the remarks about τὰ καθόλου λεγόμενα will have application only to genera. I wish to claim that this is precisely the position that Aristotle adopts in *Metaphysics Z*.

This doctrine that the form of a species is not predicated universally of the members of the species involves an obvious departure from the sort of view advanced in, for example, the *Categories*. Indeed it might be said that the theory rejected in chapter 13 is as much the theory held by Aristotle himself earlier as it is that of Plato, though it is probable that in Z 13 Aristotle has Plato mainly in mind, in view of the contents of the succeeding chapters.

In saying that Aristotle denied that a species may properly be said to be predicated universally of its members, I am not of course denying that Aristotle might have allowed that the *name* of a species was predicated of its members. Nor, perhaps, would he have said that it was for *all* purposes impermissible to speak of the form of a species as being predicated universally of its members. What he seems to have thought is that, for the problems with which he is concerned in Z, it is incorrect to say that a species form is predicated universally of a plurality of individuals. It may be helpful at this stage to specify exactly what Aristotle thought could properly be said about species and what could not, on the view that I am advancing. Firstly, he appears to be denying that a species could be predicated universally of its members, and he expresses this in various ways. No οὐσία (and therefore no species) is καθόλου λεγόμενον (1038b9): again (1038b35) none of the things καθόλου ὑπάρχοντα is an οὐσία; the reason given in the next line is that none of the things κοινῇ κατηγορομενα* is τόδε τι, earlier (1038b11) the claims of the Platonist are rejected because he allows to be a substance something which is κοινόν; it is κοινόν because πλείοσιν ὑπάρχειν πέφυκεν. At the end of the whole discussion in these chapters (16, 1041a4), his conclusion is restated: τῶν καθόλου λεγοθένων οὐδὲν οὐσία. An οὐσία is not common to a plurality of objects; it is τόδε τι. A genus is not τόδε τι but τοιόνδε (1039a1). So there is a clear contrast between the things that Aristotle is willing to say about species-forms and the things that can, in his view, be said of genera.

It is interesting to note that in the *Categories* he is unwilling to say that a secondary substance (in the

---

* "Common predicates."

terminology he then used) properly speaking signified
τόδε τι (3b14 f.). At that time he did not object to
the notion that a species was predicated of a plurality
of objects. A secondary substance is then described as
ποῖόν τι,* and the reason given is that κατὰ πολλῶν
ὁ ἄνθρωπος λέγεται καὶ τὸ ζῶον.† Thus, already at
the time when he wrote the *Categories*, he regarded
being predicated of a plurality as strictly incompatible
with being τόδε τι. In *Metaphysics* Z, where the title
πρώτη οὐσία is given to an εἶδος, he rejected the idea
that an εἶδος is predicated of a plurality along with the
idea that it cannot strictly be called τόδε τι. It is characteristic of the *Categories* to regard the difference between genus and species, in respect of right to the name
οὐσία, as merely a matter of degree; and this, I suggest,
goes with a view which regards the relation between a
species and the particulars belonging to it as essentially
the same as that between a genus and its species. In
the *Metaphysics* he thought of genera as κοινῇ
κατηγορούμενα; and this is regarded as incompatible
with saying that a genus is τόδε τι. However, in *Metaphysics* Z 13 he no longer says, as he does in the *Categories* that a genus is not τόδε τι but ποῖον; instead
he says (1039a1): οὐδὲν σημαίνει τῶν κοινῇ κατηγο-
ρουμένων τόδε τι ἀλλὰ τοιόνδε.‡ The word τοιόνδε
replaces ποῖον as the other term of the contrast with
τόδε τι. As the use of the term ποῖον in connection
with something which belongs in the category of substance is obviousy potentially very misleading, it is not
difficult to see why he should have felt the need to use
another word. But I suggest that the reasons he has in
Metaphysics Z for regarding a genus as not τόδε τι but
saying that an εἶδος is strictly not τόδε τι but ποιόν.

Another passage in Z which is worth noticing is the

*"A certain qualification."
†"For both man and animal are predicated of many things."
‡"No common predicate indicates a 'this', but rather a 'such'."

well-known passage explicitly about the Theory of
Forms in 16, 1040b27: ἀλλ' οἱ τὰ εἴδη λέγοντες τῇ
μὲν ὀρθῶς λέγουσιν χωρίζοντες αὐτά, εἴπερ οὐσίαι
εἰσί, τῇ δ' οὐκ ὀρθῶς, ὅτι τὸ ἓν ἐπὶ πολλῶν εἶδος
λέγουσιν.* It is the last phrase I am concerned with.
When Aristotle says that the Platonists went wrong in
describing, τὸ ἓν ἐπὶ πελλῶν as an εἶδος he says something which it would be difficult to square with a
view that εἴδη in one sense are properly described as
ἓν ἐπὶ πολλῶν. Admittedly, Aristotle's conception of
εἴδη was different from Plato's. But in a passage where
Aristotle tells us what is right about the Theory of
Forms as well as what is wrong, it would be strange
if he singled out as the fault in the theory that it calls
something which is 'one over many' an εἶδος if he
himself were ready to use the word εἶδος of something which was ἓν ἐπὶ πολλῶν. I suggest that Aristotle would have denied that the species man was
something 'ἐπὶ' individual men. His complaint against
Plato is that the Theory of Forms treats species and
genera as if they were alike; genera which are correctly described as ἓν ἐπὶ πολλῶν are being treated as
if they were εἴδη and therefore substances. The denial
that an εἶδος is ἓν ἐπὶ πολλῶν goes with the denial
that anything κοινῇ κατηγορούμενον is a substance.
This interpretation fits in well with the context, when
it is clear that he still concerned himself with the
evaluation of the claim of things predicated universally
to be substances.

Before I return to a detailed discussion of chapter
13, I ought to deal with a possible objection. It may
be said that Aristotle could not have denied that the
form of a species was something καθόλου and there-

---

*"But those who say the Forms exist, in one respect are right,
in giving the Forms separate existence, *if* they are substances; but
in another respect they are not right, because they say the one
over many is a Form."

fore the denial that any universal is a substance is incompatible with the view that it is εἴδη which are
οὐσίαι, if the εἴδη he has in mind are εἴδη of species
and not εἴδη distinct for each individual member of
a species. Apart from the inherent implausibility of
denying that εἴδη are καθόλου, Aristotle himself commits himself to this in Z. At 1035b27 f., he speaks of
ὁ δ' ἄνθρωπος καὶ ὁ ἵππος καὶ τὰ οὕτως ἐπὶ τῶν
καθ' ἕκαστα, καθόλου δέ etc.* The context is full of
difficulties, but it is clear that what he has in mind in
this passage are the forms of the species to which men
and horses belong. Again, it is substances which are
capable of definition in the strict sense, but definition
is only of τὸ καθόλου (cf. 1035b34, and elsewhere).

As I have indicated earlier, my reply to this is that
a distinction has to be made between the question
whether an item is something καθόλου and the question whether it is καθόλου λεγόμενον. What he is
concerned to deny is that that which is predicated universally is a substance. He is not denying that something which is καθόλου may be an οὐσία; he is saying
that nothing which λέγεται καθόλου or is κοινῇ
κατηγορούμενον is an οὐσία. Thus I think that when,
early in chapter 13 (1038b11–12) he says: τοῦτο γὰρ
λέγεται καθόλου ὃ πλείοσιν ὑπάρχειν πέφυκεν, we
should regard him as saying, not that something is
called a universal if it is such as to belong to several
things, but that something is predicated univesally if
it is such as to belong to several things. Again, when
he sums up the whole discussion at the end of chapter
16, he states his conclusion by saying not simply that
nothing universal is a substance, but that nothing
predicated universally is one.

*"But man and horse and terms which are thus applied to
(ἐπί) individuals, but universally, are not substance but something
composed of this particular formula and this particular matter
treated as universal."

It is time now to return to a detailed consideration
of chapter 13. This general discussion arose out of a
difficulty in seeing how 1038b8–15 provide an argument
against the Platonist. I shall return to this passage
later. In 11, 15–16, he offers another brief argument
against his opponent. An οὐσία is something which
is not said of a ὑποκειμένον, whereas the universal is
always said of ὑποκειμένον τι. The last statement will
have to be regarded, on the view I am defending as
claiming, not that everything universal is said of
ὑποκειμένον τι, but that everything predicated universally is said of ὑποκειμένον τι. If the sentence is taken
in context, this reading is, I think, possible. If this is
correct, Aristotle must deny that an εἶδος λέγεται
καθ' ὑποκειμένου τινός if it is to be regarded as an
οὐσία. This conflicts, apparently, with what is said in
chapter 3, at 1029a23–24: τὰ μὲν γὰρ ἄλλα τῆς
οὐσίας κατηγορεῖται, αὕτη δὲ τῆς ὕλης.* But I think
that the conflict need not worry us greatly. Since the
word ὑποκειμένον is used in several senses, the question whether something λέγεται καθ' ὑποκειμένου
τινός will also have a number of senses, and when
asked about a given item, will have different senses
according to how it is taken. The statement in chapter
13 that no οὐσία λέγεται καθ' ὑποκειμένου τινός
is to be regarded as equivalent to the denial that an
οὐσία is, properly speaking, predicated of the individuals which belong to it. This will not prevent Aristotle
from saying that an εἶδος is, in a sense, predicated of
matter.

Before returning to the argument with which we
started, I will now consider the next section, 1038b16–
30. These are taken by Ross and others to be a series
of further arguments offered by Aristotle against the
view that any universal is a substance. The first argu-

---

* "For the predicates other than substance are predicated of
substance, while substance is predicated of matter."

ment is rather obscure; in 1, 19 ἔστι is corrected by Jaeger in the Oxford Classical Text to 'ἔσται', to bring it into line with ἔσται in 1, 22. This passage, 11, 16–23, is interpreted by Ross as follows: The Platonist concedes that something καθόλου cannot be regarded as an οὐσία in the way a τί ἦν εἶναι is; none the less a genus is an element in a τί ἦν εἶναι, and thus ought to have some claim to be regarded as an οὐσία. But it itself will have to be the τ.η.ε. of something in just the way that the τ.η.ε. in which it occurs as an element is. Thus the amended suggestion of the Platonist amounts to the same as the already rejected suggestion that something καθόλου can be an οὐσία through being a τ.η.ε.; it is subject to the objections raised earlier in the chapter.

At first sight this is plain sailing. The Platonist amends his position to meet the difficulties raised by Aristotle; Aristotle then shows that the amended position is really the same as the original one. But if we look at the actual reasons for saying that the new position is the same as the old, the passage becomes more and more puzzling. The reason given is that it will be ἐκείνου οὐσία ἐν ᾧ εἴδει ὡς ἴδιον ὑπάρχει* (if we follow Jaeger and excise 'οἶον τὸ ζῷον'). But surely if it is conceded that it is the οὐσία of something to which it belong ὡς ἴδιον, then this undermines the reasons given earlier for saying that nothing καθόλου λεγόμενον can be said to be an οὐσία. The argument given earlier was that nothing which did not satisfy what I called the uniqueness requirement can be regarded as an οὐσία. But now Aristotle appears to be saying that it does after all satisfy the uniqueness requirement. It is no use to appeal to the earlier established conclusion that nothing καθόλου λεγ. is an οὐσία in the way that a τ.η.ε. as if the reason for saying

* "The substance of that in which it is present as something peculiar to it."

that it is after all a τ.η.ε. is that it belongs to a unique
εἶδος; it was precisely because this condition is not
fulfilled in the case of καθόλου λεγόμενα that it was
denied that anything καθ. λεγ. can be an οὐσία in the
earlier argument. If it now turns out that something
καθ. λεγ. can be the οὐσία of a single εἶδος, the
earlier argument is called into question. The way out
of this difficulty that I suggest is that 1038b22–23 not
only does, but is intended to, undermine the earlier
argument. The words in question are not used by
Aristotle *propria persona* but are part of a set of arguments which he represents the Platonist as advancing
in favour of his position. I think we should regard the
whole passage from lines 16 to 30 as put into the mouth
of Aristotle's opponent. Aristotle's own objections to
the position begin at line 30: 'ὅλως δὲ συμβαίνει ...'
On the usual interpretation, only ll. 16–18 are attributable to the Platonist, and from 'οὐκοῦν δῆλον'
onwards there are three arguments against his amended
position. But it seems to me that much better sense
can be made of the whole passage down to line 30
if we suppose that it is the Platonist who is speaking.
The first argument, in ll. 16–23, can then be interpreted as follows: The Platonist concedes that it is
not an οὐσία in the way that τὸ τί ἦν εἶναι is. This
concession is temporary; what he means is that it is
not an οὐσία in the way that what are agreed to be
οὐσίαι, namely species, are; it will nevertheless be an
element in a substance-species. It will have a λόγος;
the fact that the λόγος of ζῷον is not a complete
λόγος of the οὐσία *man* makes no difference; since it
has a λόγος, this λόγος will define a unique class of
species of which it is the οὐσία in just the way that
ἄνθρωπος is the οὐσία of individual men. In other
words, the Platonist is insisting that the very same
reasons that enable one to regard ἄνθρωπος as an
οὐσία consistently with the uniqueness requirement

can also enable ζῷον to be regarded as an οὐσία. He insists that species and genera be treated on the same footing. It is noticeable that in 1038b23 he says, ἐν ᾧ εἴδει ὡς ἴδιον ὑπάρχει. This would be an odd remark if Aristotle were talking in his own person; the plurality of species of which ζῷον is predicated do not fall into a single εἶδος but a single γένος. But the universalist is naturally happy to say that the various species of animal fall into a single εἶδος just as much as single men do, since he wishes to assimilate the relation of a genus to its species to the relation of a species to the individuals belonging to it.

Finally, on this section, one point of translation: Ross has to translate 'ἔστι' both in l. 19 and in l. 20 existentially: "It makes no difference if not all the elements in the substance have a definition." He thinks that Aristotle has in mind the difficulty that if the elements of a substance revealed in a definition are themselves substances, we shall be forced to allow indefinable substances, when the process of analysis is carried to its limit, if an infinite regress is to be avoided. On the view I am taking, 'ἔστι' is to be construed in l. 20 as a copula: "It makes no difference if it (sc. the λόγος of ζῷον) is not a λόγος of everything in the substance (sc. man)." Cherniss[6] takes 'ἔστι' in l. 19 and in l. 20 as a copula; on my interpretation, it has to be taken existentially in l. 19, and as a copula in l. 20.

The next argument, beginning with ἔτι in l. 23 also seems to make more sense if it is treated as an argument advanced by the Platonist. The point is that if the elements of a substance which are revealed by a definition are prior to the whole in which they occur, then, if they are not substances, they must be (e.g.) qualities; so quality will be prior to substance. Regarded as an argument in the mouth of the Platonist the

[6]Op. cit.

234 M. J. Woods

argument makes good sense. No doubt the way in which the dilemma is presented is a little simple-minded; it does not follow from the fact that genera are not, properly speaking, οὐσίαι that they belong in some other category. Aristotle's own solution, which is admittedly not easy to understand, is to invoke the notion of potentiality. He says later in the chapter that ἀδύνατον γὰρ οὐσίαν ἐξ οὐσιῶν εἶναι ἐνυπαρχουσῶν ἐντλεχείᾳ (1039a4).* Still later he invokes the matter-form model to explain the relation of genus and differentia (1045a33 f.). However, the objection that if the elements of substance are prior to the whole, they must be substances is exactly the sort of objection that might occur to someone who had read Z 10, where Aristotle is quite happy about saying that some of the parts of a λόγος (by which, presumably, he means the εἶδος) are prior to the whole; and this might readily make someone wonder how the parts of a substance can fail to be substances themselves.

To turn briefly to the third argument in this section, at 1038b29–30, he says that τῷ Σωκράτει ἐνυπάρξει οὐσία, ὥστε δυοῖν ἔσται οὐσία. Ross⁷ glosses this as follows: " 'In Socrates, himself a substance, there will be present as an element a substance (sc. animal), which will therefore be a substance of two things (sc. of the class of animals and also of Socrates)'." I think this is correct; but it makes sense in the context only if we regard it as an argument advanced by the Platonist. It cannot be an objection to regarding something καθόλου λεγόμενον as a substance that it would have to be the οὐσία of two things; for in that sense the species man is the οὐσία of two things, viz. the class of men and also Socrates. Regarded as an argument

---

*"A substance cannot be composed of actually existing substances. . . ."

⁷Op. cit., p. 211.

used by the Platonist, it makes sense. Just as the εἶδος man is the οὐσία of the class of men and, derivatively from that, of Socrates, so the genus *animal* is the οὐσία of the class of animals and also, derivatively from that, of Socrates. Considered as member of the class of men, the οὐσία of Socrates is the species *man*; considered as a member of the class of animals, his οὐσία is the genus ζῶον.

We are now in a position to explain the earlier argument in chapter 13 with which we began. It is not intended as a refutation of the Platonist's position; what Aristotle does is to draw out a consequence of it, which makes his opponent formulate it more clearly. Starting with the class of men, it is suggested that, despite appearances, if the species *man* can be said to be the οὐσία of them, so can ζῶον; Aristotle points out that if it is to be the οὐσία of the class of man, since *animal* is predicated of non-men, then other animals must be shown in some way to be identical with men. This leads the Platonist to formulate his position more carefully. Although *animal*, in relation to the class of men is not an οὐσία in quite the way the species *man* is, it is the τ.η.ε., and therefore οὐσία of a larger class. There is an εἶδος ἐν ᾧ ὡς ἴδιον ὑπάρχει.

Aristotle's own refutation of the Platonist begins at l. 30. He says, in effect, that if we allow that species are substances, then no element of a species revealed by a definition is. His reasons for this are, firstly, that no ζῶον exists χωρὶς, παρὰ τὰ τινά. (As Ross remarks,[8] when he says that there is no ζῶον παρὰ ἀ τινά, he has in mind the point that there is no animal apart from the particular species of animal, not that there is no ζῶον apart from the individual animals.) Secondly, nothing predicated in common is a τόδε τι but only τοιόνδε. I have already discussed this passage. If I am

8Op. cit.

right, he is concerned here to deny that ζῷον is genuinely predicated of a plurality of objects.

He ends by saying that if these propositions are not
accepted, ἄλλα τε πολλὰ συμβαίνει καὶ ὁ τρίτος
ἄνθρωπος.* I end my discussion of this chapter by
considering how he thought that the denial of the
doctrines led to the Third Man. We noticed a little
before that in order to refute the Platonist he makes
use of the fact that no genus exists apart from its
species. This doctrine is not argued for in chapter 13
but in chapter 12. (This, incidentally, explains why
chapter 12 comes where it does in Z; he needed to
establish this in order to disallow the claim of things
καθόλου λεγόμενα to be substances.) The idea that
no genus exists apart from its species raises many problems of interpretation, but I take it that part of what
he is saying can be stated quite simply; he is saying
that nothing can be an animal without being a particular species of animal. This may seem platitudinous but
it is certainly un-Platonic; for in our version of the Theory of Forms, Forms are construed as paradigms or ex-
emplars with only one characteristic; so the form *animal* would have to be an animal without being a
particular kind of animal, and would thus be a counter-
example to the doctrine that there is no ζῷον παρὰ
τὰ τινά in a sense which can be precisely stated. We
are by now familiar with the arguments by which
Aristotle sought to derive the Third-Man regress from
the Theory of Forms thus construed. Can we find
anything analogous relevant to the present passage?

I think we can. The Platonist, who maintains that
the genus which is an element in a species like man is
an οὐσία, is committed to holding that the word ζῷον
is predicated in the same sense both of the species *man*
and the supposed οὐσία which is an element in the

*"If not, many difficulties follow and especially the 'third
man'."

species *man*. But the common element which is present
in all species of animal cannot of course itself be regarded as belonging to any animal-species. So he has
to reject the doctrine that there is no ζῷον παρὰ τὰ
τινά. It is not difficult to see that Aristotle could have
developed a regress similar to the traditional Third-
Man regress against this position; the first step would
be to ask how the word ζῷον came to be used in the
same sense of the species *man* and the supposed common element it shared with other animal species. Something very like this argument seems to be adumbrated
in 14, 1039a30 f.

I have argued that the arguments of chapter 13
against those who say that things καθόλου λεγόμενα
may be substances are not incompatible with Aristotle's
own doctrine that εἴδη are substances. Εἴδη are things
which are not λεγόμενα κατὰ πολλῶν. However, it
may be thought that this remains no more than a
verbal maneuver unless some justification is offered for
treating species differently from genera. What justification is there for Aristotle's denial that *man* κατὰ
πολλῶν λέγεται? The answer, I think, is along the
following lines: It is the species-form *man* which supplies us with a principle for individuation for man:
it is only in virtue of possessing the form *man* that
bits of matter which constitute men are marked off
from one another. To speak of a plurality of objects
I need some means of marking off each member of the
set from other things; I do this, according to Aristotle,
by recognizing occurrences of a certain form in matter.
Thus I must already regard things as possessing the
form before I can think of objects as a genuine plurality. In so far as the statement that the form of a species
is predicated universally of its members implies the
contrary of this, it is incorrect. Aristotle refused to say
that ἄνθρωπος was καθόλου λεγόμενον because that
would suggest that you could distinguish men inde-

pendently of their possession of the form—as if you could first distinguish individual substances and then notice that the predicate applied to them which supplied a basis for distinguishing them in the first place. With species in relation to genera, on the other hand, it is the other way round. The genus does not itself supply a basis for distinguishing species; the species are distinguished by appropriate differentia; in Z a species is virtually equated with its differentia (e.g. at 1038a19), so that species are in a certain sense self-individuating; hence the genus to which they belong is predicated universally of them.

IV. ETHICS

THE MEANING OF ἈΓΑΘΟΝ IN THE *ETHICS* OF ARISTOTLE

H. A. PRICHARD

I have for some time found it increasingly difficult to resist a conclusion so heretical that the mere acceptance of it may seem a proof of lunacy. Yet the failure of a recent attempt to resist it has led me to want to confess the heresy. And at any rate a statement of my reasons may provoke a refutation.

The heresy, in brief, is that Aristotle (in the *Nicomachean Ethics*, except in the two discussions of pleasure—where ἀγαθόν is opposed to φαῦλον and μοχθηρόν) really meant by ἀγαθόν conducive to our happiness, and maintained that when a man does an action deliberately, as distinct from impulsively, he does it simply in order to, i.e. from the desire to, become happy, this being so even when he does what is virtuous or speculates. Of this heresy a corollary is the view that Aristotle, being anxious to persuade men first and foremost to practise speculation and secondarily to do what is virtuous, conceived that, to succeed, what he had to prove was that this was the action necessary to make a man happy. This corollary, how-

From *Moral Obligation* (Oxford, 1949), pp. 40–53. Reprinted by permission of the Clarendon Press, Oxford. Originally published in *Philosophy*, Vol. X, No. 37 (January 1935). For the convenience of the reader, the editor of this volume has added some translations in footnotes, using the Ross version current at the time the essay was written.

ever, which may seem only a further heresy, I propose to ignore. The heresy, in my opinion, is equally attributable to Plato, and for much the same reasons. But for simplicity's sake I propose to confine consideration to Aristotle, with, however, the suggestion that the same argument can be applied to Plato.

In attributing this view to Aristotle I do not mean to imply that he does not repeatedly make statements inconsistent with it. Nor do I mean to imply that the question of the consistency of these statements with the view simply escapes him; it seems to me that it does not, but that owing to a mistake he thought they were consistent with it. Nor do I mean to imply that his acceptance of this view appears on the surface; but rather that it becomes evident once we lay bare certain misleading elements in his account of the motive of deliberate action.

The first two chapters of the *Ethics*, and especially its opening sentence, are undoubtedly puzzling. Aristotle begins by saying: πᾶσα τέχνη καὶ πᾶσα μέθοδος, ὁμοίως δέ πρᾶξίς τε καὶ προαίρεσις, ἀγαθοῦ τινὸς ἐφίεσθαι δοκεῖ διὸ καλῶς ἀπεφήναντο τἀγαθόν οὗ πάντ' ἐφιέται. 'Every art and every inquiry, and similarly every action and purpose, is thought to aim at some good; and for this reason the good has rightly been declared to be that at which all things aim'. Then after pointing out that certain aims or ends are subordinate to others, he contends that there must be one final end to which all others are subordinate, and that this will be τἀγαθόν, the good, and that, consequently, knowledge of this final end will have great influence on our lives, since if we have it, we shall have a definite mark or goal to aim at. And he goes on to say that, this being so, his object in the *Ethics* is to discover what this final end is.

Here, as the rest of the first book shows, Aristotle, in his first sentence, is not simply stating a common opinion, but stating it with approval and on the assumption that it is an opinion which his hearers will accept and so which can be used as a basis for his subsequent argument. And, so regarded, it is very sweeping.

Even if he had said that in every deliberate action we have an aim or are aiming at something, we should have regarded the statement, put forward as expressing a fact obvious to everyone, and so as needing neither elucidation nor discussion, as sufficiently sweeping. But what he does say is more sweeping. In effect, taking for granted that there is always something at which we are aiming, he commits himself to a general statement about its nature, stating that it is always ἀγαθόν τι, or, as we may translate the phrase, a good.

But besides being sweeping it is obscure. Even if Aristotle had said that in all action we are aiming at something, we should have felt that the statement needed elucidation. But saying as he does that we are aiming at something good, we have an additional puzzle. If, instead, he had said that we are always aiming at a pleasure, or at an honour, or at doing some good action, then we should have at least suspected we knew what he meant, whether or not we agreed. But the meaning of ἀγαθόν is not clear.

Consequently to discover his meaning we have to find out not only what he means when he speaks of us in a deliberate action as aiming at something (ἐφίεσθαί τινος) or as having a τέλος or end, but also what he means by ἀγαθόν. And of these tasks, plainly the former has to be accomplished first.

The idea, which of course underlies the *Ethics*, that in all deliberate action we have an end or aim, is one the truth of which we are all likely to maintain when we first consider action, 'action' being a term which, for shortness' sake, I propose to use for deliberate action. The idea goes back to Plato; and Mill expresses it when he says that all action is for the sake of an end. We take for granted that in doing some action

there must be some desire leading or moving us to do
the action, i.e. forming what we call our motive, since,
as we should say, otherwise we should not be doing
the action; or, for this is only to express the same idea
in other words, we take for granted that in doing the
action we have a purpose, i.e. something the desire of
which moves us to do the action. And, taking this for
granted, we are apt to maintain that our purpose in
doing the action always consists in something, other
than the action, which we think the action likely to
cause, directly or indirectly, such as an improvement
in our health which we expect from taking a dose of
medicine.

Further, taking this view of the motive of action,
we are apt to express it metaphorically by saying that
in any action we have an aim or that there is something
at which we are aiming. For when we consider, e.g.,
taking a drug from the desire to become healthy, we
are apt to think of the thing desired, viz. our health,
as that by reference to which we have devised the
action as what is likely to cause it, and so as similar
to the target by reference to the position of which a
shooter arranges his weapon before shooting. We are
also apt to speak of our purpose metaphorically as our
end, as being something which we think will come
into existence at the end of the action. In either case,
however, it is to be noticed that the terms 'end' and
'aim' are merely metaphorical expressions for our purpose, i.e. for that the desire of which is moving us to
act. No doubt further consideration may afterwards
lead us to abandon this view. For certain actions and
notably acts of gratitude or revenge seem prompted by
the desire to do the action we at least hope we are
doing, such as the desire to inflict an injury on another
equal to that to which he has done us. Yet we may
not reflect sufficiently to notice this, or even if we do
we may fail to notice that such actions require us to

modify the view, or may even think, as Aristotle did, that the doctrine may be made to apply to them.

Plato, it may be noticed, expressly formulates this view in the Gorgias. In trying to show that orators and tyrants have the least power in States, he lays down generally[1] that a man in doing what he does wishes not for the action but for that for the sake of which he does it, this being implied to be some result of the action. And in support he urges that a man who takes a drug wishes not for taking the drug but for health, and that a man who takes a voyage wishes not for the sailing and the incurring of dangers but for the wealth for the sake of which he takes the voyage. He is, however, here obviously going too far in asserting that the man does not want to do the action itself, for if the man did not want to do the action, he would not be doing it. What Plato should have said and what would express the view accurately is this:

> A man undoubtedly wants to do what he does, and this desire is moving him. But the desire is always derivative or dependent. His having it depends on his having another desire, viz. the desire of something to which he thinks the action will lead, and that is why this latter desire should be represented as what is moving him, since it is in consequence of having this latter desire that he has the desire to do the action.

The view, therefore, implies the idea that the desire to do some action is always a dependent desire, depending on the desire of something to which we think the action will lead. But, as we soon notice, this latter desire must either be itself an independent desire, i.e. a desire which does not depend on any other, or else imply such a desire, since otherwise, as Aristotle put it, desire would be empty and vain. We are therefore

[1]Gorgias, p. 467.

led to draw a distinction between an independent desire and a desire depending on a desire of something which we think the thing desired will cause. Aristotle, of course, recognized and even emphasized the distinction, but unfortunately he formulated it with a certain inaccuracy. He implies that it should be expressed as that between τὸ βούλεσθαί τι δι' αὐτό, or καθ' αὐτό, and τὸ βούλεσθαί τι δι' ἕτερον. But the latter phrase must be short for τὸ βούλεσθαί τι διὰ τὸ βούλεσθαι ἕτερόν τι, and, this being so, the former phrase must be short for τὸ βούλεσθαί τι διὰ τὸ βούλεσθαι αὐτό, which, meaning wishing for something in consequence of wishing for itself, is not sense. The distinction should have been expressed as that between τὸ βούλεσθαί τι μὴ διὰ τὸ βούλεσθαι ἕτερόν τι and τὸ βούλεσθαί τι διὰ τὸ βούλεσθαι ἕτερόν τι or, to be more accurate, between desiring something not in consequence of desiring something else, and desiring something in consequence of desiring something else to which we think it will lead. And in this connexion it should be noticed that the English phrase for an independent desire, viz. the desire of something for its own sake, which is the equivalent of Aristotle's βούλεσθαί τι δι' αὐτό, has really only the negative meaning of a desire which is not dependent on any other desire.

Further, having reached this distinction, we are soon led, as of course Aristotle was, to hold that in every action we must have some ultimate or final aim, consisting of the object of some independent desire, and to distinguish from this aims which we have but which are not ultimate.

Having drawn this distinction we do not ask: 'Of what sort or sorts are our non-ultimate aims?' since obviously anything may be such an aim. But we do raise the question: 'Of what sort or sorts is our ultimate aim in various actions?'

To this question Aristotle's answer is ἀγαθόν τι, since his opening statement covers ultimate as well as non-ultimate aims. And the most obvious way to ascertain what Aristotle considers our ultimate aim is, of course, simply to find out what he means by ἀγαθόν. But, as should now be obvious, there is also another way. Like ourselves, he must really mean by our ultimate or final aim that the independent desire of which, or, as he would put it, that the desire of which καθ' αὑτό, is moving us to act. Consequently, if he says of certain things that we desire and pursue, i.e. aim at, them καθ' αὑτά, we are entitled to conclude that he considers that in certain instances they are our ultimate aim. Now in chapter 6 of Book I he maintains that there are certain kinds of things, viz. τιμή, φρόνησις, and ἡδονή, which are διωκόμενα καὶ ἀγαπώμενα καθ' αὑτά;* and to these he adds in chapter 7, § 5, νοῦς and πᾶσα ἀρετή,† of which, together with τιμή and ἡδονή, he says that though we choose them for the sake of happiness, we also choose them δι' αὑτά, i.e. as being what they severally are, since we should choose them even if nothing resulted from them. And to say this is only to say in other words that in some instances our ultimate end is an honour, in others it is a pleasure, in others our being φρόνιμος, and so on. Consequently, if we hold him to this, the only possible conclusion for us to draw is that he considers (1) that in such cases our ultimate end is not ἀγαθόν τι, whatever he means by ἀγαθόν, and also (2) that our ultimate end is not always of the same sort, so that no single term could describe it. We thus reach the astonishing conclusion that Aristotle, in insisting as he does that we pursue these things for their own sake, is really ruling out the possibility of maintaining that

---

*"Honour, wisdom, and pleasure, which are pursued and loved for themselves"—Ed.

†"Reason and every virtue"—Ed.

our end is always ἀγαθόν τι, or indeed anything else,
so that we are in a position to maintain that he has
no right to assert that our ultimate end is always an
ἀγαθόν, even before we have attempted to elucidate
what he means by ἀγαθόν.

Further, if we next endeavour, as we obviously
should, to do this, we get another surprise. Aristotle's
nearest approach to an elucidation is to be found in
chapter 6, §§ 7–11, and chapter 7, §§ 1–5. There he
speaks of τὰ καθ' αὑτὰ διωκόμενα καὶ ἀγαπώμενα
as called ἀγαθά in one sense, and gives as illustrations
τιμή, φρόνησις, and ἡδονή; and he speaks of τὰ
ποιητικὰ τούτων ἢ φυλακτικά πως* as called ἀγαθά
in another sense, and he implies that these latter are
διωκτὰ καὶ αἱρετὰ δι' ἕτερον[2] and that πλοῦτος is
an illustration.[3] Further, he appears to consider that
the difference of meaning is elucidated by referring to
the former as ἀγαθὰ καθ' αὑτά and to the latter as
ἀγαθὰ διὰ ταῦτα, i.e. ἀγαθὰ διὰ ἀγαθὰ καθ' αὑτά.
But this unfortunately is no elucidation, since to state
a difference of reason for calling two things ἀγαθόν is
not to state a difference of meaning of ἀγαθόν, and
indeed is to imply that the meaning in both cases is
the same. Nevertheless, these statements seem intended
as an elucidation of the meaning of ἀγαθόν. And the
cause for surprise lies in this, that if they are taken
seriously as an elucidation, the conclusion can only
be that ἀγαθόν includes 'being desired' in its meaning,
and indeed simply means τέλος or end. For if they
are so understood, Aristotle must be intending to say
(1) that when we say of something that it is ἀγαθόν
καθ' αὑτό what we mean is that it is διωκόμενον καὶ
ἀγαπώμενον καθ' αὑτό, i.e. simply that it is an ulti-

---

*"Those which tend to produce or to preserve them somehow."
[2]*Ethics*, I 7, 4. ["Pursued and desirable for the sake of something else."—Ed.]
[3]Ibid. I 5, 8. ["Wealth"—Ed.]

mate end, and (2) that when we say of something that it is ἀγαθὸν δι᾽ ἕτερον, what we mean is that it is διωκόμενον καὶ ἀγαπώμενον δι᾽ ἕτερον, i.e. simply that it is a non-ultimate end. In other words, if here he is interpreted strictly, he is explaining that ἀγαθόν means τέλος, and by the distinction between an ἀγαθὸν καθ᾽ αὑτό and an ἀγαθὸν δι᾽ ἕτερον he means merely the distinction between an ultimate and a non-ultimate end. Yet if anything is certain, it is that when Aristotle says of something, e.g. πλοῦτος, that it is an ἀγαθόν he does not mean that it is a τέλος, i.e. that it is something at which someone is aiming, and that when he says of something, e.g. τιμή or φρόνησις, that it is an ἀγαθὸν καθ᾽ αὑτό, he does not mean that it is someone's ultimate end, i.e. what he speaks of in VI 9, 7 as τὸ τέλος τὸ ἁπλῶς. Apart from other considerations, if he did, then for him to say, as he in effect does, that we always aim at ἀγαθόν τι would be to say nothing, and for him to speak, as he does, of the object of βούλησις as τἀγαθόν would be absurd.

But this being so, what *does* Aristotle mean by ἀγαθόν? Here there is at least one statement which can be made with certainty. Aristotle unquestionably would have said that where we are pursuing something of a certain kind, say, an honour, καθ᾽ αὑτό, we are pursuing it ὡς ἀγαθόν, i.e. as a good. Otherwise there would not even have been verbal consistency between his statements, that we pursue, i.e. aim at, things of certain stated kinds, and that we always aim at ἀγαθόν τι. Again, unless we allow that he would have said this, we cannot make head or tail either of his puzzling statement in Book I, chapter 2 that since, as there must be, there is some end which we desire for its own sake, this end must be τἀγαθόν, or, again, of its sequel in chapter 7, where he proceeds to consider what that is to which the term τἀγαθόν is applicable by con-

sidering which of our various ends is a final end. For
we are entitled to ask: 'Why does Aristotle think that
if we discover something to be desired and pursued
for its own sake, we shall be entitled to say that it is
τἀγαθόν?' And no answer is possible unless we allow
that he thought that in desiring and pursuing something for its own sake we are desiring and pursuing it
ὡς ἀγαθόν.

But Aristotle in saying, as he would have said, that
in pursuing, e.g., an honour, we are pursuing it
ὡς ἀγαθόν could only have meant that we are pursuing it in virtue of thinking that it would possess a
certain character to which he refers by the term
ἀγαθόν, so that by ἀγαθόν he must mean to indicate some character which certain things would have.
Further, this being so, in implying as he does that in
pursuing things of certain different kinds καθ' αὐτά
we are pursuing them ὡς ἀγαθά, he must be implying
that these things of different kinds have, nevertheless,
a common character, viz. that indicated by the term
ἀγαθόν. It will, of course, be objected that he expressly
denies that they have a common character. For he says:
τιμῆς δὲ καὶ φρονήσεως καὶ ἡδονῆς ἕτεροι καὶ διαφέροντες οἱ λόγοι ταύτῃ ᾗ ἀγαθά.[4] But the answer is
simple; viz. that this is merely an inconsistency into
which he is driven by his inability to find in these
things the common character which his theory requires
him to find, and that if he is to succeed in maintaining that we pursue these things of various kinds
ὡς ἀγαθά, he *has* to maintain that in spite of appearances to the contrary they have a common character.

Nevertheless, though we have to insist that Aristotle
in fact holds that in pursuing any of these things

[4]*Ethics* I 6, 11. "But of honour, wisdom, and pleasure, just in
respect of their goodness, the accounts are distinct and diverse."
—Ed.]

καθ᾽ αὑτό, i.e., as we should say, for its own sake, we are pursuing it ὡς ἀγαθόν, we cannot escape the admission that in doing so he is being inconsistent. For to maintain that in pursuing, e.g., an honour, we are pursuing it καθ᾽ αὑτό, or, as we should say, for its own sake, is really to maintain that the desire of an honour moving us is an independent desire, i.e. a desire depending on no other. And, on the other hand, to maintain that in pursuing an honour, we are pursuing it ὡς ἀγαθόν, or as a good, is really to maintain that the desire of an honour moving us is a dependent desire, viz. a desire depending on the desire of something which will possess the character indicated by the word ἀγαθόν, i.e. that we desire an honour only in consequence of desiring something which will possess that character and of thinking that an honour will possess it. It is, in fact, really to maintain that in pursuing an honour, our ultimate aim, i.e. that the independent desire of which is moving us, or what Aristotle would call that which we are pursuing καθ᾽ αὑτό, is not an honour but a good, i.e. something having the character, whatever it may be, which is indicated by the word ἀγαθόν, i.e. that we desire an honour only in consequence of desiring a good. The principle involved will become clearer, if we take a different illustration. In chapter 6 Aristotle speaks of ὁρᾶν as one of the things which are pursued for their own sake; and if he had said that we pursue ὁρᾶν ὡς αἰσθάνεσθαι he would in consistency have had to maintain that what we are pursuing καθ᾽ αὑτό is not ὁρᾶν but αἰσθάνεσθαι,* and that the desire of ὁρᾶν moving us is only a dependent desire depending on our desiring something else which we think ὁρᾶν will be.

It will be objected that there is really no inconsistency, since Aristotle conceives the characteristic referred

---

*"Sight . . . perception."

to by ἀγαθόν as a characteristic of an honour and of
anything else which he would say we pursue καθ' αὑτό,
and that to speak of us as desiring something in respect
of some character which it would have is not to represent our desire of it as dependent. In illustration
it may be urged that to speak of us as, in desiring to
do a courageous action, desiring it as a worthy or virtuous action is not to represent our desire to do a
courageous action as dependent. But the objection cannot be sustained. For if we desire to do a courageous
action, as something which would be a virtuous action,
i.e., really, a something which we think would be a
virtuous action, although our desire does not depend
on a desire of something which we think a courageous
action would *cause*, it does depend on the desire of
something which we think it would *be*. And as a proof
of this dependence we can point to the fact that if,
while having this desire, we were to do a good action
of another sort, e.g. a generous action, the desire would
disappear.

What is in the end plain is that Aristotle cannot
succeed in maintaining that our ultimate end is always
ἀγαθόν τι without abandoning his view that we pursue such things as τιμή and ἀρετή καθ' αὑτά, or, as
we should say, for their own sake, and maintaining
instead that we pursue them as things which we think
will have the character to which the term ἀγαθόν
refers. Nevertheless, in spite of having to allow that
we are thereby attributing inconsistency to Aristotle,
we have to admit that he, in fact, holds that in desiring
and pursuing certain things for their own sakes we are
desiring and pursuing them in respect of their having
a certain character, viz. whatever it be to which he
refers by the term ἀγαθόν.

So far the only clue reached to the meaning of
ἀγαθόν is the idea that Aristotle used it to refer to
a certain character possessed by certain things, the

thought of the possession of which arouses desire for them, and indeed is the only thing which arouses desire for anything, except where our desire depends on another desire.

We have now to try to get to closer quarters with the question of its meaning. The question is really: 'What is the character which Aristotle considered we must think would be possessed by something if we are to desire it, independently of desiring something else to which we think it will lead, that character being what Aristotle used the word ἀγαθόν to refer to?'

Here it seems hardly necessary to point out that the answer cannot be 'goodness'. To rule out this answer it is only necessary to point out two things. First, if Aristotle had meant by ἀγαθόν good, he would have had to represent us as desiring for its own sake any good activity, whether ours or another's, whereas he always implies that a good activity which we desire is an activity of our own, and in addition he would have had to drop, as he never does, the idea of a connexion between a good activity and our own happiness. And second, Aristotle's term ἀγαθόν is always ἀγαθὸν τινί, as appears most obviously in the phrase ἀνθρώπινον ἀγαθόν and in the statement in IX 8, 8–9, where he says that reason always chooses what is best for itself—πᾶς γὰρ νοῦς αἱρεῖται τὸ βέλτιστον ἑαυτῷ—and goes on to add that the man who gives wealth to a friend assigns the greater good, the having done what is noble (τὸ κάλον), to himself. Once, however, we regard this answer as having to be excluded once for all, there seems to be no alternative to attributing to Aristotle a familiar turn of thought to which we are all very prone and which is exemplified in Mill and T. H. Green.

When we consider what we desire we soon come to the conclusion, as of course Aristotle did, that there are things of certain kinds which we desire, not in consequence of thinking that they will have an effect which we desire, but for themselves, such as seeing a beautiful landscape, being in a position of power, helping another, and doing a good action. We then are apt to ask, 'What is the condition of our desiring such things?' and if we do, we are apt to answer—and the tendency is almost irresistible—'It is impossible for us to desire any such thing unless we think of it as something which we should like, since, if we do not think of it thus, we remain simply indifferent to its realization.' Then, if asked what we mean by its being something we should like, we reply: 'Something which would give us enjoyment, or, alternatively, gratification, or, to use a term which will cover either, pleasure.' The tendency is one to which Mill gives expression when he says that desiring a thing and finding it pleasant are two parts of the same phenomenon; and Green exhibits it when he maintains, as in effect he does, that we can desire something only if we think of it as something which will give us satisfaction, i.e. gratification. In maintaining this we are really maintaining that the thing which we at first thought we desired for its own sake, such as seeing a beautiful landscape, or doing a good action, is really only being desired for the sake of a feeling of enjoyment or gratification, or, to put it generally, pleasure, which we think it will cause in us. And correspondingly, where we think of the desire as moving us to act, we are really maintaining that what we at first thought our ultimate end is really only our penultimate end or the proximate means, and that our ultimate end is really a pleasure which we think this will cause. We are, however, apt to think of a thing's giving us enjoyment, or alternatively gratification, as if it were a quality of the thing, just as we think of the loudness of a noise as a quality of the noise. And our tendency to do this is strengthened by the fact that the ordinary way of stating the fact that something X excites a feeling of pleasure, or of gratification, is to say that X is pleasant or gratifying, a way of speaking which suggests that what is in fact a property possessed by X of causing a certain feeling is a quality of X. The tendency is mistaken, since, as anyone must allow in the end, something's giving us enjoyment is not a quality of it, and when we say that something is pleasant, we are not attributing to it a certain quality but stating that it has a certain effect. Nevertheless, the tendency exists. And when it is operative in us, we state our original contention by saying that in desiring to see a beautiful landscape for its own sake, we desire it as something which will be pleasant, and that when we are acting on the desire, our ultimate end is the seeing a beautiful landscape as something which will be pleasant, thereby representing what on our view is really the proximate means to our end as our end.

This being the line of thought to which I referred, it remains for me to try to show that it was taken by Aristotle. Before we consider details we can find two general considerations which are in favour of thinking that he took it. In the first place, if we assume it to be indisputable that he thought that there are things of a certain sort which we desire for their own sake, but that in desiring them we desire them in respect of having a certain character to which he refers by the term ἀγαθόν, and then ask 'What can be the character of which he is thinking?' the only possible answer seems to be: 'That of exciting either enjoyment or gratification.' And in particular two things are in favour of this answer. First, it is easy, from lack of consideration, to think of exciting pleasure as a quality of the thing desired—as indeed Aristotle appears to do when he speaks of virtuous actions (αἱ κατ' ἀρετὴν πράξεις) as φύσει ἡδέα and as ἡδεῖαι καθ' αὐτάς,[5]

[5]*Ethics* I 8, 11.

i.e. as pleasant in virtue of their own nature; and second, the perplexity in which he finds himself in chapter 6 when trying to elucidate the meaning of ἀγαθόν would be accounted for if what he was referring to was something which is not in fact a character common to the various things said to be ἀγαθά, although he tended to think of it as if it was. In the second place he applies the term ἀγαθόν not only to the things which we desire for themselves, but also to the things which produce or preserve them, and it is difficult to see how he can apply the term to the latter unless ἀγαθόν means productive of pleasure, whether directly or not. In fact, only given this meaning is it possible to understand how Aristotle can speak not merely of τιμή but also of πλοῦτος as an ἀγαθόν.

To pass, however, to special considerations, we seem to find evidence, and decisive evidence, in a quarter in which we at first should least expect it. At the beginning of chapter 4 he directs his hearers' attention to the question: τί (ἐστι) τὸ πάντων ἀκρότατον τῶν πρακτῶν ἀγαθῶν, i.e. 'What is it that is the greatest of all achievable goods?' and he proceeds to say that while there is general agreement about the name for it, since both the many and the educated say that it is happiness, yet they differ about what happiness is, the many considering it something the nature of which is clear and obvious, such as pleasure, wealth, or honour, whereas, he implies, the educated consider it something else of which the nature is not obvious. Then in the next chapter he proceeds to state what, to judge from the three most prominent types of life, that of enjoyment, the political life, and that of contemplation, various men consider that the good or happiness is, viz. enjoyment, honour, and contemplation. And later he gives his own view, contending, with the help of an argument based on the idea that

man has a function, that happiness is ψυχῆς ἐνέργειά
τις κατ' ἀρετὴν τελείαν.[6]

Here it has to be admitted that Aristotle is expressing himself in a misleading way. His question 'What
is the greatest of goods?' can be treated as if it had
been the question 'What is a man's ultimate end?' i.e.
τὸ τέλος τὸ ἁπλῶς. For as I 2, 1 and I 7 show, he
considers that to find what is the greatest good, or the
good, we must find a man's final end, i.e. that which
he desires and aims at for its own sake, and in I 5 he
judges what men consider the good from what their
lives show to be their ultimate aim. And his answer
to this question, if taken as it stands, is undeniably
absurd. For, so understood, it is to the effect that,
though all men, when asked 'What is the ultimate
end?', answer by using the same word, viz. εὐδαιμονία,
yet, as they differ about what εὐδαιμονία is, i.e., really,
about the thing for which they are using the word
εὐδαιμονία to stand, some using it to designate pleasure, others wealth, and so on, they are in substance
giving different answers, some meaning by the word
εὐδαιμονία pleasure, others wealth, and so on. But of
course this is not what Aristotle meant. He certainly
did not think that anyone ever meant by εὐδαιμονία
either τιμή or πλοῦτος; and he certainly did not himself mean by it ψυχῆς ἐνέργειά τις κατ' ἀρετὴν
τελείαν. What he undoubtedly meant and thought
others meant by the word εὐδαιμονία is happiness.
Plainly, too, what he thought men differed about was
not the nature of happiness but the conditions of its
realization, and when he says that εὐδαιμονία *is*
ψυχῆς ἐνέργειά τις κατ' ἀρετὴν τελείαν, what he really means is that the latter is what is required for the
realization of happiness. Consideration of the *Ethics*
by itself should be enough to convince us of this, but

---

[6]*Ethics* I 13, 1 ["an activity of the soul in accordance with
perfect virtue."—Ed.]

if it is not, we need only take into account his elucidation of the meaning of the question 'τί ἐστιν;' to be sure that when he asks 'τί ἐστι ἡ εὐδαιμονία'; his meaning is similar to that of the man who, when he asks 'What is colour?' or 'What is sound?' really means 'What are the conditions necessary for its realization?' We must therefore understand Aristotle in chapter 4 to be in effect contending that while it is universally admitted that our ultimate aim is happiness, there is great divergence of view about the conditions, or, more precisely, the proximate conditions, of its realization.

But, this conclusion reached, we can plainly take one step farther and conclude that Aristotle himself is in agreement with the view that our ultimate end is happiness, and that, taking its truth for granted, his *Ethics* is concerned first to prove that it is by virtuous action that it will be realized, and then to work out in detail the character of virtuous action, so that we shall be better able to obtain our aim. In other words, we can conclude that his real answer to the question, 'What is τὸ τέλος τὸ ἁπλῶς, i.e. our ultimate aim?' is not, as we may at first think, ψυχῆς ἐνέργειά τις κατ' ἀρετὴν τελείαν but εὐδαιμονία, i.e. happiness. Putting this otherwise, we can say that the accurate statement of his own view is to be found in I 12, where he gives as a reason why εὐδαιμονία is τίμιον, whereas ἀρετή is merely ἐπαινετόν, that it is for the sake of εὐδαιμονία that we all do everything.[7]

Now, if by thus going behind Aristotle's terminology we are driven to conclude that Aristotle really considered our ultimate end to be always our happiness, or alternatively some particular state of happiness on our part—for sometimes he seems to imply the one view and sometimes the other—we are also driven to

---

[7][ταύτης (i.e. εὐδαιμονίας) γὰρ χάριν τὰ λοιπὰ πάντα πάντε πράττομεν, *Ethics*, I 12, 8.]

conclude that, though he at times makes statements to the contrary, he also holds that where we are said to have as our ultimate end τιμή or ἐνέργειά τις κατ' ἀρετήν or anything else of a kind which we consider a condition of happiness, the thing in question is really according to him only our penultimate end, and the desire of it is only a derivative desire depending on our desire of happiness. And then it becomes obvious that when he implies, as he always does, that in desiring one of these things we desire it as an ἀγαθόν, what he means by ἀγαθόν is 'productive of a state, or rather a feeling, of happiness', i.e., as I think we may say in this context, a feeling of pleasure. Further, this being so, we have to allow that he fundamentally misrepresents his own problem. Assuming that we all always have either a single ultimate aim, or at least, alternatively, an aim of one sort, what he ostensibly maintains is that we are uncertain about its nature, and that therefore he has to discover its nature in order to help us to achieve it. But, as we must now conclude, what he is really maintaining is that though the nature of our ultimate aim, happiness, is known to us, for we all know the nature of that for which the word 'happiness' stands, we are doubtful about the proximate means to it, and that consequently he has to discover the proximate means. In other words, in maintaining ψυχῆς ἐνέργειά τις κατ' ἀρετὴν τελείαν to be our ultimate end of the nature of which we are uncertain, he is putting what on his view is really the proximate means to our end in the place of what on his view is really our end. And if we ask 'How can he have come to misrepresent his own view so fundamentally?', then, if the contentions already advanced are true, we have at hand a satisfactory answer. We can reply that the misrepresentation is due to his making two mistakes to which we are all prone: first, that of thinking of the property of causing happiness as a quality of what

causes it, and secondly, that of thinking that where
we are aiming at something of a certain kind for its
own sake, and so having it as our ultimate end, we are
nevertheless aiming at it in respect of its having a
certain character.

By way of conclusion it may be well to refer to an
objection which will inevitably be raised, viz. that I
have been, in effect, representing Aristotle as a psychological hedonist, and that to do this is absurd. I admit
the charge, but do not consider the representation
absurd. It seems not only possible, but common, to
hold that there are a number of things other than
pleasure which we desire for their own sake, and then
when the question is raised, 'How is it that we desire
these things?', to reply: 'Only because we think they
will give us pleasure.' In my opinion, the reply is mistaken, and is made only because we are apt to think of
the gratification necessarily consequent on the thought
that something which we have desired is realized as
that the thought of which excites the desire. But the
mistake is a very insidious one, as, if I am right, is
shown by the fact that Green, in spite of all the trouble
he takes to point out that Mill falls into it, falls into
it himself.

ΑΓΑΘΟΝ AND ΕΥΔΑΙΜΟΝΙΑ IN THE *ETHICS* OF ARISTOTLE*

J. L. AUSTIN

This article takes its start from an article by Professor H. A. Prichard (*Philosophy*, X [1935], 27–39 [241–60 above]) on "The Meaning of ἀγαθόν in the *Ethics* of Aristotle." It will be seen that I disagree with him, but I think his article has the great merit of raising serious questions.

Statement of Prof. Prichard's conclusions. Prof. Prichard begins by stating his "heretical" conclusions, as follows:

(1) Aristotle really meant by ἀγαθόν "conducive to our happiness."

(2) Aristotle maintained that when a man does an action deliberately, as distinct from impulsively, he does it simply in order to, i.e. from the desire to, become happy, this being so even when he does what is virtuous or speculates.[1]

---

*This paper was composed by the late Professor John L. Austin before World War II, while Professor Prichard was still alive. Some changes and additions were made after World War II. Its publication was made possible by the kind consent of Mrs. J. L. Austin. The author's footnotes are numbered. For the convenience of the reader some translations have been supplied by the editor of this volume. The translation employed is that of W. D. Ross, since his was the version current at the time this paper was written.

[1]This distinction between "speculating" and "doing what is virtuous" is not strictly Aristotelian: θεωρία *is* ἐνέργεια κατὰ τὴν τελειοτάτην ἀρετήν.

(2.1) A corollary: Aristotle, being anxious to persuade men first and foremost to practice speculation and secondarily to do what is virtuous,[1] conceived that, to succeed, what he had to prove was that this was the action necessary to make a man happy.

(The corollary Prof. Prichard ignores, and, at least for the present, I shall do the same.)

His reason for excluding certain passages from consideration invalid. We must first direct our attention to a curious and important reservation, which Prof. Prichard makes in stating his view. Aristotle, he says, means by ἀγαθόν conducive to our happiness "in the *Nicomachean Ethics* [abbreviated *NE* hereafter—Ed.] except in the two discussions of pleasure—where ἀγαθόν is opposed to φαῦλον and μοχθηρόν." We are not here concerned with the restriction to the *NE*, but it is necessary to examine the further restriction, by which we are precluded from using *NE* VII xi–xiv and X i–v.

The argument implied in Prof. Prichard's words seems to be as follows:

(a) In these passages ἀγαθόν means something different from what it means in the rest of the *NE*.

(b) This is shown by the fact that it is, in these two passages opposed to φαῦλον and μοχθηρόν.

With regard to (a), it is most unfortunate that Prof. Prichard does not tell us what ἀγαθόν *does* mean in these two passages.

As to (b), we clearly need further explanation. I hope that the following is a correct expansion of Prof. Prichard's argument.

(1) Throughout the *NE*, with the exception of these two passages, ἀγαθόν is never opposed to φαῦλον or μοχθηρόν, but to something else, presumably κακόν.

(2) In these two passages alone, ἀγαθόν is opposed, not to κακόν, but to φαῦλον and μοχθηρόν.

(3) Since we know on independent grounds that κακόν has a different meaning from φαῦλον or μοχθηρόν, it follows that ἀγαθόν, in these two passages, must have a meaning different from that which it has throughout the rest of the NE.

(To take a parallel case. Suppose that I do not know the meaning of the adjective "green": and that throughout a certain work I find it opposed to the adjective "experienced," except in two passages where it is opposed to "red" and "yellow." Then if I know on other grounds that "experienced" means something sufficiently different from "red" or "yellow," I can infer that "green" must, in these two passages, have a meaning different from that which it has throughout the rest of the work.)

If this is actually the sort of argument on which Prof. Prichard is relying, I think there are considerations which will lead him to abandon it.

(1) ἀγαθόν is opposed to μοχθηρόν elsewhere in the NE—e.g. in IX viii 7—where pleasure is not under discussion. (Not to mention passages in other works, e.g. *Met.* 1020b21). I have not found a case of ἀγαθόν being explicitly opposed to φαῦλον elsewhere, but cp. (3) *infra*.

(2) ἀγαθόν is constantly opposed to κακόν in the two discussions of pleasure: VII i 1–2, xiii 1 and 7, xiv 2 and 9, X ii 5. In VII in particular, the discussion is introduced and terminated by an opposition between ἀγαθόν and κακόν, and in xiv 2 we read: κακῷ γὰρ ἀγαθόν ἐναντίον.

(3) I do not know of any clear distinction between the meaning of κακόν and the meanings of φαῦλον and μοχθηρόν (or πονηρόν) any more than I can clearly distinguish between ἀγαθόν, ἐπιεικές, and σπουδαῖον. The words seem to be used almost indifferently, or at least for "species" of one another which would be equivalent in certain contexts.

Very many passages in the NE, such as III v 3, are evidence of this. But the point seems clear even from the two discussions of pleasure. σπουδαῖον seems equivalent to ἀγαθόν in VII xiv 4, ἐπιεικές to ἀγαθόν in X ii 1, μοχθηρόν seems equivalent to or a species of κακόν in VII xiv 2, φαῦλον to κακόν in X i 2. Pleasures are called ἀγαθαί, σπουδαῖαι, ἐπιεικεῖς (also καλαί, etc.) in apparently the same sense or senses not sufficiently distinguished: and similarly οὐκ ἀγαθαί, μοχθηραί, φαῦλαι (also αἰσχραί, etc.) in apparently the same sense. And these adjectives seem opposed to one another indifferently, cp. e.g. X v 6. (It must be admitted that Aristotle does not use the expression κακαί ἡδοναί: if this requires some explanation, I think one could easily be found.)

It is, of course possible that some distinction can be drawn between κακόν on the one hand and φαῦλον and μοχθηρόν on the other. But (a) It is clearly incumbent on Prof. Prichard to draw it—which he does not do. (b) Even so he would by no means be out of the wood, for (i) it does not seem to be true that ἀγαθόν is, in these passages on pleasures more commonly opposed to φαῦλον and μοχθηρόν than to κακόν. μοχθηρόν only occurs once in each book, and is only used as opposite of ἀγαθόν in VII xiv 2: and there it is only so opposed because it is equated with κακόν. φαῦλον is opposed to ἀγαθόν only once in X i 2, a rather popular passage: and there, as section 5 of the same chapter shows, it is equivalent to κακόν. (ii) Actually ἀγαθόν is in these same passages much more commonly opposed to κακόν, and so presumably has its 'normal' sense. (But we shall see that it is vital for Prof. Prichard that, when Aristotle says "ἡδονή is an ἀγαθόν," ἀγαθόν should never have its 'normal' sense of "conducive to our happiness.") (iii) In a most important passage, X ii 1, exactly the same remarks are made about ἀγαθόν as in I i 1, a passage

on which Prof. Prichard relies in arriving at his interpretation of it as "conducive to our happiness." Here
then ἀγαθόν must presumably have that meaning:
but this is one of the places where ἡδονή is said to be an
ἀγαθόν, which, on Prof. Prichard's interpretation of
ἀγαθόν, does not make sense. *v.i.*

It would seem then that Prof. Prichard's ostensible
argument for excluding these two discussions of pleasure from consideration will not bear examination. And
it is in any case so very recondite that we may be
tempted to think he would never have chanced upon
it, unless he had been *searching* for some reason to
justify the exclusion of these passages.

*Why does he wish to exclude these passages? His
interpretation of* εὐδαιμονία. Why then, we must ask,
should it be important for Prof. Prichard to secure the
exclusion from consideration of the two discussions of
pleasure? In order to understand this, we must first
understand that the whole argument of Prof. Prichard's
paper is based upon a premise which is never expressed,
no doubt because it seems to him obvious; namely,
that "happiness" (his translation of εὐδαιμονία) *means*
a state of feeling pleased. This may be shown as follows:

(1) On p. 39, line 16 [p. 259, l. 37 above] "causing
happiness" is substituted without remark for "causing
pleasure," which was the expression used in the parallel argumentation on e.g. pp. 35–36.

(2) On p. 38, [p. 259)] at the bottom we read "what
he means by ἀγαθόν is productive of a state, or rather
a feeling, of happiness, i.e. as I think we may say in
this context, a feeling of pleasure." This remark is interesting, since it seems to imply that "in other contexts" being happy does *not* mean feeling pleased.
However, we need not worry, I think, about these
other contexts, for it is quite essential to Prof. Prichard's argument at a crucial point that the word

εὐδαιμονία, or in English "happiness," should be and should be known by all to be, at least for purposes of Ethics, entirely clear and unambiguous in meaning: so that, if being happy means feeling pleased in some contexts in the *NE*, it clearly must do so in all thought that concerns the moral philosopher.[2] (The crucial point referred to is found on p. 37 [p. 257] at the bottom, and repeated on p. 39 [p. 259] at the top. Prof. Prichard there maintains that Aristotle cannot be really asking the question he "ostensibly" asks, viz. "What is the nature of happiness?" for there is no uncertainty about that—"the nature of . . . happiness is known to us, for we all know the nature of that for which the word 'happiness' stands.")

(3) On p. 39 [p. 260], in summing up his own contentions, Prof. Prichard says that he has in effect represented Aristotle as a psychological *hedonist*; i.e., I understand, he claims that, according to Aristotle, all deliberate action is done from a desire to produce in ourselves feelings of *pleasure*. Now on p. 27 [p. 241], quoted above, Prof. Prichard said that, according to Aristotle, all deliberate action is done from a desire to become *happy*. Hence being happy and feeling pleased are evidently, for Prof. Prichard, equivalent expressions. (And this enables us to see why he considers his view, as he says on p. 27 [p. 241], "heretical," although, at first sight and as here stated, it does not appear very extraordinary: if we realize that "become happy" means "feel pleased" the view certainly is very strange.)

It is, therefore, clear that Prof. Prichard does not distinguish what we call "being happy" from what we

---

[2]Prichard's reservation, "in this context" whatever it means, is not important here; nor is the contrast between state ("disposition") and feeling. Similarly, on p. 38 [p. 258], a distinction is drawn between "happiness" and "some particular state of happiness": but I do not think that concerns us here.

call "feeling pleased": and he has in fact been good enough to tell me that that is so.

It now becomes evident why the two discussions of pleasure in the NE should have a peculiar interest for him.

For if ἀγαθόν means "conducive to our happiness," and if "happiness" is equivalent to "pleasure"—then how can we ask, as Aristotle does in these passages, whether ἡδονή is an ἀγαθόν? For ἡδονή must presumably be translated "pleasure": so that the question we are asking becomes "Is (our) pleasure conducive to our pleasure?" which is absurd, or at least absurdly limited. Further similar difficulties arise, if we ask, for instance, what could be meant by saying that some ἡδοναί are ἀγαθαί, and, odder still, that some are not ἀγαθαί.

Hence it is essential for Prof. Prichard to maintain that ἀγαθόν has in these passages a meaning different from "conducive to our happiness": but, as we have seen, his reason for saying ἀγαθόν has a new meaning in these two passages is invalid (nor does he explain what ἀγαθόν does mean in them).

But Prof. Prichard has another and quite radical difficulty to face in connection with Aristotle's discussions of pleasure, which in his paper he appears not to appreciate. For Aristotle there discusses the relation of ἡδονή to εὐδαιμονία in such a manner as to make it quite plain that these two Greek words do not mean the same.[3] Whereas Prof. Prichard's whole argument depends on translating εὐδαιμονία "happiness," and taking "happiness" to be equivalent to "pleasure" which must (we assume) be the translation of ἡδονή: so that ἡδονή and εὐδαιμονία ought to mean the same. Hence Prof. Prichard must hold that, in these discussions, not merely ἀγαθόν, but also either

---

[3] εὐδαιμονία is τὸ ἄριστον, ἡδονή is not τὸ ἄριστον: and so on.

εὐδαιμονία or ἡδονή changes its meaning from the normal. Otherwise his view is untenable. As to which alternative he would choose, I do not know: but both are very difficult. He can scarcely hold that εὐδαιμονία changes its meaning, for, as we shall see, much of his argumentation depends on his view that the meaning of εὐδαιμονία was clear and unambiguous. As to ἡδονή, he does hold, as we shall see, that the word is sometimes used in a special restricted sense to include only the σωματικαὶ ἡδοναί: but it is obviously quite impossible to hold that it has only this restricted sense throughout the two fulldress discussions of pleasure. Unfortunately, Prof. Prichard does not notice this additional difficulty.

Even the exclusion of these passages would not suffice to save Prof. Prichard's view from refutation. It would still be open to Prof. Prichard to maintain (and in view of his low opinion of Aristotle's *Ethics*, I think it possible he might do so) that, even apart from other arguments such as that about φαῦλον and μοχθηρόν, these very facts which I have just mentioned are themselves sufficient to show that the two discussions of pleasure are inconsistent with the rest of the *NE* and may therefore be neglected. It need scarcely be pointed out how dangerous this would be: for we are trying to discover the meanings of ἀγαθόν (and εὐδαιμονία) and it is scarcely permissible to eliminate a large part of the evidence, not otherwise known to be incompatible with the rest, on the ground that it will not square with our interpretation of those meanings. At least it would be necessary to prove that εὐδαιμονία *must* elsewhere mean "pleasure": but, it seems to me, Prof. Prichard does not prove this, he assumes it.

However, it would in any case be of no use to exclude from consideration the "two discussions of pleasure." For pleasure is mentioned in many other parts of the *NE*, and precisely the same difficulties for Prof. Prichard's view are to be found in them also.

Let us confine ourselves to Book I, since it is upon that book that Prof. Prichard principally relies, including chapters v and xii, which he cites.

In I v we are told that οἱ πολλοὶ καὶ φορτικώτατοι maintain that εὐδαιμονία is ἡδονή and that Aristotle himself *rejects* this view. According to Prof. Prichard's interpretation, it would seem that he ought to accept it, as tautological. Prof. Prichard did reply, when faced with this, that ἡδονή here, being the end of the ἀπολαυστικὸς βίος, has a special restricted meaning which includes only the σωματικαὶ ἡδοναί (cp. VII xiii 6).[4] This is scarcely obvious, and we should have expected Aristotle's rejection to take a rather different form, if he himself held that our end *is* ἡδονή, although not merely the σωματικαὶ ἡδοναί. However, we need not insist on this passage; others are plainer.

In I xii 5, what Eudoxus said about ἡδονή is compared with what Aristotle himself says about εὐδαιμονία: clearly, then, ἡδονή and εὐδαιμονία are distinct. And, whatever may be true of Sardanapallus, there is no reason whatever to suppose that Eudoxus meant by ἡδονή merely the σωματικαὶ ἡδοναί.

Finally, in I viii the relation of ἡδονή to εὐδαιμονία is discussed very much as in books VII and X: εὐδαιμονία is μεθ' ἡδονῆς ἢ οὐκ ἄνευ ἡδονῆς,* but quite clearly it is distinct from it. (Even if they are necessarily connected, we must not confuse one with the other: cp. *EE* I ii 5.)

We do not, naturally enough, find in Book I, a discussion as to whether ἡδονή is an ἀγαθόν. But the

---

[4]Just as, when Aristotle says ἡδονή is ἀγαθόν, Prof. Prichard says ἀγαθόν has a meaning different from the ordinary, so, when Aristotle distinguishes ἡδονή from εὐδαιμονία, Prof. Prichard says ἡδονή has a meaning different from the ordinary.

*"Accompanied by pleasure or not without pleasure."—Ed.

views that it is τὸ ἀγαθόν or τὸ ἄριστον are mentioned, and, though rejected, not rejected as absurdities
(I v and xii). Moreover, as was pointed out above,
Eudoxus' views are mentioned in I i and xii in pretty
much the same words as in X ii, so that it would seem
that the meaning of ἀγαθόν ought to be the same in
each case.

We see then, that Prof. Prichard cannot exclude
VII xi–xiv and X i–v from consideration, and that they
are fatal to his view. But even if we do exclude them,
other passages, equally fatal, can be produced even
from Book I, on which he relies. So that, if he still
maintains the view, it would seem that he must be
prepared to attribute to Aristotle even more and graver
inconsistencies and oversights than those, already so
numerous, which he attributes to him in his article.
Myself, I am not yet prepared to do this: though I am
only too well aware how imperfect the *Ethics* is in
these respects.

Present state of the problem. So far our results are
negative. εὐδαιμονία does *not* mean a state or feeling
of pleasure and ἀγαθόν does *not* mean conducive to
our pleasure. (It is, however, still possible that ἀγαθόν
may mean conducive to our *happiness*, if "happiness"
is not equivalent to "pleasure.") It certainly is important to discover, therefore, what these two words
do mean. Of the two, εὐδαιμονία is, for reasons which
will appear, considerably the easier to elucidate, and
accordingly I shall consider it first.

Τί ἐστιν εὐδαιμονία; *the meaning of the question.*
Once again I shall take my start from Prof. Prichard's
article. In a passage extending from p. 36 at the bottom
to p. 38 [pp. 256–58 above], he argues that evidence
for his view is to be found in *NE* I iv. I must quote,
I am afraid, at some length.

> At the beginning of Chapter IV he [Aristotle]
> directs his hearers' attention to the question...

"What is it that is the greatest of all achievable goods?" and he proceeds to say that while there is general agreement about the name for it, since both the many and the educated say that it is happiness, yet they differ about what happiness is, the many considering it something the nature of which is clear and obvious, such as pleasure, wealth, or honour, whereas, he implies, the educated consider it something else, of which the nature is not obvious. Then in the next chapter he proceeds to state what, to judge from the most prominent types of life, that of enjoyment, the political life, and that of contemplation, various men consider that the good or happiness is, viz. enjoyment, honour, and contemplation. And later he gives his own view . . . that happiness is ψυχῆς ἐνέργειά τις κατ' ἀρετὴν τελείαν.

Here it has to be admitted that Aristotle is expressing himself in a misleading way. His question, "What is the greatest of goods?" can be treated as if it had been the question, "What is man's ultimate end?" . . . And his answer to this question, if taken as it stands, is undeniably absurd. For, so understood, it is to the effect that, though all men, when asked "What is the ultimate end?" answer by using the same word, viz. εὐδαιμονία, yet, as they differ about what εὐδαιμονία is, i.e. really, about the thing for which they are using the word εὐδαιμονία to stand, some using it to designate pleasure, others wealth, and so on, they are in substance giving different answers, some meaning by the word εὐδαιμονία pleasure, others wealth, and so on. But of course this is not what Aristotle meant. He certainly did not think that anyone ever meant by εὐδαιμονία either τιμή or πλοῦτος; and he certainly did not himself mean by it ψυχῆς ἐνέργειά τις κατ' ἀρετὴν τελείαν. What he undoubtedly meant and thought

others meant by the word εὐδαιμονία is happiness.
Plainly too, what he thought men differed about was
not the nature of happiness but the conditions of
its realization, and when he says that εὐδαιμονία *is*
ψυχῆς ἐνέργειά τις κατ' ἀρετὴν τελείαν, what he
really means is that the latter is what is required for
the realization of happiness . . . this meaning is similar to that of the man who, when he asks "What is
colour?" or "What is sound?" really means "What
are the conditions necessary for its realization?"

Here is the passage, I iv 1–3: Λέγωμεν . . . τὶ τὸ
πάντων ἀκρότατον τῶν πρακτῶν ἀγαθῶν, ὀνόματι
μὲν οὖν σχεδὸν ὑπὸ τῶν πλείστων ὁμολογεῖται· τὴν
γὰρ εὐδαιμονίαν καὶ οἱ πολλοὶ καὶ οἱ χαρίεντες λέγουσιν, τὸ δ' εὖ ζῆν καὶ τὸ τῷ πράττειν ταὐτὸν ὑπολαμβάνουσι τῷ εὐδαιμονεῖν. περὶ δὲ τῆς εὐδαιμονίας,
τί ἐστιν, ἀμφισβήτουσι καὶ οὐχ ὁμοίως οἱ πολλοὶ τοῖς
σοφοῖς ἀποδιδόασιν. οἳ μὲν γὰρ τῶν ἐναργῶν τι καὶ
φανερῶν, οἷον ἡδονὴν ἢ πλοῦτον τιμήν κτλ.*

Whence does Prof. Prichard derive his confidence
that Aristotle is misrepresenting his own problem? If
he is, it must be admitted that the misrepresentation
is pretty consistent. Right through to Book X Aristotle
always purports to be telling us "what εὐδαιμονία is."
(He summarizes the present passage in almost the same
words again in I vii 9.)[5] Moreover, Aristotle is, of course,
aware of the very kind of misrepresentation of which
Prof. Prichard accuses him: compare what he says about

---

*"Let us state . . . what is the highest of all goods achievable
by action. Verbally there is very general agreement; for both the
general run of men and people of superior refinement say that it is
happiness, and identify living well and doing well with being
happy; but with regard to what happiness is they differ, and the
many do not give the same account as the wise. For the former
think it is some plain and obvious thing, like pleasure, wealth, or
honour; etc."—Ed.

[5]The only reasonable alternative is to hold that in both passages it is really τὸ ἄριστον ἀνθρώπῳ which is being elucidated.

pleasure in VII xii 3 and X iii 6, rebuking those who maintained that pleasure *is* a γένεσις, when they really meant that a certain γένεσις is the condition of the realization of pleasure.

The real reason for Prof. Prichard's confidence is to be found in his unquestioned assumption that εὐδαιμονία means pleasure. This assumption is stated in the passage above: "What Aristotle undoubtedly meant and thought others meant by εὐδαιμονία is happiness." (This is, of course, rather odd as it stands, since Aristotle did not know English: it would lose its plausibility if we substituted ἡδονή for "happiness.") For if εὐδαιμονία were the Greek word for 'pleasure', it might well be contended that to ask τί ἐστιν εὐδαιμονία; *must* be misleading: for it might very well be held[6] that 'pleasure' stands for something unanalyzable and *sui generis*, which we either know, and know with entire adequacy, from experiencing it, or do not know at all. Pleasure might, on these lines, very well be considered to be in the same case as colour and sound, to which, accordingly, Prof. Prichard without hesitation compares εὐδαιμονία. In such cases, one who asks "what is so-and-so?" will very probably be found to be asking "what are the conditions for its realization?" And whether or not 'pleasure' could in any sense be analyzed, at least e.g. the person who said pleasure is honour or wealth would obviously be suspect of only really intending to give conditions of realization.

However, εὐδαιμονία does not mean pleasure, as we have seen. And this very passage proves as well as another that it does not. This is not merely because the theory that εὐδαιμονία means or "is" ἡδονή is rejected, but also because in a most important clause omitted in Prof. Prichard's paraphrase, εὐδαιμονία is said to be equivalent to τὸ εὖ ζῆν καὶ εὖ πράττειν which can-

[6]I do not enquire whether this would be correct.

not mean "feeling pleased." To this we shall return shortly.

Prof. Prichard seems to make out that, apart from the fact that the Greeks did not disagree about what εὐδαιμονία stands for, Aristotle's actual presentation of his question makes it in general an absurd one. Certainly, Prof. Prichard's ostensible argument for maintaining that Aristotle here misrepresents his own problem is not very explicit. According to him, Aristotle says that men agree only on the *name* for the τέλος, viz. εὐδαιμονία, but disagree about what it is used to stand for, or to designate. This, he says, is undeniably absurd. Now why? Has Prof. Prichard any other reason for saying so, except his belief that there could, in fact (owing to the unanalyzable nature of what εὐδαιμονία does stand for), be no disagreement about what εὐδαιμονία stands for?

He seems to suppose that, according to Aristotle, (1) men agree *only* on the name; (2) that is a substantial measure of agreement; (3) what is being (mistakenly) asked for is some *synonym* for εὐδαιμονία, in the simplest sense—some other word or phrase which stands for precisely the same as εὐδαιμονία stands for. (Somewhat as though, when asked for the answer to a mathematical problem, all should agree that the name for the answer was '*k*' while disagreeing as to the number which '*k*' stands for.) I do not know whether even this would be undeniably absurd (always assuming that in fact all did *not* know εὐδαιμονία to stand for 'pleasure'): but in any case, Aristotle does none of these things.

(1) According to Aristotle, men agree, not merely on the name εὐδαιμονία, but also that εὐδαιμονία is equivalent to τὸ εὖ ζῆν καὶ εὖ πράττειν. (This statement Prof. Prichard omits in his paraphrase.) Moreover, it transpires later that they also agree on a number of other propositions about the characteristics

of εὐδαιμονία, which are listed in chapters viii and ix–xii.

(2) As is shown by I vii 9, Aristotle does not think that the agreement on the name alone is very substantial. And indeed it is clear even from chapter iv that this agreement could cover most radical disagreements.

(3) Aristotle is not, I believe, searching for some simple synonym for εὐδαιμονία, but rather for an 'analysis' of its meaning. While satisfactory as a preliminary statement, this does not make it sufficiently clear what exactly Aristotle is doing.* All men know more or less vaguely what is meant by εὐδαιμονία or τὸ εὖ ζῆν καὶ εὖ πράττειν, and agree on many propositions about it: but when they attempt to clarify that meaning, they disagree. Cp. I vii 9: ἀλλ᾽ ἴσως τὴν μὲν εὐδαιμονίαν τὸ ἄριστον λέγειν ὁμολογούμενόν τι φαίνεται, ποθεῖται δ᾽ ἐναργέστερον τί ἐστιν ἔτι λεχθῆναι.†

To search thus for an analysis of the meaning of εὐδαιμονία does not seem to me absurd, except on the false assumption that its meaning was, and was known to be, simple and unanalyzable. We might, to take a similar case, agree that the aim of the statesman is "liberty" or "justice," and yet, in a perfectly intelligible sense, disagree about "what liberty is" or "what justice is."

**There is no doubt, however, that this account of what Aristotle is asking when he asks τί ἐστιν εὐδαιμονία; is far from entirely satisfying. For we need to distinguish from the analysis of the meaning of εὐδαιμονία another procedure altogether, namely the

---

*At this point, in view of the state of the manuscript, some editing by Mr. Urmson was required.—Ed.

†"Presumably, however, to say that happiness is the chief good seems a platitude, and a clearer account of what it is is still desired."—Ed.

**See below under the same sign.

"discovery" of those things, or that life, as he would rather ordinarily say, which satisfy the definition of εὐδαιμονία when that has been discovered. As Moore has insisted, in the case of 'good' (which will occupy us later), it is important to distinguish the discovery of what a word means from the discovery of those things in which the characters meant by the word in fact reside. (Of course this latter procedure is still not what Prichard means when he speaks of discovering 'the conditions for the realization' of something.) This is too simple a view for modern times, since few will accept that goodness is a character in this simple sense. But we still would distinguish the meaning of εὐδαιμονία—the best life for man, etc.—from what we may call the specification of the good life: what the good life allegedly consists in concretely. The whole problem arises over the connection between these two.

There is justice in Prichard's remark that Aristotle "certainly does not think that anyone ever *meant* by εὐδαιμονία either τιμή or πλοῦτος." They were capable of having *said* that they meant this, but would have more plausibly claimed that τιμή or πλοῦτος was what satisfied the specification of εὐδαιμονία. But it is not so clear that "he certainly did not himself mean by it ψυχῆς ἐνέργεια τις κατ' ἀρετὴν τελείαν," at least ἐν βίῳ τελείῳ. It is hard to discover, especially in I vii, where the analysis ends and the other process begins. It is perhaps impossible to judge how much is meant to be analysis. Certainly εὐδαιμονία is analyzed (ταὐτὸν ὑπολαμβάνουσι) as τὸ εὖ ζῆν καὶ εὖ πράττειν. Then ἐν βίῳ τελείῳ (ambiguous phrase!) also seems clearly part of the meaning of εὐδαιμονία. I *believe* that the whole of I vii 9–16 is intended to be an analysis of that meaning. And it results, as it should, in a clear and full definition, referred to as ὁ λόγος of εὐδαιμονία or of τὸ ἄριστον. Moreover *EE* II i 10 says that ψυχῆς ἐνέργεια κατ' ἀρετήν is τὸ γένος καὶ τὸν ὅρον εὐδαιμονίας. If it had been said that Aristotle did not mean by εὐδαιμονία θεωρία, that would, I think, be certainly true: and it is θεωρία which, in Aristotle's theory, occupies the place of ἡδονή and πλοῦτος in rival theories, as chapter v plainly shows.

But when Aristotle discusses what are in fact the special virtues, and which is the most perfect, he cannot be said any longer to be analyzing the meaning of εὐδαιμονία. He is asking τί ἐστιν εὐδαιμονία; in a different sense: what are the virtues that fill the bill. Even in X viii 8, where the conclusion is reached: ὥστ' εἴη ἂν ἡ εὐδαιμονία θεωρία τις, it is evident that εὐδαιμονία does not mean θεωρία—ἐφ' ὅσον δὴ διατείνει ἡ θεωρία καὶ ἡ εὐδαιμονία, καὶ οἷς μάλιστα ὑπάρχει τὸ θεωρεῖν καὶ τὸ εὐδαιμονεῖν οὐ κατὰ συμβεβηκὸς ἀλλὰ κατὰ τὴν θεωρίαν.**

So Aristotle's distinction between analysis and specification is most unclear. But there is some excuse for Aristotle perhaps, in that εὐδαιμονία does not stand for some character, such as goodness might be, but for a certain kind of life, or ἐνέργεια (Aristotle is unclear as to which): in such a case it is not so easy clearly to observe Prof. Moore's distinction, or even one such as Hare's or Urmson's between meaning and criteria. Suppose we were to ask, for instance, "What is golfing?" But there is this finally to be said. If Aristotle had thought that εὐδαιμονία, like golfing, resided in fact in only one activity of one kind of creature, there would have been more excuse for him than is

**The material included between the double stars required extensive editing by Mr. Urmson because the manuscript on these pages was complicated by notes, corrections, and revisions. Ross's translation of this Greek passage reads: "Happiness extends, then, just so far as contemplation does, and those to whom contemplation more fully belongs are more truly happy, not as mere concomitant but in virtue of the contemplation; . . . Happiness, therefore, must be some form of contemplation."—Ed.

actually the case. For actually he does think that
εὐδαιμονία is achieved, in different ways, by gods and
by men: hence εὐδαιμονία cannot mean those activities in which human εὐδαιμονία is found. (Unfortunately, of course, his statements on divine εὐδαιμονία
are rudimentary, and it is very doubtful, e.g. how
ἐν βίῳ τελείῳ can be a part of the meaning of εὐδαιμονία if the gods are also εὐδαίμονες!)

Some distinctions, however, though not this requisite
one, Aristotle does draw: in a way he was perhaps on
his way to it. In Rhet. I v ad init. he says we must ask:
τί ἐστιν εὐδαιμονία καὶ τὰ μόρια αὐτῆς; and this distinction is common, though not in the NE. In EE I v
13–14, he calls the particular virtues μόρια τῆς
ἀγαθῆς ζωῆς, which συντείνουσι πρὸς εὐδαιμονίαν.
(This does not, of course, mean that they are "the
conditions for the realization" of εὐδαιμονία: in NE
1129b18, where the μόρια εὐδαιμονίας are mentioned,
they are distinguished from τὰ ποιητικὰ καὶ
φυλακτικὰ εὐδαιμονίας [cp. VI xii 5], a distinction
insisted on in e.g. EE I ii 5. There is a similar distinction in EE I i of ἐν τίσι τὸ εὖ ζῆν from
πῶς κτητόν; compare also MM I ii 9–11:
οὐ γὰρ ἐστιν ἄλλο τι χωρὶς τούτων ἡ εὐδαιμονία
ἀλλὰ ταῦτα.)[7] Now in effect, the discovery of the
μόρια εὐδαιμονίας is the discovery of the activities
which together make up the life which, for man, satisfies the definition of εὐδαιμονία; and we can in a sense
say, as Aristotle does, that this life is εὐδαιμονία.
Nevertheless, εὐδαιμονία does not mean that life, and
its discovery is posterior to the analysis of the meaning
of εὐδαιμονία. Two erroneous presuppositions were,
however, encouraged by Aristotle's failure to be clear
what question he is asking when he writes τί ἐστιν

---

[7]It is important to remember this when interpreting such a
passage as I vii 5. Compare EE II i 12, a better statement.
[Austin's MM is a reference to Magna Moralia—Ed.]

εὐδαιμονία; first, the presupposition that εὐδαιμονία—
the ideal life—is not a will-o'-the-wisp, and that there
is only one possible ideal life; second, that the question
of what fills the bill is throughout purely factual.

Summing up then, the question τί ἐστιν εὐδαιμονία;
is sensible but ambiguous. Aristotle means to ask
firstly: what is the analysis or definition of εὐδαιμονία?
and secondly: what life, in particular for man, satisfies
that definition or specification? (A subsidiary and distinct question is: What are the conditions ὧν οὐκ
ἄνευ, and the methods necessary for the realization of
such a life?)

*What does εὐδαιμονία mean? Some general con-
siderations.* We must now concern ourselves with the
first of these questions: What does εὐδαιμονία mean
in Greek and incidentally what is its translation in
English? But I cannot enter into details of Aristotle's
own analysis: I shall only attempt to show what, according to him, was the vague and common notion
of εὐδαιμονία from which his analysis starts.

According to I iv 2, τὸ εὐδαιμονεῖν was admittedly
equivalent to τὸ εὖ ζῆν καὶ εὖ πράττειν. (In I vii 4 there
is a weaker statement: it is admitted "that the εὐδαίμων
lives and acts well"—but, as Aristotle remarks, on his
own account εὐδαιμονία is living and acting well: and
in both the other *Ethics* the statement is given as in
I iv 2; cp. *MM* I iii 3; *EE* i 10 and I i 7.) εὐδαιμονία,
then, means living a life of a certain kind—of *what*
kind can of course only be discovered by analyzing the
word εὖ, and hence ἀγαθόν (so that the full analysis
of εὐδαιμονία includes that of ἀγαθόν). εὐδαίμων,
I suppose, means literally or, what is often the same,
etymologically, "prospered by a deity": and what the
deities prosper is lives or careers or activities or parts
of these. Aristotle insists on two further points—
εὐδαιμονία means a *complete* life of *activity* of a certain kind. On the latter point, that the reference is to

ἐνέργεια not to ἕξις, he is always firm (cp. also I xii).[8]
On the former point he is not so happy: not only is
βίος τέλειος hopelessly ambiguous (cp. MM I iv 5),
but Aristotle often omits to remember this qualification. So much so that in the end he never explains how
the βίος is made up—only the ἀρεταί which predomi-
nate it.

At any rate, what is important in all this is, that,
though of course we can speak of a man as εὐδαίμων,
the substantive with which εὐδαίμων naturally goes is
βίος or a similar word: a man is only called εὐδαίμων
because his life is so. Hence the discussion in chapter
v of the various βίοι which lay claim to being
εὐδαιμονία.[9] And hence the saying "call no man
εὐδαίμων until he is dead" (I x i).

Similarly the forms εὐδαιμονίζειν and εὐδαιμονισμός,
which seem to mean "to congratulate," "congratula-
tion." That whereon I congratulate someone is an
achievement, an activity and normally a completed
one (though normally also, of course, of less extent
than his whole career). With reference to this point
consider I v 6 and viii 9.

These considerations show conclusively that εὐδαιμονία could not mean "pleasure": pleasure is a feeling,
not a life of a certain kind nor an achievement: nor do
I congratulate someone on his feeling pleased: and it

[8]On p. 38 [p. 258], Professor Prichard makes what seems to me
serious misstatements about I xii. "In other words . . . everything
else." The contrast in the first sentence I, of course, consider
mistaken. As for the rest, the quotation given is actually from
section viii where εὐδαιμονία is not contrasted with ἀρετή at
all. The contrast with ἀρετή is in ii and vi: ἀρετή is ἐπαινετὸν
qua τὸ ποῖον καὶ πρὸς τι εἶναι — viz. the ἐνεργείαι (πράξεις,
ἔργα) which are εὐδαιμονία: the ἐνεργείαι are τίμια and are
εὐδαιμονία. Professor Prichard talks as though in xii ἐνεργείαι
κατ' ἀρετήν were ἐπαινετά: they are τίμια!

[9]And when in I iv the suggestion is made that εὐδαιμονία is
ἡδονή or πλοῦτος, that is loose language (as V shows) for
the life in which most pleasure or most wealth is gained.

would be silly to say "call no man pleased until he is dead."

There is, however, Aristotle's own remark in I iv that many people do maintain that εὐδαιμονία *is* ἡδονή, as others πλοῦτος or τιμή. This is a loose remark—as Prof. Prichard claims, though not in his way. His explanation, that Aristotle meant that some maintain that εὐδαιμονία is *produced* by ἡδονή, also πλοῦτος. etc., is incorrect. Aristotle himself shows what he meant more fully in chapter v. The view was that εὐδαιμονία is the ἀπολαυστικὸς βίος, the life in which most pleasure is felt. Likewise the identification with πλοῦτος should be taken as "the life in which most wealth is gained" (not, of course "is by definition" but "in fact resides in").

If we want a translation of εὐδαιμονία which will not mislead, as "happiness" appears to mislead Prof. Prichard, we might use as a prophylactic "success." "Success" is at least a word of the same *type*, so to say, as εὐδαιμονία. "Success" does mean living and acting well: a life or a part of it is "successful": and with some hesitations I do congratulate on "success"; it might well be said "call no man successful until he is dead." Furthermore, success demands just that fortunate supply of εὐτυχία, εὐημερία, which Aristotle admits in I viii 15–17 is also a necessary condition for εὐδαιμονία.

It is true, however, that "success" is not a moral notion for us. Perhaps this is no great disadvantage, for it is doubtful how far a pagan ethic, such as the Greek (or the Chinese) gains by a translation which imports our own moral notions: εὐδαιμονία is certainly quite an unchristian ideal. Still, we do require a word to import some form of *commendation*, as εὐδαίμων did, and to certain non-personal standards.

**That εὐδαιμονία did mean life of activity of a certain kind is almost certainly the correct analysis;

and that it did further mean life of ἀρεταί seems equally correct. So we may say that the analysis in I vii 8–16
is correct and is supported by I viii. However we must
also say: (a) That roundabout way of bringing into
the discussion ψυχή and ἔργον is a piece of unnecessary Aristotelian metaphysics. It is not really made use
of until the very end, in the argument for the su-
premacy of θεωρία; the argument proceeds straight on
to the ἀρεταί. (b) The whole discussion here is *not*
purely factual; its nature is disguised by the trans-
ference of commendation to the ἀρεταί. (c) Of the
three lives suggested none accords with the popular
view which was that of Tellus the Athenian.* His
ideal is omitted altogether except when allowed in by
the back door suddenly in Book X. (d) It might be
argued that he omits to give sufficient consideration to
μεθ' ἡδονῆς ἢ οὐκ ἄνευ ἡδονῆς and it might be argued further that not enough deference is shown to
ψυχικόν—people may have meant by this something
genuinely internal, as did later the Stoics. Quite possibly εὐδαιμονία *did* have this "meaning" too.**

Nevertheless, "happiness" is probably after all to be
preferred as a translation, partly because it is traditional,
and still more because it is fairly colourless.[10] It seems
to me very rash to assume that in common English
"happiness" obviously means feeling pleased: probably
it has several more or less vague meanings. Take the
lines:

---

*Tellus the Athenian is mentioned by Plutarch in his *Life of
Solon*, where Solon is said to describe him as a happy man on
account of his honesty, his having good children, his having a
competent estate, and his having died bravely in battle for his
country. Tellus appears to have been a plain man whose happiness, nevertheless, Solon holds up to Croesus.—Ed.

** . . . ** This passage appears to be a later addition by Austin,
which we inserted here in a somewhat expanded form.—Ed.

[10]Success also does not always or usually refer to life *as a whole*:
and it has perhaps a nuance of *competitiveness*.

> "This is the happy warrior, this is He
> That every Man at arms should wish to be."

I do not think Wordsworth meant by that: "This is the warrior who feels *pleased*." Indeed, he is

> "Doomed to go in company with Pain
> And fear and bloodshed, miserable train."

(Though no doubt his life is μεθ' ἡδονῆς ἤ οὐκ ἄνευ ἡδονῆς as Aristotle likes to assume or feebly to argue his own chosen one must be.) What every man at arms is being incited to wish, is not so much to get for himself *feelings* comparable to those of the paragon, as to imitate his *life*. I think, then, that if we are on our guard against misleading nuances, "happiness" is still the best translation for εὐδαιμονία.

The question of the relation of εὐδαιμονία to ἡδονή has not, it should be noticed, yet been cleared up. It to a great extent coincides with the equally difficult problem of the relation of τὸ ἀγαθόν to τὸ ἡδύ. Both must be reserved for a separate discussion later.

ἀγαθόν—Does Aristotle tell us what its meaning is? Prof. Prichard's contention is, it will be remembered, that Aristotle really means by ἀγαθόν "conducive to our happiness." Not concerning ourselves for the moment with the precise interpretation given, we may notice, *firstly*, that he is purporting to give Aristotle's answer to a question which Aristotle himself expressly declines to answer, viz. what is the meaning of ἀγαθόν? And *secondly*, that the answer given, implying as it does that ἀγαθόν *does* have a *single* meaning, is of a kind which Aristotle himself is at pains to prove impossible.

Let us take the translation of ἀγαθόν as "good" here for granted, and let us once more, following Prof. Moore, distinguish between two very different sorts of question, which are commonly asked in books on ethics. We are investigating, we may say, the Good:

but we may intend to ask: (1) What does the word
'good' mean?[11] or (2) What things are good, and in
what degrees? Of course, these two questions may be
formulated in a variety of ways. For (1) we may substitute: What is the nature of goodness? or: In saying
of anything that it is good, what am I saying about
it? even: What sort of a predicate is 'good'? and so
on. For (2) we may substitute: Of what things may
it be truly said that they are good? And which is the
best of them? and so on.

To these two different sorts of question, as Moore
claimed, we shall get two correspondingly different
sorts of answer. To (1) the answer might be: Goodness is a simple unanalyzable quality like yellow, or:
"Goodness" means "approved by me," or: To say of
anything that it is good, is to say that it is conducive
to happiness, or: 'Good' is an evaluative word. Whereas
to (2), the answer might be: Friendship is good, or:
Violence is better than justice, and so on. Note here
that it is assumed that the only sense in which ἀγαθόν
has a "meaning" is in some "factual" sense. Aristotle
assumes this too.

Now we must ask, on this distinction does Aristotle
concern himself with both these questions or with
one only? And if the latter, with which? And I think
that we must answer, that he concerns himself pro-
fessedly with the second only.[12]

For Aristotle himself is aware of and draws this distinction between the two questions, and says that, in
the *Ethics*, he is concerned only with the second. This
he does in the celebrated chapter I vi. He there con-

[11]Which is itself probably an ambiguous question, but we may
let this pass for the moment. (We also have to distinguish (a)
how to translate a word? (b) what does someone say about the
analysis of the meaning or of the definition of a word? and both
of these from (c) possibly different senses of 'mean'.)

[12]And with that only in the more special form: "What particular things are good, and in what degrees, *for man*?"

futes those who had supposed that the word ἀγαθόν
always stands for a single identical predicate.[13] But in
proving this, he does not tell us what are the various
meanings of ἀγαθόν—the furthest he goes in that direction is to give us a hint as to how the various meanings
may be related to one another, i.e. how the variety
yet forms a unity. He then dismisses the matter,
1096b30: ἀλλ' ἴσως ταῦτα μὲν ἀφέτεον τὸ νῦν.
ἐξακριβοῦν γὰρ ὑπὲρ αὐτῶν ἄλλης ἂν εἴη φιλο-
σοφίας οἰκειότερον.* He then turns to his present
problem: What is that good which is πρακτὸν καὶ
κτητὸν ἀνθρώπῳ, that is: What particular things are
good for man, (and in what degrees)? Unfortunately,
as is well known, he does not in fact discuss "the
meaning of ἀγαθόν" elsewhere.

It is clear, then, that Aristotle declines in general
to discuss the meanings of ἀγαθόν but argues that it
has no single meaning. In both respects Prof. Prichard's
view conflicts, prima facie, with Aristotle's statements.
Nevertheless, it may be urged, both that Aristotle is
unjustified in declining to explain the meaning of
ἀγαθόν and that he must himself attach some meaning
to it in using in throughout the Ethics, which we may
be able to discover. And further, that meaning might
be identical in all important cases (this will be
explained later).

If asked to justify himself, there is no doubt how
Aristotle would reply.[14] The NE is only intended as

---

[13]Compare [H.W.B.] Joseph, Some Problems in Ethics [Ox-
ford, 1931], p. 75.: "That goodness is not a quality is the burden
of Aristotle's argument in NE I vi.": but this is not quite correct.
Aristotle is anxious to say that ἀγαθόν has no single meaning—
whether a quality, a relation, or anything else. As a matter of fact,
he says it does sometimes stand for a quality.

*But perhaps these subjects had better be dismissed for the
present; for perfect precision about them would be more appropriate to another branch of philosophy."—Ed.

[14]Aristotle does to some extent reply to this objection in I vi
14–16.

a guide for politicians, and they are only concerned to know what is good, not what goodness means. Probably Platonists would have said that I cannot discover what is good until I have found the definition of goodness, but Aristotle would claim that the definition, if possible at all, is only necessary if we wish to *demonstrate* scientifically that certain things are good. So much ἀκρίβεια is not called for in the *NE*, and in any case one can know what things are good without knowing the analysis of 'good'.[15] Whether this reply is satisfactory is doubtful. Certainly there is much to be said on Aristotle's side. Firstly, as Moore pointed out, we can know something to be true without knowing its analysis. Secondly, as Aristotle pointed out in I vi 4, if goodness is an isolable, definable property we should be able to study it in isolation from all subject matters, whereas in fact there is no such study. Thirdly, even those who, like Moore, find goodness "unanalyzable" still go on to discuss what is good. But in any case it must be admitted that his method has its dangers; and whether they are serious can best be judged by its results in the body of the *NE*. (In at least two cases, those of ἡδονή and φιλία and perhaps also in that of τιμή the lack of a clearer account of the meaning or meanings of ἀγαθόν is in fact most serious.)

The extent to which Aristotle does in fact attach a discoverable, and even single, meaning to ἀγαθόν will, of course, concern us largely. But before proceeding, it is worth considering an example of the extreme lengths to which Prof. Prichard is prepared to go in imputing inconsistency to Aristotle. His view, we said, implies that ἀγαθόν does have a single meaning, i.e. does always stand for an identical common character in the subjects of which it is predicated. (Note that

---

[15] I do not, however, accept Burnet's exaggerated view of the "dialectical" method of the *NE*.

we need 'character' here, not 'quality'; for, of course, one of Prof. Prichard's main contention is that Aristotle mistakes "being conducive to our happiness" for a *quality* of that which is so conducive, whereas it is not.) And this, we said, conflicts with Aristotle's own statement that ἀγαθόν does not do this.

Now it may be thought that I have been wasting unnecessary words over this, since Prof. Prichard himself notices this objection and answers it on pp. 32–33 [p. 250.]

But Aristotle in saying, as he would have said, that in pursuing, e.g. an honour, we are pursuing it ὡς ἀγαθόν, could only have meant that we are pursuing it in virtue of thinking that it would possess a certain character to which he refers by the term ἀγαθόν, so that by ἀγαθόν he must mean to indicate some character which certain things would have. Further, this being so, in implying as he does that in pursuing things of certain different kinds καθ᾽ αὑτά we are pursuing them ὡς ἀγαθά, he must be implying that these things of different kinds have, nevertheless, a common character, viz. that indicated by the term ἀγαθόν. It will, of course, be objected that he expressly denies that they have a common character. For he says: τιμῆς δὲ καὶ φρονήσεως καὶ ἡδονῆς ἕτεροι καὶ διαφέροντες οἱ λόγοι ταύτῃ ᾗ ἀγαθά (*Ethics* I vi 11).* But the answer is simple; viz. that this is merely an inconsistency into which he is driven by his inability to find in these things the common character which his theory requires him to find, and that if he is to succeed in maintaining that we pursue these things of various kinds ὡς ἀγαθά, he *has* to maintain that in spite of appearances to the contrary they have a common character.

---

*"But of honour, wisdom, and pleasure, just in respect of their goodness, the accounts are distinct and diverse."—Ed.

We are not concerned for the moment with this doctrine about "pursuing things ὡς ἀγαθά."[16] But what we must notice is that Prof. Prichard quotes the sentence about τιμή, φρόνησις, and ἡδονή, as though it were an *unwilling admission*, into which Aristotle's honesty drives him: as though Aristotle is admitting that in certain cases he *cannot* find the common character, which he *must* find. Yet a glance at the context will show that, on the contrary, the whole passage is designed to *prove* that there is no such common character: and the sentence quoted clinches the argument.[17] It is not too much to say that, if τιμή and the rest are possessed of a common character denoted by ἀγαθόν, the whole argument against the Platonists is undermined: and Prof. Prichard must accuse Aristotle not so much of inconsistency as of bad faith.

In any case, this passage cannot be thus lightly dismissed. The objection retains, it seems to me, very considerable weight.

ἀγαθόν—*Does it mean "that which is desired"?* We may now turn to the main problem, the meaning of ἀγαθόν. It must, I think, be agreed, that there is some chance of our being able to discover what Aristotle does in fact believe about the meaning of the word: but, since Aristotle appears to decline to assist us, that chance is small.

It is on p. 31 [p. 248] that Prof. Prichard begins his attempt to elucidate the meaning of ἀγαθόν: and he says that "Aristotle's nearest approach to an elucida-

---

[16]ὡς ἀγαθά does not in Greek mean "in virtue of their possessing a certain characteristic, 'goodness.' " It means rather "pursuing them *in the way in which we pursue things we say are good*." Thus the phrase is noncommittal as to whether there is a common quality or not. Cp. in English 'stating as a fact,' 'stating as a matter of opinion.'

[17]Aristotle does not say he "cannot find" a common character denoted by ἀγαθόν in these instances: he says that he knows ἀγαθόν stands for *different* characters.

tion" is to be found in I vi 7–11[18] and vii 1–5. Certain statements there made, he says, "seem intended as an elucidation of the meaning of ἀγαθόν"; nevertheless they fail, even formally, to constitute such an elucidation: and moreover, if they are "taken seriously as an elucidation," the result is to render absurd other well-known doctrines in the *NE*.

I suppose it cannot be denied that Aristotle is capable of getting himself into pretty tortuous confusions; but this time, at least, I think he can be exonerated.

In the first place, it seems to me that the statements in question are not intended at all as an "elucidation of the meaning of ἀγαθόν" in Prof. Prichard's sense.[19] It is, consequently, not surprising that they fail formally to constitute such an elucidation: what is surprising, I think, is Prof. Prichard's reason for saying that they so fail. In the second place, if they are "taken seriously as an elucidation," they do not so much render absurd the doctrines mentioned by Prof. Prichard as others which it is easy to find.

In these passages, says Prof. Prichard, Aristotle speaks of τὰ καθ' αὑτὰ διωκόμενα καὶ ἀγαπώμενα as called ἀγαθά in one sense ... and he speaks of τὰ ποιητικὰ τούτων ἢ φυλακτικά πως as called ἀγαθά in another sense, and he implies that these latter are διωκτὰ καὶ αἱρετὰ δι' ἕτερον (*Ethics* I vii 4) ... Further he appears to consider that the difference of meaning is elucidated (sic) by referring to the former as ἀγαθὰ καθ' αὑτά and to the latter as ἀγαθὰ διὰ ταῦτα, i.e. ἀγαθὰ διὰ ἀγαθὰ καθ' αὑτά. But this unfortunately is no elucidation, since to state a difference of *reason* for calling two things ἀγαθόν is not to state a difference of mean-

---

[18]For "7–11" we should read "8–11."

[19]If any passage deserves the description "Aristotle's nearest approach to an elucidation," it is probably I vii 10 (not mentioned by Professor Prichard); on this *v.i.*

ing of ἀγαθόν, and indeed is to imply that the meaning in both cases is the same. Nevertheless, these statements seem intended as an elucidation of the meaning of ἀγαθόν. And the cause for surprise lies in this, that if they are taken seriously as an elucidation, the conclusion can only be that ἀγαθόν includes 'being desired' in its meaning, and indeed simply means τέλος or end.

It will, I am afraid, necessarily take some considerable space to clear this matter up.

Let us, as a preliminary, remark that the passage vii 1–5 is not concerned with at all the same matter as vi 8–11. In vii 1 he asserts that τὸ ἀγαθόν of any activity whatsoever is τὸ τέλος (incidentally this passage implies that τὸ ἀγαθόν and τὸ τέλος do not mean the same): he then proceeds to ask, what is the τέλος τῶν πρακτῶν ἁπάντων? And the word ἀγαθόν is not so much as mentioned again. Moreover, though he does proceed to distinguish a τέλος καθ' αὑτὸ διωκτόν (αἱρετόν) from a τέλος δι' ἕτερον διωκτόν (αἱρετόν) he does not assert that the word τέλος has (in any sense) two meanings, only that there are some τέλη which are τέλεια (complete or final), others which are not. Still less, of course, does he assert that ἀγαθόν has two meanings, or endeavour to elucidate its meaning: he says nothing about it at all; just as, in vi 8–11, no mention is made of τέλος at all.

We may confine ourselves, therefore, to vi 8–11. Upon what is Aristotle there engaged? In the earlier part of the chapter he has been arguing that ἀγαθόν cannot have always an identical meaning. But now he produces an attempted answer to his own objections, which is to be understood by referring to his own logic (*Categories* I a1). A word (ὄνομα) may be used either συνωνύμως, ὁμωνύμως, or παρωνύμως. If, on each occasion of its use, its connotation (ὁ κατὰ τοὔνομα λόγος τῆς οὐσίας) is identical, then the word is used συνωνύμως. If, on different occasions of its use, its connotations are different, then the word is used ὁμωνύμως: e.g. κλείς may be used to mean "key" or "collarbone," ζῷον "animal" or "picture." But there is a third possibility: on different occasions of its use, the word may possess connotations which are *partly* identical and *partly* different, in which case the word is said to be used παρωνύμως.[20] There are evidently many ways in which a word can be used paronymously: Aristotle names some of them, and gives examples (τὸ ὑγιεινόν in *Met.* 1003a33 τὸ ἰατρικόν and τὸ ὑγιεινόν in *Met.* 1060b37. Also notoriously τὸ ὄν with which ἀγαθόν here is again compared, and τὸ ἕν. For more details, the reader may refer to those passages, or to Burnet's notes on p. 29 of his edition of the *Ethics*).[21]

One such type of paronymity is known as the "πρὸς ἕν." When we speak of a "healthy exercise" the word 'healthy' has a connotation which is only partly the same as that which it has in the phrase "a healthy body": a healthy exercise is an exercise which produces or preserves healthiness in bodies. Hence healthiness[a], when predicated of an exercise, means "productive or preservative of healthiness[b]" i.e. of healthiness in the sense in which it is predicated of bodies. Thus "healthiness[b]" and "healthiness[a]" have connotations which are partly identical and partly different.

Now, in our present passage, vi 8–11, Aristotle is producing as an objection against himself the fact (admitted elsewhere, cp. *Rhet.* 1362a27) that ἀγαθόν is paronymous in this way. His opponents are supposed

[20]Compare the traditional classification of terms as *univocal*, *equivocal*, and *analogous*.—Joseph, *An Introduction to Logic* (Oxford, 1916), p. 46: "analogous" is unsatisfactory, since κατ' ἀναλογίαν is only one form of paronymity.

[21]This supplements and amends *Cat.* I. a bit; homonymy and paronymy are defined by very limited examples there. Consider also Rhet. 1362a21 ff. with regard to this point.

to claim that, although ἀγαθόν does not always have an identical meaning, that is *merely* because it is paronymous in the above manner. Sometimes it means "x," sometimes "productive, etc. of x," etc.; and clearly it is only the "*nuclear*" meaning of "x" which is common to both, with which they are concerned. And it *is* always identical. To which Aristotle replies as follows. First, let us distinguish ἀγαθόν as used in the one sense, from ἀγαθόν as used in the other, by substituting for it, in the one case ἀγαθὸν καθ' αὐτό, and in the other ἀγαθὸν διὰ ἀγαθόν τι καθ' αὐτό.[22] Then let us disregard all cases where ἀγαθόν is used in the latter sense. And finally observe that, even in cases where it is used in the former sense only, it *still* has not always an identical meaning.

Now let us ask, with reference to Prof. Prichard's argument quoted above, does Aristotle intend here to "elucidate the meaning" of ἀγαθόν? It is clear that there is no simple answer, Yes or No, to this question. He does intend to point out that it has at least two meanings, at least in a reasonably strict sense, and to explain how those two meanings are related, and to show how they are in part identical. But he does not intend to elucidate that identical part. Moreover, he proceeds to assert that in fact ἀγαθόν, used in the nuclear way, has at least three different meanings (so that there may be at least six meanings of ἀγαθόν in general): but he does not mean to elucidate any one of the three, nor even to explain how they are related to each other. It is not, then, surprising that Prof. Prichard should feel dissatisfied; if we ask his oversimplified question, the passage must "seem intended as an elucidation" of the meaning of ἀγαθόν, and yet fail to *be* one—for plainly, Prof. Prichard would only count as a *real* elucidation, an elucidation of the mean-

[22]πρὸς might have been expected rather than διά: but διά is more general.

ing of ἀγαθόν in the nuclear sense of senses, which Aristotle is not concerned to give him.

Prof. Prichard's remark, that "to state a difference of reason for calling two things ἀγαθόν is not to state a difference of meaning of ἀγαθόν, and indeed is to imply that the meaning in both cases is the same," remains to me obscure. But it seems clear that he has not appreciated the doctrine of παρώνυμα, since he uses the rigid dichotomy "same meaning—different meaning" whereas παρώνυμα are words which have meanings *partly* the same and *partly* different. His "difference of reason" might be the point about, say, healthy. Then Aristotle would accept the claim, and say that what he offers is *not* an elucidation and is not intended to be one. We have seen, however, that Prof. Prichard is prepared to believe that the passage may be seriously intended as an elucidation of ἀγαθόν in the "nuclear" sense. Seeing that he has already dismissed the distinction between ἀγαθά καθ᾽ αὑτά and ἀγαθά διὰ ταῦτα as "no elucidation," and seeing that Aristotle makes no attempt to elucidate the meaning of ἀγαθόν in the nuclear sense, and further states that it has at least three nuclear senses, it is clearly bound to be difficult for Prof. Prichard to find anything in the passage which could be described as "an elucidation of *the* meaning of ἀγαθόν." He fastens upon the words διωκόμενα καὶ ἀγαπώμενα, διώκεται, διώκομεν and concludes that, according to Aristotle here, ἀγαθόν "simply means τέλος or end."[23]

Let us proceed to consider first Prof. Prichard's arguments to prove that ἀγαθόν does *not* have that meaning. After asserting that it quite certainly is not used by Aristotle with that meaning [which in a way is true: but surely then, it is unlikely that he intends

[23]It seems to me doubtful whether τέλος means simply "something desired": but for present purposes it will do no harm to suppose it does so.

to ascribe that meaning to it in this passage?] he proceeds as follows: "Apart from other considerations, if he did [mean by ἀγαθόν simply τέλος], then for him to say, as he in effect does, that we always aim at ἀγαθόν τι would be to say nothing, and for him to speak, as he does, of the object of βούλησις as τἀγαθόν would be absurd."

The first of these arguments is perhaps too concise to be clear. "We always aim at ἀγαθόν τι" may perhaps mean

(1) whenever we *act*, we aim at ἀγαθόν τι, or

(2) whenever we *aim*, we aim at ἀγαθόν τι

If (1) is meant, I very much doubt whether Aristotle would maintain it; for we sometimes act from ἐπιθυμία or θυμός, and then we aim at ἡδύ τι or at ἀντιλύπησις. But he might say[24] that in all *deliberate* action we aim at ἀγαθόν τι, as he implies in the first sentence of the *Ethics*.[25] However, this qualification need not concern us here (though, since he *would* certainly have said that every action aims at some τέλος, it is clear enough that ἀγαθόν does not mean τέλος). If, then, (1) is meant, and if ἀγαθόν τι *means* τέλος τι, Aristotle will be saying "Whenever we act, we aim at some end." But to say that is not to say *nothing*: indeed, it is to say something which Prof. Prichard declares, on p. 29 [p. 243], to be false.[26] At most the sentence is *pleonastic*: for we could write τινός for τέλους τινός (or ἀγαθοῦ τινός) without loss of meaning. But that is a very minor matter. And this would serve, e.g., to define ἀγαθόν.

If (2) is meant, the sentence is certainly emptier: "whenever we aim, we aim at some end." It might be said to be a matter of definition. But it might well be

[24]Wrongly.

[25]The importance of which should not be exaggerated.

[26]Because he understands by τέλος *only* what Aristotle calls a τέλος παρὰ τὴν πρᾶξιν, I confess that his criticism at this point seems to me perverse.

said, for emphasis, in explaining the notion of "aiming," or in otherwise explaining the use of words. However, for reasons similar to those given in the preceding paragraph, I do not consider that Aristotle would ever have made such a remark about ἀγαθόν, though he might well have made it about τέλος. If we change it to "whenever we aim *deliberately*, and only then, we aim at ἀγαθόν τι," Aristotle might agree: but *then*, if we substitute τέλος τι for ἀγαθόν τι, the statement would simply be *false*. Thus proving, though not by Prof. Prichard's argument, that ἀγαθόν does not mean τέλος.

Now take Prichard's second argument. Here, no such objection applies as in the case of the first argument, for Aristotle certainly *would* say that the object of βούλησις is τἀγαθόν. If ἀγαθόν means τέλος, the statement becomes: "the object of βούλησις is τὸ τέλος." Now this is not, as a matter of fact, as it stands, absurd—it is in fact a remark which Aristotle often makes, with good sense (cp. e.g. 1111b26, or 1113a15, ἡ βούλησις τοῦ τέλους ἐστίν). However, τὸ τέλος is there being contrasted with τὰ πρὸς τὸ τέλος, and βούλησις with προαίρεσις: whereas it is clear that Prof. Prichard means, and fairly enough, to refer to a context where βούλησις is being contrasted with ἐπιθυμία and θημός, and τἀγαθόν with τὸ ἡδύ and ἀντιλύπησις. In such a context, it is clear enough that we cannot substitute τέλος for ἀγαθόν. For in the case of the other two types of ὀρέξεις we are also aiming at a τέλος, and we need ἀγαθόν not τέλος to provide the contrast. Prof. Prichard's arguments, then, reduce to one, which I think is sound: ἀγαθόν cannot mean "that which is desired," because Aristotle holds that there are *other* objects of desire besides τὸ ἀγαθόν.

Apart from this argument, it is absolutely clear from I vi itself that ἀγαθόν does not, for Aristotle, mean (or at any rate *merely* mean?) "that which is desired."

It is not merely that he says that ἀγαθόν has no single meaning, and hence a fortiori, not that suggested. But further, he says of τιμή φρόνησις and ἡδονή that they are all διωκόμενα καθ' αὐτά, so that, presumably, their λόγοι ᾗ διωκόμενα καθ' αὐτά* are identical: whereas their λόγοι ταύτη ᾗ ἀγαθά are different. So that being ἀγαθόν cannot mean being desired.

I expect the reader has found the proof of this tedious. But it is important to establish the point, since the relation between "being ἀγαθόν" and "being desired" is one of the most baffling puzzles in Aristotle's, or for that matter Plato's, ethical theory. This puzzle, like that of the relation between ἀγαθόν and ἡδύ, must be reserved for a separate discussion.

*Their accounts as things pursued for their own sake." (Ed. transl.).

THE FINAL GOOD IN
ARISTOTLE'S *ETHICS*

W. F. R. HARDIE

Aristotle maintains that every man has, or should have, a single end (τέλος), a target at which he aims. The doctrine is stated in *NE* I 2. 'If, then, there is some end of the things we do which we desire for its own sake (everything else being desired for the sake of this), and if we do not choose everything for the sake of something else (for at that rate the process would go on to infinity, so that our desire would be empty and vain), clearly this must be the good and the chief good. Will not the knowledge of it, then, have a great influence on life? Shall we not, like archers who have a mark to aim at, be more likely to hit upon what is right?'[1] (1094a18–24). Aristotle does not here prove, nor need we understand him as claiming to prove, that there is only one end which is desired for itself. He points out correctly that, if there are objects which are desired but not desired for themselves, there must be some object which is desired for itself. The passage further suggests that, if there were one such object and one only, this fact would be important and helpful for the conduct of life.

From *Philosophy*, XL (1965), 277–95. Reprinted by permission of the author and the editors of *Philosophy*.

[1]Here, and in quoting other passages, I have reproduced the Oxford translation. I refer to the *Nicomachean Ethics* as *NE* and to the *Eudemian Ethics* as *EE*.

The same doctrine is stated in *EE* A 2. But, whereas in the *NE* the emphasis is on the concern of political science, statesmanship, with the human good conceived as a single end, the *EE* speaks only of the planning by the individual of his own life. 'Everyone who has the power to live according to his own choice (προαίρεσις) should dwell on these points and set up for himself some object for the good life to aim at, whether honour or reputation or wealth or culture, by reference to which he will do all that he does, since not to have one's life organised in view of some end is a sign of great folly. Now above all we must first define to ourselves without hurry or carelessness in which of our possessions the good life consists, and what for men are the conditions of its attainment' (1214b6–14). Here, then, we are told that lack of practical wisdom is shown in a man's failure to plan and organise his life for the attainment of a single end. Aristotle omits to say, but says elsewhere, that lack of practical wisdom is shown also in a man's preference for a bad or inadequate end, say pleasure or money. We learn in *NE* VI 9 that the man of practical wisdom has a true conception of the end which is best for him as well as the capacity to plan effectively for its realisation (1141b31–33).

How far do men in fact plan their lives, as Aristotle suggests they should, for the attainment of a single end? As soon as we ask this question, we see that there is a confusion in Aristotle's conception of the single end. For the question confuses two questions: first, how far do men plan their lives; and, secondly, so far as they do, how far do they, in their plans, give a central and dominating place to a single desired object, money or fame or science? To both these questions the answer that first suggests itself is that some men do and some do not. Take the second question first. It is exceptional for a life to be organised to achieve the satisfaction of one ruling passion. If asked for ex-

amples we might think of Disraeli's political ambition
or of Henry James' self-dedication to the art of the
novel. But exceptional genius is not incompatible with
a wide variety of interests. It seems plain that very few
men can be said, even roughly, to live their lives under
the domination of a single end. Consider now the
first question. How far do men plan their lives? Clearly
some do so who have no single dominant aim. It is
possible to have a plan based on priorities, or on equal
consideration, as between a number of objects. It is
even possible to plan not to plan, to resolve never to
cross bridges in advance. Hobbes remarked that there
is no 'finis ultimus, utmost aim, nor summum bonum,
greatest good, as is spoken of in the books of the old
moral philosophers. . . . Felicity is a continual progress
of the desire, from one object to another, the attaining
of the former being still but the way to the latter'
(*Leviathan*, ch. xi). But even such a progress may be
planned, although the plan may not be wise. Every
man has, and knows that he has, a number of independent desires, i.e. desires which are not dependent
on other desires in the way in which desire for a means
is dependent on desire for an end. Every man is capable,
from time to time, of telling himself that, if he pur-
sues one particular object too ardently, he may lose or
imperil other objects also dear to him. So it may be
argued that every man capable, as all men are, of
reflection is, even if only occasionally and implicitly,
a planner of his own life.

We can now distinguish the two conceptions which
are confused or conflated in Aristotle's exposition of
the doctrine of the single end. One of them is the
conception of what might be called the inclusive end.
A man, reflecting on his various desires and interests,
notes that some mean more to him than others, that
some are more, some less, difficult and costly to achieve,
that the attainment of one may, in different degrees,

promote or hinder the attainment of others. By such
reflection he is moved to plan to achieve at least his
most important objectives as fully as possible. The
following of such a plan is roughly what is sometimes
meant by the pursuit of happiness. The desire for happiness, so understood, is the desire for the orderly and
harmonious gratification of desires. Aristotle sometimes,
when he speaks of the final end, seems to be fumbling
for the idea of an inclusive end, or comprehensive
plan, in this sense. Thus in *NE* I 2 he speaks of the
end of politics as 'embracing' other ends (1094b6–7).
The aim of a science which is 'architectonic' (1094a26–
27; cf. *NE* VI 8, 1141b24–26) is a second-order aim.
Again in *NE* I 7 he says that happiness must be 'most
desirable of all things, without being counted as one
good thing among others since, if it were so counted,
it would be made more desirable by the addition of
even the least of goods . . .' (1097b16–20). Such considerations ought to lead Aristotle to define happiness as
a secondary end, the full and harmonious achievement
of primary ends. This is what he ought to say. It is
not what he says. His explicit view, as opposed to his
occasional insight, makes the supreme end not inclusive
but dominant, the object of one prime desire, philosophy. This is so even when, as in *NE* I 7, he has in
mind that, *prima facie*, there is not only one final
end: '. . . if there are more than one, the most final
of these will be what we are seeking' (1097a30). Aristotle's mistake and confusion are implicit in his formulation in *EE* A 2 of the question in *which* of our
possessions does the good life consist (1214b12–13).
For to put the question thus is to rule out the obvious
and correct reply; that the life which is best for a man
cannot lie in gaining only one of his objects at the
cost of losing all the rest. This would be too high a
price to pay even for philosophy.

The ambiguity which we have found in Aristotle's

conception of the final good shows itself also in his attempt to use the notion of a 'function' (ἔργον) which is 'peculiar' to man as a clue to the definition of happiness. The notion of function cannot be defended and should not be pressed, since a man is not designed for a purpose. The notion which Aristotle in fact uses is that of the specific nature of man, the characteristics which primarily distinguish him from other living things. This notion can be given a wider interpretation which corresponds to the inclusive end or a narrower interpretation which corresponds to the dominant end. In *NE* I 7, seeking what is peculiar to man (1097b33–34), Aristotle rejects first the life of nutrition and growth and secondly the life of perception which is common to 'the horse, the ox and every animal' (1098a2–3). What remains is 'an active life of the element that has a rational principle' (1098a3–4). This expression need not, as commentators point out, be understood as excluding theoretical activity. 'Action' can be used in a wide sense, as in the *Politics* VII 3 (1325b16–23), to include contemplative thinking. But what the phrase specifies as the proper function of man is clearly wider than theoretical activity and includes activities which manifest practical intelligence and moral virtue. But the narrower conception is suggested by a phrase used later in the same chapter. 'The good for man turns out to be the activity of soul in accordance with virtue, and if there are more than one virtue in accordance with the best and most complete' (1098a16–18). The most complete virtue must be theoretical wisdom, although this is not made clear in *NE* I.

The doctrine that only in theoretical activity is man really happy is stated and defended explicitly in X 7 and 8. Theoretical reason, the divine element in man, more than anything else is man (1177b27–28, 1178a6–7). 'It would be strange, then, if he were to choose not the life of his self but that of something else. And what we said before will apply now; that which is proper to each thing is by nature best and most pleasant for each thing' (1178a3–6). Man is truly human only when he is more than human, godlike. 'None of the other animals is happy, since they in no way share in contemplation' (1178b27–28). This statement makes obvious the mistake involved in the conception of the end as dominant rather than inclusive. It is no doubt true that man is the only theoretical animal. But the capacity of some men for theory is very small. And theory is not the only activity in respect of which man is rational as no other animal is rational. There is no logic which leads from the principle that happiness is to be found in a way of living which is common and peculiar to men to the narrow view of the final good as a dominant end. What is common and peculiar to men is rationality in a general sense, not theoretical insight which is a specialised way of being rational. A man differs from other animals not primarily in being a natural metaphysician, but rather in being able to plan his life consciously for the attainment of an inclusive end.

The confusion between an end which is final because it is inclusive and an end which is final because it is supreme or dominant accounts for much that critics have rightly found unsatisfactory in Aristotle's account of the thought which leads to practical decisions. It is connected with his failure to make explicit the fact that practical thinking is not always or only the finding of means to ends. Thought is needed also for the setting up of an inclusive end. But, as we have seen, Aristotle fails to make explicit the concept of an inclusive end. This inadequacy both confuses his statement in *NE* I 1 and 2 of the relation of politics to subordinate arts and leads to his giving an incomplete account of deliberation.

I have represented Aristotle's doctrine as primarily a doctrine about the individual's pursuit of his own good, his own welfare (εὐδαιμονία). But something should be said at this point about the relation between the end of the individual and the 'greater and more complete' end of the state. 'While it is worth while to attain the end merely for one man, it is finer and more godlike to attain it for a nation or for city-states' *NE* I 2, 1094b7–10). This does not mean more than it says: if it is good that Smith should be happy, it is even better that Brown and Robinson should be happy too.

What makes it inevitable that planning for the attainment of the good for man should be political is the simple fact that a man needs and desires social community with others. This is made clear in *NE* I 7 where Aristotle says that the final good must be sufficient by itself. 'Now by self-sufficient we do not mean that which is sufficient for a man by himself, for one who lives a solitary life, but also for parents, children, wife and in general for his friends and fellow-citizens, since man is born for citizenship' (1097b7–11). That individual end-seeking is primary, that the state exists for its citizens, is stated in Ch. 8 of *NE* VI, one of the books common to both treatises. 'The man who knows and concerns himself with his own interests is thought to have practical wisdom, while politicians are thought to be busybodies.... Yet perhaps one's own good cannot exist without household management, nor without a form of government' (1142a1–10). The family and the state, and other forms of association as well, are necessary for the full realisation of any man's capacity for living well.

The statesman aims, to speak roughly, at the greatest happiness of the greatest number. He finds his own happiness in bringing about the happiness of others (*NE* X 7, 1177b14), especially, if Aristotle is right, the happiness of those capable of theoretical activity. Speaking in terms of the end as dominant Aristotle, in *NE* VI 13, sets a limit to the authority of political wisdom. 'But again it is not supreme over philosophic wisdom, i.e. over the superior part of us, any more than the art of medicine is over health; for it does not use it but provides for its coming into being; it issues orders, then, for its sake but not to it' (1145a6–9). This suggestion that science and philosophy are insulated in principle from political interference cannot be accepted. The statesman promotes science but also uses it, and may have to restrict the resources to be made available for it. If the secondary and inclusive end is the harmonisation and integration of primary ends, no primary end can be sacrosanct. But, even if Aristotle had held consistently the extravagant view that theoretical activity is desired only for itself and is the only end desired for itself, he would not have been right to conclude that there could be no occasion for the political regulation of theoretical studies. For the unrestricted pursuit of philosophy might hinder measures needed to make an environment in which philosophy could flourish. It might be necessary to order an astronomer to leave his observatory, or a philosopher his school, in order that they should play their parts in the state. Similarly the individual who plans his life so as to give as large a place as possible to a single supremely desired activity must be ready to restrain, not only desires which conflict with his ruling passion, but the ruling passion itself when it is manifested in ways which would frustrate its own object.

In *NE* I 1 and 2 Aristotle expounds the doctrine that statesmanship has authority over the arts and sciences which fall under it, are subordinate to it. An art, A, is under another art, B, if there is a relation of means to end between A and B. If A is a productive art, like bridle-making, its product may be used by a superior art, riding. Riding is not a productive activity, but it falls under generalship in so far as generals use cavalry, and generalship in turn falls under the art of the statesman, the art which is in the highest degree architectonic (1094a27; cf. VI 8, 1141b23–25). Thus the man of practical wisdom, the statesman or legislator, is compared by Aristotle to a foreman, or clerk of the works, in charge of technicians and workmen of various kinds, all engaged in building an observatory to enable the man of theoretical wisdom to contemplate the starry heavens. In the *Magna Moralia* the function of practical wisdom is said to be like that of a steward whose business it is so to arrange things that his master has leisure for his high vocation (A 34, 1198b12–17). Perhaps the closest parallel to the function of the statesman as conceived by Aristotle is the office of the Bursar in a college at Oxford or Cambridge.

This account of statesmanship as aiming at the exercise of theoretical wisdom by those capable of it is an extreme expression of the conception of the end as dominant and not inclusive. The account, as it stands, is a gross over-simplification of the facts. When he speaks of a subordinate art as pursued 'for the sake of' a superordinate or architectonic art (1094a15–16), Aristotle should make explicit the fact that the subordinate activity, in addition to serving other objects, may be pursued for its own sake. Riding, for example, has non-military uses and can be a source of enjoyment. Again two arts, or two kinds of activity, may each be subordinate, in Aristotle's sense, to the other. Riders use bridles, and bridle-makers may ride to their work. The engineer uses techniques invented by the mathematician, but also promotes the wealth and leisure in which pure science can flourish. Aristotle does not fail to see and mention the fact that an object may be desired both independently for itself and dependently for its effects (*NE* I 6, 1097a30–34). He was aware also that theoretical activity is not the only kind of activity which is independently desired. But he evidently thought that an activity which was never desired except for itself would be intrinsically desirable in a higher degree than an activity which, in addition to being desired for itself, was also useful. It is, so to say, beneath the dignity of the most godlike activities that they should be useful. Aristotle is led in this way, and also by other routes, to give a narrow and exclusive account of the final good, to conceive of the supreme end as dominant and not inclusive.

Aristotle describes deliberation, the thinking of the wise man, as a process which starts from the conception of an end and works back, in a direction which reverses the order of causality, to the discovery of a means. Men do not, he asserts, deliberate about ends. 'They assume the end and consider how and by what means it is to be attained; and if it seems to be produced by several means they consider by which it is most easily and best produced, while, if it is achieved by one only, they consider how it will be achieved by this and by what means *this* will be achieved, till they come to the first cause, which in the order of discovery is last' (*NE* III 3, 1112b15–20). Such an investigation is compared to the method of discovering by analysis the solution of a geometrical problem. Again in VI 2 practical wisdom is said to be shown in finding means to a good end. 'For the syllogisms which deal with acts to be done are things which involve a starting-point, viz. "since the end, i.e. what is best, is of such and such a nature" . . .' (1144a31–33).

This is Aristotle's official account of deliberation. But here again, as in his account of the relation between political science and subordinate sciences, a too narrow and rigid doctrine is to some extent corrected elsewhere, although not explicitly, by the recognition of facts which do not fit into the prescribed pattern.

Joseph, in *Essays in Ancient and Modern Philosophy*, pointed out that the process of deciding between alternative means, by considering which is easiest and best, involves deliberation which is not comparable to the geometer's search (pp. 180–81). But he remarks that Aristotle does not 'appear to see' this. What the passage suggests is that the agent may have to consider the intrinsic goodness, or badness, of the proposed means as well as its effectiveness in promoting a good end. A less incidental admission that there is more in deliberation than the finding of means is involved in Aristotle's account of 'mixed actions' in *NE* III 1. Aristotle recognises that, if the means are discreditable, the end may not be important enough to justify them. 'To endure the greatest indignities for no noble end or for a trifling end is the mark of an inferior person' (1110a22–23). 'It is difficult sometimes to determine what should be chosen at what cost, and what should be endured in return for what gain' (1110a29–30). Alcmaeon's decision to kill his mother, on his father's instruction, rather than face death himself is given as an example of a patently wrong answer to a question of this kind. This kind of deliberation is clearly not the regressive or analytic discovery of means to a preconceived end. It is rather the determination of an ideal pattern of behaviour, a system of priorities, from which the agent is not prepared to depart. It is what we described earlier as the setting up of an inclusive end. It is a kind of practical thinking which Aristotle cannot have had in his mind when he asserted in *NE* III 3 that 'we deliberate not about ends but about means' (1112b11–12).

I have argued that Aristotle's doctrine of the final human good is vitiated by his representation of it as dominant rather than inclusive, and that this mistake underlies his too narrow account of practical thinking as the search for means. But to say that the final good

is inclusive is not to deny that within it there are
certain dominant ends corresponding to the major interests of developed human nature. One of these major
interests is the interest in theoretical sciences. Of these,
according to Aristotle, there are three; theology or first
philosophy, mathematics and physics (*Metaphysics* E
1, 1026a18–19, cf. *NE* VI 8, 1142a16–18). His account
of contemplation in the Ethics, based on the doctrine
of reason as the divine or godlike element in man (*NE*
X 7, 1177a13–17; 8, 1178a20–23), exalts the first and
makes only casual mention of the other two. Elsewhere,
in the *De Partibus Animalium* I 5, he admits that
physics has attractions which compensate for the relatively low status of the objects studied. 'The scanty
conceptions to which we can attain of celestial things
give us, from their excellence, more pleasure than all
our knowledge of the world in which we live; just as
a half-glimpse of persons that we love is more delight-
ful than a leisurely view of other things, whatever their
number and dimensions. On the other hand, in cer-
titude and in completeness our knowledge of terrestrial
things has the advantage. Moreover their greater near-
ness and affinity to us balances somewhat the loftier
interest of the heavenly things that are the object of
the higher philosophy' (644b31–645a4).

I cannot here discuss the theological doctrines which
led Aristotle to place 'the higher philosophy' on the
summit of human felicity. But there is an aspect of
his account of the theoretic life which has an immediate
connection with my main topic. He remarks in *NE*
VII 14 that 'there is not only an activity of movement
but an activity of immobility, and pleasure is found
more in rest than in movement' (1154b26–28). This
doctrine that there is no 'movement' in theoretical
contemplation, and the implication that its immobility
is a mark of its excellence, is determined primarily by
Aristotle's conception of the divine nature. The latest

commentators on the *NE*, Gauthier and Jolif, say, with justification, that he here excludes discovery from the contemplative life. 'On pourrait même dire que l'idéal, pour le contemplatif aristotélicien—et cet idéal le Dieu d'Aristote le réalise—ce serait de ne jamais étudier et de ne jamais découvrir...' (855–56). In *NE* X 7 we are told that 'philosophy is thought to offer pleasures marvellous for their purity and their enduringness' and that it is 'reasonable to suppose that those who know will pass their time more pleasantly than those who enquire' (1177a25–27). It is not reasonable at all. It is a startling paradox. I shall now suggest that Aristotle's apparent readiness to accept this paradox, like his confusion between the dominant and the inclusive end, is to be explained, at least in part, by his failure to give any explicit or adequate analysis of the concept of end and means.

Aristotle states in *NE* I that an end may be either an activity or the product of an activity. 'But a certain difference is to be found among ends; some are activities, others are products apart from the activities that produce them. Where there are ends apart from the actions, it is the nature of the products to be better than the activities' (1094a3–6). The suggestion here is that, when an activity leads to a desired result, as medicine produces health or shipbuilding a ship or enquiry knowledge, the end-seeking activity is not itself desired. As he says (untruly) in the *Metaphysics*, 'of the actions which have a limit none is an end' (Θ 6, 1048b18). But an activity which aims at producing a result may be an object either of aversion or of indifference or of a positive desire which may be less or greater than the desire for its product. It is necessary to distinguish between 'end' in the sense of a result intended and planned and 'end' in the sense of a result, or expected result, which, in addition to being intended and planned, is also desired for itself while the process of reaching it is not. It is true that travel may be unattractive, but it may also be more attractive that arrival. A golfer plays to win. But, if he loses, he does not feel that his day has been wasted, that he has laboured in vain, as he would if his only object in playing were to win a prize or to mortify his opponent or just to win. Doing crossword puzzles may be a waste of time, but what makes it a waste of time is not the fact that we rarely get one out. It would be a greater waste of time if we never failed to finish them. In short, the fact that an activity is progressive towards a planned result leaves quite open the question whether it is the process or the result which is desired, and, if both, which primarily. If Aristotle had seen and said this, he might have found it more difficult than he does to suggest that the pleasures of discovery are not an essential element in science as a major human interest. Philosophy would be less attractive than it is if only results mattered. God's perfection requires that his thinking should be unprogressive. But men, who fall short of perfect simplicity, need, to make them happy, the pleasures of solving problems and of learning something new and of being surprised. For them the best way of life leads, in the words of Meredith,

> 'through widening chambers of surprise to where
> throbs rapture near an end that aye recedes'.

We have seen that Aristotle's doctrine of the final human good needs clarification in terms of a distinction between an end which is inclusive, a plan of life, and an end which is dominant as the satisfaction of theoretical curiosity may be dominant in the life of a philosopher. No man has only one interest. Hence an end which is to function as a target, as a criterion for deciding what to do and how to live, must be inclusive. But some men have ruling passions. Hence some inclusive ends will include a dominant end. I shall now try to look more closely at these Aristotelian notions, and to suggest some estimate of their relevance and value in moral philosophy.

It will be best to face at once and consider a natural and common criticism of Aristotle; the criticism that his virtuous man is not moral at all but a calculating egoist whose guiding principle is not duty but prudence, Bishop Butler's 'cool self-love'. Aristotle is in good company as claiming that rationality is what makes a man ideally good. But his considered view, apart from incidental insights, admits, it is said, only the rationality of prudent self-interest and not the rationality of moral principle. Thus Professor D. J. Allan, in *The Philosophy of Aristotle*, tells us that Aristotle "takes little or no account of the motive of moral obligation" and that "self-interest, more or less enlightened, is assumed to be the motive of all conduct and choice" (p. 189). Similarly the late Professor Field, a fair and sympathetic critic of Aristotle, remarked that, whereas morality is 'essentially unselfish', Aristotle's idea of the final end or good makes morality 'ultimately selfish' (*Moral Theory*, pp. 109, 111).

When a man is described as selfish what is meant primarily is that he is moved to act, more often and more strongly than most men, by desires which are selfish. The word 'selfish' is also applied to a disposition so to plan one's life as to give a larger place than is usual or right to the gratification of selfish desires. But what is it for a desire to be selfish? Professor Broad, in his essay 'Egoism as a theory of human motives' (in *Ethics and the History of Philosophy*), makes an important distinction between two main kinds of 'self-regarding' desires. There are first desires which are 'self-confined', which a man could have even if he were alone in the world, e.g. desires for certain experiences, the desire to preserve his own life, the desire to feel respect for himself. Secondly there are self-regarding desires which nevertheless presuppose that a man is not alone in the world, e.g. desires to own property, to assert or display oneself, to inspire affection. Broad further points out that desires which are 'other-regarding' may also be 'self-referential', e.g. desires for the welfare of one's own family, friends, school, college, club, nation.

A man might perhaps be called selfish if his other-regarding motives were conspicuously and exclusively self-referential, if he showed no interest in the welfare of anyone with whom he was not personally connected. But usually 'selfish' refers to the prominence of self-regarding motives, and different kinds of selfishness correspond to different self-regarding desires. The word, being pejorative, is more readily applied to the less reputable of the self-regarding desires. Thus a man strongly addicted to the pursuit of his own pleasures might be called selfish even if his other-regarding motives were not conspicuously weak. A man whose ruling passion was science or music would not naturally be described as selfish unless to convey that there was in him a reprehensible absence or failure of other-regarding motives, as shown, say, by his neglect of his family or of his pupils.

The classification of desires which I have quoted from Broad assumes that their nature is correctly represented by what we ordinarily think and say about them. *Prima facie* some of our desires are self-regarding; and, of the other-regarding desires, some are and some are not self-referential. But there have been philosophers who have questioned or denied the reality of these apparent differences. One doctrine, psychological egoism, asserts in its most extreme form that the only possible objects of a man's first-order independent desires are experiences, occurrent states of his own consciousness. Thus my desire to be liked is really a desire to know that I am liked; and my desire that my children should be happy when I am dead is really a desire for my present expectation that they will be happy. The obvious criticism of this doctrine is that it is preposterous and self-defeating: I must first desire popularity and the happiness of my children if I am to find gratifying my thought that I am popular and that my children will be happy. To most of us it seems that introspective self-scrutiny supports the validity of this dialectic. We can, therefore, reject psychological egoism. A *fortiori* we can reject psychological hedonism which asserts that the *only* experiences which can be independently desired are pleasures, feelings of enjoyment. This further doctrine was stated as follows by the late Professor Prichard. 'For the enjoyment of something which we enjoy, e.g. the enjoyment of seeing a beautiful landscape, is related to the thing we enjoy, not as a quality but as an effect, being something excited by the thing we enjoy, so that, if it be said that we desire some enjoyment for its own sake, the correct statement must be that we desire the experience, e.g. the seeing of some beautiful landscape, for the sake of the feeling of enjoyment which we think it will cause, this feeling being really what we are desiring for its own sake' (*Moral Obligation*, p. 116). Surely most of us would be inclined to say that we can desire for its own sake 'the seeing of some beautiful landscape' and that we do not detect a distinct 'feeling of enjoyment'.

Was Aristotle a psychological egoist or a psychological hedonist? A crisp answer would have been possible only if Aristotle had explicitly formulated these doctrines as I have defined them. So far as I can see, he did not do so even in his long, but not always lucid, treatment of friendship and self-love in *NE* IX. This being so, he cannot be classed as a psychological egoist in respect of his account of first-order desires. When Aristotle confronts the fact of altruism, he does not

refuse to accept benevolent desires at their face value
(*NE* VIII 2, 1155b31; 3, 1156b9–10; 7, 1159a8–12).
But he shows acuteness in detecting self-referential
elements in benevolence. Thus he compares the feelings
of benefactors to beneficiaries with those of parents
for their children and of artists for their creations. 'For
that which they have treated well is their handiwork,
and therefore they love this more than the handiwork
does its maker' (*NE* IX 7, 1167b31–1168a5).

The nearest approach which Aristotle makes to the
formulation of psychological hedonism is, perhaps, in
the following passage in *NE* II 3. 'There being three
objects of choice and three of avoidance, the noble,
the advantageous, the pleasant, and their contraries,
the base, the injurious, the painful, about all of these
the good man tends to go right and the bad man to go
wrong, and especially about pleasure; for this is common to the animals, and also it accompanies all objects of choice; for even the noble and the advantageous appear pleasant' (1104b30–1105a1). But there are
passages in his discussion of pleasure in *NE* X which
show that, even if he had accepted psychological egoism, he would not have accepted psychological hedonism. 'And there are many things we should be keen
about even if they brought no pleasure, e.g. seeing,
remembering, knowing, possessing the virtues. If pleasures necessarily do accompany these, that makes no
odds; we should choose them even if no pleasure resulted' (1174a4–8). This reads like a direct repudia-
tion of the doctrine in my quotation from Prichard. In
NE X 4 he asks, without answering, the question
whether we choose activity for the sake of the attendant
pleasure or vice versa (1175a18–21). The answer which
his doctrine requires is surely that neither alternative
can be accepted, since both the activity and the attendant pleasure are desired for their own sake. But it

is open to question whether, when we speak of a state or activity, such as 'the seeing of some beautiful landscape', as pleasant, we are referring to a feeling distinct from the state or activity itself.

The charge against Aristotle that his morality is a moraliy of self-interest is directed primarily against his doctrine of the final good, the doctrine which I have interpreted as a conflation of the distinct notions of the 'inclusive end' and the 'dominant end'. But the critic may also wish to suggest that Aristotle overstates the efficacy of self-regarding desires in the determination of human conduct. To this the first answer might well be that it is not easy to overstate their efficacy. The term 'self-regarding' applies, as we have seen, to a wide variety of motives; and there is a 'self-referential' factor in the most potent of the other-regarding motives. Altruism which is pure, not in any way self-regarding or self-referential, is a rarity. The facts support the assertion that man is a selfish animal. But the criticism can be met directly. Aristotle does not ignore other-regarding motives. Thus, while he points out that the philosopher, unlike those who exercise practical virtue, does not need other men 'towards whom and with whom he shall act', he admits that the pleasures of philosophy are enhanced by interest in the work of colleagues. 'He perhaps does better if he has fellow-workers, but still he is the most self-sufficient' (*NE* X 7, 1177a27–b1). When, in the *EE*, Aristotle speaks of philosophy as the service of God, he seems to imply that the love of wisdom is not directed merely to the lover's own conscious states (1249b20). Again, in *NE* IX 8, he can attribute to the 'lover of self' conduct which is, in the highest degree, altruistic and self-sacrificing. 'For reason always chooses what is best for itself, and the good man obeys his reason. It is true of the good man too that he does many acts for the sake of his friends and his country, and, if necessary, dies for them; for he will throw away both wealth and honours and in general the goods that are objects of competition, gaining for himself nobility (τὸ καλόν); since he would prefer a short period of intense pleasure to a long one of mild enjoyment, a twelvemonth of noble life to many years of humdrum existence, and one great and noble action to many trivial ones. Now those who die for others doubtless attain this result; it is, therefore, a great prize that they choose for themselves' (1169a17–26).

But it is not enough, if we are to do justice to the criticism that Aristotle makes morality selfish, to quote this passage, or the passage in *NE* I 10 where Aristotle speaks of the shining beauty of the virtue shown in bearing disasters which impair happiness (1100b30–33). Such passages, it may be said, show Aristotle's moral sensibility and moral insight. But the question can still be asked whether their commendation of the ultimate self-sacrifice, and of endurance in suffering, is consistent with Aristotle's doctrine of the final human good. Perhaps he is speaking more consistently with his own considered views when, again in *NE* IX 8, he makes the suggestion (or is it a joke?) that a man may show the finest self-sacrifice, the truest love, by surrendering to his friend the opportunity of virtuous action (1169a 33–34). Perhaps Aristotle's commendation of the surrender, in a noble cause, of life itself needs to be qualified, from his own point of view, as it was qualified by Oscar Wilde:

> And yet, and yet
> Those Christs that die upon the barricades,
> God knows it I am with them, in some ways.

To this question I now turn. My answer must and can be brief.

We have found two main elements in Aristotle's doctrine of the final good for man. There is, first, the suggestion that, as he says in *EE* A 2, it is a sign of 'great folly' not to 'have one's life organised in view of some end'. Perhaps it would be better to say that it is impossible not to live according to some plan, and that it is folly not to try to make the plan a good one. The inevitability of a plan arises from the fact that a man both has, and knows that he has, a number of desires and interests which can be adopted as motives either casually and indiscriminately or in accordance with priorities determined by the aim of living the kind of life which he thinks proper for a man like himself. But in an agent naturally reflective the omission to make such a plan is not completely undesigned: the minimal plan is a plan not to plan. To this side of Aristotle's doctrine I have applied the term 'inclusive end', inclusive because there is no desire or interest which should not be regarded as a candidate, however unpromising, for a place in the pattern of life. Wisdom finds a place even for folly. The second element which we have found in Aristotle's doctrine is his own answer to the question what plan will be followed by a man who is most fully a man, as high as a man can get on the scale from beast to god. Aristotle's answer is that such a man will make theoretical knowledge, his most godlike attribute, his main object. At a lower level, as a man among men, he will find a place for the happiness which comes from being a citizen, from marriage and from the society of those who share his interests. I have called this the doctrine of the dominant end. The question whether Aristotle's doctrine of the final good can be reconciled with the morality of altruism and self-sacrifice must be asked with reference both to the inclusive end and to the dominant end.

To say that a man acts, or fails to act, with a view to an inclusive end is to say nothing at all about the comparative degrees of importance which he will ascribe to his various aims. His devotion to his own good, in the sense of his inclusive end, need not require him to prefer self-regarding desires to other-regarding desires, or one kind of self-regarding desire to another. All desires have to be considered impartially as candidates for places in the inclusive plan. To aim at a long life in which pleasures, so far as possible, are enjoyed and pains avoided it is a possible plan, but not the only possible plan. That a man seeks an inclusive end leaves open the question whether he is an egoist or an altruist, selfish or unselfish in the popular sense.[2]

While a man seeking his inclusive end need not be selfish, he can be described as self-centred in at least three different ways. First and trivially his desire to follow his inclusive plan is his own desire; it is self-owned. Secondly, a man can think of a plan as being for his own good only if he thinks about himself, thinks of himself as the one owner of many desires. His second-order desire for his own good is self-reflective. Thirdly, this second-order desire, being a desire about desires, an interest in interests, can be gratified only through the gratification of his first-order desires. Even the martyr plans to do what he wants to do. We can express this by saying that the pursuit of the final good is self-indulging as well as self-reflective. But 'self-indulgence' as applied to a way of life in which pleasures may be despised and safety put last carries no pejorative sense. That action in pursuit of an inclusive end is self-centred in these ways does not mean

[2] I owe this point, and less directly much else in my discussion of the criticism of Aristotle's ethical system as egoistic, to Professor C. A. Campbell's British Academy Lecture (1948), "Moral Intuition and the Principle of Self-Realisation" (especially pp. 17–25). Professor Campbell's lecture discusses the ethical theory of T. H. Green and F. H. Bradley, and I do not know whether he would think of his arguments as being relevant to the interpretation of Aristotle. But I have found his defence of 'self-realisation' as a moral principle helpful in my attempt to separate the strands of thought in Aristotle's doctrine of the final good.

that the agent is self-regarding or self-seeking in any sense inconsistent with the most heroic or saintly self-sacrifice.

To the question whether the pursuit of the human good, understood in terms of Aristotle's conception of the dominant end, can be reconciled with the morality of altruism, and in particular the extreme altruism of the man who gives his life for his friends or his country, a different answer must be given. Here reconciliation is not possible. In order to see this it is necessary only to reflect on Aristotle's definition in *NE* I 7 of the dominant end, which he calls happiness, and to compare this definition with what is said about the self-love of the man who nobly gives up his own life. 'Human good turns out to be activity of soul in accordance with virtue, and if there are more than one virtue, in accordance with the best and most complete. But we must add "in a complete life." For one swallow does not make a summer nor does one day; and so too one day or a short time does not make a man blessed and happy' (1098a16–20). How then can the man who, to gain nobility (τὸ καλόν) for himself, gives his life for his friends or his country be said to achieve happiness? Aristotle's answer, as we have seen, is that such a man prefers 'a short period of intense pleasure to a long one of mild enjoyment, a twelvemonth of noble life to many years of humdrum existence, and one great and noble action to many trivial ones' (1169a22–25). But the scales are being loaded. For why should it be supposed that the man who declines to live the final, if crowded, hour of glorious life will survive to gain only 'mild' enjoyments and a 'humdrum' or 'trivial' existence? If such existence is, or seems, humdrum *because* the 'intense pleasure' of self-sacrifice has been missed, then Aristotle's thought here is circular and self-stultifying. The intensity of the brief encounter, it is suggested, is such that by contrast the remainder of life

would be humdrum. But, unless the alternative would
be humdrum in its own right, the encounter would
not be intense enough to compensate for the curtail-
ment of life and happiness. A 'complete life' either is, or
is not, a necessary condition of happiness. Aristotle as a
theorist cannot justify the admiration which, as a man,
he no doubt feels for the 'one great and noble action'.
Confronted with the facts he would have to admit that
the man who, whether by good fortune or design, sur-
vives a revolution or a war may live to experience intense enjoyments and to perform activities in accordance with the best and most complete virtue. He may
become a professor of philosophy or at least a prime
minister. We must conclude, therefore, that Professor
Field was right: the doctrine of the good for man, as
developed by Aristotle in his account of the dominant
end, does make morality 'ultimately selfish' (*Moral
Theory*, pp. 109, 111).

Aristotle offers us in his *Ethics* a handbook on how
to be happy though human. To some it may seem that
a treatise on conduct with an aim so practical and so
prudential can do little to clarify the concepts with
which moral philosophy is mainly concerned, the concepts of duty and of moral worth. 'He takes little or
no account', Professor Allan tells us, 'of the motive of
moral obligation' (*The Philosophy of Aristotle*, p.
189). Perhaps not. The topic is too large for a concluding paragraph. Certainly most men feel moral ob-
ligations which cannot be subsumed under the obligation, if there is one, to pursue their own happiness by
planning for the orderly satisfaction of their self-regarding desires. But 'obligation' and 'duty' are words with
many meanings, meanings variously related to the concept of moral worth. Perhaps Aristotle is not wrong,
as he is not alone, in connecting the concept of moral
worth with the fact that man is not just the plaything
of circumstance and his own irrational nature but also

the responsible planner of his own life. This aspect of
Aristotle's teaching is what I have called his doctrine
of the 'inclusive end', and I have argued that there
is no necessity for the doctrine to be specified and
developed as a recommendation of calculated egoism.
Aristotle himself, as we have seen, does not adhere
consistently to his own exaltation of self-regarding aims.
He is, indeed, always ready to notice facts which are
awkward for his own theories. Thus in *NE* I 10 he
recognises that the actual achievement of happiness,
virtuous activity, is largely outside a man's control. 'A
multitude of great events if they turn out well will
make life happier ... while if they turn out ill they
crush and maim happiness; for they both bring pain
with them and hinder many activities' (1100b25–30).
He adds that, even when disaster strikes, 'nobility
shines through, when a man bears with resignation
many great misfortunes, not through insensibility to
pain but through nobility and greatness of soul'
(1100b30–33). 'The man who is truly good and wise',
he goes on to say, 'bears all the chances of life be-
comingly and always makes the best of circumstances
as a good shoemaker makes the best shoes out of the
hides that are given to him' (1100b35–1101a5). The
suggestion of this passage is that a man's worth lies
not in his actual achievement, which may be frustrated
by factors outside his own control, but in his striving
towards achievement. In an earlier chapter (5) of *NE*
I he speaks of the good as something which 'we divine
to be proper to a man and not easily taken from him'
(1095b25–26). Aristotle's doctrine of the final good is
a doctrine about what is 'proper' to a man, the power
to reflect on his own abilities and desires and to conceive and choose for himself a satisfactory way of life.
What 'cannot be taken from him' is his power to keep
on trying to live up to such a conception. Self-respect,

thus interpreted, is a principle of duty. If moral philosophy must seek one comprehensive principle of duty, what other principle has a stronger claim to be regarded as *the* principle of duty?

ARISTOTLE ON PLEASURE

J. O. URMSON

Aristotle's most mature and careful account of pleasure or enjoyment—he uses the noun ἡδονή and its cognates and the verb χαίρειν without any apparent discrimination—is to be found in Book X of the *Nicomachean Ethics* (1174a13 ff.). I propose to summarize this very acute account and then to discuss some of the problems arising out of it.

Like sight, Aristotle holds, pleasure is not a process (κίνησις) but an activity. As such, it is complete at any time. When you build a temple, you begin, continue, and perhaps finish it, and until you have finished it, you have not built a temple; but if at any moment you see or are enjoying something, then you have seen or enjoyed it. Sight and enjoyment cannot be left half-finished.

Perception, of which sight is an example, thought, and contemplation have objects. When the perception or thought is high-grade and its object is worthwhile, then the perception or thought or contemplation is enjoyable (pleasant). The higher grade the perception and the more valuable its object, the more pleasant and more perfect the activity. But the excellence of the perception or thought and its object make the activity perfect in a different way from that in which enjoyment perfects it; the former are constitutive of its perfection while the enjoyment is a manifestation of it as the grace of youth is a manifestation of physical prime. We might say that it adds zest to the activity. When, through tiredness or illness, the activity is impaired, so is the enjoyment of it. Again, novelty commands effortless attention and therefore enjoyment, but when novelty wears off, the attention wanders and enjoyment wanes. So activity and life itself are bound up with enjoyment (pleasure); there is no enjoyment without activity enjoyed and enjoyment is the mark of activity at peak performance.

Different activities (1175a21) are differently enjoyable. Just as perception and thought are different species of activity, so the pleasures of perception are different in species from the pleasures of thought. Every activity has its own 'proper' (οἰκεῖα) pleasure; one could not chance to get the pleasure of, say, reading poetry from stamp collecting. The enjoyment proper to an activity promotes that activity, whereas the enjoyment of something else impedes it. If we are doing two things at once, perhaps arguing and listening to music, the more enjoyable gets in the way of the other. So when we enjoy something very much, we do not do anything else at the same time; we only eat sweets at the theater when we are not enjoying the plot very much. So, if two enjoyments can conflict, they must be distinguishable. Just as the enjoyment of something else maims the enjoyment of an activity, so does the 'proper pain', that is, the dislike of that activity. We are disinclined to draw or reason if we find it disagreeable.

As activities differ in worth (1175b23) so do their enjoyments (proper pleasures). Even desires for the worthwhile or the base are praised and blamed, although the appetite is not so intimately bound up with the activity of pursuing them; how much more so are the enjoyments of these activities which are scarcely distinguishable from the activities themselves.

This very acute analysis of the enjoyment of activities can be supplemented from elsewhere in the *NE*. As a prologue to his discussion of temperance in Book III, Aristotle says that the pleasure of the soul need be distinguished from the bodily pleasures, instancing the love of honour and love of learning. He adds that the lover of each of these "enjoys what he loves, his body being in no way affected, but rather his intelligence." This remark puzzled the commentator Aspasius to the point of exasperation: "What does he mean," he protests, "when he says that the enjoyment of lovers of learning or honour involves a condition of the intelligence? For enjoyment and the pleasures are not in the intelligence but in the affective (παθητικῷ) part of the soul." Aspasius never understands Aristotle's view that enjoyment of learning is exhibited in the effortless concentration of the intelligence on its problems rather than in getting some feeling as a result or concomitant of one's study.

It has, indeed, been commonplace in the history of philosophy to regard doing something for the pleasure of it as doing something for the sake of gaining some sensation or feeling named 'pleasure'. Psychological hedonists have typically assumed this analysis and concluded therefrom that mankind has only one goal of action which they call pleasure. Sometimes their opponents have seemed to think that to reject psychological hedonism, they must say that we do not do things for pleasure but for their own sake, thus consenting to the analysis; they take the pleasure of an activity to be a feeling resulting from it but claim that the pleasure is a mere bonus resulting from gaining what one wanted rather than the end for the sake of which the activity was performed. It is not surprising, perhaps, that the fascination of this analysis should have made Aspasius and many of his successors among the commentators on Aristotle's ethics unable to see that Aristotle has no inclination to accept it. The enjoyment of an activity is for him not a result of it but something barely distinguishable from the activity; it is more like the effortless zest with which the activity is performed than a result or concomitant of it. His account is, indeed, very similar to the account of enjoyment given by G. Ryle in his *Concept of Mind* (London, 1949), a fact which should surprise nobody. Ironically enough, we shall find that Aristotle is at his weakest in discussing just those aspects of pleasure to which the 'traditional' analysis is most plausibly applicable. He is in the end most interested in the enjoyment of intellectual activities, and it is here that his view is most obviously attractive.

But what of the bodily pleasures? It is clear that in Book X Aristotle wishes to give the same general account of them as of intellectual enjoyment. Thus, bodily pleasures (σωματικαί ἡδοναί) are construed as the enjoyment of activities of sense-perception. Aristotle gives the same account of them in general in Book III. He makes it clear that he is thinking of the enjoyment of colors and shapes and pictures (sight), of music (hearing), and smells. But the objects of taste and touch have a special position among the objects of bodily pleasure, so that usually when Aristotle speaks of bodily pleasures (e.g. at 1104b5, 1153b33, 1154a8, 1154a10, 1154a26, 1177a7) he seems to have them alone in mind. They also are the only objects of bodily pleasure which fall within the sphere of temperance.

Aristotle, we have said, allots a special position to the objects of taste and touch; at times he was little inclined to distinguish between them, as when he treats χυμός as a ἁπτόν in *De Anima* 414b6–11. But in a remarkable passage (*NE* 1118a26–33) he makes it clear that touch is the true sphere of temperance: "They [the intemperate] seem to make little use of taste. For to taste belongs the judgment of flavors, as is done by wine-tasters and cooks. But it is not these that people enjoy, intemperate ones at any rate, but the experience which is all a matter of touch, whether in the field of food or drink or sex." Here, it seems to me that Aristotle is on the brink of making a distinction far more important than his distinction of the enjoyment of perceptual and intellectual activities. To this further distinction, that he never quite makes clear even, I think, to himself, we must now turn.

The account of the enjoyment of activity, whether it involves the exercise of thought or the senses, given in Book X seems to me to be remarkably acute; it is surely, at least in general, correct. But Aristotle appears to offer it as an account of pleasure in general and as such it raises problems, of which we shall immediately raise the most acute.

One is inclined to say that it is a correct account of the enjoyment of an activity in contrast to those accounts of it which make such enjoyment the obtaining of pleasant experiences which accrue from the activity, accounts such as, apparently, Aspasius and Prichard in his essay in this volume [pp. 241–60] would be inclined to give. But surely there is such a thing as gaining pleasant experiences as a result of activity, even if this is not what it is to enjoy that activity? Let us suppose that I am engaged in geometrical thinking and on the verge of completing an important proof. Certainly such a situation as this could result in a glow of excitement and elation welling up within me, though this is not the enjoyment of the activity, which Aristotle held to be scarcely distinguishable from the activity itself. Moreover, this excitement might well intercept and impede my geometrical thought in the way that 'foreign pleasures' are said by Aristotle to do; I might have to light a pipe and pace about until the pleasurable excitement died down and I could again become absorbed in my geometry. Yet in his account of pleasure Aristotle seems to leave no room for this sort of pleasurable feeling. Even the bodily pleasures are regarded as the enjoyment of activities of sense perception; they are less clear or pure than the pleasures of intellectual activity and arise from painful conditions such as thirst, but Aristotle seems to think that they can be subsumed under the same general analysis.

But it is pretty clear that the pain of thirst, which is alleged to be the opposite of the pleasure of drinking, is not like the disagreeableness of doing geometry, which is also in some way the opposite of finding geometry enjoyable. When we find geometry disagreeable, Aristotle tells us, we tend to avoid geometry and can attend to it only with difficulty. But Aristotle cannot wish to claim that the pain of thirst is such that we find it hard to pay attention to our thirst, nor does he speak of the 'proper pleasure' of thirst or the 'proper pain' of drinking. And the reason for these facts is clear; thirst is not an activity, and the pangs of thirst are an unpleasant sensation unconnected with activity; similarly when Aristotle refers to the pleasure of drinking he is not referring to the enjoyment of the activity of drinking but the pleasant feeling engendered by drinking when thirsty.

Certainly Aristotle's account of enjoyment can be applied to activities essentially involving sense perception. One can, as he points out, be interested in tastes (enjoy tasting things) in the way that an expert cook or connoisseur of wines is likely to be; one might be interested in tastes as one is interested in geometry and enjoy tasting things as one enjoys doing geometry. Or, again, watching plays and looking at colors, shapes, and pictures are activities which essentially involve sense perception, as also does listening to music. If these are to be called bodily pleasures, as involving the senses, we do not have to exclude them from the field happily covered by Aristotle's account.

But we should notice that the activities are looking at (or watching), listening to, tasting (as understood in wine tasting), and smelling (understood as sniffing at things), not merely seeing, hearing, having a taste in one's mouth or an odor in one's nostrils. There could be a comparable pleasant activity of active touching, a quasi-aesthetic enjoyment of textures; touch is not essentially different here from the other senses.

Now surely if we look attentively at Aristotle's discussion of temperance and intemperance in Book III, especially the passage from it quoted earlier, it is clear that when the intemperate man eats, drinks, and indulges in sexual activity, he is characterized not as enjoying these activities, but as performing them for the sake of the pleasant feelings they produce. It is the feelings that are enjoyed by the intemperate, not the activities that engender them. But Aristotle fails to make explicitly clear to himself the central point; he persuades himself that the intemperate pleasures are to be distinguished from the pleasure of looking at pictures because they involve the sense of touch and thus fails to see that he has really made a distinction between enjoying activities essentially involving use of the senses and doing things which produce a pleasant feeling. Pleasant bodily feelings such as those engendered by food, drink, and sex are merely conspicuous examples of the latter. We must surely recognize that one might smell roses not because one enjoyed smelling roses but because one enjoyed the smell —a passive experience to which the activity of smelling is but a means. Similarly, one might, though the possibility is remote, do geometry not because of an interest in geometry and enjoyment of geometrical work, but in order to produce the feeling of exhilaration which successful work can sometimes give rise to, the feeling being what was enjoyed.

In the Topics (106a36 ff.) Aristotle remarks that "the pain from thirst is opposite to the pleasure from drinking, but there is none opposite to the pleasure from contemplating the incommensurability of the side and the diagonal. So the term 'pleasure' is used ambiguously." But in the NE, he has rightly noticed that there can be a 'proper pain' of thinking; I might find the contemplation of this incommensurability infinitely tedious. In the same way, I might find the activity of drinking tedious. Moreover, abstinence from geometrizing, like abstinence from drinking, might produce pangs of deprivation akin in principle to the pangs of thirst. What again we need is what Aristotle only half sees, a distinction between the pleasantness (welcomeness) and unpleasantness (unwelcomeness) of things, in particular feelings, which may be produced by or be otherwise concomitants of an activity and the pleasantness or unpleasantness of the activity itself. No doubt the pleasantness of the feelings produced by drinking is causally dependent on their being preceded by unpleasant feelings of thirst, whereas the pleasure of geometrizing is not so closely bound to the unpleasantness of anything. But these are contingent facts, for we might conceivably have pleasant sensations from drinking until we burst and enjoyed doing geometry only after a toothache.

So it would seem that Aristotle, having adumbrated a distinction between the enjoyment of perceptual activity (bodily pleasure in the wider sense), and the enjoyment of feelings produced by the bodily, but scarcely perceptual, activities of eating, drinking, and sex; fails to recognize its proper significance, making it, wrongly, a question of what sense is employed. It is remarkable that while most philosophers have wrongly assimilated the enjoyment of activity to the enjoyment of feelings, a mistake for which Aristotle duly castigates them, he himself makes the uncommon error of assimilating the enjoyment of feelings to the enjoyment of activity.

Yet at times, it seems that Aristotle effectively has the distinction clear, particularly in Book VII of the *NE*. There he is attacking the views of those who denigrate pleasure and it seems that he has two main contentions to make. First, he sees in such views a mere excess of asceticism; the activities from which pleasant feelings arise are essential features of human life and thus have their place if not cultivated in excess. Further, if one wishes to engage in theoretical work a neutral state is no doubt preferable to either pleasant or unpleasant bodily feeling; but no one would wish to regard this as a reason for a general attack on pleasure who did not think of pleasant bodily feeling as the whole of pleasure so that (1153b33) "the bodily pleasures have gained a proprietory right to the name." As he duly points out (1153a22), the enjoyment of speculative thought can hardly be claimed to impede speculative thought. Throughout these discussions in Book VII, one has to take the term 'bodily pleasure' as meaning 'pleasant feelings' rather than 'enjoyment of activities involving use of the senses'. And yet even in Book VII, he gives a summary definition of pleasure as 'unimpeded activity', which I take to be essentially similar to that of Book X; that is, I take him to mean that an activity is enjoyable when it is unimpeded (by, for example, "foreign pleasures").

To sum up, then, I should contend that Aristotle gives us a clear and valuable account of the enjoyableness of an activity. What leads to the obscurity and insufficiency in his position is an ambiguity in his use of the term 'bodily pleasure' of which he himself is unaware. At times, he uses it to refer to the enjoyment of any activity essentially involving the use of any of the senses, including listening to music and watching plays. At other times, he uses it to refer, sometimes quite clearly, to the pleasant sensations which can be gained by activity. But, since he draws his examples from localized bodily feelings resulting from contact, and since there are no familiar examples of enjoying active employment of the sense of touch, he gives a mistaken formal account of the matter as if there were no ambiguity but the generic case of enjoyable use of the senses and the specific case of enjoyable use of the sense of touch. Thus, in Book X of the *NE*, he gives a final account of pleasure which is appropriate as an account of enjoyable activity in general, including those involving the senses, but, failing to see the ambiguity of 'bodily pleasure', he falsely believes that he has given a general account of pleasure in giving an account of the enjoyment of activity.

I would like to add a few remarks about the terminology employed by Aristotle and its translation. It is plain that at times, particularly outside his official discussions of 'pleasure', Aristotle is referring to pains and other very unpleasant bodily feelings when he uses the word λύπη; obvious examples can be found in Book VII, chapter 7. But the verb λυπῖσθαι frequently cannot be idiomatically translated 'be pained', but means rather 'find distasteful' as when Aristotle says that the musician λυπεῖται by bad songs—he is repelled by them, finds them distasteful. It is abundantly clear that to speak of the 'proper pain' of an activity is highly suggestive of just that analysis of enjoyment and its opposite which Aristotle rejects; to perform an activity λυπούμενος is not to perform it with pain but finding it disagreeable, irksome, boring, or repulsive. Moreover, while λύπη is used by Aristotle as the opposite of ἡδονή, pain is not the opposite of pleasure. It is not even the opposite of pleasant feeling, a position occupied by unpleasant feeling (there are many unpleasant feelings which are not pains). It is hard to translate λύπη because there is no obvious opposite in English to 'enjoyment' or 'pleasure'; 'displeasure' will only do in certain rather special contexts; but we ought to abandon the word 'pain' as a translation. Pains have no opposite; in this respect they resemble tickles. It is also notable that while the word ἡδονή is common, and sometimes refers to a pleasant feeling, the verb ἥδεσθαι is far less common in the NE than χαίρειν, which is the usual opposite of λυπεῖσθαι; I have noticed no case where ἥδεσθαι could mean 'have a pleasant feeling', and I suppose nobody would suggest that χαίρειν has such a meaning, though one can χαίρειν σωματικῇ ἀπολαύσει. It would seem that for Aristotle χαίρειν is the verb most commonly corresponding to the noun ἡδονή rather than ἥδεσθαι and if this is so, it is surely suggestive for our understanding of the word ἡδονή in Aristotle.

NOTES ON CONTRIBUTORS

John L. Ackrill is Professor of Ancient Philosophy at Oxford University and Fellow of Brasenose College, Oxford.

Miss G. E. M. Anscombe is Lecturer in Philosophy and sometime Research Fellow in Somerville College, Oxford.

John L. Austin was White's Professor of Moral Philosophy at Oxford University and Fellow of Corpus Christi College from 1952 until his death in 1960.

John Cook Wilson was Wykeham Professor of Logic at Oxford University and Fellow of New College, Oxford. He died in 1915.

Irving M. Copi is Professor of Philosophy at the University of Michigan.

W. F. R. Hardie is President of Corpus Christi College, Oxford.

K. J. Hintikka is Professor of Philosophy at the University of Helsinki and at Stanford University.

G. E. L. Owen is Professor of Philosophy at Harvard University.

Father Joseph Owens teaches at the Pontifical Institute of Medieval Studies at Toronto.

H. A. Prichard was White's Professor of Moral Philosophy at Oxford University. He died in 1947.

Manley Thompson is Professor of Philosophy at the University of Chicago.

J. O. Urmson is Fellow of Corpus Christi College, Oxford.

M. J. Woods is Fellow of Brasenose College, Oxford.

SELECTED BIBLIOGRAPHY

This is a bibliography relevant to the topics discussed in this anthology. The selections are designed primarily for the student of philosophy.

(A) TRANSLATIONS

Oxford Translation under the editorship of J. A. Smith and W. D. Ross. 12 vols. Oxford: Oxford University, 1908–52.

Clarendon Aristotle Series, ed. by J. L. Ackrill. Oxford: Clarendon, 1963–   (translations and commentaries of selected portions of the *Organon, Metaphysics,* and *Physics,* with most volumes still under preparation).

(B) GENERAL

Allan, D. J., *The Philosophy of Aristotle.* Oxford: Oxford University, 1952.

Anscombe, G. E. M., and Geach, P. T., *Three Philosophers.* Oxford: Blackwell, 1961.

Bambrough, R. (ed.), *New Essays on Plato and Aristotle.* London: Routledge & Kegan Paul, 1965.

Bonitz, H., *Aristotelische Studien,* I–V. Vienna, republished 1962–67.

Cherniss, H. F., *Aristotle's Criticism of Plato and the Academy.* Baltimore: Johns Hopkins, 1944.

Düring, I., and Owen, G. E. L. (eds.), *Aristotle and Plato in the Mid-fourth Century*. Göteborg: Almquist & Wiksell, 1957.

Jaeger, W., *Aristotle*. 2d ed.; Oxford: Clarendon, 1950.

Mansion, A., (ed.), *Aristote et les problèmes de méthode*. Louvain: Publications Universitaires de Louvain, 1961.

Mure, G. R., *Aristotle*. London: E. Benn, 1932.

Ross, W. D., *Aristotle*. 5th ed.; London: Methuen, 1949.

(C) LOGIC

Bochensky, I. M., *Ancient Formal Logic*. Amsterdam: North Holland Publishing Company, 1951.

Hintikka, K. J., "An Aristotelian Dilemma," *Ajatus*, XXII (1959), 87–92.

——, "Aristotle and the Ambiguity of Ambiguity," *Inquiry*, II (1959), 139–51.

——, "Necessity, Universality, and Time in Aristotle," *Ajatus*, XX (1957), 65–90.

Joseph, H. W. B., *An Introduction to Logic*. 2d ed.; Oxford: Clarendon, 1916.

Kneale, W. C. and M., *The Development of Logic*. Oxford: Clarendon, 1962.

Lukasiewicz, J., *Aristotle's Syllogistic*, 2d ed.; Oxford: Oxford University, 1957.

    review of Lukasiewicz (1st ed.) by J. L. Austin, *Mind*, LXI (1952), 395–404.

McCall, S., *Aristotle's Modal Syllogisms*. Amsterdam: North Holland Publishing Company, 1963.

Patzig G., *Aristotelische Syllogistik*. 2te Aufl.; Göttingen: Vandenhoeck & Ruprecht, 1963.

    review of Patzig (1st ed.) by J. L. Ackrill, *Mind*, LXXI (1962), 107–17.

(D) "CATEGORIES" AND "DE INTERPRETATIONE"

Albritton, R., "Present Truth and Future Contingency," *The Philosophical Review*, LXVI (1957), 29–46.

Bonitz, H., *Über die Kategorien des Aristoteles*. Vienna: Staatsdruck, 1853.

Butler, R. J., "Aristotle's Sea Fight and Three-Valued Logic." *The Philosophical Review*, LXIV (1955), 264–74.

De Pater, W. A., *Les Topiques d'Aristote et la dialectique platonicienne. Etudes Thomistes*, X. Fribourg, 1965.

Hintikka, K. J., "The Once and Future Sea Fight," *The Philosophical Review*, LXXIII (1964), 461–92.

Husik, J., "The Categories of Aristotle," in *Philosophical Essays*. Oxford: Blackwell, 1952.

Owen, G. E. L., "Inherence," *Phronesis*, X (1965), 97–105.

Owens, J., "Aristotle on Categories," *Review of Metaphysics*, XIV (1960–61), 73–90.

Saunders, J. T., "A Sea Fight Tomorrow," *The Philosophical Review*, LXVII (1958), 367–78.

Steinthal, H., *Geschichte der Sprachwissenschaft*. 2d ed.; Hildesheim: Olms, 1890 (1961).

Strang, C., "Aristotle and the Sea Battle," *Mind*, LXIX (1960), 447–65.

Taylor, R., "The Problem of Future Contingencies," *The Philosophical Review*, LXVI (1957), 1–28.

Trendelenburg, A., *Geschichte der Kategorienlehre*. Hildesheim: Olms, 1846 (1963).

(E) METAPHYSICS

Albritton, R., "Forms of Particular Substances in Aristotle's Metaphysics," *Journal of Philosophy*, LIV (1957), 699–708.

Cook Wilson, J., "Aristotle *Metaphysics* 1048a30 sqq.," *Journal of Philology*, XXXII (1913), 300–1.

Cousin, D. R., "Aristotle's Doctrine of Substance," *Mind*, XLII (1933), 319–37; XLIV (1935), 168–85.

Eslick, L., "What Is the Starting Point of Metaphysics?" *Modern Schoolman*, XXXIV (1957), 247–63.

338

Guthrie, W. K. C., "The Development of Aristotle's Theology," *Classical Quarterly*, XXVII (1933), 162–71; XXVIII (1934), 90–98.

Harring, E. S., "Substantial Form in Aristotle's *Metaphysics Z 1*," *Review of Metaphysics*, X (1956), 308–32; XI (1957), 482–501, 698–713.

Heidel, W. A., *The Necessary and the Contingent in the Aristotelian System*. Chicago: Chicago University, 1896.

Lacey, A. R., "OUSIA and Form in Aristotle," *Phronesis*, X (1965), 54–69.

Mansion, S., "La doctrine aristotélicienne de la substance et le traité des Catégories," Library of the Tenth International Congress of Philosophy. Amsterdam: North Holland Publishing Company, 1949.

McMullin, E. (ed.), *The Concept of Matter in Greek and Medieval Philosophy*. Notre Dame: University of Notre Dame, 1963.

Mure, G. R., "Aristotle's Doctrine of Secondary Substances," *Mind*, LVIII (1949), 82–83.

Owen, G. E. L., "A Proof in the PERI IDEOON," *Journal of Hellenic Studies*, LXXVII (1957), Pt. I, 103–11.

———, "Aristotle on the Snares of Ontology," in R. Bambrough (ed.), op. cit.

———, "Logic and Metaphysics in Some Earlier Works of Aristotle," in I. Düring and G. E. L. Owen (eds.), op. cit.

Owens, J., *The Doctrine of Being in the Aristotelian Metaphysics*. 2d ed.; Toronto: Pontifical Institute of Medieval Studies, 1963.

Sachs, D., "Does Aristotle Have a Doctrine of Secondary Substances?" *Mind*, LVIII (1948), 221–25.

Sellars, W., "Substance and Form in Aristotle," *Journal of Philosophy*, LIV (1957), 688–99.

Solmsen, F., *Aristotle's System of the Physical World*. Ithaca: Cornell University, 1960.

Sorabji, R., "Function," *Philosophical Quarterly*, XIV (1964), 289–302.

Tugendhat, E., *TI KATA TINOS*. Freiburg: K. Alber, 1958.

(F) ETHICS

Adkins, A. W. H., *Merit and Responsibility*. Oxford: Clarendon, 1960.

Allan, D. J., "The Practical Syllogism," *Autour d'Aristote*. Louvain: Publications Universitaires, 1955.

Anscombe, G. E. M., *Intention*. Oxford: Blackwell, 1958.

Burnet, J., *The Ethics of Aristotle*. London: Methuen, 1900.

Cook Wilson, J., *On the Structure of the Seventh Book of the Nicomachean Ethics*. Oxford: Clarendon, 1912.

Frankena, W. K., *Three Historical Philosophies of Education*. Chicago: Scott, Foresman & Co., 1965.

Gauthier, R., *La morale d'Aristote*. Paris: Presses Universitaires de France, 1958.

Grant, C. K., "AKRASIA and the Criteria of Assent to Practical Principles," *Mind*, LXV (1956), 400–7.

Horsburgh, H., "The Criteria of Assent to a Moral Rule," *Mind*, LXIII (1954), 345–58.

Jackson, R., "Rationalism and Intellectualism in the Ethics of Aristotle," *Mind*, LI (1942), 343–60.

Joachim, H. H., *The Nicomachean Ethics*. Oxford: Clarendon, 1951.

Mothersill, M., "Anscombe's Account of the Practical Syllogism," *The Philosophical Review*, LXXI (1962), 448–61.

Owens, J., "The Ethical Universal in Aristotle," *Studia Moralia* III (Rome: Desclée, 1965), 27–47

Ritchie, O. G., "Aristotle's Explanation of AKRASIA," *Mind*, VI (1897), 536–41.

Robinson, R., "L'acrasie selon Aristote," *Revue Philosophique*, CXLV (1955), 261–80.

Walsh, J., *Aristotle's Conception of Moral Weakness*. New York: Columbia University, 1963.

Williams, B. A. O., "Aristotle on the Good; A Formal Sketch," *Philosophical Quarterly*, XII (1962), 289–96.

(G) CONTEMPORARY PHILOSOPHY
RELATED TO ARISTOTLE

Austin, J. L., "A Plea For Excuses," *Proceedings of the Aristotelian Society,* LVII (1956), 1–30.

Bennett, J., "Substance, Reality, and Primary Qualities," *American Philosophical Quarterly,* II (1965), 1–17.

Copi, I., and Gould, J. (eds.), *Readings on Logic.* New York: Macmillan, 1964.

Frankena, W. K., *Ethics.* Englewood Cliffs: Prentice-Hall, 1963.

Gauthier, D., *Practical Reasoning.* Oxford: Clarendon, 1963.

Geach, P. T., *Reference and Generality.* Ithaca: Cornell University, 1962.

———, "Subject and Predicate," *Mind,* LIX (1950), 62–83.

Grice, H. P., "Some Remarks about the Senses," *Analytical Philosophy,* ed. by R. Butler. Oxford: Blackwell, 1962.

Hamlyn, D. W., "Categories, Formal Concepts, and Metaphysics," *Philosophy,* XXXIV (1959), 111–24.

Hampshire, S., *Thought and Action.* London: Chatto and Windus, 1959.

Harrison, B., "Category Mistakes and Rules of Language," *Mind,* LXXIV (1965), 309–25.

Hart, H. L. A., "A Logician's Fairy Tale," *The Philosophical Review,* LX (1951) 198–212.

Jarvis, J., "Practical Reasoning," *Philosophical Quarterly,* XII (1962), 316–28.

Ryle, G., "Categories," *Logic and Language* (2d ser.), ed. by Flew. Oxford: Blackwell, 1955.

———, "Pleasure," *Dilemmas.* Cambridge: Cambridge University, 1954.

Strawson, P. F., *Individuals.* London: Methuen, 1959.

———, *Introduction to Logical Theory.* London: Methuen, 1952.

von Wright, G. H., "Practical Inference," *The Philosophical Review,* LXXII (1963), 159–79.

———, *The Varieties of Goodness*. London: Routledge & Kegan Paul, 1963.

Williams, D. C., "The Sea Fight Tomorrow," *Structure, Method, and Meaning*, ed. by P. Henle. New York: Liberal Arts, 1951.

ANCHOR BOOKS

PHILOSOPHY

AESTHETICS AND HISTORY—Bernard Berenson, A36

THE AMERICAN TRANSCENDENTALISTS: THEIR PROSE AND POETRY—
Perry Miller, ed., A119

ARISTOTLE—ed. by Julius Moravcsik, AP1

BASIC WRITINGS ON POLITICS AND PHILOSOPHY—Karl Marx and
Friedrich Engels; Lewis Feuer, ed., A185

BERDYAEV'S PHILOSOPHY: The Existential Paradox of Freedom and
Necessity—Fuad Nucho, Introduction by Richard Kroner, A539

THE BIRTH OF TRAGEDY AND THE GENEALOGY OF MORALS—Friedrich
Nietzsche, A81

THE BROKEN IMAGE: MAN, SCIENCE, AND SOCIETY—Floyd W. Mat-
son, A506

CRITIQUE OF PURE REASON—Immanuel Kant, trans. by F. Max
Müller, A551

CRITIQUE OF RELIGION AND PHILOSOPHY—Walter Kaufmann, A252

EITHER/OR, Vol. I—Soren Kierkegaard, A181a

EITHER/OR, Vol. II—Soren Kierkegaard, A181b

ESSAYS ON POLITICS AND CULTURE—John Stuart Mill; Gertrude
Himmelfarb, ed., A373

ESSAYS IN PHILOSOPHICAL PSYCHOLOGY—Donald F. Gustafson, ed.,
A417

ETHICS AND SOCIETY: Original Essays on Contemporary Moral
Problems—Richard T. DeGeorge, A512

THE FAITH OF A HERETIC—Walter Kaufmann, A336

FEAR AND TREMBLING AND THE SICKNESS UNTO DEATH—Soren
Kierkegaard, A30

FIVE STAGES OF GREEK RELIGION—Gilbert Murray, A51

FOUR EXISTENTIALIST THEOLOGIANS—Will Herberg, A141

FROM SHAKESPEARE TO EXISTENTIALISM—Walter Kaufmann, A213

FROM THE STONE AGE TO CHRISTIANITY—W. F. Albright, A100

THE GENESIS OF TWENTIETH CENTURY PHILOSOPHY: The Evolution
of Thought from Copernicus to the Present—Harry Prosch,
A536

HEGEL: A Reinterpretation—Walter Kaufmann, A528a

HEGEL: Texts and Commentary—Walter Kaufmann, A528b

Philosophy (continued)

THE HUMAN CONDITION—Hannah Arendt, A182

THE HUMAN USE OF HUMAN BEINGS: Cybernetics and Society—Norbert Wiener, A34

HUME—ed. by V. C. Chappell, AP2

INDIVIDUALS—P. F. Strawson, A364

IRRATIONAL MAN—William Barrett, A321

LOGIC AND LANGUAGE—Antony Flew, ed., A449

MAN IN MODERN AGE—Karl Jaspers, A101

MARXISM AND EXISTENTIALISM—Walter Odajnyk, A443

THE MARXISM OF JEAN-PAUL SARTRE—Wilfrid Desan, A507

THE METAPHYSICAL FOUNDATIONS OF MODERN SCIENCE—Edwin Arthur Burtt, A41

MODERN SCIENCE AND MODERN MAN—James B. Conant, A10

MYSTICISM AND LOGIC—Bertrand Russell, A104

THE ONTOLOGICAL ARGUMENT—Alvin Plantinga, ed., A435

PATTERNS OF ANARCHY—Leonard I. Krimerman and Lewis Perry, eds., A501

PERCEIVING, SENSING AND KNOWING—Robert J. Swartz, ed., A460

THE PHILOSOPHY OF HISTORY IN OUR TIME—Hans Meyerhoff, ed., A164

PHILOSOPHIES OF JUDAISM—Julius Guttman, A509

THE PHILOSOPHY OF TIME—Richard Gale, ed., A573

PRAGMATIC PHILOSOPHY—ed. by Amelie Rorty, A538

PSYCHE AND SYMBOL—C. G. Jung, A136

SELECTIONS FROM THE WRITINGS OF KIERKEGAARD—Lee M. Hollander, ed. and trans., A210

SOCIALIST HUMANISM: An International Symposium—ed. by Erich Fromm, A529

SOCIAL AND POLITICAL PHILOSOPHY: Readings from Plato to Gandhi—John Somerville and Ronald Santoni, eds., A370

SOCRATES—A. E. Taylor, A9

THE SPIRITUAL HERITAGE OF INDIA—Swami Prabhavananda with Frederick Manchester, A419

THREE WAYS OF THOUGHT IN ANCIENT CHINA—Arthur Waley, A75

WITTGENSTEIN AND MODERN PHILOSOPHY—Justus Hartnack, A469

WITTGENSTEIN: The Philosophical Investigations—ed. by George Pitcher, AP3

ZEN BUDDHISM—D. T. Suzuki, A90

ZEN FLESH, ZEN BONES—Paul Reps, ed., A233

ZEN: Poems, Prayers, Sermons, Anecdotes, Interviews—Lucien Stryk and Takashi Ikemoto, eds., A485

ANCHOR BOOKS

RELIGION

AMERICAN DIALOGUE—Robert McAfee Brown and Gustave Weigel, S.J., A257

THE AMERICAN PURITANS: Their Prose and Poetry—Perry Miller, ed., A80

THE AMERICAN TRANSCENDENTALISTS: Their Prose and Poetry—Perry Miller, ed., A119

ANCIENT LIBRARY OF QUMRAN—Frank Moore Cross, Jr., A272

THE BIBLE AND THE ANCIENT NEAR EAST—G. Ernest Wright, ed., A431

THE BIBLE FOR STUDENTS OF LITERATURE AND ART—G. B. Harrison, ed., A394

BIBLICAL ARCHAEOLOGIST READER I—G. Ernest Wright and David Noel Freedman, eds., A250a

THE BIBLICAL ARCHAEOLOGIST READER II—Edward F. Campbell and David Noel Freedman, eds., A250b

BOOK OF THE ACTS OF GOD—G. Ernest Wright and Reginald H. Fuller, A222

CHRISTIAN SOCIAL TEACHINGS: A Reader in Christian Social Ethics from the Bible to the Present—George W. Forell, A535

CHRISTIAN SCIENCE: Its Encounter with American Culture—Robert Peel, A446

CHURCH AND STATE IN LUTHER AND CALVIN—William A. Muller, A454

CREEDS OF THE CHURCHES: A Reader in Christian Doctrine from the Bible to the Present—John H. Leith, ed., A312

CRITIQUE OF RELIGION AND PHILOSOPHY—Walter Kaufmann, A252

THE DEAD SEA SCRIPTURES IN ENGLISH TRANSLATION—T. H. Gaster, Revised edition, A378

THE DOGMA OF CHRIST—Erich Fromm, A500

THE EARLY CHRISTIAN CHURCH—J. G. Davies, A566

THE EASTERN ORTHODOX CHURCH: Its Thought and Life—Ernest Benz, Richard and Clara Winston, trans., A332

EITHER/OR, Vol. I—Soren Kierkegaard, A181a

EITHER/OR, Vol. II—Soren Kierkegaard, A181b

EVANGELICAL THEOLOGY—Karl Barth, A408

THE FAITH OF A HERETIC—Walter Kaufmann, A336

FEAR AND TREMBLING and THE SICKNESS UNTO DEATH—Soren Kierkegaard, A30

FIVE STAGES OF GREEK RELIGION—Gilbert Murray, A51

FOUR EXISTENTIALIST THEOLOGIANS—Will Herberg, A141

FROM RITUAL TO ROMANCE—Jessie Weston, A125

FROM THE STONE AGE TO CHRISTIANITY—W. F. Albright, A100

MAGIC, SCIENCE AND RELIGION AND OTHER ESSAYS—Bronislaw Malinowski, A23

MAKER OF HEAVEN AND EARTH—Langdon Gilkey, A442

MAN IN THE MODERN AGE—Karl Jaspers, A101

MARTIN LUTHER: Selection from His Writings—John Dillenberger, ed., A271

MARTYRDOM AND PERSECUTION IN THE EARLY CHURCH—W. H. C. Frend, A546

PHILOSOPHIES OF JUDAISM—Julius Gottmann, A509

PORTRAIT OF KARL BARTH—Georges Casalis, A422

THE PROPHETIC VOICE IN MODERN FICTION—William R. Mueller, A510

PROTESTANT, CATHOLIC, JEW—Will Herberg, A195

PROTESTANT CONCEPTS OF CHURCH AND STATE—Thomas G. Sanders, A471

THE QUIET BATTLE: Writings on the Theory and Practice of Non-Violent Resistance—Mulford Q. Sibley, ed., A317

RELIGIOUS CONFLICT IN AMERICA—Earl Raab, ed., A392

THE RELIGIOUS FACTOR—Gerhard Lenski, A337

THE SPIRITUAL HERITAGE OF INDIA—Swami Prabhavananda with Frederick Manchester, A419

THE THEOLOGY OF JONATHAN EDWARDS—Conrad Cherry, A542

THREE WAYS OF THOUGHT IN ANCIENT CHINA—Arthur Waley, A75

THE TREASURE OF THE COPPER SCROLL—John Marco Allegro, A412

TWO SOURCES OF MORALITY AND RELIGION—Henri Bergson, A28

VARIETIES OF UNBELIEF—Martin E. Marty, A491

ZEN BUDDHISM—D. T. Suzuki, A90

ANCHOR BOOKS

FICTION

THE ANCHOR ANTHOLOGY OF SHORT FICTION OF THE SEVENTEENTH CENTURY—Charles C. Mish, ed., AC1

BANG THE DRUM SLOWLY—Mark Harris, A324

THE CASE OF COMRADE TULAYEV—Victor Serge, A349

CHANCE—Joseph Conrad, A113

COME BACK, DR. CALIGARI—Donald Barthelme, A470

THE COUNTRY OF THE POINTED FIRS—Sarah Orne Jewett, A26

DREAM OF THE RED CHAMBER—Chin Tsao Hseueh, A159

THE ENGLISH IN ENGLAND—Rudyard Kipling; Randall Jarrell, ed., A362

ENVY AND OTHER WORKS—Yuri Olesha; trans. by Andrew R. MacAndrew, A571

HALF-WAY TO THE MOON: New Writings from Russia—Patricia Blake and Max Hayward, eds., A483

HEAVEN'S MY DESTINATION—Thornton Wilder, A209

A HERO OF OUR TIME—Mihail Lermontov, A133

IN THE VERNACULAR: The English in India—Rudyard Kipling; Randall Jarrell, ed., A363

THE LATE MATTIA PASCAL—by Luigi Pirandello, trans. by William Weaver, A479

LIFE OF LAZARILLO DE TORMES—W. S. Merwin, trans., A316

A MADMAN'S DEFENSE—August Strindberg, trans. by Evert Sprinchorn, A492b

THE MASTERS—C. P. Snow, A162

REDBURN: HIS FIRST VOYAGE—Herman Melville, A118

THE SECRET AGENT—Joseph Conrad, A8

THE SHADOW-LINE AND TWO OTHER TALES—Joseph Conrad, A178

THE SON OF A SERVANT: The Story of the Evolution of a Human Being (1849–1867)—August Strindberg; trans. by Evert Sprinchorn, A492a

THE TALE OF GENJI, I—Lady Muraski, A55

THREE SHORT NOVELS OF DOSTOEVSKY: The Double, Notes from the Underground and The Eternal Husband, A193

UNDER WESTERN EYES—Joseph Conrad, ed. and introduction by Morton Dauwen Zabel, A323

VICTORY—Joseph Conrad, A106

THE WANDERER—Henri Alain-Fournier, A14

WHAT MAISIE KNEW—Henry James, A43

THE YELLOW BOOK—Stanley Weintraub, ed., A421

YOUTH, HEART OF DARKNESS and END OF THE TETHER—Joseph Conrad, A173

CLASSICS AND HUMANITIES

THE AENEID OF VIRGIL—C. Day Lewis, trans., A20

A BOOK OF LATIN QUOTATIONS—Compiled by Norbert Guterman, A534

THE ECLOGUES AND GEORGICS OF VIRGIL—In the Original Latin with Verse Translation—C. Day Lewis, A390

FIVE COMEDIES OF ARISTOPHANES—Benjamin Bickley Rogers, trans., A57

FIVE STAGES OF GREEK RELIGION—Gilbert Murray, A51

GREEK TRAGEDY—H. D. Kitto, A38

A HISTORY OF ROME—Moses Hadas, ed., A78

THE ILIAD, THE ODYSSEY AND THE EPIC TRADITION—Charles R. Beye, A521

THE ODYSSEY—Robert Fitzgerald, trans., illustrated by Hans Erni, A333

SAPPHO: Lyrics in the Original Greek with Translations by Willis Barnstone, A400

SIX PLAYS OF PLAUTUS—Lionel Casson, trans., A367

SOCRATES—A. E. Taylor, A9

SOPHOCLES' OEDIPUS THE KING AND OEDIPUS AT COLONUS: A New Translation for Modern Audiences and Readers—Charles R. Walker, A496